Praise for International Bestselling Author Eric Lustbader's Nicholas Linear Novels

SECOND SKIN

D0311461

FLOATING CITY

"*Floating City* is a penetrating look into drugs, nuclear weaponry and industrial espionage.... Lustbader is a stunning writer whose words flow strikingly from page to page. ... The plot is as coiled and deadly ... as the writhing sex scene set amid an aquarium of live serpents...."

—Florence Gilkeson, *The Southern Pines Pilot* (NC)

"Action, intrigue, Oriental philosophy and romance.... Lustbader is a clever wordsmith who can paint vivid pictures."

—*USA Today*

THE KAISHO

"If ... international ... action-adventure mystery spy novels are not your normal fare, but secretly you long for such, then start with *The Kaisho*.... [which] reflect[s] the author's respect and careful research into ancient Oriental mysticism.... The plot in *The Kaisho* ... keeps on surprising.... It's great to get hold of a book that consumes your imagination, filling your head with a myriad of visual images and anticipation—like Cinerama in the mind ... good, solid entertainment."

—Suzanna Phelps-Fredette, *The Commercial Appeal* (Memphis)

"High-intensity action and intrigue.... Lustbader possesses enormous powers of both sensory and sensual detail.... He is decidedly not predictable, another fine gift."

—Emmett Gard Pittman, *South Bend Tribune*

ERIC LUSTBADER

A NICHOLAS LINNEAR NOVEL

SECOND SKIN

POCKET BOOKS

New York   London   Toronto   Sydney   Tokyo   Singapore

Thanks are due to the following authors, publishers and agents for permission to use the material included.

"Constant Craving" by k. d. lang and Ben Mink, published © 1992 Polygram International Publishing, Inc., Bumstead Productions U.S., Inc., and Zavion Ent. Inc. Used by Permission. All Rights Reserved.

The haiku of Taniguchi Buson from *An Introduction to Haiku* by Harold G. Henderson. Copyright © 1958 by Harold G. Henderson. Used by permission of Doubleday, a division of Bantam Doubleday Dell Publishing Group, Inc.

The two haîku—the second is the "song" Honniko sings at the end of the novel—by Izumi Shikibu from *The Ink Dark Moon* by Jane Hirshfield and Mariko Aratani. Copyright © 1990 by Jane Hirshfield and Mariko Aratani. Reprinted by permission of Random House, Inc.

In addition, the author would like to acknowledge two books that were of particular help in formulating Michael Leonforte's neo-Nietzschean philosophy:

Beyond Good and Evil by Friedrich Nietzsche, translated by Marianne Cowan.

The Birth of Tragedy and the Genealogy of Morals by Friedrich Nietzsche, translated by Francis Golffing.

This book is a work of fiction. Names, characters, places and incidents are products of the author's imagination or are used fictitiously. Any resemblance to actual events or locales or persons, living or dead, is entirely coincidental.

POCKET BOOKS, a division of Simon & Schuster Inc.
1230 Avenue of the Americas, New York, NY 10020

ISBN: 0-671-86811-X

First Pocket Books paperback printing March 1996

10 9 8 7 6 5 4 3 2 1

POCKET and colophon are registered trademarks of Simon & Schuster Inc.

Cover design and typography by James Wang
Cover illustration by Don Brautigam

Printed in the U.S.A.

Grateful acknowledgment is made to:

Frank Panico
Frank Capone, for insight and research into Ozone
Park and East New York
Virgil England, for the design of Mick's push dagger
Jim Schmidt, for his scholarly treatise on Damascus steel

Maybe a great magnet pulls
All souls towards the truth
Or maybe it is life itself
That feeds wisdom
To its youth

—"Constant Craving"
k. d. lang/Ben Mink

Until the day of his
death, no man can be sure
of his courage.

—Jean Anouilh

Dead Can Dance

Time is a storm
in which we are all lost.

—William Carlos Williams

Tokyo

"What is it that you've always wanted?"

Mick Leonforte stared across the table at the tall, elegant woman who sat unmoving as she slowly smoked a thin, black cigar. Giai Kurtz was Vietnamese, a daughter of one of Saigon's elite families. She was married, of course, but that was part of the kick. Alone and unattached, she would not have seemed nearly as desirable. She was also the kind of woman Mick had wanted to be with since he had come to Asia more than twenty years ago. Even before that, if he were to be perfectly honest with himself.

Staring at the jewel-shaped face with its high cheekbones, unblemished skin the lush color of teak, the heavy cascade of blue-black hair, he understood that this exquisite creature—or someone very much like her—had inhabited his dreams before he had ever known the first thing about Asia. It was no wonder that having come in-country for the war, he had never returned home. Vietnam *was* his home.

"Tell me," he said with the hint of a smile at the corners of his mouth. "Tell me and it's yours."

The woman smoked her cigar, letting the gray-brown smoke drift languidly from her partly opened lips, and if one was not as well versed in the peoples of Southeast Asia as Mick was, one could easily miss the metallic glitter of fear far back in her depthless eyes.

"You know what I want," she said at last.

"Anything," Mick said. "Anything but that."

They were in the rearmost booth of Pull Marine, a chic French restaurant that Mick had bankrolled in the posh Roppongi district. It was one of many burgeoning businesses throughout Asia—legitimate and otherwise—that he controlled. Mick was involved in numerous such ventures that he had kept secret from his late, unlamented partner, Rock.

"I want *you*."

No, he thought, *that is what I want. At least what I want you to feel.*

"You have me," he said, spreading his hands wide. "See?"

In the opposite corner from where Mick and Giai sat, a rail-thin Vietnamese woman warbled the songs of Jacques Brel, filled with melancholy and the black sails of death. She expressed Brel's profound sadness like the wounds of war; the room was burnished as much by her serpentine voice as it was by the low, artful lighting.

"You know what I mean. I want us to be together always."

"But I won't be here," he said with deliberate emphasis on each word, "always."

The chanteuse was accompanied by a guitarist and a synth player who made his instrument sound, at times, like a cathedral organ. This churchlike overtone caused Mick to remember the many stories of Joan of Arc his father had told him. Apocryphal or not, they stayed with the young Mick, perhaps because they were so much a part of his father's worldview; saints as warriors for righteous causes had been a major theme in Johnny Leonforte's subconscious.

"Then I will go with you wherever you go." She sucked on her cigar. "That's what I want."

Mick stared into her dark eyes for a long time, calculating. "All right," he said at length, as she smiled, smoke escaping from between her ripe lips.

The restaurant was a piece of Saigon reproduced whole-cloth in Tokyo, a reflection of Saigon's deliberate air of change and newfound prosperity. Gold-leaf walls gleamed and sparked, a black marble floor reflected the midnight-blue domed ceiling. The candles on the tables gave off the faint incense of a temple's interior. Bathed in the cool bluish wash of spotlights, a highly stylized mask fashioned out of crimson lacquer from a traditional Vietnamese design dominated one wall.

Smartly dressed waiters were overseen by Honniko, a spectacular bare-shouldered blonde in a golden velvet bustier and form-fitting raw-silk skirt that came down to just above her ankles. She spoke perfect French and Japanese. She also spoke Vietnamese, and her air of authority was absolute. Normally, at this time of night, one would have been impressed by her genuine warmth in greeting patrons and adeptly steering them to their candlelit tables, but tonight she stood immobile behind her bronze podium, gazing slit-eyed at the chanteuse. In truth, she had nothing else to do, since the couple in the far corner were her only customers. Behind her, the front door to the second floor restaurant was locked, its lace curtains pulled tautly over the narrow cut-glass panes. Through the glass bubble of the terrace, the brilliant Roppongi night glittered like a shower of diadems.

A waiter, his face as cool and detached as a doctor's, brought plates of fish *en croûte* and whole unshelled tiger prawns in a delicate garlic and cream sauce.

Without a word, Mick reached for his fork while Giai continued to draw on her cigar. "I wonder if you mean it," she said.

He began to eat with the relish of a man too long deprived of decent food. Giai watched him while two long fingernails lacquered the same color as the walls flicked against each other. *Click-click. Click-click.* Like beetles doing battle with a window screen.

"Eat. Aren't you hungry?" Mick asked, though from his tone he seemed indifferent as to whether or not she would answer. "Personally, I'm starving."

"Yes," she said at last. "I'm well aware of your appetites." She regarded him with the scrutiny of an angel or a devil. She saw a man with a rugged, charismatic face fronted by a prominent Roman nose and odd gray and orange eyes that gave him a fierce and feral aspect. His salt-and-pepper hair was long and he wore a neatly cropped beard. It was a face born to give orders, the face of a man who harbored radical philosophies and dark secrets in equal number, whose personal worldview was iconoclastic and unshakable.

"Where is it?" she asked in a voice that with considerable effort managed to remain calm. "Show it to me."

Of course he knew what she meant. "How do you know I have it with me?" He popped the head of a prawn between his lips and crunched down on it.

"I know you." She made to light another cigar, but he put his hand over hers, took it away. Momentarily startled, her eyes locked with his and something akin to a shudder could just be discerned in her shoulders. She nodded briefly, took up her fork, and obediently began to eat. But there was no gusto in her movements, merely a mechanical tempo. Mick thought it a shame she was so careful; he could not see the motion of her even, white teeth.

He found he very much needed to see those teeth, and he brought out from beneath the table the push dagger, holding it obliquely in the air so that the candlelight sent long glistening flashes along the black length of its Damascus-steel blade.

Giai was transfixed, her hand pausing in midair, flaky strata of fish sliding between the slick tines of her fork. Her nostrils flared like an animal scenting the fresh spoor of its prey.

"Is that it?" But of course she knew that it was. It was an odd-looking weapon, a bronze shield sculpted into the shape of a lotus leaf covering the top of his fist, a vertical bar attached to its underside from which the grip was formed, and two narrow, wicked blades seeming to bloom from the middle fingers of his fist.

"Wiped carefully clean." He waggled the blades before her gaze. "Dipped in a bottle of Château Talbot '70, his favorite wine and vintage. Fitting, don't you think?"

She shivered, her shoulders convulsing once and then again, but her face showed no distaste. On the contrary, her eyes were shining and her lips were still apart.

"Yes," she said softly, though what question she was answering was a mystery. "We drank a bottle last night. He toasted our fifth anniversary by licking the first sip out of my navel. I lay on the carpet willing myself not to vomit. I wound my fingers through his hair, in passion, he thought. And all the while I was thinking . . ."

Her gaze left the push dagger to settle on Mick with the kind of shocking intimacy that comes only during sex. "I was thinking it was his heart I had squeezed between my hands."

"He was a bastard, no doubt about it," Mick agreed. "He tried to fuck me over in the TransRim CyberNet deal. He thought he'd been clever enough to hide behind a phalanx of front men and lawyers, but all of them owe me or are terrified of me and they gave him up, willingly I might add, almost gleeful in their relief." He shrugged. "But that's the way Saigon is: influence, contacts, money—they're all you need there, but they're the most difficult to obtain." He turned his fist over, slammed the points of the double blades into the tabletop. Neither the chanteuse nor the maître d' missed a beat. "You've got to spill blood—more than a little, eh, Giai?—to get what you want. That's Asia. Life is cheaper than a kilo of rice, isn't that what you drank in with your mother's milk?"

Giai's eyes clung to the quivering push dagger as if it were a puff adder about to strike. It was impossible to tell from her face whether she despised or coveted its absolute power. Her cheeks were flushed and a thin sheen of perspiration was on her upper lip.

"You killed him yourself, didn't you?"

"No, Giai, *you* killed him."

"I? I did nothing."

He regarded her for some time. "Astonishing. I think you really believe that. But here's the truth. You sit on the sidelines, open your legs, and let your sex give the orders, pretending it has a mind of its own, as if you are not accountable for those decisions of life—and of death."

"I cannot stand the sight of death," she said in a reedy whisper. Her eyes slipped out of focus, went to that spot over his left shoulder, and now he knew what she saw there: the past. "Ever since I found my mother on the floor of her room . . . The blood, the blood . . ." She took a quick sucking breath. "All of her insides slithering over the floor like a nest of serpents." Refocusing in a flash, she sent him an accusatory stare. "You know this—you *know*. And yet you judge me by your own standards."

He leaned forward a little, his gray and orange eyes glittering. "That's all I know how to do, Giai. It's nothing personal." He skewered a prawn on his fork. "Eat your food. It's getting cold."

Giai ate with a degree of eagerness now. Once or twice, he had the pleasure of seeing her tiny teeth as they flashed like lights behind her lips. In a way, he was sorry her husband was dead. Part of the pleasure he had in taking her was the knowledge that she belonged to someone else. He remembered once at an intimate dinner party, he had had her in the pantry, pushed up her skirt, hands pressing her jiggling breasts, impaling her again and again, listening to her mounting gasps while her smug husband, oblivious, drank his wine and made deals on the other side of the wall. There was a certain kick to cuckolding a man who had tried to fuck him over, and now that was gone. Pity. But, then again, Mick mused, it was time to move on. The intervention of Nicholas Linnear in Floating City had precipitated that.

Floating City had been a fortress, a city-state hidden in the northern highlands of Vietnam from which Mick and Rock had directed an unprecedented worldwide network of international arms trading and drug distribution. Floating City was just a memory now, nuked out of existence because of Linnear. That was okay with Mick; he'd known for some months it was time to move on; he'd just needed a kick in the ass to get him going—and Nicholas Linnear had provided that. Linnear had penetrated Floating City and had killed Rock. He might have worked his particular brand of magic on Mick as well had it not been for the nuclear explosion of the handheld experimental weapon known as Torch.

Mick had come face-to-face with Nicholas at last in Floating City, and it had come as a profound shock to him—like meeting the legendary Colonel Linnear, Nicholas's father. Like meeting your own other half, your—what did the Germans call it?—doppelgänger.

There was a unique bond between the Colonel and Mick's father, Johnny Leonforte—and thus a connection between the sons. But Nicholas did not know that yet. Mick had barely believed it when he had discovered it and had worked diligently—and fruitlessly—for months to disprove it. Accepting it had altered his life forever, just as it would change

Nicholas's someday in the not too distant future. But Mick, forever aware of playing all the angles, was determined that Nicholas should learn this particular bit of knowledge at the time and place of his own choosing.

Mick had spent years researching the life and personality of Colonel Linnear's son, until he had felt more intimate with him than any lover he had taken to bed. But when they had come face-to-face in Floating City, Mick's fantasy had burst like a soap bubble. The real Nicholas Linnear was someone more than Mick had ever imagined. Looking deep into Nicholas Linnear's clear, clear brown eyes, he had felt the stirring of the short hairs at the back of his neck. In that moment when investigation and reality had come together, he knew this man's fate was inextricably entwined with his.

In Nicholas Linnear, Mick Leonforte had recognized the ultimate adversary he had been searching for all his restless life. That was why he had provided the necessary means for Nicholas to escape the bamboo prison cage into which Rock had thrown him. In the endgame of the killing ground he knew he would need every advantage he could bring into play to counteract Nicholas's Tau-tau, the secret knowledge of ancient psycho-necromancers. Mick had seen for himself the power of Tau-tau when Nicholas had overcome his guards and had killed Rock, a huge beast of a man who had outthought and outfought every dangerous opium warlord in the uplands Golden Triangle of Burma's Shan States.

He could still remember barreling out of Floating City in a truck on which Nicholas had hitched a ride. (Had Nicholas's powers allowed him to know that Mick had been driving that truck?) He could still see clearly Rock's wounded body in the rearview mirror as he aimed Torch at Nicholas, could still feel the cold breath of Tau-tau as Nicholas redirected the path of the missile upward with the power of his mind.

Soon after, Nicholas had leapt from the back of the truck, plunging hundreds of feet into the roiling waters of the cataract far below. He did not know, of course, that Mick had had the truck lead-lined or that they were already out of the four-square-city-block radius of Torch's ground zero detonation zone. Floating City had been incinerated, but Mick had not died and neither, he believed, had Nicholas Linnear. Mick had had a hand in Nicholas's escape from Rock's cage.

Nicholas had had a hand in keeping Mick from being incinerated by Rock's final attack.

They had an appointment in the future, a day of reckoning, a moment toward which, Mick now knew, he had been moving all his adult life. That was why he had come to Tokyo, and why, if he were brutally honest with himself, he was with Giai Kurtz now.

"Excuse me," he said, pushing himself out of the banquette. On his way back to the men's room, he turned to glance at Giai, who was finishing the tiger prawns, using her long, delicate fingers like chopsticks. He paused, watching her insert one long nail between head and torso to crack a prawn open. Then he went down a short corridor and into the men's room. He urinated, checked all the stalls even though he knew no one was there. Then he pulled out his cellular phone and made a call.

"Time to go," he said, when he returned a moment later.

"Don't you want dessert?" Giai asked, staring up at him with those huge eyes that had captivated him nearly fifteen months ago at the embassy fete in Saigon. Such bores, those political parties, unless you knew the right people, and Mick knew them all. Having asked the Japanese trade legate about her, he had set about separating her from the pack with the obsessive single-mindedness of an Australian Border collie. Her husband, a ruddy-faced, blond-haired Aryan businessman from Köln, arrogant and tormented, who fancied he knew all about Southeast Asia, was interested only in making deals. Mick had had the impression that if he had taken Giai there and then on the Persian carpet, Rodney Kurtz would not have blinked an eye. As it was, they did it in the powder room with a crystal bowl of heart-shaped soaps crashing to the marble floor as she came.

"Later," he said. "Not now."

He held out one hand and she took it, rising. As they crossed the floor, he waved to Honniko, the blonde in the gold bustier. The chanteuse had finished her set, otherwise he would have saluted her as well.

"Where are we going?"

"Home," he said. "To Hoan Kiem."

She pulled up, looking at him quizzically. "*My* villa? I haven't been there all day."

He knew what she meant. "Don't worry," he said, shepherding her along, "he's not there anymore." He smiled. "And whatever blood was spilled has been cleaned up."

"Where is he, exactly?"

"Nowhere you want to know about," he said as they swung out the door into the riotous Roppongi night. Immediately, they were hip deep in tourists and tripped-out teenagers. Just looking at them could give you a nosebleed, Mick thought. Tattooed heads, branded hands, and metal impedimenta pierced through noses, eyelids, tongues, lips, and nipples were the stuff of nightmares. The breakdown of society was everywhere evident. The hardworking races endure leisure only with great difficulty, Friedrich Nietzsche had said. Which was why, Mick supposed, he admired the Japanese. But look at them now! Lolling around, disfigured, grotesque as sideshow freaks.

The rain-washed street seethed with the peculiar hormonal vibrancy of youth. Crowds of people thronged the sidewalks, pushing off into the traffic-clogged streets. A permanent pall of diesel fumes hung in the air, giving the neon colors a lurid hue. In windows were displayed the cream of this year's crop of designer clothes, some of which, Mick judged, were not meant for the human form.

They picked up a cruising taxi on Roppongi-dōri, took it to Giai's villa in the Asakusa temple district. Hoan Kiem—Returned Sword—was a beautifully conical concrete and wood structure, more spacious than most Tokyo residences. Its cool, crisp interior was filled with dark-stained rattan in the grand Saigon manner, giving rise to the speculation that both Kurtzes were ultimately more at home there than in Tokyo. The rooms were illuminated at night by brass lamps and during the day by bars of sunlight filtering in through the wide jalousied windows. Through them, one had a spectacular view across the river to the futuristic Flamme d'Or, the Phillippe Starke–designed building of black glass, a kind of tetrahedron on acid, surmounted by a vaguely flamelike shape derisively christened by Tokyoites "the Golden Turd."

Giai hesitated as she unlocked the door and Mick swung it open.

"I told you he isn't here," Mick said, stepping past her

and, grasping her hand, pulling her over the threshold. "Here, I'll show you where it happened."

"No!" she cried, and almost succeeded in pulling her hand from his fierce grip.

He stood in the center of what had been, until just after midnight this morning, Rodney Kurtz's domain, smiling slyly at Giai. He raised his arms in an expansive gesture. "This is what you wanted, isn't it?"

Giai glared at him darkly. "Bastard. Yes."

He went to the mirrored bar, took down a pair of cut-glass snifters. "It isn't me who's the bastard, darling." He poured generous measures of Napoleon brandy, turned around, and handed her one. "It was your husband, Rodney. Remember?" He clinked his glass against hers, took a sip, watching her all the while. He liked seeing her this way: nervous and a bit unsure. But then he liked to engender those emotions in everyone he met.

"The nights I would call you up, after he beat me, raped me, spit on me."

"And you came back for more."

"He always apologized. He was so repentant, like a little child."

Mick hid his disgust behind the mask he had perfected, thinking of what was to come.

"You took it all."

"Not all," she said defiantly. Now she downed the brandy in two hard swallows. Her eyes watered. "Not *now*. I made my stand. He's dead and I'm glad of it."

"So you did." Mick nodded. "Long life and health to both of us," he said, then took more brandy into his mouth and savored it. One thing you had to say for old Rodney, he thought, he did know how to live.

"And so," he said, putting down his empty snifter and rubbing his palms together, "to bed."

Mick took her in his arms, feeling her melt against him. He was a man who believed himself to be, in the words of Nietzsche, predestined for victory and seduction. Like Nietzsche, his wartime idol, he understood the profound connection between the two. He was a man bent on controlling and outwitting himself. Like two of Nietzsche's own idols, Alcibiades and Napoleon, he had the craftsmanship and subtlety for war. He was, in sum, continually challenging life.

She tasted like burnt sugar and he crushed her to him. He stripped her of her clothes and inhaled her musk. As usual, she wore no underwear. Her breasts reared into his hands and she moaned deep in her throat. He lifted her by her buttocks and her legs wrapped around him. Neither of them could wait for the bed. Her fingers, which had so skillfully cracked the prawn's translucent shell, now deftly unbuckled his belt, pushed down his trousers. She brought him hotly against her, her eyes flying open with the sensation, then closing slowly, languorously, as they began their rhythm.

Quidquid luce fruit, tenebris agit, Mick thought between mouthfuls of dusky flesh. Whatever is started in the light continues in the dark. It was one of Nietzsche's favorite sayings, and his as well. How true it had proved itself in his life!

He pushed her roughly against the wall—just *here*—where he had made the first thrust with the push dagger, where the arrogance on Kurtz's face had been supplanted by disbelief and, then, fear. Oh, the ecstasy of it! He, the true Nietzschean superman, bringing down the Aryan prey.

He was grunting now, not with the effort but with the images flooding his mind. Giai licked his ear and hunched frantically against him. While his body worked, his mind sang! Of course Kurtz was tormented, of course he beat his wife regularly. There are countless dark bodies that must be *inferred* to lie near the sun; we shall never be able to see them, Nietzsche had written. Kurtz was one of them. Obviously, in marrying Giai he had crossed the line. Dissolution, the base shuttling and rearranging of the races, was intolerable to the proud and pure Aryan in him. Yet he would not leave her. So he beat her, punishing her for the sin he dare not admit to himself he had committed.

Giai was soon to reach her pinnacle. She groaned, her eyes rolling, her belly rippling, the muscles of her thighs and buttocks clenching furiously. And, like a house plucked up by a tornado, he was brought along with her. She stroked the nape of his neck, his damp hair, crooning wordlessly like a child in delirium.

It was Mick's firm and abiding belief that morality was merely timidity tricked out in a philosophical overcoat. Even if he had not read this in *Beyond Good and Evil*, his own experiences in the war in Vietnam would have taught him the same thing. As it was, they merely made Nietzsche's words resonate in his mind all the louder. *And like all men of prey*, he thought, *I am misunderstood*. What was morality but a recipe against passion, an attempt to castrate the dangerousness in which man lives with himself?

"Yes," Giai breathed. "Oh, yes!"

He held her, light as a feather, as she shivered and moaned, trembled and clung in great gasping sighs, then started all over again as he put his head down, his white teeth sinking into the tender flesh of her shoulder as he skewered her—once, twice, three times—gushing as he thought of life—Kurtz's life—bleeding away in a mass of stinking, steaming innards.

He opened his eyes. Giai was staring at him.

"I'm free, aren't I?"

He could feel her hot fluids—and his, too, perhaps—sticky on his thighs.

"Had enough?"

"No," she cried. "No, no, no!"

Of course not. It was part of their game.

Before his erection could subside he rubbed cocaine into the reddened skin. He felt the familiar tingling, then the curious numbness through which only sexual desire could burn like a beacon in dense fog. Then he entered her again, walking her across the room, her heels bouncing against the tops of his buttocks.

Giai, always wild with him, was particularly frenzied. In fact, her freedom, as she called it, had made her almost insatiable, and for once Mick thanked the lucky star under which he had been born for the cocaine-induced numbness. Otherwise, even he would not have been able to last.

He had her on Kurtz's dining room table, a polished teak affair from Thailand, on Kurtz's desk, the cordless phone clattering to the floor, on Kurtz's prize Isfahan rug, in Kurtz's bed, and finally in Kurtz's shower. And after Giai thought it was over, he did what he had wanted to do all along: he took her from behind.

She wanted to sleep after all that exertion, but he was still wired. The cocaine, he told her, urging her to dress quickly while he struck a match and lighted his cigar. So instead of crawling between Kurtz's silk sheets, they returned to the rainy, neon-lighted Tokyo night.

The taxi he had called was waiting for them. It was after midnight and they made the trip to the warehouse district of Shibaura in short order. They emerged into Kaigan-dōri, and Mick told the taxi to pull over. He paid the fare and they got out, heading for Mūdra, one of the many hip dance clubs that had bloomed here like weeds in the early nineties.

They had not walked more than a block when a black Mercedes rounded a corner behind them, heading along Kaigan-dōri. Mick glanced over his shoulder and saw it coming up behind them, swerving dangerously up onto the sidewalk, sideswiping a couple of moonfaced bohemians, chicly garbed in grunge, purple-black hair in exaggerated Woody Woodpecker top knots, their lips glossed in black.

"What is it?" Giai asked.

Up ahead, two bikers in luminous trench coats and multiple nose rings sat astride luridly painted Suzukis, swigging beer and trading lewd stories of mutilated flesh. Incensed, Mick walked a couple of paces on, shouting at the drunken teenagers, while Giai stood waiting. He turned. "Morons," he said, but he was looking straight at the oncoming Mercedes, which, having cleared the cars ahead of it, now put on a last furious burst of speed.

Mick shouted something incoherent and Giai turned, her eyes opened wide, just as the front fender of the Mercedes plowed into her. Instantly, she was slammed backward with such force that when she landed her back broke. But by then she was drowning in her own blood.

The Mercedes had already taken off as people on line for the clubs came out of their shock and started to scream. There was a mad jostling, an almost carnivorous mass convulsing through which Mick slithered, heading up Kaigandōri, avoiding the jammed sidewalk, after the Mercedes. The familiar high-low police Klaxon could be heard, still some distance away but closing fast on the scene of panic behind him.

He saw the Mercedes swerve left at the last possible instant, into a narrow alley, and he followed, his legs churning easily, his heart racing nicely, his lungs pumping in exhilaration. He turned the corner, saw the black Mercedes had come to a stop, rocking on its heavy-duty shock absorbers. The alley was deserted; even its usual denizens had headed toward the site of the screams.

One of the black Mercedes's rear doors flew open and he accelerated toward it, his heart singing. What was it Nietzsche had said? Ultimately one loves one's desires, not the desired object.

Then he was there, slinging his body into the backseat, hearing the gears crash, the tires squeal, the car accelerating down the alley as he leaned over, slamming the door shut, and he said to the driver, "Jōchi, well done!"

Book 1

Between Dog
and Wolf

The best way to keep one's word
is not to give it.

—Napoleon

1
Tokyo/New York

Nicholas Linnear looked out at Tokyo, its pink-and-acid-green neon signs creating an aurora that blocked the night. Far below, a soft parade of black umbrellas bobbed and weaved, filling the sidewalks of Shinjuku as the steady rain filled the gutters of the wide, traffic-clogged streets.

It was a familiar view from his corner office on the fifty-second floor of the Shinjuku Suiryu Building. But almost everything now seemed different.

It had been fifteen months since he had been in Tokyo, fifteen months since he had taken on *giri*, the debt he had promised his late father, Col. Denis Linnear, he would honor. Fifteen months since he had been contacted by a representative of Mikio Okami, his father's closest friend and, as it turned out, the Kaisho, the *oyabun* of *oyabun* of all the clans of the Yakuza, the powerful Japanese underworld.

Okami had been in hiding in Venice, under a death threat from his closest allies within his inner circle of advisers. He had needed Nicholas's help, so he had said, to protect him. Nicholas had his own very private reasons for hating the Yakuza and could have turned his back on Okami and his obligation to his late father. But that was not his way. Honor meant everything to him, but the irony of helping keep alive the living embodiment of the Yakuza was not lost on him.

19

On the contrary, in pure Japanese style, it added to the poignancy of his mission.

Eventually, he had found and dispatched the would-be assassin, a particularly frightening Vietnamese named Do Duc Fujiro, along with the *oyabun* who had hired him. Now, with Tetsuo Akinaga, the only *oyabun* of the inner circle still alive, awaiting trial on charges of extortion and conspiracy to commit murder, Okami had returned to Tokyo, and Nicholas with him to face an entirely new threat.

Fifteen months and to Nicholas it seemed as if Tokyo had changed beyond recognition.

These changes revolved around the great Japanese depression that had begun in 1991 and showed little sign of lifting. Today, there were more homeless in the streets than ever before, every company's profits were either sharply off or in negative figures. Layoffs—a hitherto unknown practice—had begun in earnest, and those remaining in jobs had not seen a pay raise in four years. On the way to Shinjuku that evening, Nicholas had seen outside food shops long lines made up of housewives who insisted on buying Japanese rice instead of the imported American variety.

The trade war with America was intensifying almost every day. In addition, there was an increasingly militant and belligerent North Korean regime to consider. Japan's pachinko parlors, traditionally run by native Japanese, were now in the hands of Koreans, many of whom had ties to North Korea, and it was becoming an increasing source of embarrassment to the Japanese government to have these profits going directly to the dictatorial and paranoid regime that ruled the north.

For the first time since the advent of the great economic miracle in the early 1950s, Japan seemed on the brink of losing both momentum and purpose. People were dispirited and fed up, and the media, trained at birth to emphasize bad news while minimizing the good, could see only a dark, downward spiral.

Nicholas felt a hand softly stroking his back, and he saw Koei's face reflected in the rain-streaked window. With her huge, liquid eyes, small mouth, and angular cheekbones, it was far from a classically beautiful face, but he loved it all the more for that. She was the daughter of a Yakuza *oya-*

bun. They had met in 1971 and had fallen madly, magically in love. And out of that mad love, Nicholas had killed the man who he thought had raped and tormented Koei, only to discover that the man was innocent. The miscreant was her father. Shame had caused her to lie, and this had forced Nicholas to walk away. He had not seen her until last year, when Okami had arranged for them to meet again so Nicholas could heal the rage he felt toward her and all Yakuza.

Over the years, she had turned her back on the world of the Yakuza, losing herself in the syncretic Shugendo Shinto sect in the mystical hills of Yoshino, where she might have remained but for a summons from her father. He needed to broker an alliance, and to seal it Koei was obliged to marry a man she had not met. After spending six months with the man she wanted out, but he was unwilling to let her go. In desperation, she turned to Mikio Okami, the Kaisho, the one man who had more power than this man and would be willing to stand up to him. Okami had spirited her away, sending her into the hinterlands of Vietnam where this man could not find her, though he tried hard enough. The man she had been with, whom she had been duty-bound to marry and had come to despise and fear, was Mick Leonforte.

"Nangi-san isn't here yet," she said, "and the dinner is scheduled to begin in ten minutes." Tanzan Nangi was the president of Sato International, the high-tech *keiretsu*—the Japanese-American conglomerate Nicholas owned with Tanzan Nangi—that had been created from the merger of Sato Petrochemicals with Tomkin Industries, the company Nicholas owned and ran. "I hope this won't be too much for him." Six months ago he'd had a minor heart attack and, since then, had become somewhat more reclusive.

"It had better not," Nicholas said, checking his tie in the mirror. "The Japanese launch of the TransRim CyberNet has been his dream ever since my people came up with the technology."

Koei turned him around, worked on his tie herself. "The VIPs are arriving and Tōrin is getting nervous. He's wondering why you're not already down at Indigo to greet them."

"I've still got to make a last check at research and development on the fortieth floor." Nicholas kissed her lightly.

"The proprietary CyberNet data are being transferred to the central computer."

The CyberNet, a multimedia highway for trading and instantaneous communication throughout Southeast Asia, had the potential to lift Sato International out of its recessionary spiral and return it to profitability. But if anything went wrong with the CyberNet—if it crashed and burned—Sato International was sure to follow it down. The unique combination of Nangi's calculating mind and Nicholas's brilliant leaps of intuitive ingenuity had been the main reason for Sato's success. But these days Sato, like all Japanese *keiretsu,* had been undergoing a painful restructuring.

Keiretsu—holdovers from the prewar family-run *zaibatsu*—were groups of interlinked industrial companies composed around a central bank. In boom times this gave each *keiretsu* the major advantage of being able to lend itself money for expansion and research and development at highly competitive rates. But during a recession—as now—when banks ran into the twin difficulties of deflated values on their real estate portfolios and rising yen rates, they became a major liability to the *keiretsu.* Lately, it had been up to Nicholas's American arm to provide the R&D for new Sato products like the supersecret CyberNet technology. Despite this revolutionary breakthrough he was racked by guilt. If he had not been with Mikio Okami these past fifteen months, he might have helped his company avoid the worst ravages of the deep recession. Instead, he had insisted that Sato International be at the forefront of fiber-optic telecommunications, and to that end, the vast majority of the *keiretsu*'s capital reserves had gone into expansion into not only Southeast Asia and China, but also South America. This was the smart long-term bet of the visionary, but it had created a short-term crunch that the recession had exacerbated almost beyond Sato's tolerance. Now the company was forced to rise or fall on the success of the CyberNet, and Nicholas knew it was his doing.

"Nicholas."

He smiled and, taking her in his arms, kissed her harder this time. "Don't worry. I'll see to it," he said.

She stood there, in her dark, sequined dress, looking impossibly lovely. "I know you," she said. "Such a man of action. Wining and dining corporate guests cannot be your favorite thing. But consider the source and honor your promise. It was Nangi-san who requested you attend this dinner. You don't need me to remind you of its importance. It will officially launch the TransRim CyberNet in Japan while representatives from America, Russia, Vietnam, Thailand, Singapore, and China look on. The Net is so important to Nangi-san—and to Sato International as a whole."

She was right, of course, to remind him to return to this time and place. Nangi was far more than Nicholas's business partner. He was also his mentor. The two had shared so many life-or-death situations that their fates were now inextricably entwined.

Koei picked up a phone, spoke briefly into it. When she turned to Nicholas, she was frowning. "Nangi-san still hasn't arrived. It isn't like him; he's never late." She touched his arm. "And, Nicholas, you've told me how tired and drawn he's looked of late."

He nodded. "I'll get in touch with him, then come right down. All right?"

"All right." She left him alone in the semidarkness of his office.

He turned to his desk, asked the voice-activated autodialer to get Nangi's home phone. It rang ten times before he told it to hang up. No doubt, Nangi was on his way.

He dug in the pocket of his tuxedo, drew out a small matte-black rectangle slightly smaller than a cellular telephone. He thumbed a tab and it flipped open to reveal a small screen, which soon burned luminescent green. This was Kami, a prototype of the communicator that would soon be on-line for the CyberNet. The Kami had been keeping the two men in touch during the last part of Nicholas's absence from Sato International's boardrooms. He was about to use the touch screen to dial Tanzan Nangi's personal number when the unit began to vibrate. He had it set to silent running and this meant a call was coming in. He pressed the touch screen.

"Linnear-san." Nangi's face appeared on the flat liquid-crystal-display screen, incredibly clear via the digital video pathway. This vid-byte bandwidth communication was the technological breakthrough that made the CyberNet so valuable—and vulnerable to corporate espionage.

The opening of the TransRim CyberNet in Southeast Asia and Russia had generated an almost feverish scrutiny from Sato International's rivals. In an age when the speed of information was everything, whoever controlled so-called cyberspace on the Pacific Rim would reap billions of dollars of benefits for the foreseeable future.

"Nangi-san, where are you? The TransRim launch dinner is about to begin."

"I am aware of the time," Nangi interrupted in uncharacteristic fashion. He passed a hand across his face. Where was he? There was not enough background showing on the screen for Nicholas to tell. He only knew he wasn't home. "But I have had something of a dizzy spell—"

"Are you all right?" A stab of fear went through Nicholas. "Have you called the doctor?"

"There's no need, I assure you," Nangi said hastily as his eyes flicked briefly to one side. Was someone in the room with him? "I am being well taken care of."

"But, Nangi-san, where are you? The guests are waiting."

"Yes, yes, I understand your concern," Nangi said as a small cup of tea was placed in front of him by someone unseen. "But I am not indispensable. The party can go on without me."

Why was he keeping his whereabouts secret? Nicholas wondered. "Perhaps we should postpone the opening of the Net."

"Nonsense. It must be opened tonight." For a moment, some of Nangi's old spark and fire returned. "We have far too much riding on its success. Postponement will only send rumors through the industry that would surely undermine confidence. No, no. I trust you and Tōrin to do the honors. Whatever help you need, he'll provide. As my new right-hand man, he can be of extraordinary use to you."

Nangi was about to disconnect from the CyberNet when Nicholas said, "Nangi-san, at least hear me out." He'd gotten an idea, but would Nangi go for it? "Perhaps there is a way to use your absence to work for us."

Ill or not, this got Nangi's attention. He lifted a hand. "Go on, please."

"Let's make the first use of CyberNet in Japan a link from the dinner to you."

"No."

Nicholas was puzzled. "But it's perfect, Nangi-san. You can stay where you are, and everyone can see you blown up on the special screen that's been erected downstairs."

"I said no and that's final," Nangi snapped, and without another word, he disconnected from the Net.

Nicholas, whose loyalty to Sato was now joined with his loyalty to Mikio Okami, did not know whether he felt more puzzled or concerned. He could not imagine Nangi acting in such a cold and irrational manner. What was happening to his friend? These abruptly ended communications were fast becoming the rule rather than the exception. He knew Nangi was under extreme pressure in putting the CyberNet on-line, and at seventy-six he was no longer young. But Nicholas suspected these conversations could not merely be explained away by Nangi's age. Had the heart attack somehow changed his personality? Nicholas resolved to see him in person when tonight's dog and pony show was over.

As he checked his tuxedo, he took one last moment to evaluate his recent decision to join Mikio Okami, the Kaisho.

The Yakuza's role in Japan was significant. Unlike in America, where the underworld was outcast from society, the Yakuza were, in a very real sense, a part of it. Even though they might still see themselves as outcasts, they were an unspoken part of what was known as the Iron Triangle that, since 1947, had ruled Japan: bureaucracy, business, and politicians. The Ministry of International Trade and Industry, MITI, had emerged as the most powerful of the postwar bureaucratic entities. It was MITI that dictated economic policy and allowed the *keiretsu,* the interlocked trading groups run by the top industrial families, tax breaks and incentives to move into fields that MITI determined would be best for Japan as a whole. It was MITI, for instance, that decided in the 1960s to encourage the trading companies to switch from the manufacture of heavy goods such as steel to computers and semiconductors. In this way MITI orchestrated Japan's economic miracle and, simultaneously, made billionaires of the industrialists. MITI perpetuated its absolute control over business by sending its ex-ministers out to work at the very *keiretsu* for which it created policy.

But MITI had help. The Liberal Democratic Party, which had dominated Japan's political scene from the forties through to its ouster in 1993, worked hand in hand with the ministry to keep Japan, Inc. on an even keel. This was relatively easy, since the Japanese people have been used to leaders taking care of them. Before the war, they had looked to the emperor for this. Afterward, it was a series of prime ministers from the LDP.

As for the Yakuza, they were the intermediaries who greased the wheels. For the proper remuneration, they ensured that the LDP remained in power by brokering each prime minister's constituency. For the proper remuneration, they saw to it that the "political contributions" the *keiretsu* made influenced the politicians to enact legislation favorable to business. And so it went for decades, an endless wheel of staggeringly swift progress and deeply entrenched corruption.

Until the great recession of 1991 brought everything Japan, Inc. had worked toward to a screeching halt.

Nicholas was about to go down to R&D when his Kami buzzed him. This time, he saw Mikio Okami's face in the screen. Even with the fine lines at the corners of his eyes, accentuated now by the exhaustion evident on his face, he looked at least ten years younger than his ninety years.

"Nicholas," he said without the usual ritual of formality, "I have momentous news." Without anybody else knowing about it, Nicholas had given him a prototype Kami so the two could keep in touch at all hours. CyberNet Communications were far more secure than most cellular phone conversations. "Tomorrow morning the prime minister will announce his resignation."

Nicholas, feeling suddenly deflated, sat down on the edge of his burlwood desk. "That makes six in just over three years."

Okami nodded. "Yes. As I predicted, without a strong LDP, the coalition of lesser parties cannot hold the center. There are too many different and mutually exclusive agendas for a true consensus to form. The Socialists, especially, have proven difficult, and this has weakened every new prime minister because he has been, in one form or another, something of a compromise."

"What are we to do now?"

"That's why I've called. This latest resignation will come as a complete shock to all parties. There is no one waiting in the wings, no strong foreign minister or trade representative ready to step up as has been the case before. There will be a power vacuum. This means political chaos and we cannot allow that."

"I think we should meet."

Okami was nodding. "My thoughts precisely. The Karasumori Jinja the day after tomorrow at seven P.M. I will be tied up in urgent meetings until then."

"Agreed."

"Good." Okami looked visibly relieved. "How is the reception going?"

"I'm about to find out."

"Good luck."

Nicholas thanked him, then disconnected from the Net. He left his office, heading through the reception area, toward the private chairman's elevator that would whisk him at high speed down to mezzanine level. He glanced at his watch. No time now to stop at R&D on the way down. Maybe he could break away during dinner so he could check on the CyberNet data transfer. As he fitted his key into the slot in the scrolled-bronze elevator door, he again heard Okami's voice as the Kaisho had told him the real reason he had called in Nicholas's debt of honor:

When you came to me last year and I saw how full of hate you were for the Yakuza, I could find no way to tell you the truth about your father. That he and I—the Kaisho, the head of all the Yakuza clans—were partners from 1946 until his death in 1963 in the creation of the new Japan. Then I was obliged to carry on his vision virtually alone.

Your father was the most remarkable visionary, and because you are his son, I finally summoned you to my side. Not to protect me as I told you—you have now seen that I am well capable of doing that with my own resources. It was merely the trigger to begin your healing, first, your rage at Koei's mistake, and because of it, your unreasoning hatred of the Yakuza. So you could begin to understand the truth

that lies behind your father's carefully composed mask. And
for you to accept that truth. It is time for you to continue the
work Colonel Linnear and I planned together.

Two years before, Nicholas and Nangi had decided to buy
the long-term lease of the stuffy French restaurant that had
occupied the mezzanine level of the Shinjuku Suiryu Building when it had gone bust. For eighteen months, architects,
technicians, and designers had been at work transforming
a rather austere space into an opulent nightclub-restaurant
suitable for entertaining on the grandest scale.

Indigo had opened three months ago to great fanfare and,
so far, extraordinary success. But, tonight, it was closed to
the public so that Sato International could have its
TransRim CyberNet launch party.

The impressive three-story space was composed of an ascending series of flying-carpet-like platforms each occupied
by three or four boomerang-shaped tables with semicircular
banquettes facing onto a dance floor that had been laser-
etched to resemble a vast Persian rug. Soft lights shone from
high above the tables and, embedded in the dance floor,
from below, giving the sensation of floating in a pool of
blue-green light. Panels of cherrywood, stained indigo, rose
in tiers at the restaurant's curvilinear sides, and along one
of them a long bar snaked, the lights glinting off its blued
stainless-steel top. Bottles of spirits, liqueurs, and imported
beers from Southeast Asia, the Philippines, and microbrew-
eries in the States were arrayed on glass shelves hung against
a long mirror.

When Nicholas entered, the dance floor was alive with
extravagantly dressed people and the hubbub of a hundred
conversations in at least a dozen languages. People were
three deep at the bar, the three bartenders kept humming
with a constant barrage of orders. The cool jazz of Miles
Davis was drifting from the sixty-six speakers sunk flush into
the walls, ceiling, and floor.

Heads turned at his approach, and it was no wonder. The
guests saw a powerfully built man, graceful as a dancer with
wide shoulders and narrow hips. What was most impressive—and intimidating—about him, however, was his fluidity
of motion. He did not walk or turn as other people did but

appeared to be skating on thin air, operating in very low gravity. When he moved, it was with all his weight in his lower belly, the place of power the Japanese called *hara*. He had dark, thickly curling hair that was at odds with the distinct oriental cast to his face—the high flat cheekbones, the almond-shaped eyes. Despite that, the face was long and bony, as if some English influence deep in his genes would not be denied its due.

Nicholas picked out Kanda Tōrin, headed toward him through the crowd. Still in his early thirties, Kanda Tōrin was a tall, slender man with a long, handsome face and the cool, calculating demeanor of a man with a decade's more experience. Nicholas's opinion of him was still not completely formed. He had apparently proved to be an invaluable aide to Nangi during Nicholas's absence. So much so that Nangi had recently promoted him to senior vice president, an unprecedented level for a man his age.

To be truthful, Nicholas resented the younger man's presence. It compromised his special relationship with Tanzan Nangi. That Tōrin was astute, perhaps even, as Nangi believed, brilliant, was beyond question, but Nicholas suspected he was also gifted with an overweening ambition. His power grab at the CyberNet was a prime example. Or was Nicholas being too harsh with his judgments? Tōrin could simply have had Sato International's best interests at heart, filling the vacuum Nicholas had left. Still, Nicholas could not entirely shake the impression, admittedly hastily gleaned, that Tōrin was a team player only so long as it suited his own needs. That was a potentially dangerous trait.

As Nicholas approached, he saw that Tōrin was being harangued by a florid-faced American with curly red hair and the belligerent demeanor of a man too long frustrated by Japan's arcane and maddening protective barriers. Unfortunately, this was the attitude of too many Americans these days. Nicholas recognized this one as Cord McKnight, the trade representative of a consortium of Silicon Valley–based semiconductor manufacturers.

Nicholas circled around until he was standing behind Tōrin's right shoulder.

"You poor bastard," McKnight was saying. With his strong face and stronger ideals he would not have looked out of place on the athletic field of an Ivy League campus. His pale eyes, set wide apart, gave nothing away. "Was it only three years ago you guys bought into Hollywood, Manhattan, Pebble Beach, and two-thirds of Hawaii at prices no sane businessman would touch? Yeah, it's gotta be 'cause now that your bubble economy's burst, you can't afford to hold on to anything you bought."

Tōrin said nothing, either out of good sense or an acute sense of humiliation. The recession had had an incalculable emotional effect on the younger men of Japan, Inc. These men had become used to their supreme power—their *ichiban,* their number-one-ism. The concept of Japan as number two, inconceivable only four years ago, had caused a severe shock to their egos.

"I mean, look what's happening now," McKnight went on as a small crowd began to form. In among the curious onlookers Nicholas saw Koei and Nguyen Van Truc, the Vietnamese head of marketing for Minh Telekom, a company that had been trying to interest Nicholas and Nangi in accepting a capital infusion in exchange for a piece of Sato. "Japan's already a second-rate power. Remember when you were bashing our education system? You don't hear any of that crap now." His lips cracked a superior smile. "Wanna know why? You guys are turning out computer-illiterate graduates. While we use computers in our schools from the ground up, you find them too impersonal. Your elaborate and cumbersome rituals of doing business are impossible to carry out via computer, so you think of it as a symbol rather than as a tool." He laughed raucously. "You'd rather use a fucking abacus, for Christ's sake."

His laughter kept on building. "My God, what you and your pals are missing back in the States, Tōrin. Locked into your monopolistic system, you can't do what we're doing so successfully. We're forging our own kind of *keiretsu*—for the twenty-first century—built from alliances between telecommunications, consumer electronics, electronic media, and computer companies that have downsized. They've shed the fat of the last decade, become more productive and competitive while the Jap companies are still overstaffed and overdiversified."

"Don't you think you've rather overstepped the bounds

of good manners, old man?" Nguyen Van Truc said in his evenly modulated voice. He had been educated in England and, thus, possessed the exaggerated accent the foreigner often brings to the language.

"Who the hell are you?" McKnight asked. "I'm only saying what's right. Unless you have something constructive to say, butt out."

Van Truc looked around the crowd. He knew just about everyone and was in his element. He gave the American a superior smile. "I think you're being overly emotional and over—"

"Not constructive," McKnight snapped, and returned his attention to Tōrin. "Here's what I mean. We Americans have changed. We're lean, mean fighting machines now. We can already transmit billions of digital bits of multimedia information to millions of households throughout the United States because we've got the most advanced cable system in the world." His laugh was a derisive bark this time. "And what've you got? Zip. Hey, you know you're the only developed country without a mature cable industry? Your manic desire to keep closed your telecommunications and broadcasting industries will be your downfall. The closed field has put you at an insurmountable disadvantage.

"Ever hear of competition, buddy? It's the American way and it's going to beat you back into the sea. You need only look at high-definition TV to see the future. You've had to abandon an industry into which you've sunk—what?— hundreds of billions of dollars. Why? Because Japanese HDTV is analog and, therefore, obsolete. Ours is digital, so superior to your version there is no contest."

"You're speaking of the past, Mr. McKnight," Nicholas said. His voice caused a stir, and Tōrin glanced briefly over his shoulder. Nicholas wondered whether Tōrin was happy to see him. "Here, tonight, the future is now. The TransRim CyberNet is already on-line in Russia where it has far exceeded our expectations within an exceptionally short time. Check with Tōrin-san, he has all the most up-to-date figures."

The younger man nodded stiffly. "I will be presenting the full-range of statistics during dinner."

McKnight scowled. "You're Nicholas Linnear, am I right?

Well, Linnear, correct me if I'm wrong, but isn't there a cybernet already active in Russia? Who needs another one?"

"Tōrin-san can answer that better than I can." It wasn't true, strictly speaking but Nicholas needed to give Tōrin back some of the face McKnight had taken from him.

"True enough, in Russia, the CyberNet was not first as it is in Southeast Asia, but that is irrelevant because it is the best," Tōrin said, right on cue. "It is fast gaining on the indigenous Relkom, which lacks the many proprietary features of the CyberNet that your American cyberjockeys came up with. The CyberNet's bandwidth—that is, the amount of information that can be transmitted along it—is far greater than Relkom's, or any other current net, for that matter. The CyberNet is already on-line there and in Southeast Asia with the Kami's next-generation communication: digital video."

Nicholas spotted Sergei Vanov, a young black-haired man with a Slavic face and soulful eyes. He pulled the Russian over and, smiling winningly at McKnight, said, "Let's hear it from the horse's mouth."

"I don't know about a horse, but this Russian's in love with TransRim," Vanov said with a chuckle. As an inveterate cyberjockey, he loved Americanisms or any foreign jargon, for that matter. It made him feel relevant, like a part of the world community. "My country is particularly ripe for the CyberNet, because it is filled with people like me, twenty-first-century entrepreneurs who understand how valuable the Net is to them, even with only a cheap clone of the first-generation IBM-PC and a modem. All we need do is plug into the Net for a fee and wheel and deal without any governmental influence or regulation."

Nicholas spread his hands wide. "Imagine. They trade everything from crops of potatoes to trainloads of potash, from rights to a portion of a new Siberian oil pipeline, Ukrainian wheat, to Bulgarian fruit."

Tōrin nodded, at last warming to the one-two-punch offensive that Nicholas had devised. "Anything and everything is possible—all one needs is the hardware, a commodity with which to barter, the imagination to close the deal—and, of course, the CyberNet.

"Electronic mail, the current darling of Net-jockeys, will soon be a thing of the past," Tōrin added. "Why type words into a computer when you can simply send the message via a video image? In our world, speed is of the essence. In that regard, nothing can beat a vid-byte. With the Kami one can word process, do update spreadsheets, downlink and uplink to office computers, receive and send vid-byte faxes and vid-mail, buy, sell virtually anything, transact business on all the financial bourses."

"So great, but will the digital vid-thing really work?" McKnight said sourly. The wind had been taken out of his sails.

"That," Nicholas said, "is why we're all here tonight."

"I, for one, already applaud the CyberNet," Raya Haji said. He was a tall, dusky-skinned Muslim, the Singapore government's representative. Nicholas had worked with him several years ago on Sato's fiber-optic project in his country. He had been one of the Net's most enthusiastic supporters from its very inception. "I can attest to its worth." He pulled out a prototype Kami. "After the official opening, I plan to call the prime minister himself. And I can tell you I look forward to seeing his astounded face."

There was general laughter and applause from the crowd.

"My workload has been cut by a third because of the CyberNet," the Vietnamese Nguyen Van Truc chimed in. "Throughout Vietnam, now there is a reliable means of communication. No more blackouts or constant busy signals on overloaded, outmoded phone lines for me."

"Now that we've given you the unsolicited testimonial portion of tonight's program," Nicholas said lightly, "why don't we get on with dinner? I don't know about anyone else, but I'm starved."

There was general and enthusiastic assent. The guests consulted the small cards they had been given on arriving that indicated their tables and slowly milled toward the respective places. Koei stood by Nicholas as he shook hands and mouthed pleasantries with this VIP or that. When they were, at last, alone for a moment, she took his hand discreetly and squeezed it.

"Quite a good showing for someone who despises this sort of thing," she whispered.

"Someone had to come to Tōrin's defense. The man may be a first-rate administrator, but he's still got a lot to learn about diplomacy."

"So, apparently, does McKnight."

Nicholas nodded. "He's quite a bear, all right. But, in a sense, he's only doing his job. It seems that one of the avowed goals of the current American administration is to push, bully, threaten, and goad the Japanese into opening as many of their businesses as possible."

Koei frowned. "We opened our rice market to the Americans, after months of bitter dispute and near riots by our farmers, and you've seen for yourself all that's done is cause rice lines at the shops. Any more of this and we'll turn into a third-world country just like Russia."

Nicholas and Koei were seated at a group of tables with many of the top Japanese politicians and bureaucrats. He wondered what their reaction would be come tomorrow morning when their prime minister delivered his resignation. Tōrin, who was with McKnight, Raya Haji, and several others some distance away, glanced darkly—and covetously—in Nicholas's direction.

"Poor Tōrin," Koei said as they greeted their tablemates and sat down, "he looks as miserable as a drenched kitten."

Nicholas, who assumed the seating arrangements had been decided upon by Nangi, grinned and said, "It'll do him good to enter the bear's den. He's got to master difficult people, and sooner is always better than later. Anyway, McKnight is essentially harmless. Even if Tōrin blunders and further angers him, there'll be no real harm done."

Waiters were already circulating with the first course, poached tiger prawns with Chinese-herbed aioli. The striped shells were so thin and translucent no one bothered taking them off. They all crunched down, munching heads and all. Next came wooden trays piled with fresh cold soba noodles. The pale, buckwheat pasta was something of a delicacy, and Nicholas's guests slurped noisily and appreciatively. Sake was served, along with beer and wine.

Following this course, the room darkened and Tōrin took his position on a spotlit area of the dance floor. Just above him, a large screen had been lowered. He looked quite dashing, tall and handsome with his thick hair slicked back and his ramrod-straight demeanor. He looked, once again, the cool, unflappable executive.

"Ladies and gentlemen, much as I hate interrupting your enjoyment of the wonderful food we've prepared tonight, it is my pleasure to preside over the opening of Sato International and Denwa Partners' Japanese-based TransRim CyberNet."

Denwa Partners? Nicholas thought. *Who or what the hell are they? Sato has no partners in TransRim!*

Down on the dance floor, Tōrin was holding a Kami, using the touch screen to dial a number. "Ladies and gentlemen, this is a historic occasion and I am honored that all of you are here to witness the first official digital video communication via the TransRim CyberNet. Please direct your attention to the screen."

"Moshi-moshi." The screen had lit up. It was filled with the face of the prime minister of Japan. The clarity and detail of the digital image was astounding.

Nicholas glanced over at the table Tōrin had been seated at, wanting to see the look on McKnight's face, but he could not find him. His place was empty. No one seemed to notice he was missing except Nicholas.

"Prime Minister," Tōrin said. "This is Kanda Tōrin, vice president of CyberNet Operations for Sato International speaking to you from the nightclub Indigo in Shinjuku."

"Greetings, Tōrin-san," said the prime minister. He looked gray and tired. Nicholas was not surprised. "This is Prime Minister Takanobu, speaking to you from the floor of the Tokyo Stock Exchange in Nihonbashi. My word, Tōrin-san, but you look your best in that tuxedo. Would you or any of your distinguished guests care to execute a trade on the New York Stock Exchange?"

His comment was greeted by a roar of laughter from the assembled guests, which was quickly followed by a long round of thunderous applause. As the demonstration proceeded, to the continuing delight of the audience, Nicholas slipped out of his seat and, keeping to the shadows, exited the nightclub. He crossed the mezzanine lobby and had entered the chairman's elevator to go up to check on the CyberNet data transfer when he saw McKnight striding quickly out of the men's room on the far side of the lobby.

McKnight, who had no view of Nicholas inside the private elevator car, went into Indigo.

Nicholas pressed the button for the fortieth floor and the bronze door began to close. At the last instant, he shoved his foot between the door and the frame, punched the DOOR OPEN button. He peered across the lobby. Another man had come out of the men's room. He had gone immediately to the bank of public elevators, pressed the UP button.

Now, as Nicholas strode quickly out of the chairman's elevator, the man slumped against the wall and would have collapsed completely had Nicholas not caught him. Still, he was all but dead weight.

Nicholas thought he had recognized him from across the lobby, and now he was sure. This was Kappa Watanabe, one of the R&D techs in charge of making the CyberNet data transfer. He should have been on the fortieth floor. What was he doing coming out of the men's room on the mezzanine? And what had happened to him?

"Watanabe-san," Nicholas said, but there was no response. The tech's eyes were mere slits, but the pupils were dilated and unfocused.

Nicholas listened to Watanabe's heartbeat and pulse. Both were unnaturally slow, as if he were slipping into a coma. And unless Nicholas was mistaken, a faint bluish tinge was coming into Watanabe's lips. Nicholas was about to call for an ambulance when he noticed the fingers of the tech's right hand. They were curled inward in a curious kind of claw-like gesture.

Quickly, with some alarm, Nicholas pried open the stiff digits in order to get a look at the palm. He had seen these same symptoms before on someone lying along Vung Tau, the beachfront southeast of Saigon. Peering at Watanabe's palm, he found what he was looking for: a tiny puncture wound, dark blue around its edges.

Nicholas remembered the oddly clawed hand on the snorkler who had washed up on that beach in Vung Tau. The man, already dead, created not a ripple of notice.

He had asked a local fisherman what had happened and he was told that the unfortunate man had been lanced by a Banh Tom. The innocuous-sounding "prawn pancake" was, in fact, a dangerously poisonous stingray, indigenous to the

Andaman and South China Seas, whose skin was striped like a tiger prawn's—or the ocean bottom where it lay flat as a pancake and camouflaged, waiting to paralyze and kill its prey.

Perhaps the snorkler had reached out for a particularly beautiful shell lying on the ocean floor. Whatever, he'd had the singularly bad joss to touch a Banh Tom and had been stung on the hand. "See here"—the fisherman had pointed at the palm of the snorkler's hand—"the blue spot shows the poison."

Kappa Watanabe had been poisoned by the venom of a Banh Tom through a tiny needle that had punctured his palm. Why? Nicholas used a nail to strip open the skin at the wound site, bent over it, and began to suck out as much of the venom as he could, spitting the stuff onto the floor. Then he stripped off his bow tie, used it as a tourniquet around Watanabe's wrist. Had he done enough to save the man's life? There was only one way to tell for sure.

Bending over Watanabe, Nicholas closed his eyes. And opened his *tanjian* eye. The world appeared to go into eclipse as he plunged into Tau-tau. A kind of darkness descended like a veil. Nicholas opened himself to Akshara, the Path of Light, whose philosophy was built around the ability to transmogrify energy, more specifically thought, into physical deed.

The discipline taught that there was at the center of all things *kokoro,* a membrane upon which certain repeating rhythms were beaten. Like chants or mantras, these rhythms excited the membrane *kokoro,* causing in the adept an altered state in which psychic energy could be harnessed. In the end, Tau-tau was not so different from the power of Tibetan mystics, Chinese ascetics, or the shamans of many different tribal cultures. All drew energy from the same ancient source from which man, as he became ever more civilized, had been driven.

But for Nicholas, Akshara was imperfect because embedded within the esoteric psychic discipline were dark kernels of Kshira, Akshara's black other half, a discipline that had killed many of its adherents—or turned them mad. Nicholas had made this terrifying discovery while battling Do Duc Fujiro. Since then, his inner struggle—and urgent search—

had been to overcome Kshira by merging it into Akshara in a fusion known as Shuken, before the dark path overtook him. Shuken—the so-called Dominion—sought to negate Kshira via integration into a whole that was at least partially mythical. *Tanjian* scholars disagreed on whether Tau-tau had ever been a whole of darkness and light or was ever meant to be. Those skeptics doubted that Shuken had ever existed.

But Nicholas had to believe because there was a great danger, growing like an evil flower inside him. Each time he involved Akshara more fragments of Kshira loosed themselves in his psyche. Soon, he knew, if he did not find the path to Shuken, it would be too late. Kshira would claim him as it had his *tanjian* mentor, Kansatsu.

Sounds echoed and re-echoed, suspended in the liquid of time. It was like being underwater, being able to hear as whales did over a distance of miles, sounds so acute they impacted upon the skin with a physical presence. The world itself seemed simultaneously close and far away, a bowl from which Nicholas could pluck a single element—a voice, an insect's flight, the path of a vehicle—and dissect it with the most minute scrutiny.

And in this state he reached into the bowl of the world and plucked out Watanabe's psyche, attaching himself like a lamprey to a shark's sandpaper skin. He was with the tech now—though he could not know it—a part of him. And Nicholas knew he was dying. The dose of venom that had been introduced was far more concentrated than that found in nature. Enough of it had already moved past the entry point, the tourniquet's barrier, and had entered Watanabe's bloodstream.

Element by element, as he had been taught by Kansatsu, he went through the tech's blood, observing as the nerve toxin swept along, until he isolated the substances he needed. Moving his psyche to different organ sites within Watanabe's body and brain, he stimulated the production of antibodies, hormones, complex neuropeptides that would naturally inhibit the poison. Only when he was certain the tech was stable did he ascend backward into the cool, monochromatic light of normal reality.

Nicholas, emerging fully from Tau-tau, called for security and, when the three men came at a run, had them move

Watanabe to the company infirmary. "Get some ice on this as soon as you get him upstairs," he told one of the security officers. "When the ambulance arrives, tell them this man has been poisoned with a form of nerve paralyzer. And I want you and another man with him at all times, even in the hospital. Don't leave his side. Got it?"

"Yes sir," the officer said as the elevator doors closed.

Nicholas sprinted for the chairman's elevator, used his key, punched up the fortieth floor. An icy dread gripped his heart. Watanabe should not have been off the R&D floor. What was he doing in the men's room on the mezzanine at the same time that the American Cord McKnight was in there? Nicholas thought he knew, but he needed confirmation, and that would only come at Watanabe's workstation in R&D.

The elevator door opened and he stepped out onto the main floor of Sato International's Research and Development division. He found the night-shift manager, told him in broad strokes what had happened. "Get a security detail up here on the double," he said. "I want the main corridor manned night and day. I'm going to be fiddling with Watanabe-san's computer, probably taking it off network, so make sure the internal alarm is overridden."

"Yes, sir," the stricken man said. "Right away."

"Also, get me the man in charge of transferring the CyberNet data."

"That was Watanabe-san."

"His supervisor, then. Tell him to meet me at Watanabe-san's office."

"I'll find Matsumura-san immediately."

Nicholas followed the night manager's directions and found Watanabe's office without difficulty. The tech's computer was on. It showed that the downloading of the CyberNet data was still in progress. On the other hand, when Nicholas accessed the menu for the main data bank and punched in his access codes, he discovered that the CyberNet data had already been transferred to the core. That meant despite all the safeguards that had been put in place, someone had made an unauthorized copy of the proprietary CyberNet data.

Returning to Watanabe's program, he saw that it was off-line the R&D network. Watanabe had somehow run the CyberNet data through his own program. That meant he could have made a minidisc copy. Theoretically, this should have been impossible. Nicholas's own techs stateside had assured him the version they were sending contained an encryption that prohibited unauthorized copying. He could not, however, refute the evidence of his own eyes. Watanabe had found a way to defeat the encryption.

"Linnear-san?"

A slender, pale-faced man with wire-rimmed glasses and almost no hair had appeared. "I am Junno Matsumura."

"You are Watanabe-san's supervisor?"

"Yes, sir."

Nicholas brought him up to speed.

His eyes were wide behind the lenses. "I can't believe what has happened."

"That makes two of us. I've found that Watanabe-san took his terminal offnet. Can you tell me if any other terminal was offnet at the same time?"

"Let me check." Matsumura bent over the terminal and, using the trackball mouse with lightning speed, went into the core data banks. "None, sir. Only this one was offnet."

Nicholas breathed a bit easier. That meant that whatever Watanabe was up to, he did it on his own. So now Nicholas knew what Watanabe had been doing in the mezzanine men's room: passing the copy he'd made of the TransRim CyberNet data to Cord McKnight.

"Should I destroy the CyberNet data on RAM here?" Matsumura asked.

Nicholas thought a moment. "I have a better idea." He told the tech what he needed done.

"No problem," Matsumura said eagerly. "It'll be my pleasure."

Nicholas left him to it and went back downstairs. As he headed to the bank of elevators, he was pleased to see two security men on guard. Downstairs, he spoke briefly to another security guard. He learned that Watanabe had been taken to the hospital under tight security. He gave the guard instructions, then reentered Indigo. The demonstration had concluded, most successfully he imagined, and the guests were busy digging into the main courses. He located

McKnight, sitting next to Tōrin, calmly dissecting his brace of lacquered whole roast squab.

Nicholas slipped back into his seat, murmuring his excuses. Koei was tuned to his psyche and, though sensing his tension, knew not to question him in public.

The dinner proceeded without incident. Koei, a charming and accomplished hostess, had kept Nicholas's guests entertained in his absence. Now he did his part, all the while keeping an eye on McKnight. The ministers were predictably ecstatic about the digital video network. After the HDTV debacle they were relieved to have a Japanese project launched so successfully.

"What happened to your tie, Linnear-san?" Kanioji Nakahashi asked. He was one of the ranking Socialist Party representatives in the Diet, the Japanese legislature.

"I lost my napkin, Nakahashi-san, and had to wipe the squab grease off my mouth before the American McKnight could accuse me of being a glutton."

Everyone at the table roared with laughter, especially Nakahashi, who enjoyed a good joke at the American's expense better than the next man.

The dishes were cleared, dessert was served along with coffee and liqueurs, and conversation devolved into that form of meaningless small talk endemic to all receptions of any nationality.

It was past eleven when the guests began to depart. Nicholas had surreptitiously dropped the keys to their car into Koei's hand and had whispered in her ear that he would be home later. Keeping well back in the throng, he followed McKnight and a whole band of people out into the mezzanine and down the wide, sweeping metal staircase into the lobby.

Outside, the rain had turned to mist. Still, a field of umbrellas flowered open as the guests waited for their cars and limos to pull up. McKnight was no exception, stepping to the curb to take possession of his white BMW. As he did so, Nicholas looked for the security guard he had spoken to earlier. He found him a hundred yards from the jammed building entrance, standing over a big black Kawasaki motorcycle with a futuristic, swept-wing silhouette.

"Your bike's all ready for you, sir," the guard said to

Nicholas. "I got it out of the storage lot, topped off the tank, and fired it up as you asked."

"Do you have the package?"

"Straight from Matsumura-san." The guard handed over a small Styrofoam-wrapped parcel. "He said he thinks you'll be more than pleased with the results."

Nicholas thanked him, donned the helmet draped over one handlebar, and stepping on the throttle, took off after McKnight's white BMW. The American was alone in the car.

Nicholas kept well back in the traffic as he trailed McKnight through Tokyo's clogged streets. He fit right in with the fleets of sleek motorcycles, as kids, joyriders, and gang members swept through the rain-slicked streets with a wild thrumming of powerful engines. Now and again, a pale, crescent moon peeked out from behind wispy clouds. The mist remained.

It looked as if McKnight was headed for the crowded Ginza. If he made the Ginza Yon-chōme crossing, which was so vast it was like the intersection of the world, Nicholas knew there was a chance he might lose him. But instead, McKnight turned off before he got to the wide avenue, doubling back toward a different area of Shinjuku.

In the seedy Kabukichō area, he headed across the railroad tracks, then swerved abruptly. His tires screeched as they slid on the wet tarmac, then the BMW made the cut and, rocking on its shocks, disappeared into a narrow side street.

Nicholas nosed into what was known locally as *shomben-yokochō*, Piss Alley. It was lined with bottomless bars, sleazy nightclubs with raunchy sex shows, and none-too-clean *yaki-tori* shops, which stood as slack-jawed as the vagrants who drifted by outside. Halfway down the block, Nicholas saw the white BMW being driven off by a valet. He didn't know such services were available from the establishments of *shomben-yokochō*.

He parked the Kawasaki, began to walk down the block. Which place had McKnight gone into? There were so many of them, jammed side by side, it was impossible to tell from the street and he did not think he had the time to poke his head into every dump.

But there was another way.

He entered into Akshara, reality sliding away like a dream turned sideways, colors coronaed, then bleached out by the inner light. And he was with McKnight as he cruised a sleazy bar filled with gunmetal smoke, dark swirls of mingled conversation, and very bad drag queens.

He was with McKnight as he wended his way around tables filled with men dressed as women, businessmen and adventurous tourists, settled himself into a tiny corner table whose only other chair was occupied by the Vietnamese Nguyen Van Truc. McKnight ordered a whiskey.

Nicholas entered the club. It was called Deharau, which meant to have nothing left.

The drink came and McKnight tossed it down and ordered another.

"Didn't get enough at the reception?" Nguyen asked archly.

McKnight eyed him. "I don't know about you, buddy, but killing someone is not my everyday activity."

Nguyen pursed his lips. "You Americans are so fastidious. I told you. I should have done it."

"And I told you," McKnight said, downing his second drink, "Watanabe's deal was with me. He'd never have gone near you."

"And look what his trust of Americans got him." Nguyen had to laugh. These Americans. So righteous in all they did and said. It got old quickly. "He should have known better."

Apparently, that ended the entertainment portion of the program.

"Were you successful?" Nguyen said, leaning forward.

McKnight's third drink was served by a waiter with a huge set of false breasts and a wig like Dolly Parton, and both men waited until they were again alone within the convivial babble of the bar. "Yes, yes. Of course," McKnight said. He was feeling that exultant rush of adrenaline that follows a close look at death's face. Also, he was enjoying turning the tables on the Vietnamese. For the moment, he was holding all the cards, and he was going to milk the moment for all it was worth. He would, Nicholas knew as he circled his prey, be at his most indiscreet, and therefore, Nicholas concentrated all the more.

"I am merely following orders. My superior wants—"

"I *know* just what your *superior* needs," McKnight said with a sneer that Nicholas could easily imagine. "And I have it."

"Time is of the essence."

"Really?" McKnight stretched his long legs. "Why?"

"That is no concern of yours."

"No?" McKnight lit a cigarette, watched the smoke rise lazily toward the ceiling. "But I am in a position to help your *superior.*"

"You were hired to do a job. If you were successful, then you will be paid—handsomely, as you know. Otherwise—"

"Listen, errand boy," McKnight hissed suddenly, "I'm an *American,* see? You don't talk to me like that. No one does, not even your boss. I'm tired of sitting on the sidelines, being fed a peanut salary by guys raking in millions in stock options. I want a piece of the action and what I have on me is my ticket."

"The data, please," Nguyen said stonily.

"All in good time. I want a meeting with Mick Leonfor—"

"*Please,* no names," Nguyen said with some urgency.

McKnight laughed. "Yeah, I know, I'm not playing the good little spy. But I *did* get your attention, didn't I?" He released smoke through his nostrils. "Anyway, who's around here to hear us, huh? A bunch of Jap pansies with wigs and eyeshadow." He guffawed. "Watch out, Van Truc. They might hit you with a falsie."

"Nevertheless, you will refrain from using any names, is that clear?"

"Tell me why your *superior* needs this shit so quickly."

At the mention of Mick Leonforte's name Nicholas had gone as still as a statue. Gone was the aura of satisfaction at having successfully tracked a spy and a thief, replaced by a dark empty space into which he preferred not to look. While in the Vietnam War, Mick had been picked by a group of spies working inside the Pentagon to secure for them the major drug pipeline from the Shan States. They sent him into the badlands of Laos where Mick had promptly commandeered the pipeline and gone AWOL. Later, he had taken on Rock and a Vietnamese named Do Dur as his partners. Together, they had built Floating City in the nearly inaccessible highlands of Vietnam to house their fortune and the immense stockpile of armament they regularly sold to the burgeoning number of feudal warlords worldwide.

Nicholas had thought Mick dead—incinerated or rotted with radiation poisoning during the detonation of Torch in Floating City. Now he knew that Mick was alive and behind the theft of the TransRim data, and his thoughts were filled with the same kind of static he had felt in Floating City when the two of them had come face-to-face.

"This is not your business," Nguyen said at last.

"But, you see, I'm making it my business." McKnight flicked ashes from the tip of his cigarette. "This is a requisite for delivery."

"We did not contract for—"

"I just changed the terms, asshole. Now deal with it."

Nguyen waited a beat while he looked around the crowded bar. When he spoke, his voice had lowered almost to a whisper so that McKnight had to lean far across the table to hear him. "All right. But I daren't tell you here. I know someplace more private." He threw some yen on the table and they pushed back their chairs.

By the time they stepped out onto the street, Nicholas was nowhere in sight. Standing in the shadow of a doorway to a sex club, he watched as the valet ran to fetch the white BMW.

"You bring a car?" he heard McKnight ask.

"Took a taxi over," Nguyen replied. "That way, should anyone ask, there's nothing to tie me to this place."

As they got into the car, Nicholas looked past the gamy stage shots, clustered like pustules on the doorframe, of women bound and gagged on a small spotlighted stage.

The BMW's engine sounded and he went across the street to the Kawasaki and climbed aboard. Still attached to McKnight, he moved in far behind them as Nguyen directed the American down a series of streets. They were heading east, toward the exclusive Shinbashi district where geishas still plied their ultracivilized trade. But Shinbashi was also home of the gargantuan Tsukiji Fish Market where the land abutted the wide Sumida River. The moon was obscured by thickening clouds, and the lights of the city bloomed like phosphorescent plankton in the ocean, white and ethereal, haloed in the inky night.

Nicholas watched as McKnight parked the BMW by the water and the two men went along the dockside, stepping onto a small boat. Nicholas, physically marooned on the sidewalk, was obliged to rely solely on his psychic link to McKnight while he searched for a boat to follow them.

There was none around and he began to run along the slick, deserted streets of the market, paralleling the boat's progress. Just past the market, where the only lights came from across the Sumida, Nguyen slowed the boat so that only intermittent ripples veed out from its prow.

Nicholas, deep in Akshara, heard voices coming over the water almost as if the two men were directly beside him.

"Okay," McKnight said, "this is as private as it gets in Tokyo. Now tell me—"

Nguyen, stepping carefully down the center of the boat, struck him hard in the carotid nerve plexus at the right side of his neck. McKnight fell into Nguyen's arms as if he had been poleaxed.

While the Vietnamese went methodically through McKnight's pockets, Nicholas sprinted down the quay. He was still a good distance away, and it was now not a matter of getting there in time but just how late he would be.

Nguyen was an expert, and McKnight had not been particularly clever. The Vietnamese found the stolen TransRim data encoded on a minidisc within moments of rendering the American unconscious. It had been hastily pushed into the lining of one shoulder of McKnight's tuxedo jacket, hidden by the padding.

Nguyen pocketed the minidisc, then hauled McKnight by his jacket. Spreading his legs to brace against the inevitable rocking, he dropped McKnight's head and shoulders into the water.

Nicholas felt a cold ripple of recognition through his psyche and redoubled his efforts. He ran along the quay, passing through the reflections of lamplight that looked like a handful of tiny moons that had been thrown down from the sky.

Ahead, in the Sumida, Nguyen kept one hand on the back of McKnight's neck and began to whistle a low tune, a snippet of a Jacques Brel song. Nicholas recognized it—it encapsulated all the dehumanization the world underwent during the war in the image of the whore, lying on her back, her legs spread, calling, "Next!" to her soldier client.

The melody served as a tangible line in the darkness, an umbilical cord linking him to the terrible act in progress. Closer now, he felt the imminence of death—not his own, but McKnight's. It was eerie and unsettling to be a fly on the shoulder of death as it advanced to claim another victim. He was at once aware of McKnight's psyche and the essence of what was coming to claim him. He could feel the cold and the dark as if they were moving toward an unseen void.

There was a resonance in the air as of a winter wind blowing through a forest of icicles. This note combined with those Nguyen was whistling to create an entirely different melody that unexpectedly expanded into a dark symphony.

This was, Nicholas knew, the moment of McKnight's death, when something inside him screamed or sighed, in any case breathed its last, evaporating out of the corpus like light freed from a labyrinth. Nicholas's heart clamped so tight he felt a pain in his chest. All the breath went out of him, and for a moment, he slumped limply, his eyes squeezed shut.

The purity of the sound was absolute, and it continued to fix him in his tracks, his boat gliding silently across black, purling water, past huge facades that looked with blank-eyed stares at the death that had stolen silently across the water.

When the sound vanished without the hint of an echo, Nicholas felt diminished. Perhaps it was only that the psychic connection had been abruptly severed, but he suspected there was something more. McKnight was gone and there hadn't been a thing he could have done about it. Frustration mingled with the thought that even a bastard like McKnight did not deserve that kind of death.

Now there was only the Vietnamese Nguyen, who, having ascertained that McKnight had breathed his last, tied him down with blocks of concrete, launched him over the side, and was on the move again.

Nicholas had to deal with Nguyen. But how? Instead of returning to the dock by Tsukiji, he was continuing down the river. This further reinforced Nicholas's suspicion that

Nguyen had planned this all along. He had taken a taxi to the Kabukichō, he'd had this boat with the concrete blocks in its bottom ready and waiting. Nicholas felt certain that if McKnight hadn't forced the issue, Nguyen would have found some way to lure him on board. Any way the deal went down, McKnight hadn't been meant to live through the night.

Nicholas took a deep breath; he had come to the place where the American had so recently been drowned. Extending his psyche, he could feel the black weight sinking down, down into the muck of the Sumida from which he would never resurface. Wherever Nguyen was headed, Nicholas reasoned he'd have to pull into shore sometime. Doggedly, gritting his teeth, he continued running, following Nguyen, paralleling the river lights and the dark blight heading down it, his mission now set firmly in his mind.

Margarite Goldoni DeCamillo emerged from her shiny new Lexus onto Park Avenue and Forty-seventh Street. New annuals had been planted in the avenue divider, and halos of green were just beginning to wreathe the English plane and ginkgo trees. Though it was after five, the afternoon light was still strong, a surer sign than the still chilly wind whistling among the skyscrapers that spring was on its way. She told Frankie, her armed driver, to wait, then, accompanied by Rocco, her bodyguard, she entered the glass and steel skyscraper.

On her way up to the thirty-sixth floor she had time to collect her thoughts. This respite, even so brief, was a blessing because over the past fifteen months she had had little time to devote to her business. Ever since her brother, Dominic Goldoni, had been brutally murdered, she had been thrust into a maelstrom of another life so alien and anathema to her that it had initially set her reeling. Even though Dom had tried his best to tutor her, introducing her to many of his most important contacts in New York and Washington, still she had been unprepared for the Machiavellian complexities of taking over his position as capo of all the East Coast families. Her husband, Tony D., the highly successful show biz lawyer, had been her mask. Ostensibly, Dom had chosen him to be his replacement, but all along it was Margarite who was pulling the strings like a ghost from the shadows. She not only had to keep the peace among her own galaxy of Families but continually to fend off the advances of Dom's bitter enemy, Bad Clams Leonforte, who, now that Dom was dead, was avariciously bent on expanding his domain from the West Coast eastward. In the last several months, he had, over Margarite's protests and best defenses, maneuvered and manhandled his way to controlling the Chicago and midwestern Families. She knew he would never have dared attempt such an usurpation of power—let alone been successful at it—had Dom still been alive. Always now, there was the metallic taste of bile in her mouth as she struggled with the fact that she had failed her brother and all the Families he had devoted himself to shepherding.

The elevator slowed to a stop, a tiny bell rang, and the doors slid open. As she and Rocco strode down the gray and beige hallway toward the offices of Serenissima, her highly successful cosmetics company, she felt with a physical pang the heavy burden of responsibility Dom had placed on her shoulders. How she had missed being immersed in the excitement of her own business, the thousand daily decisions that would keep it on course, the triumphs and, yes, the failures, as well, because they were also part of the learning process.

She and her partner, Rich Cooper, had built Serenissima up from a small two-person mail-order business to the burgeoning international organization it was today. The company now had boutiques in Barneys, Bloomie's, Bergdorf, and Saks in New York and all across the country through a newly formed subcompany that doles out franchises. The French loved the products, as did the Italians and the Japanese. Later this year, Rich was planning an all-out assault on Germany, and there was talk of going into the former Eastern Bloc countries.

Thank God for Rich, she thought. He had been minding the store while she had been busy battling Bad Clams and continuing Dom's business partnership with Mikio Okami.

Serenissima's offices were low-key and elegant. Colors of toast and burnt rose predominated. The furniture in the reception area was actually comfortable—Margarite had insisted on it. The walls were dominated by enormous glossy blowups of the internationally renowned model she and Rich had chosen to be their sole figurehead. She had been with them from the beginning and had given the product line an instant recognition and cachet. Like Lancôme, they had decided to ignore fashion trends. One year the zaftig look was in among models, the next year the waif was all the rage. None of this mattered to Serenissima, whose net profits soared 25 percent per year.

Rich was waiting for her in the conference room, a sconced, heavily curtained rectangle softened by floor-to-ceiling bookcases and the Old World cornices and moldings she had had put up. The room was dominated by a highly polished teak table in the shape of a boomerang, behind which was a long credenza on which stood a Braun coffeemaker and cappuccino machine, twin carafes of ice water, a bottle of sambuca. Behind its carved teak doors lay a small fridge and well-stocked minipantry. You never knew. Experience had taught them that when they got into a brainstorming session it could go all day and well into the night.

Rich sprang up as she arrived through the double pocket doors. She took a last look at her bodyguard as he took up station just outside the boardroom. She hoped a day would come when he or someone like him would not be a necessity.

"*Bella,* it's been so long!" Rich opened his arms and embraced her, kissing her warmly on both cheeks in the European style. "I was getting worried about you. It was like you had fallen off the ends of the earth. I got so tired of speaking to your answering machine I blew a raspberry at it!"

"I know," Margarite said, laughing. "I heard it last night when I got home." She disengaged herself. "I'm sorry I've left you in the lurch, but—"

"I know, I know," he said, putting up his hands. "You've had a helluva time with Francie."

This was the cover story she had chosen because, like all the best lies, it contained more than a grain of truth. Her teenage daughter, Francine, caught in the middle of Margarite and Tony D.'s abusive relationship, had become depressed and bulimic. Francie's encounter with Lew Croaker, the ex–NYC cop and Nicholas Linnear's best friend, seemed to have turned her around. Her deep-seated rage at her parents still existed, but Croaker's influence had shaken it from the dark recesses of her subconscious. Francie loved Croaker with an absolute devotion that sometimes made Margarite jealous. She might love Lew—a sad, ironic love, since Lew's overdeveloped sense of right and wrong was immutable—but his harmonious relationship with her daughter was sometimes so maddening that she cried herself to sleep. How she longed to have a normal, loving relationship with Francie. She wondered whether that might ever be possible.

"She's better, Rich, really," she said, sitting down in the chair he had pulled out for her.

Rich Cooper was a dapper-looking man. He was fluent in all the Romance languages and was currently breezing through his Japanese lessons. He had a certain adaptability to different cultures and mind-sets that others sometimes mistook for glibness. But to underestimate him was to give him an advantage he would exploit to its fullest. He was in his early forties but his unruly sandy hair and quick blue eyes gave him a boyish air. He was small and compact and possessed of a seemingly inexhaustible nervous energy. He was the only man she knew who could spend five days working the Milan couture show, fly off to Tokyo, then jet to Paris for a week and return to the office ready to work. His favorite thing was to travel, to meet new faces and win them over to his cause.

He was fervid about Serenissima—always had been—and he took great pride in its enormous success. From time to time, he had brought up the idea of going public, but Margarite was firmly against it. "Think of all the added capital that will flow in!" Rich would say excitedly. "A virtual avalanche, *bella!*" But, no, she would tell him. Going public meant a board of directors, answering to investors, the threat of being taken over or, worse, ousted from their own company. Margarite had seen it happen time and again. "What's ours is ours," she had told him firmly. "And I intend to see that it stays that way."

"So, bring me up to date," Margarite said now as she opened her overstuffed Filofax.

For the next hour, Rich gave her a rundown on sales—up 30 percent for the quarter; research and development—

a new overnight cream that dissolved the puffiness of too much alcohol and not enough sleep; the franchise division—seventy-five and counting; the German putsch—the department store experiment at Kaufhof and Karstadt had been wildly successful, and their first two stand-alone boutiques were scheduled to open in the spring in Berlin and Munich. In fact, Rich, told her, he had just wrapped up the deal with the German partners who were going to build and manage the boutiques.

There was not a negative note to Rich's profit aria, and yet, watching him, Margarite could not shake the feeling that something was amiss. He played nervously with his silver Pelikan fountain pen—a gift from the Germans—and seemed to rush through his presentation instead of drawing it out, relishing every moment as he had every right to do.

When he was finished and she had initialed the papers and co-signed every contract he had placed before her, she looked over to him and said in her usual blunt style, "Okay, what's up?"

For a moment, Rich said nothing. He rolled the Pelikan between his fingers like a drum majorette with a baton. Then, abruptly, he shoved his chair back and went to the windows. He pulled apart the heavy drapes, peered out across the city to the Hudson River and, beyond, the smoky haze of industrial New Jersey.

"Rich . . . ?"

"I wish to God you hadn't come back."

"What?"

He let go of the drapes, turned to face her. "I had the letter all drafted. It was going to be typed up this morning, sent over to Tony's office."

She stood up, her heart pounding in her chest. "What letter?" She could see him take a deep breath, bracing himself, and she felt a painful constriction in her throat.

"I've sold my share, *bella.*"

Margarite stared at him, her mind in a numbed state of shock. She could not think of even one word to say except "Shit!" The kind of unconscious expletive you come out with when you see a car coming at you broadside and you know it's too late to do anything but brace yourself for the impact and hope the seat belt and air bag are enough to save you. What was going to save her now? she wondered.

At last, as the shock dissipated, she found her voice. "You bastard. Why?"

He shrugged, looking sheepish now in the face of her growing anger. "Why else? Money."

"Money?" Outraged, she could hardly believe what she was hearing. "You mean you aren't getting enough *money,* enough *perks,* now?"

He shrugged again. "There's always more money, *bella."*

Bella. "Stop that! You've no right to call me that anymore."

He went white, and stricken, he turned back to the window. "You see now why the letter would have been better."

Margarite put her fingers to her throbbing temples. She went to the credenza, poured herself a glass of water, fumbled in her purse for some extra-strength Dufferin, downed them with a gulp. Then, blotting her lips, she turned to him. "Why didn't you discuss this with me before—"

"Because," he said, rounding on her, "you haven't been here in months!"

They stood close together, panting like two animals caught in a crossfire of headlights, terrified, unsure what step to take next.

"Rich"—she put out a hand—"let's talk about this now. It's not too late to—"

"It *is* too late, Margarite. I signed the papers late yesterday. It's a done deal."

She looked into his blue eyes, trying to fathom the truth. This was so unlike him. It was as if she were seeing an entirely different person from the one she had come to know over the course of their twelve-year partnership. How many times had he been over to the house? He had come to Francie's Communion, had bought her that six-foot, cuddly bear she still loved, had presented her last year with that massive multimedia system—stereo speakers and all—for her top-of-the-line MAC. And now this: betrayal. Why? For money?

"Who did you sell out to?"

"Oh, come on, *bella,* nothing's going to change. I'll still be working here. I signed a personal services contract—"

"A contract!" He reacted to the sneer in her voice. "A paid employee in your own company." She shook her head, raked fingers through her dark, thick hair. "Madonna, listen to yourself. You still don't get it. These *petzinavanti*, whoever they are, *own* you. The minute they don't like the job you're doing or disagree with it or, even, don't like the suits you're wearing or the smell of your breath, you're out of here, no recourse. Everything you've worked for for more than a decade, down the drain, over, *finis*." She stared at him. "Oh, Rich, what have you done?"

"What had to be done," he said, turning away from her, "believe me."

"Right now I don't believe anything or anyone." She finished the rest of the water, poured herself more. Her throat was so dry. "So who is it? Perelman? Am I now co-owned by Revlon?"

"No, no one like that," he said, biting his lower lip. "In fact, this is the company's first foray into cosmetics. It's name is Volto Enterprises Unlimited. They're out of West Palm Beach in Florida, but they have offices all over the globe. They flew me down to West Palm," he continued, in a pathetic attempt to attach his enthusiasm to her. "Christ, you should see the layout they have there. This huge white stucco mansion over the Atlantic—breathtaking."

"So they had people schmooze you, probably fuck you till you couldn't see straight, then greased you," Margarite said, the disgust evident in her voice. "What was Volto's head honcho like?"

"I don't know. I never met him. Just a bunch of upper-management people—the board of directors, I believe—and, yeah, some good-time, um, people." Rich was bisexual, which was often something of an asset in Europe. "And a shitload of lawyers. It was unbelievable."

"Breathtaking . . . unbelievable," she said bitterly. "I can't wait to meet my new partners."

"Nothing's going to change." But he had already turned away from her, as if even he could not believe his words. "The Volto people will be in tomorrow to take a meeting with both of us. You'll see, then, that this isn't going to be the disaster you anticipate."

"Madonna, what cabbage patch did you grow up in?" She

found herself on the verge of laughing, which was okay because it stopped the tears from forming. She finished her water, went straight for the sambuca. "You betrayed me, betrayed everything we had together."

Silence. Air rushing through the vent like a live wire, buzzing like the blood singing in her temples.

"I *trusted* you and you sold me out." She swung the empty glass at his head. "Bastard!"

Every Thursday at five Tony D. had a massage. Even when he was out of town—which he often was, in L.A.—work stopped on that day at that hour so he could relax. Relaxation was one of Tony D.'s requirements of life. He found deal-making impossible without it. A clear mind enabled him to conceive of new ways to fuck people over with impenetrable paragraphs of legalese that, like soft time bombs, would tie his adversaries into knots one, two, or five years hence.

When, as now, he was working in his New York office, he retired at four forty-five to a back room adjacent to the gym he had had installed during the recent renovations.

It was just four-thirty and Tony was on the phone with the head of Trident Studios in L.A.

"Listen, Stanley, my client has a legitimate beef." He nodded his patrician head. "Sure, I know all about it. I negotiated that sonuvabitch contract with your legal department. There's three months of my blood in it and that's why I'm telling you it's not gonna work. . . . Why? I'll tell you why, Stanley, that prick of a producer is stepping all over my client. He wants him gone. . . . That's right, outta there. . . . Good, Stanley, scream all you want, get it out of your system now. Because if you don't do as my client asks, I'm gonna see that your studio is closed down tighter than a duck's ass. The unions will . . . A threat, Stanley? Are you serious?" He pushed a toothpick to the other side of his mouth. "You know me better than that. But I *am* what might be called a weatherman. . . . Yeah, that's right. And at the moment from where I sit there's a storm front heading your way so my advice to you is pull in your sails—all of them—before you capsize."

Tony D. slammed down the phone with an exhaled

"Schmuck!" He thumbed his intercom. "Marie, when Stanley Friedman calls back, I'm not in. And call Mikey in L.A. Tell him three days at Trident, he'll know what you mean." That ought to clean Mr. Stanley Friedman's clock, he thought. What would three days without a working studio cost Friedman? Plenty.

He glanced at his slim gold Patek Philippe. Four forty-five. He stretched, rose, and went through a door at the rear of his office, kicking off his handmade loafers. All things considered, it had been a good day.

Padding through the gym, he entered the massage room. He went to the window, stood looking out at Manhattan with blind eyes. Then he closed the thick curtains against the twilight glare of the city, disrobed, took off his jewelry, and lay facedown on a padded table with a freshly laundered towel draped over his hairy buttocks.

The masseuse, the same one he had used for five years, entered the outer office, was sent by his receptionist down the long, richly paneled hallway smelling of new paint and a tweedy Berber carpet to the reception area of his own suite of offices. There, she and all her equipment were thoroughly searched by a pair of bodyguards. Then, and only then, was she escorted into the massage room.

She entered today as always without a word, placing an audiotape in the stereo—Enya's "Shepherd Moons." He heard the water running as she washed up, then the soothing scent of rosemary as she opened a bottle of oil and, warming her hands by rubbing her palms briskly together, got down to work.

The placid music washed over him as her strong, capable hands began kneading the tension from his neck and shoulders. As always, as he sank deeper into the growing lassitude, memories of his childhood surfaced like long-buried artifacts at an archaeological dig. The comforting smell of bread baking as his mother hummed a Sicilian tune under her breath; her forearms covered with flour and confectioners' sugar, white as a ghost's, thick as a plowshare.

The sharp odor of rosemary reminded him, too, of the acrid smoke of the crooked, hand-rolled cigars his father used to make from Cuban leaf down in the dank cellar. The one time he snuck down there to have a look around, his father beat him senseless. That was okay; he had been stupid, straying into a man's world before he was a man. His taciturn father, who spoke infrequently about sports but never about his job in a dingy factory across the river in Weehawken where he was daily exposed to the chemicals that one day killed him like that, wham! Better than a decade of emphysema or a year or two of lung cancer, Tony overheard a neighbor say to his mother at the funeral. Later on, when he got into Princeton, Tony D. realized that his father never spoke about his job because he was ashamed of it, ashamed of his lack of education. And when Tony graduated law school, his only wish was that his father had been there to witness his triumph.

He grunted now as the masseuse's fingers dug into the nerve complex at the base of his neck. His breathing deepened as he relaxed even more.

The rosemary reminded him of Sunday dinners at his brother's. Marie knew how to cook, you only had to look at her to know. But she was sweet and she had given Frank two strapping boys. More than Margarite ever gave him. Besides, Marie didn't know the meaning of back talk. She knew a woman's place and kept to it, let Frank bring home the bacon. While he was just a glorified messenger boy, a stooge, fronting for Margarite. God *damn* Dominic and his obsession with women!

"Relax, Mr. Tony," the masseuse said in a gentle whisper. "You're tensing up again."

Yeah, well, who wouldn't, Tony thought as he felt her fingers kneading deeper. Christ almighty, the humiliations he had to put up with. A bossy wife who thought she was a man, who couldn't—or, worse, wouldn't—give him a son. A daughter who was happier away from home in some place in Connecticut where Margarite had stuck her, wouldn't even tell Tony where. And then there was this thing she was having with that fucking ex-cop Lew Croaker. It was enough to drive any real man insane.

But Tony D. knew he had to be cool. Patience, never his long suit, was the key. If he could be as patient with Margarite and Francie as he was in his contract negotiations with the studios, he'd be okay. In like Flynn. The bitches would have to respect him, after a time. A reconciliation would come. Margarite would see how idiotic this fling with Croaker was and he could bed her again, maybe even get her to pop out the son he wanted so dearly. You weren't really a man until you sired a male child, that's what the old man had said, his hands filthy from the Weehawken chemicals, and he was right.

He turned his head from one side to the other to ease the strain, and that was when he saw the heavy curtains move. He lay very still, his heart thudding slowly and heavily. He blinked, looked again. Stirring still. But that was impossible. This building was like so many of the city's modern skyscrapers: the windows did not open. A breath of fresh air came to him, stinking of soot and car fumes. He moved his arm, so slowly the masseuse did not detect it.

"Doris," he said softly, "I think I'd prefer the lavender."

"Yes, Mr. Tony," the masseuse said, lifting her hands off him and moving silently to her equipment bag where her containers of oils were grouped with a thick rubber band.

As she bent over her capacious bag, the curtains billowed outward and Tony sat up. They parted to reveal a large circular hole cut in the window glass. The precisely cut glass lay like a gigantic lens, gripped by a pair of powerful suction cups, on a wooden scaffold that window washers use.

The man who had cut the glass took one step into the room. He was dressed in the anonymous denim overalls of a window washer. His right hand was filled with a .38 fitted with a snub-nosed silencer. He grinned at Tony D.'s nakedness, showing crooked yellow teeth. "Bad Clams says, 'Good-bye, Tony.'"

Phut! Phut! The sounds were insignificant, much as if Tony had passed wind, but their effect was anything but. The grinning man spun backward, his mouth frozen in that same smirk but his eyes opened wide, registering shock at the silencer-equipped Colt .45 in Tony's oily fist. He grabbed onto the curtains, pulling them half off their track, blood spurting from chest and throat. Then he pitched to the floor.

"Too bad you won't be able to tell Bad Clams anything," Tony said into eyes already beginning to film over.

He heard heavy gasping and turned, seeing Doris with one hand in her mouth, the other clutching something white, perhaps the bottle of scented oil she had just taken from her bag. Her eyes were wide and staring as she backed up against one wall.

"It's okay," he said reassuringly. "It's all over." He got off the table and, holding the .45 at his side, walked toward her. "You're safe now." He tried a smile, but still panicked, she was fixated on the gun. Just like a woman. The last thing he wanted was anything to alert the building security. His was a strictly legit business, and any event to the contrary could kill his reputation. Hence the silencer on his .45.

He lifted it, placing it gently on the massage table, coming toward her with his hands raised and open. "See? There's no problem. It's over."

He was within a pace of her and he could see her breathing calm. She took her hand from her mouth. Tiny white ovals were imprinted on the skin where she had almost drawn blood.

"Doris?" He touched her. "Okay? Are you all right?"

"It's not me I'm thinking of," Doris said as she buried the four-inch stiletto blade in his sternum.

"Oh, fuck! Wha—?" He fell against her, then opened his mouth to scream and found her fist jammed into it.

"Bad Clams says you should take better care of yourself, Mr. Tony," she said, staring intently at him as if he were a frog she was about to dissect.

He wanted to curse her, to reach for his weapon, but he could manage neither. His legs had turned to jelly and his extremities had turned to ice. He grunted instead, as she quite expertly dragged the small but razor-sharp blade up through his lungs and into his heart and his full mass came against her.

Dead weight, Doris thought as she pushed him down to the floor. She wiped the handle of the blade, then dragging the would-be assassin over, pressed his still-warm fingers around the folding handle. Looking around, she used a towel to drop the Colt between the two bodies. She picked up the white tampon within which she had secreted the stiletto. She jammed it into her bag, gathered up the rest of her equipment. Shouldering her bag, she ducked through the neat hole in the windowpane, clambered out onto the scaffolding, and was gone.

2
Tokyo/Palm Beach/ New York

"So you followed him all the way back here."

"Yes," Nicholas said.

"What kind of place has this mysterious Vietnamese gone into?"

Nicholas looked at the bat-winged glass and ferroconcrete building in the center of the arty, tourist area of Roppongi. "See that buttressed glass bubble terrace on the second floor? He went into the French restaurant there called Pull Marine. It's new, I'm told. Ultra-opulent place with prices to match."

Tanzan Nangi had not turned to face Nicholas. Instead, he continued to sit in the leather backseat of his Mercedes limousine, staring through the smoked-glass window out at the steel-gray skyline of Tokyo that rose above Roppongi's rooftops.

Five minutes ago, the Mercedes limo had slid to a stop behind Nicholas's black Kawasaki. Earlier this morning, he had had Koei drive him back to the dockside near Tsukiji where he had left it. From the car, he had phoned the hospital and was told that Watanabe was in stable but guarded condition, so weak that he had not yet regained consciousness. When he did, Nicholas knew he would have to question him.

Nangi had come in response to Nicholas's video summons via the Kami. Nicholas supposed he might not have emerged from his unknown den were it not for the startling news that the CyberNet data had been stolen.

What did Nangi see, Nicholas wondered, in Tokyo's rain-befogged cityscape? Individual signs and shapes were blurred into a giant pachinko parlor, a riot of neon colors and loud whirs and whistles, nothing more than an approximation of reality, which was what this city of symbols really was.

"And whom did he contact there?" Nangi said.

"A woman," Nicholas said. "Her name is Honniko."

"She has the data now?" Kanda Tōrin said.

"Yes."

Nangi had not come alone and this surprised Nicholas. He was accompanied by his new vice president. The many things Nicholas wished to discuss with Nangi could not be brought up with Tōrin here, and again he felt the change in his special relationship with his friend and mentor.

So long from Nangi's side, he could not shake the concern he felt for him. Nangi was no longer as vigorous as he had once been. Last year's lightning trips to Russia, Ukraine, Singapore, mainland China, and Hong Kong had taken their toll on the older man. Perhaps they had even had some cause in his heart attack. But there was still the question of his behavior.

True, he was obsessed with saving Sato and, therefore, with the success of the CyberNet. But this very obsession made Nicholas all the more guilty for deserting him during the onset of this crisis.

Nangi moved uneasily, and pale light flared off his artificial eye. He had been through much in the war, not the least of which was losing his best friend, the man who had willed him Sato International. "This is a disaster of incalculable proportions," he said, shaking his head slowly back and forth. "We must get the CyberNet data back at all costs."

"Still, it is inconceivable to me how the data were stolen at the reception," Tōrin said. "It speaks of a gross lapse in security." Of course, he was comfortable criticizing an area not currently under his control. Was he angling for that cut of the pie, as well? Nicholas wondered. "This is the second such breach within eighteen months. Another tech, Masamoto Goei, was found selling Sato secrets. I suggest a full-scale investigation be launched." Yes, he was.

"Linnear-san did well to save Watanabe-san's life," Nangi said without enthusiasm. He sighed and raised a hand, perhaps in acquiescence to the young vice president's suggestion. "Perhaps, Tōrin-san, we erred in rushing the TransRim CyberNet into service more quickly than was prudent."

Tōrin was silent. He was smarter than to try to answer that loaded question. No matter what he said, he'd look bad. But Nicholas used his reticence to ask the question most on his mind since the reception last night.

"Nangi-san, could you explain to me who or what Denwa Partners is? Tōrin-san introduced their name at the presentation as the co-owners of the CyberNet."

Nangi passed a hand over his face, just as he had last night when he had video-logged on the CyberNet to Nicholas at the office. "Ah, yes. I have not had time to tell you, Nicholas-san. But during your long absence, in order to accelerate the start-up date we were forced to bring in several partners."

"Partners? Why wasn't I advised of this? We had an agreement."

Tōrin's brow furrowed in consternation. "Nangi-san, pardon this unforgivably rude question, but didn't you inform Linnear-san of the partners' agreement via the Kami?"

Nangi closed his eyes, ignoring Tōrin's query. "But, you see, we didn't have any choice." He gestured to the young man on his left. "Actually, it was Tōrin who came up with the idea."

Nicholas gave a brief glance at Tōrin, who sat ramrod straight, his handsome face a complete cipher.

"I think it was quite brilliant, really," Nangi said. "Bringing in corporate partners spreads goodwill, which along with the success of the CyberNet, is what we most need now." He shook his head like an old terrier. "Terrible about the prime minister. Did you hear? It was broadcast early this morning. What a shock. And now this CyberNet disaster. But Tōrin-san is good, very clever, indeed, and now that the

CyberNet is operational, I've given him the task of running it day to day."

As if this were a signal, Tōrin leaned forward and pulled down a small, polished burlwood door, revealing a bay, equipped with a mini-hibachi and all the accoutrements for making tea. He began to prepare green tea for the three of them. Nangi, though he had his head turned away from the two men, must have known what was happening because he kept silent.

Nicholas watched Tōrin as he beat the powdered tea to a fine bitter froth with a bamboo whisk. He placed the first cup in Nangi's hands. Nicholas received the second. Then he lifted his own. He watched Nangi with the anxious covetousness of a nanny with her sickly charge, as if his good or bad health would directly reflect on him.

Nangi finished his tea, but apparently it failed to calm him. He said, "The launch of the CyberNet was all perfectly orchestrated. Perfect. But now that the data have been stolen, I don't know what will happen."

Nicholas stared out the window while sooty rain slid slowly down the pane. He did not care for Tōrin's attitude. It was almost as if he were indicating that Nangi's brain was deteriorating, that his memory was not what it had once been. He worked to clear his mind of anger and concentrate on the matter at hand.

Everything had changed at the moment he had discovered that Nguyen was working for Mick Leonforte. What did Leonforte want with the TransRim CyberNet data? He wasn't foolhardy enough to attempt to start his own competing cybernet with the information; Sato's lawyers would slam him with so many infringement suits he'd be out of business in a matter of months. What then?

Nicholas had no idea, but he knew he had to find out. His encounter with Mick in Floating City had been profoundly disturbing. And, if he were to be brutally honest with himself, it had been preying on his mind ever since. There was something strange about Mick—and terrifyingly familiar as well. It was as if he had known Mick long before they had ever met. But that was impossible, wasn't it?

"More tea?"

Nicholas turned to see Tōrin, solicitous as a geisha, bending over Nangi, but Nangi shook his head, turned to Nicholas, said, "Find that data. You must bring it back to us. The CyberNet is our only hope."

"Nangi-san, we must speak—"

But his friend was waving him away. "I am tired. We will talk later, yes?"

Nicholas looked up, saw Tōrin holding open the limo's door. As he stepped out into the drizzle, Nicholas said to Tōrin, "Please come with me a moment." The younger man nodded in that curiously obsequious manner that Nicholas suspected he trotted out to hide his rapacious appetite for advancement and power.

Nicholas watched Tōrin fastidiously open a black umbrella over both of them. Nicholas said, "Now I think you had better bring me up to speed on everything."

Tōrin, who continued to industriously play the servile manqué, said, "Of course, Linnear-san. You were so helpful to me last night. I want to be of as much assistance as I can."

Nicholas was aware that Tōrin was baiting him, playing to his impatient occidental side. It was a common tactic by which canny Japanese most often trapped Westerners. He was certainly prepared to play this the Japanese way, but that did not mean he wouldn't have some surprises for the younger man.

"As you know, my absence from the office has put me at something of a disadvantage. I am going to have to rely on your reports to make certain I am fully briefed on Sato business."

Tōrin nodded, a ghost of a smile playing across his pressed-together lips. "I am honored, Linnear-san. Though there is, doubtless, no replacement for your legendary first-hand impressions, I will endeavor to provide an inadequate substitute."

Despite himself, Nicholas was impressed. Tōrin had managed to insult him in the guise of praising him. On the other hand, he did not like being chided for his absence, especially by Tōrin, who had no business rebuking anyone of superior status.

Putting his growing personal animosity firmly aside, Nicholas said, "Nangi-san is acting oddly. He seems cold, distant. Also, he was supposed to have informed me of the CyberNet partners agreement but he did not. Have you any idea why?"

"Perhaps the heart attack has changed him. I have read this sometimes happens." Having delivered this fleshless answer in a clipped manner, Tōrin stood erect as a soldier, his free hand placed demurely at the small of his back. Again, this slick mask of the loyal manservant was delivered with the artistry of a No performer.

Nicholas waited a beat while he scanned Tōrin's blank face, before continuing, "Have you any opinions of your own?"

"Any personal opinions would be presumptuous of me."

Nicholas, who had begun to get the measure of him, said, "I take that to mean that you *do* have an opinion of Nangi-san's condition. If that is so, I'd be very much obliged if you would share it with me."

"As you wish, sir." Tōrin cleared his throat. He seemed more relaxed now, perhaps only intent on what he was about to say, but also because the interview was going in the direction he had set it on. "My opinion is that over the course of the past year Nangi-san has suffered a series of—I don't know what—mini-strokes."

Again, Nicholas felt a clutch of fear. Life without his mentor seemed impossible. "Is there any medical evidence to support this theory?"

"No, sir. There is not." Tōrin's head swiveled as he tracked the movements of two men who came abreast of them and then, in a double halo of black umbrellas, walked past. "And it is just a personal opinion. Frankly, I would not repeat it to anyone other than you."

"That's very good of you, Tōrin-san." Nicholas nodded, hiding how disturbed he was by this news. "That will be all. Oh, and I want all pertinent particulars on the Denwa Partners as soon as possible."

Tōrin, appearing as obedient as ever, nodded. "Yes, sir." With his hand on the limo's door handle, Tōrin turned back to Nicholas. "If I may ask, sir . . ."

"By all means."

"Nangi-san spoke to me of the theft of the TransRim data. May I inquire as to how you could leave the stolen material in the hands of someone you have identified. Would it not have been more prudent to take her—and the data—into custody?"

Nicholas spent a moment reassessing the acuity of this young man. He had asked a very pertinent question, and it was imperative that Nicholas allay any suspicions he might harbor. "The material would be safe, that's true," Nicholas said carefully. "But we would know nothing of the people who have stolen it. And, sooner or later, they would try again and we might not be so lucky that time."

"I see." Tōrin nodded like a student absorbing a beloved professor's theories. He opened the car door and furled his umbrella. Drizzle turned his slicked-back hair shiny as a samurai's helmet. With impeccable timing, he said, "By the way Nangi-san wished me to tell you that he has called in a favor on our behalf. A member of the Tokyo prosecutor's office—a man named Tanaka Gin—will join you on this investigation."

"I don't need a Tokyo prosecutor or anyone else for that matter. I work best alone. Nangi-san knows that."

"I am sure he does." The ghost of the smile lingered on the corners of Tōrin's mouth as he climbed into the limo. "I am the messenger in this matter, nothing more."

Before Nicholas had a chance to reply, Tōrin slammed shut the armor-plated door and the Mercedes nosed out into traffic, rain sizzling on its highly polished surface.

"We're closed."

Nicholas eyed Honniko. She was dressed in a lustrous green-gray Tokuko Maeda suit of *shingosen,* a new Japanese synthetic that was highly tactile, could be manufactured to have any texture imaginable. This one appeared to be a cross between silk and linen. It also covered her gray heels. Her pale blond hair was done in a short bob, and her lips, a frosted bow, were painted the palest pink. She wore a wide cuff of incised, brushed gold on her left wrist but was otherwise devoid of jewelry. She looked slim and elegant, just what you would expect from the hostess of a restaurant like Pull Marine.

The interior walls were a muted gold-leaf, except for the bar, which was copper-topped, reflecting the light in distorted sections. A small stage projected from one corner, and each table had on it a thick, saffron-scented candle. There were so many Vietnamese artifacts the place looked like any of the new upscale restaurants sprouting up in newly affluent Saigon.

"I'm not here to eat," Nicholas said. Perhaps it was a trick of the light, but the room appeared to curve, much like the shell of a nautilus.

Honniko was perhaps thirty, but her dark, slightly almond eyes seemed older than that. She possessed a sweetness that was leavened by a no-nonsense air that made you believe she knew her way around demanding people and thorny situations.

"You don't look like a salesman and we're not appreciably behind in any payments, so you can't be a process server." Her eyes widened. "Are you a cop?"

"Now why would a cop come in here?"

"I can't imagine."

"I'd like a drink." He stood in the doorway, filling it up in spirit rather than in bulk.

"Beer all right?" she asked, leaving her podium and going behind the bar. She was smart enough to figure out she wasn't going to get rid of him any other way.

"Suits me." He pulled up a barstool, watching her long, slender fingers as she pulled the bottles of Kirin Ichiban out of the ice chest, popped the tops. Instead of drinking hers, she made water rings on the bartop with the bottle.

"Been here long?"

She looked up. "Are you speaking of the restaurant or of me?"

"Why don't you choose."

"Three months for the place, but of course it's been under construction for a year before that."

"Your place?"

She laughed, a soft, throaty sound. "Hardly. But I can't complain. I get my piece."

"I suppose it isn't enough."

"What a curious thing to say." Her lips pursed and she could not help keeping the smile on her face. "But, you're right. It's never enough."

"You know a man named Van Truc? Nguyen Van Truc."

"That's a Vietnamese name."

"It is."

Her brows furrowed as she made a show of searching her memory. "We have a couple of Vietnamese who come in on a regular basis, but none with that name."

"Are you sure? Nguyen's the Vietnamese equivalent of Joe Smith."

"Still, it's not familiar to me." She pushed her Kirin away. "You *are* a cop."

"Van Truc owes me money. I've followed him all the way from Saigon to get it back."

Behind him, the door swung open and a deliveryman wheeled in a cart of soft drinks. Honniko excused herself, signed the manifest, then called to the back of the restaurant. A bent-backed Japanese emerged in rolled-up sleeves and a dirty apron and took possession of the shipment.

"If this man comes in here, I will be certain to tell him you are looking for him." Honniko turned back to Nicholas. "Is there anything else?"

"You move with the relaxed grace of the true geisha." He saw that he had astonished her. He had given her the highest compliment and she knew it.

"Thank you."

He slid off the barstool. "What do I owe you?"

"On the house." She smiled, but something dark was swimming far back in her eyes. Perhaps it was curiosity. "What are you, part American?"

"Brit, actually. My father served with MacArthur."

"My father was an MP stationed here after the war. We never went home."

There was a moment then between them when the unspoken bond of their oriental mothers passed between them like DNA from cell to cell. Perhaps she was about to say something, but at that moment, the phone rang. He bowed as she spoke briefly into the cordless receiver, giving her a traditional Japanese farewell. Putting down the phone, she seemed about to say something, then giving in to protocol, she bowed him out the door.

The white sun was at its zenith in Palm Beach, the full blast of its light spread across the water. The royal palms clattered in the heat. It was just past one in the afternoon, but Vesper Arkham and Lew Croaker had been hard at work since three-thirty the previous morning.

In fact, for Vesper, the work had begun years before. Originally spying clandestinely for the Kaisho, Mikio Okami, Vesper had been inserted into Looking-Glass, the top-secret federal espionage and assassination bureau. While there, she had discovered that someone was stealing ultra-high-tech weaponry from the Pentagon's Defense Advanced Research Projects Agency, known as DARPA, and selling it on the worldwide black market. This was very bad news for America as a whole and the Pentagon in particular. The thought of the U.S.'s most highly advanced experimental weaponry in the hands of Saddam Hussein or the Colombian drug cartel was nothing short of terrifying. And it became even more so when Vesper discovered that the leak within DARPA appeared to lead back to someone inside Looking-Glass.

Ever since she had discovered that Leon Waxman, the late head of Looking-Glass, had been Johnny Leonforte, she had been trying to discover whether it had been the Leonfortes who were behind the consistent theft out of DARPA. DARPA was black-budgeted, which meant that Congress did not vote on appropriations for it. In fact, officially DARPA did not exist. And yet, someone had breached its defenses and was selecting plum weapons from its arsenal.

Caesare Leonforte? Vesper suspected as much. It made sense, since Caesare's father, Johnny Leonforte, had had access to DARPA through Looking-Glass. If the elder Leonforte had been Caesare's entrée into DARPA, Caesare was smart and clever enough to maintain the pipeline through bribes or extortion or both to keep it going even though Johnny was dead.

In Vesper's mind, the need to plug the leak in national security, to bring Caesare to justice, had turned into something of an obsession. She had been conned by Johnny Leonforte, just like everyone else at Looking-Glass, and she was determined to make the son pay for the sins of his father, along with those of his own evil making.

To that end, she had gotten herself reassigned within the Federal government, into the Anti-Cartel Task Force, and had asked to have Lew Croaker hired as an independent field operative assigned to her. This was not so difficult as outsiders might think. For one thing, the federal agencies were a labyrinth of overworked, undermotivated bureaucrats handling a mare's nest of paperwork each day. If you knew which routings to use, assignments with the proper signatures could be manipulated without undue strain. Vesper's old boss, Leon Waxman—Johnny Leonforte—was dead. And Vesper herself had an extensive network of supporters—shadowy people for whom an operative with her abilities was an invaluable asset. These men were so high up in government their word was akin to God's.

Once outside the ACTF, she had quickly discovered that it had already targeted a company named Volto Enterprises Unlimited. It was a Bahamian shell corporation that the ACTF believed was a conduit for hundreds of millions of dollars annually of IGG, ill-gotten gains. And the man getting filthy rich from the IGG, the man behind Volto itself, Vesper had read with a certain quickening of her pulse, was believed to be Caesare Leonforte, Johnny's son.

That's when it all came together for Vesper. She had always wondered how Johnny Leonforte had successfully masqueraded as Leon Waxman. It was true that Johnny had obtained a superbly forged legend—official documents such as a birth certificate, high school and college records, credit history, even Army records, and for verisimilitude, a divorce decree from the State of Virginia. He'd also had extensive plastic surgery performed on his face overseas. Still, Vesper had asked herself, how had Leonforte passed the sophisticated vetting set up by Looking-Glass?

A little digging gave her the answer. During the time of Leonforte's hiring the entire federal government was on one of its periodic austerity kicks. Squadrons of lower-echelon workers were laid off, including the vetting staff, who only worked part-time anyway. In their place, he hired National Security Services, an independent security vetting service. Scouring a maze of computer records, Vesper had subsequently discovered that NSS was a wholly owned subsidiary of Volto Enterprises Unlimited. No wonder Johnny Leonforte had beaten the elaborate security system. In effect, he'd cleverly short-circuited it: he'd been "vetted" by his own son!

And still the pieces of the puzzle kept fitting together. Lew Croaker had told her how Nicholas Linnear, who was also working with Mikio Okami, had stolen highly classified computer data from Avalon Ltd., one of the most notorious international arms-dealing organizations, that showed hundreds of millions of dollars in payments to Volto.

And last year, Avalon Ltd. had somehow gotten hold of Torch, an antipersonnel nuclear device shot out of a hand-held rocket launcher that had been developed by DARPA, the Defense Advanced Research Projects Agency. Then she had unearthed the fact that Caesare Leonforte owned Avalon.

That someone had to have access to the most secret documents in Looking-Glass. Now that she'd unraveled the puzzle, Vesper had to admire how beautifully it was put together. Caesare put Johnny in place; perhaps he had been the one who provided Johnny his bogus bona fides as Leon Waxman. In return, it looked likely that Johnny gave Caesare the information he needed to infiltrate DARPA's security system and plunder its riches. Now it looked as if Caesare was using Volto to launder and warehouse the enormous profits from illicit arms trading he made through Avalon.

Vesper and Croaker had had the white mansion in West Palm under surveillance for a week. During that time, she had made careful note of everyone who had come and gone: the suits, the sentries, the lawyers, the businessmen visitors, the gangster-type visitors, the party girls—and, interestingly, boys. Then there were the regular services: daily deliveries of rolls and bread from La Petite Bakery, fresh flower arrangements by Amazonia, twice weekly pool maintenance by Blue Grotto, weekly pest control, tree and lawn care, the list went on for two single-spaced pages.

Vesper's thoughts snapped back to the present. She was sitting at a table in a trendy Palm Beach restaurant with Lew Croaker. Outside, along Worth Avenue, the heart and soul of Palm Beach, the inveterate shoppers needed something to stoke their second wind. In twos and threes, they staggered in out of the oppressive heat, shopping bags clutched between lacquered talons as long as finishing nails.

Vesper, preparing herself mentally, looked into the enormous mirror that ran along the side wall so she could keep an eye on the entrance without turning her head. The restaurant was ostensibly owned by a pair of enterprising Argentine brothers, dark and smoldering, who loved women more than they did business. Which was just as well, because they were a front. Il Palazzo was, in fact, owned by Caesare Leonforte—or, to be perfectly accurate, one of his subsidiary corporations.

Vesper crossed her legs, ordered another martini. She was heart-stoppingly beautiful with cornflower-blue eyes and hair like spun gold, blunt cut, that hung over one side of her face. She wore a sleeveless Hervé Leger dress that showed her long legs—and every other part of her—to their best advantage. That was, she reflected, what a $3,000 outfit could do for you—make you look drop-dead sexy instead of cheap.

An hour ago, Croaker, looking like a high-living dude on the prowl, had picked her up at the marble-topped bar that snaked its way down one side of the restaurant. Plenty of people had seen him do it, which was the point—they were not supposed to know one another.

He was a bear of a man with a rumpled, almost pushed-in face that somehow made him seem resolute rather than plain. You could also be intrigued by that weird polycarbonate and titanium biomechanical hand the Japanese surgeons had given him. They were sharing a huge bowl of Manila clams and a Caesar salad, and to anyone who looked their way they certainly seemed to be having a time of it. He told jokes and she laughed.

Speak of the devil, she thought, as in the mirror she saw Caesare enter Il Palazzo with his entourage, larger than usual today. This was her cue.

Caesare apparently was a creature of habit. He had come here for lunch every day this week, which was why Croaker had suggested they make contact here. Initially, Vesper had been against his plan. Croaker had told her about his run-ins with Caesare. Leonforte had tried to use Croaker against Margarite, knowing that they had been having an affair, and when Croaker had tried to get away, had made an attempt on Croaker's life.

This is nuts. Bad Clams'll kill you on sight, she had said.

But Croaker had shaken his head. *Not this bastard. That's too direct. Trust me, he'll want to torture me first.*

Caesare was swaggering into the restaurant. Vesper closed her eyes now and, one sense at a time, detached herself from the world around her. Soon enough, she was enveloped by the beating of her heart, thundering like the beat of ceremonial drums. She could feel the air rushing in and out of her lungs as they inflated and deflated. As she concentrated on this, her heartbeat receded until there was only the peculiar silence of thought. The *beat-beat-beat* as the wings of unseen birds filled her up as if she were a crystal vessel.

She turned her head, her eyes snapped open, and she found herself gazing into Caesare Leonforte's eyes. Croaker had been correct. In person, there was something feral, almost deranged, flickering in their depths. Even from across the large room he seemed impressive. He had powerful arms, a narrow waist, and an unruly shock of coarse hair. This, combined with his wide, wry grin, gave him the aspect of a reckless adolescent. Then, you came to the eyes and a chill went through you.

While Caesare stared at her, she sat by Croaker's side, entirely relaxed, waiting. She was fully briefed on Caesare; she knew he was not your typical gun-toting hood. Smart and perhaps half-mad, Bad Clams ruled the West Coast families without quarter or remorse. Ever since he had come to power, he had coveted Dominic Goldoni's hold on the East Coast, and with Dom's assassination fifteen months ago he had begun to probe for weaknesses.

"He's seen us," Vesper whispered to Croaker, and for Caesare's benefit, threw her head back and laughed at something clever Croaker might have said.

Then she whispered, "All your backups have been set." She was talking of their unit of the Anti-Cartel Task Force.

Something in the tone of her voice warned him. "If you're getting cold feet, forget it. And for Christ's sake don't worry about me. I've been around feds almost all my life. I can handle them."

"Forrest's a good man but hardheaded—like you."

"I said, don't worry. I'll handle Wade Forrest and all my other fed playmates at the ACTF. They're bureaucrats at heart—political and ruthless. That makes them predictable."

Croaker was right about her. Like a bride just before her wedding, she had begun to have doubts about this whole scheme. She had had to make a deal with Forrest, who headed the special group within ACTF that had been after the Leonfortes for years: his intelligence and backup in exchange for sharing whatever they learned and letting him in on the kill—if there was one. Forrest had had to admit that the plan she and Croaker had cooked up, though unorthodox and dangerous, was the best shot at getting inside the Leonforte organization. *If Bad Clams is the one siphoning off the country's most advanced weapons out of the DARPA labs, I'll find out,* she had confidently told him. Forrest was impelled to believe her, not only because of her record with Looking-Glass but because he had to. He had run out of other options. So he had agreed to play backup, which was fine as far as it went. But as Vesper had taken great pains to point out to Croaker, though Forrest was absolutely reliable, as a fed he was sure to have his own agenda.

She was going to use Bad Clams's vulnerable spot—his love of beautiful women—to get inside his organization, get close to him. But in doing so, she was putting her neck on the chopping block; as Forrest had pointed out, she'd be totally vulnerable and beyond immediate help should the scam blow up in her face. It was a daring and dangerous plan, but it was their only chance to bring Bad Clams down. Or it was going to get all of them dead.

"He's coming over," Vesper said.

Caesare disengaged himself from his entourage as they were being seated at a round table laden with flowers on the upper level and, like a moth to a flame, headed toward Croaker and Vesper. He waved away two of his bodyguards who had begun to follow him. Still, they quartered the room with their narrow, blank eyes, like hunting dogs on point.

"And the signal," Vesper said with a false laugh.

"Don't for God's sake worry," Croaker said. "Your luscious body at the window. How could I forget that?"

Vesper, smiling sweetly at Croaker, felt Bad Clams' proximity. It was as if she had spent too much time in the Florida sun. Her skin prickled, burning slightly as if it had been rubbed raw.

"Croaker," Caesare rumbled, "fuck're you doing here?"

Croaker looked up into Bad Clams' face to see that he was unabashedly staring down Vesper's cleavage.

"What does it look like?" Croaker spread his hands. "I'm taking a vacation before I get back to my sportfishing business in Marco Island."

"You're blowing smoke up my ass," Caesare said in his most charming voice. "Your business is *morto,* dead." His head swung around and he fixed Croaker with a steely gaze. "Shouldn't you be back in NYC, trying to get into Margarite's panties?"

"Who the hell is Margarite?" Vesper said, playacting in a small, hurt voice.

Caesare's face opened up into his most charming grin. It was the one he used when he wanted to win over and influence people. "I don't know what line this wise guy's been feeding you, but he's got a steady squeeze back home. A *married* squeeze, to boot."

"Shit!" She threw down her napkin. "And I thought you were being straight with me."

"Sit down!" Croaker blazed, continuing their charade. He was actually enjoying it, Vesper was a born actor. "Don't listen to this guy. He's got a hard-on for me."

Caesare's grin got wider as he bent over Vesper. "The only thing I got a hard-on for, my dear, is you." He extended a hand. "How about you join my company over there. I'll show you a really good time."

"Butt out," Croaker said.

At which point, Caesare turned on him. "You better watch your mouth, wise guy, before you find yourself eating outta your neck."

Croaker moved his biomechanical hand, the stainless-steel nails beginning to extrude from the finger ends, when Caesare slammed down a knife with a short, thick blade. The point pierced the hand's titanium back, pinning it to the table.

Caesare put his face up against Croaker's. "I told you once before not to fuck with me, asshole, but you just go along whistling your own tune. Now you'll see how stupid that was."

He gave an oddly courtly bow, looking like an Old World

doge as he presented Vesper with a red rose from an adjoining table. "A beautiful flower for a beautiful woman."

Vesper inhaled its fragrance as Caesare took her hand. She smiled up into his face as he led her away. As he did so, he turned back to Croaker. That demented light in his eyes flared like a nova as he grinned broadly. "Know what, asshole? I'm gonna take my time an' think of what else I can take away from you."

It took all of Croaker's resolve to sit tight, stare at a spot behind and above Leonforte's left shoulder, and ignore his manic cackle. *What next?* he thought. *Will he kick up his feet and click his heels in delight?*

Bad Clams might laugh as he took Vesper away. But the laugh was on him, wasn't it? Croaker thought, pulling the blade out of his hand. He flexed his fingers, one by one, testing their response. He felt no pain, and of course there was no blood. Many of the hand's circuits were self-repairing, but there were others that could be damaged. He put on a sour glance as he saw Bad Clams seating Vesper next to him at the large round table. His plan had worked. Vesper, posing as a Florida bimbo, was inside, as close to Leonforte as you could possibly get. Now, she would have to use all her skills to stay there. Caesare was attracted to her, that much was obvious, but she would have to work to ensure that he did not view her as simply a one-night stand.

Margarite, preoccupied with Rich Cooper's betrayal, was heading toward her Lexus. Memory was so odd. Afterward, she could recall only seeing Frankie, her driver, swing out of the Lexus where he had been reading the *Daily News*'s racing pages. She could see his smile as he headed around the front of the car. She could even remember seeing the bulge under his jacket where his .38 was holstered in his armpit.

Then it seemed everything happened at once. Her body-guard, Rocco, appeared to slip, going down by her side. She looked down, saw one leg crumpled under his body. He was clawing for his gun when his head blew backward, spraying blood and brains all over a dowager walking down the block. She screamed and Margarite turned to see Frankie crouching down beside the offside fender of the Lexus. He was shouting for her to get down. Then he was running toward her, stretching out, leaping in front of her, twisting in midair as a bullet caught him beneath the chin, destroying his cricoid cartilage. Another shattered his right shoulder blade, but as a practical matter, he never felt it because he was already dead.

Margarite felt a hot spurt as Frankie fell against her. She tried to catch him but he was dead weight and she went to her knees.

"Frankie! Jesus and Mary, Frankie!"

Her hand, trapped under him, felt the cool metal edge of his .38. Instinctively, she pulled it out from under him. She was already aware of a swirl of movement, of people screaming, yes, the beginning of chaos, but within that the outlines of three thugs running toward her, guns drawn. Who were they? Imported talent. Out-of-town professional hit men, she'd bet. Her heart was pounding painfully. *He's coming after me,* she thought. *First the Leonfortes murdered Dom and now it's my turn.*

She tried to stand up, but the .38 was caught in a fold of Frankie's coat. Margarite cried out, used the heel of her shoe to roll him over, his dead eyes turned upward, a line of red spittle running from the corner of his mouth down his chin.

One of the three thugs was on his knee, leaning against a parked car in a sharpshooter's stance, a .45 aimed at her. Margarite got the gun free, swung it at the end of an iron-straight arm, squeezed the trigger. The kneeling man was blown backward by the shot, his arms upraised. His two pals stopped dead in their tracks, momentarily stunned.

She got off another shot, then she was up and running, swinging into the Lexus through the open driver's door, switching on the ignition even before she had fully slid behind the wheel. One foot found the accelerator, slid off it in her near-panic as she threw the Lexus in gear. She screamed as a shot shattered her rear window and she stamped on the accelerator, swinging out into traffic without checking the side mirror, clipping the headlight of an oncoming taxi. Horns shrilled angrily along with brakes.

Another shot ripped through the interior of the Lexus and she was off, correcting for the overswing caused by the crash, speeding through a red light, almost broadsiding a dilapidated truck that was lumbering along, clearing it and almost running over a delivery cyclist, stamping hard on the brakes, making the U-turn on Park Avenue in a welter of flying safety glass and torn chrome and plastic, heading downtown like a bat out of hell toward the Midtown Tunnel and home in Old Westbury.

The driver turned the bulletproof limo into the crushed-shell driveway of the huge white mansion in West Palm Beach with its Tara-like columns, Old World porte cochere, thick hedges, and pristine manicured lawn. It stood at the end of Linda Lane where it debouched onto Flagler Drive. Its site was not as flashy, perhaps, as one on Ocean Boulevard just to the northeast of West Palm in Palm Beach proper, but then it was far more secluded, and just as important, its approach was through a solid middle-class residential district, rather than the black ghetto just west of Palm Beach.

In overlooking the bright blue water of Lake Worth, the mansion did not have a view of the Atlantic, but it also lacked the flocks of tourists and curiosity seekers that drove by the glitzy areas in an almost unending stream.

"Here we go," Bad Clams said with what Vesper thought was an inordinate amount of glee. "Weimaraner alert."

The limo came to a halt just inside the iron gates while Bad Clams slipped down a window, said, "New blood."

A gimlet-eyed sentry glowered, while another bearlike man slammed open the rear door. He had with him a powerful Weimaraner on a short choke chain. The Weimaraner stuck its ugly snout into the interior where Vesper was sitting beside Leonforte. A genuinely scary monster, it looked as if it had been fed a diet of bloody meat and steroids for the past six months. As it brought its powerful forepaws onto the carpeted floor, the sentry eyed Vesper with sullen lust.

"Open your bag," he ordered.

Vesper snapped open her handbag so the dog's muzzle could root around in her personal possessions. *So this is how it's going to be,* she thought. Bad Clams, crude but magnetic, was no dummy. He had presided over the large table, regaling his entourage with stories ranging over many topics. All the while, his hand was exploring Vesper's thigh beneath her tight dress. Before he went too far she had clamped her fingers over his. This had astonished him and, not unexpectedly, had increased his ardor. It was Vesper's experience that men coveted most what they could not have, so it had come as no surprise to her when Bad Clams had cut the luncheon short to invite her home.

The sentry grunted as the Weimaraner strained to sniff her. "Out of the van."

Vesper looked over at Bad Clams, who was staring at her with such fixed intensity it would have made her blood run cold had she not been prepared for him.

"You gotta problem with my security, babe?"

She smiled sweetly. "Not a one."

Clambering out, she drew on dark glasses, stood perfectly still in the Florida harsh sunlight while the sentry slipped the Weimaraner's chain. The dog almost skipped in its elation to be free. Sunlight sheened its sleek gray coat. It stalked around her, then buried its nose in her crotch. The sentry, watching her face, broke out into a smile.

Nobody said a word. Vesper's cool blue eyes held the sentry's until he was forced to look away.

Bad Clams laughed. "Some pair of balls on her, right, Joey?"

"Yeah, sure, Mr. Leonforte," Joey said, re-leashing the Weimaraner.

Bad Clams gestured. "Come on back inside, babe. You passed." He watched her as she ducked her head to get inside the limo. "You okay?"

"Sure. As long as that dog doesn't mistake me for lunch."

"Leave that to me," Bad Clams chuckled. He covered her knee with his hand as they went up the drive to the porte cochere. Vesper sat back, content for the moment.

The mansion was as white inside as it was on the exterior. *It must be a bitch to clean,* Vesper thought. Not that that would mean anything to a sport like Bad Clams Leonforte. Curving walls made of blocks of translucent glass gave the sunlight a kind of explosive echo. The furniture, which looked made-to-order, had that low, sleek, frictionless look of ultramodern Milanese fashion. A pair of white leather sofas crouched like a pair of commas around a sunken pool in which spotted carp swam with lazy indifference. A ridiculous bronze fireplace large enough to stand in was filled with an enormous display of fresh flowers, the riot of colors startling in the stark formality of the room.

Music was playing: Jerry Vale on one of those CD endless loops. "You like this shit?" Bad Clams asked rhetorically as he strode to the stack of matte-black audiovideo equipment that glowed like the control in an airplane cockpit. "Personally, I can't stand it," he said, taking the CD off-line, "but the staff, you know, it's kind of like a tradition. Reminds 'em of mom and pop or somethin'."

"Does Jerry Vale remind you of your father?"

He paused, turning slowly to look deep into her eyes. Perhaps he was just paranoid about whether she knew who his father was. She slowed her heartbeat with the same method she used to fool a lie detector. That kind of thing was fun for her—a challenge worthy of her extraordinary mind. She was a Phi Beta Kappa graduate of Yale, and of Columbia University with a degree in clinical psychology, plus a doctorate in parapsychology. She had also been a member of Mensa.

"My old man never listened to Jerry Vale," Bad Clams said with exaggerated care. "Opera was his bag. Give him a good aria an' within minutes he could be in tears."

Vesper, feigning disinterest, was scanning his CD collection. She pulled out a jewel box. "How about this?"

Bad Clams took the CD from her, looked at it. "Gerry Mulligan? Really? You like jazz?"

She nodded. "Some, like Mulligan and Brubeck and Miles. Not the pop-fusion crap." She had done her homework, memorizing his CD collection in the time it would take other people to register the names of a few titles.

"Me, too." Bad Clams slipped the disc into the player, and Mulligan's elegant baritone sax drifted through the room.

Without warning, he swung her around and, taking her in his arms, began to dance. He was surprisingly good at it, light on his feet, looser, more open to the beat than most men. His hips swiveled opposite hers. He had drunk quite a bit at the restaurant but he showed no signs of being high. She felt him, weighty as a dark star, pulling her inward with a force not unlike gravity. For a moment, she felt frightened, out of control, as if, like the Weimaraner outside, something inside her had slipped its leash. Whirled around, she took a deep breath, swallowing whole the disconcerting feeling.

For Vesper, a self-imposed orphan, a child of the streets who knew what it was like to be savage and homeless, her worst nightmare was to feel out of control. She had been born in Potomac, Maryland, to Maxwell and Bonny Harcaster, but they were no longer a part of her life, if they ever had been. Gifted or doomed with a mind outpacing her body and her emotions, she had early experimented with drugs, sex, alternative lifestyles, everything and anyone she could lay her hands on. Nothing was too outré or taboo. She knew very well about AIDS—one of her friends had died of it long before it hit mainstream America between the eyes—and still she did not stop experimenting. She could not. Remaining still was her only fear, back then. Totally out of control, she careened from one bizarre encounter to another, self-destruction part of an alien vocabulary she could not recognize.

Like a discarded coin, scarred and grimy, she had been plucked off the mean streets by Mikio Okami. She had been absolutely alone when he found her, severed from humankind as if she had been a leper. In her feral and fear-driven state she had tried to bite him, to scratch his eyes out, believing with the fevered paranoia of the streets that he meant to rape her. It took time to purge her delirium, and still she distrusted him because she was convinced he wanted to tame her, to break her spirit, when all he wanted to do was to set it free.

Now, dancing groin to groin with Bad Clams Leonforte, Vesper's old fear of losing control welled up once again, threatening to strangle her. She had for so long kept her wild emotions in check that the thought of returning to that ungovernable state had seemed unthinkable even a half hour ago. But in Caesare's arms she seemed to have been taken up by a primal force, thrown sideways out of herself—the self she and Mikio Okami had painstakingly built through three years at Yale and four at Columbia, then five years in Okami's service. He had forged high school grades for her, and she in turn had scored full marks on the SATs, had wowed college examiners in interviews. She had had her pick of colleges, all at full scholarship. Mikio Okami had been right, the whole world had been waiting to take her up in its arms.

Caesare's hand was at the small of her back, moving in an almost imperceptible circle. She stared into his eyes as he drew her hips against his. She saw the red spark; the scent of dementia was upon him, and it was so recognizable to her that her nostrils flared. If he were, indeed, mad, then it was an insanity with which she was intimately familiar. The very thought of it, a triumphant yowl in the night, caused a shiver to run down her spine.

Mulligan's sax blew through the pockets of soft shadow and blazing light, bouncing off the glass blocks as if they were mirrors. Outside, the royal palms dipped as if in three-quarter time, and the shore lights blazed in the hot, spangled afternoon.

Vesper, swaying back and forth in Caesare's arms, felt caught in the magnet of time, drawn inexorably back to when she was in her teens, tight as a rubber band, when she had managed to exceed every limit society put upon its denizens. She was a citizen of no land, accountable to no one, feverishly fucking one woman after another, loving them harder, treating them more roughly perhaps than any man would. Which was why her recruitment by Mikio Okami had been a godsend, because he had offered her a legitimate outlet for all her birds in flight, their talons drawn, their beaks open in a perpetual screech.

For the longest time, she had thought of her—well, her *mind* for want of a better word—as a flock of falcons, borne on the night wind, driving her aloft. Of course, this was probably drug-induced imagery, but it stuck with her nonetheless.

Now, as Caesare's lips came down over hers, she felt the stirring of her falcons as they shifted restlessly on the dark perch where she had relegated them when she had seen Mikio Okami for what he was, had accepted him. And she knew if she did not find some way to deflect them, they would soon take wing and take her where she had promised herself she would never go again.

Caesare was whispering her name and she closed her eyes.

She was aware that he was backing her toward one of the curving glass-brick walls, and her heart rate climbed. She felt the cool glass against her back and Caesare came against her. She was flooded in green light, diffused through the translucent brick, diamondlike sunlight bouncing off the water in the pool, casting a rippling funnel of illumination on the ceiling.

She drew one leg up along his thigh, surrendering, and his hand was at the place she had been denying him all afternoon long. He cupped her, then pressed his middle fingers gently in, splitting her open.

Her head went back and she released a low moan as her falcons took wing from out of the darkness, the exile into which she had plunged them. Talons extruded, they began to scream in her ears. Once, when she was seventeen and in the full grip of her madness, her lust for women had caused her to consider undergoing the operation that would have completed the transformation she believed already begun. Strange as it might seem, Caesare Leonforte was the first man she had been with who made her forget that she had ever wanted to be a man.

He was panting now as he peeled her elasticized dress up over her hips. Her fingers unbelted and unzipped his trousers. When she freed him, he was hard and heavy and she could not wait. She rubbed him against her and almost fainted with the sensation. Then she guided him inside, all the breath rushing out of her at once, to be replaced by a liquid heat that filled her up.

At the feel of him inside her, she began to spasm, losing herself in the ecstasy of orgasm that made her cry out. She bit the meat of his shoulder, pulling him hard against her, coming again, shuddering and slipping down the glass wall. He followed her, on top of her, the weight feeling good, making her feel protected and whole. Somewhere, deep down, a tiny part of her that was still rational quailed at such insanity. But it was soon drowned out by the crying of the falcons, which merged with Vesper's sobbing moans as she was shaken by yet another orgasm.

This was too much even for Caesare, who felt himself ejaculating. The feeling was quite beyond his control, and stunned, he hunched against her spasming body, wanting nothing more than to get more deeply inside her than he already was. That was the moment he knew he was in trouble.

She slept where she lay, wet with her own fluids and his, for the moment drained. While Caesare rose to start making his phone calls, while Mulligan's eternal sax continued to drift through the mansion, Vesper dreamed she was back at Columbia, immersed in the parapsychology program, but in the curious symbology of dream she was thinking of Caesare. She had entrapped him by using the force of her personality, drawing him to her at the restaurant with a silent beckoning. But, this time, her charism—the charism that had terrified her, that she had been running from, that Okami had forced her to face and to manipulate—had backfired. It had somehow opened her up to his magnetism, letting the falcons free. And now she was in the most dangerous position of her life.

3
Tokyo/New York

"The French have a saying: Between the hour of the dog and the wolf lies the end of all things."

"Is that a real time?"

Mick Leonforte smiled. "Indeed, yes. It is the hour between twilight and dusk, when the sun has slipped behind the horizon but the night has not yet arrived, when the goat herders of the Luberon mountain range instruct their dogs to bring their charges from the grazing lands before the wolf can strike them down." Mick pursed his lips. "It is the hour when anything is possible."

Ginjirō Machida, the chief of the Tokyo Prosecutor's Office, sucked on teeth stained by tobacco the color of old ivory. "The end—"

"Or the beginning," Mick said. "The *mutability*. You see, it all ties in."

"How so?"

"History is constantly being rewritten by the present." Mick moved restlessly around the rhomboid-shaped room, prowling like a caged animal. "Great minds are defined by their ability to reinterpret the past, reject the lies propounded by a conspiracy of so-called historians, and extract the hard truths buried there. After all, what is history but a synthesis of language and text. But language, by its very definition, is notoriously unreliable, and texts are by and large ambiguous, open to interpretation, and therefore, distortion."

The two men were in Machida's Tokyo house. It was a cultural landmark, having been built in the 1920s after designs of Frank Lloyd Wright. It was constructed entirely of concrete blocks that had been carved in a vaguely Mayan pattern. The result was both otherworldly and wildly futuristic, a combination that most people found forbidding, oppressive, and much too intense.

Machida, however, adored it. Restrained in every other way, the house was his one passion in life, and keeping it in pristine condition had become an obsession.

"I am a deconstructionist," Mick was saying. "By careful textual analysis I dismantle history piece by piece until, by peeling away the layers of misinterpretation, misrepresentation, and manipulation—in other words all subjectivism—I come upon the truth."

Machida stared into the varnished stone and polished bronze hearth while he considered this. He was a dark-complexioned man with a flat face, slicked-back hair, and the predatory manner of a successful litigator, which is precisely what he had been before ascending to the exalted apex of the Tokyo Prosecutor's Office. He had a wide mouth and huge, coal-black eyes that seemed to see everything at once.

At length, he turned to Mick, who stood slouched in a black Issey Miyake suit, looking every inch a visitor from another planet. "You deny everything that has come before. You manipulate. In effect, you murder the past."

"No, no, no. Just the opposite," Mick said. "I seek a reinterpretation, a forum to show—as in the case of the so-called holocaust—how past events have been misinterpreted—in some cases, as with the Jews, systematically manipulated to portray a victimization that never actually occurred."

Machida possessed that form of stillness, a serene authority, most prized by the Japanese. Without it, one could never ascend into the starry firmament of business or bureaucracy. "Six million Jews did not die by Nazi hands. This is your contention."

"Yes."

"And all the documentation—"

"Staged, doctored, faked." Mick made a gesture, the flat of his hand cutting diagonally through the air. "I told you, the systematic manipulation of past events is endemic. The *science* of history is only now making itself heard all over the globe. But its time is coming. I promise you, it will not be denied."

Machida allowed himself the ghost of a smile, as he went to a silver and black marble deco bar decorated with a frieze of borzois and whippet-thin women. "Yes, your philosophy is quite dynamic, quite ... compelling." He laughed. "You won me over in a single sitting, and these men ... well, so as not to be indiscreet, let me just say that they are predisposed to this body of thought."

As if you're not, Mick thought as he strode across the room. Putting his face close to the chief prosecutor's, he said, "You know what clay pigeons are? That's it, exactly. You take care of getting me in to see these bozos and I'll do the rest."

Machida, who did not care for close proximity to others, did not give so much as an inch. "Often, you know, I wonder at the wisdom of entering into an alliance with you."

"Then get the hell out," Mick snapped. "I don't care for partners with dancing feet."

Machida, who had poured them both large glasses of Suntory Scotch, now handed one to Mick. "I can't get out. Not at this late date. I have gone to a great deal of trouble to locate and identify all the members of Denwa Partners who would be, er, responsive to your message. Promises have been given, deals have been struck, compensation has changed hands. You have been in Asia a long time; you understand these things."

Mick politely took a sip, then put the glass down. "Yes, I do." He didn't much care for Japanese Scotch.

"Good." Machida made no physical movement, but something inside him seemed to extend out, pushing against Mick like a negative charge, making his skin tingle and the little hairs at the back of his neck quiver. "Because I know you have had partners in the past. None, I believe, have survived. Those are bad odds." Machida shrugged without seeming to move his shoulders. "This does not faze me. I have made and maintained my reputation on situations with bad odds. They are, so to speak, my rice."

"Is this a threat?"

That ghost of a smile returned to play at the corners of Machida's wide mouth. "When you know me better, you will see that I never make threats. I make predictions."

Mick had also been in Asia long enough to understand this game of who had the larger *katana*. The Japanese were absolutely passionate about seeing how far you would allow yourself to be pushed before you held the line. It was only then they might grant you a measure of respect.

"Everywhere around me," Machida continued, "I see the closed faces of those who fear the changes proposed by the so-called reformers. I, alone, am unafraid of these reformers because they have no power. I am the power. I buy and sell deals, I purchase people the way other people buy rice. This is the way it has been in Japan since the war in the Pacific and it is how it will remain. The reformers are not only powerless, they are naive. Their 'coalition' is a joke. Already, it has fallen apart so many times that defections have made its face unrecognizable. Special interest is what, in the end, makes Japan run like a well-oiled engine. The old Japan will abide; *I* will abide, despite the ineffectual efforts of the reformers—political or otherwise."

Mick knew all this, of course. It was why he had come to Machida in the first place. "As Nietzsche said, 'If you want the bond to hold, bite on it—free and bold.' If I have had no partners who survived their bond with me, it was because they lacked the will—or the courage—to bite on it boldly."

Machida clacked his white teeth together loudly. Possibly he was amused, although it was difficult even for Mick to tell. At that moment, the doorbell rang, and without moving at all, Machida said, "An unfortunate but necessary interruption." He gestured. "There is a wide range of interesting books in the library down the hall. Some of them are even in English."

"I read Japanese," Mick said, instantly regretting the admission. You never knew when such an advantage would come in handy, whether among friend or foe.

Nodding to Machida, he went down the hall, out of sight.

*   *   *

When he had made certain Mick was out of sight, Machida went into the entryway and opened the front door.

"Chief Prosecutor," Takuo Hatta said, bowing deeply.

Machida ushered him inside. He was a small, compact man with iron-gray hair cut so short his scalp gleamed through. He wore round, steel-rimmed spectacles, his watery eyes magnified by the thick lenses. He carried a battered leather attaché case, which he clutched as if it held all the secrets of the state.

"I thought I told you to buy yourself a new attaché case," Machida said with some distaste. "This one looks as if the dogs got to it."

"Yes, Chief Prosecutor," Hatta said in the midst of an orgy of continuous bowing, "I simply haven't the time to—"

"Are you complaining about the workload?"

"No, Chief Prosecutor."

"Because I did you a great favor by naming you my administrative adjutant. The way you botched the Noguchi prosecution was enough for serious reprimand. I cannot understand how you failed to conduct a proper set of interviews. It is inexcusable that you missed Noguchi's illicit connection with Tora Securities. You are a competent administrator, but when it comes to people . . . pah!"

With that sound of disgust, Hatta winced, watching from the corner of his eye as Machida went to the bar, drank a sizable gulp of Scotch. There was another glass there and he almost downed that, as well. "Every time I see you my stomach turns over," he said unkindly. "Noguchi is still laughing at your incompetence. You dishonored the entire office." He turned around. "And I *would* have demoted you save for the fact that my former adjutant resigned to move to Kyoto the day your debacle came to light. I needed an adjutant and there was no one else available. Bad luck for me, perhaps; good luck for you." He came back across the room. "When I tell you to do something, do it. Get a new attaché during your lunch break tomorrow."

"Yes, Chief Prosecutor."

"Now, have you reviewed the brief Tanaka Gin submitted on Tetsuo Akinaga?"

Hatta dived into the open attaché. "Right here, Chief Prosecutor."

Machida took the folder from his adjutant, grunted as he read. "Perhaps I did not make such a blunder with you, Hatta-san. You demonstrate you are not stupid. Plus, your single status affords you the luxury of working my late hours."

Hatta bowed. "I do not deserve such praise, Chief Prosecutor," he said, watching as Machida went through the brief, which was to be filed the next morning. Machida was notorious for nitpicking a brief until it was virtually unassailable in court.

Machida was frowning. "I'm only on page two and I already see problems." His forefinger stabbed out. "Here, here, and here. Ministerial signatures are missing, noted testimony is missing or incomplete." He looked up. "We cannot bring Akinaga into court with the brief in this state. Where is Tanaka Gin?"

"He is working the Kurtz murder, Chief Prosecutor."

"Ah, yes. Gin-san has a reputation for piling his plate high, eh, Hatta-san?"

"Yes, Chief Prosecutor."

"This Kurtz matter is high profile. The man was an *iteki*, a foreigner, and a fabulously wealthy one at that, involved in business all over Asia. I need Gin-san on that case and I have no one else for reassignment." His forefinger stabbed out again. "I have an idea, Hatta-san." He pushed the folder into his adjutant's hands. "You rework the Akinaga brief, obtain the missing material. I have marked the trouble spots. Then I will review it with you." He nodded, settling the matter in his mind. "In the meantime, you will have to petition the court for a postponement."

"Akinaga-san's attorneys are apt to make the most of it. Gin-san has already been granted two delays in order to get the brief to this state."

"Just do it," Machida said dismissively. "Keep me informed if you run into trouble."

But by Machida's tone Hatta knew he was expected to gain the delay on his own. "Yes, Chief Prosecutor. First thing in the morning."

Machida saw Hatta out, shutting the door firmly behind him. When he turned around, Mick was already standing in the living room.

"Trouble in paradise, Chief Prosecutor?"

"Nothing a few more billion yen would not cure." Machida sighed, pouring himself another Scotch. "This recession is becoming tiresome."

"Even for the Dai-Roku, I imagine," Mick said, bringing the conversation back to where it had been going when they were interrupted.

Machida turned. "It is not, perhaps, a good idea to mention this word aloud."

"What, here?" Mick guffawed. "This is your own home, for Christ's sake. Lighten up, will you? We're talking a group of guys here."

Machida looked as if he were chewing on a lemon wedge. "Dai-Roku is more an ideal than a group. There are no meetings, no notes taken, only verbal exchanges made, never over any electronic media. Dai-Roku is a way of life, a continuation of traditions of strength and value prevalent in samurai Japan before the Meiji Restoration of the nineteenth century stripped away their power and influence."

Mick shrugged. "Group or ideal, it makes no difference to me. I struck a deal with you because I had been told that you could make contact with the Dai-Roku, that you could identify those within it who were also Denwa Partners in Sato International's TransRim CyberNet. And that you have done with admirable efficiency."

Machida bowed deferentially. "You did the right thing," he said with a warning note. "Dai-Roku does not take kindly to gaijin—to Westerners. If you had been foolish enough to attempt to contact them yourself, you would have run into a stone wall. Those who adhere to Dai-Roku all have great power and influence and insight into the way the world will be tomorrow and tomorrow. They trust me implicitly. Why, how many services have I done them—and they me." He chuckled a moment. "With me as an intermediary, they will see you. As for the rest . . ." He shrugged, indicating that the rest would be up to Mick.

"That is why they're perfect for my plan," Mick said. "I need visionaries, people who are as concerned with all the tomorrows as they are with today."

They had come to a kind of understanding, at least an equilibrium. But Mick did not for a moment believe Machida's assertions of humility. That, he knew, was just the Japanese way of communicating, that damnable Confucian thing all Asians had of being humble, of saying "can do" when they meant "can't do" or "won't do." Everything was possible in Asia, if you were foolish enough to believe it.

Mick suspected that Machida was not the Dai-Roku's lackey runner, as he apparently wanted Mick to believe. Mick believed that he was one of the men he needed to win over, to sell his potent brand of deconstructionism.

If, as Machida maintained, Dai-Roku was a kind of philosophy of samurai purity, it functioned as a loose-knit alliance of businessmen and bureaucrats who not only believed in this almost mythical purity of purpose but, in more practical terms, had come together out of mutual necessity.

The recent evolution in Japanese politics had proved that business could no longer go on as usual—the kickback schemes to keep politicians in one's back pocket were no longer feasible as a simple solution to getting favorable legislation passed or assuring tax breaks or industry incentives that would give one's company an edge over all one's rivals.

More subtle forms of influence peddling were required if those who believed in Dai-Roku were to maintain their positions and continue to build their wealth and suzerainty. These men—all captains of multibillion-dollar *keiretsu* or chief ministers of their respective bureaucracies—were akin to the feudal lords of seventeenth-century Japan. Each had his particular fiefdom from which he derived his power and status in society. Therefore, those domains were of paramount importance to them.

Mick knew that for all their vaunted influence, deep down these men were running scared. Yet they maintained the disposition of a glacier. Change came to them in infinitesimal degrees, if it came at all, and then only after an earth-shattering struggle.

The endless stream over the past six years of political and business influence peddling, illegal-contribution and kickback scandals that had ruined companies, brokerage firms, and had, at last, brought down the long-ruling Liberal Democratic Party, had rattled them. They saw, in the increasing scrutiny not only by law enforcement officials but also by the normally placid and indifferent public, a threat to their mini-empires.

The inevitability of change was what these men refused to grasp. Mick and Machida had gone into partnership in order to capitalize on these men's fear, to harness their power and influence in ways they had never conceived of. To exploit them in the way they spent their lives exploiting those beneath their social station.

Machida seemed a willing confederate in this scheme perhaps because of all those who adhered to Dai-Roku, he lacked the requisite moneyed background to be considered fully an equal. Also, Mick believed, Machida secretly felt the others tolerated him simply because of his position. As chief prosecutor he was in the ideal position to keep them abreast of the latest investigations and to warn them of impending crackdowns, raids, and sting operations—all ever-widening nets in which these men or their cronies, associates, and those they kept on secret payroll might one day be caught.

Now, with the scheme in place, it was Mick's job to convince the Dai-Roku change was not only continuing to occur but that—surprise!—it could actually be used to make them wealthier and more influential. In one sense, it could be said that Mick was selling them nothing, using a sophisticated version of the con game. But, on another level, he would refute that. Because his own passion was as strong—possibly even stronger—than theirs. Mick wanted nothing less than to change history, to move the Nietzschean philosophy into the twenty-first century: the complete control of the commerce of business and thought. It was his right and due as an *Übermensch,* a Nietzschean Superman; who better than he to control the destiny of the world. And to think that the very technology of this new age would bring it to him. As more and more Japanese companies became comfortable with the vid-byte technology of the CyberNet, they would use it more and more to instantaneously transmit data over lines that would be proclaimed secure. A veritable treasure trove of secrets would come spilling into Mick's lap: Sony's newest digitized electronic breakthroughs, Masushita's technology for a tiny video camera worn inside the rim of a pair of eyeglasses, which companies were currently on MITI's most favored list, even which way the yen would go. So many, many ways to make money, to gain a crucial edge over a competitor. So much to do and so little time to do it in.

This ambitious takeover of international commerce he had no doubt he could do, assuming he had enough money, leverage, and the right people behind him. He had already had a number of years building his underground arms and drug networks throughout Southeast Asia from his former base of Floating City. Now it was time to get into the legitimate end of commerce. This he meant to do here in Tokyo, where the tenor of the times—militancy—the temperament of the people—subservience—seemed to him ideal. And, of course, Tokyo was where Sato International was; Sato with its TransRim CyberNet. If all went as planned, he would be inside Sato within a matter of weeks—if he could convince the Denwa Partners to go along with him. They would, of course, because he had done his homework, he knew these men and what made them tick. What he would offer them, they would find irresistible. These men feared change above all else because it was the status quo in Japan that lent them their power. They could see cracks forming in their power—political scandals, bribery links to brokerage houses, giant construction companies they owned—a vast and swelling outcry from the media and the public. These things they feared and reacted against instinctively.

Mick would give them what they needed to allay their fears—an establishment of a new status quo that enhanced their power base. How could they resist? Once they made that crucial decision, he would control them. They would be his entrée into Sato International. And once there, he would exert his influence, quickly, decisively, in true Nietzschean fashion, causing the ruin of the man he had come to view as his nemesis, his doppelgänger: Nicholas Linnear.

Margarite awoke from a dream-stalked sleep cramped and grimy-eyed. She uncurled herself from the backseat of the Lexus. She got out of the car and stretched. It was just past noon, not surprising since she had not fallen asleep until— what?—four, five in the morning? Then she got behind the wheel, drove out of the telephone rest stop, and hit the first 7-Eleven she came to.

Over a steaming hot coffee and a Drakes cake, she pondered her situation. Perhaps she had carried paranoia too far by not checking into any one of a number of anonymous-looking motels that dotted the Long Island Expressway, but she had not wanted to take a chance. She took another sip of overroasted coffee and massaged the back of her neck.

Late last night she had been within a couple of miles of her mansion in Old Westbury when it occurred to her she was doing just about the most foolish thing she could do. Wasn't it logical that the people who had tried to kill her would have her house staked out? Sure. She had been in such a panic leaving the scene of the abortive strike against her that she had not been thinking straight. Clearly, she needed to get away and to implement a well-considered course of action. She had to call Tony, and this she did while she kept driving on the Long Island Expressway past her customary exit.

"Call Tony's office," she had said to the phone mounted on the center console of her car. She glanced at her watch, gave a little scream. She had to wipe away blood—Rocco's or her driver Frankie's—before she could see the numerals. It had been seven-thirty. Tony would be finished with his massage by now and back at work, making his most important West Coast calls.

"Hello. Who's this, please?"

A strange voice on the other end of the line. When she identified herself and asked for Tony, he said gruffly, "Hold a sec', don't go away." She heard a muffled word on the phone, something that sounded like Lew Tennant, and she automatically thought of Lew Croaker. *My God, how I miss him,* she thought. *He'd know what to do in this crisis.*

"Mrs. DeCamillo? That you?" Another voice, deeper, a whiskey baritone.

When she answered, he said, "My name's Jack Barnett, Mrs. DeCamillo. I'm a detective lieutenant with the NYPD." That was it, she thought. Lew Tennant. Lieutenant. "I'm afraid I have some bad news regarding your husband."

An icy chill gripped Margarite's insides. She swerved off

the expressway onto the trash-strewn grassy verge where she braked to a halt, watching her hands shake. "Is he dead?"

"I'm afraid so, Mrs. DeCamillo. Murdered in his office."

Bad Clams. So many emotions rushing through her like a wind blowing down a canyon. Tony dead. She felt as if her soul were being scoured clean by the hand of God. She slowed her breathing into deep inhalations, struggling to clear her mind, so she could ask the right questions.

"Mrs. DeCamillo? Are you still there?"

Concentrate, damn it! "When did it happen?" she said, slamming the door shut.

"I beg your pardon?"

"What time was Tony killed?" She was impatient now because this information was crucial.

"I'm not sure. But it couldn't have been more than an hour ago. The blood hasn't yet fully coagulated."

"I see."

There was a small pause. "Mrs. DeCamillo, I wonder where you are. You've had quite a shock, maybe someone should be with you. Plus, it would be helpful if we could talk to you."

"I'm afraid that's impossible, Lieutenant . . ."

"Barnett, ma'am. Jack Barnett."

"I'm on the road right now and it will be some time before I can get back to the city." She looked around her at the cars whizzing by as she listened to the silence build at the other end of the line.

"Do you think that's wise, Mrs. DeCamillo? I mean, your husband has been murdered. The people who did this could be looking for you. At the very least, I'd think you'd want protection."

He is right about that, she thought. *Cars and more cars swimming by like schools of fish, blurred and indistinct, each carrying passengers with their own life stories. An uncaring cavalcade of metal and flesh ignorant of what's happening to my life. First, my partner betrays me, selling my company out from under me, then my bodyguard and driver are gunned down and I am almost killed at just about the same time that Tony is murdered.*

"Mrs. DeCamillo?" Lieutenant Barnett's voice broke into her thoughts. "If you know anything about the circumstances of your husband's murder or you believe you have any information regarding the perpetrator or perpetrators, it would be in your best interests to tell me. Plus, it could help stave off a potential bloodbath."

"What the hell is that supposed to mean?"

"A lawyer like your husband with a lotta different business interests, it's only natural he'd made some very powerful enemies. Mrs. DeCamillo, I wonder whether we're connecting."

"Go to hell."

"I know you're upset. But, see what I'm doing, Mrs. De-Camillo? I'm reaching out to you the best way I know how. Do you think you could take even one step in my direction?"

Margarite suddenly felt vulnerable, sitting on the side of the LIE with her rear window a spiderweb of broken glass. *I've got to get out of here,* she thought.

"If you want to know who killed my husband, talk to Caesare Leonforte," she said, severing the connection.

That was when the full brunt of the paranoia had taken hold, and instead of pulling into a motel, she had stopped at the telephone drive-by and had stayed there.

The way the ground had been systematically cut from under her was all too much of a coincidence, she thought now as she finished her too sweet Drakes cake. It had been as meticulously coordinated as a military campaign. Who the fuck were the people Rich sold out to? What a schmuck. Bad Clams had played him like a Steinway. She had little doubt now that Caesare Leonforte must own or at least control Volto, the company to which Rich had sold his half of Serenissima. She was shaking with rage and fear.

I've got to try calling Lew and Vesper again, she told herself as she caught a window in the traffic flow and accelerated into the right-hand lane with a screech of tires. She'd tried them last night with no success. But first, she had to get to Francie. Her daughter was the most important person in her life, and now that danger had appeared at every side, her primary instinct was to get to her as quickly as possible. She'd tried calling last night, had gotten the answering machine. She'd checked her datebook and had seen that

Francie was coming back from a horseback riding show sometime today.

Margarite exited the LIE and reentered heading westbound, on her way to the Throgs Neck Bridge. She turned on the CD player, needing some music to calm her nerves, but nothing happened. She turned to a classical radio station, instead.

For the past nine months Francie had been living with Julie Longacre, Margarite's friend in Connecticut. Julie was a horse fanatic and a first-rate rider, and Francie had taken to her right away. Lew's advice to Francie had convinced Margarite to keep her daughter out of the family situation that had caused her problem in the first place.

So Margarite had secreted her at Julie's. Not even Tony knew her whereabouts. And Julie, a divorced heiress with horses, hunting dogs, and all the paraphernalia to go with it, treated secrets like a sacred trust.

Margarite knew she had been foolish and out of touch, believing that she and Tony could hide their problems from Francie. Children had a way of being far more clever than their parents could possibly believe. And that, of course, made them more vulnerable to pressures and evil forces within the family.

Tony DeCamillo had been just such an evil force, but it was still possible for Margarite to understand how she had fallen in love with him. He was handsome, bright, and best of all, had access to a different level of society than she had been brought up with. The glitterati of Hollywood all knew Tony—many had been his clients. Margarite, on Tony's arm, had met them all. She would never forget attending her first Oscar telecast. It was like being picked up by a whirlwind and being deposited in Oz. Of course she had been blown away. Of course she had looked up to Tony as some kind of God. Of course she had married him.

Then had come the nightmare.

She paid her toll, went across the bridge, and picked up Route 95.

Tony had wanted a baby machine. He'd told her on their honeymoon that he expected her to give him a child a year. And sons! My God, how he flew into a rage when Francie was born! He had changed the moment of his daughter's birth, shunning the infant and physically punishing the wife who in his mind had betrayed him by depriving him of his son, his heir, the continuation of his branch of the DeCamillos.

She rocketed past the Pelhams, the Lexus humming happily while the wind whistled eerily through the shattered glass.

How did she feel now that Tony was dead? Could she mourn him? Not really. Truth to tell, she felt lighter than air, as if a long-standing ache with which she had learned to live had suddenly vanished. It astonished her how easy it was to breathe, how sweet each breath she took in now seemed. She felt dizzy with relief. But behind all that crept the anxiety of the many pronged attack on the Goldoni family and on herself.

Bad Clams was behind this, she was sure of it. No wonder he had waited so long to make his move. He needed the time to coordinate all the pieces of the attack, and he needed to lull her into thinking he might never attempt to take over the East Coast Families, what had been Dominic's territory.

So far every phase had worked to perfection, save the hit on her. That she had managed to escape was, she knew, something of a miracle. She must have her own personal angel looking over her shoulder. But now, as she entered Connecticut, the fear for her—and for Francie—intensified. Whom could she trust? She no longer knew. It occurred to her that no matter how much power Bad Clams had managed to muster, he would still need help from inside her own Family. Who had betrayed her and Tony? Probably one of the Family *capi* who had been promised more territory and influence under the Leonforte regime.

Abruptly, she swerved to the curb, braked to a halt. For a moment, she sat slumped over the wheel, trying unsuccessfully to slow her breathing. *Oh my God,* she thought. *Oh my God!*

She stared into her side mirror, scrutinizing the street behind her. What if she was being followed? Given the nature of the recent well-coordinated events, it was more than possible. She was driving her own dark red Lexus with gold trim and her MGDC vanity license plate. She would be all too easy to spot. She scrabbled in her handbag, extracted the .38. She opened it, thankful Dom had insisted she take lessons, and checked the cartridges. She found she had only fired one. One? It seemed as if she had emptied all the chambers at her would-be assassin. She closed it, hefted it in her palm.

Once again, she felt awash in paranoia and wondered if Dominic had lived his entire adult life in this state. But paranoid notion or not she had given it credence, because if she was being followed, she was taking them right to Francie's doorstep. She wasn't about to make the mistake Tony had made in underestimating Bad Clams. He was smart enough to know that Francie was Margarite's weak spot. If he had a fallback plan now that the murder had failed, it would surely entail Francie.

If he could find her.

She was damned if she was going to give him his chance. Still scanning the street, she said, "Call Julie," and the phone dialed the number. While it rang, she prayed that Francie would answer. But, instead, her heart sank as she got the answering machine. After the beep, she said, "Francie, darling, it's me. Hope you had a good time at the horse show. If you'd call me when you get home, I'd appreciate it. I'm in the car and I'll be here till very late. Speak to you soon, baby." She broke the connection, hoping that her terror hadn't been apparent in her voice. Then she said, "Call Lew," dialing Croaker's portable-phone number, but it just rang and rang.

Damn, now what? Next Saturday night she was expected to be the guest of honor at the Joey Infante and Kate Dellarco wedding. She knew that, come what may, she needed to make an appearance there if she had any hope of holding on to Dominic's domain. The Sicilian Infantes and the Neapolitan Dellarcos were two families that had been at each other's throat, and their escalating war was destabilizing the entire East Coast operation and bringing down fleets of homicide cops to deal with the corpses piling up in East New York and Ozone Park.

How to handle this inflammable situation had been Margarite's first test of power management. She had discovered that Joey and Kate had been seeing each other secretly, like

Romeo and Juliet. But unlike Shakespeare's star-crossed lovers, Margarite was determined to bring about a happy ending.

She and Tony had called a meeting with the heads of the two families and, at it, had brought in the two lovers. Vitriolic invective had almost turned to physical violence. Tony had quelled that soon enough, and then, slowly and quietly, Margarite had outlined just how the love between these members of the two families could help heal the wounds. She had given them the emotional underpinnings for a permanent truce, and then Tony, with his relentlessly logical litigator's brain, had provided the practical framework.

Now, after months of negotiations and diplomacy the deed was about to be done. At the wedding of Joey and Kate the Infantes and Dellarcos would finally bury the vendetta that was decimating them and weakening the East Coast Families alliance.

This was why she had to be there. The wedding was the cornerstone of the new regime. If it fell apart, so would Dominic's legacy, which he had entrusted to her. She was already at a loss as to how to operate in the male-dominated world of the Mafia without her husband as her mask. Ostensibly, he had been Dominic's successor, but it was she who knew all of Dom's secrets, she who made all the decisions. Now, with Tony gone, she was naked in the light. Which one of the Family heads would follow her, a woman? None. This was why her role had been such a well-kept secret. Only Tony had known, and she suspected he hated her for usurping what he saw as rightfully his.

Dominic, however, in his usual brilliant manner, had seen matters entirely differently. To this day, Margarite had no idea why he had asked her to take over his position as head of all the East Coast Families. He must have known what an impossible task he was leaving her with. And yet he had persisted. And she, partly as dutiful sister, partly as fascinated initiate, had acquiesced. But now look where it had got her, alone and exiled, betrayed from within and under attack, bereft of her power. Surely, Dom could not have envisioned this bleak future.

Putting her face in her hands, she wept, her shoulders shaking, engulfed by self-pity. When, at last, she was cried out, she turned her head, willing the phone to ring, but it remained silent as a serpent.

Francie, where are you? Please, God, keep her safe from harm.

She jumped as the phone rang. For an instant, she hesitated, then she breathed a little sigh. Francie.

She opened the line. "Hello?"

"Hello, sweetheart."

Her heart constricted. "Who is this?"

"They messed up, Margarite. They were supposed to take out your bodyguard and snatch you—no fuss, no muss. Oh, well, it's getting harder to find competent help."

"Caesare?"

"In another time, another place, we could have been pals," Caesare Leonforte said. "Closer even, maybe. Pity."

She closed her eyes. "What do you want, Caesare, my death?"

"Oh, no. Not only your death, Margarite. I want it *all*. Everything Dominic built, everything that is yours." He chuckled. "Not so much to covet, in the scheme of things. But I *will* have it all, Margarite."

"Not if I have anything to say about it."

"But you don't, sweetheart. You're nothing: a skirt, a twist, a *woman*. Now that Tony's gone I've cut off the head. The Goldonis only have you." He laughed. "And I've put an end to you."

Her hand tightened on the grip of the .38. "I put a bullet through the heart of one of your assassins. I'll do the same to you."

"Oh, I believe you, sweetheart. Even though you're a woman you're a damn fine shot. I can't afford to have you barreling around like a loose cannon, so I'm going to order you in from the cold."

"You'll never be able to order me to do anything."

"Never say never, Margarite. Dominic would have told you that."

"Don't use my brother's name."

"Come in, Margarite. I promise you won't be harmed. I'll give you directions right now—"

"Fuck you!"

"How ladylike. Well, darling, you force me into the distasteful position of using leverage. Did you wonder why your CD player isn't working? That's because we outfitted your Lexus with a phone monitor. Your daughter is at Julie's, isn't she? We ran Julie's number through a contact at the phone company and came up with the address. Want to hear it?"

Margarite's blood had run cold. Francie! "Bastard."

"Thirty-eight thirty-seven Fox Hollow Lane in New Canaan."

Margarite screamed.

"Are you all right, sweetheart? I think I heard a noise."

Margarite leaned over the phone. "Caesare, if you harm Francie in any way, I promise you I will hunt you down no matter where you are, no matter how long it takes."

"I don't doubt you'd try, which is why I haven't the slightest intention of hurting her. Assuming you give yourself up. You have an hour, Margarite." He gave her an address in Sheepshead Bay, off the service road of the Belt Parkway near Coney Island Avenue. "If you're not at this location at that time, I'm afraid I cannot take responsibility for what happens to your daughter."

She was weeping despite biting her lip in an effort to hold it back. "Oh, Caesare, she's just an innocent child." There was no answer and she ground her teeth. Her eyes felt hot, stinging with tears. "You'll have to bring her or I won't come in."

"Forgetaboutit."

"I need proof."

"This is war, Margarite. I give no quarter."

"Neither do I."

"You fuckin' bitch, you give me any more trouble an' I'll bring her fuckin' finger to the meet, get me?"

"You do that, Caesare, and I promise you I'll personally gouge your eyes out and make you eat them."

Perhaps the tone of her voice made him relent. Maybe he meant to give in all along and had just been torturing her. "Okay, okay. You come in an' she'll be there. Satisfied?"

"In one piece?"

"In one piece, sure."

Her mind was awhirl in shock and grief. "I need more time."

"No, you don't."

"I won't make it, I know it. There's traffic, the bridges, I'm almost out of gas. Plus, I have to find a pharmacy."

"A pharmacy? What for?"

"What do you think, idiot. I just got my period. I need—"

"Enough! I don't want to hear this."

"For the love of God, Caesare, we're talking about my child's *life.*"

There was a brief pause, during which Margarite just had time for a quick, silent prayer.

"All right, sweetheart, I'll give you three hours. But that's all the time Francie has."

Tokyo's mistlike drizzle had turned into a metallic rain that bounced off vertical neon signs and Shinto shrine torii gates alike. There were plenty of the latter in the Asakusa temple district where Nicholas met Tanaka Gin. He was standing in front of a conical private residence, beneath a single cryptomeria set into a grating of concrete blocks.

Tanaka Gin was a slender, dark-faced man with the kind of laconic grace one often found in Japan's cinema detectives or samurai heroes. He had about him an air of mystery, as if his mind were a safety deposit box filled with secrets. His hooded eyes were deceiving. He seemed half-asleep, but Nicholas felt certain that he would appear this way even if he was running full tilt after you down an alley or putting the pressure on you in an interrogation cell.

"Linnear-san," Tanaka Gin said, bowing formally, "it is an honor to meet you."

"The honor is all mine, I assure you," Nicholas said, returning the bow. He stowed away his Kami. The ever-efficient Kanda Tōrin had digi-faxed him the information on the dozen or so members of Denwa Partners. The data had come into his Kami as a stream of ones and zeros, which the unit had translated into Japanese kanji. "Your reputation precedes you—especially the cases you put together against Tetsuo Akinaga and Yoshinori." He was referring to two men—one a prominent Yakuza *oyabun*, the head of a Japanese underworld family; the other the most influential unaligned politico with the reputation of making or breaking the last eight prime ministers. "Your reputation as *the* latter-day reformer is formidable."

The success of the prosecution of Akinaga's case was of particular importance to Nicholas. Tetsuo Akinaga was the *oyabun* of Tokyo's powerful and murderous Shikei clan. Yakuza, who proudly considered themselves outsiders in Japanese society, preferred ironically fatalistic names of their clans. Shikei meant capital punishment. Akinaga had been a member of the Kaisho's inner circle, a purported friend and disciple of Okami's, but in fact his bitterest enemy. All of Okami's other enemies were gone, washed away in a tide of blood. Only Tetsuo Akinaga remained.

"I have an excellent and dedicated staff," Tanaka Gin said. He stood in the rain without the protection of an umbrella. His sole concession to the weather was the lapel of his iridescent green trench coat, which he had turned up to keep the water from running down his back. "It was good of you to meet me at such short notice."

"I am as anxious as you are to discover the identity of the people involved in the theft of the CyberNet secrets."

Tanaka Gin used a key to open the patined bronze door, in the process stripping off three lines of bright orange police tape. WARNING! POLICE CRIME SCENE! ENTRY FORBIDDEN! they had printed on them in kanji. He stepped inside and Nicholas followed.

Nicholas found himself in an astonishing replica of a colonial-Saigon villa. Aqueous light, tinged by neon, seeped in through the jalousied windows. The smell of incense and star anise wafted in the air. But something hanging like the web of a giant spider made Nicholas start involuntarily.

Tanaka Gin closed the door behind Nicholas. "Let us be frank, Linnear-san. I have agreed to help your investigation because Tanzan Nangi asked it of me. He is a man for whom I have great respect." He went to a long side table, turned on two bronze lamps. "As it happens, I have much on my plate. I am investigating the murder of a German businessman, Rodney Kurtz, and the subsequent hit-and-run death of his wife, Giai, a Vietnamese national." He spread his hands. "This is where Mr. Kurtz was killed."

Nicholas nodded. "As long as we are being frank, Prosecutor, allow me to say that I never asked for your help and, in fact, prefer to work alone."

"That is a dangerous occupation in Tokyo. Officially, I would not advise it."

"And unofficially?"

Tanaka Gin smiled. "I know something about you, Linnear-san. Nangi-san speaks of you in the manner one would talk about his progeny. This I take as significant." He paused a beat. "I am willing to offer you assistance as you need it. But it would be . . . unfortunate if your investigation caused me or my office any embarrassment."

"I take your point, Prosecutor. And I appreciate the advice." Nicholas could sense Tanaka Gin, behind his half-lowered lids, sizing him up.

"Yes, I believe you do."

Nicholas watched Tanaka Gin using a pocket flashlight with a powerful beam to illuminate the walls one by one. It lingered on a section speckled with what could be dried blood. "Do you wish me to leave, Prosecutor?"

With the beam still full on the blood spots Tanaka Gin said, "I believe you knew the deceased, Linnear-san."

So this was what he meant, Nicholas thought. *I know something about you.* "I met him perhaps once or twice. I did not know him."

Now Tanaka Gin turned on his heel and his hooded eyes fixed Nicholas. "No? But he was a partner in the Trans-Rim CyberNet."

Damn Kanda Tōrin and his overweening desire to get the CyberNet on-line, Nicholas thought. *This prosecutor knows more about the partnership deal than I do.*

"If he was, it comes as news to me," Nicholas said. "If you have done your homework, Prosecutor, you know that I was not involved in the TransRim partnership itself."

Tanaka Gin's eyebrows raised slightly. "Can this be possible? Your own American computer techs developed the CyberNet technology. How is it possible you have been kept out of the loop?"

Ask Tōrin, Nicholas thought. To Tanaka Gin, he said, "Nangi-san made that decision while I was otherwise occupied overseas. As I understand it, the business climate dictated we get the CyberNet on-line as quickly as possible.

Since Sato itself was unable to raise that much capital so quickly, Nangi-san decided to turn to outside partners. I think it was a good idea. Right now the *keiretsu* can ill afford to take on the onerous debt the TransRim start-up costs would impose."

Tanaka Gin made no reply, but walked toward the wall. "I wonder whether it was here, near the bar. In any case, some wicked blade—nothing our people have ever seen before—pierced his flesh, not once, but many times. Over and over."

"A slasher."

Without turning around Tanaka Gin slipped a couple of photos out of his breast pocket, handed them to Nicholas. They were of Rodney Kurtz's corpse in situ, Nicholas saw by the light of one of the bronze lamps. Close-ups of his face, neck, and shoulders.

"Where did you find the body?"

"Not here in the house. He had been dumped near Tsukiji." Tanaka Gin meant Tokyo's enormous fish market. The light, brighter now with Tanaka Gin's proximity, wavered slightly. "Arcane weapons, I believe, are a specialty of yours, Linnear-san. Can you tell me what kind of weapon the murderer used, a spike or—"

"Not from these photos. This body is too ripped up to make a guess. But if you'd keep your people on the lookout for any new murders that fit this pattern—"

"Done," Tanaka Gin said, making a note on a slim pad. "Perhaps not a slasher, then. There is a pattern carved into his forehead."

Indeed, there was. "A vertical crescent," Nicholas said, studying the photos in greater detail.

"Precisely."

In one of them, Nicholas saw the beginning of a curious dark blotch in the lower right corner of one photo, where Kurtz's chest began. What could that be? Another wound?

He looked up to see Tanaka Gin watching him. A look of intense curiosity was on the prosecutor's face.

"They say that even at the point of death you could will yourself to show no emotion." Tanaka Gin cocked his head to one side. "Is this true? I wonder."

Nicholas handed back the crime-scene photos. "Why would this concern you?"

"It is you I am dealing with now, Linnear-san. Before I do, a common ground must be struck." Tanaka Gin made a gesture that might be construed to be conciliatory. "I think you would agree all relationships work best this way."

"All except those with women."

"So? I would have said *especially* with women."

"I can see you are no romantic, Prosecutor," Nicholas said, walking out of the lamplight into the darkness to stand beside the other man. "Where love is concerned, *not* knowing what is ahead is often most important."

"Ah, I see the difficulty. You were speaking of love and I was referring to sex." Tanaka Gin played the beam of light slowly across the speckled wall. "Too often the two are not compatible."

Nicholas took a look around the room. "Gin-san, I wonder whether you would allow me access to the rest of the house?"

"As you wish. I have no objection. The place has already been dusted for fingerprints and photographed."

Nicholas went off through the house. He looked through rooms filled with a mortal silence, but in his inner mind he heard a screaming, an echo perhaps of the pain that had existed in this house for some time. He opened his *tanjian* eye, on the lookout for anything out of the ordinary. Black fingerprint powder lay everywhere like soot from a leaky furnace. He went through the dining room, Kurtz's study, all the bedrooms. The marble master bathroom was ultraluxe. It contained a shower, a Japanese cedar bathtub, and a fiberglass Jacuzzi. The juxtaposition of the traditional and the modern was jarring.

He sat down on the edge of the Jacuzzi. Where it abutted the wall was an access panel for the Jacuzzi plumbing. Something about the panel caught his eye. Bending over, he examined one of the four screws that held it in place. Was that a scratch on the plate near it? No. He unscrewed the screw, saw a human hair carefully wrapped around the threads. Its end, sticking out slightly, had looked like a scratch. There was no doubt in his mind that it had been deliberately set there. Why? To let someone know if the plate had been tampered with?

He unscrewed the plate, put it aside. Inside, he found an expensive, hardened-steel combination wall safe. That explained the carefully wound hair. He ran his fingertips around the door and discovered that it was unlocked. He swung it open and peered inside. Empty. Ransacked by Rodney Kurtz's murderer? It would seem so. And whoever it had been had been meticulous enough not to disturb the hair and clever enough to have seen it.

When he returned to the living room, he found Tanaka Gin standing in exactly the same position.

Tanaka Gin said, "There were pubic hairs on the dining room table and on Kurtz's desk. Curious, don't you think?"

"Sex and death. A strong, almost uncontrollable connection among certain people."

Tanaka Gin turned. "Certain people?" He nodded slowly, as if divining a hidden meaning to Nicholas's words. "Can't you just see the man as he held Kurtz while he drove the blade in, quite deliberately, again and again. The man was passionate but there was, I think, no red haze, no frenzy. It was all quite well thought out."

"Was this before or after he had Kurtz's wife in the dining room and Kurtz's office?"

Tanaka Gin appeared to be doing no more than counting the blood spots. He took a deep breath. "That depends, doesn't it?"

"On what?"

"Whether or not she was involved in the murder." His eyes slid sideways to gather Nicholas into their web. "Witnesses to Giai Kurtz's death say that she was with a man— a Westerner. After the black Mercedes hit her he took off after it and no one saw him again."

It was at this moment that Nicholas realized just how good a detective this man was. "You're certain it was a Mercedes?"

"Absolutely. We found it early this morning at a building site in Shibuya, abandoned and burned to a cinder." He snapped off the light. "By the way, the medical examiner has determined that Kurtz was murdered ten to twelve hours before the wife was struck by the Mercedes."

"Do you think she was deliberately killed?"

"Hit-and-runs are not routine in this city. But perhaps this one was different." Tanaka Gin shrugged, his thin frame outlined like a charcoal sketch by the lamplight. "This is my working hypothesis, anyway."

In the dimness, the two men stood shoulder to shoulder, breathing in the scents of sex and death.

"Tell me, Linnear-san, what does the image of vertical crescent mean to you?"

Nicholas hesitated. He had seen that symbol before. It was *ngoh-meih-yuht*, a phrase in an obscure Chinese dialect that meant "the crescent moon." It was the Gim, the Two-Edged Sword, the initiation symbol into a cult of myth and magic. It was part of a Vietnamese Nung tribe tattoo he had seen on the Messulethe, Do Duc Fujiro, the man who had tried to murder Mikio Okami. The Messulethe were terrifying psycho-magicians; so ancient legend had it, they were descended from the Cycladeans and the Titans. It was even rumored that their magic had been the precursor to Tau-tau.

But Okami was not a part of this investigation and Nicholas did not want him involved in any way. Also, he had killed Do Duc on Japanese soil and he did not want that incident investigated. He said, "I don't know."

"This man who destroyed the Kurtzes, I think, is exceptionally dangerous." Tanaka Gin's head swung around, his eyes glittering in the low lamplight. "Would you tell me if it did mean anything to you?"

He was an excellent interrogator, as well, Nicholas thought. "Of course. I have nothing to hide." But he could not shake the terrible sensation that had hit him like the stink of a charnel house the moment he had stepped through the Kurtzes' front door: that another Messulethe had been loosed.

He was very close to the blood-spattered wall and he felt himself sinking down, inward toward *kokoro* almost despite himself. Something dark and inexplicable seemed to be calling to him like echoes beneath a deep-water lake.

"Interesting. I would imagine a man who is sworn to protect the Kaisho would have much to keep secret." Tanaka Gin shrugged. "But perhaps I am mistaken. After all, what can I, a civil servant, know of such things?"

Nicholas felt a kind of schizophrenia come over him. Part of his mind reacted, dismayed that Tanaka Gin knew something of his relationship with Mikio Okami. That could prove dangerous. But part of him was already adrift from the bonds of time and space.

He had put the flat of his hand against the wall. The fingers, barely curled so their ends made contact, acted like a fiber-optic cable, transmitting data. The world had canted over on its side, diminishing in Akshara as if he were flying away from a spit of land. Time dissolved like a lozenge in the mouth, and he was back in this room as it had been the day before.

Tanaka Gin was right in at least part of his hypothesis. "He was here," Nicholas whispered.

Tanaka Gin's torso swayed forward as if drawn by the suck of time collapsing in upon itself. "Who? Who was here with Giai Kurtz? Her husband?"

"At first, yes. Then, later . . ."

Tanaka Gin was breathless. He had heard of Nicholas Linnear's arcane powers, but he had been loathe to believe the stories. However, looking at Nicholas's drawn face, he knew this was no illusionist, no rigged freak-show exhibit. Whatever was happening was real, and he thought, *there is real hope here for me.* "Yes, what happened later?"

"Kurtz was murdered here."

"In this house, you mean."

"Right here." Nicholas moved his hand over the wall. His face seemed even more twisted, deformed, as if it were being illuminated from below. "Someone else. Some . . ." Abruptly, he shuddered. He was quite white.

"Linnear-san are you all right? What is it you saw?"

"I . . ."

"Who was with Giai Kurtz?"

"The same person who murdered her husband."

Tanaka Gin emitted the smallest sigh. "Did you see him?"

There it was again, that familiar static in his mind that he associated with Mick Leonforte and with—what?—a feeling or sensation like a host of insects crawling inside him, tiny pincers clipping his flesh. Perhaps dark presentiment described it best. But he could not say any of this to Tanaka Gin. "I saw . . . something."

"What was it, a shadow?" *He is still not himself,* Tanaka Gin thought. What had happened to him? "Linnear-san, you must tell me everything."

Nicholas stared at the prosecutor for a long time, but his eyes were oddly focused, as if he saw something *inside* Tanaka Gin's body. Outside, cars hissed by and trucks making nighttime deliveries ground their gears and passed on to unknown destinations.

"You can trust me, Linnear-san. This I swear to you."

Nicholas nodded, a spastic jolt of his head.

"Tell me what your Tau-tau revealed to you. We will come to an understanding, you and I, because I think we can help one another."

Nicholas was staring out the jalousied window where lights sparked and danced on the river. "How can I help you?"

Tanaka Gin lifted his arm. "Shall we sit down a moment?"

They sat on a rattan sofa, while the light from the Golden Turd across the Sumida filtered through the jalousies.

But almost at once, Nicholas jumped up. "This is a violent place, filled with hatred and rage."

"So I've heard. There are rumors that Mr. Kurtz beat his wife."

"Did she ever file charges?"

"No. But unfortunately that is the norm in pattern physical-abuse cases."

Nicholas, silhouetted by the lights, seemed all alone and a little bit lost. Tanaka Gin could understand just how he felt. It had only been a month since Ushiba's death. Friendship such as theirs had been should not be so abruptly severed. He was still trying to recover.

"I want to trust you," Nicholas said. "Now is a time when I must trust *someone.*"

"About Kurtz. There's something about the body I haven't told you." Tanaka Gin's steady gaze regarded Nicholas with equanimity. "Some of his organs were missing— heart, pancreas, liver." So that explained the dark smudge at the bottom of one of the photos, Nicholas thought. It had been part of the hole through which the organs had been removed. "They had been excised with surgical precision.

the medical examiner assured me. The vertical crescent, the missing organs, do these mean anything to you?"

They did. Dominic Goldoni's heart had been taken from him when the Messulethe killed him, but Nicholas was not going to tell Tanaka Gin about that. "No, but I'm willing to do some research."

"That would undoubtedly be helpful."

Nicholas wondered how much irony to read into that comment. Again, he had the impression that the prosecutor knew more than he was letting on. But he had not time to dwell on this because he was trying to work out something significant. And physically shocked as he was, he knew he needed to solve this problem to clear his head, to try to forget what he had seen while he had been in contact with the death wall. It was like a new wound, pulsing in the center of his mind.

We will come to an understanding, you and I, because I think we can help one another. That was what Tanaka Gin had said, and Nicholas could see his point: this was no ordinary murderer and the prosecutor's instincts had told him so. Obviously, he knew something about Tau-tau, knew some potent stimulus left at what he believed to be the murder site might bring on the psychic dislocation of time and space that allowed Nicholas to "see" what had happened here. That was why he had asked Nicholas to meet him here at the Kurtzes' instead of at his office, which would have been standard operating procedure.

He must be desperate for my help, Nicholas thought.

The two men were silent for some time, Nicholas because he was working out the vectors of this new situation, the prosecutor because he wanted to give Nicholas time to recover his inner equilibrium.

At length, Tanaka Gin stirred. "When I arrested the *oyabun* Tetsuo Akinaga, I did so in public. He lost a great deal of face. Perhaps that was a tactical mistake on my part. Akinaga-san is a formidable enough foe without enraging him. But I was very angry myself because, in a way, he caused the death of an honorable man and a good friend."

Tanaka Gin looked away, at the wall and its tiny constellations of blood spots.

"In any event, he warned me, 'There are mechanisms in

113

place within your own department that will lead to your destruction.' Those were his words exactly. I have not forgotten them nor the look in his eyes."

"Bluster from a man trying to regain some face."

Tanaka Gin inclined his head. "My thoughts also, Linnear-san. Except that Akira Chosa, another of the Yakuza *oyabun,* told me much the same thing. 'If it's corruption you're after, look to your own department,' he said. As you have said, I have developed some small repute as a reformer. Understandably, this has alienated me from more people than you would imagine. Also, it has spawned some powerful enemies in highly unexpected places." Tanaka Gin cleared his throat. "Someone is hindering my case against Akinaga and I cannot tell who it is."

"You think I can?" At last it was becoming clear: Gin's acquiescing to Nangi's request, allowing Nicholas the run of a murder crime scene, his deliberately leaving provocative clues in situ. Here was Gin's need, spread out on the table.

"I know it, Linnear-san." Tanaka Gin's eyes glittered. "It is the Tau-tau. How you were able to see—the violence here, the rage inside the marriage."

"Perhaps there was that between Rodney and Giai Kurtz, but what I see, what I feel here, is far stronger. It is from someone else."

"The murderer, Linnear-san!"

"Yes, perhaps."

Tanaka Gin, his eyes alight, leaned forward. "You saw him, didn't you? Tell me who he is."

"I don't know. I can scarcely believe what I . . ." Nicholas had to start all over again, but his voice was now a harsh whisper as the psychic wound that had been opened at the death wall regathered its force. "Gin-san, I reached out with Tau-tau, with my mind to see who murdered Rodney Kurtz and perhaps Giai Kurtz as well . . . and it was like looking into a dark mirror." He pressed his fingertips to his temple. "I saw myself."

Experiment in Terror

The man who sees two or three generations
is like one who sits in the conjuror's booth
at a fair, and sees the same tricks two or
three times. They are meant to be seen
only once.

—Schopenhauer

Ozone Park, N.Y.

Spring 1961

For as long as he could remember, Mick Leonforte had had the same dream. He was a young man—not the boy he had been when he first started having the dream—and he looked nothing like the darkly handsome Mediterranean-blooded person he saw in the mirror every morning. He was blond and blue eyed, smartly dressed in white—always white—and he was a long way from his family apartment on 101st Avenue and Eighty-seventh Street in the Ozone Park area of Queens.

Exactly where he was he could not say. Maybe it was Florida or Europe or something because there were palm trees and cool trade winds and sunlight sparkling off a green ocean studded with luxury yachts. But maybe it wasn't Florida after all because everyone was speaking a foreign language, not Italian, not English, even him. Anyway, come to think of it, he'd been to Florida once with his father and his brother, Caesare, and this wasn't it.

For sure, it was someplace exotic and he was with someone heavenly, a girl tall and lean with long brown limbs so shapely you didn't want to take your eyes off them, and blond hair tied back off her oval face in a French braid and green eyes cool and deep as that ocean.

She was sitting next to him on the buffed tan leather of the gold and black Stutz Bearcat's seats, and her tan knees were visible below the hem of the silk skirt she'd had to hike up to get into the car. She was smiling at him while a few wisps of hair by her ear fluttered against her cheek. The sight of those knees and just an inch or two of thigh above was enough to give him heart palpitations.

"Michael," she said into the wind. "Michael."

She always called him Michael, never Mick, and he loved her for it. But then he adored everything about her, so much so that the feeling was like an ache in his heart, as if she were part of him, inside him, privy to all his thoughts, all his secrets. All the darkness.

And still she loved him.

He felt lighter than air, as if he could scale the white clouds painted on the sky like cartoons.

In the dream, he drove her in his Stutz Bearcat along a road that wound through dark green cypresses that rose thin as pencils out of a white cliff that hung at the water's edge. Every so often they'd pass a house, bright with a tomato-colored tiled roof, its stucco walls white and pristine as milk.

The feeling of freedom was like a drug in his veins. It pulsed like a tropical moon over water, shivering his spine. He reached out to touch her and she grabbed his hand, engulfing his fingertips with her ripe red lips.

Then they were on a slate dance floor at an open-air nightclub that hung high above the ocean on a cantilevered terrace, lined with heavily scented roses. A band in tuxedos was playing "Moonlight Becomes You," and the girl was in his arms, warm and syrupy, as if she were made of honey. Her eyes held his and in them he could see reflected the line of Chinese lanterns strung diagonally across the dance floor, tiny saintly auras through which they passed, one by one, as they danced.

What he particularly loved was that the band was playing just for them. There was no one else in the nightclub and no one else would come. This was his place, and tonight, he did not want to be disturbed.

As if reading his mind, the band segued into "Moonlight Serenade" and he drew the girl closer to him so that he felt her hard body from breasts to knees, felt her like an electric current as her thigh slipped between his, felt himself getting hard, not just his penis, but his entire body—his mind, as well, until she was all he could think of, even the band and the Chinese lanterns and the ocean fading into a pale distance, leaving him there with her, united.

He could recall with an almost suprareal clarity the first time he had had this dream. Upon waking, he lay staring up at the ceiling with blind eyes, watching the play of light thrown off by the Chinese lanterns, strains of "Moonlight Serenade" still in his ears, the ineffably exquisite feel of her resilient thigh rubbing his crotch to unbearable smoothness like a sculptor's cloth.

Then a sharp rap on his door dissolved the dream's last residue, and he turned his head as the door of his bedroom opened inward and his sister, Jaqui, poked her head in.

"Time to get up, Michael."

That moment was, for him, frozen in time, as with an immense erotic charge and a superhot gush of mortification he realized that she was the girl in his dream.

Michael Leonforte's grandfather, for whom his older brother, Caesare, had been named, had emigrated to the New World in 1910. He had lived in an area of East New York called the Old Mill. It was a Sicilian ghetto at the bottom of Crescent Street at Jamaica Bay known familiarly by the younger generation as the Hole on account of the fact that its streets were twenty to thirty feet lower than any other in Brooklyn, or anywhere else in the five boroughs of New York, for that matter. At the turn of the century, the city fathers had declared all streets had to be a certain height above river level and they raised those found wanting. All except those in the Hole. No one knew exactly why. Perhaps there were too many existing houses there already or, more likely, because it was a ghetto and no one gave a shit.

In the early days, Mick's grandfather raised goats, selling their milk and their flesh to his fellow immigrants. Soon, though, he graduated to protection, which was far more lucrative. He also emigrated for the second time—out of the Hole and into a spacious third-story apartment in a brown-brick building on 101st Avenue and Eighty-seventh Street in Ozone Park, an area of Queens within which Sicilians and Neapolitans resided as uneasy neighbors.

Even in those days, moving from East New York to

Ozone Park was not an easy thing. Both areas were populated by hooligans, wiseguys, toughs, and just plain crazy button men in training. East New York was dominated—and always had been, it seemed—by the F&R, the Fulton-Rockaway Gang. They owned the turf bounded by Rockaway Avenue and Fulton Street, south of Atlantic Avenue. In Ozone Park, the Saints held sway, a newer but no less savage group of young men and pimply teens that had been born in the 1950s. Not to be outdone by their older enemies, the Saints even boasted a six-man suicide squad—point men in any turf rumbles. These certified madmen rode Cross Bay Boulevard in a prized Ford, full-panel, low pickup truck and were armed at all times with tire chains, handguns, and a variety of unpleasant-looking knives.

It was in this highly charged atmosphere that Mick grew up. Every time you went out into the street you had it in mind to defend yourself. But if outside life was violently confrontational, his family life was no less so. As the younger of the two brothers—he was also younger than his sister, but in the family scheme of things she didn't count—he was constantly tormented by thoughts of his father, John. In those days, no one spoke about Johnny Leonforte, not Johnny's older brother, Alphonse, not Johnny's own father, Grandfather Caesare, for whom Mick's older brother had been named.

What had happened to Johnny Leonforte? No one would speak of it. If he was dead, his children had not been told; if he was alive, he had never contacted them. To be sure, there were rumors in the neighborhood of humiliation and disgrace of such magnitude that it had broken Grandfather Caesare's spirit. Some said the Leonfortes were never the same again. But if anyone knew the exact nature of the secret, they would not say. Mick did not know what to believe, but Caesare, always the hothead, was constantly on guard, ready to get bloody to defend his absent father's honor. The fact that Mick would not join him, was in fact silent on the subject, only served to further inflame him.

Grandfather Caesare was slim and very tall, and he was so smart it didn't matter that he lacked the usual Sicilian trait of physical intimidation. Everyone was automatically terrified of him. As for Alphonse, he was as big as a bear and just as tough. Many was the bruising fight he'd get into just for the sheer pleasure of mauling another human being. Mick's older brother, Caesare, wished for that ability, but all he got for it was a series of bloody noses and, worse, Uncle Alphonse coming to his rescue. This constant humiliation he took out on Mick, who seemed to lack all the skills at petty perfidy that Caesare possessed in spades.

Caesare, having been named after his beloved grandfather, was the favorite, that was common knowledge inside the household, and perhaps as things fell out, outside as well. Uncle Alphonse had a strap hanging on the inside of the door to the bathroom that he used on Mick and Caesare with liberal and gleeful intent, recalling, perhaps, the beatings his father had inflicted on him in the "backhouse," as the outhouse was called.

In this situation, Mick had two choices: he could hew to the traditional upbringing his odd family provided and continue to love his father's memory as Caesare did, or he could rebel and hate his father for abandoning the family. What it was inside Mick that caused him to choose the latter path it was impossible to say. But the fact was, by the time he was fourteen, he was already inwardly estranged from a father he could not remember and was immutably bonded to his grandfather.

Old Caesare, in his ubiquitous black suit and fedora, looked like a Sicilian crow on a fence rail. His black eyes, ringed by squint lines, peered out from the penumbra of the fedora's brim with a startling clarity. He had these enormous square hands that invited attention. He would sit at the kitchen table, a water glass of valpolicella in front of him, smoking cigarettes, which he placed between the pinky and ring finger of his right hand. Yellow with nicotine, this right hand felt like a bear's paw when it gripped Mick, which was often. Grandfather Caesare was animated when he spoke or lectured on topics that were dear to him. He could come to an important point in his narrative, jam his cigarette into his mouth, and clamp Mick's shoulder with a viselike grip whose terrible intensity at first made Mick tremble.

"You're a good boy," he would say. "You're smart enough, but it's a different kind of smart. This work—the biziness—it is not for you— unnerstand?"

Mick would come to understand what the old man meant, but all he got from his grandfather then was that he was loved even though he was different. For the moment, that was enough, though it wouldn't be for long.

Mick's brother, Caesare, was a complete mystery to him. Looking in Caesare's eyes, Mick could see a light that seemed not very distant from the one he observed in red stars as he peered through the telescope his grandfather bought him that year for Christmas. Each night he'd throw the telescope over his shoulder and climb up to the roof, setting it up on the black asphalt to peer through the big-city light-haze into the night-darkened sky. What he saw there fascinated him because in imagining himself far, far away he could look down upon Earth and see continents other than his own.

He was also as far away as possible from Uncle Alphonse, who was, in any case, increasingly away setting up his family in his new home base of San Francisco.

Every so often, up on the roof, as he was folding up his telescope for the night, he'd hear a heavy car door slam, and looking over the parapet, he'd see Grandfather Caesare walking across the courtyard, coming home after being driven from a nighttime meeting at his office or perhaps at the Fountainbleu Florists on Fulton and Pine streets, where a lot of heavy-duty meets were set. Seeing the old man from above with his black fedora and the spring still in his step after so many years gave Mick the sense of continuity he'd never received from a father who was entirely absent.

What Mick liked best was to visit his grandfather at work. His office was above the Mastimo Funeral Home on Conduit Avenue. Tony Mastimo was an old-time funeral director with four daughters and no son to carry on the business. He was old and tired when he sold out to Grandfather Caesare, but perhaps not as old and tired as he made out to the world at large. Caesare made him an offer he was smart enough to accept. Now he lived with his new wife in a small but neat row house in Bay Ridge and played boccie when he wasn't taking her on trips to Europe.

It was a good deal for everyone involved. Within six months of taking over, Grandfather Caesare had magically turned the funeral parlor into a cash cow. Within a year, he had opened two other Mastimo Funeral Homes in Queens, all of them instantly successful. Such was his charisma and his repute.

Grandfather Caesare's rise in Ozone Park was altogether meteoric, but not without its rough spots. Jealousies quite naturally erupted both from those who were his rivals and from the family remnants of those who had been displaced. Those latter were no longer around. Most had simply disappeared, although it was true that several of the most vocal and openly antagonistic had been found in the backseats of anonymous cars in the junkyards at the end of Pennsylvania and Fountain avenues. To a man, they displayed a single bullet hole through the backs of their heads, which was enough to subdue or at least silence the rest of Grandfather's enemies.

Grandfather liked three lumps of sugar in his espresso and a generous dollop of anisetto. This and many other minuscule peculiarities Mick memorized instantaneously so that after school, when he visited Grandfather at his place of business above the Mastimo Funeral Home on Conduit Avenue, he could provide these services for the old man. Most often Mick took the Green Bus Line, but sometimes in good weather he biked over.

Naturally, his brother, Caesare, scoffed at such servitude, since he was already out on the street with a gun he knew how to fire, but Mick ignored his brother. Unlike his older brother, who was eager to make his bones, daily violent confrontation with the dangerously low IQ *gavonnes* of either Ozone Park or East New York held no special interest for Mick. And when he was with Grandfather while he was working, he could silently observe all that went on: the *capi* who came to do business and to genuflect before the old man, the friends who gathered at the round oak table to smoke hand-rolled cigars and drink wine, clear spirits, and espresso, and to talk. He learned from his grandfather the nuances of command, the necessity for humor and the darkness of life. Gradually, he discerned something that fascinated him: his grandfather had many acquaintances and, it seemed by the number who sat with him, even more enemies, but almost no friends, or at least people in whom he could confide with openness.

"Friendship is a strange and unruly animal," his grand-father once said to him as he stirred the sugar into his espresso. "Like a lame dog you take offa the street and nurse back to health who then bites you onna hand, you must treat friendship with equal amounts of apprehension and skepticism."

They were alone in Grandfather's office, which when it didn't smell of espresso and anisette and fear, smelled strongly of sickly sweet embalming fluid. Outside, it was pissing down rain, the traffic along Conduit hissing like serpents aroused from slumber.

He took a long drag of his cigarette and seized Mick's shoulder in his bone-crushing grip. The smoke, let out in a soft sigh, closed one eye. "Me, I prefer the company of my enemies and I'll tell you why. I know who they are and what they want from me." He turned Mick around so that he could fix the teenager with his black eyes. "Besides, the more time you spend with your enemies, the better you get to know 'em." He smiled then, and it was as if Mick's whole universe expanded exponentially. "But you, you smart dunce, you already know that, don't you?"

Grandfather then did an extraordinary thing. "Here, sit down nexta me," he said. He pulled over a cup and poured espresso into it. He plopped in three cubes of sugar, stirred it with a small spoon, then pushed it over in front of Mick. "Drink up. It's timea you enjoyed a little of what you bring to me."

It was the first and only time that Grandfather Caesare in any way acknowledged that he knew why Mick so often visited him at work.

Mick's older brother, Caesare, may have had no respect for Mick, but he was not above using him when the need arose. Mick was not then so much the rebel that he could refuse his brother, but somehow, he always ended up regretting his involvement.

Take the incident of the turquoise Fairlane. One day Caesare comes to Mick and he says, "Hey, kid, I need ya t'do somethin' for me. It's easy, don't worry. Even a civilian like you can do it, no sweat." He put two sets of keys into Mick's hand, one for a car. "I wancha to go inta Manhattan.

There's this faggoty blue Ford Fairlane parked ata meter on Tenth Avenue. By Fiftieth Street, okay? All's you gotta do is get in an' drive it to this here address around the corner from the Jamaica Avenue post office, right?" He told Mick an address. "This other key'll open an apartment ona fourth floor. Piece of cake." He put a twenty-dollar bill in Mick's hand. "There's twenty more when you deliver both keys to the man'll be there, okay?" Mick nodded. "Right. Got that driver's license I gotcha says you're eighteen?" Mick nodded again. "Fuck you waitin' for? Get goin'."

This Mick did. Not that he didn't resent being spoken to this way. Not that he didn't have misgivings about anything his brother asked him to do. But family was family. The Fairlane—actually a beautiful turquoise—was parked just as Caesare had said. The meter still had time on it and it had a full tank of gas. It was some beautiful set of wheels, and Mick spent a half hour admiring every line, every dazzling inch of chrome. At last, he started her up and pulled out into traffic. Everything was fine until some schmuck ran a red light at the big intersection at Thirty-fourth Street and cut him off. He almost accordioned the front end of the Fairlane, and although he was able to keep the car from being scratched, he was royally pissed off.

The other guy, a civilian in a brown suit, was so shaken up he shook his fist in fury at Mick. That was not the smartest thing for him to have done because it got Mick even more pissed off. All the pent-up anger at his father and his brother erupted out of him like a volcano blowing its top, and he strode over to the other motorist, hauled him out through the open window, and beat the back of his head against the chrome of his white Chevy until blood started to run.

Perhaps it was the sight of blood running, but he suddenly came to his senses, and letting the motorist fall against the car, he strode back to the Fairlane on rubbery legs, slammed it in gear, and roared away.

He arrived in Jamaica without further incident, passing by the grimy stone facade of the post office on Jamaica Avenue. He parked across the street from the apartment, locked the car, and went up the brownstone stoop into a dim vestibule that smelled of garlic and rosemary. He took the stairs two at a time, thinking about what he was going to do with his forty dollars, and rapped on the appropriate door.

When there was no answer, he used the keys and let himself in. He was in a sparsely furnished one-bedroom that smelled of old gym socks. An old Norge hummed in a linoleum-covered kitchen. In the tiny bathroom, a tap dripped into a sink whose bottom was the same color as the Fairlane.

No one was home. Back in the living room, he went around the brown tweed couch, glanced out the window at the Fairlane parked beneath a Dutch elm tree, dusty with soot. He put the keys on the kitchen table, which was covered with a faded patterned piece of oilcloth, and opening the Norge, put some ice on the knuckles of his right hand, which were sore and skinned from his altercation with the motorist on Thirty-fourth Street. He wanted to leave but he also wanted his second twenty. Out in the living room, the telephone began to ring.

After a moment's inner debate, he went and picked up the heavy black receiver.

"Mick, that you?" said a familiar voice in his ear.

"Caesare?"

"Fuck you do? I tol' you zackly what you had to do. Fuck you do?"

"Do?" Mick said, bewildered. "What did I do?"

"Fuck do I know? But I getta call from our man inna precinct, cops is after the man that drove the Fairlane. Seems some insurance salesman called the police once he got to the emergency room of Roosevelt Hospital, gave the cops the license plate number ova Ford."

"Jesus."

"You tellin' me," Caesare said. "Look out onta the street, kid, tell me whatcha see."

Mick craned his neck. "Ah, fuck, a cop car's what I see."

"Yeah, you do, you little prick. An' you know what's inna trunka that Fairlane? Ten poundsa pot an' the same of heroin."

Great, Mick thought. *That fuckin' brother of mine. Now I'm in the same sackful of shit he's in.* "Fuck you doin' with that shit?"

"Fuck you think I'm doin'? Makin' a fuckin' living while you're playing busboy down by the funeral."

"Grandpa says drugs have no part of our biziness," Mick said, somewhat judiciously.

"Listen to the big shot," Caesare said, his voice dripping contempt. "Fuck you know about the biziness, kid? Fuck all, is what. So you leave makin' the money to me. Times is changin' but Grandpa he's still got one foot inna Hole. All due respect to the old bird, but the world's passin' him by."

If Caesare had been in the same room with him instead of connected by voice through a telephone cable, Mick was quite certain he would have wrung his neck or at least tried to for that kind of remark. As it was, all he could muster was, "Fuck you."

"Hey, watch that fuckin' mouth, kid." Caesare chuckled. "Well, now you know what's what, here's what you gotta do. You gotta get the shit outta the trunk without the cops knowin'."

"But Caesare—"

"Just do it, kid," Caesare barked, "or I swear I'll come over there myself and beat you black-an'-blue."

Mick slammed down the receiver and stood with his hands jammed in the back pockets of his trousers. He peered out the window. Fuckin' cops. They'd be sitting there all night waiting for him to show. What the hell was he gonna do?

The light was fading. At six o'clock, he was still wondering how he was going to get Caesare's stash when he saw the cop car take off. A couple of minutes later, another one took its place. He sat up and paid careful attention. Sure. He should have thought of it before: shift change. When was the next one? He racked his brain for the information he had picked up on the street. Four in the morning.

He settled into the apartment, made himself some pasta with tomato sauce, then got a couple of hours of sleep. He was up at one and then three. After that, he couldn't fall back to sleep. Besides, there was no time. He had to be in place when the shift changed. And he knew he had to be lucky. If the four A.M. car arrived before this shift was up, he was fucked.

It didn't. At four on the nose, the cop car swung out of its spot, cruised off down the street. As it turned the corner, heading up to Jamaica Avenue, Mick was tearing across the street, key in hand. He fumbled at the Fairlane's trunk lock, got it open. He filled his arms with Caesare's shit, slammed the trunk shut, and hotfooted it out of there.

It should have been that Mick was happy to drop the shit into his brother's lap and Caesare pissed at how he'd fucked up, but the funny thing was, it turned out just the opposite. In fact, Mick was so scared by his brush with the cops, he was in a towering rage when he came into the house.

After a brief glance to make sure they were untouched, Caesare put the packages aside and, grabbing Mick around the shoulders, bent his head so he could kiss the top of it. "Kid, I gotta admit I never thought I'd say it, but you're so okay you should come work for me."

"Hey, cut it out," Mick said, flailing his arms like a windmill. He stood back from his brother, looked around to make sure their mother or Jaqui wasn't in the vicinity. Then he pointed a finger at his brother and, with heretofore unknown storm clouds beetling his brow, said, "You sonuvabitch, if you ever get me involved in your stinking drug runs again, I'll cut off your balls."

Instead of taking offense, Caesare laughed. Why wouldn't he? This was his younger brother talking, a skinny kid who preferred hanging out with their grandfather than making his bones on the street like every other male his age. Who could take anything he said seriously? But Caesare did object to one thing. "Keep your fuckin' voice down. Fuck'samatta wich you? Ya wanna broadcast this alla way to the women?"

Mick knew what Caesare really meant. He didn't give a shit about the Leonforte women, who were, in any case, nonentities as far as the biziness was concerned. He was terrified Grandfather Caesare would get wind of what he was up to, and then, the favorite or not, he'd really catch it.

"I want my money," Mick said.

"Sure, sure, kid." Caesare drew out a roll of bills, which he carried just like the older made men they saw around the neighborhood. He peeled off a bill. "Here's your twenty."

But Mick shook his head. "I deserve more than that."

"Fuck for?"

"Hazardous duty, Caesare." Mick held out his hand. "I got your shit past the cops. You owe me."

Caesare looked hard into his younger brother's eyes and saw he wasn't kidding. He also knew the kid was right and he laughed. "Fuck you. I tol' you forty an' that's what you gettin'."

Mick grinned at him. "I wonder what Grandpa would say to all these drugs you're selling."

"You know fuckin' well what he'd say." Caesare's eyes squinted hard. "You little extortionist." But he was grinning as he forked over another two twenties. "Here, fuckface, don't spend it all in one place."

"Eighty dollars," Grandfather Caesare said, staring down at the four twenty-dollar bills Mick had laid on the round table in his office. The place stank of formaldehyde, cigar smoke, and stale sweat. Mick had watched for three hours while the old man negotiated with his allies and enemies for pieces of turf that had been under dispute so long they were known as a battle zone for the Saints and the Fulton-Rockaways to let off steam. Now, with increased vigilance by the cops, that no longer seemed like such a good idea.

The settlement had been hammered out at last, but it hadn't gone down well with all parties. The dark-faced Frank Vizzini of Bay Ridge, known as the Importer, and the sausagelike Tony Pentangeli of the Rockaways, who controlled the truckers, both afraid of change and dissensions within their families, were adamantly opposed to the plan. Paul Vario, who took a piece of everything that went in and out of Kennedy Airport, was neutral, as was Black Paul Mattaccino from Astoria, who, like Grandfather, controlled segments of the insurance and fire protection industries, as well as the Fulton Fish Market and the humongous import-export business owned by the Venetian, don Enrico Goldoni. All of them were into the unions. That was one pie big enough to go around the table.

Grandfather's negotiating skills, however, had won the day, along with the solid support he got from Gino Scalfa, one of the dons from East New York, who looked like a puffer fish and commanded a great deal of respect. He was one of the first dons Grandfather had gone to see when he had moved out of the Hole.

During the murderously tense session, Mick had observed

how his grandfather had cleverly preyed upon the various dons' personalities in order to manipulate their votes. Cataloging this skill more than compensated for his scurrying around the table, serving men who didn't even know he existed. Now, at last, they were all gone.

"Openna window," Grandfather Caesare said. "It's close in here."

He sighed deeply as Mick let the fresh air in. "Makes me kinda sad," he mused, almost to himself.

"What does, Grandfather?" Mick asked as he poured some anisette into a cordial glass and stuck it in front of the old man.

Caesare picked up the glass, watching how the light played off the crystal and the liquor. He took a deep breath. "That's the smell that makes it all worthwhile." He downed his anisette, sighed again. "Fix it inna you mind, Mikey, because it's the most important smell in life, more important even than the smell ova woman." He pursed his lips. "It'sa smell of fear and it'sa good smell."

He looked down at the twenties spread out in front of him. "This money?"

Mick, relieved that he hadn't been asked where he got the eighty bucks, said in a rush, "I wanna invest it."

"S'matta, you haven't gotta bank account?"

"Banks is for goofballs. I wanna invest it with you."

Mick went to pour him more anisette, but Grandfather waved him off. He rose, stretched, then put on his hat. "C'mon, I wanna show you somethin'." Then he pointed to the four bills. "Take that whicha."

Grandfather liked to drive. He had a '59 emerald green Caddy that was kept in pristine condition for him. He had a driver, of course, but truth to tell he preferred to drive. That was one of the great things about America, he had always said. Driving. As he aged, he had taken even more pleasure in driving that Caddy, and only Mick suspected part of the reason he did was that he could still do it, and a skill like that was becoming increasingly important to him.

This evening, he took Mick west about ten miles along the Belt Parkway down to Sheepshead Bay. In those days, a couple of country clubs and a hotel, the Golden Gate Inn, were down there by the Belt Parkway right at the bay, catering to the ginzoes. They liked the water. Who knows, maybe it reminded them of Italy.

Grandfather parked the car off the service road at the verge of where it got thick with overgrown weeds and the ferocious, unlovely underbrush of the city, and they got out. The sun was just going down. Seagulls were wheeling, calling to each other from out of a sky the color of mother-of-pearl. Grandfather stared down at the water, which, in taking on the color of the sky, had disappeared.

"Beautiful, isn't it?"

Mick nodded.

Grandfather pointed. "Know how many people I know about inna bay tied to cement blocks? Twenty. And that's just me." He laughed, a dry sound like the scraping of boots against a cement sidewalk. "You know, that Gino Scalfa, you remember him, the fat one. He comes down here by himself every evening, stares inna water. Why? It keeps him sharp, he says, because it reminds him what happensa guys who get too greedy or too wise or too ambitious too soon. An' he's right. That's our world." He sighed as he took the twenties out of Mick's hand. "You know, whatchew asking me?"

"I know."

"Well." The old man made quite a show of folding the bills and pocketing them. "Let 'em grow, just like seeds, right?" He touched the brim of his fedora. "Not only enemies out there inna water, you know. Friends, too. Some of 'em I even miss." He turned to Mick and quite suddenly in a very low voice said in Italian, "Mikey, I'm gonna tell you the secret of life. Not *my* life, but *yours*. Don't wind up sounding like a mick. Educate yourself. Education is the key to knowing yourself, and without that you'll be lost like all these penny-ante hoodlums looking to make a name for themselves. Education is history and history can teach us everything we need to know because in history all the serious mistakes have already been made. A student of history is bound never to repeat them, and let me tell you, *not* making mistakes is what it's all about."

Grandfather Caesare's enormous hands pumped up and down. "This is America and it's a mistake to think of it like it's Sicily. It isn't, not even the Hole, much as we wanted it to be. Now I see even the wanting was wrong."

He pushed his hands apart, palms up, and switched back to English. "I mean, why'd we come here, anyway, to do the same things we were doing inna old country? No. We came for opportunity, yeah. But we also came to change." He winked at Mick. "Not too many *paisans* understand this, and inna end they're the ones'll die like dogs with their faces inna pavement."

Looking at the milky stars through the lens of his telescope, Mick heard his grandfather's voice. *Educate yourself.* There were the Big Dipper and Orion, the weaker stars made smudgy by the city's glow. He wished his brother had heard Grandfather. *We came for opportunity, yeah. But we also came to change.* Maybe then Caesare wouldn't think Grandfather was over the hill. Then, again, maybe not. Caesare had his own way of looking at the world—his own kind of philosophy—that, like it or not, Mick had to admire. He didn't agree with it, and he certainly didn't like his brother any more for it, but he was already three steps ahead of the wiseguys and would-be wiseguys all around him. Caesare was destined for great things, Mick knew, if he didn't die like a dog with his face in the pavement.

One night, a month or so after Grandfather had taken him down to Sheepshead Bay, Mick was up on the roof of his building staring at the stars. His eye ached with the strain of peering through the city's light at the pristine sky above.

He heard the door open behind him and took his eye away from the telescope. Rubbing it to get some circulation back into it, he saw a small figure emerge onto the tarred roof.

"Jaqui?"

"Hi, Michael," she said.

It was the beginning of June, had been one of those quintessential New York days that was as scorching as midsummer. Night had brought only minimal respite. Mick stared at his sister, who was dressed in a thin white cotton halter dress and sandals. Her shoulders and legs already glowed with the inner light of summer.

"How's it going?"

"Okay," he said, choking off the specter of his recurring dream. He pointed upward. "Just stargazing."

"I think it's great that you do that."

"You do?"

"Sure. You're not on the streets with those bums."

"I have no interest in bums," Mick said brazenly.

"Good for you."

Jaqui, who had been named by her mother in atypical Italian fashion after someone she had read about in *Life* magazine, did not speak like anyone else in Ozone Park. She was studious and conscientious and, in her quiet way, proud of both traits. It was rumored in the family—though Mick had never heard it spoken of—that she might become a nun. Certainly, she was a regular Mass-goer and often disappeared into the Sacred Heart of Santa Maria Convent in Astoria.

She was beautiful, it was true, with her wide-apart green eyes and luscious lips, but what Mick loved most about her was that she moved through Ozone Park as if it did not exist. She was immune to the daily violent altercations, the gangland turf wars, the guns and cigars in the house, even— and perhaps most importantly—the closed doors behind which the men met to discuss the biziness.

At nineteen, she was absolutely untouched by the savage world of the uneducated men, so different from their mother, who, after all, cooked for Grandfather Caesare and his cronies. In living by their rules, their mother had in some way become like them. But Jaqui was as isolated from them as the twinkling stars were from the streetlights of Ozone Park. In a way, she was already in that place where Mick longed to be, on another continent, unknown and far away.

Somewhere, from some other rooftop or perhaps an open window, Doris Day was singing "Love Me or Leave Me." *Never deceive me,* Mick thought. There was a sentiment not well known in Ozone Park.

When Jaqui walked, it seemed to Mick as if she were dancing, and as she moved dreamily toward him, he could not help picturing a cantilevered terrace, a tuxedoed band, a string of Chinese lanterns, elements resurrected from the dream he'd had so many times it had the substance of reality.

"Can I look?" she asked.

"Sure."

He beckoned and she put her eye to the lens. "What you're looking at is Orion. It's a constellation."

Jaqui looked at him with her cool green eyes and laughed. "I know that, dummy." But it was a gentle laugh, not anything like Caesare's, which was like a cattle prod in his ribs. Then she put her eye back at the telescope.

"How many stars in Orion?"

"Seven," he said. "Two shoulders, see 'em? And then three dimmer ones, those're his belt. And then, lower down, two more are his knees."

"I can't find the belt."

As he bent over her, he smelled the clean citrusy odor of her hair, and he felt his knees grow weak. Immediately, his cheeks burned with shame. How could he feel this way about his sister? But it wasn't just a physical thing, it was more. He knew that, and somehow the knowledge calmed him somewhat. She was like a part of him that had broken off, a piece he had been searching for.

He put his hands on her soft shoulders, moved her just slightly. "There."

"Yes. I see them now. Oh, Michael, how beautiful."

Of course it was so. Beautiful stars as opposed to ugly Ozone Park. How he longed to be with her on that cantilevered terrace on a continent far, far away. His fingers moving over her shoulders felt her skin raised in goose bumps, and her hair drifted onto his knuckle.

"Jaqui?"

She took her eyes from the lens. "Yes, Michael?"

"Nothing." He looked away and swallowed hard. What was he going to say to her? What madness had been about to escape his mouth? He put his hand up to his forehead to see if it was still burning with blood.

She clasped her hands behind her back and smiled. "You know what I also think is great?"

"What?"

"That you're sticking it out in school." She pursed her lips and shook her head. "That brother of ours is going to flunk out. I just know it. He's more interested in using a gun than in using his brain."

"What brain?" It was easy to make a joke at Caesare's expense when he wasn't around.

Jaqui frowned. "He isn't stupid, you know, not like the rest of those *gavonnes* he runs with. They're like the gang that couldn't shoot straight. If they had half a brain between them, they'd be dangerous."

Mick laughed, delighting in her insight. "Yeah, well, you know how Caesare is."

"I sure do. Tough as a bull and twice as stubborn. But inside that big bark of his lies a first-rate mind." She sighed. "If only he'd take your lead for once and apply himself to learning."

"Caesare? Not a chance. He's too busy lapping up all the street has to give him."

Jaqui stood very close to him. Her breath smelled like the roses in his dream, and for a dizzying moment it seemed to him as if they had been magically transported inside his dream, that it was real and the rooftop in Ozone Park was, in fact, the dream. Someone else's nightmare.

"Michael, this life makes me afraid. I'm not like Mom, just sitting still while all the wildness, the death, swirls around me, I can't imagine myself waiting patiently for a man to return home from that war. The fear, it's like something sleeping in my bones, you know?—like a disease that I'm fated to have but hasn't yet come to life." She shuddered and Mick could do nothing else but hold her. Her head on his shoulder was almost more than he could bear.

"I want out, Michael," she whispered in his ear, "so badly it's a taste in my mouth." She pushed away from him so her beautiful green eyes could meet his. "It's crazy, isn't it, what I just said?"

Tell her, stupid, a terrifying voice inside him begged. *If there ever was a time, this it is. Tell her everything.* But all he said was, "Not at all. I understand."

"You do? Really and truly?"

It was one of her favorite phrases. Where she had picked it up, he had no idea. "Really and truly."

Her smile was radiant as she hugged him to her. "Oh, Michael, thank God there's someone in the family I can talk to."

Now he understood the dilemma that bound them together as closely as did his recurring dream. *I'm not like Mom*. The men were off limits to her, and their mother was too traditional to understand the radical thoughts in Jaqui's head. But he understood, better than she would ever know.

"You can always talk to me," he said, "about anything."

"You're not like any of them." She sat on the parapet, ran a hand through her hair, and the lights of the city were reflected in her eyes. "No wonder you come up here every night. It's so far away from everything *down there*. All the evil energy, the stupid violence." She looked up at him, the naked, innocent look in her eyes stabbing at his stomach. "Why are men so violent, Michael? It's a question I ask myself over and over."

"I don't know. Maybe it's in the genes, you know, a territorial thing, like in the old days protecting the family."

He had caught her interest. "War is in men's blood, is that what you mean?"

"Yeah, kinda. They can't help it."

"But you're not like that."

"Maybe I got a genetic deficiency," he joked. They laughed together and he felt them drawing even closer, the dream and reality overlapping, exchanging places, reality and unreality fusing with the intoxicating scent of roses.

Then she shivered. "This discussion sounds eerily like a part of Friedrich Nietzsche's philosophy. Have you heard of him?"

"No."

"He was a nineteenth-century German philosopher whose theories on the nature of man were expropriated and maybe even distorted by the Nazis. They used him to, in part, justify their aims of ethnic cleansing. He was all for the primitive man—who lived in the tropics and the primeval forests of the soul. Nietzsche had only contempt for those men who dwelled in the temperate zones, whose morality was, in his mind at least, timidity."

"In other words, he believed that war lived in men's blood and souls."

Jaqui nodded. "I'd say so. And he'd also say that the most warlike men, like, for instance, Napoleon and Cesare Borgia, were misunderstood. Nietzsche believed that these men were condemned by moralists looking for evil, but in fact, Napoleon and Borgia were merely acting out the true nature of man."

Mick found this ideology irresistible since it at once made clear to him two points of view he had up to now found irreconcilable. Grandfather had said that education was the key to success because it showed you who you were, and Mick believed him. But what about Caesare? He was largely self-educated, having terrorized the local school into submission. He came and went there of his own volition. And yet, in his own despicable way, he was already successful. He had a fully formed outlook on life, an inner perspective, and now in Nietzschean terms, Mick could understand his success without education. He lived in the tropics, the primeval forests of the soul. He was like Napoleon and his namesake, Cesare Borgia.

At that moment, he heard the slam of a heavy car door and he looked over the parapet on which Jaqui was sitting. She turned to look down also, and they both saw Grandfather Caesare walking across the courtyard as his driver took the Caddy to the parking spot across the street that, by common consent, was always left vacant for it.

Mick was about to call out to the old man when he heard a sound. It might have been a voice, harsh and piercing in the night. It might have said, "Caesare Leonforte!"

The old man must have heard it as well because he halted, turning back toward the street. And that was when Mick saw the two shadows stride into the courtyard. At the same instant he yelled a warning, they opened fire. Bright yellow flames leaped from the muzzles of their handguns, and a great booming echoed off the stone facade of the courtyard. Blood spurted from the old man's chest and head as he was thrown backward.

Jaqui put her hand to her mouth and screamed. Mick had the presence of mind to pull her down from the parapet where she could be seen by the assassins. He crouched down with her, feeling the involuntary tremors rippling through her. Her green eyes were wide and staring, and she was biting on a knuckle in order not to scream again. A tiny rivulet of blood trickled between her fingers, and when Mick pulled her hand away, he saw the series of small crescent marks her teeth had made as they punctured her skin.

He felt her trying to stand up and he kept a tight hold on her. She opened her mouth to protest, but he put a hand across her lips, shook his head, making a gun out of his forefinger and thumb so she would get the idea that they were in danger unless they remained hidden.

A voice began to wail from an open window fronting the courtyard. Voices began to shout. Mick stood up, peered over the parapet. The courtyard was alive with people, but of course the assassins were nowhere in sight. Mick let go of his sister, ran to the side of the building facing 101st Avenue. He saw a dark-colored Cougar pulling out, heading very fast toward the light at Eighty-eighth Street. It was going to run the light, which had just turned red, but at almost the last instant the driver saw the cop car nosing up the side street and screeched to a halt.

Mick ran for his telescope, lugged it back to his vantage spot. Swinging the barrel over and down, he peered through the lens at the back of the dark-colored Cougar. The cop car had turned on its siren and flashing lights, headed directly for his house. He just had time to make out the license plate number of the Cougar when the driver threw it in gear and hot-rodded down the avenue as the light hit green.

"Did you see anything?" Jaqui said, her eyes wide. "The police are here. Can you help them?"

Mick, thinking of how she had said he wasn't like all the other males in Ozone Park, said, "There's wasn't anything to see."

He could see the disappointment in her eyes. "Really and truly?"

"Really and truly."

He folded down the telescope, put his arm around her. "Let's go downstairs."

They came out into the courtyard, having first deposited the telescope in the apartment. Sadly, it was an all too typical scene for Ozone Park. Women were weeping. The cops had already cordoned off the body and were interviewing everyone for potential witnesses. Caesare, in a rage of frustration and fear, was shouting at the cops. John was gone and Alphonse was three thousand miles away in San Francisco. Jaqui went immediately to their mother, who was sobbing in the arms of several other women.

Mick moved through the crowd until he was at the closest perimeter. His grandfather lay facedown in the courtyard in a pool of blood and brains and feces. It was a more horrifying sight than he could ever have imagined, and he stared fixedly at it, drinking in the horror as if for fortification. Slowly, he began to tremble.

Behind him, in ones and twos, the people dispersed as they were let go by the police. Caesare, vowing revenge, had stormed off. Mick's mother, half-fainting with shock, had been led into the house, and now Mick and Jaqui, having endured the cops' indifferent questions, stood together as police photographers took flash photos of the crime scene. Soon enough, the coroner arrived.

"You don't have to stay for this," Mick said quietly.

Jaqui took his hand, squeezing her fingers between his. "Yes, I do."

And there they stood, in the stone courtyard. No band was playing, and instead of the glow of Chinese lanterns the night was filled with the harsh light of flashbulbs popping. And with the stench of death instead of the attar of roses in his nostrils, Mick was left with his grandfather's ironically prophetic words: *And inna end they're the ones'll die like dogs with their faces inna pavement.*

"You want what?"

"I told you, Caesare, a trace of this license plate number."

Caesare Leonforte squinted at his younger brother. "You're a cute kid, ya know that, but I got no time for you now. I'm tryin'ta run down every fuck inna Fulton-Rockaways. I don't know who to whack first, the Vizzinis or the Pentangelis. Not to mention I'm not too sure where this young don, Dominic Mattaccino, stands. Y'know, with his father, Black Paul Mattaccino, to this day no one knows how he died. Then the widow takes up with Enrico Goldoni, it's not even a year since Black Paul kicked the bucket. And her brat Dominic takes over, thinks his shit don't stink. Maybe he ain't even Black Paul's son." Caesare threw up his hands. "An' what's Goldoni anyway, a fuckin' Venetian, for Christ's sake, that's maybe not even Italian." The hands spun like pinwheels. "What the fuck's he know from *la famiglia*, uh? Grandpa might've trusted him, but not me. This is fuckin' war. I got suspects comin' outta my ears, an' now *this.*"

The two brothers, along with perhaps a dozen of Caesare's

cronies, button men and minor family heads, were in Grandfather's office above the Mastimo Funeral Home. Despite the clamor and grim tension, it seemed cold and lonely, and Mick was just now realizing how much Grandfather Caesare's presence filled it up.

"I know that."

"Okay, you wanna be useful," Caesare said, "gimme an espresso."

"But I need this. It's very important. I think these wiseguys stole my telescope off the roof, the telescope Grandpa gave me."

Caesare tore at his hair. "Stolen telescopes? Madonna, Richie, whattam I gonna do with this kid?"

"Whyint I make the fuckin' call?" Richie said. "Get'em off our backs."

Caesare snapped his fingers. "Go on. Fuck not?"

An hour later, the call back came from one of the Leonfortes' contacts at the 106th Precinct. Richie, the receiver held between his shoulder and ear, scribbled frantically on a scratch pad. "Yeah, yeah, got it. Thanks." He cradled the receiver, ripped off the sheet, gave it to Mick.

"Here, kid, don't get inta no trouble wid dis or your brudda will kill da bothuv us."

"Thanks," Mick said, pocketing the paper.

Outside on the street, the late-afternoon sun was shining and a small breeze was ruffling the leaves on the elms and plane trees. Cars whooshed by on Conduit Avenue, and a bus spewed diesel fumes into the air. Mick took a look around his world and found that it all looked different. There was a sheen, no, more like an aura, like the halo around a saint's head, over everything. The outlines of buildings and people came to him with the superreal crispness of things seen through the lens of his telescope. Colors were so vivid they almost made his eyes water. He would have slipped on his sunglasses, but the sensation felt too good.

Back home, he went into his brother's bedroom and, reaching into the back of the closet, pushed aside the neat stack of winter clothes. Behind that, he took down an olive-colored metal ammo case from World War II. He had been with Caesare when he had bought it at a war-surplus store and, curious as to why his brother would want such a useless item, had spied on him as Caesare had filled it and had carefully hidden it away.

Now he brought it over to the bed and opened it. Inside, wrapped in oilskin, was a .45-caliber handgun and rounds of ammunition. Mick took out the gun, hefting it in his hand. He loaded it as he had seen his brother do many times, slipped extra ammo into his trousers' pocket, and replaced the ammo case inside the closet. Before he left the apartment, he took a wire coat hanger out of his own closet and slipped his mother's long-bladed paring knife into the waistband of his trousers at the small of his back.

Only then did he open the slip of paper on which Richie had written the name and address of the person who owned the dark-colored Cougar he had seen racing away from the scene of his grandfather's murder. A name he did not know, an address in East New York. But they meant everything to him now, because he realized that the moment his grandfather had been killed his whole life had changed. Standing there with Jaqui in the bloody courtyard, he had felt it, intangibles swinging on an invisible axis, canting the world—*his* world—over on its side. Nothing would ever be the same again. He did not know why, but he knew it was so.

He walked more than a mile from his apartment before he stole the car. He broke in using the wire hanger and hot-wired it without any trouble. Then he set off for East New York.

He pulled up across the street from the address, nosing into a parking spot. He did not see the dark-colored Cougar anywhere around, so he got out, scouted around to get the lay of the land. Then he returned to the stolen car and sat back, folded his arms across his chest, and waited. Into his mind swept the darkness of his grandfather's fate: to be walking across the familiar pavement of home one instant, to be ripped asunder by assassins' bullets the next. To die like a dog with his face in the pavement.

Oh, Christ!

Tears stood in the corners of Mick's squeezed-shut eyes, and he felt a red rage filling him. He would not—could not—allow this to be his grandfather's fate. He was a great man, not a dog. Vengeance would be his salvation. Mick was no longer living in the temperate zone of his youth.

He had crossed over to the tropics, the primeval forest of the soul.

A cool, clear wind blew through Mick when he opened his eyes. A dark blue Cougar was heading down the street as if looking for a parking spot. He spotted the license plate in his rearview mirror and it matched up. He started his engine, pulled out so the Cougar could park. It was a joke. The driver actually waved at him in thanks as he took the spot.

Mick double-parked around the corner. He hurried back and was in time to see a tall, dark-haired individual with deep olive skin locking his car. He was in his early twenties and, on closer inspection, had a scar separating one eyebrow.

"Hey, there!" Mick called, putting a smile on his face as he jogged toward the man. "Vinnie Mezzatesta."

He turned. "Fuck you want, kid?"

"Not much," Mick said as he put all his weight into a solid punch to Vinnie's solar plexus.

Vinnie doubled over and Mick hauled him into a dank and narrow alley he had discovered on his reconnaissance. He slammed Vinnie into the wall and slapped his face. "Hey, fuckface! Hey, Vinnie Halfahead, you with me? My name's Michael Leonforte." He put his lips against Vinnie's ear. "That's *Leonforte*, asshole."

"So fuckin'what?" Vinnie said.

"So fuckin'*this*," Mick said, kneeing him in the groin.

Vinnie groaned and slumped so that Mick had to pin him against the wall. He slapped the man until his bloodshot eyes opened and he could see the .45 in Mick's left hand. "So you killed my grandfather."

Vinnie stared, entranced, at the muzzle of the gun. "Kid, you're fuckin' outta your mind."

"You and someone else."

"You little fucknuthin', you know who I work for? Gino Scalfa. Sure as I'm standin' here, you're a fuckin' dead man."

Mick pushed the gun against the side of Vinnie's neck, and as he stared him in the eye, he reached into his waistband and in one fluid motion drew the paring knife and jammed the entire blade into the outside of Vinnie's right knee.

Pop! Pop! The joint made all kinds of interesting noises as Mick slashed the blade horizontally through tendons and ligaments.

Vinnie yelped as he jumped like a frog hit by a lightning bolt. Mick actually saw his pupils contract with the pain as he let him go and he slid down the wall.

"Oh, Jesus and Mary," Vinnie cried, rocking himself, "look at my fuckin' knee."

"Yeah, Vinnie Halfahead, now you ain't standing anymore." Mick knelt beside him, ignoring the blood and the fragments of bone sticking up through the slit skin. "You killed my grandfather and I don't give a fuck who you are, where you go to church, or who you work for." He put the muzzle of the .45 against Vinnie's left temple. "I'm gonna fuckin' blow your brains out."

Vinnie Mezzatesta finally got it through his half a head that this was no mere kid, that he meant what he said and was not to be fooled with. The cheap hood's bravado with which he had applied Gino Scalfa's muscle in injudicious quantities evaporated like mist in the sun. What it left behind was what had always been there: a none-too-bright young man without any sense of himself.

"I didn't fuckin' do it," he said, still rocking back and forth. "I only drove the fuckin' Cougar. You're right, there was someone else."

"Who, Vinnie?"

"Jesus, kid, you know what you're asking me t'do?"

Mick, calmly and deliberately, drove the blade of the paring knife into Vinnie's kneecap so that he screamed and squirmed to get away. Mick slapped him hard across both cheeks with the barrel of the .45.

"Who pulled the trigger?" He already knew Vinnie was lying about only driving the car because he had seen two shadows, flames jumping from two guns. Vinnie and who else?

Vinnie put his head down and mumbled something at his bloody shoe.

"What was that?"

Vinnie was beginning to shiver and shake as he went into shock. "Was Gino himself," he whispered. "Jesus, it hurts." His eyes were tearing. "Gino pulled the trigger on your grandfather. He fuckin' had no respect for that Sicilian ginzo, comin' inta turf Gino wanted, making deals wid Gino's enemies. He hated that fuck from the moment he walked into Gino's place of business. Know why? 'Cause he went to Black Paul Mattaccino first, didn't give Gino the respect he deserved. But Gino was patient, he bided his time. He saw how your grandfather could organize the neighborhood for him. Now he's gonna step in nice 'n' easy and have everything set up for him."

Perhaps it was a renewal of the ethnic hatred that gave Vinnie back his braggadocio. Or perhaps, as he was named, he only had half a brain. In any event, as he spoke, he lunged for Mick's gun.

Mick, who was watching him with such intensity that he saw the intimation of the movement in Vinnie's bloodshot eyes, let him get his bloody hand on the gun. That was okay by him because while Vinnie was occupied, Mick drove the blade of the paring knife into his chest.

He must have hit a main artery because blood began to fountain out of the wound almost immediately, and he had to jump back in order not to get drenched. Vinnie's eyes were wide with fear. His mouth flopped open and closed like a fish gasping in the bottom of a boat. He made a vain effort to cover the wound, then he fell over in a heap.

It was astonishing, really, how calm and clearheaded he was. He could feel the blood pumping in his veins and there was a feral smell in his nostrils. He had never killed before, had never even contemplated it. Shouldn't this monumental act have changed him in some way? He had the blood of another human being quite literally on his hands. But his metamorphosis had already occurred. He was merely following through on this particular strand of what he now knew to be his destiny. It was right and proper—merely business.

Mick wiped the knife on Vinnie's clothes, then put both weapons away. He found the keys to the Cougar. It was parked almost directly across from the alley. He went around, popped the trunk, went back into the alley, and making sure he was alone, hefted Vinnie's corpse and dumped it in. He slammed down the trunk's lid, then he drove off.

A light drizzle was falling across Sheepshead Bay as Mick pulled up. He sat in the Cougar and listened to the drone of jets from the airport. There was a soft, dank smell here that was unique. Probably, you didn't want to know what was causing it. Maybe it was all those bodies Grandfather and Gino Scalfa had dumped into the bay.

Scalfa was already there, standing near the water, as Grandfather had said, gazing out over the water. Mick beeped the horn several times until Scalfa turned slowly around.

"Hey, Vinnie, whatta you doin' here? I tried ta call ya before but there was no ansa."

Mick got out of the car, came down to where the don stood, fat as a moon.

"You ain't Vinnie." He scowled, his puffer-fish face contorted in the effort to remember Mick's face. "I know you, don't I?"

"Vinnie sent me," Mick said to allay Scalfa's fears and give him just enough time. He had the .45 in his right hand and was now close enough to press its muzzle against the fat don's heart.

"The name is Leonforte," he said, pulling the trigger. "Mick Leonforte."

The bullet tore clean through Scalfa, boring a good-sized hole in him and completely obliterating his heart. He dropped to his knees, but Mick saw there was no reason to shoot him again: the light was already out of his eyes.

Gulls rose, crying and circling, from either the gun's report or the smell of blood. Mick's hand ached from the .45's heavy recoil. As Scalfa fell over, face first, Mick launched the gun far out into the bay. The gunshot had sounded like nothing more than a truck backfire, and in this isolated spot, no one was likely to notice. On the other hand, he had no intention of hanging around to find out. He dragged Scalfa's fat form back to the Cougar, did some rearranging of limbs in the trunk, and got him in beside Vinnie Halfahead.

Mick looked around. Except for the voracious gulls, the spot was deserted. Overhead, a large jet was streaking silently across the sky. Suddenly, its sound rose like a bird from the bay, a deep rumble like a portent from heaven.

"You did *what?*" Caesare shook his head. "Fuck're you tellin' me?"

Mick, in the somber foyer of the Mastimo Funeral Home, went through it all again, how he had been up on the rooftop when Grandfather had been murdered, how he had used his telescope to get the license plate number, how he had pumped Vinnie Mezzatesta, how he had gone to Sheepshead Bay.

"Whatta you askin' me t' believe, that you, you little pissant, bidda-bing, bidda-bam, bidda-boom, whacked this Vinnie Whatsis and *Gino fuckin' Scalfa?*" Caesare threw up his hands. *"Marrone,* kid, you gotta some imagination, I'll grant you that."

"Come downstairs. I've got the bodies in Vinnie's Cougar. I didn't want to leave them lying around for the cops to find and give them an excuse to come down even harder on us."

Ten minutes later, a white-faced Caesare called for Richie and two of their buddies. As they gathered at the rear of the Cougar, he said, "Drive this crate around to the service entrance. There's cargo in the trunk. Get 'em out and prepare 'em in the usual way. Then, get rid of the car. Incinerate it."

"Who's in there?" Richie asked.

Caesare leered at him. "You'll find out soon enough. An', take it from me, you won't believe your fuckin' eyes."

As they drove off, Caesare stood in the street with Mick, with the last of the drizzle coming down. "You're one crazy bastard, you know that, kid?" He cuffed Mick roughly. "I should be pissed at you for not cuttin' me in onna action." He grinned. "But Jesus *Christ,* you whacked these two real good. Just like a professional."

That was as close as he could come to saying he was proud of his brother. Mick, who was only now realizing how long he had waited for this moment, felt somehow deflated. Instead of feeling proud, he found himself wondering what Jaqui would think of a world where recognition came from whacking people. Trouble was, he knew very well what she would think. She despised it with every fiber of her being.

"Fuckin' Gino Scalfa." Caesare was shaking his head. "I never would have figured. He was the old man's best friend."

"Friendship is a strange and unruly animal," Mick said, recalling his grandfather's words. "Like a lame dog you take off the street and nurse back to health who then bites you on the hand, you have to treat friendship with equal amounts of apprehension and skepticism."

Caesare looked at him. "What the fuck does that mean?"

"It means," Mick said, "that in the biziness you *have* no friends, only enemies."

There was a different tone in Caesare's voice, a kind of respect he'd never showed before for his brother. "Where, allova sudden, you get to know so much about the biziness, kid?"

"From serving espresso and anisette to Grandpa."

They went back into the funeral home. Mick had never been to the rear where the bodies were prepared. In the four hours he was there he learned a great deal. Vinnie Mezzatesta and Gino Scalfa were cleaned up, embalmed, then placed in the bottom of cherrywood coffins paid for by legitimate customers.

That was because the rightful deceased were placed in these coffins, directly on top of the mobsters. In that way, the whacked men were disposed of without anyone knowing what had happened to them. And there was no possibility of their corpses appearing six months or a year later in the Pennsylvania and Fountain avenues junkyards or washing up in the bay.

It was a foolproof way of making people disappear, and as Mick discovered that night, it was the innovative method by which Grandfather Caesare had turned a lackluster business into a booming franchise.

"Kid, you did one fuckin' job whacking the bastards who killed Grandpa," Caesare said. "He woulda been prouda you." He shook his head sadly. "I gotta admit it, I miss the old bird."

"Me, too," Mick acknowledged.

"Yeah, but the difference is you spent all this time with him. Looks like you were the smart one."

They were upstairs in Grandfather's old office. Mick was making espresso while Caesare sat at the round table around which so many men of power and respect had sat and drank and smoked and played cards and lied to one another. It would never be the same again in here or anywhere else in Ozone Park, both men knew that. Uncle Alphonse had no use for New York. He had come for the funeral and had gone back to California, where the younger Leonfortes' mother would soon go. Caesare, as well, as it turned out.

Caesare wasted no time in telling Mick how it was going to be. The Leonfortes were pulling up stakes in New York. Times were changing. With Grandpa gone there was no reason to stay on. Besides, there was more opportunity on the West Coast.

"I'm gonna go inta Uncle Alphonse's biziness," Caesare said. "Won't be long before I'm his right-hand man. He's got no sona his own so ..." He stirred sugar into the espresso Mick had brought over. The two brothers sat in silence for some time, sipping their coffee and thinking their own thoughts. "You're welcome ta come an' help out."

Mick, who had been around this table long enough to separate the lies from the truth, found the offer amusing. It was as phony as a three-dollar bill. Caesare could not possibly want a potential rival for Alphonse's affection and respect, especially not his brother.

"Be your gofer, you mean. No way. I have my own ideas. I'm going into the Army."

"What?" Caesare's cup clattered loudly into its saucer. "Are you mental, or what?"

"I've got to get out of here."

"So, okay," Caesare said, digging into his hip pocket and coming out with a wad of bills. He began to peel off hundreds. "So how much do you need, kid? Say the figure an' it's yours. You sure earned it."

"No, no." Mick raised his hands. He caught his brother's eyes. "Caesare, listen to me. What I did I did out of love and respect for Grandpa. I did it because I *had* to. I *didn't* do it for money, understand?"

"Hey, kid, don't take offense. We're not talking blood money here, if that's your worry. The family owes you and I want to—"

"Forget it. The family owes me zip." Mick rolled up the hundreds, put them into his brother's hand. "See, it's not just Ozone Park I want to get out of. It's everything."

Caesare cocked his head. "Everything? I don't unnerstand."

"I'm not sure."

Caesare scowled. "Kid, you're starting to piss me off. First, you don't accept my offer of money—made free an' clear as one brother to another. Now, you're starting to talk crazy. I don't like any of it."

"It's not for you to like or dislike," Mick said, getting up. "Good-bye, Caesare."

Caesare pushed his chair back so roughly it toppled over. "Hey, not so fast, wise guy. What about Mom? You can't just leave her like this. She's expecting you to come with us to San Francisco. With Jaqui staying here and all, this'll break her heart."

"Sorry."

"Sorry?" That weird manic light like a red star had come into Caesare's eyes. "Is that all you can say, you ungrateful sonuvabitch." He took one step toward Mick. "I'll fuckin' break your neck for you, kid."

"That time's past." Mick put up a warning hand, and astonishingly, Caesare halted in midstride. Mick could see it in his eyes, that uncertainty, that knowledge of what Mick had done to the two men in the cherrywood coffins.

"Do what you fuckin' want, then," Caesare said, his hands stuck in his pockets. "But don't come to me for help. I won't know you."

The Convent of the Sacred Heart of Santa Maria dominated a quiet, tree-shaded street in Astoria. Although it was by far the largest structure on the block, it was flanked by a bakery and a dry cleaner's. On the opposite side of the street stretched a row of neat attached brick-faced houses, all with small aluminum awnings over the front doors.

The convent was actually quite a beautiful building. It was constructed of large blocks of white stone off which the sunshine sparked and cascaded like rippling water. There was a carved alabaster statue of Mary alone on one side of the gated entrance and another of Her and the baby Jesus on the other.

Mick, pulling the brim of the black fedora down over his forehead so the wind wouldn't take it, rang the bell at the side of the gate and was admitted. Not knowing the proper protocol, he took the fedora off as soon as he was in the grounds.

A nun in habit met him at the front stoop. She smiled quietly at him as he approached.

"I'm here to see Jaqui," he said, his throat suddenly tight. And when the nun looked at him quizzically: "Jaqui Leonforte."

The nun smiled and bowed him in. "You must be Michael," she said in her soft voice. "Follow me, please."

She led Mick down a series of dark stone corridors whose walls were completely unadorned. He passed a pair of French doors that led out onto a small courtyard opulently bedecked with flowering shrubs and vines. He caught a glimpse of a stone bench and a small fountain before the nun led him farther down the corridor. At its end, she opened high wooden double doors but did not go in herself.

"The mother superior will see you."

Mick went into a surprisingly small room that had been turned into something of an office. A small niche held a plaster Madonna, and on the wall behind the desk hung a wood and gilt crucifix.

"I am Bernice," a woman in her late fifties said as she rose from her chair. "You must be Michael Leonforte." She stuck out her hand, shook his forthrightly with a grip as firm and dry as a man's. "Marie Rose has spoken of you often."

"Who?"

Bernice took off her steel-rimmed spectacles so that he could feel the full impact of her extraordinary pale blue eyes. "I thought you knew. Your sister is a full novitiate, a permanent member of the convent now. Her new name is Marie Rose."

Mick, holding his grandfather's fedora tightly in both hands, shifted nervously from one foot to the other. "Does this mean I can't see her?"

"It is not usually allowed," Bernice said in her steady voice that neither rose nor fell.

"But, see, I'm going away. For a long time, maybe." He ground the brim of the fedora against his thighs. "I gotta see her."

"Sit down a moment, won't you, Michael?" Bernice said, indicating a straight-backed chair. And when he had done so, she smiled. "I don't mean to make you uneasy."

"Oh, it's not you," Mick said hastily. "It's this place. It's so quiet."

"Deliberately so." Bernice paused for a moment, as if debating with herself whether to go on. "I understand you had a close and unusual relationship with your grandfather."

Mick nodded. "Jaqui, um, Marie Rose told you."

"No," Bernice said, sitting down at her desk. "I knew your grandfather quite well."

"You did?"

Bernice smiled again. "You seem surprised."

"Well, uh, you know, Astoria, it's a little out of his territory," Mick said, recovering quickly.

Bernice laughed, a low, astonishingly joyous sound. "I suppose that is one way of putting it." She reached into a drawer, took out something that she spread upon the desktop. "Four twenty-dollar bills," she said, and those pale blue eyes impaled him again.

"I asked him to invest them."

"Are you surprised that he chose to invest your money with me rather than with the funeral home or the insurance companies he controlled?"

Mick squinted at her. "What do you know about all that?"

"Everything," Bernice said, swiping the money off the desktop as deftly as a Las Vegas dealer. The smile wreathed her face. "I think, in the end, you will be pleased with the return on your investment." She stood up. "Now, go back the way you came to the meditation garden. Novitiate Marie Rose is waiting for you there."

"Thank you, Mother Superior," Mick said, stumbling to his feet.

"You're quite welcome, Michael." At the door to her office, she said in the hushed voice of a confidante, "I loved him, you know." Then she softly closed the door.

As Mick went down the corridor, he heard the soft chanting of prayers. What on earth had the mother superior meant by that last cryptic statement? In what way had she loved Grandfather Caesare? And why would she tell Mick?

He was still pondering these questions when he opened the French doors. The sound of songbirds greeted him, along with the heavy perfume of roses, and he was immediately plunged into his dream. He walked out into the courtyard, and though it was in Queens, it might just as well have been that terrace cantilevered out over the unknown coastline of his dream. The prayer, stronger now because it emerged from an open window fronting the courtyard, was like music.

As he walked down the narrow, mossy brick path to the single stone bench, Jaqui turned toward him. Her face was radiant and he felt his heart lurch in his chest. Nothing had changed on this score, he saw. He felt about his sister as he always had.

She smiled and, instead of embracing him, took his hands in hers. "Michael, it's so good to see you. I wasn't certain you'd come before you left." She shook her head. "I've tried to talk to Caesare. But you know our brother." She gave him an almost embarrassed smile. "He never listened to a word I said." She put a hand to his cheek. "You look tired."

She led him to the bench, where they both sat in silence for some time. All Mick could smell were the roses. For a time, he tried not to breathe, but that didn't work, either.

"Jaqui, you sure this is what you want?"

"It's right for me, Michael."

He sighed. "I guess I just don't understand." He gestured up at the white stone walls. "All this." He shook his head in bewilderment.

"You met Bernice."

"The mother superior. Sure."

"Then you know why I'm here." She squeezed his hand. "Grandfather knew."

"He did?"

She nodded. "From the very beginning. And Mom's been very understanding." She glanced away, at a songbird that flitted among the vines, looking for something to eat.

"Jaqui—"

She turned back to him. "I'm Marie Rose now."

"Yeah, sure." He disentangled his fingers from hers and stood up. This wasn't how it was supposed to end. This wasn't what he wanted. "I gotta get going." Why had he come here, anyway?

"I know." She continued to sit on the bench as if willing them both to remain here in this odd limbo for at least a while longer, and for a flash, he had the profoundly disquieting sense that she was aware of his dream.

"I don't know when I'll be back."

She turned her face up to him. "But we'll see each other."

"You bet."

He turned, leaving her there with the sun in her eyes, but in all the years afterward of never seeing her, the deep Mediterranean green of her eyes never left his mind or his dreams.

Book 2

Smoke and Mirrors

A thousand hearts are great within my bosom.
Advance our standards, set upon our foes!

—Richard III, act 5, scene 3
Richard III, William Shakespeare

4

New York/Tokyo

A mockingbird's insouciant calling ushered in Margarite Goldoni DeCamillo's return to Astoria. Despite her apprehension and fear over her current predicament, the sight of the familiar streets and stores began a flood of memories inside her.

She parked in front of the bakery and went in just as it was closing. It looked the same as it always had, with its sawdust over the tiny white floor tile, so scratched and cracked it might be somewhere in Italy. Fluorescent lights bounced off the large glass cases, though oddly they didn't seem as huge as they once had.

"Can I help you?" asked a chubby little woman who bustled out from the back. Her gray hair was tied back in a bun. She had a doughy face with thick eyebrows that arched like a clown's. She broke into a smile. "Margarite?"

"Yes, Mrs. Paglia. It's me."

"Madonna!" Mrs. Paglia cried, coming around from behind the cases. "*Bella!* So good to see you! Poor darling, how are you?" She pulled Margarite's head down to her ample bosom. She smelled of flour and starch. "Such a tragedy about Tony. It was on the news this morning, so terrible I couldn't believe it! I said to Luigi, 'Can you believe this about our Tony D.?'" She bit a knuckle. "It's an *infamia!*"

"I know. I'm still in shock."

Mrs. Paglia waved her pudgy hands. "But don't worry, *Bella*. You're here now. You're home." She hurried back behind the counter, began picking through the bread and rolls. "But you're so thin." She handed a fistful over the countertop. *"Mangia, angel. Mangia!"*

Margarite, far from hungry, took several bites of the roll. It would have been disrespectful to do otherwise, but she could already feel her tightly knotted stomach rebelling.

"Now don't you worry about a thing," Mrs. Paglia was saying, as she brought some grappa from the back and poured it into a water glass. "Here, angel. Fortification. Drink up." She waved her hands again, as if with the gesture she could get the rim more quickly to Margarite's lips. "Drink it all, *Bella*, it will do you good!"

Then she bustled around the cases again to put her arm around Margarite. "I know why you're here," she whispered with a glance toward the back where her husband, Luigi, must have been working on the bakery's books. "Instinct, angel. That's why you've come here in your hour of need." She squeezed Margarite's shoulders. "The men think they have it all figured out, right? But we know better. All they've figured out is what we give them." She cackled a little. "You finish your roll and then you go next door like you planned. It's the right thing."

"She's there?"

Mrs. Paglia nodded and crossed herself. "Thank God. He looks after her. Though she's in her nineties, you'd never believe it." She tapped the side of her head with her stubby forefinger. "She's no longer mother superior, of course; another has taken up those duties. But she is sharp as ever, angel. You'll see."

Outside, the mockingbird's clear notes pierced the night air. Margarite glanced at her watch. Two hours left before she had to make the meet so she could save her daughter's life. But what would happen to them then? Nothing good. Far from ending things, turning herself over to Bad Clams would be just the beginning. He wanted all of Dominic's secrets: his contracts with truckers, wholesalers, judges, cops, bankers, and manufacturers across the country, his contacts in Washington, and most of all, he coveted the power of the Nishiki network, which had provided Dominic with personal dirt on enough high-level government officials to get whatever he wanted from them. Mikio Okami was Nishiki, mysteriously providing the secrets of other people's lives in order to keep them under the Goldonis' thumb.

The complex mechanism for gaining this information Margarite now had in her head. Bad Clams would use Francie for as long as he could as the goad that would make her spill her guts to him.

She staggered as she walked down the street. Then, rushing to the curb, she doubled over, vomiting up everything she had just eaten and drunk. When the spasms had subsided, she opened her purse, wiped her mouth with a couple of Kleenex. The gun glinted evilly in the sodium streetlights.

Christ, she thought. *What am I going to do?*

She knew exactly what she must do at this moment. She went to the wrought-iron gate protecting the large white stone building that took up most of the block. The images of Mary and the baby Jesus flanked the gate, just as they had when Dominic had first taken her here six years ago to begin her education.

She rang the bell and was admitted at once.

A strange kind of peacefulness stole over her as she stepped into the grounds of the Sacred Heart of Santa Maria Convent. Above her head, sitting high in a magnolia tree, she saw the mockingbird peering down at her with its head cocked at a comical angle. Then it began to sing, sounding like one, two, three, four other birds. The master of disguise, protecting its young with its ventriloquist's voice.

She walked up the marble steps and the doors opened inward.

"Welcome, my child," a familiar voice said from the shadows.

Margarite, who had for a moment been lost in the past, said, "Bernice?"

"Yes, my child." Bernice wrapped her in her loving embrace.

"Oh, Bernice!" Margarite began to sob. The tenderness of those arms, the warmth of that body in her moment of crisis, were too much for her. "God in heaven, what is happening to my life?"

"That is what you have come to find out, my child."

Bernice closed the wooden door behind them, walked with her arm around Margarite down the corridor. Once again, Margarite was struck by the almost magisterial silence of the convent. What other, less attuned visitors mistook for austerity, she recognized as an absolute serenity at the center of the spirit.

"Everything that's happened—I just feel so helpless. It's all spinning out of control—" She broke off, unable to go on.

Bernice stopped before a mirror. Her strong hand grasped Margarite's chin, turned her face up so that she was staring at her reflection. "Look. What do you see? Your face is stained with tears," Bernice said softly. "But I see deeper than that. Your soul is choked with tears. This is not just from the events of the past few days, my child. You must recognize this before you can go on."

"I can't. I—"

"Ah, Margarite, you can. And do you know why? It is because you are your brother's sister. You have so much of him inside you, though you are not of the same blood. No doubt, he saw that kinship of temperament in you."

Margarite and her sister, Celeste, who lived in Venice, were the daughters of Enrico Goldoni, a manufacturer and exporter of fine Venetian silks and brocades, who had residences in Venice and Astoria, Queens. In 1964, when his daughters Margarite and Celeste were nine and six respectively, he remarried. The woman, Faith Mattaccino, came to him with a son, Dominic, whom he adopted a year later. Faith had been married to Black Paul Mattaccino, by all accounts an exceptionally scary New York Mafia don, who died under mysterious circumstances. One of the many rumors that had swirled around Black Paul was that Dominic was not his son.

"I doubt if he was ever this out of control."

"But control is why Dominic first came here, Margarite," the old mother superior said. "And it is why you have come." Her pale blue eyes grew round and depthless in that charismatic way of hers as she gathered herself for power. "Never forget that your inner strength is why Dominic chose you to succeed him."

"I don't know. What if he was wrong?"

"But *I* am not wrong," Bernice said in that tone she used that brooked no rebuttal. She took Margarite's tear-stained face in her smooth hands. "Now listen to me, child. I advised your brother on his successor and he agreed. We were not wrong about you. But your path is difficult, you knew that when you began your journey."

"But I didn't know *how* difficult it was going to be."

"None of us do. But that is God's will, believe me. He is always testing us, that is His way." She patted Margarite on the arm. "Now come. Dry your eyes. It is time for a council of war."

There was something immensely comforting about Bernice's office. Perhaps it was the size or shape, like a room in one of the fairy stories Margarite used to read to Francie when she had been young.

Francie!

"That evil monster has my baby!" she blurted out as soon as she stepped across the threshold. "What have we wrought with the Leonfortes, Bernice? They murdered Dom. Now Tony has been killed, I am almost gunned down on Park Avenue, and Bad Clams has my Francie! And to top it all off, I may have lost control of my business!" The tears were coming again, even though she had promised herself that she must be calm. Hadn't it been Bernice herself who had taught her that serenity in crisis was the only path that would take her safely to victory? But there was no path to safety here, at least none that she could see. She clenched her fists and her voice was clotted with emotion. "That animal, that troll! I'll kill him!"

Bernice sat beneath the wood and gilt crucifix, wrapped in her serenity. Age had given her face lines and an almost absolute absence of fat, so that the skin was stretched slackly over the bones of her skull seemingly without the intervention of flesh or sinew. But even time could not diminish the fierce intensity of those pale blue eyes, whose fire had unerringly guided so many over the years. "My dear, if you truly think like that, then Caesare has already won his most important victory.

"You are terribly frightened. And you have every right to be. Believe me when I tell you I understand what you're feeling, Margarite." She placed her hands on Margarite's fists, and slowly, inexorably, their warmth opened the clenched fingers like petals turn to the sun. "But that feeling must end, *now*. Fear breeds hate, and hate is ignorance. People such as Caesare Leonforte count on the ignorance of their adversaries."

"But look what he has done to me!" Margarite cried. "In one concerted strike, he has taken my whole life from me. I have lost the battle, the war, everything. In less than two hours I have to be in Sheepshead Bay or he will kill Francie!"

"He won't kill your daughter," Bernice said with such finality that, at last, Margarite was forced to believe her.

"How can you say that?"

"Think about it rationally and logically, my dear. What can he gain from Francine's death? She is the one form of leverage against you he can be certain of. Once he lets go of that, you will slip away from him, and he knows it."

Margarite could feel her teeth grinding together. Bernice said she knew what Margarite was feeling, but how could she? She'd never had a child. And now that that child was in jeopardy, Margarite knew she would do *anything* to get her back. "With all due respect," she said, "this is Caesare Leonforte we are talking about. I don't believe that he is either rational or logical. He lives purely on emotion and we both know it." Beneath Bernice's warmth, Margarite could feel her hands curling back into fists.

"Margarite!"

Bernice leaned forward, pouring her psychic energy into the younger woman until she was enfolded in Bernice's charismatic power. "Listen to me now because it is crucial you understand what I am about to say. Right now your mind is locked within the cage of revenge." Margarite's head shook from side to side. "Don't bother to deny it. I can see the venom in your eyes, feel it in the clenching of your fists. You *must* let go of such poisoned thoughts, my dear. It is what started the vendetta between the Leonfortes and the Goldonis. Otherwise, as surely as night follows day, suffering and death will ensue."

For a moment, Margarite said nothing. She felt Bernice's aura bathing her, that strange and unique quality she found both comforting and exhilarating. This was not a power that

Bernice used indiscriminately. In fact, it was safe to say that most visitors to the convent had no idea she possessed anything other than a kind and generous spirit.

"I can't just bow my head and acquiesce, Bernice," she whispered. "You can't ask me to do that because I won't. I won't, I tell you!"

Bernice gave off the semblance of a smile. "Spoken like Dominic. 'Always take the offensive,' he said. 'The minute you curl up in a ball, you're dead.' That was why he hated the Federal Witness Protection Program so passionately. Why he kept in contact with you, against their rules. Dominic played life by his own rules, and damn what anyone thought of him."

Margarite found herself mesmerized by those electric blue eyes. "At this moment Caesare has taken the one thing you hold most dear," Bernice went on. "I am not asking you to fold, Margarite. On the contrary, I believe we have embarked on the last phase of the long and bloody vendetta between the Leonfortes and the Goldonis. Now is the darkest time, my child, but it is also the time for you to be strongest. The time for you to make your stand."

"I don't know. My world has been torn apart; I no longer recognize it."

"That is Caesare's goal. It is up to you to see he does not achieve it." Bernice's grip tightened on Margarite, the heat of her power infusing the younger woman. "Judicious use of all forms of power is what we are about. Isn't that what you were taught during your time here?"

For a moment, Margarite's face clouded with remembrance, then she nodded.

"It isn't power itself that corrupts us," Bernice said. "It is the *abuse* of it. This is what makes the Leonfortes so strong; but it is also what will bring them ruin."

"Then let the two brothers kill each other," Margarite said bitterly.

"Revenge is God's province, not your own. I want you to remember that in the days to come." Bernice rose. "Now I will leave you to prepare yourself mentally. As usual, all the considerable facilities of the convent are at your disposal, should you need them."

Once more, her charismatic power enfolded Margarite in

its loving embrace. "Remember everything you have learned here." She leaned down, kissed Margarite's forehead. "God bless you and watch over you always, my child."

Morning mist rose from the Sumida, wrapping Tokyo in a damp haze that made it seem like a picture postcard. The exhaust from Nicholas's black Kawasaki rumbled off the facades of the prewar warehouses that closely lined the streets of this business district. A mournful foghorn from a boat heading downriver outlasted the liquid cough of the motorcycle's enormous engine as he rolled to a stop, then cut the ignition.

He dismounted, stood gazing at the front of a small town house wedged between two warehouse behemoths. It was an unremarkable facade, so much so that it would surely remain unnoticed by any but the most penetrating glance.

So this was the home of Kisoko, Mikio Okami's sister, Nicholas thought. The place where Nangi had chosen to recuperate. Just what did he think he was doing? Nicholas wondered as he placed his helmet beneath his arm and, quickly crossing the cracked pavement, went up the stairs to the front door.

There was no bell, and the first thing he noticed when he used the brass knocker shaped like an animal's paw was the sound it made against the door. He put his hand out experimentally and discovered that the door was metal, most likely steel. Very odd in a private dwelling such as this. Was it for security?

But there was no time for further speculation as the door opened inward and he found himself face-to-face with Mikio Okami's sister.

Nicholas had heard stories of Kisoko, but she was highly reclusive, and despite the fact of his closeness with Okami he had never before met her. Despite this, he recognized her immediately.

"Won't you come inside?" she said in a musical voice, as naturally as if he were an old friend. "There's more rain coming, I fear, and you will get soaked if you stand on the stoop much longer."

When he hesitated, she added, "I know who you are, Linnear-san. I would recognize you anywhere."

He stepped into the foyer and she swung the steel door shut behind him. It closed with the heavy clang of a prison door.

"You have your father's face," she said. "And some of your mother's, as well."

"You knew them?"

"In a manner of speaking, yes."

He found himself in an oval foyer, painted a rich cream color with wainscoting of pale gold. In the center was a small, elegant marble console on which was a large crystal bowl filled with sprays of bright flowers. Beyond was the kind of grand staircase that hadn't been built with such expertise since the turn of the century.

Though the house was, as far as Nicholas could discern, entirely Western in aspect, Kisoko was clad in traditional silk kimono and underkimono. Her hair was intricately coiffed, held up with a set of long, curved silver pins. Her kimono was the color of a blood-orange sunset; the under-kimono, which could only be seen at cuff and collar, was the indigo blue the Japanese had justly made famous.

Nicholas knew Kisoko was in her seventies, but she looked twenty years younger. She had the pale, unblemished skin, glossy as porcelain, of the pure-blood samurai woman. Hers was an odd face, asymmetrical with sensual, bow-shaped lips. Nevertheless, it was almost wholly dominated by her utterly black eyes, which, so he had heard, had the ability to extrapolate conclusions about people from their seemingly insignificant physical movements. It was said that she was never surprised by anything. It was also whispered that she was *kanashimi de nuitori shite aru*. Literally, this meant that she was embroidered in sadness. What it implied was that she had experienced a terrible tragedy sometime in her past. What that tragedy was, Nicholas had no idea; given the secrecy surrounding her, he doubted that anyone other than Kisoko and perhaps her brother knew.

She led him soundlessly down a corridor paneled in gleaming cherrywood. At intervals, *surimono*—Japanese prints from the 1700s that had originally been greeting cards—were hung in gilt frames. Their authors, scorned in their day, had now achieved the status of world-class artists, sought after by collectors, auction houses, and museums the world over.

In a sitting room painted persimmon with gold trim, Nicholas found Tanzan Nangi. He was half-reclining on a pale yellow brocaded settee of French manufacture. He looked tired and drawn, and when Nicholas tried to make eye contact, he looked away.

"I am honored that you are finally here, Linnear-san," Kisoko said quickly and lightly, as if trying to defuse a potentially thorny situation. "I realize I have been remiss in not inviting you."

A palace-sized Persian carpet covered the wood floor. The furniture was all period pieces, with wide seats and low backs, but made comfortable by a plethora of voluptuous, tasseled pillows in damask, chintz, and more brocaded silk. The walls were without paintings. In their place, suits of samurai armor for full battle regalia stood at eternal attention within glass cases. The pristine collection was as stunning as it was extensive. Many museums, Nicholas knew, did not have this range.

"The armor does not belong to me," Kisoko said, watching the direction of Nicholas's gaze. "It belongs to my son, Ken."

"It's astonishing. Magnificent."

She bowed slightly. "Such effusive praise cannot fail to please him." She smiled suddenly and, as if they were alone in the room, said, "Would you care for tea?"

"Thank you, no."

"It is poor fare, I know, but . . ."

"Thank you, no."

She asked one more time and he declined, after which, in this heavily Confucian society, he was allowed to accept the offer. Kisoko bowed and, with a secret smile, said, "If you will excuse me for a moment, it is the servants' day off."

Left alone in the sitting room with Nangi, Nicholas crossed to the settee.

"Nangi-san."

"How did you find me?" he said curtly.

"Through your Kami transmission."

An odd, cool silence ensued, during which Nicholas sat

next to his friend and mentor. "Nangi-san, there are many matters that urgently need our attention."

"Discuss them with Tōrin-san. That's why he's there."

"Tōrin is no substitute for your expertise. I cannot say that I trust him overmuch."

"He has my complete trust," Nangi said emphatically. "You must find a way to work with him." He lay back as if exhausted. "I grow old, Nicholas-san." He smiled. "Or perhaps I am merely melancholy."

Nangi's head turned and his good eye peered at Nicholas. "You're far too clever a detective for me to think I could hide from you for long." He nodded. "You see what I mean? A simple miscalculation, but five years ago I would not have made it." He sighed.

"I have to talk with you, Nangi-san," Nicholas pressed. "Sato-Tomkin without a working president will soon be in disarray. I'm afraid I need to go to New York to sort things out, and I don't know how long I will have to stay. Sato needs you here at the helm."

Nangi hitched himself higher on the settee. "Listen to me, Nicholas-san. I won't always be here. Don't you think I know your nature? I never expected you to tie yourself down to Tokyo, to overseeing the day-to-day running of Sato International. You have more than enough on your plate as it is with the American affiliate. And then there's been your involvement with Okami-san and the Yakuza."

His head swung away and that odd, cool silence crept into the room again. "That's why I have been bringing Tōrin-san along. He's young but he's smart and quick. You *must* overcome your prejudices and learn to trust him."

"I don't *want* to trust him."

"Yes. You've made that eminently clear."

Nicholas was aware that a gulf had formed between them, as if they were at odds over a key issue, and this was something for which he was totally unprepared.

"Nangi-san, if I have—" He turned his head, abruptly aware of Kisoko standing in the doorway, observing them. When she saw Nicholas's head turn, she came into the room, gliding as if with no movement or effort.

Nangi had averted his head again. "I wish you hadn't come."

Kisoko stood staring down at the tea service for a moment before looking to Nicholas. She smiled sweetly, and Nicholas had a brief glimpse of the sensual woman she had once been. Then she put the tray down on the art nouveau iron and lacquer coffee table. Out of her pocket she took a small vial, shook out a pill. This she put carefully and tenderly under Nangi's tongue.

Nangi sighed, his good eye going out of focus for a moment.

"Nangi-san," Nicholas insisted gently, "we have to talk. I need your advice regarding the Denwa partnership."

Nangi spread his hands. "As always, anything I can do, I will."

"Now don't tire him out, Linnear-san," Kisoko said softly as she served them green tea.

Nicholas sipped the pale, bitter brew, then put the tiny cup down. "Nangi-san, you tell me that I must trust Tōrin-san, but how can I when he helped put this partnership together? You and I have had many offers of partnership in the past and we have refused them all. Neither of us have wanted to be responsible—or answerable—to outside people. For this reason, the Denwa partnership makes me profoundly uneasy. We have gone too far out on a limb. We are so financially strapped that even the smallest miscalculation will end in disaster."

"You don't understand," Nangi said. "The CyberNet *is* the future. We had to put it on-line in Japan before anyone else managed similar technology."

"But don't you see what you have done?" Nicholas cried. "You've gambled everything on one roll of the dice. And if we stumble now, it will be the Denwa Partners who gather up the pieces. Everything we have worked for will have come to nothing."

"This isn't about Denwa or the CyberNet, is it, Nicholas-san? It's about Tōrin-san. You don't like to see him in a position of such responsibility."

"It's true he's very young to be a vice president, but that isn't without precedent," Nicholas said, carefully feeling his way among the minefield of new and unknown relationships. How close had Tōrin bonded with Nangi while Nicholas had been away? It seemed like years rather than fifteen months.

"Please try to see it from my point of view. When I left for Venice to fulfill my obligation to the Kaisho, I had not even met Kanda Tōrin. Now, a year and a half later, I return to find he's not only overseeing our most important project but has helped you structure a deal with outside partners—which *is* precedent for Sato."

Nangi nodded, but his good eye had slipped half-closed and Nicholas could see he was tiring. Kisoko flashed him a warning glance.

Nangi said, "I quite understand your apprehension, but the world turns, Nicholas-san, with or without you." He gave a wan smile as he shifted in the sofa. "This is not meant as a rebuke, merely as a statement of fact. Another fact: I needed you here, but I know you are a man of honor and your father's *giri* had become yours. I know you are racked with guilt, but that is wasted emotion. I would have done the same had I been you. Honor above all else, Nicholas-san. This is what marks us, sets us apart, defines the nature of our existence." His hand began to tremble and Kisoko took the teacup from him.

His blind eye with its fixed stare seemed to give off an air of defiance and empathy. "The fact remains *you were not here* and I could not do this deal alone. I needed someone younger, with good instincts, a fresh perspective, who knew the playing field and could look into the future as you do. Someone who would not look back, who was not afraid to act—to dare to be the future. I found that in Kanda Tōrin.

"His dossier had crossed my desk some time ago and I had been keeping an eye on him ever since. His quarterly evaluations had been nothing short of spectacular, so I reached into the resources of our company and pulled him up into the executive suite. Since then, he's risen to every challenge I've set before him."

There was silence for some time. Like a tableau or an image stuck in time, the three of them ceased to move. It seemed to Nicholas that his breathing, even the beat of his heart, had been suspended, and he experienced an abrupt sense of discontinuity, or tearing free of time, and he thought, *No, no! Not now!* But the Kshira was rising, ripping through his consciousness like high winds scattering gauzy clouds, and he was falling, falling . . . seeing, as one does in a dream, his own body, along with theirs, like husks of corn in a field, ready for the reaper's rapacious blade. He experienced then the ascendancy of Kshira, and though it was momentary, it was like an iris opening onto the portal of death, and every dark thing that lay beyond. Deep inside himself he began to scream. . . .

Nangi was drifting off to sleep. Kisoko sat still as a statue, as if waiting for some unheard signal. Eventually, she stirred. "I'll see you out," she said.

Nicholas stood on trembling legs. He breathed silently, trying to center himself, then followed Kisoko to the front door. There, she turned to face him.

"Nangi-san has told you about us, though he has kept me secret from everyone else."

This was true. Last year, Nangi had told him a bit about his relationship with Kisoko. They had met eleven years ago and had had a torrid, though ultimately tragic, affair. Nangi had never forgotten her, and when they had met again, it seemed it was, at last, their time.

Nicholas understood her meaning. "I will not speak of you, even to Tōrin-san."

She bowed her head in thanks. When she looked up, she said, "Don't think ill of him. This was hard, having you come here. He had no wish for you to see him like this, weak and ill."

"But I had a meeting with him yesterday in his car."

"Yes. But he was prepared for you then, dressed as he has always dressed, buttressed by drugs, and I will bet the interview was brief."

"It was."

She nodded and smiled. "It is his way, Nicholas-san, do not be downcast. He loves you like a son. Indeed, he thinks of you as his own flesh and blood. Which is why he is ashamed for you to see him old and helpless."

"I had to come."

"Of course you did," she said kindly. "I appreciate it, and believe me, beneath his shame, he does as well." She looked into his sad eyes. "Six months ago, you were not here when he had his heart attack."

He nodded. "That has never been out of my mind. I cannot forgive myself—"

"I forgive you," Kisoko said unexpectedly. "As for Nangi-san, he sees nothing to forgive you for." She took a step closer to him. "My point was not to make you feel guilty, but to make the confession he could not bring himself to make. The truth is his heart attack was more serious than anyone—even Tōrin-san—knows. Now, don't worry. He will recover without any permanent impairment, the doctors have assured us. But it will take time."

Her voice was reduced to a whisper. "This is what I must ask of you, Nicholas-san, though I know it is rude and presumes too much on a relationship that has just begun. But, after all, I did know your parents and I was very fond of them."

"I will do what I can, Kisoko-san."

She nodded with a sense of relief. Oddly, at that moment, he felt as if she were about to touch him. But that was, of course, nonsense. Such a breach of etiquette in a woman of her age was unthinkable.

The moment passed, and she smiled up at him. "You remind me so much of your father. So strong of will, so handsome." She put her long-fingered hand on the door, opened it so that a dank breeze blew across their faces and entered the house. "Do whatever you have to do, but give him the time he needs to recuperate fully. If this means working with Tōrin-san, I beg you to do it."

A gust of wind brought a spray of rain onto the front steps, and a foghorn lowed mournfully out along the river.

Nicholas nodded. "I appreciate your candor, Kisoko-san."

She smiled. "How could I be otherwise? You are dear to the two most important men in my life." She gazed into his eyes, and once again he had a flash of the magnificent woman she had been decades ago. "You are my brother's angel. Isn't that how Westerners would say it?"

He nodded again. "I will do what has to be done, Kisoko-san."

She gave him a curiously informal bow. "I know you will and I am grateful." Again he had the curious sensation that she wanted to reach out and enfold him in her arms.

"Godspeed," she whispered after him into the wind.

* * *

Nicholas caught Honniko as she was coming down the staircase to Pull Marine.

"Isn't this your day off?" He was perched on his Kawasaki.

Honniko paused halfway down the stairs, then laughed, continuing her descent. "It is, but how did you know that?"

Nicholas shrugged. "I asked Jōchi, the other maître d' at the restaurant."

She came across the crowded Roppongi sidewalk. She was wearing a cool blue-green linen skirt and a crisp pearl-gray blouse beneath a black-and-green-striped bolero jacket. Her small feet were in black flats, and a thin gold chain was wrapped around her throat. "That doesn't explain how you knew where to find me."

"He also told me you'd be coming in for an hour or so today for the staff meeting."

"Jōchi said that?"

"I told him I was in love. I guess he took pity on me."

"Better him than me."

She put on a pair of dark glasses. The sun was beginning to break through a widening rift in the misty clouds, but Nicholas wasn't at all sure this was her motivation. In tone as well as physical proximity she was keeping her distance.

"Ouch. I'm not all that bad."

Honniko scrunched up her face. "You want something. Trouble is, I can't figure out what."

"I already told you. I'm trying to find Nguyen Van Truc."

"Oh, yeah. He owes you money."

"That's right."

She took one step toward him. "You're a liar."

"I'm not lying."

She leaned forward. "And I can't be intimidated."

"I never said you could. Take off those glasses, why don't you."

"Even by a handsome man on a dashing black motorcycle," she added with a perfectly straight face.

He smiled. "Now that you've drawn the line in the sand and stepped across it, the least I can do is take you to lunch."

Honniko thought a moment. "Or I could take *you*."

"There's that line again," Nicholas said, patting the back

of the Kawasaki. "We'll eat and then do whatever you say, does that suit you?"

By way of reply, Honniko swung aboard, clasping him tightly around the waist. He could feel the press of her breasts against his back.

She did take off the sunglasses, but only after they were seated in the restaurant, a small café called Third Stone From the Sun, after the Jimi Hendrix song, he supposed. It was on the terraced third floor of the Gorgon Building, just down the street from "Little Beverly Hills," where one could eat at the Hard Rock Cafe or Spago's.

Nicholas liked this place because it was an unpretentious island in a sea of self-conscious French and Chinese restaurants and because it overlooked the Gorgon Building's glass-walled wedding hall, where outlandishly hip Western-style weddings were always in progress. Today, a Japanese couple improbably dressed as Elvis and Priscilla Presley were in the midst of their nuptials. These recessionary days, the lavish excesses of Las Vegas–style bad taste had been replaced by the curious Japanese propensity to maladroitly appropriate icons of American pop culture. When the loudspeaker system gushed forth the King's red-hot rendition of "Burning Love" as the couple walked down the aisle, Honniko burst into laughter.

"So it seems you have a sense of humor after all," Nicholas said.

"Jesus," she sputtered, wiping her eyes, "did you know about this place?"

He nodded, laughing. "I figured with someone who works all night in a top restaurant the show would be more important than the food."

Her dark, almond eyes regarded him with great care. "That was thoughtful." Then, as if the small compliment had been some kind of gaffe, she snatched up the menu, buried her head in it. With her blond hair and oriental eyes, she provided a mix as potent as a double sake martini.

After a moment, she noticed that he wasn't reading his menu. "Aren't you hungry? Or is the food here that bad?"

"You order for me. I'm sure I'll like whatever it is."

Honniko put down her menu. "You are the most self-assured man I have ever met. How do you do it?"

"What do you mean?"

"Look at the world. There's no stability anywhere. I used to think, well, that's one thing Japan has: stability. But look what's happened in the last four years. We're plunged into an endless recession, bankruptcies are at an all-time high, our major banks are going under, the strong yen is killing us, our real estate is next to worthless, there's massive unemployment for the first time in memory, the ruling party gets bounced out of power, people are more concerned with the price of rice than with how government is failing, and now we have resurrected on our doorstep the specter of another nuclear attack."

Across the terrace, Elvis and Priscilla had come out into the pallid sunlight, surrounded by their joyous guests. "Burning Love" had been replaced by "I Want You, I Need You, I Love You." Someone had dragged out a microphone, which the groom had good-naturedly grabbed. He swung his hips, lip-synching the lyrics. Priscilla clasped her hands and rolled her eyes. The guests applauded.

Honniko was applauding, too. "That's why I admire anyone with such self-assurance. It speaks of a strong philosophy of life." She turned her eyes on him. "It reassures me there's still a North Star up there in the sky to be guided by."

"Like the samurai daimyo—the warlords who used to live here in Roppongi."

"Yes, exactly. Their purity of purpose seems overly harsh, even at times incomprehensible to most Westerners."

The waiter came with their drinks and Honniko ordered goat-cheese salads and stir-fried vegetable plates for both of them. "I'm a vegetarian," she said to Nicholas. "I hope you don't mind."

He shook his head. "Do you know how Roppongi got its name? Once upon a time, it belonged to six of those daimyo I was speaking of. They all had the Chinese character for 'trees' in their names, hence Roppongi—Six Trees. In the middle of the nineteenth century, when their status as samurai ceased to be a shield, their property was confiscated by the Meiji government and given over to the Imperial Army."

"I know the more recent history. After the war, it was requisitioned by the American Occupation, and gradually it became an entertainment quarter." Honniko fiddled with her dark glasses. "I know that because my father was stationed here in those years."

"He was Army, right?"

Around and around the tabletop the dark glasses went. "Military police." She glanced up at him. "He went after the bad buys, you know, the users: the currency runners, arms merchants, drug dealers, black marketeers."

It was interesting. She was giving off two conflicting signals. She didn't want to talk about her father, but she did.

"Tell me about your mother," he said as the salads were served. Maybe that would take some of the pressure off.

"There's nothing much to tell. My father met her here in Roppongi." Honniko was watching a new marriage party—this group in black leather motorcycle jackets and silver studs—make their way across the terrace under the direction of a rather hyper photographer.

"And that's the end of the story."

As the photographer placed the party in the sunlight, Honniko looked down at her salad and said nothing.

"Forget it," Nicholas said. "It's none of my business."

Across the terrace, the party was shedding their leather jackets, revealing skin so covered with tattoos that there was hardly a flesh-colored patch anywhere to be seen.

Honniko, studying the array of tattooed flesh like a careful housewife picking over fresh fish, said, "Actually, there *is* more to the story."

While the wedding photographer worked in a flurry of movement, Nicholas waited for her to continue.

"My mother worked not far from here, in a *toruko*," she said after a long pause. Her eyes caught his, flashed away. "Do you know what that is?"

"Yes. Nowadays, it's called soapland." He took up a forkful of radicchio, mâche, and goat cheese. "The word is a bastardization of the English *Turkish bath*."

"Then you know that men went to a *toruko* not merely to get clean."

"I suppose it had to do with how much money they were willing to part with."

"And the imagination of the woman getting you clean." She looked down at her untouched salad. "My mother was a *halo*." The word was slang. Literally, it meant box, but the meaning was pussy. It was also the nickname of the women who worked the old-time *toruko*.

"Your father knew this?"

"Yeah. It was called Tenki." *Tenki* was Japanese for a profound secret. "He got a call to raid the place and dig out a black marketeer who was getting his genitals soaped. Everyone in the *toruko* was hauled out and arrested, my mother included."

"And they fell in love."

"Like hell." Honniko laughed uneasily. "My father was all-American and a pure, cross-eyed romantic. Also, he knew nothing about the Japanese." Finding no good use for her fork, she finally put it down. "He wanted to take her away from all that."

"And, of course, she went." He pushed his salad away; he'd had enough. "Because he wanted her to, not because *she* wanted to."

"She became his wife." Honniko watched the waiter take their plates away. "She became what he wanted her to be."

"Did she have a choice?"

Honniko shook her head. "Not really. He was the one who sprung her from jail. Her family, who lived in Ise, did not even know she was in Tokyo." The plates of brightly colored vegetables were set in front of them. "He paid her fine, got the authorities to wipe her record clean—so she could start fresh, he told her." She stabbed a piece of asparagus with more force than was required. "His life, not hers." She stared at the asparagus on her fork as if it might be alive and squirming. "Still, as you can imagine, she was immensely grateful."

On the sun-splashed terrace, the photographer was nervously rearranging the wedding party into so many designs it was dizzying.

"From that day forward the *giri* she owed him was so great she could refuse him nothing. The ironic thing is that if my father ever suspected, it would have blown his mind. Of course, he never did."

Nicholas pushed the food around on his plate. Maybe her lack of appetite was contagious. "Did she come to love him in the end?"

Honniko gave him a wistful smile as she gave up on her food. "We all wish for happy endings, don't we?" She put down her fork. "The truth is I don't know. I never will. She died last year and my father . . ." She let out a long breath. "I don't know where my father is, whether he's alive or dead. He walked out on us when I was twelve and we never heard from him. He never sent my mother money for me. Nothing. It's like he never existed, and from that time on my mother never spoke his name." She looked at him. "So I guess, yeah, she must have loved him in some fashion because he sure as hell broke her heart."

Looking at the wedding party now filing inside for the ceremony, Nicholas thought maybe it hadn't been such a good idea to bring her here, after all.

Abruptly, the world canted over on one side. The disappearing wedding party looked like stretched-out bars of Turkish taffy and the sky had turned the color of bubble gum. Nicholas, alarmed, looked down at his right arm. Had it gone *directly through* the table, as it now seemed? He shook his head, but the buzz of 10 million bees refused to abate. He sensed Honniko looking at him oddly, but he could not actually see her. The bubble gum was coming down from the sky.

Then, like a rubber band snapping back into place, reality returned to its previous form.

"—all right?" Honniko was saying. "You went white there for a moment, and now you're sweating."

Nicholas wiped his forehead with his napkin. His tongue felt as thick as a log. What had happened? Another small seizure of Tau-tau, but not Akshara, no. Kshira. His power rising, unbidden. Toward what end? The question made him shiver.

"It's nothing. I'm all right." But even as he said it, he knew it for a lie.

Thirty years ago, the Golden Gate Inn had been a hip and happening place. Despite its unlovely exterior, the six-story building had the right location for the wiseguys of Queens and East New York. It overlooked Sheepshead Bay at Coney Island Avenue and the Belt Parkway. As such, it was prime location for what the wiseguys favored most: beach, boats, and bodies.

The bodies—all dead, all, in one form or another, enemies—were discovered from time to time in the section of overgrown weeds and steel-woolly underbrush where, in 1961, Mick Leonforte had whacked Gino Scalfa. Scalfa was by no means the first to get it there and he certainly wasn't the last.

Nowadays, the hotel was no longer hosting wiseguys to drinks, broads, and braggadocio. It was, in fact, closed up and all but derelict. But the area next to it that had never been developed, wild with weeds, grasses, and goldenrod in summer, enriched over the years with their blood and brains, still abided by the side of the service road.

It was at this place that Caesare Leonforte had set the meet with Margarite. She arrived in the vicinity ten minutes early and sat in her car waiting. It was not cold, nevertheless her arms were crossed over her chest in order to keep herself from trembling.

To calm her wildly beating heart, she took the time to review all the ways in which Bad Clams had turned her life upside down. And at once she saw how much she had been in shock these last two days. They seemed like days, weeks, so paralyzed had she been. Caesare—brilliant bastard that he was—had struck her heart three times in succession and had succeeded in robbing her of her best defense: her mind. She was in an intense state of fear for Francie's life even while she had been mourning for her beloved business—and, yes, even for Tony, with whom she had shared at least some good times and a sense of intimacy. Tony might have abused her, but he had loved her as well, of this she had no doubt. She also knew that she had grown where he had not. And, in doing so, she had become a person with whom he could not cope. For men like Tony, women with aspirations were bad enough. But those who turned those aspirations into success were intolerable. Where, in his mind, she should have stayed at home banging out a succession of little De-Camillos for him, she went out, got educated, went into her own business. But for all that, she was a failure as a woman, as far as Tony had been concerned. And then had come the topper. Dominic had made Tony his successor as don in name only. All the real power had devolved onto Margarite. It was Margarite whom Dom trained, Margarite to whom he whispered all his secrets. It had driven Tony wild.

Now he was dead and though Margarite could mourn him in the traditional sense, she wondered whether a day would come when she would miss him.

She stared hard at the slashed and gaping hole in the dashboard where the CD player had been. She had used the crowbar in the trunk to gouge it out, had thrown it out the window as she had sped along the Belt Parkway. Then and only then, when she was certain that Caesare could not trace her calls, did she phone the beeper of the high-level Goldoni contact at City Hall. She had told the official to pull Jack Barnett, the cop who was investigating Tony's murder, off that case and any others he was currently on. "This is what I want Barnett to do," she told the official, and had then given the man a specific set of instructions.

The official did not complain. He was one of literally hundreds of municipal, state, and federal government officials on whom Dominic Goldoni had compiled dossiers. The Nishiki network constantly updated these dossiers, and when Dom had been murdered, Margarite had inherited these files and the power they brought anyone who possessed them.

This particular man, Margarite knew, was a cross-dresser, not a peccadillo that would be condoned if it were made public. A man—especially a government official—dressing up in women's clothes would cause a scandal of epic proportions if it hit the news media.

The phone rang and she jumped just as if a shot had been fired at her.

"Yes?" she answered warily. What if it was Caesare calling to torment her again?

"Mrs. DeCamillo? Barnett here."

Her eyes closed in relief. "Where are you, Detective?"

"Close. Very close."

Margarite glanced at her watch. "It's time."

"I know."

"My daughter, Francine—"

"You've made yourself very clear, Mrs. DeCamillo. You pull some extremely powerful strings at City Hall."

"All in a day's work."

"Your work, Mrs. DeCamillo. I'm only brought in to clean up the messes you and people like you make."

Her face was a mask of concentration as she put the Lexus in gear. "I'm going in."

"Understood."

She broke the connection as she nosed down the service road toward the patch of weeds and underbrush. Beyond, the bay twinkled with lights and reflections. The lights of the city bounced eerily off the underside of low clouds. The air was heavy and wet with incipient rain. A plane following a flight path into Kennedy roared by, sounding like thunder.

Bernice was wrong, Margarite thought, as she kept her eye out for the other car. And, anyway, it was impossible to put aside thoughts of vengeance. This was Francine, her baby, they were talking about! Business was one thing, but Bad Clams had violated every code of their world: he'd gone after her family. That was, as Mrs. Paglia had said, an *infamia,* and now, whatever Bad Clams's fate, he had brought it down on himself.

She knew she was taking a terrible risk. But this situation wasn't that cut-and-dried. In snatching her daughter Caesare had crossed a line. His unspeakable act had branded him for destruction, and Margarite was determined to be the agent of that annihilation.

Up ahead, in the tarmacked space between the service road and the place where the weeds began heading down to the bay, she could see a dark Lincoln, lying low and in wait like a hunter. It had kept dark all this time, but as she approached, its golden running lights were switched on. She rolled to a stop, the Lexus's engine ticking over like a clock, like her pulse. She stared hard at the car, as if she had X-ray vision that could penetrate its armor plate and see her daughter.

Francine! Her mind screamed in her agony. Oh, Bernice, for all her wisdom, could not know such profound fear and pain!

She blinked several times, then slowly and methodically disengaged her white fingers from their death grip around the steering wheel.

"Mrs. DeCamillo." A voice, disembodied by distance and darkness, made her shiver.

Breathe, she commanded herself. *Breathe.*

"Yes," she called out of the open window. "I'm here."

"Please get outta the car an' open all four doors."

It will all be over in a minute, she told herself as she got slowly out of the Lexus. *That's what Barnett said and I believe him. I have to believe him.*

"Now step away from the car so we can see inside an' make sure you're alone."

"I told Caesare—"

"Gotta make sure, Mrs. D. You know how it is. I got my orders."

She walked carefully out of the headlight beams.

"Stay where we can see ya. Right in fronta the car."

She did as she was told, but she had the .45 in her hand, hanging at her side, hidden by her body and her handbag. She had already killed once in defense of her life, and she knew she was prepared to kill again to get Francie back. She had become the agent of Caesare's annihilation.

"She's clear," the voice said, "an' so's the car. It's like she said, she's solo."

A car door slammed and Margarite squinted through the glare of the headlights at a bloblike shape. This was not going to be so easy; seeing wasn't so good from where she was standing. As she took a step toward the darkness, a voice stopped her.

"It would not be wise to move, Mrs. D.," another voice, deeper, thicker, said. "I have your daughter here an' I know you wouldn't want anything bad to happen to her at this late date."

Margarite's heart flipped over painfully. "Francine!"

"Mom!"

Thank God! Margarite breathed. *She's here!*

"Are you okay?"

"Mom, what's going on?"

Margarite's heart went out to her daughter. She'd gone through so much already. "Don't worry, angel. This is just business. Caesare wants to—"

"That's enough wid the chitchat, you two," the deep voice said. "Mrs. D., my name's Marco. Now that you know we have your daughter, I want you to walk straight toward me. I'm standin' next to the rear door to the black Lincoln. Get

in an' I'll put your daughter in beside you an' that'll be that.
We'll take carea the Lexus."

"But I—"

"Mrs. D., you do just as I say, nothing more, nothing less.
I wancha t'know your daughter is standing directly in fronta
me. Vinnie's at the wheela the Lincoln an' he's armed. So'm
I. I gotta gun against the backa your daughter's head." He
lowered his voice. "Go ahead, kid, tell 'er."

"He's got something pressed against my head, Mom!"
Francine piped up in a voice quivering only slightly with
held-in tension and fear.

"All right, all right!" Margarite called. "I'm coming
straight toward you." She stepped out of the headlight
beams, heading toward Marco and Francine. "I'm doing just
what you said."

"That's good, Mrs. D.," Marco said. "Makes my job easier
an' your daughter—"

He never got to finish his thought because, at that instant,
Margarite had come abreast of him and, whipping the muzzle of the .45 beneath his jaw, pulled the trigger and blown
the top of his head off.

Francie screamed from the sharp report of the pistol's
discharge and from the spastic jerk of Marco against her.
Margarite grabbed her daughter, shoved Marco's heavy
corpse away, and trained her gun in Vinnie's direction. But
she needn't have bothered. There was another sharp report,
echoing over the bay, and a surprisingly small section of the
Lincoln's windshield shattered inward. The rest of it had
turned into a vast and complex spiderweb behind which Vinnie could be seen spread-eagle against the seatback, staring
upward at the large hole in his forehead.

Margarite threw down her .45, kicked it beneath Marco's
body as the form of Detective Lieutenant Jack Barnett
picked its way fastidiously across the tarmac.

"Mrs. DeCamillo, are you and your daughter okay?"

She raised her voice long enough to say, "We are,
Detective."

She cuddled Francine and whispered urgently in her ear.
She devoured Francie with her eyes, and seeing her own
face reflected in her daughter's, she thought, *She's all right*,
She kissed both her cheeks, stroked her curling red hair,

which she wore long and wild. She stared into Francie's hazel, quicksilver eyes, trying to read a world in a split second. *She's so beautiful,* Margarite thought, *the only good thing to come out of my marriage to Tony. But she's pure Goldoni. If there's any DeCamillo in her, I can't see it.* The long-legged, coltish body trembled like a fawn's in Margarite's embrace. Francie, in wide-legged Gap jeans, well-worn Tony Lama cowboy boots, an inside-out black tee, and a rumpled denim jacket with the sleeves rolled up her forearms, pressed herself against her mother, but she was staring wide-eyed at the dead men. *How fragile youth is,* Margarite thought. *And how precious. It's snatched away in the blink of an eye and then it's gone forever.*

"That first shot gave me quite a start." Barnett, coming up on mother and daughter, squinted through the hole his shot had made through the Lincoln's windshield. He was holding a Husqvarna rifle, outlined with a nightscope, in his left hand; in his right was his service revolver. He was a dapper-looking man in his early forties with sandy hair and light eyes, although in the glare of the headlights Margarite could not tell their exact color. He possessed the face of a man who had seen many things and passed through them all as a fakir walks over hot coals, with a mixture of faith and practical knowledge of the way the universe works. He was dressed in a dark suit with surprisingly few creases. His tie, which now flew over his shoulder in the freshening wind, was elegant rather than loud.

He came around the side of the Lincoln where Margarite stood with Francine tucked protectively into her body and stared down at Marco's crumpled form. "Hmm. Two down and only one shot fired." He sniffed. "I'm good but, much as I hate to admit it, I'm not that good." His eyes swung up to fix Margarite in a gaze as hard as the glare from sodium lights. "You wouldn't know anything about that, would you, Mrs. DeCamillo?"

Margarite was thinking of an answer when Barnett was slammed against the side of the Lincoln. The Husqvarna flew from his grip and he leaned against the shiny black metal with a confused and slightly sad expression on his face. He looked up at her and his eyes crossed. That was when she noticed the rapidly expanding boutonniere of blood damaging his beautiful suit. She gripped Francie more tightly as she felt a choked-off scream burning her throat like acid.

She wanted to reach out to poor Barnett even though the flower of blood emanated from over his heart, but a low moan escaped Francie's lips and her daughter began to tremble in earnest. Margarite kissed the top of Francie's head. She couldn't let go of her, and yet, as Barnett slid to the blood-spattered ground, she felt she had to do something. She began to reach out toward his service revolver, but a voice made her freeze.

"Oh, do try for it. Shooting an armed woman is much less problematic than killing an unarmed one. And so much more fun."

She turned then and saw a man coming through the Lexus's beams. He walked with a peculiar hip-tilting gait, as if one leg didn't work right or was shorter than the other. He had compensated for this disability by employing an almost skipping motion in his walk, so that he moved quickly and at sharp angles, reminding Margarite of the small, colorless sand crabs she had seen on the beach in the Caribbean.

There was nothing colorless, however, about this man. Though he was somewhat short, he was nonetheless imposing. He had a wide face, square as a block of ice, with mackerel eyes that seemed dead, yellow as yesterday's marrow. He wore a neat, unfashionable goatee that gave him something of the aspect of Bacchus, the Greek god of wine, women, and song, who was said to be part animal. Like Bacchus, he had jet-black, curling hair that fell in shiny ringlets across his forehead and down the nape of his neck, a wide, sensual mouth, and a long, straight, Roman nose. A striking man, though the heaviness of some features prevented him from being handsome.

He was dressed in a striped, collarless shirt beneath a handsome pig suede jacket dyed the color of whiskey, black jeans, and boots of whiskey-colored alligator with high Cuban heels and custom toes shod in what looked like stainless steel.

"I know you, don't I?" Margarite said.

"You do an' you don't. I'm the ghost of Black Paul Mattaccino. I'm his son, Paul Chiaramonte."

"I know that name. You're part of the Abriola family my husband trusted with his life. The Abriolas have served the Goldonis faithfully for decades."

While he smiled a lopsided grin, he lifted a leg and, with the finesse of a ballet dancer, flicked Barnett's weapons away into the darkness. He held a long-barreled gun in his left hand.

"Bad Clams warned me not to trust you and he was right. But then he's always right." Paul Chiaramonte clicked his tongue against the roof of his mouth in that reproving sound old ladies make during sex scenes in the movies. "Well, we can say good-bye to Vinnie and Marco." He shrugged. "Not the best of talent, anyway." He gave her that lopsided grin again. Because of his sensual lips, it was almost a leer, and Margarite found herself putting her hand over Francie's face to shield her further. "In the old days they called soldiers like Vinnie and Marco cannon fodder because they were gonna die on the battlefield." He shrugged again. "That's gotta happen to someone. Why waste A-list talent when it's so hard to find these days?" He chuckled, showing teeth like a wolf's, sharp as paring knives.

His eyes fell upon the body of Detective Lieutenant Jack Barnett. "But who's this?" His stainless-steel boot toe kicked Barnett in the side and Margarite winced even though the detective was dead. Paul Chiaramonte grinned up at Margarite as he knelt down. "Bodyguard or boyfriend? Maybe both."

He carefully used one long fingernail to peel back the blood-sodden jacket, reached inside, and opened the small plastic wallet he found there. "Not much of a sport, I see." Then, he let out a little cry and dropped the thing as if it had stung him.

His eyes, black and ripe as grapes, goggled at Margarite. "Are you fucking mental? This guy's a *cop*, for the love of Mary!" He did a tiny jig, making him look as if he were summoning up the woodland nymphs for an orgy. "I whacked an NYPD blue. Oh, holy shit! Who coulda figured?"

"You didn't have to kill him," Margarite pointed out. It was an inane thing to say, but she was now so terrified and so shocked at what she had done she couldn't think of anything else.

Paul Chiaramonte jumped, his face black with rage. He shoved the muzzle of his gun into the soft spot beneath the point of her chin, making her cry out.

"Mom!"

"Hush, angel," she said as tears of pain ran freely down her cheeks.

"You and your cop buddy whacked two of my crew," he shouted in her face. "I should blow the toppa your head off for you." He had gold rings on all his fingers, including his thumb, which made it look deformed, heavy with menace.

"Killing a woman. That would be just your speed," Margarite said.

Paul Chiaramonte hit her backhanded across both cheeks, his gold rings gouging her flesh and making her bleed.

"Shut up and stand like a statue!" he said with his lips pulled back from his teeth. "Christ Jesus, I haven't seen so much trouble since your stepmother lived here."

"What do you know about Faith Goldoni?"

"Plenty." Paul Chiaramonte sneered. "My mother was Sara Chiaramonte. She was the only woman Black Paul Mattaccino ever loved." He was staring at Francine, who seemed as mesmerized by him as she would be by an exotic animal. "He was locked in a loveless, lifeless marriage with Faith, the bitch. But he was Catholic, from the old school, and wouldn't divorce her." His eyes, quick as an adder's tongue, flicked to Margarite's face. "So she killed him slowly with poison in the black figs he adored, so she could marry your father, Enrico Goldoni."

"Are you trying to frighten me? Everyone knew that rumor about her. But that's all it was. She told me. People were jealous of her, marrying my father. Faith was incapable of killing anyone."

"I know better. But who gives a shit, anyway? She's dead now so at least she can't lie to you anymore."

Fright and disgust mingled so thoroughly in her Margarite could no longer look at him. So she stared at Jack Barnett's face, which was no help at all. It was a handsome face, especially with that sandy hair lying across his eyes. Did he have a wife? A child, maybe Francie's age? She didn't know, never would know, and after all, it was irrelevant because he was dead. In the name of revenge, she had brought him into this, and to this end. *As surely as night follows day, suffering and death will ensue,* Bernice had said. But Margarite had thought she was smarter than that, was sure that she could beat the odds, change the rules, and upset the game. Instead, look what had come of it. She had reached out with her power—the power of the Goldonis—and had brought death to an innocent man.

What was it Bernice had told her? *It isn't power itself that corrupts us. It is the abuse of it.* She had abused her power, and suffering and death was the result.

Everyone thought Faith was dead—even apparently Paul Chiaramonte. But the truth was she had merely changed identities. She was now Renata Loti, one of Washington's major power brokers. Margarite saw her stepmother infrequently. Theirs was a thorny and unsatisfying relationship. She had been nine when her father, Enrico Goldoni, had married Faith, too old to easily lose her bond with her real mother, too young to fully grasp the difficulties Faith was facing with a new husband and a new—and hostile—family.

Margarite had always kept herself aloof from the common neighborhood belief that Faith, in Machiavellian calculation and cold blood, had murdered her first husband. But perhaps that had only been out of a sense of self-preservation. What child would want to be brought up in the same house as a murderess?

Your soul is choked with tears, Bernice had said, reading her with uncanny insight. Margarite wailed inside, and she jumped as that wailing became a real sound.

Sirens ululating in the night, startling all three of them.

"Hello, we must be going," Paul Chiaramonte said, paraphrasing Groucho Marx. Using the muzzle of his gun, he roughly herded the two women up the incline and into the ghostly hotel's parking lot. Phosphorescence glistened out on the bay. It was probably best not to know its source, Margarite thought.

A fire-red, vintage Thunderbird convertible crouched in a shadowed corner of the lot. He directed Margarite to bind Francie's wrists and ankles. They bundled her into the cramped back space. Then, working swiftly and surely, he did the same with Margarite.

"This isn't necessary. I'll sit beside you in the front. You have my daughter. You can trust me."

"Like Marco and Vinnie could trust you?" Paul Chiaramonte sneered. "Your stepmother raised you well. You're a fuckin' viper, lady."

He stuffed his handkerchief into her mouth, pressed her head down, pushed her on top of Francie. Then he slammed the door shut, got behind the wheel, fired up the T-bird, and swung out of the lot.

Out on the Belt Parkway, with the cassette deck cranked up, cruising easily under the speed limit, he passed a fleet of blue-and-white cop cars, top lights revolving, sirens screaming, heading for the Golden Gate Inn.

"So long, suckas," Paul Chiaramonte called over Brian Wilson's choirboy voice singing "Don't Worry Baby."

5
Tokyo/West Palm Beach

Nicholas met Tanaka Gin in Kappa Watanabe's hospital room. The cyber tech looked like hell. His skin, pulled tight against his bones, had been tainted an alarming greenish yellow by the Banh Tom nerve toxin. A ventilator was assisting his breathing, and a plethora of plastic tubes snaked in and out of him. His heart and pulse rate were being monitored, and a nurse stood by his side, adjusting the levels of the many chemicals being pumped into him.

"You may have five minutes with him, no more," the obviously annoyed physician had told them in the corridor just outside. "He's still very weak, so don't upset him in any way."

"We appreciate the assist," Tanaka Gin had said as he bowed respectfully.

Inside, however, he was brisk, all business, as he quickly introduced himself to Watanabe. "This is a criminal investigation," he concluded, ignoring the nurse's silent disapproval. "Your involvement has put you at great risk, as you must already have guessed. But if and when you get out of here, I am authorized to tell you that you will be charged with multiple counts of espionage, piracy, and grand larceny. Other charges are currently being drawn up as the investigation continues." Tanaka Gin stared down at Watanabe's yellow eyes as he waved away the increasingly frantic motions of the nurse. Judging by the noises from the monitors, the cyber tech's vital signs were becoming elevated. As Tanaka Gin and Nicholas had discussed, now was the time to press him even harder. "Watanabe-san, you have willfully stolen copyrighted and proprietary material from Sato International. I am afraid that all you have to look forward to is a lifetime in jail. If you don't die in here, that is."

"Just a moment," Nicholas said, adhering to their prepared script. "I have an idea, Gin-san, an alternative."

"There *is* no alternative," Tanaka Gin said, his steely eyes boring into Watanabe's wide-apart eyes.

"At least hear me out. What if Watanabe-san makes a full confession and cooperates fully with this investigation?"

"Yes," Watanabe said in a wan but desperate tone. "Yes."

Tanaka Gin snorted. "Linnear-san, this man is a thief. He tried to bankrupt you. I cannot believe you are defending him."

"Not defending. But I want to get to the bottom of this. Don't you see? I am convinced by the evidence we have so far that Watanabe-san did not steal the CyberNet data on his own. If he can lead us to the others, I am not interested in prosecuting him."

"You may not be, but I certainly am!" Tanaka Gin thundered so loudly that even the nurse cowered into her corner. "By God, the Tokyo Prosecutor's Office will not tolerate industrial espionage. Damn it, it's a matter of national security."

Watanabe was trembling and his heart rate was going crazy. "But I have the information, Linnear-san," he pleaded. "I can never forgive myself for what I have done, but at least I can try to make amends."

"No deals!" Tanaka Gin's voice rose to a crescendo.

"I don't want him in jail if he helps us," Nicholas said. "You know what it's like inside. He'll never survive."

Now Watanabe was goggling at them both. Terror such as he'd never known filled his very soul. And he struggled to get everything out at once.

At that moment, the door swung open and the doctor

strode in. "What in the name of heaven is going on here? I told you—"

"This is official business," Tanaka Gin said, pinning the doctor with that patented steely glare. "Out until I tell you otherwise."

"You can't talk to me that way. I am in charge here."

"When I'm finished, you are." Tanaka Gin drew out a folded sheet. "Otherwise I am authorized to remove your patient to the medical facility in Metropolitan Prison. Is that your wish, Doctor?"

The doctor stared at Tanaka Gin for a moment to allow himself to regain some face with the nurse, then he let the door close.

Tanaka Gin, with a quick glance at Nicholas, turned back to Watanabe just in time to see Nicholas bending over him. "It's going to be all right, Watanabe-san, I promise you."

And with a great deal of satisfaction, Tanaka Gin heard Watanabe squeak, "I am prepared, Linnear-san. It is quite clear in my mind. I want to tell you everything I know."

Tanaka Gin flipped on a pocket recorder, spoke into it the date, time, location, and those present. Then he set the recorder down in the swinging tray in front of Watanabe's mouth, and Watanabe said he was making this statement of his own free will.

"You admit to making an unauthorized copy of Sato International's TransRim CyberNet data?" Tanaka Gin began.

"I do."

"And you acknowledge knowing that said data were the sole property of Sato International?"

"I do."

"Did you perpetrate this crime on your own?"

"No. I was approached by a man named Nguyen Van Truc. He's the vice president of national marketing for Minh Telekom, a Vietnamese company."

"Just a moment," Nicholas interjected. "You weren't approached by the American Cord McKnight?"

"No. As I told you, it was Van Truc."

"But you made the data transfer with McKnight," Nicholas said.

"As far as I know, he was just an intermediary. A cutout so Van Truc could keep his hands clean." Watanabe put his head back on the pillow. His hair was shiny with the sweat of exertion.

"Let me get you some water," Nicholas said. They watched as Watanabe sucked ice water through a straw, his eyes closed with the intense pleasure of a child.

"Tell us a bit more about the Vietnamese," Tanaka Gin said.

Watanabe nodded. "Van Truc works for Minh, as I said. But he was being paid by someone else. An industrialist I'd heard of named Kurtz."

Tanaka Gin and Nicholas exchanged glances. "Rodney Kurtz?" Nicholas asked.

"Yes."

"How could you know this?" Tanaka Gin said. "By your own admission, these people were extremely careful. Van Truc used McKnight as a cutout."

"Yes, yes. But, you see, Van Truc had to use something of sufficient value to entice me to steal the CyberNet data. What he offered me was my own R and D lab with Sterngold Associates. I did some digging and discovered that Sterngold is one of half a dozen companies in Asia owned by Rodney Kurtz. How else would a vice president of marketing of a Vietnamese telecommunications company be offering me such a plum job unless Kurtz was financing the whole thing?"

"You should have come to me with all of this before the fact," Nicholas said. "I would have helped you and you wouldn't be lying here now, poisoned by the people who hired you."

Watanabe, who was clearly exhausted by his ordeal, closed his eyes. His hands were trembling and the nurse seemed truly alarmed by the readings coming off the monitor.

"I might have," he said in a voice that had become thin and reedy, "because everyone at Sato talks about how kind and intuitive you are. But you weren't around, were you?"

In a *kissaten*, a coffee shop nearby the hospital, Nicholas and Tanaka Gin sat staring out the window at the rest of the world rushing home to dinner and TV. Cars and buses clogged the street to the point of immobility, and a sea of pedestrians spooled by as if on moving walkways.

"Are you okay?" Tanaka Gin asked. "You look almost as bad as Watanabe."

"I'm fine," Nicholas said, sipping his coffee.

"Well, I'm not." Tanaka Gin rubbed his eyes with the pads of his thumbs. "Just before we met at the hospital, I got word that Tetsuo Akinaga's lawyers sprung him."

"You mean the charges have been dropped?" The thought of the Yakuza *oyabun* who was Okami's most powerful and implacable enemy being set free was unthinkable. "But he was awaiting trial."

"Akinaga's lawyers claimed there were irregularities in my prosecutorial brief and apparently they were right." Tanaka Gin shook his head. "The brief was sabotaged, Linnear-san. As I told you, I had been warned of corruption within my department. Now I am seeing direct evidence of it."

"I will make some inquiries in areas off limits to you."

Tanaka Gin bowed formally. "Thank you, Linnear-san. I am in your debt."

They ordered more coffee and stared out at the traffic and the rain. The slick sidewalks seemed lacquered with neon reflections.

"I sure would like a word with Nguyen Van Truc," Tanaka Gin mused, "but it's as if he fell off the face of the earth. Neither his company nor his relatives have heard from him since the night of the CyberNet launch dinner, and Immigration informs me he hasn't tried to leave the country. So where the hell is he?"

Nicholas stared at the rush-hour traffic and said nothing.

"You were right about Kurtz," he said at last. "Sterngold Associates appears on the list of the CyberNet's Denwa Partners."

"But why would Kurtz want to steal data from a project he'd just invested in?"

"Interesting question," Nicholas said. "It also puts a whole new spin on Kurtz's murder."

"How so?"

"Look at it this way. Kurtz was incredibly reclusive from a business perspective. He never let any of his businesses go public, even though it's a matter of public record from numerous stories in *Stern, Time,* and *Forbes,* to name just three, that his accountants, lawyers, and business associates had been urging him to do just that and make a killing on the international markets. He was something of a genius. People would fall all over themselves to buy into the Kurtz empire."

"Yes. So what?"

"So all his holdings are personal," Nicholas said. "If he dies, his wife inherits them. And if she dies . . ."

"They had no children."

"No." Nicholas drained the rest of his coffee. "So Kurtz likes the CyberNet prospects so much he buys into Denwa Partners. Two weeks later, he's murdered, and the next day his widow is killed by a hit-and-run. Cosmic coincidence or hidden connection?"

"I don't believe in coincidences where murder is concerned. I think I'd better find out who gets the estate now that both principals are deceased."

Tanaka Gin threw some bills on the table. "Linnear-san, about what happened last night at the Kurtzes', I know that in some way your Tau-tau allowed you to feel the presence of the killer. Have you any more impressions of who he might be? I have to discount your sensation of looking into a mirror and seeing yourself. You didn't kill Kurtz."

"No, of course not. I—"

The world canted over and was sliding into a rain-puckered ocean. Red and blue mixed, becoming magenta columns rising out of the *kissaten*'s floor, a forest of taffy. He heard his heartbeat, quick and fast, filling up his ears with pulsing fluid. He looked down, felt himself sinking through the floor, passing through solid objects as if they were made of ether.

A roaring colored the fluid in his ears, the massed buzzing of 10 million bees, a hive of kinetic activity that made him wince as he fell and kept right on falling . . .

"—near-san! Linnear-san!"

Someone was shouting, trying to drown out the bees' cross-pollinated conversations. Quiet, please!

"Linnear-san!"

It was Tanaka Gin's familiar face close by as he pulled Nicholas off the floor.

Nicholas put his hand to his throbbing head. The columns had disappeared and the floor seemed solid enough, but there was still the aftermath of the bees to contend with. "What happened?"

"You tell me," Tanaka Gin said. "You suddenly went white and slid off your chair."

Nicholas thought of the end of his lunch with Honniko. Those damned bees buzzing in his head, trying to be heard.

"Let's get out of here," he said.

Out in the rain-dark streets, it seemed quieter. The incessant crowds, the familiar chirping of the crosswalk units for the blind, provided a sense of continuity and lulled him back into reality.

"Linnear-san?"

"I slipped."

"Slipped? I saw you in a Tau-tau trance at the Kurtz house, and that was no normal slip."

"You're right," Nicholas said bleakly. "I'm very much afraid it was a slip from one reality to another."

Bad Clams had a forty-foot Cigarette—one of those ultrafast, ultraslim power boats so coveted in Florida. Its hull was painted the color of the ocean at night, a muddy shade in sunlight, but by moonlight it virtually disappeared. Of course, that was the point. Cigarettes were smugglers' boats.

Caesare's Cigarette was fast, even by the souped-up standards of the craft. Vesper's skin turned to gooseflesh within minutes of taking off from the dock in West Palm, and she had to hold on to the railing for support. The noise was almost insupportable, like being in the center of a jet engine. Her white-knuckle grip was secure on the gunwale as it had been as a kid on roller coasters that took her breath away just like this. Craning her neck, she saw the front of the boat was on plane, all the way out of the water, spray caroming off the sleek sides, hard and solid as hail.

"You need a sweater, babe? I think there's a couple stowed away below," Bad Clams shouted over the roar of the wind and the gigantic twin engines.

Vesper, her body vibrating with the throb of the engines, shook her head. "How fast are we going?"

"Faster than anything else afloat," Bad Clams confided, "and that includes those Coast Guard dicks."

It was just past seven and he still seemed agitated. He had been pacing the floor, looking at the phone, and when it had rung, he almost broke his hip lunging for it. He'd seemed initially disappointed, as if this business call was not the one he'd been waiting for. Nevertheless, he'd told her to get dressed as he hung up. "I got too much energy to stay in," he'd told her. He was jumpy and elated all at once, and she wondered what had happened.

As she tumbled out of bed, she wondered how Croaker was making out with Wade Forrest, the head of the Leonforte unit of the Anti-Cartel Task Force. Had it been crazy to involve Croaker? He was tough and smart, but she knew the ambitious Forrest very well, and if Croaker didn't handle himself just right, Forrest would blow him off without a second thought. She did not want that. She had come to be quite fond of him. Being with him was like hanging around a Robert Mitchum film character. She'd always been a sucker for Mitchum.

"There's a man maybe coming tomorrow, friend of mine," Bad Clams said as he headed out along the scimitared line the moonlight made on the ocean. "Real character, this guy. I think you'll get a kick outta him. He's gonna stay couple days, maybe. Bringing his girlfriend, she's okay." He waited a moment. "Not that it matters, she's a sickly broad, so you won't be seein' mucha her."

"Does this mean we can't go to South Beach?" Vesper drew wisps of hair off her face. "You promised me we'd go tomorrow."

"No, South Beach it is. My friend, Paulie, he won't be here till sometime inna afternoon. We'll go for lunch, 'kay? I'm sick of Il Palazzo, anyway."

About three miles from shore, he abruptly cut the engines and they began to drift.

"Look at that sunset," he said, pointing to the green and orange fire beyond the western horizon. "Makes you glad t'be alive, doesn't it?"

It was preternaturally quiet out here, beyond the seabirds

and out of the shipping lanes. The pleasure boats were all riding at anchor or safely in their slips. Only the distant drone of a plane could be heard wafting over the water. Far off, the lights of Palm Beach had come on, a spangle, part of another world, a reflection of the sunset riding the waves.

"You hungry?"

"Not really." She noticed a large Styrofoam chest that had been stowed beside the wheel.

"Hey, you know what I did today?" he said, his tone still light and conversational. "I checked you out. And y'know what I found?" He was coming toward her and Vesper had sense enough to stand her ground. Not an easy thing given the pissed-off look on his face. "I found out that you worked for the federal government." He was close now. "Not only that, you worked for a virtually unknown unit called Looking-Glass." She could smell him, that curious, spicy animal scent with which he scared people. "Not only that, you worked for my father, John."

"It's all true," Vesper said quietly.

He snorted. "I know that, lady. What I *don't* know is what you're doing here." His hands gestured. "I mean, it's too much ova coincidence you showin' up in Il Palazzo just in time for me to walk in and see you."

Vesper was walking through a lethal minefield without a diagram of where the explosives were located. Being with Caesare Leonforte was like that. Not that she minded such an assignment. Almost all her life, it seemed, she had been a sister to risk. And to her credit or her damnation, depending on your point of view, she clove to it like a moth to a flame.

The essential attraction of risk was that it took you out of yourself. Like acting, it was the antithesis of self-contemplation, which had never been one of Vesper's attributes. In being someone else, actors had no time to be themselves, and it was the same for risk. In those situations that entailed the greatest risk, you had to be whatever it was the other person needed you to be. Up to a point. Then you turned the tables on them in order to get what you wanted out of them.

Vesper's relationship with Bad Clams was still in the first, and most dangerous, stage. For if she was found out, there would be no other stages to follow on. Everything would be lost.

On the risky theory that the best defense was offense, Vesper pushed herself against him, encircling him with her arms. She kissed him hard on the lips. Then she pulled her head away so she could see his eyes and grinned up at him. "Did I somehow magically make you come over and pick me up?"

"No, of course not, but—"

"But I *was* there hoping to run into you."

His eyes narrowed. "Yeah, why?"

"Because of the Pentagon investigation into your father's dealings with DARPA, I need a secure place to hide." She was talking about the Pentagon's Defense Advanced Research Projects Agency. DARPA was so ultrasecret it was black-budgeted, which meant that Congress never knew about its funds and, therefore, never had to vote appropriations. "Your father was dipping his fingers into the DARPA experimental weapons cache virtually at will. When that came to light, it got a lot of people at the Pentagon really pissed off because it made the generals look foolish and compromised the entire fast-track advanced weapons research program."

"So okay, what's that got to do with you?"

"I needed to get out of Washington permanently before the investigation got around to me."

Now he seemed really suspicious. "Yeah, why? You had nothing to do with the DARPA procurement network."

Like most things in life, it was a trade-off. She'd gotten him more pissed off and suspicious of her, but in the process he'd given her a vital piece of the puzzle she was trying to solve. Now she had confirmed that Caesare had been involved in his father's scheme to raid DARPA of its best weapons ideas.

"No, but I worked closely with your father."

"On what?"

"Drugs."

For a moment, Caesare was too shocked to say anything. Then he began to laugh. He laughed so hard he held his sides and tears came to his eyes. "You?" he gasped. "A beautiful, intelligent broad like you involved in the macho sleaze of the drug world? You gotta be kidding."

"I'm not."

Caesare sobered up quickly. "Don't you fuckin' try to scam me, I'll skin you alive." When he spoke like that, his street voice overrode everything.

"No scam. I was your father's administrative assistant, on the books, that is. What I *really* did for him was coordinate his drug operation from inside Looking-Glass."

"How come I never heard of you?"

"Because I took care of the Asian side of things. Besides, Johnny had more secrets than a small town."

"Yeah, you could say that again." Caesare was calmer now. "That sonuvabitch never told anybody anything more than he thought they needed to know. Was always like that. Never trusted anybody—not even his kids." He snorted again. "Hey, shit, what am I talkin' about—*'specially* his kids. Nobody, an' I mean *no*fuckingbody, was close to Johnny Leonforte." This was said with a certain admiring machismo, but Vesper felt an undercurrent like a wisp of a breeze against her cheek, a dark and brooding hurt like a bruise that had never healed.

He sat down on the stern of the Cigarette, looked at her. "He keep you a secret 'cause he was boffing you?"

For a moment, Vesper wondered which way to play this. She knew now that Caesare would be intensely jealous if she said yes. The question was whether she wanted that.

"Well, he certainly tried," she said, going solely on instinct. "And tried and tried and tried."

Caesare stared at her in a kind of reverie. He had never met a woman even remotely like her, and he was intoxicated. Much to his astonishment, he found that he admired the way she stood up to him almost as much as he adored the fury with which she made love. For him, whose needs required that everything be larger than life, she was like a gift from heaven. Everything about her was larger than life—her passion, her humor, her intelligence, her fury. Rather than being intimidated, as most men would be, he embraced these things in her. After spending his life dismissing women as second-class citizens who did no more than inhabit the vast backdrop of his life, he had discovered a kind of soulmate who, by sheer force of her animal personality, had pushed herself to the foreground where he had always stood alone.

Not surprisingly, this revelation set up a series of ripples in his mind. Like unknown currents, they branched out, chilling him, firing him, taking him to places he had not known existed.

He shook his head. "You're some fuckin' broad, you know that? Whatta pair of *cojónes* on you."

Then they were laughing together and she knew she had made the right decision because she felt one of his internal walls crumbling. She was further inside than she had been.

It was growing dark now, the string of lights on shore more brilliant. The eastern half of the sky was already black.

"Y'know, I never met a broad before my father wanted who he didn't get."

"That must've been hard on your mother."

"Ah, my mother." Caesare crossed himself. "God rest her soul. She hung in there, gotta give her all the credit inna world. She loved my father until the day she died, and nothing was gonna shake that love apart. But he was nevah there, y'know?" He looked out over the waves. "But sometimes I think he sure did his best." He put his elbows on his knees, stared down at the deck. "Why'd he hurt her so to leave her like that? I mean, us kids, we were alla time runnin' around so we hardly so we had time t'miss him. Leastwise I nevah did." But something far back in his eye told Vesper he was lying—not only to her but perhaps to himself as well.

Caesare shook his head. "What'd she ever do to him but love him, make him the only man inna world? An' then he skips out. But he hadda job t'do, y'know, she knew that, I mean, she had to, right? It was business, but she hadda miss him something fierce and it must've killed her inside, the love eating right through her. Anyway, I used to ask myself these questions when I was young an' stupid, running around the streets of Ozone Park."

His eyes flicked up to hers. "And, y'know, I never could come up with the answers until one day I had to do this errand, take my sister to Astoria, to this convent she was crazy for." His fingers laced and unlaced as he spoke. "She was so odd, my sister, Jaqui. Talk about someone I never understood, Jesus! Anyway, Jaqui, her dream was to be a nun, that's why she was always going off to this convent, the Sacred Heart of Santa Maria. I was only there the once but I never forgot the name."

He sighed. "Anyway, I was driving Jaqui there and we were talking. Poor thing, she was always trying to talk to me, only I don't think I ever paid attention. I mean she was my *sister,* for Christ's sake, what could she have t'say, alla time talkin' about stuff I knew nothin' about? 'Cept this time. I asked her those questions that were driving me batty. 'When's Pop coming home?' I asked her. 'I mean, Mom's gotta broken heart already from waiting for him.' An' she said, 'Don't you get it yet? He's never coming back.'"

Caesare's hands opened wide. "Naturally, I got pissed off and yelled at her. I mean, what the fuck, she was talking bullshit, like she always did, no wonder I never listened to her. Of course, Pop was coming back. We were his family, right?"

He was staring down at his feet. "But, funny thing, y'know, she was right. Pop never did come back."

Caesare's head came up suddenly and he guffawed. His mood change was startling. "She could really be something, Jaqui. You remind me of her maybe a little 'cause she was big—in here." He tapped his temple meaningfully with a forefinger. "Y'know, she never called Pop Pop, or Dad or Father, even. Father was for the priests, anyway, far as she was concerned. I guess she hated him or maybe pitied him 'cause she felt abandoned."

"Didn't you?" Vesper asked. "I mean it'd be only natural."

"Who, me? Nah, I was too busy learning the family trade, so to speak, from Uncle Alphonse, that rat bastard." She heard that same dark undercurrent in his voice. He grew unaccountably melancholy again and she felt she was on one end of an emotional yo-yo. "An' I always, y'know, stuck up for the old man. Not like Jaqui. She had some fuckin' mouth, my sister. An' no fuckin' respect for family, either." He rubbed his palms together slowly as if he needed to warm them and looked out to sea.

"What happened to Jaqui?" Vesper put a hand on his back, rubbing in circles. As she did so, she detached herself from her physical moorings as Okami had taught her until even the beating of her heart receded down a long crystalline corridor, until she was enveloped in the singular silence of thought. The *beat-beat-beat* of the wings of unseen birds pushed outward, past the barrier between humans, and entered Caesare's psyche. Connected in this tenuous fashion, she did her best to push him on. Revelation would follow revelation, the first one being the most difficult. This Bad Clam shell was beginning to open.

"That's the really shitty thing, see." He took a breath even as he waved a hand dismissively. "She died inna car crash when she was twenty. Year after she joined the convent." He continued to stare bleakly out to sea. "Twenty, Jesus." He turned to her. "Y'know, the funny thing is, I miss her now. Never did when she was alive and inna convent. Never even thought of her much, 'cept to be pissed at her for not respectin' Pop. But now I think of her all the time. Weird, isn't it?"

"Not really, and I think it's good. It's good that you can appreciate her now. She'd like that, don't you think?"

"I dunno." Caesare seemed so sad. "I think of that time I yelled at her inna car onna way to the convent, y'know? Truth is, I didn't just yell—I slapped her. I hit her hard, y'know. I hurt her, outside and inside. I know it. I feel it"—he curled one hand into a fist, pounded his chest over his heart—"here."

"But now you're sorry you did it."

"Course I am. Jesus, what a fuckin' monster I was then, trying so hard to be like Pop, 'cause he was gone and I had to be the head of the family, there was no one else. I mean, my brother, Mick, forgetaboutit, he always had his brains up his ass."

Mick Leonforte, Vesper thought. What role had he played in the family dynamic—then and now? She was about to lead him into this territory when he abruptly rose and went to the wheel and switched on green running lights. This sudden burst of physical energy snapped Vesper's delicate psychic threads, and he was gone.

"See that out there?" He had grabbed a pair of binoculars and was peering through them out into a dark part of the ocean.

Vesper walked to where he stood. She could just make out a pair of red sparks. "What are those, running lights?"

Caesare grinned. "Smart girl. Yeah, we're meeting a boat out here."

"I'm flattered you took me with you."

"Don't be," he said flatly. "This is an ideal place to dump a body. Sharks'll make sure there's nothing left to find."

Vesper's heart flipped over. "Is that what you plan to do with me?"

"It was inna beginning." Caesare took the binoculars from his eyes. "But now I gotta bettah idea. It depends on whether I believe your story or not."

This was not a good position for her to be in and she knew it. She got up on the rail, spread her arms wide, balancing there. "Then push me in. As you said, it'll all be over in minutes."

The red running lights were coming closer, and now the deep throbbing of engines could be heard faintly.

"Nah. I'd rather let you think about it some."

"Why wait, Caesare? Do it now. You can get back to your life and forget all about me."

He looked at her for a long time. Behind her, she heard the engines quit as the unknown boat slid silently toward them. Only the faint wash of the waves could be heard.

"I'm curious," he said. "I wanna see if you're bullshitting me."

"Really?"

Caesare held out a hand but he did not touch her. "That and I don't want to forget about you."

But now she knew what he was really saying, though at the moment he might not have understood. *I don't want to forget about Jaqui.*

"You've hurt me. I'm not one of your bimbos. Do you think you can just put on one of your macho shows, announce that you're thinking of plopping me in the water, and watch while my insides turn to jelly?" She kept her voice on a steadily rising pitch. "You think that's amusing or fun?"

"Look at it from my point of view. What if you're the heat?"

"You're still the fucking monster you were when you hit your sister!" she shouted.

"Naw, c'mon, babe. Cut out the crap."

"You *like* fucking with my mind, you sadist."

"Don't—Jesus, don't, for God's sake, use the f-word."

"Why the hell not?" Of course she knew why not. She'd bet the farm Jaqui had never used the f-word. "You do. Besides, you've scared the piss out of me. How the hell do you think I feel?"

"Yah, well ..." He shrugged, took a step toward her, enfolded her in his arms, and she let him take her down from there, hold her close to him. He kissed her on both cheeks, on each eyelids, on her forehead. Very formal, very tender. Then his lips pressed against hers, opened, and their tongues met briefly.

A soft hail came on the night air, and Caesare put her down. "Business now," he whispered. As he gently touched her cheek, he returned the hail.

She nodded. "I'll go below."

But as she turned, he grasped her hand, pulled her back. "No, stay here." He neatly and efficiently tied off the lines thrown to him. "You say you were in the business."

"I *was* in the business," she whispered fiercely as a man thin as a whippet climbed over the side from a dinghy lying to.

"Okay, then." He turned back to her. "I want you to give me your opinion of this motherfucker."

Vesper turned to see a Coast Guard cutter off the starboard bow. It was showing no lights, which was highly unusual. She checked its markings, saw the designation: CGM 1176. The whippet-thin man was dressed in the standard uniform of a lieutenant in the U.S. Coast Guard. He was carrying a blue and white nylon gym bag.

"Caesare," he said. His smile showed about an acre of gold-capped teeth. He had the close-set nervous eyes of a rodent, and he had a twitch in his right shoulder as if he had a gun butt digging into his armpit.

"Milo." Caesare lifted a hand. "This's Vesper. She's gonna check the shipment. Okay with you?"

Milo shrugged. "Me, I don't give a shit if you want the pope to taste it. Alla same t'me."

He unzipped the gym bag, handed over a clear plastic bag filled with a white powder. Vesper took it and the knife Caesare handed her. She made a small X in the bag, drew out some of the white powder on the flat of the blade, tasted it. Then she turned her head, spat over the side. She looked hard into Caesare's eyes for a moment before nodding.

"Bring the shit over," Caesare said.

The transfer took approximately seven minutes. During that time, Caesare brought out an attaché case in which Vesper assumed was the money to pay for the cocaine. With her back to Milo, she whispered to Caesare, "Don't pay him yet. Just follow my lead."

"Is this all of it?" Vesper asked as Milo counted out the last of the 150 bags.

"That's it. I'll take the money now."

"Just a moment." Vesper stood in front of the shipment and, kneeling down, plucked out two bags at random from the inside of the pile.

"What's she doin'?" Milo said in mild alarm. "We gotta deal."

"I'm checking the merch," Vesper said as she slit open the bags.

"You already done that." Milo looked at Caesare. "She already done that." His mouth screwed up. "Now you lettin' a broad wear the pants, Bad Clams?"

"Shut your fuckin' yap," Caesare said.

Milo looked down to see a MAC-10 machine pistol in Caesare's right hand. "Jesus Christ," he cried, "take it fucking easy, would you? I didn't mean anything."

Vesper stood up. She was careful to keep out of Caesare's line of fire. "The bag on the left's okay. But the one on the right's laced with something really nasty: arsenic."

Caesare hefted the MAC-10, pointed his chin at Milo. "Well?"

Milo dipped his pinky into the open bag on the right, tasted off the tip. He nodded, his face expanded with astonishment. "Damned if she isn't right on the money, boss."

All at once Caesare leapt across the deck and jammed the muzzle of the MAC-10 into the soft spot between Milo's neck and chin. "I wanna know right now, you lying, cocksucking sonuvabitch if you're tryin' t'fuck me ovah, because if you are an' deny it now, you'll be singin' alto inna girls' choir." A red madness was in his eyes, like that of a berserk or rabid beast, a vast and burning rage not wholly under his control. *"Answer me,* you fucking weasel nothing!"

"Jesus Christ, don't kill the messenger just 'cause the news sucks. I'm not the source, for Christ's sake. Besides, you know drugs aren't my thing. I haven't touched your shit an' I'll kill the motherfucker what says I did." Milo almost choked on his fear. "This's the first I'm hearin' of it, I swear!"

Caesare drew himself up slightly, and taking a deep breath, he turned to glance at Vesper. She nodded to tell him she believed Milo was telling the truth.

In a way, Caesare seemed disappointed. He wanted immediate satisfaction for this outrage, and Vesper could see he was just itching to go after Milo.

"Okay," Caesare said at length. He let Milo up. The whippet-thin man was drenched in sweat and his knees almost buckled when Caesare let go of him. He knew just how close he had come to disaster.

"Someone's trying to fuck me over, Milo." Caesare kept the MAC-10, but now held it muzzle down at his side. "Let's see, there's a delivery set up for tomorrow night, right?"

Milo nodded numbly.

"We'll take carea this mess then."

Milo began to breathe again. "Inna meantime, I'll get this gahbidge outta here. Let the fuckin' sharks choke on it."

"Shut the fuck up," Caesare snapped. "Who told you to think?" He pointed to the bag of arsenic-laced dope. "Wrap that up an' make sure it's on the boat tomorrow night. I'm goin' with you."

"You, boss, but nevah—"

"Get outta here!" Caesare screamed at him and Milo scrambled to obey.

When they were alone, Vesper turned on Caesare, her eyes blazing. "You set me up. This was a test."

He shrugged. "Yeah, well, can you blame me? A broad too good t'be true drops outta the sky inta my lap, I gotta wonder 'bout that. Problem?"

"No problem."

"Good. Anyway, looks like you did me a big one, fingering the shit with the arsenic." He broke out the Styrofoam chest, which was filled with food and iced champagne. "Let's eat. I'm starved."

The pink and acid-green neon glow of Tokyo radiated like the heart of a gigantic generator. But here amid the modern concrete shell of Karasumori Jinja, the soft nineteenth-century light of lanterns cast a flight of hazy circles within the environs of the Shinto shrine. Despite the looming bulk of the nearby New Shinbashi Building, the Jinja was set within a series of narrow alleys whose appearance harked back to a different Tokyo before war and economic miracle had made of it another country.

"Japan is now without a political leader," Mikio Okami said. "In this time of economic chaos it lies adrift and rudderless in violent seas. As with all vacuums nature will not long tolerate this one."

"But you told me that there are no leading candidates to become prime minister," Nicholas said.

"That was then," Okami said as he stepped from lantern light into relative darkness. "This afternoon, the name Kansai Mitsui was put forward by the coalition as a kind of compromise."

"I don't know him."

"Not surprising. Not many people who aren't on the political inside do. But he's a dangerous man. It's his contention that the rape of Nanking was nothing more than a fabrication." Okami was speaking of one of Japan's most notorious—and bestial—war crimes. In 1937, Japanese soldiers massacred hundreds of thousands of Chinese civilians. More than twenty thousand women were raped and the city was torched. Eleven years later, a war crimes tribunal sentenced the commander of the Japanese forces in Nanking to death.

"Kansai Mitsui is a deconstructionist, pure and simple," Okami continued. "He's intent on remaking history in his own image. To that end, he's made threats against the current prime minister for trying to heal the wounds of the war in the Pacific. He claims our invasion of the Asian mainland should be remembered—lauded as an act of liberation. In denying that Japan was ever intent on expanding her territory, he insists that we were merely liberating the Asian people from their enslavement by Western colonial aggressors."

Okami stopped just out of another circle of lantern light. "Also, what almost no one knows is that Mitsui is backed by Tetsuo Akinaga. But that may be of little moment. Akinaga is destined to rot in prison."

Nicholas's eyes glittered. "Late this afternoon I received word that our old friend Akinaga will be walking free within days. His lawyers have sprung him on a series of technicalities."

"Akinaga is going free?"

"Someone or some people within the Tokyo Prosecutor's Office are in his pocket. I am working with a prosecutor named Tanaka Gin. He's a good man, a dogged and dedicated detective. Akinaga was his case. He believes his brief was sabotaged by someone in his office. Maybe you could look into this."

Okami grinned fiercely. "It will be my pleasure."

They came upon a local musician, who took up his samisen and began a haunting melody. They walked on, needing the space in which to talk, but the music followed them, drifting like smoke amid the lanterns.

"How big a threat is this man, Mitsui?" Nicholas asked.

"That remains to be seen. But, undoubtedly, the greatest threat is Akinaga himself. I want to see if he still has the muscle to push Mitsui's nomination through."

"By then it may be too late."

"Not really." Okami resumed walking. "Akinaga's the key. Without him, Mitsui will fall into line, another weak prime minister who won't accomplish much. Right now, I think it's worth biding our time and letting Akinaga run out his skein."

"The talk of threats has made more urgent something that happened to me twice this afternoon." Nicholas related the odd and disquieting sensations of Tau-tau he had experienced while with Honniko and Tanaka Gin without having consciously summoned it up.

"I have never known Akshara to manifest itself in this manner," Okami said, clearly concerned.

"But it was strangely different from Akshara." Nicholas

had not told Okami about the eerie doppelgänger sensation he had experienced at Rodney Kurtz's, and he had no plan to until he could better sort it out for himself. It was too personal, too intimate in a way Nicholas had yet to define, to confide it in anyone—even Okami.

"What was it like?"

"I'm not sure. Like the sky was melting, like ten million voices speaking to me at once." He shook his head. "I know. All of that sounds crazy."

"Not at all. But I do believe we ought to continue with our attempts to heal the defects inside you." Okami reached out a hand. "Are you prepared?"

Nicholas nodded, though after the unsettling experiences of the last few days, he approached this session with a heightened sense of trepidation. He stood very still, listening to the city sounds around him first growing unnaturally loud, then fading into the distance, as normal reality fled through a hole in the universe.

"That's right," Mikio Okami said, "drink in the night."

He watched as Nicholas, head thrown back, stared into the void that was Akshara. High above and with each heartbeat growing more distant were the lights of Tokyo, a dome of neon, receding into darkness.

"Enter deeply into Akshara," Okami said. "So deeply that you begin to see the dark patterns in the void. Here is Kshira."

Kshira was the dark path, the other half of Tau-tau, the part almost never spoken of because those who dared try to master it either died or went mad. Such had been the case with Kansatsu, Nicholas's Tau-tau *sensei*, who had embedded pieces of Kshira inside Nicholas's mind like cunning time bombs.

Nicholas had been told that Okami possessed *koryoku*, the Illuminating Power. It was said among the ancients who practiced Tau-tau centuries ago that *koryoku* was the sole path to Shuken, the Dominion, where the two halves of Tau-tau could be united into a working whole. But others insisted that Shuken was merely a myth, that Akshara and Kshira were never meant to meld into a whole.

Nicholas fervently believed in Shuken. He needed to. Otherwise Kshira, the soul destroyer, would eventually take him over and drive him mad as it had done to Kansatsu.

Abruptly, he felt the jellied sky covering his limbs, heard the chittering of 10 million voices speaking in unknown tongues directly at the center of his mind. It was as it had been this afternoon. It was Kshira, and it was too much. It—

"No," Okami said sharply, "do not pull away from Kshira. You will only draw the dark patterns closer to you, and once they attach themselves to your conscious they cannot be severed."

Deep within the trancelike state of Tau-tau, Nicholas was beyond time and space. He existed as a point of light in a void without dimension. All around him the cosmos breathed like a beast in the forest, but now instead of being encased in the armor of Akshara, he felt the unquiet darkness all around as the shards of Kshira swirled in the void. Once, they seemed almost harmless, distant clouds on a limitless horizon. But now they circled him so swiftly that at any given moment they blocked out increasing sections of the void, impairing his psychic vision. All too soon, he knew, they would link up, making a continuous band around him, cutting him off from chunks of Akshara until all he could see and feel would be their black weight, and then the madness would set in.

His psyche was directed toward a newly erected coruscating column of light, beautiful filaments floating off it now and again to touch the black bits of Kshira his mind had summoned up. Behind the light, he could sense Okami's psychic presence. They had been at this for over a week, ever since they were reunited in Venice, and still the Kshira raged within Nicholas, blinding him psychically at odd moments, at others distorting Akshara so badly it frightened him on the most profound level.

And his fear increased as he was reminded of another moment like this one in the forest of Yoshino three weeks ago when he and Tachi Shidare, the young Yakuza *oyabun* who had befriended him, had attempted just such a psychic union. Tachi also possessed *koryoku,* but when he attempted to make contact with Nicholas, he faltered. *I can't. Something . . . I don't know . . .* There had been an odd look on his face. *The Kshira is so strong . . .* And Tachi had pulled away. Moments later, he was killed and Nicholas never solved the riddle. Had Nicholas's Kshira been too strong for Tachi? But how was that possible? *Koryoku* was meant to handle Kshira.

Okami's face was forming within the column of light, and perhaps Nicholas would get his answer.

He could feel the psychic emanations from within the glittering light source, and he was drawn to it. He felt a heat and a crawling on his skin as of sweat or insects as the ionized particles interacted with his psyche.

Now, as Nicholas moved toward the swirling column of light, it began to iris open to admit him, and his heart leapt with elation. At last, he was beginning his journey to integration; at last, the dark power of Kshira, which had been haunting him, would be put to rest.

But the moment he reached out to embrace the particles of light, he heard Okami's voice in his mind, as he had heard Tachi's at this point in the ritual: *No, no . . . Too much. I cannot hold the line. . . . It is falling inward, imploding. . . . Get clear! Quickly now! It has come undone. Get clear!*

Like a band snapping, Nicholas's hold on Akshara broke, and he was bounced back into specific time and space. He crouched in the grounds of the shrine, panting, the unearthly neon glow of Tokyo spreading over him like a mechanized Milky Way.

Nicholas, still dizzy from the abrupt severing of Akshara, looked around for Okami. He found him sprawled on the ground as if he had been shot with a high-powered rifle. Nicholas dragged himself over, listening for breath, checking the eyes beneath the closed lids.

Okami began to convulse. His blood pressure was dangerously high. What had happened at *kokoro?* What had Okami seen? What had sent him into spastic shock, made him lose hold on the column of light, on *koryoku?* Was it the same mysterious occurrence that had made Tachi pull abruptly away from psychic contact with Nicholas? Had Kansatsu somehow psychically poisoned him? He had to know.

Using Akshara, he extended his psyche until it entered Okami's bloodstream. There he adjusted adrenaline levels downward while getting Okami's body to pump out a more potent mix of nucleopeptides to help fight off the shock, calm the convulsions, and bring him back to consciousness more quickly.

Okami quieted in Nicholas's arms, the last of the spasms dissipating, and his eyes opened.

"How do you feel, Okami-san?"

"Tired." He tried to smile but did not quite make it. "I am not as young as I used to be."

"You're ninety."

"Who told you that? Celeste?" He licked his dry lips. "Even she does not know my real age. Just as well." He gestured. "Help me up, please."

As Nicholas began to move him, Okami held his head and groaned, and Nicholas set him carefully back on the ground. "What did you do to me? I haven't had this amount of endorphins running through me since I was in my seventies."

"You went into violent convulsions."

"I do not remember."

Nicholas watched Okami carefully as he went into prana, breathing deeply and evenly to continue the bodily cleansing.

When Okami's eyes fluttered open, they were looking directly at Nicholas. "I do not believe I can help you, my friend, though I very much want to."

I cannot be hearing this, Nicholas thought. "But you have *koryoku*. It is the only way to integration. You are my last hope."

"Let us pray to whatever God we believe in that this is not so. Because then you are doomed." Okami sighed, grabbing on to Nicholas as they rose. "You see, all the time Kshira has been inside you, you have had no access to it. I cannot get close, either. When I tried, I was almost killed. And from what you have told me about your experience with Tachi Shidare, he was stymied in the same manner. From these unfortunate encounters we must conclude that *koryoku,* the Illuminating Power, is of no help to you."

Nicholas fought a vertiginous sensation of panic. "What, then, am I to do, Okami-san? I cannot tolerate Kshira much longer inside me. Lately, I have felt its strength growing. It is like a shadow on my soul."

"I know, my friend, and I sympathize. But Kshira must

be approached in just the right manner otherwise it will be like disarming a booby trap without knowing how the mechanism works. Disaster." Okami shook his head. "Pity that Kansatsu, the *sensei* who trained you, is dead. He is the one man who would know how to save you." He spat. "What a twisted, diabolical brain he had. He must have hated you with all his soul to have done this to you."

Okami walked on legs made stiff by shock. "Come. It is time we left this place. The psychic echoes of the near catastrophe are disturbing."

As they walked out into the bustle of West Shinbashi, Okami looked at Nicholas's ashen face. "I am too old and tired to help you, but do not give up hope, Linnear-san. I know the answer exists. There *is* someone out there who possesses the means by which you can escape the unique prison into which you have been placed."

6

New York/Tokyo

"Everyone comfy?"

"Mom's asleep," Francine Goldoni DeCamillo said.

"Yah, I know," Paul Chiaramonte said. "I gave her something so she should rest."

It was dark in the belly of the private plane, and cold. They sat on facing seats while outside the small, scarred Perspex windows clouds rolled by, illuminated eerily by moonlight. They looked like smoke from the dry-ice machines used in rock videos, Francie thought. She was trying to be brave, trying with all her might to still the painful fluttering of her heart. She moved a little until she felt the warmth of her mother's shoulder and felt a little better.

"Where are you taking us?"

Paul's eyes glittered in the semidarkness. "South. Where it's warm. You'll like it. Plenty of swimming, maybe even surfboarding."

"Who are you trying to kid? You're taking us to Bad Clams."

Paul regarded her for some time. "Kid, you're a smart cookie."

"Don't talk down to me. I'm not seven years old."

"I can see that." He eyed her appreciatively. "I think you threw out your training bra a while ago, hah?"

"You like them," she said, arching her back slightly, "my breasts?"

Paul shrugged. "What's not to like?"

Francie smiled. "Want to touch them?"

Paul reacted as if she had burned him with the end of a cigarette. "Jesus, kid, what the hell kinda question's that?"

"That's not how you acted back at Sheepshead Bay."

He waved a hand dismissively. "I was fuckin' pissed off. An' didn't I have a right t'be? Your mother was responsible for whacking the men I hired."

"They were going to kidnap us."

"An' she made me whack a cop. A *cop,* kid, you unnerstand? My ass is grass back in NYC. You kill a fuckin' cop, they catch you, you're a goner. They lock you up an' throw away the key."

"He was only trying to protect us."

Paul eyed her with what could only be termed a grudging kind of respect. "What're you, seventeen?"

"Almost."

Paul snorted. "Goin' on twenny-eight. Take my advice, kid. Give it a rest, okay? You got plenty of time t'grow up, you don't need t'do it in one gulp."

Francine thought about this for some time. "How come you put my mother to sleep and not me?"

"Y'know, Jesus Christ, I bettah watch what I say around you."

"Why did you want to talk with me alone?"

Paul put a fingernail to his mouth, tore off a thin sliver with his teeth. "I like you, kid. You ask a straight question, no bullshit. So I'll answer you straight. Your mother, she, y'know, like hates my guts 'cause of how things worked out. Also, I roughed her up a littlc I was so pissed, an' for that I am truly sorry. So I know right off for sure I can't talk with her because whatevah I say, she'll go, 'Fuck you,' an' she'd be right, I guess. But I figure maybe you are, like, different. You, bein' almost seventeen and all, might listen to what I have to say."

"I'll listen, unless I think what you're saying is bullshit. Then you can fuck yourself."

" 'Kay, I can respect that." Paul tore another thin strip of nail off the end of his finger. "You evah met Bad Clams, kid?"

"No."

"Well." He looked away, as if that weren't at all what he had meant to ask her. "Hey!" He jumped up, startling her. "You hungry? How about I make us some pasta?"

Francie looked around. "There's a kitchen on the plane?"

"Sure, sure, whaddaya think? 'Cept it's called a galley, like onna boat." He led the way down the aisle to a small space where he turned on a light to reveal a compact stainless-steel galley.

"Aren't there any flight attendants?"

"Nah. This's a *private* flight, y'know?"

He took down a box of pasta, set water to boiling on the two-burner electric stove. Then he set about making a sauce from tomato paste, stewed tomatoes, parsley, oregano, olive oil, and sautéed onions. "A little salt and pepper," he said, "and we're done." He set the pot of sauce on the second burner.

"What happened to your leg?"

Paul automatically glanced down at his shorter leg. "Was an accident happened a long time ago when I was a kid. Nineteen sixty-two. In Astoria, near where I lived." He stirred the sauce and shook his head. "It was kinda crazy, like a dream, y'know? If not for my leg I'd be *sure* it was a dream. I saw a car speeding down the street, an' for some reason I knew something terrible was about to happen. It was comin' right at this girl. I'd been watching her, y'know, 'cause, my God, she was a beauty.

"I shouted a warning an' she turned. I leapt off the curb just like someone inna movies, thinking I could save her, but the car clipped my hip and thigh."

"What happened to the girl?"

"She died. I was inna hospital a long time. I had three operations an' they still couldn't get me back to the way I was. Said I was lucky t'be walking on two legs. In between times, that's when I tried to find out about the girl an' was told she didn't make it. Her funeral'd already happened." Then he pointed. "Hey, look, the pasta's done. Trick is not t'let it overcook, y'know?"

"Yeah. I know."

He made a fluttering gesture with his hand. "That's what everyone says. But the *real* secret's to make a sauce that coats the pasta just right." He looked down at her and was disappointed that she wasn't smiling. "You scared?"

For a moment, she did not answer. "A little, I guess. I've heard a lot about Bad Clams."

Paul snorted. "Who hasn't?" He shook his head. "You know how he got his name?"

Francie shook her head. "Uh-uh."

"Well, the first guy he whacked, it was like a contract job, y'know? Guy was eatin' inna restaurant an' Bad Clams he comes in, levels the gun and—wham!—plugs the guy. Then, like he's got no nerves at all, he looks down at the guy he just whacked, whose face is inna bowl of pasta with white clam sauce he's been eatin' from, an' he says, 'Must've been the bad clams that killed 'im.' " Paul was laughing. "Jesus, Christ, can ya picture it?"

His smile faded a bit as he regarded Francine's serious face. "A little scared, that's okay. But, hey, kid, nothing bad's gonna happen t'you."

"How do you know?"

"I know, that's all." He dumped the pasta and boiling water into a colander he had wedged into the small sink. "I know a lotta things." With a deft twist of his wrist he slid the pasta back into the pot, then added the sauce and tossed it.

"Beautiful. Good pasta is a masterwork." He portioned out the pasta into two bowls. "Nothing like it to restore the soul and the spirit, that's what my mother used t'say." He handed her one bowl, along with a fork and large spoon. "Sorry I don't have any fresh-baked bread, kid."

"That's okay." The smell coming out of the bowl was heavenly, and suddenly Francie realized that she was ravenous.

They sat in facing seats, feasting. He had turned on one of those small overhead lights that shone between them with a pure, brittle beam, half-illuminating their faces like in the mirrored room of a fun house.

"When it comes to cooking, this's the only thing I do well. Learned it from my mother."

"Who *was* your mother?"

"Belissima. A beautiful woman," Paul said in a voice tight with tension. "That's all you gotta know."

Francie gave him a quick glance and went back to eating her pasta. Paul looked at her head pulled down into her shoulders, and he put down his fork onto which he had twirled just the right amount of sauce-coated pasta.

"I get a little, y'know, uptight about her because, well, because she was Jewish—outside *la Famiglia.* But, well, I guess that's what my old man figured. Woulda been too complicated to have an Italian mistress, hah? With a Jew, it was a no guilt kinda thing, right? I mean she could never be considered family, so even if Faith—y'know, your, what?—stepgrandmother kinda thing—she was married to my father then—so even if she found out, no threat, no sweat, justa roll inna fuckin' hay."

Francine risked a glance at him. He looked so sad at that moment she felt an urge to hug him. She knew better than most what it was like to have fucked-up parents.

"Faith found out, didn't she?"

"It wasn't that, really." He put aside his bowl, locked his arms behind his head, and stared up at the dark ceiling of the plane. "Thing is, she found out that for my father it hadn't been just a roll inna hay. He felt something for this other woman—this *Jew*—and she put her foot down. 'It's her or me,' she said, knowing full well he couldn't divorce her in the eyes of God." He gave Francine a meaningful stare. "Catholicism, right? It's a fuckin' pain inna ass, you ask me."

"I don't know much about it."

"There, y'see. What I said." His eyes returned to the ceiling. "My old man, he might've been a terror onna streets of Astoria, but he was a devout Catholic. Went to church, donated money, did, y'know, good deeds for the diocese, even ate fish on Fridays even though he hated it like poison. Useta cough it all up inna toilet, afterwards. But he nevah ate more food till the next morning.

"So he, y'know, took what Faith said as gospel. The Church said divorce was a sin an' that was that."

"So then what happened?"

"Faith, she said to him, 'What does it matter, anyway? She's a Jew. She knew what she was getting into when she seduced you. She won't feel a thing.' Trouble was, she'd got it ass backwards. It was my father who had seduced my mother; it was my father who didn't know what he was getting into."

"So he *did* see her again," Francine said, hoping for a happy ending.

"I dunno, really." Paul blinked several times as if he had something in his eye. "My mother married John Chiaramonte, a Renaissance-history professor from City College, where she was going to night school twice a week. She'd known him for some time and he had already proposed to her once. She did it very fast, I guess, because she knew she was pregnant.

"My mother was a practical woman, always using her head," he said with a good deal of admiration. "When I was born six months later, John never asked her who the father was. According to my mother, he just accepted me as his own."

He sighed deeply. "A love like that . . ." He broke off for a moment. Then looked across at Francine. "That was the kind of love Black Paul Mattaccino felt for her." He put his ragged nail between his teeth once more. "He must've seen her somehow, some way, 'cause she got money regularly." He gripped his short leg. "My stay inna hospital, the operations an', afterward, the rehab, my mom got the money from him for that."

"But why do you work for Bad Clams?" Francine asked, putting her bowl on top of his. "Why do you hate my mother so much?"

"I don't hate your mother so much now, an' I don't hate you at all. You believe that, don't you?"

Francine shrugged.

"Well, it's true. Hey, remember what you said before about bullshit? This is not bullshit, okay? Whatever's going down, it's between families, the Leonfortes and the Goldonis. You and your mom just, like, got caught in the gears, is all. She shoulda kept her nose clean, stood bya sideline like a woman should."

"Then they would have shot her down, just like they did my father," Francine said fiercely.

"I don't know 'bout that, I swear." Paul flicked a piece

of nail into the darkness. "Was imported talent did that, an' I was kept inna dark." He waved a hand. "Between you an' me, I think it was a wrong decision to try to whack your mom. She's a tough cookie, just like you." He gave her a little smile. "But she sure fucked up my life now."

"Occupational hazard."

He stared at her wide-eyed, then gave a little snort of astonishment. *"Marrone,* whatta mouth on you, kid."

She looked at him with a steady gaze. "Maybe this isn't just family. You hated Faith, I know that."

"Sure I hated the fuckin' bitch. She killed my father, Black Paul."

"Is that story true?"

Paul held up a hand. "On the soul of my sainted mother." He grimaced. "I hope Faith got what was comin' to her. I hope she's fryin' in hell."

"I smell revenge."

"Where d'you get that kinda talk, kid, the fuckin' movies?"

She climbed up on the seat, turned to look back down the seatbacks to where Margarite lay in darkness. "You think she's all right?"

"Sure, she's all right."

Francine turned back as he tapped her lightly on the arm. She slid down into the seat.

"Kid, tell me something. Your mom ever, like, take you to Santa Maria in Astoria?"

"The convent, you mean?"

Something passed behind Paul's eyes. "The convent, yeah. The Sacred Heart of Santa Maria."

Francine nodded. "Lots of times."

"You met the old lady, the mother superior?"

"Every time I was there."

"What'd you guys talk about? Religious stuff or what?"

"Yeah. Religious stuff."

But her eyes slid away from his and he knew she was lying. It didn't matter, he wasn't interested in what they talked about. He leaned forward, his hands clasped in front of him. "You meet anyone else?"

Francine could sense the tenseness come into his face because she could see all squinty lines at the corners of his eyes and mouth get harder, more defined. "Sure, lots of others. Nuns, right? Who else would be in a convent?"

"Of course. Who else?" he said so softly she had to strain to hear him. "But, I mean, could you tell me if you'd met one specific nun if I described her?"

"Why do you want to know?"

He leaned even closer. "It's important, kid, okay?" His voice was no louder than the harsh whisper she used while talking to a friend in the library.

Because she believed him, she said, "Okay."

"Right, she's kinda tall, lean, with, like, great legs." He waved his hands as if to erase the message. "But that wouldn't mean nothing, 'cause she'd be wearing a habit, wouldn't she? But she'd be real pretty and have dark, wavy hair. And the most unusual green eyes, the kinda green you see inna ocean, not close in, like, but far out where the water's deep." He sat back abruptly as if he had realized he had said too much. "You seen anyone like that at Santa Maria?"

"No."

He squinted at her. "You sure, kid? You're telling me the truth?"

"Yes."

"Really?"

"Really and truly."

"Oh, Jesus," he whispered. *Really and truly.* That was the phrase Jaqui used. He sat for a long time staring at Francie before his eyes went out of focus. Even in the semidarkness, she could see she'd hit a nerve, and she'd remember that. At length, his eyes snapped into focus and he slapped his thighs with the flats of his hands.

"Okay, kid," he said in a completely different voice. "What say we see how your mom's doing back there?"

"Come to bed."

"Not yet," Nicholas said.

Koei, who slept in the nude, wrapped herself in the bedclothes and stepped off the futon. As soon as her feet touched the wooden floor, she shivered. "It's cold." She pressed herself against him. "Aren't you cold?"

"Only up here," Nicholas said, tapping his head. "I had

two incidences of Kshira burning through my conscious state today, time and light shifting. I was out of control, my mind felt as if it had been taken over."

"And how do you feel now?"

"Fine. Perfectly normal."

Her eyes, huge and dark and full of life, seemed to hold reflected the whole of Tokyo's nighttime dazzle. "Okami-san will help you."

"I don't know." He felt her near him, felt how much he desired her near him. "He was hurt this evening trying to help. He's old, Koei. His mind's sharp enough, but it's turned elsewhere, on the politics consuming the country, and I think he lacks the intrinsic strength to help with my inner battle."

For a long time Nicholas said nothing. He stared out the window at the nighttime lights of Tokyo. They were high up in an ultramodern high-rise with a sculpted facade in the center of the city. Nicholas had bought a duplex, huge by Japanese standards, then hired the architect who had designed the building to redo the interior. The result was a combination of pink, gray, and black granite surfaces softened by chunky expanses of light cherry and darker, deep-grained *kyoki*-wood.

"I'll make us some tea," Koei said, unwinding herself from him.

Nicholas stared down at the Naigai Capsule Tower. It seemed close enough that a leap to its top was possible. It was a holdover from the 1970s Metabolism movement, which separated permanent structures like roads and freeways with the temporary, like housing. It had been a brave but unsuccessful stab at integrating the two halves of an urban whole.

The tower of spiderweb scaffoldings and elevator banks was like an exoskeleton within which were arranged like boxes of chocolates, premade apartments of different sizes into which people moved as their economic status evolved. What had been a fad twenty years ago was now a relic, the impractical and unlovely Metabolism movement having died a deserved death. Only a few people made their homes there now. He wondered why it hadn't been razed to make way for new ideas in architecture.

After a moment, he followed Koei down the wide staircase with the stainless-steel banister, which led from the second floor with its two bedrooms and baths, done in traditional Japanese style.

Downstairs was almost entirely Western in aspect, save for Nicholas's museum-quality collection of artifacts from all over Southeast Asia and China, which filled the walls and cabinets, covered the sleek granite and marble tops of coffee tables, sideboards, and commodes.

As he watched her deft, concise motions, he said, "Do you ever think about him?"

This form of verbal shorthand might have stymied another woman, but not Koei. Her active, intuitive mind absorbed every nuance and tonal quality of the person she was with.

"I almost never think of Michael Leonforte." She measured out the pale green tea with a thin bamboo ladle, her beautifully formed arm passing through darkness into spangled light so that diamonds danced along her skin. "When I do, it's to remind myself how truly miserable a human being can be." She looked up at him and the light in her eyes was electric. "So I will never forget how lucky I am to have found you again."

Nicholas watched her finish fixing the tea in the midst of the *kyoki*-wood and porcelain kitchen. Her deftness came from happiness, an inner knowledge of self. How different she was from the teenaged girl he had fallen in love with so many years ago, different as night from day. As different as this kitchen was from the large one he'd had in his house on the outskirts of the city. He had been very fond of that kitchen, but this one was infused with Koei's small, ordinary movements, and the other was dark and dead as a grave.

"How much do you miss the house?" Koei asked with her usual perceptiveness.

"I was raised there," Nicholas said, taking the fired-clay teacup from her. "There are so many memories. It's hard to let go."

"Are you sorry you sold it?"

He sighed. "I don't think so, no. There were bad memories there, also. The house felt glutted with Justine's unhappiness. And then when she was killed in that car accident . . ." He paused for a moment, sipping his tea. "She never was able to adjust to living here. She wanted so badly to return to New York."

Koei looked at him over the rim of her teacup. "So, I think, do you."

"I don't know."

"Oh, but you do," she whispered. "It's always in the back of your mind, even though you may not want to admit it."

"Japan is my home."

"Perhaps." Her face, knowing and serene, seemed to float in the light-infused darkness, a beacon of sanity in an increasingly insane world. "But maybe you weren't meant to have just one home. Not everyone is. I feel your longing, Nicholas. I know how much you miss it."

"I have no time now to go back."

"That remains to be seen. Perhaps you will return sooner than you think."

He looked deep into her eyes. "I *will* have to go, and soon. The American affiliate is still without a president. Terrence McNaughton, my high-powered lobbyist in Washington, is conducting the prelims with a corporate headhunter right now, but I'm going to have to do the final interviews myself. But how did you know?"

She laughed, holding out one palm to him with the openness of a child. "I am only responding to what I feel from you."

"Even so, how can I think of going back to New York when I've lost touch with what's happening at Sato? This new man, Kanda Tōrin, has inveigled his way into the company and Nangi-san's trust."

They went into the living room. Koei pulled the drapes back, revealing the spectacular view of a city as if caught in the midst of a stellar fire. They sat together, touching, two tender animals in the comfort of the night.

"I take it you don't trust him."

"Frankly, I'm not sure what to make of him," Nicholas said. "Something is rotten inside the company, and right now Tōrin's my prime suspect. But I know whatever opinions I might have are colored by the fact that I'm jealous of his position with Nangi-san."

"Then I think it's time you had another talk with Nangi-san."

"Nangi's heart attack was worse than he let on." Nicholas, finished with the tea, felt the hand-fired clay cup sturdy beneath his palm. "He's getting better, but what I'm told he needs most now is time. Besides, he told me to trust Tōrin."

"Then give them both the benefit of the doubt."

Nicholas shook his head. "Sounds good in theory, but in practice ..." He looked at her. "I get the distinct impression something is happening I know nothing about."

Koei put the tip of her forefinger in the center of his forehead. "Do you feel it from here with your *tanjian* eye?"

"Yes."

"Then you may very well be right." She sighed. "On the other hand, the older you get the more precious time becomes, my darling. I think you must give Nangi-san that time." She reached up, smoothed the lines on his forehead, then kissed him on the cheek. "Don't look so perplexed. You already know what you will do. Follow your heart and you will find yourself close to the mark."

He turned abruptly away from her and she felt his withdrawal. It was not the first time, nor would it be the last. She was neither offended nor worried. She knew these acrid emotions had turned Justine's relationship with him rotten. Time was her only ally here, and she knew she needed to make the most of it.

"It's all right that you're thinking of her," she said softly. "It's only right and natural. Justine was your wife."

Nicholas turned back to her, the pain so evident in his face her heart broke. "It isn't that she died; I've come to terms with that. It's the guilt. I left her alone and desperately unhappy. She pleaded with me not to go. She had come to hate Japan and I knew it. I just didn't believe it. I chose to ignore all the warning signs."

"Her death was an accident, nothing more. She and a friend were driving back to the house from Tokyo. You were in Venice with Mikio Okami."

He nodded. "I tried to call her. Twice. It was the middle of the night but the phone just rang and rang. She was so angry at me, she probably didn't want to talk."

"That's not the point. Even if you had been in Tokyo, you couldn't have saved her. It was her karma."

He took her in his arms and kissed her. She was right, as

always. He had to let it go. "Let the past be the past," he whispered. "Karma that you and I met again." He stroked her, breathed in the scent of her hair, closed his eyes, and felt a kind of peace steal over him. "I'm so lucky to have found you."

The underground food courts of Tokyo's enormous department stores were jammed throughout the shopping day. But after five o'clock, when the stores closed, they were deserted. The court at the Ginza branch of Tamayama on the Harumi-dōri was a vast marketplace arrayed like an English garden maze, an orderly design of formal structures and aisles in order to make shopping at the panoply of different stations that much easier.

There was something eerie about this sub-street-level floor at night. Even the cleaning people were gone, and surfaces shone and glittered dimly in the service lights, empty of wares and, therefore, of meaning. Transformed into form without substance, the stations, so alive with transactions during the day, were now cast adrift like the growing number of homeless on Tokyo's sidewalks.

But behind the food court was another, far more private gathering place. In contrast to the food court, however, it was generally deserted during the day. Used mainly at night, it served Mick in good stead. The fact was he—and a number of Korean partners—had bought Tamayama two years ago. The recession at retail had ground down the reserves of a store that had been dedicated to delivering high-fashion names at top dollar to the Japanese consumer. The recession had transformed Tamayama's success into bankruptcy almost overnight. Mick and his partners had come in, thrown out nine-tenths of the fashion names, and substituted house brands imported from Taiwan, Malaysia, and mainland China.

The response had been nothing short of miraculous. A populous formerly fixated on brand names were more than happy to buy quality items at half the price. So the dresses, skirts, suits, trousers, and blouses didn't have Chanel or Armani couture labels. They looked good and the prices were right. Now Tamayama's new regime was applying the same principle to durables and electronic goods made in

Southeast Asia, mostly by Mick's own companies. Vertical retailing had come to Japan with a bang.

Tonight, Mick had arrived early to oversee every phase of the dinner that would be served to the members of Denwa Partners whom Ginjirō Machida, the chief prosecutor, had invited. Unlike most such business gatherings, the food was every bit as important as the speech-making.

When Mick emerged from the kitchens, he saw that the wood-paneled room was decorated in the muted colors he had prescribed. The long cherrywood table shone magnificently beneath the huge cut-glass chandelier. Cutlery and stemware glittered and sparkled like diamonds in a Tiffany's window, and at each place a calligraphied card rested with the name of the designated attendee.

Twelve men were in the room, along with Machida. The chief prosecutor made the introductions, one by one, in the formal Japanese manner, while waitresses in kimono and obi circulated with glasses of Louis Roederer champagne, beluga malossol caviar, and toro, the fat-webbed sushi Japanese loved. The room was already blue with cigarette smoke, and a haze not unlike the smog hovering over the city outside collected just below the ceiling, trembling in the eddies of chill air from the air-conditioning ducts.

Soon thereafter, Machida called the room to order, and the men, peering at the place cards, worked their way to their assigned seats. When, at length, they were all seated, Mick took his place at the head of the table. Machida sat opposite him, at the other end of the table. One setting remained vacant.

This was a signal for the attentive serving staff, who uncorked bottles of Corton Charlemagne. Mick gazed down the long table much as a benevolent dictator looks to attending his satraps, with a certain but unmistakable steely charm. The golden French wine flowed as freely as the water in the fountains of Paris. Everyone was in a receptive mood, expectant and in good spirits. Mick had not been wrong. To these men, the recession had only reinforced their almost obsessive love of everything rare and expensive.

"Good evening, gentlemen," Mick said, making eye contact with each man ranged around the table. "I am honored that you have agreed to attend this momentous gathering.

And may I say it was a distinct pleasure to meet each and every one of you." So much for the soft part of the evening, he thought.

The waitresses placed a small plate of salad in front of each man. Honniko appeared through the kitchen door, pushing a small cart in front of her. On it was an outsize tureen of chased silver and a large ladle. She stopped before each setting and ladled out a heaping portion onto the center of each salad.

To a man, the attendees glanced down at what she had served them, trying to identify it. The food looked like large beans, striped black and yellow, steeped in some kind of clear and viscous glaze.

"Our first course comes from China, from inside the walls of the Forbidden City, in fact." Mick lifted his hands and broadcast his most electric smile. "Tonight, gentlemen, we eat like emperors!"

The men took up their forks and began to eat. Mick gave Honniko a brief nod as she left the room after serving his portion. He did not, however, look down, but rather cast his countenance around the table at all the well-groomed and impeccably dressed men.

"I had a prepared speech to make tonight," he began, "but yesterday I chanced to overhear a debate in Ueno Park between two elderly gents who seemed quite knowledgeable about the current state of the world. One claimed that the masses are destined to kowtow before any ideology that appeals to their baser instincts.

"What does he mean by that? Consider: home, hearth, self-preservation. These are elemental instincts in man—good instincts, we would all agree, correct? But how many racial and ethnic wars the world over have been started and kept going by the rallying cry of home, hearth, and self-preservation.

"This is not a coincidence. Look at the proliferation of Fascism in the wake of Communism's worldwide demise. In Germany, the neo-Nazis are inexorably on the rise. In Italy, voters have brought to power a coalition dominated by men who consider Mussolini their idol. In Russia, dissatisfaction with the chaos of a free-market economy has brought to prominence a man who says, 'Russia first. Burn all others!'—

who says he is determined to go to war to reclaim Alaska from the United States. Today, there are millions who call these men great!

" 'Well,' said the second man, 'perhaps there *is* greatness in men prepared to risk everything to break away from the old order, the corrupt ways, the cozy coalitions that have kept each other in power since the end of the War in the Pacific. Corruption that is so well entrenched requires extreme measures. Can such endemic evil be rooted out any other way? Do not the ends justify the means?' "

Mick raised a hand. "Do we automatically condemn those charismatic men who have the power to galvanize large masses of people to carry out their vision? Or are the means these men employ—sometimes ruthless, coldly efficient, absolute—justified by their vision of a future ethically streamlined and supremely productive by the codification and enforcement of law? Do we—as acknowledged leaders, the elite of society—stand by and do nothing while society devours itself like a mongrel dog? Or do we seize society by the throat and impose the necessary harsh rule in order to properly govern and guide the masses? This is an age-old question. It has been debated by philosophers, politicians, generals, and theologians through the ages without having come to any definitive conclusion."

Mick opened wide his arms as if to embrace the entire room as the waitresses took away the salad plates. "I hope you have enjoyed your Imperial appetizer. Now as we take a break between courses, I wish to go around the table and ask each of you in which camp you place yourself." He nodded deferentially to the gray-haired man on his immediate left, who was head of a well-known electronics trading firm. "Perhaps we can begin with you, Asada-san."

"The debate seems clear enough," Asada said. "Just after the war we created the Liberal Democratic Party by unacknowledged mutual consent. It remained the unchallenged ruling party, and until three years ago, it had absolute control over Japanese politics and policy. Without the leadership of the LDP and its handpicked prime ministers, Japan would not have achieved the great economic miracle that transformed it from a defeated nation on the brink of crippling inflation and unemployment to an economic colossus."

He nodded. "At times, the means the LDP used to maintain control of the country were ruthless and—yes, cruel, by some standards. But we all agreed it had to be done; it was in the best interests of Japan. History has spoken most eloquently. Therefore, I say the ends *do* justify the means."

One by one, the men around the table answered in much the same words.

When they were done, Mick said, "I congratulate all of you for understanding the nature of true greatness."

"But what does it matter?" Asada asked. "Those were the old days, and as we all know, the old days are gone. The LDP has been deposed and we are left with a ruling coalition so fragile, so devoid of a consensus on how to govern, that we have a new prime minister every six months. I defy anyone in this room to tell us where in this time of constant compromise our future lies. Nowhere, that's where. If only we could return to the way things have been."

Mick leaned forward on his arms, his eyes alight with a religious fervor. "You are wrong, my friend. Think again of the debate between these two men. The first one, who decries the progress of history *in whatever form it takes,* is living in the past. He takes comfort in the way things have been. Perhaps that is you, as well. Conversely, the man who seeks to justify men whose primary rallying cry is 'I hold the future in my hand!' is living in the future. He thinks only of the way things should be.

"But I tell you this, gentlemen: neither of them have a *today,* and so they are doomed to be relics of history's inexorable march."

Mick waited a beat, luxuriating in the scent of tension perfuming the air. "As are you all, unless you can take that great leap of faith to change the way you view your life and the world. Unless you join me in the most audacious—and lucrative—venture of the coming century!"

He spread his arms again, and now the gesture had the effect of taking them all inside his protecting embrace. The doors to the kitchen opened and the waitresses flowed in, Honniko at their head. Mick's voice softened from its proselytizing edge as he said, "Gentlemen, this is the all-important decision I leave you with while you take time to savor your main course. Please enjoy yourselves!"

A new round of wine was uncorked, a deep, rich red this time, a 1960 Pétrus. Then the entrée was served, a dark meat stew, pungent with aged balsamic vinegar and sautéed onion. Japanese rice, of course, on the side, along with slender stalks of baby asparagus.

Mick raised his wineglass high, toasted their health, and watched them dig in. He found Honniko's eyes from across the room. He gave her a slight nod again, and she shooed her charges back into the kitchen.

"Consider the masses, slaves of the media. Now consider yourselves—men of such intelligence and will that you are *above* the rest of mankind. You are slaves of no one." He used the mesmerizing rhythm of the righteous, the incantatory rhythm of the political polemicist, the Baptist minister, the rapturous televangelist. "You are the overlords."

It was a dark and charismatic human stream from which he was drawing, one that knew no boundary of race, creed, or religion, but that resided somewhere within all men, slumbering like a serpent, all too ready to slither to the surface.

"The cultural and philosophical diversity now considered politically correct in countries such as the United States is the ideal medium for breeding the overlord," he continued. "In this atmosphere of openness and creativity, he becomes stronger and richer than he could possibly have been under more oppressive societies. Prejudice—the bane of the politically correct individual—would cut off the overlord's development in the bud. Universities—filled with potential acolytes—are now *paying* rich fees to propounders of racial hatred in the name of diversity and freedom of speech. In just such an atmosphere does the overlord thrive.

"And what do I mean by an overlord? One meant to rule the masses." He reached out his hand, extending a forefinger, dramatically moving it around the room as it settled in turn on each man ranged around the dinner table. "You, Asada-san ... you, Morimoto-san ... you ... and you ... and you."

His finger cut through the air like a scythe. "*All* of us here who are special, who live our lives by different rules, who come and go as we please, who gather power around us as the emperor gathers his ermine cloak. We see the future, a future the common man crawling by beyond these walls cannot even imagine. *This* is what we all have in common. Japanese or Caucasian, it matters not, for we speak a common language."

As he lowered his voice, he could feel them leaning forward so as not to miss a word. "We have a right—no, no, a *responsibility* to take advantage of the freedom a politically correct society offers us." He raised a forefinger. "Which we can do—beginning right here, right now at this table." His hand swept over the food. "It is no coincidence that we eat like emperors tonight, gentlemen. It is a form of initiation, a magical rite." He smiled winningly. "You know, in the jungles of Vietnam and elsewhere in the real world, there is a strong belief that the first step to the true defeat of your enemy is to devour him whole!"

"What nonsense is this?" Ise Ikuzo said. He was a beefy man on Mick's immediate right, the head of a steel and metallurgy conglomerate with shadowy ties to the Yakuza—the Shikei clan, if Mick's sources of information were accurate. "You told us the first course was from China. It was sweet enough to be Chinese!"

"Yes, indeed," Mick said, his smile widening. "Our appetizer consisted of Imperial bees sautéed in their own honey and liquor. Were they not delicious?"

"Indeed," Asada said, nodding. "It is rare for a Westerner such as yourself to have such sophisticated taste in food. I, for one, had expected french fries and Bigu Makus for dinner."

There was general laughter around the table and a nodding of heads. Of course, they had liked the Imperial Chinese bees. That was to be expected, Mick thought.

"And what about the main course?" Ikuzo asked.

"Was that not also to your liking, Ikuzo-san?" Asada asked from across the table. "Most unusual flavor, do you not agree?"

Ikuzo shrugged. "I have been to Venice. I have tasted their *fegato* specialty."

"Ah, yes, liver cooked in the Venetian manner," Mick said "But *what* liver!" He looked around the table at each man. "We all remember the late Rodney Kurtz. So sad about him." He gestured to the empty seat. "In his memory, we have kept a place for him." His voice was building again in that charismatic way. "And in memory of his attempt to subvert Denwa Partners to serve his own ends, it is *his* liver we have just eaten."

Mick, having delivered his coup de théâtre with the skill of a surgeon, stood back and watched the ensuing uproar with delight.

"This is outrageous! A monstrous jest!" Ikuzo shouted, and Asada looked blood-choked, as if he were about to be sick on the spot. He was not alone. All twelve were on their feet, shouting, shaking fists, pale as ghosts. Amid this chaos, Machida sat still as a statue, neither responding to angry queries nor looking at his colleagues.

At last, Machida pushed his chair back and stood with all the rest. "It is no jest." His commanding voice cut through the babble. "And I suggest we listen to what Mr. Leonforte has to say."

In ones and twos, the men sat back down. Most pushed their plates away into the center of the table, some would not even look at them.

"Now we are all one!" Mick cried as all the heads in the room turned his way. "Now we have supped on Power and are bound together in a modern-day version of a blood oath!" He took up a forkful of the dark stew and, shoving it in his mouth, chewed happily. Swallowing, he said, "We have devoured our enemy whole. Now we must ban together to use Denwa Partners in the manner for which it is ideally suited."

Ikuzo threw down his fork with a harsh clatter. "I'll have none of this fairy tale! I have been deceived and made a fool of." He jumped up. "You have abused your responsibilities as a host. I have no obligation to you."

"I think it would be best if you stayed long enough to hear me out," Mick said softly. "Then you will be free to leave."

"I am free to leave now!" Ikuzo said, incensed. "Who are you to dictate terms to me? You are *iteki,* a foreigner with no influence over me."

"Ikuzo-san, it pains me to see us so at odds," Mick said. "Of course you are free to leave now if that is your preference."

"It is," Ikuzo said, puffing out his chest. He looked around the table, made his ritual bowing.

Mick waited until he was almost at the door when he said, "Ikuzo-san, I would appreciate it if you would answer one question."

Ikuzo turned back to the room. "And what is that?"

"You are a silent partner in Sterngold Associates, aren't you?"

"Why ask a question to which you obviously know the answer?" Ikuzo snapped. "Sterngold was owned by Rodney Kurtz."

"Do you know that Mr. Kurtz was working on squeezing you out of Sterngold *and* Denwa Partners?"

A look of consternation flickered across Ikuzo's face. "What are you talking about?"

"Kurtz wanted you out as a partner so he agreed to swap your minority interest in Sterngold for half his share in Denwa. But you hadn't made your last payment to him, so, technically, you're in breach of your contract. In that light, Kurtz made certain arrangements in the event of his death—and that of his wife. Sterngold is now in the hands of Bates and Bates, an American law firm. According to Kurtz's will, *all* of Sterngold's interest in Denwa has been taken over by Worldtel, Inc., a shell corporation which I have just bought."

"What? But that's impossible!" Ikuzo sputtered. "He couldn't have done that. He knew I was in a cash crunch. I met with him last week. He expressly told me I had six more weeks to pay him the rest of the money I owed him. The deal was all set."

"Guess what?" Mick said, taking out the contracts and spreading them on the table. "He lied. You know what they said about Kurtz in Germany? Don't stand downwind of him when he pisses." He watched as Ikuzo's eyes were inexorably drawn to the contracts. "Well, what are you waiting for, Ikuzo-san? You are free to leave." He waited a beat. "Or you can return to the table and we can renegotiate your partnership in Denwa." He broadcast that winning smile again. "I assure you I am a more trustworthy partner than Kurtz ever was."

He was aware of the entire room riveted on Ikuzo as he slowly made his way back to his seat and slipped silently into it. Mick graciously passed down the contracts to him.

Then Mick raised his voice. "Asada-san was quite correct

in his lament. The good old days are gone, gentlemen; they sang themselves out in Mozart, as Friedrich Nietzsche would say. Or, in our case, in the shogun Iyeyasu Tokugawa. When the Meiji government stripped the samurai of their status and rank in the 1800s, they deprived Japan of its history—of its very soul.

"Which is why the TransRim CyberNet is so vital to Japan's future. Right now, you are a computer-illiterate society. Your children go through school without learning how to use the one tool that will bring them into the twenty-first century. Japanese need to learn to move all forms of information along the CyberNet superhighway like the Americans and the Europeans do. And this Japan will do in its own formidable way. It will do it because it is essential in order for Japan to compete effectively in the coming years.

"The CyberNet is the first such worldwide superhighway in Japan— and therefore it will be adopted as the computer net of choice for the country as a whole. Further, with its digital video capabilities I can assure you it will have a monopoly on information transmission and dissemination for the foreseeable future.

"Frankly, I'd like nothing better than to start my own CyberNet, but, as you all know, the TransRim vid-byte technology is proprietary—patented, locked up tight against theft."

"If any such competing net came on-line, we would sue its owners and win, bankrupting them," Asada-san said.

"Precisely," Mick replied. "That is why I bought into Denwa Partners. The vid-byte technology is going to be worth billions and billions of dollars in the coming decades—not only from TransRim itself but from subsequent licensing deals that are sure to follow."

He raised a forefinger. "But the fact is the CyberNet is not being utilized to its ultimate potential, which is why we are all here tonight. *Dissemination of information.* Think about that phrase for a moment. The CyberNet is going to be the single most influential tool by which people in Japan and in the entire Pacific Rim move information. But it can also be used to *influence* people, business deals, and the like. It is the next generation up from satellite TV. And it has a great advantage over satellite TV, which, we have seen, cannot pass with impunity across all national boundaries." Mick looked from face to face. "I need hardly remind you of the example of Rupert Murdoch's Star TV, which had to stop beaming the BBC news broadcasts into China because of programs critical of the Chinese government's civil rights position. The CyberNet will have no such problems because it is not transmitted in any conventional way. No one can regulate what is disseminated on a computer on-line service. We will become the architects—the gods, if you will—of our own information autobahn."

He paused to allow the concept to sink in. "There will be no secrets from us; we will have control of communication, of commerce. Owning the system, we will be able to dictate the programming to the drones who log on. Imagine twenty-four-hour-a-day advertising that is masquerading as programming. If, for instance, we want to initiate a resurgence of the Liberal Democratic Party, we need only begin a daily forum on the CyberNet skewed toward LDP policies. Pounding them home day after day, night after night, will have its effect—and will effectively stifle anti-LDP sentiment in the media."

He paused a moment to let that concept sink in, then leaned forward, like a figurehead into the wind. "Consider, as another example, that we want to know what our rivals are doing at Mitsui Heavy Industries or at the Bureau of Foreign Affairs or within the Metropolitan Police Department. Do you think that within twelve months any Japanese *keiretsu* or bureau will be able to conduct business without the CyberNet? Not if it wants to be globally competitive! Imagine it! You will have the control—no, much *more* than you have had in the past, than you are clinging to now with the old ways of bribery and extortion under attack by the police, under the scrutiny of the media and the public. With control of the CyberNet you can discard the old ways, which have become increasingly dangerous for you through repeated investigations by both the police and the media. The web which you have so effectively spread since the end of the war is outdated, a dinosaur that takes more time and effort than you can afford to give it in this day and age." He spread his arms wide. "It all comes to you—and *more,* much more—electronically; deal-making made simple, quick, efficient, and, best of all, absolutely untraceable."

"This is revolutionary thinking, without doubt. But inspiring as all this may seem, isn't it impossible?" Asada said. "With knowledge comes sophistication. Companies won't begin to move their secret data along the Cybernet until they're sure they can do it confidentially. Right now the CyberNet communication is not secure; anyone can read anyone else's communications."

"Asada-san is as right as he is wrong." Like a magician, Mick opened his right hand. In the center of his palm was a tiny computer chip gleaming like platinum. "Gentlemen, allow me to present the Kyron Algorithm Lithium Chip. The KALC is a refined version of the U.S.-designed Slipjack algorithm, a so-called unbreakable coding device that will make eavesdropping on the CyberNet impossible—or so we will prove to everyone. We will give the KALC to all companies going on-line within the first six months. It will be a promotion, a way to induce them to use the CyberNet."

A slow smile spread across Mick's face. "What we *won't* tell them is that the KALC can also *break* any code, no matter how complex. It is the ultimate eavesdropping device because it works for both audio *and* video encryption."

From beneath the table, he drew out two electronic devices. He pointed to the one on his left. "Here is a machine that has recorded a conversation encrypted with the American Slipjack algorithm." He spoke the word "Play," and a spew of gibberish emanated from the recorder.

"Can anyone tell me what was being said on the tape?" Silence.

Mick looked up as he ran the tape back. "I have no doubt that any of you could take this tape and run it through your mainframes from now until the end of the year and you'd be no closer to decoding the Slipjack algorithm. It is, indeed, powerful."

He then connected the machine on his right to the first one. "This machine contains the KALC. I will now run the tape through its circuit." He turned on the KALC-loaded recorder, spoke, "Play," to the machine on his left.

"We have no such initiative on the boards at this time, Mr. President."

"Then we should have."

Mick watched intently as everyone around the table leaned forward as they recognized the slightly nasal accent of the president of the United States.

"You tell Mitchelson at Commerce that we've got a policy gap and I don't like it. The Japanese ought to be buying more rice from us. That's the bottom line."

"Uh, Mitchelson's going to want to know what kind of leeway he's being given, sir."

"Any way Mitchelson wants to handle it is okay with me. We've gotten tough with the Japanese before and it works. I want them buying our rice. Got it?"

"Absolutely, sir."

Mick switched off the recorders. There was a kind of stunned silence in the room. "All we need do is incorporate this chip into the CyberNet matrix. It will allow us to key into any and all encoded data run on the CyberNet."

At last, Morimoto, the head of MITI's Industrial Policy Bureau, cleared his throat and said, "Sato International is the majority partner in the CyberNet." He looked around the room. "Like everyone here, I know Tanzan Nangi. He would not allow such a chip to be incorporated in the CyberNet. Even were we to go along with you, Nangi-san will not."

"Nangi-san is an old man," Mick said. "Furthermore, he's been ill. His recent heart attack—"

"We have been assured that Nangi-san's illness is minor," Asada said.

"Yes, and we will assure everyone that the KALC will make electronic eavesdropping impossible. Does that make it so?" Mick allowed his words time to sink in. "Yes, yes, his heart attack was minor, so we have heard. But what if it was worse? What if Nangi-san's abilities have been permanently impaired?" Mick said carefully. "Would you want such a man leading Sato International?"

"Do you know something we don't?" Asada asked.

Mick seemed to ponder a moment, a theatrical gesture underscoring what he was about to say. "He had his attack, what . . . ?"

"Six months ago," Morimoto said.

"Is he back at his desk yet?" Mick asked in all innocence.

"No," Asada said thoughtfully. "And his infirmity would explain why he was not at the CyberNet launch dinner."

"If he is so unwell," Morimoto said, recognizing his chance and seizing it, "then he should no longer be guiding a *keiretsu* of Sato's size and influence." Heads nodded in agreement. Everyone in the room knew his views on Tanzan Nangi. Morimoto thought Nangi had too much power, but that might simply be because of jealousy. Before "retiring" into the business community, Nangi had been a high-ranking minister of MITI. Though he had made his mark at the Ministry of International Trade and Industry, he had become far more well-known as head of Sato.

"Now we have come to the crux of the matter," Mick said. "Control of the parent company, Sato International. Up to now Sato, as a privately held *keiretsu,* was untouchable for takeover even by such an exalted group such as we have here." His eyes sparked and his words ramped up in speed and emotion. "But the CyberNet and Denwa Partners has changed all that. Sato is in such dire financial straits it had to seek outside financial backing in order to launch the CyberNet."

"But we are only minority shareholders," Asada pointed out. "Sato still has majority ownership."

"Only under certain conditions," Mick said. "Under the agreement, a bridge loan Denwa made to Sato must be repaid within ninety days. If it is not, we can gain a foothold into the company. I intend to see that the loan is not repaid. In fact, I can guarantee it. In return, I ask that you elect me president of Denwa Partners. In that capacity, as part of our agreement with Sato, I will automatically go on Sato's board of directors when they are in default of the loan payment. That is all I need to eventually gain complete control of Sato and the CyberNet. Once on the board, I can work on the other members individually until I get a majority to vote Nangi out and elect me as the new chairman of Sato International."

Again, a silence enveloped the room. As Mick watched the expressions on their faces, he knew he had gambled and won. He had gambled that these men—the Dai-Roku— would have no love for the well-known liberal Nangi, that they were jealous of his power, and that they feared Nangi's partner, Nicholas Linnear.

Everything he had told them was the truth, up to a point. But he had another, hidden agenda. He wanted control of Sato International. Despite its current financial woes, it remained the single most influential *keiretsu* in Japan and overseas, and its clout could do wonders for opening the legitimate doors of business for Mick. Sato was his ticket into the real world, a world in which he longed to become a player—a mover and a shaker. Too long had he pulled the strings of clandestine activities from the shadows of mountainous Vietnam. That Sato International was co-owned by his nemesis, his dark twin, Nicholas Linnear, made his longing all the more potent. That he was becoming the seed of Linnear's destruction was an irresistible lure.

Having given them enough time, Mick now said, "Here is our chance to seize the present for Japan and to break Sato International's stranglehold on the future."

"What about Linnear-san?" The naked fear in Asada's face bespoke their capitulation. They wanted in; they wanted Mick to guide them. They had seen his future and had made it theirs.

Mick smiled, said softly, "Leave Linnear to me. I know how to handle him. I promise you, he won't interfere with our plan." He leaned forward. "Now which of you are with me? Think it through. This is, without hyperbole, the opportunity of a lifetime. Do we use Denwa to seize control of Sato?" He looked around the table. One by one, they nodded solemnly. There was not a dissenting vote among them.

Later, when they had all gone, including Machida, Mick sat smoking a cigar, staring up at the ceiling. The table was bare, save for a multicolored runner down the middle. Its gleaming cherrywood surface gave off the sharp, pleasing odor of lemon wax. In the kitchen, Honniko was supervising the last of the staff cleanup.

It was at times like this that he thought of Koei. His six months with her had been difficult, painful even, in some ways. But, like prison, he would never be able to forget. She had despised him, of this he was certain, and it should have been enough for him to turn her out. Alliances were all well and good, but what did one need with a woman who would as soon spit at you as climb into your bed? And yet it was this very hatred that had meant the most to him. He missed it when she was gone, or anyway, he missed the menu of small humiliations and degradations he found himself composing in order to keep that black emotion burning. It became like a bitter taste at the back of his mouth, as from ash in the vicinity of an incinerator.

He was roused from this unsavory reverie by Honniko, who had reemerged from the kitchen. She had changed out of kimono and obi into a smart, smoke-gray Armani suit without lapels. She wore almost no makeup at all, and this naturalness seemed to accentuate the oriental caste of her eyes. Her blond hair was even more startling in this context.

"A masterful performance," she said.

"Do you think so?" He blew out a cloud of aromatic smoke as his head came down. "It was a good presentation, yes, but all I did was tell them what they most wanted to hear. I put a hook in their noses and led them along, but they were ripe for foment. They don't like the uncertainty of the present, they long for the past and fear for the future."

He rolled the cigar between his lips in a curiously obscene gesture. He sucked in more smoke, let it out slowly. "But I was also lucky." He snapped the minidisc Honniko had delivered to him earlier between two fingers. "The procedure I drew up to get this from Sato's R and D could have gone wrong in so many places."

"I don't see how. You were prudent at every stage."

"Prudence is the crutch by which man rationalizes defeat." Mick twirled the minidisc between his fingers. "It is an inadequate arsenal."

She came and sat beside him, ran fingers through his hair. "Does it matter? You got everything you want."

"I have the CyberNet technology, but I never wanted or needed it." He twirled the minidisc between his fingers. "I had this stolen from Sato as a ruse, to distract them from the true assault on them that will be coming through the contract Sato signed with Denwa Partners. I don't want anyone at Sato thinking about that contract now. Let them run themselves in circles trying to find out who stole their precious data—and why. For all the good it will do them."

He inhaled his cigar, blew out a cloud of blue smoke.

"But as for having everything, I don't. I don't have Linnear's head. Not yet." Then he grinned, a sudden boyish gesture she had come to know well. "Want to see the fruits of our labor?"

She hitched her chair forward. "You bet."

He drew out a soft-sided attaché case from which he took a notebook computer outfitted with a CD-ROM and mini-disc drive. He switched it on, slipped the minidisc in, and booted up. When the computer came on-line, he switched to the minidisc drive.

"This is it," he told her as his finger hovered over the ENTER key. "Once I press this, the CyberNet data will appear on the computer screen." He sucked some smoke into his mouth, savoring its bite. Then, as the smoke drifted from his partly opened lips, he hit the button. The drive light switched on and the computer began its processing.

Almost immediately, the screen was filled with lines of data: complex formulas, operating instructions, data codes, cipher overrides, the entire CyberNet matrix, along with an index of files.

"Ahhh!" Mick let out a long sigh of satisfaction as he scrolled through. Then he chomped down on his cigar so hard he almost bit it in two.

"What the fuck?"

The screen was wiping itself of the data. Mick's fingers flew over the keys, trying everything he knew to save the data to the hard drive before it was lost. He managed to save almost three-quarters of it before the screen purged itself.

He accessed the minidisc to download the rest of the data, but he got an ERROR message. He switched the screen to the minidisc itself, discovered to his consternation that the minidisc was reading devoid of data. He tried another way to access the data, same result. He removed the minidisc, closed down the computer, then rebooted it and started the procedure all over again.

This time, not only could he not get the contents of the minidisc to download, some of his own computer's commands were malfunctioning. He switched to his C drive, accessed the built-in diagnostic, discovered that a virus was busy dismantling the software on his hard drive. He booted up his antivirus program, but that had already been overridden and destroyed.

"What's going on?" Honniko asked.

"I don't know," Mick said, hunched over the keyboard. But there was nothing he could do. "Somehow a virus has been introduced into the computer that's destroying everything on my hard drive."

"Even the CyberNet data?"

As he nodded, a single word popped up onto his screen. He could not wipe it off, no matter what he did.

"SMILE."

He sat there, staring at the computer. Then, with a string of curses, he swept it off the table. It crashed to the floor. He stood up, leaving it there.

"Come on," he said. "Let's go home."

At that moment, his cellular phone rang.

"What is it?" he barked into the mouthpiece.

"I'm out at the Keiji," Jōchi, his lieutenant, said in his ear. Keiji Hakubutsukan was the Criminal Museum in Kanda, the quarter of Tokyo that is part of both the High City and the Low City.

"What are you doing there?"

"I think you'd better get over here and see for yourself."

Mick would have made a remark concerning Jōchi's enigmatic call, but he heard the degree of agitation in his voice. Jōchi knew they were on a secure line and could speak freely. Something monstrous must have hit the fan.

"We're just finishing up at Tamayama," Mick said. "We'll be there. By the way, the shipment to my brother got off on schedule?"

"Right on time. This new shipper is aces."

Mick hung up and to Honniko's inquiring gaze, said, "Jōchi's found something over at the Criminal Museum."

"At this time of night? The museum's been closed for hours."

"Let's go," Mick said, grabbing his ankle-length raincoat. "It sounded urgent."

There was something magical about Tokyo late at night, Mick thought as he roared down the rain-slicked street. The eighteen-hour-a-day crowds were gone, replaced by lumbering trucks that, by law, were allowed to make deliveries only at night. Teenagers, too, were evident, in their black leather jackets, their spiked hair and pierced flesh, thundering high and hard on their motorcycles. Mick thought he understood their obsession with self-mutilation. Everywhere, things were melding. Youths in Brussels, St. Petersburg, Saigon, and Pittsburgh were all the same. They wore the same clothes, played the same on-line games, watched MTV. Man required self-definition, and the more you peered into TV, ramped up your computer, played video games on your CD-ROM with a net-pal in Timbuktu or wherever, the more difficult self-definition became. And the more reason there was to find permanent methods of setting yourself apart.

"I am not a number. I am a free man."

That's what it boiled down to, this trend, moving from tattooing to piercing to branding and back again.

They arrived in Kanda to the roar of a group of far-off motorcycles, echoes bouncing off the high-rises like steel balls in a pachinko game. Jōchi emerged from the shadows of an alleyway at the side of the Criminal Museum. He looked both ways along the deserted street, beckoned silently to Mick, who got out of the car and followed him. Mick took Honniko's hand. Her heels clacked along the pavement, sounding unnaturally loud in the darkness.

Jōchi switched on a powerful flashlight as he led them deeper into the alley. They passed a pair of gargantuan green metal Dumpsters that looked as if they hadn't been emptied in years. Between them was a small camp of homeless men. A fire was burning through a metal grillwork. The homeless—those who were not asleep in their filthy rags—peered at them out of rheumy, incurious eyes. The reek of alcohol and rancid bodies lay like a suffocating blanket.

Mick did not hurry by, as most people would have, averting their eyes and holding their breath. Instead, he slowed, studying these folk carefully. Though he would rather slit his throat than admit it, he had more in common with them than he did with the men of the Dai-Roku. They belonged to the High City, the part of Tokyo once ruled by shoguns and their daimyo. Mick was a part of the Low City, the dark, unseemly corners where humanity crawled on its belly when it moved at all, the steaming, unsightly boils that grew without the benefit of light or privilege.

"Mick, come on!" Jōchi urged. "Now is not the time for a sociological survey of the soft black underbelly."

They continued on, and at last they came to the far end of the alley. Here, a soot- and grime-encrusted concrete wall abutted the side of the museum. Jōchi shone the flashlight's beam, revealing a figure sitting up against the wall. His position seemed so natural that at first Mick thought he was merely sleeping. But, on closer inspection, he saw the stiffness of the limbs, the bloated nature of the fingers. And then, as the flashlight's beam moved, he saw the unnatural pallor of the face.

"Jesus Christ," he breathed. "It's Nguyen."

Jōchi nodded. "It's Van Truc, all right, the man who picked up the CyberNet minidisc from the American McKnight." The beam held steady. "We've been looking for him ever since he delivered the minidisc to Honniko."

"He seem okay to you then?" Mick asked as he moved cautiously around the body. There was a smell here, coming from the corpse in waves.

"I guess," Honniko said. "He seemed calm enough. You know, cool, but then I didn't know him."

"I think you're the only one who did," Jōchi said to Mick.

"That's right. I recruited Nguyen in Saigon. He was perfect: deeply venal, committed to money." Mick glanced at Jōchi. "What the hell killed him?"

"Damned if I know. We found him and I called you. He hasn't been touched by us."

Mick moved in, used the toe of his shoe to kick Nguyen over. The stench billowed up as if from the depths of hell.

"Ugh!" Honniko said, but she stood her ground.

Mick glanced at her. She was not the kind of woman to get sick at the sight of death. She'd seen her share. Not like him, of course. But he'd been in the war in Vietnam, where monstrous atrocities became mundane.

Mick kicked the corpse around good, until he had seen all sides of him. "He wasn't shot, knifed, or garroted."

"He could have been smothered to death," Honniko said.

"Not this man," Mick said. "He'd have never let anyone get that close."

Mick kicked at the corpse one more time so that Nguyen's face was up. He directed Jōchi to move the light in closer, then he squatted down. He breathed shallowly through his mouth, feeling the stench claw at the back of his throat. Peering at the features, he said, "You know, I do believe our friend here was drowned." He pointed. "You see here—and here—there's evidence of bloating, as if he'd been in the water some."

"You mean someone drowned him then dumped him here?" Honniko asked. "But why?"

Mick had seen so many dead in his time you'd think one more wouldn't matter. But it did. Death was not like the films made it out to be, ennobling and featureless. It made you sick to your stomach, it made you examine what was inside you, question what life was all about. Maybe it didn't diminish you, as books said it did, Mick thought. But it sure as hell changed you.

"Only one reason I can think of," he said, standing up. "Look where he was dumped. At the back of the Criminal Museum. Get the message? Whoever killed him wanted us to find him."

"But no one even knew Nguyen was working for you," Jōchi said.

That was when Mick thought of the computer virus. It had been contained in the minidisc, riding piggyback on the CyberNet data. That meant one of two things: either Kappa Watanabe, the Sato R&D tech Mick had co-opted, had fucked him over, which, knowing Watanabe, he seriously doubted, or the minidisc had somehow been intercepted and switched.

"Shit!"

Mick clenched his fists in rage. Only one man had had the means and the opportunity to make the switch: Nicholas Linnear.

He looked skyward, his lips pulled back in a bloodless grin. He had found that there were moments in life when a mixture of circumstance and emotion caused the world to change shape. The evening he had spent with Jaqui up on the roof the night his grandfather had been murdered had been one such incident, and there had been a second in the highland jungles of Laos with the Nungs when he had been initiated into their tribe and had been inscribed with the Gim, the dark blue, vertical crescent tattooed on the inside of his wrist. This was yet another. Everywhere he looked, the sharp edges of buildings had taken on a preternatural clarity, the ruthless acuity of a razor blade's edge. He sucked in the humid Tokyo air, and it had the mind-expanding chill of a Himalayan night, and he rejoiced in the knowledge. So now they were into it, just the two of them. And isn't this exactly what he had wanted? A chance to pit himself against his shadow double, his doppelgänger, the man with whom he had so much in common?

Linnear was doing a number on his head. *Smile*, the computer virus had written on his screen, and having writ refused to get the hell off. So Linnear was stalking him just as he had been stalking Linnear. A dance of death, the two of them in a prescribed circle, moving from the darkness to the light and back again, tied together by the mysterious cord that linked their pasts.

Now, truly, reality seemed to fade into the hazy distance. Instead, Mick found himself in a heightened state, the entire universe traveling the path of darkness and light with nothing in between. It was as if he and Nicholas Linnear were polar opposites, proton and electron inhabiting the last atom, circling one another at higher and higher speeds, both repelled and attracted, coming inevitably closer to the clash that would mean existence for one of them—and destruction for the other.

Saints

The samurai of old were mortified by the idea of dying in bed; they hoped only to die on the battlefield. A priest, too, will be unable to fulfill the Way unless he is of this disposition—

—The priest Ryōi
From chapter 10 of *Hagakure*, the book of the samurai

Astoria

Spring 1957/Winter 1945/
Spring 1961–62

Jaqui Leonforte knew she was destined for something special the moment she met Bernice. Within the boundaries of the Convent of the Sacred Heart of Santa Maria, Jaqui felt as if she possessed a curious inner light, as if she could look straight through the mother superior's facade of warmth and wisdom to her warrior's heart.

Out of the corner of her eye, Jaqui looked at Mama, who, she was now certain, did not possess this inner light. Mama was, after all, a normal woman in every respect. Sometimes, lying in bed at night, Jaqui wondered restlessly if she had come into this family by mistake. Maybe she and another female infant had inadvertently been switched in the hospital, and somewhere across the city another girl was living the life Jaqui should have been living. At times she was so certain of this that she had become almost autistic, as if responding to any stimulus in her environment would give it a legitimacy it did not deserve.

So obsessive did this behavior become as Jaqui grew that Mama, terrified, had taken her to a specialist in Manhattan. Jaqui remembered the train ride across the bridge more clearly than she did the doctor's myopic face.

"There is nothing wrong with your daughter," he had pronounced. Mama was so relieved that she cried. "All that's really needed is for you to engage her attention more. She's just bored."

On the train ride home, Mama said, "I know you are unhappy. I've known for some time, but I've been putting off doing anything about it. I thought"—she wrapped Jaqui's hand in her own—"I thought you would grow out of it." Mama sighed wistfully staring out the grimy train window. "Instead, you've grown into it." It was time, Mama said, she took Jaqui to Astoria.

Jaqui fell in love with the Sacred Heart of Santa Maria the moment she stepped through the iron gates into the heavily treed grounds. She loved the smell sunlight made as it dried out the dew-dampened foliage, the heavy drone of the bees as they pollinated the roses, the bright twitter of the birds as they flitted through the branches of the trees.

But, above all, she felt a *presence*. Perhaps, after all, it was God, as Bernice so fervently believed. Or, then again, perhaps it was simply a lack of the quotidian violence that invaded Jaqui's world at every turn.

But whatever it was, Jaqui felt it as surely as a strong, guiding hand upon her shoulder. And Bernice knew she felt it.

The white stone facade shone in the sunlight like a polished mirror. In one of the small, slitted windows that flanked the front door, Jaqui felt, rather than saw, eyes peering at her with curiosity and keen anticipation. When Mama led her up the wide flight of steps to the iron-banded wood door and it opened inward, Jaqui knew that she was entering a world apart, that she was about to begin a journey that would last the rest of her life.

It was the spring of 1957; Jaqui was fifteen.

"Do you believe in God?"

"I believe . . ." Jaqui broke off, at a loss. It was not that she was intimidated by those piercing blue eyes, or by the peculiar iconography of Catholicism that adorned the walls of Bernice's office. The fact was that after being baptized and confirmed, after attending church regularly with her parents, after years of reciting the catechism, of staring at Jesus bleeding on the cross, of confessing in a booth that smelled of shoe polish and sweat, she had no more idea of her beliefs than she did about what would befall her a year from now.

"I don't know whether I do or not."

"Good," Bernice said with such enthusiasm that it caught Jaqui's attention instantly. Mama had remained in the rose garden, wandering, putting her face up to the sun and worrying whether she had done the right thing in bringing her daughter here.

"How is that good?" Jaqui asked now.

"You answered honestly and that's a start," Bernice said flatly. She had the gift of transforming opinion into fact.

Jaqui looked around the office at the religious paintings, the statue of the Virgin and Child, the large wood and gilt crucifix, and she was at once suffocating beneath the weighty religious symbols. "I don't want to become a nun."

Bernice leaned forward and, taking Jaqui's hands in her own, smiled. "Child, I have no intention of making you become a nun."

At that moment, Jaqui knew it had been Bernice peering at her through that very medieval window. A castle window, slitted and fortified against the arrows and spears of the enemy. And it resided here, on a quiet, poplar-lined street of Queens. She looked at Bernice and, in astonishment, saw her clad in burnished armor, a great broadsword scabbarded at her side. This armor shone with the same quality as had the white stone facade of the building in the sunshine.

Jaqui murmured something under her breath, then blinked several times. When she looked at Bernice again, the mother superior was as she had been, clothed in her habit.

"What is it, my child?"

"I thought—" Jaqui blinked again. Then she let out a small, embarrassed laugh. "I thought I saw you covered in medieval armor. Crazy, isn't it?"

Bernice let out what seemed a long-held exhalation. She was on the verge of tears as she rose. "Come, I want to show you something." But instead of leading her to the door, she took Jaqui back to a rear alcove, where floor-to-ceiling bookcases rose. She put her hand behind a row of books.

There was a soft click and one part of the bookcase opened inward.

They crossed the threshold and Jaqui found herself in a stone corridor with an arched ceiling. It was lit by small electric lights in niches in the wall where, in Europe, one would expect to find torches. Their shoes echoed against the stone flooring. At the end of the corridor, Bernice used a set of keys she drew from her pocket to open an iron door. It creaked loudly. Bernice locked it carefully behind them and, lifting her hem, marched up a metal spiral staircase.

The room they entered at the top was not large; nevertheless it was impressive. It featured one wall that, like a castle's turret, was semicircular. From perhaps three feet off the floor to just below the ceiling, the wall was a line of the most magnificent stained glass Jaqui had ever seen. Oddly, only one panel had a religious theme, and that was of Joan of Arc on a white stallion. The remainder of the panels depicted scenes from the history of France and Italy. As far as Jaqui could tell, war was the predominant motif.

The massive expanse of stained glass flooded the room with a multicolored light so extraordinary it seemed magical. It spilled over Bernice and Jaqui, and Jaqui felt transformed. A curious warmth suffused her, and it was as if the horrors of Ozone Park and East New York had ceased to exist.

"Oh, Bernice," she cried, "it's so beautiful!"

"Do you really think so?"

"Really and truly," Jaqui said, turning to face the mother superior. "I feel . . ."

Bernice gripped her shoulders, her blue eyes piercing Jaqui's flesh. "What do you feel?"

"I don't know." Jaqui was as breathless as if she had run all the way here from Ozone Park. *"Something . . ."*

"Yes," Bernice said fiercely. "I was right about you."

Then she turned Jaqui around until she was facing the one flat wall of the room. It was made of the same stone as the corridor and was unadorned save for a painting. The painting was not large, nevertheless it dominated the room as if it were ten times the size.

"My God!" Jaqui breathed.

"Indeed," Bernice said, her electric-blue eyes alight.

Jaqui found herself mesmerized by the painting. It depicted an armor-clad figure with a great broadsword strapped to one hip. The helmet was off, held in the crook of the figure's left hand, and the face could plainly be seen. It was a woman. A woman whose countenance was not so dissimilar from that of Bernice. The artist had rendered the handsome face enrobed in an inner light that burst upon the canvas.

"This is the vision I had in your office," Jaqui said with her heart pounding so hard it seemed ready to leap into her throat. "Is that you?"

"How could it be? The painting is hundreds of years old."

"And yet—" Jaqui stepped closer. She looked back at Bernice. "It *is* you!"

Bernice shook her head. "Only in one sense. This is a portrait of Donà di Piave, the founder of this order."

Jaqui continued to gaze at the painting in wonderment. "But it is my vision! Bernice, I *saw* her."

"More likely what you felt downstairs was her presence inside me."

"Look at her face. It is alight with . . ."

"Divine animation."

"Yes," Jaqui said, knowing instinctively that Bernice was right. "But she was some kind of warrior."

"Donà de Piave was a nun," Bernice said softly. "But she was also a great champion, a defender of her people. Sometimes, in a world full of fear and evil, they can be one and the same." She nodded to a pair of Savonarola chairs facing one another, glittering in the light from the stained glass. "Sit, my child. There is much you must be told before you can make your decision."

"What decision?"

"You are special, Jaqui. Part of the chosen. That is why your mother brought you here." Bernice smiled her most benign smile, but Jaqui was not fooled. Already she could see behind that mask, clever as it was, to the woman warrior who stood beside her.

Bernice said, "In our world women are dismissed as mothers or as whores. Either way, they're considered irrelevant to business." She waited until Jaqui had settled herself on the left-hand Savonarola chair. "Do you know Goethe, the German philosopher?"

"I've heard of him, but I haven't read him."

"You will read him here if you choose to join us," Bernice said, sitting opposite the girl. "He wrote that few men have imagination enough for reality." She was staring at the portrait of Donà di Piave. "But he quite rightly did not include women."

She rose, and as Jaqui watched her, she grasped the left edge of the picture frame and pulled it toward her. Behind the portrait of Donà di Piave was a niche carved into the stone wall and, inside, an object, long and narrow, covered by a purple velvet cloth, fringed in gold. Embroidered on it were words in Latin Jaqui could not understand.

Turning around, Bernice held the object in front of her and carefully removed the velvet cloth. Jaqui gaped. She held a sword in her hand, a darkly gleaming object of iron, clearly forged centuries before the advent of stainless steel.

"This is the sword of Donà di Piave," Bernice said.

And, as if drawn by magnetic force, Jaqui left her chair and reached out in wonder toward the weapon. At just that instant, Bernice lost her balance and the blade came down, slicing into the meat at the base of Jaqui's right hand.

Strangely, she did not cry out and she did not jump. In fact, she felt no pain at all, just an odd pulsing, and looking down, she saw her hands covered in blood.

Bernice, who had dropped the sword and rushed from the room, now returned with Merthiolate, sterile gauze, and first-aid adhesive.

"It doesn't hurt," Jaqui said as if to no one in particular.

And Bernice, slipping to her knees, grasped Jaqui's wrist, and as she painstakingly cleaned and dressed the wound, she thought, *Praise God. She* is *the one.*

"And your bishop agrees with your interpretation of Goethe?"

"This is 1945," Bernice said to Camille Goldoni. "My archbishop is too busy with the war effort to care one whit about what Goethe wrote, let alone what my interpretation of his philosophy might be."

Camille—who was Margarite's aunt by marriage; she had died in the early 1970s—was a big-boned woman with a wide waist, fleshy arms and shoulders. She was not pretty, but her-

face was handsome in its way. Her decidedly mannish features were offset by the resoluteness of her demeanor and
the determination in her eyes. She was also exceedingly
kind, and this generosity of spirit glowed like light from
a lantern.

She was with Bernice because her husband, Marco Goldoni, Enrico's older brother, had had a stroke. This was
unusual in a man of forty. As luck would have it, he had
been home alone with her. It had been a Sunday. She rushed
him to the hospital, and when Marco's personal physician
told her what had happened to him, she determined then
and there that no one would know about it. She bribed the
doctor and the two nurses she allowed into the room. She
lied to Marco's bodyguards, who had driven the couple to
the hospital. The don was suffering from an acute case of
food poisoning, she told them.

"I knew that if news of Marco's stroke got out, the family
would be in serious trouble," Camille said now. "Enrico is
in Venice and, in any event, Marco is the powerhouse, the
connected one, the thinker and the planner."

She was dry eyed, having wept in the privacy of her husband's bedside. She sat with her back very straight, at this
moment conscious of all the minutiae that kept her together:
her makeup, the seams in her stockings, and little more. "Of
course, I know nothing about Marco's affairs. As is the custom, he is scrupulous about separating his business from his
personal life."

Camille had not yet come around to the real reason for
her visit. It was a simple matter for Bernice to provide comfort, but she suspected Camille was here for another purpose entirely.

"You see, Bernice, I need to confide in someone, but I
did not know who to turn to. Marco met with his *capi* every
week. Most of them come to dinner once a month, but I
don't know who among these men I can trust. Who will be
loyal when they hear the news? Who will seek to betray the
family in its time of weakness?"

"My dear, this sounds like an unsolvable problem."

"No, no. I came here to the one person I can trust without question."

Bernice's heart skipped a beat. Could this be the sign in

the physical world she had been destined to find? She took a deep breath and waited for events to unfold.

"Marco has been very generous, especially to this convent," Camille continued. "And we were both so grateful and thrilled when you agreed to take in our daughter. The doctors said she would never survive in the world outside, and we could never subject her to the cruelty of an institution." Now her emotions betrayed her, and clutching her handkerchief to her eyes, she began to cry. "We will never forget such kindness, Bernice."

Bernice leaned over, stroked Camille's cheek. "There, there, my dear. Marco has bestowed his own great kindness on us. After all, it is due to him that Santa Maria will be renovated—a new facade, a new wing. We are flourishing while others are struggling and dying out." She smiled benignly as Camille clutched her hand. "Besides, my dear, you and I know each other some years. We have spent so many hours in the contemplation garden, speaking of many things while the roses grew up around us."

Camille smiled. "It's true. I remember when you were first introduced to me. Mother Superior Mary Margaret was not so old then, but she was not well. She would not relinquish her title, but instead brought you along. 'Bernice will speak for me,' she said in that sandpaper voice of hers."

Bernice nodded. "God forgive me, it will be a blessing, really, when she dies." She shook her head. "So much pain for one person to endure."

"Bernice, I must ask you. I know you are not ignorant of what the Goldoni family's real business is. Yet you have befriended us."

"Of course." Bernice took the other woman's palm, pressed hers against it, transmitting the charismatic warmth that was but one of her extraordinary gifts. She was a tall, slender woman with a startlingly expressive face. Someone once said that she had the eyes of a mathematician. They were analytical, observing patterns that most other people missed, in the minute movements of everyday life. She held no truck with blandness or indecision. Among the women in the neighborhood, she was widely known as being tough as a man but far more fair in her judgments. She was an ardent reader of books and human character; she did nothing arbitrarily. "I am a pragmatist, as the best of my kind always are," she said. "I have this flock to care for and, besides, I pray twice a day for Marco's soul. I used to laugh and say, 'Without sinners like Marco the Church would be out of business.'" She smiled. "But, my dear, you must know that you and I could not be closer were we sisters."

"So." Camille arranged her hands in her lap, her fingers twisting and untwisting her damp handkerchief. "So."

A soft chanting began, emanating from another part of the convent, penetrating the stone walls. The liturgical Latin seemed immensely comforting, the slow phrasing calming wildly beating hearts.

"Camille, tell me how I can help you." Bernice turned her palms upward. "I assure you, nothing you could ask me will be a burden."

Camille nodded, gaining courage from her friend's words. "I have come here in my hour of desperation to ask for your advice." She looked into Bernice's piercing blue eyes. "My entire family is hanging in the balance. Tell me what I should do."

Bernice sat back. Now she knew what it was she was facing: nothing less than her destiny. She could taste it, hold it in her hand, and yet she felt curiously calm. "My dear, before we go further, let me say that dispensing advice is easy. Taking it is quite a different matter."

"Oh, Bernice, I'm here, aren't I?" Tears stood in the corners of Camille's eyes. "You're the one I came to. I have nowhere else to go. Whatever advice you give me I swear I will take."

"This is a house of God. When you take an oath, it is forever."

Camille swallowed hard. "Then let it be forever."

Bernice nodded. "Very well then. My advice is for us to look to Goethe. 'Few men have imagination enough for reality.' Let me explain how this applies to us. You talk of custom, my dear. You tell me you know nothing of the details of your husband's business and I believe you. In his eyes—in the eyes of all men—that is right and proper. But taking from Goethe, I strenuously disagree.

"What I mean is that men have had their way for so long, and what has it brought us—bloodshed and war, because that is how men settle arguments. But the deaths of our sons is no way to pay for the future."

Bernice lifted her forefinger. "I want you to consider something. Perhaps your husband's illness is a sign. Three nights ago I had a vision that God stretched out His hand in the darkness and loosed a bolt of lightning. Where He directed it, I had no idea, but I do now."

Bernice's face was filled with the kind of divine animation depicted in her forebear. "This is God's work, Camille, and we must recognize His plan in what has happened. The moment we recognize this, we turn tragedy into triumph."

Camille shook her head. "I don't understand. How could Marco's stroke possibly be interpreted as a sign from God?"

"Think of Goethe's quote. Men have been bound into societies for centuries, and for centuries the world has revolved around territory and war."

"But that is the way the world works, Bernice. How can we do anything about it?"

"On the surface, we can't. And that is as it should be. But, Camille, as you well know, appearances are often not the whole story." Bernice tapped the side of her nose. "Secrets are best kept by women and dead men. It comes so naturally to us. A woman lies to her man every day of her life in order to ensure his happiness or to save him from grief, isn't that so?" She sighed. "Sometimes, I am convinced that God put the sweetness on our faces and into our voices for just this purpose."

"It's true." Camille nodded. "In the household, a man says, 'Ask me no questions and I'll tell you no lies.' But a woman's gift is to makes her lies seem like the truth."

"And so it has been down through the ages." Bernice took Camille's hand, brought her into the same turreted room to which she would bring Jaqui a decade later. Camille sighed when she entered. It was the sound one makes when inhaling the rich perfume of the first rose of summer, expressing not only contentment but pleasure.

When she had drunk her fill of the stained glass, Bernice showed her the portrait of the nun-warrior.

"Many years ago, in the fifteenth century," Bernice said, "a secret society was formed—a society of women called the Order of Donà di Piave. In those days, it was natural for the power of women to accumulate in places out of the light of day, in places, moreover, not subject to the daily scrutiny of men. A convent was a perfect place to maintain this power, don't you think?

"It was formed because those women strong enough to make the leap of faith beyond the boundaries of their sex felt it was time to take an active role in creating a future where their sons did not march off to die in war or return crippled in body and in spirit, where their daughters were not left to raise their children alone.

"Centuries later, this society came to this country, and here it has remained, waiting for a day of rebirth. And, Camille, I very much believe that *this* is the day." Bernice gestured at the painting. "We live in a time not so dissimilar to that of Donà di Piave's. It is an age of fear and evil."

She put her arm around Camille's shoulder. "The sign from God foretold not merely Marco's disability, but the transference of power from his hands to yours."

"What?" Camille looked aghast.

"Listen to me closely, my dear. You came to me because you said I am the only one you can trust. Trust me now when I tell you that this is our chance to seize the power." She lifted a forefinger. "And remember what you swore before God and His intermediaries."

Camille looked defeated. "But, even if what you say is true, how can I possibly do what my husband did? We live in a world dominated by men. And none more so than *la Famiglia*. Do you seriously believe any of Marco's *capi* would listen to a word I tell them? That is, even assuming I knew what orders to give."

"Orders are not difficult to formulate," Bernice said crisply. "One need only think in logical sequence and everything will be made clear. Take care of one problem at a time and you find they all fall like dominoes." She nodded. "As to the rest, you are quite right, the lieutenants will follow only the orders they believe come from Marco himself—or someone he has designated.

"Therefore, I suggest you contact Marco's younger brother, Enrico, in Venice and urge him to come to his brother's side."

"But Enrico is an exporter of fabrics. He knows nothing of Marco's real business."

"Then he will learn along with you. The important thing is, up until now you have made all the right decisions. No one knows how ill Marco is and, God willing, they will never know. Enrico will become his emissary and then his mouthpiece and, finally, it will be Enrico who takes over for Marco. Only we will be making the decisions, behind the scenes, in the sanctity of the convent, and no one will ever know."

Camille was trembling. "Oh, Bernice, I don't know. The whole idea is so frightening!"

"Of course it is. But think, my dear, what a force for good you can become! Rein in the fears for yourself. Come from a place of light and truth. Put your thoughts beyond the boundaries of home and hearth. Set your goals beyond Marco and the family. Think only of God and the dazzling opportunity He has presented you. And remember that the full resources of the Order of Donà di Piave will be at your disposal forevermore."

After she saw Camille out, Bernice went to the kitchen and returned to the turret room with a tray of food. She pushed through another hidden door into another, more spacious room furnished as a bedchamber. Thick curtains were drawn across the two windows that overlooked the inner courtyard with its central meditation garden. Fresh flowers in glass vases festooned the room. A single lamp glowed dimly on a small wooden table beside a well-worn easy chair pulled up to the curtained window. On the other side of the room was an enormous four-poster bed made of mahogany and ebony. It was a masterful bit of carpentry, very old, and had been shipped in pieces from Europe.

Bernice stood in the room, waiting for her eyes to accommodate to the semidarkness.

"Bernice, is that you?" The voice was dry and brittle as a broom sweeping a sidewalk.

"Yes, Mary Margaret."

"What has happened?"

"Marco Goldoni has had a stroke."

"How bad is he?"

"Quite bad, apparently."

"Was he so evil?"

"Evil enough, I imagine," Bernice said. "But, as in all things, it is in the eye of the beholder."

"Indeed, he's always been most generous with us. Most generous. And now Camille has come to us."

"Yes."

"Praise God."

Bernice approached the bed. Despite her best efforts, the room held the cloying sweet smell of sickness and of encroaching death. "I will praise Him when He gives you some rest."

Mary Margaret sighed. "Such anger. You should have a sword at your side." Her cackle broke down into fitful coughing. Bernice had tissues waiting for her sputum. "Pull me up."

She was bald now, her face sunken by age and by ravaging illness. She wore a baby blue satin bed jacket, a present from the women on the street who knew her. It was a sickening color, but she loved it just the same. Her dark eyes looked enormous in that cadaverous face that seemed all skull. Long ago, Bernice had had all mirrors removed from this room and the adjacent bathroom.

Mary Margaret's face scrunched up so that she looked like a wizened doll that had been abandoned by her owner. "It must have been terribly difficult for her, to come here."

"I think it was more difficult for her to do nothing. Also, she knows we love her. And now she knows we can help her." Bernice kissed Mary Margaret's cold forehead. "Those things are what she needs most."

As Bernice arranged the pillows behind her, Mary Margaret said, "It's happened. We have our chance, don't we?"

"Yes."

Mary Margaret put a clawlike hand out, tapped a horny fingertip against the back of Bernice's hand. "This is what we have prayed for, and yet you do not seem happy."

"Oh, I am." Bernice brushed a thread of hair off her forehead. "But I am also worried."

"As long as you're in the mood, worry about my food."

Bernice brought over the tray and, setting it down, perched on the edge of the bed. "Are you hungry?"

"Not particularly. But I need to eat, don't I?"

Bernice commenced to feed her, dipping a small chased-silver spoon in a mélange of steamed vegetables, depositing them into Mary Margaret's mouth.

"I was dreaming when you came in."

"I'm sorry if I disturbed you."

"Oh, you didn't. In my condition, time and place have collided. I dreamt I was a child, and in my dream I knew I was in this room and that you were coming. Odd, isn't it, that the closer one gets to death the more one understands the nature of time. It doesn't exist. Not really. At least, it doesn't for me. It's like a wheel that revolves constantly. What happened two years ago is no less clear than what transpired two minutes ago. And what happened twenty years ago—forty—is just as clear. They're all on the wheel, you see, and it keeps revolving."

Mary Margaret closed her eyes while she ate. Chewing was an effort for her, Bernice knew; perhaps she could concentrate better this way.

"I was a child again, in this dream," she continued. "Except that it wasn't a dream. Not really. I *was* a child again, far from this decaying body." Her eyes snapped open. Perhaps she wanted to be sure that Bernice was paying attention. She had always been full of these kinds of tricks. "Do you believe that?"

"Yes, Mary Margaret, I do."

Satisfied with this exchange, Mary Margaret accepted another spoonful of cauliflower and peas and closed her eyes, chewing slowly and methodically like a soldier trudging through virgin jungle.

"But as this child, I knew everything I know now. It was so extraordinary! To be so young and so knowledgeable. Can you imagine it?"

There were times Mary Margaret asked questions to which no answer was appropriate. From long and intimate experience, Bernice knew this was one such. She fed her another spoonful and kept quiet.

"No one could imagine it unless they had experienced it, and that's the truth," Mary Margaret said. "God works in mysterious ways. You see, I have my recompense for my pain. I can roam through life without restrictions, and I can find God in all the little places one never has the time to look when one lives one's life from day to day."

She had stopped eating for the moment, and her eyes were open, shining very clear, as Bernice remembered them before they had become perpetually clouded by pain.

"You see, there is faith and then there is *faith*," Mary Margaret whispered. "Oh, one's faith in God never wavers. Never. But it is so thrilling to actually *see* His handiwork and to experience all over again how one was shaped by His hand and His wisdom."

She was still for a moment, resting, and in that moment the clarity in her eyes was again occluded by pain.

"Mmm," she whispered. "No more food for me. No matter what you give me it tastes like library paste."

Bernice put down the spoon and wiped Mary Margaret's lips. She knew better than to argue with the older woman even at this late stage.

"Lest you think my mind has been wandering," Mary Margaret said abruptly, "this is all in aid of saying no matter how much you worry, no matter what disasters befall—and there *will* be setbacks, of that you may be certain—you must persevere. God is with us. It is by His will that the Order of Donà di Piave was founded. It was by His will that Donà di Piave was obliged to take up the sword. The doge of Venice sent Donà di Piave and her nun soldiers to guard the Sacred Heart of Santa Maria when the Serene Republic was under siege by Charles VIII of France in 1495. After the soldiers were wiped out, it was Donà di Piave who received a divine vision. God directed her and her fellow nuns to take up the soldiers' weapons and defend the Sacred Heart themselves.

"Thirteen years later, when Pope Julius II, Louis XII of France, Ferdinand of Aragon, and the Emperor Maximilian formed the League of Cambrai to greedily carve up the Venetian territory on the mainland, Donà di Piave and her order were able to judiciously apply the influence she and her adherents had amassed from the shadows, the ragged edges of history where women have resided and, it seems, are destined to remain, to divide and defeat Venice's enemies."

Mary Margaret smiled. "Serenissima's doge and council

took credit for the diplomatic coup, but we know the truth of it. That it was the women of our order who changed history by applying pressure in a French monarch's bed, an emperor's boudoir, in a pope's ear. It was the order who trained Lucrezia Borgia, nearly all the wives of the Mocenigo family, so influential it produced no less than seven doges, along with uncountable other women notable only in select secret circles for their influence in political intrigue.

"We inveigled national policy, inveighed successfully against our enemies, getting the regal men of pomp and power, the dim-witted and the inbred, to do our bidding. Yes, we developed to a high art the business of power by proxy. We learned our lesson well: that the direct approach is, for us, forbidden. But there are so many other ways to apply influence at which women excel."

Mary Margaret stroked the coverlet as she spoke in the same slow rhythm by which she chanted her Latin prayers. "Men have no use for artful flattery and so cannot detect it even when it floats right under their nose. They'd much rather see it as the truth, especially when it comes from someone with a pretty face and an enticing body. That is why we take no vow of celibacy in our order, though this omission is kept secret from every archbishop to whom we report. God gave us certain tools by which we may accomplish from the shadows what we could not do in the light."

She was quiet for some time, and Bernice could hear her breathing as stentoriously as a grandfather clock counting time. Bernice began to weep, even though she had promised herself that she would reserve her tears for when she was alone.

She felt the old, dry hand on hers. "Why do you cry, my child?"

Bernice's hands clamped into fists hard as steel. "It is so unfair, this suffering."

"Spoken like a true warrior. But swords are not always the answer. Faith is."

"Faith." Bernice said it as if it left a bad taste in her mouth.

"Listen to me." Mary Margaret struggled to sit up higher, her satin bed jacket rustling like an insect's wings. "A person who serves when treated kindly by God is no retainer. But one who serves when God is seeming heartless and unreasonable has fulfilled her purpose."

Bernice bowed her head, willing her tears to cease.

"Now tell me why you are worried," Mary Margaret asked briskly.

Bernice took a deep breath, let it all out before she began. "I will come after you, to continue the order's work. But who will come after me? There are no candidates among the nuns. Not a one."

Mary Margaret's face was set in stone. "That is the least of your problems now." Her horny finger tapped the back of Bernice's hand again. "Stop trying to do everything yourself. Remember, think only of the task at hand and you will be able to accomplish anything. And let God do His part. You will see. He will bring you your successor, just as He brought you to me."

"How will I know her, Mary Margaret?"

For the longest time, the old woman said nothing. Her eyes had again gone out of focus, and Bernice knew she was seeing events on the wheel of life.

"You will know her," she said at last, "because her hands will be covered in blood."

During the time Bernice had been reciting this story of Camille, the sun had gone in, and now the turret room was emblazoned in a deep, jewel-toned dusk that seemed to seep into every corner of the room. A mockingbird began its caroling song, the notes piercing even the stone walls and stained glass.

"So the Goldonis endow the convent," Jaqui said. She gave Bernice a quizzical look. "Enrico Goldoni and my father, John, do not see eye to eye."

"To put it more bluntly, they're enemies," Bernice said.

"Then why am I, a Leonforte, here?"

Bernice smiled. "It is as I said. You are special, part of the chosen. In that regard, the enmity between Goldoni and Leonforte is irrelevant." She took Jaqui's hands in hers and Jaqui could feel the heat of her inner power. "On the other hand, the Goldonis' role here is not well known." Her piercing blue eyes bore into Jaqui's. "Nor should it be."

"I understand," Jaqui said after a time. "I will tell no

one." Somehow, saying this made Jaqui feel at once closer to Bernice, and she liked that very much.

In the small silence that followed, Bernice gave a small smile. "I suppose you're wondering how I came to know about you. Your grandfather Caesare and I are old friends."

"Friends? Does he know about the Goldonis' involvement in the Sacred Heart of Santa Maria?"

"Oh, yes. But I can assure you he was the only one. You see, Jaqui, your grandfather is an extraordinary man. He was one of the very few down through the ages who has understood the role we have played. He wanted only to help us. That was why he talked to me about you."

"What?"

Bernice nodded. "Yes. He spoke to me about you many times."

"Grandpa Caesare did that?" Jaqui was stunned. She knew the old man had loved her, but she had assumed that, like all Italian grandfathers, his attention had been focused on his grandsons.

"He had his eye on you as you grew up. He was well versed in the power of the order."

Jaqui looked to Bernice for some time. "So now you think God has sent me to you, just as He sent you to Mary Margaret."

Bernice said nothing for the longest time, sunk so deeply in thought was she. "I believe what my heart tells me," she said at length. "Lies and false visions come in all forms and guises. But you had the vision of Donà di Piave, just as I did when I came here, and every beat of my heart confirms the truth in God's order of things." Her eyes focused on Jaqui and she smiled. "That is my roundabout way of saying, yes, God is the messenger here. I believe that with every fiber of my being." Her hands lifted, then fell back into her lap. "But experience also tells me that what I feel is meaningless—if you don't feel it, as well."

"But I do," Jaqui blurted. "I mean I've felt *something* from the moment I stepped through the front gate. What is it? Is it Donà di Piave speaking to me or is it God touching me with His hand?"

Bernice shook her head. "I can help you with many things, my dear, but not this. You must discover the nature of the *presence* for yourself because it is different for everyone." She looked deeply into Jaqui's eyes. "Is this something you think might interest you?"

She said this as if she were asking Jaqui if she'd like to come with her for a lovely evening stroll, but Jaqui knew better. Pursuing the nature of the *presence* would be a lifetime commitment. In a sense, the enormity of it terrified her. And yet, she felt a curious kind of elation she had never before known. Wasn't this kind of enigma just what she had been searching for? It was something unconnected with the dull and frightful world into which she had been born, from which she had been desperately trying to flee almost all her young life.

"Yes," she said in a hoarse whisper. "It interests me greatly."

"Ah, greatly," Bernice said with a nod. "That is good, because from the first I have known that you are—as I am—an agent of change." She offered her hand, and when Jaqui took it, she allowed the charismatic warmth to transfer itself to the girl.

"There," Bernice said. "The compact has begun."

What Jaqui always thought about her brother Michael was this: that there was a wolf inside him, eating at him, desperate to get out. And it was this desperation that frightened her. She could admire his innate intelligence, she could applaud his decision to keep his distance from the family business that had already ensnared Caesare, but she recognized the danger of this beast inside him and it made her tremble.

And yet.

What was it about Michael that made him seem to her as if he were a kindred spirit? All alone in the night, she dreamed of him. In her dream, they stood in a glade of a vast woods. All around them was chittering darkness where beasts of prey prowled. The glade shone whitely in moonlight, but the dense canopy of treetops would not let the light penetrate the woods.

Michael stood tall and handsome and absolutely unafraid, but she could feel her terror like a second skin, crawling over her like a skein being drawn by an invisible insect.

Michael, she cried. *Help me, I'm afraid!*

He smiled at her with that peculiar, goofy smile he directed only at her.

Michael! she screamed, more loudly.

But he could not hear her, and now she realized that she was mute. She heard the rhythmic liturgical chanting of Latin prayers, and she grabbed Michael's hand and fled with him into the darkness of the woods.

And in that darkness, she could hear the twin beatings of their hearts, synchronized and harmonized, like the choral voices of the liturgical song. Deeper and deeper into the dangerous woods she drew him until both glade and moonlight were but a memory. Why? Why? What was she seeking?

She awoke knowing they were about to be attacked, and the thought in her head, revolving like a wheel: I've done this to him. It's all my fault.

This dream was alive and glowing in her mind that hot June night in 1961 when she found Michael up on the roof of their apartment building in Ozone Park. Grandpa had given him a telescope, the perfect present for a boy longing to outpace the boundaries of his limited world. But then Grandpa always seemed to know just what his grandchildren wanted most. On her last birthday, Valentine's Day, when she had turned nineteen, he had given her a book on the birth of Italy. For Caesare's birthday, he had chosen a gun.

There was a peculiar kind of fever coming off Michael that night, as if he, too, possessed that second skin beneath which a hitherto unknown person was thirsting to emerge. That night, he was by turns avid and unresponsive, as if a central question in his mind had not yet been resolved.

She had evinced an interest in the stars even though they seemed as remote and dead as Latin. But even Latin, when sung in chant, possessed a certain formal beauty that the stars, in their coldness, could not. They were far too alien for her. Still, she was desperate to talk and she did not know how else to prolong her presence up on the roof. Michael liked to be alone; perhaps he even thrived in his solitude. This was another element about him that frightened her. Solitude was too demanding; it required a certain concentration she was only now beginning to explore with Bernice in her studies at Santa Maria.

She had been so stupid that night! She had gotten so close to him, she could feel all her defenses crumbling. She longed to confide in him, to tell him about the extraordinary journey on which she was about to embark, but at the last instant, she had wrenched herself back from the brink. What had she been thinking of? Living with secrets was now an integral part of her life. If she could break her vow to Bernice and the order so easily, then she had made a terrible mistake and must abandon her training now.

But she knew she would do no such thing. The order was for her. It was her destiny to replace Bernice, she knew that as surely as she drew each breath. But what was it about Michael that made her want to confide in him?

That night, in the intimacy of the rooftop encounter with him, in the aftermath of the subsequent tragedy, she came to know. Seeing how he responded so instinctively, so much more *intelligently* than Caesare did to Grandpa's murder, convinced her that the beast in him had been released by some mysterious alchemy. Perhaps being an eyewitness to Grandpa's death had given birth to the creature of the second skin lurking beneath the surface. And standing with him in the bloody courtyard while the flashbulbs lit the walls of the buildings with their lurid light, she understood everything. Her dream and reality merged to form an entirely new reality. She was standing with him in the darkness of the chittering woods, and she knew why she had taken his hand, had run with him from the softness of the moonlight into the dangerous dark. It was this very beast, so terrifying to her, that drew her to him.

Caesare, on the other hand, was an open book. He was scary to everyone on the street, but he wasn't to her, even though he yelled at her. Often, she suspected it was because he knew she could see right through him. Understanding Caesare was simple: he adored their mother and was almost destroyed by his conflicting feelings about their father. It was typical of him that he conveniently ignored their mother's failings—her extreme passivity, the long-suffering mask that had become part of her. She thought she was nurturing her family, but all she was doing was stifling them. Her passivity threatened to make them passive or—as in Caesare's case—excessively violent.

If only Johnny had not abandoned them to his wild schemes, Jaqui thought, for in her heart she was certain that her wayward father had found himself a woman younger and prettier than Mama and was living with her somewhere warm and tropical. How else to explain the rumors and innuendos of great humiliation? How else to explain the fact that Grandfather Caesare never spoke of him? It was as if Johnny Leonforte never existed. If Grandfather knew his son's dreadful secret, he kept it locked away inside his heart.

And what of Mama? Did even she know what had happened to her husband, whether he was alive or dead? Jaqui had asked herself those questions so often that when one long and dreary afternoon she discovered her mother sitting on their big four-poster bed, weeping, she had no inkling that the answers were merely a hairbreadth away.

It was a year before she entered the Convent of the Sacred Heart of Santa Maria, and Mama had started when Jaqui came in the room and slid something behind her into the bedclothes. Thinking at first that it was some kind of game, Jaqui had scrambled across the bed and, making an end run around Mama, had snatched from beneath the coverlet an opened letter.

"No!" Mama had cried with such unexpected ferocity that Jaqui allowed her to snatch it back. Mama immediately crumpled it between reddened hands.

"Who is the letter from, Mama? Tell me."

"I can't." Mama's face was filled with a kind of anguish Jaqui had only read about in books.

With the teenager's preternatural sense of emotion, she blurted the first thing that entered her mind: "It's from Johnny."

Even as she said it, it sounded absurd. Johnny Leonforte, if he was still alive, was at this moment no doubt sunning himself on some beach with a blonde with big breasts and—

But then something that was odd about the scene hit her. "It *is* from Johnny."

"I wish you'd call him Papa." Now Mama's eyes were filled with tears. Jaqui, who had become frightened without quite knowing why, kneed across the bed to wrap her arms around Mama's shaking shoulders.

"My little girl." Mama wept. "You see too much. You know too much." She shook her head. "It's not right, you're all I have to confide in."

Jaqui put her head close to her mother's. "Johnny's alive?"

"Swear to me, Jaqui. Swear before God and the Virgin Mary that you will tell no one."

"But why not?"

"Swear!" Again Jaqui felt that unexpected force of will from her mother, and she swore even while she was wondering from what deep well that force sprang.

"He's alive." Mama said it in a sigh, and Jaqui, her heart unaccountably breaking, used the pad of her thumb to wipe the tears from her mother's eyes. "No, darling, leave them. It's good for me to cry. So much feeling bottled up inside for so long—it's not healthy. Ask your grandfather."

"He knows Johnny's alive?"

Mama nodded. "He knows everything. Every detail. But don't ever ask him to admit it. He'd rather slit his own throat. And he'd be terribly angry with me if he knew I'd told you."

Jaqui clutched her mother's meaty shoulder. "But what *happened?* Where *is* Johnny?"

Mama had put her head down, defeated. "I don't know. His letters used to come from Japan, but now the postmarks are from here, cities all around the country. But I don't think he's in any of them."

"Is he coming back?"

"I don't know." The whisper was so low, Jaqui had to lean closer to hear it.

"Mama, why did he go away?" She took her mother by the shoulders and shook her. "Why did he leave us?"

Mama was shaking her head as if she were a dripping dog coming in out of the rain.

"Mama!" Jaqui screamed, and her mother shook as if jolted by lightning.

"He—you know your father was in the Army during the war. Afterward, he—stayed on in Japan for a time." Mama was sobbing, but Jaqui felt no inclination to stop her. She felt as if she were standing in a drought-dry stream bed looking up at a long-awaited torrent of water about to inundate her. "He tried to do something. It was business, so don't ask me what, I was never told. It was clever, it was stupid. It would have made the entire Leonforte family, Grandfather said."

None of this made any sense to Jaqui. "What happened?"

"I don't know. Events fell out the wrong way or someone was more clever—in any case, it was a terrible disaster from which your grandfather never quite recovered. Neither did the family."

So the rumors and innuendos were true—at least part of them, Jaqui thought. "But what does it matter? Why isn't Johnny here where he's needed?"

Mama's head came up and her bloodshot eyes looked bleak. She tried to smile, stroking her daughter's gleaming hair. "You're so beautiful, you remind me so much of—"

"Mama!"

"It was your grandfather's wish, that's all I can say."

"You mean Grandfather banished him for life?"

"For life?" Mama's eyes had gone vague. "I don't know. It's business and that's the end of it. I have accepted it and now so must you."

After she had burned the letter—she would not let Jaqui read it—Mama felt better. She went about her household chores as if nothing had happened. And that night, when Grandfather Caesare returned home, to Jaqui's astonishment, Mama greeted him at the front door with her customary warmth and effusiveness.

"When the hell is Pop coming back?" Caesare said to Jaqui the morning after Grandfather Caesare's funeral as he drove her to Santa Maria. "If he was here now, I wouldn't be havin' t'make a deal with Uncle Alphonse."

Jaqui was so astonished that he had confided in her that she did something stupid—she told him the truth: "Johnny's never coming back. Face it, he left us, Mama, you, me, Mick—all of us. He just walked out. Why should he come back now?"

Which was when Caesare hit her.

Afterward, she could see that he had had no other choice.

In Caesare's black-and-white world, Johnny was not merely his father, but the head of the family, his idol—not to mention a don who commanded a whole other kind of respect and loyalty.

They sat in silence the rest of the way to Astoria. Jaqui was acutely aware of her flaming cheek. It was the heat she felt, not the pain. And when the car drew up in front of Santa Maria, she was so humiliated she could not summon up the Christian kindness to offer him her other cheek and forgive him. Bernice would, no doubt, have been disappointed in her.

But, later, she understood so clearly the lesson she had learned that day. The truth, like everything else in life, had its place. It was not to be dispensed indiscriminately like cannoli at a street fair because it could cause as much pain and suffering as a well-placed lie.

She had been halfway out the door of his car when he said to her, "This is the last time you go to Santa Maria."

She turned back to him, stunned. "What?"

"I'm only letting you go this time because of Mama."

Jaqui shook her head as if she could not believe her ears. "What are you saying?"

"Fuck you mean?" he snapped. "Santa Maria is in Goldoni territory."

"So what?"

His patience gave out. "So we fuckin' hate the Goldonis!" he shouted with such ferocity that Jaqui flinched.

"I'm not involved in your stupid vendettas," she said after a moment. Her heart was beating so fast she was quite certain it would burst through her chest. "This is a *convent*. A place of God."

"Maybe so, but the Goldonis have made it theirs." Caesare sat back with that self-satisfied expression he got when he knew something you didn't. "They give a ton of money to Santa Maria's. Christ, it wouldn't even be in existence today if it wasn't for the Goldonis."

"Don't talk like that here," she said evenly. "It's sacred ground."

He stared at her for a minute. "You really believe in all this, don't you?"

"Yes, I do."

He launched himself forward on the seat. "But you're a Leonforte, damn it!"

"Not inside Santa Maria's. Don't you get it? That's why I want to be there."

He threw up his arms, his big hands banging off the inside of the car's roof. "Those nuns!" He shook his head. "Forget the nuns for a minute and use your head that's supposed to be so smart. The Goldonis will never let you forget who you are."

"You're wrong."

Caesare sighed. "Mom made a mistake bringing you here. Jaqui, this comes straight from the top. From Uncle Alphonse. He wants you back home."

They stared at each other for a long time, and who could say what images of their father ran through their minds.

At last, Jaqui said, "I don't care."

"Well, you'd better care," he said, returning to the well-worn role of unthinking bully.

"Why?" She slid off the seat and out of the car. "You're the one who wants to be like him, not me."

"Hey, Sis, you can't run away!" he shouted at her through the window. "You were born a Leonforte and you'll die a Leonforte! Goddamn it, there's no escape! Not at Santa Maria's or anywhere else!"

Jaqui was lost in prayer. It was a prayer for the dying, a prayer of the order that had been taught her by Bernice because it did not exist in Scripture.

Light like liquid honey filtered lazily through the chapel's stained-glass windows. Tall and narrow as spears, there was about them a certain medieval quality and more: a hint of fortification, an ancient garrison's slitted window. The chapel held all sound as if it were sacred, preserving even the most minute echo.

Jaqui, praying in Latin, as was the habit of the order, formed the words and felt as clumsy as a drunken bluejay. Often, as now, she was struck with the awesome asceticism of the life she had chosen. Or had it chosen her? This was her fear, that she had lost all control over her life. Which, of course, she had. As Bernice so accurately pointed out, one entered the order ceding all control to God.

Jaqui prayed, and as she did so, doubt crept in. She knew—because Bernice had told her—that doubt was the work of the devil. Belief in God was the Shining Path, but her fear was that that divine belief was a sham, nothing more than blind, unthinking obedience, and Jaqui hated anything blind and unthinking.

She tried not to hate her father, she tried not to hate her brother Caesare for being blind and unthinking about her and their father and the world at large. She knew hate was the work of the devil; that if she hated she was not worthy of being in the order, not worthy of Bernice's trust, not worthy of God. To hate was like dying inside, and yet she could not help what she felt. These were evil men and in her heart she knew it. God could never smile upon these men of her family as, surely, He smiled upon Michael.

She was not pure; but Bernice had told her purity was not a component of human nature. Purity was for the saints and for God. The object—surely the only real object in submitting to God's will—was to strive for that purity.

Jaqui, her head bent, kneeling within the sight of God, felt His presence sweep through the chapel like the rush of wings across treetops. She felt a warmth and closed her eyes. It was as if a great hand squeezed her shoulder, and she was reassured.

Perhaps Bernice was right—perhaps she was destined for great things.

In the turning of the solstice, with the coming of spring, Jaqui met Paul Chiaramonte at the small bakery on one corner of the block in Astoria dominated by Santa Maria. Mrs. Paglia was gathering up six loaves of bread for the convent when Paul walked in. Jaqui, who was counting out the money on Mrs. Paglia's crumb-strewn glass countertop, looked up to see a dark-faced, dark-eyed young man regarding her.

He sauntered to the counter with the exaggerated air of a drunkard or a kid wanting to act older than he was. He did not reek of liquor and he could not take his eyes off her. Jaqui smiled at him and he looked as if he would faint. His knees seemed to buckle and he clutched the edge of the counter with the desperation of a drowning man.

Mrs. Paglia, ever the worrier, eyed him and said, "Paulie, are you okay?"

"Sure, Mrs. Paglia," Paul croaked. "I could use a drinka water, though."

She nodded, put Jaqui's bags down, and bustled into the back.

Paul grinned at Jaqui, said, "Hi! My name's Paul Chiaramonte."

She extended her hand. "Jaqui Leonforte."

Paul seemed so stunned he did not know what to do with her hand. He continued to stare at her as if she were made of porcelain. Then, as if regaining consciousness, he grasped her hand, pumped it twice, then let it go as if it had been a hot poker. He seemed disappointed he had done that.

"I live around heah," he said. "You?"

She shook her head. "Ozone Park. But in a few weeks I'm going to be staying at Santa Maria."

He goggled at her. "You're going to be a nun?"

"Is that so odd?"

"Oh, God." He seemed so crestfallen. "I haven't even gotten to know you yet."

At that moment, Mrs. Paglia returned with a glass of water. Paul drank and Jaqui paid for her bread.

"Nice meeting you," she murmured, and could not help giggling as he almost choked on the water.

She also could not help thinking about her effect on him. He was no kindred spirit. She did not feel drawn to him in the same way she did Michael. She and Michael shared the same emotional wavelength; that kind of intimacy she did not believe could be repeated.

But she felt something else for Paul. Jaqui had never had a boyfriend, had never, in fact, gone out on a date. Boys bored her with their groping sweaty hands and their lethargic brains. Michael's brain was agile and unpredictable and she loved him for it. This was, she supposed, why she had not tried to stop him from going after Grandpa's murderer. She could not in any way condone his thirst for vengeance, but at least she could understand it. Nietzsche wrote that the greatest danger to mankind is that he will choke on compassion.

This was, in a way, what Bernice had taught her: that

valor was a matter of fanaticism. In the end, compassion had been an inadequate defense of the Sacred Heart of Santa Maria. Therefore, God had shown Donà di Piave and her warrior-nuns another way. They took up the swords of the soldiers and had beaten back the enemy. And then God had shown them another way: what Bernice liked to call the diplomacy of fanaticism. "But our own kind of fanaticism," Bernice said. "In those days females needed fanaticism in order to rise above their traditional lot in life, to gain the strength to free themselves from the bondage of drudgery. But God showed Donà di Piave a divine truth: that fanaticism is inherently dangerous because it can so easily blind the faithful to facts."

When God struck the soldier's bloody sword from Donà di Piave's fist when the Sacred Heart of Santa Maria had successfully been defended, He ordered her never to take it up again. God blinded her for the space of thirty seconds, and in that time He showed her the path she dare not take. Fanatics, God revealed to her, are blinded to the truths all around them because they are fixated on the one truth by which they set their sails.

In light of all Bernice had taught her, it did not seem odd to Jaqui that Michael had become something of a hero when he killed the two men responsible for Grandpa's murder. On the other hand, she knew Michael could not long tolerate notoriety in the world he had come to loathe, and she knew, deep in her soul, that he would soon be going far away.

Paul, too, seemed different, though not in the same way. Thus, to her utter astonishment, she found herself standing outside the bakery, waiting for him to emerge. When he did, he seemed as astounded as she. He carried her bags to the convent and, after she had deposited them in the kitchen, was still waiting for her outside the iron gates.

They walked together in the gathering twilight. Cars passed by, their headlights sweeping past them in brief golden flares. Streetlights dropped puddles of bluish light on the pavement.

They spoke very little, of nothing and everything. Jaqui had no desire to open herself up to him in the way she did with Michael. Besides, that was a kind of sacred relationship that she would not violate, even with Bernice. Her desire for Paul was like an acute hunger in the pit of her stomach. And, though it was an entirely new sensation for her, she suspected it was foolish for her to attempt to satisfy it. Within weeks, she would be locked away from Michael's world—and Paul's—within the white stone walls of Santa Maria. She had pledged herself to the order, and far from causing her to doubt that vow, her feelings for Paul only made them stronger.

And yet she wanted him. It was foolish because it was so selfish. He was smitten with her now, but in time he would get over it. To go deeper than this innocent walk, to explore this longing in her lower belly, and then to turn her back on him was more than selfish. It would be cruel. But hadn't she already warned him about her intentions? Yes, yes. And still he took her hand, gazed into her eyes with such naked hunger that her knees turned to jelly.

She had never been naked in front of a man. As a small child, she had run naked with her brothers, but that had stopped long, long ago. And once in a while they would catch a glimpse of one another through the steamy bathroom they shared. But, anyway, that was different, all curiosity.

There was none of this liquid heat she felt as Paul opened the buttons of her dress, none of this breathless anticipation as her stiff fingers fumbled at his belt. But when his hands pushed aside her bra and closed over her breasts, it was she who almost fainted from the sensation. Her eyes fluttered closed and her body went limp in his arms.

He carried her through the damp grass of his backyard to the toolshed, kicking open the door. The sharp tang of well-oiled steel mingled with his own scent, making her nostrils flare. She gave a tiny moan and kissed the skin of his bare shoulder.

He loomed above her like a god. The experience, so unearthly up until now, assumed a supraclarity she would carry with her for the rest of her days. He did not press down on her, he did not fumble and hurt her with his powerful hands. Instead, he waited for her to reach up to him, to bring his heat down to her quivering flesh.

He did not enter her at once, but played with her, kissing

her all over—on her forehead, her cheeks, her eyelids, her lips, his tongue slipping between her partly opened lips. She panted into his mouth, arching her breasts against him.

When his mouth enclosed a nipple, her thighs rippled open, and when he slipped to her belly, licking her there, she gasped, kneading the powerful muscles of his shoulders.

"Oh, no!" she cried when he reached her sex, but she had no idea what she meant by that. He opened her with his lips and tongue, and she smelled the roses from Santa Maria, as if her petals were giving off the same rich scent. She was immersed in sensation she had not been able to imagine. She felt a growing heaviness between her thighs, spiraling outward through her whole body. It was as if they had been transported off the earth and were lying on a planet whose gravity drew them down, sucked them inward to its glowing core.

He slipped into her and she wanted him so completely she twined her arms around him, bringing him to her, lifting her thighs as he tore past her ribbon of membrane, and then he was inside.

Her eyes flew open and she licked the sweat from his forehead. Her eyes, big as moons, were all pupil in the darkness of the shed. She saw rakes and pruners, hedge clippers, a metal can of three-in-one oil, two pairs of soiled garden gloves, piles of wooden stakes, bags of lawn seed and Hollytone, and these became like stars, like constellations floating in a mist of ecstasy. She wanted him with every fiber of her being, right now, right here, and it was happening. Afterward, she wept for the exquisite beauty of it and for the loss, because she knew she would never have it again.

Jaqui knelt in the chapel, waiting. It was almost midnight. Outside, a full moon rode in a clear sky. Its light fell through the long, slender stained-glass window, painting pale patterns on the stone floor and wooden pews. The altar before which Jaqui knelt was draped in purple velvet upon which sat a chalice of chased silver. She could hear chanting.

She was dressed in robes of white linen with an overdress of heavy black muslin, on which was stitched a cross in gold thread. It was an exact replica of the garments worn by Donà di Piave centuries ago. The last time it was worn was when Bernice had knelt before a similar altar to be initiated by Mary Margaret.

Jaqui, head bowed, eyes closed in prayer, felt Bernice enter the chapel. She carried with her the broadsword of Donà di Piave. Bernice took her place and began the Latin prayer. She poured sacrificial wine into the chalice and, as she recited another prayer, anointed the tip of the sword with the wine. She wiped it clean with a white cloth, then held the newly stained material aloft.

"Here is the blood of those who died in the service of the order. We remember and honor them," Bernice intoned. "Here is the blood of Donà di Piave. We honor and cherish her memory." She carefully folded the cloth three times and placed it beneath the silver chalice.

Then she stepped down off the dais of the altar and stood before Jaqui. "Sister Marie Rose, you have been chosen by God, you have been touched by Donà di Piave to continue her work in God's name." She brought the flat of the blade onto Jaqui's left shoulder and let it rest there. "Swear before God that you will serve His will wherever it may lead you."

"I swear," Jaqui murmured.

Bernice moved the flat of the blade to her right shoulder. "Swear that you will serve the order. Swear that you will do whatever is required of you."

"I swear."

Bernice moved the flat of the blade to the top of her head. "Swear that your life, your mind, and your heart belong to the order and to God."

"I swear."

Bernice removed the blade, and she and Jaqui recited a Latin prayer. Then Bernice bade Jaqui rise and, grasping her shoulders, kissed her on first one cheek, then the other.

Bernice's eyes were shining with the light of God. "It is done," she said.

Of course, at the last moment it threatened to all come undone. It was her fault, Jaqui knew that, but it was a kind of divine intervention, as well, as Bernice said. She had said her good-byes to Michael, who had come to see her, as she knew he must, before he shipped off to God only knew where. Jaqui was unsurprised by his leave-taking—or that he was taking the radical step of joining the military. He needed to get as far away from Ozone Park as he could. Besides, John had been in the military during World War II, stationed in Tokyo. It would not surprise her if Michael ended up there, as well.

But the farewell proved far more difficult than she had imagined. Michael was choked with emotion. He would have loved taking her with him, so that they could continue their journey to far-off climes together. But that was Michael for you, always wanting his cake and eating it, too.

She was far too happy for him to immediately feel the loss. But he seemed so melancholy she knew that despite his facade he was missing Grandpa with an almost palpable pain. He had been the closest to the old man, had understood him far better than either of Grandpa's sons. Perhaps, though, that was the way of the world.

She was also happy to see him go because he would not be around when she died. She did not think she could bear knowing that he was standing above her grave as they lowered her coffin into the ground. She had almost withered and died to see the look on his face when they had stood over Grandpa's sprawled body in the bloody courtyard. She never wanted to see that expression again.

As for Caesare, they never spoke again after the incident in the car. It was just as well. He had never cared to take the time to understand her. Caesare had inherited too much of his father. He felt about women as he did about furniture: they were useful when and where they were needed.

But it was her one lubricious evening with Paul Chiaramonte that almost undid everything. She and Bernice had been plotting her death ever since Caesare had made this threat to her. It seemed excessively extreme—at first, all Jaqui could think about was the pain she would cause Mama and Michael—but Bernice, ever the warrior-nun, convinced her that only an extreme solution would have any chance of success.

Though Caesare had not come back to Santa Maria, Jaqui's uncle had. Alphonse, annoyed at having to come all the way east from his home in San Francisco, had pushed himself into Bernice's chambers as if assaulting the very gates of heaven. But, in the end, he had been defeated.

"It is Jaqui's choice to be here," Bernice had told him with all the fierce determination at her disposal. "And it is God's will. Neither you nor anyone can take that away from her." The divine charisma was upon her, and Alphonse, usually so clever and forceful, could do nothing but retreat to the street, where he climbed into his limousine without a backward glance, returning to the airport from which he had come.

But Bernice was not fooled. "You are a Leonforte," she told Jaqui, eerily echoing Caesare's phrase. "Your family will never forget you are here—and never forgive. There is only one way to put an end to it. You must die."

As it happened, there was a young nun, Sister Agnes, at the convent who was dying. The doctors could do nothing for her, and rather than being left to the inconsiderate ministrations of hospital personnel, she had requested that she live out her remaining days in a place of God's radiance. Of course, Bernice had acquiesced.

"She is not so dissimilar to you in physique or in features," Bernice said. "Though no one would ever mistake you for sisters, still there is enough of a resemblance for our purposes."

"But—"

"No buts. I have discussed the entire matter with her. She has no family of her own and she has agreed to everything. It is God's will."

Jaqui, after speaking to Sister Agnes herself, had reluctantly agreed. But in the deepest recesses of her mind she wondered whether the plan was indeed God's will—or merely part of Bernice's byzantine design.

She and Bernice continued to discuss the plot until they believed they had covered every angle, aspect, and contingency. But, as Mary Margaret had liked to say, God dislikes plots and so does His best to unravel them in one way or another.

The way He contrived to unravel this one was to make sure that Paul Chiaramonte was on his way to the bakery when the car that was meant to hit Jaqui came hurtling down the street. She had made certain that she had been coming back from errands to the greengrocer and the bakery at precisely the same time each day for the past six months.

The day of the staged accident, however, she had been at the corner window of the convent that had an unobstructed

view of the scene. In her place was the person they had
secretly hired to dress up like her—a stunt woman who got
"killed" every day of the week in the incomprehensible
world of films and television.

Intent on carrying out the complex timing of the plot, the
stuntwoman had not seen Paul until it was too late. He had
cried out, she had turned, and for a split instant he was
staring straight at her.

Dear God! No one was supposed to see her face.

Then he was leaping toward her, knocking her sideways,
dear Lord, the car striking him, twisting him in midair so
that even from a distance Jaqui imagined that she heard the
bones snap.

It was Bernice who took care of most of the arrangements—Jaqui's mother being too overcome with grief. It was
she who spoke to the police—the beat cops who first responded and then the plainclothes detectives, all of whom
she knew personally. She spoke to the coroner, and to the
funeral director, making absolutely certain that the coffin's
lid remained closed, hinting to the world at large in hushed
tones that the face had been mangled beyond the repair of
even the finest mortician.

It all went smoothly, as Bernice had predicted.

Afterward, following the funeral, when the world believed
that Jaqui was really and truly dead—when Sister Agnes's
body was buried in the coffin the Leonfortes had picked
out—was when it almost came undone. Bernice assured
Jaqui that Paul was receiving the best care. The convent had
anonymously sent the money to pay for his operations, and
it all seemed to be working as they had plotted.

Then one day Bernice told Jaqui that Paul had been asking questions about the accident.

"I don't think he believes you're really dead," Bernice said.

"Leave it alone," Jaqui counseled. "Do nothing."

"But he could cause problems. He's saying he saw someone else, that it wasn't you who got hit by the car. He thinks
there's a conspiracy of some kind."

"It's just a reaction," Jaqui insisted. "I know him. He was
almost killed himself, and now he has come out of the hospital a changed person. He *wants* to believe, that's all."

But, when she was left alone, her resolve failed her and she was consumed with guilt. Look what her one evening of bliss had created. Paul knew what he knew. He had seen the stunt-woman's face, had known something was wrong with the entire picture. No wonder he was conjuring up conspiracies.

She hoped to God that he would leave it alone, as she had told Bernice. Perhaps, as the sense of trauma faded, his memories of the moment would become less reliable until doubts would creep in and he would begin to suspect that he saw only what he wanted to see. Yes. His troublesome questions would soon subside and he would get on with his life. He would forget all about her.

But alone in her night, the question returned again and again to haunt her: what if he didn't? They had gone to so much time and trouble to assure Jaqui's place at Santa Maria, and now one man, one night of passion, was threatening to unravel what she had come to think of as a lifetime of commitment: to God, to the Sacred Heart of Santa Maria, and to its legendary protector, Donà di Piave. But, as is God's way, the crisis had an altogether different side to it. And this led her, inevitably, to thoughts of her mother.

On a beastly day in the July following her "death," when, at eight P.M., the thermometer still hovered near ninety, Jaqui slipped to her knees in the chapel and clasped her hands in fervent prayer. The truth was, beneath her innate love for her mother festered an unmistakable contempt. In accepting the family's way of life, in turning a blind eye to the extorting, intimidation, and murder, Jaqui had seen her as no better than the men who perpetrated those despicable acts. They were sinners, all of them.

But now God had revealed the truth, as He always did in His own time and in His own way: that her mother, in bringing her to Santa Maria, had shown extraordinary courage. What kind of punishment had she received at Uncle Alphonse's hands for what she had done: taking her daughter into the den of the Goldonis and leaving her there for permanent indoctrination?

Alone in the chapel, sweating beneath her habit, Jaqui shuddered. Her own courage seemed a small and unformed thing next to that of her mother. The bells of the chapel began to toll, the echoes filling the stone space, and Jaqui continued her prayers, for her mother and for herself.

Book 3

Doppelgänger

One has not watched life very observantly
if one has never seen the hand that—kills
tenderly.

—Friedrich Nietzsche

7

Tokyo/South Beach

Kisoko's town house looked stark and bare in the early-morning light. All the huge warehouses near the Sumida River loomed over it, as if frowning in disapproval. The rain had stopped, and as Nicholas dismounted his Kawasaki, sunlight, pink as the inside of a seashell, streamed through a break in the clouds. Green leaves, blown off the trees during the night, skittered along the pavement like the footsteps of unseen spirits.

A young woman in uniform opened the door and Nicholas introduced himself. She let him into the vestibule with, he felt, some reluctance.

"The mistress is not yet seeing guests." Her voice was a mere wisp, like a reed in the wind.

"No need to bother Kisoko-san," Nicholas said. "My business is with Nangi-san."

"I'm afraid the old boy isn't awake yet," came a commanding voice from the far side of the foyer. "Perhaps I can be of assistance."

Nicholas saw a man in his early forties wheel himself through into the vestibule. He had a long, brooding face, with large liquid brown eyes that seemed soft but soon proved otherwise. The muscles of his powerful upper body flexed as he swung into the room on the chrome wheelchair.

It glided across the marble with not so much as a whisper of its rubber tires. The maid gave him one look and vanished up the stairs.

"I gave Kisoko-san—"

"My mother."

As Nicholas continued to look at him, the man grinned. "She didn't tell you anything about me, eh?" He shrugged his massive shoulders. "Typical. My name's Ken and I already know yours, Linnear-san." He did not bow or hold out his hand. In fact, he gave no sense of greeting at all.

"Even though I gave your mother my word, I must speak with Nangi-san. There are a number of business matters I don't understand."

Ken laced his fingers together. Their calluses were like armor plate. "That is the prevailing creed of the human condition. Ignorance." He grinned again. "Some people are simply more ignorant than others."

Nicholas stared at Ken. Whom did he remind Nicholas of? "I am concerned about Nangi-san."

"I expect you are. Nasty disease, old age." Ken arranged his huge hands in his lap. "But he'll be fine, never fear." He cocked his head to one side. "You know that they were once—and future—lovers."

He had the disconcerting habit, not unlike an expert interrogator, of jumping from one topic to another without using subject names as guideposts.

"I had no idea." This was a lie, but Nicholas had no difficulty telling it.

"Well, don't worry. Hardly anyone else does." He appeared to consider a moment. "They met in 1948 at a *toruko,* one of those odd places—the Japanese version of a Turkish bath—that catered to American soldiers in the occupation years after the war."

Nicholas felt a tiny thrill of recognition go through him at Ken's mention of the *toruko.* Honniko's mother had worked in such a place after the war called Tenki. "Where was this *toruko?*"

Ken shrugged. "In Roppongi. That was where most of them were in those days."

Nicholas could not contain the creeping along his flesh. What was he feeling? The present and past swirling together in a nexus of unanswered questions. Nangi and Kisoko had met only eleven years ago. Ken was lying to him, but for what purpose? "What was the name?"

Ken rolled his eyes up to the ceiling as he called up his memory. "Let me see. I think it was called Tenki."

Nicholas shivered slightly. The same *toruko* where Honniko's mother had worked. It was as if Ken were trying to tell Nicholas something.

"Ken!"

The sharpness of Kisoko's voice caused Ken to stare silently at Nicholas.

"You have pressing obligations elsewhere!" Kisoko came down the staircase up which the maid had fled a moment ago. Perhaps she had told her mistress what was going on down here.

Ken was facing away from his mother, and as she came toward them, he gave Nicholas a swift and inexplicable grin that was more like a grimace of pain. Then, without saying another word, he wheeled himself around and disappeared down the hallway to the rear of the house.

"I can make no adequate excuse for my son's rudeness," Kisoko said as she came toward him. "All I can offer is that his . . . disability has made him something of a social misfit." She wore an informal kimono of indigo-dyed cotton, but her hair and face were, as usual, exquisitely made up.

"He's quite a handful."

"Forgive me." She smiled. "I haven't had time to explain him to you, and Ken requires so much explaining. Why, you and I have only begun to get to know one another." Her arm swept toward the back of the house. "You're just in time for breakfast. Would you care to join us? I'm afraid Nangi-san is still in bed."

Nicholas felt a momentary stab of fear. "Is he all right?"

"Perfectly." Her smile softened. "I told you, Linnear-san. All he needs is time. He will be fine, don't worry."

Nicholas opened his mouth to reply and felt as if a wooden stake had been jammed between his jaws. Darkness came down like dirt into an open grave, and he felt the marble floor bubbling, turning molten beneath his feet. He slipped, tried to regain his balance, but as the Kshira seizure gripped him, he fell to his knees.

Darkness all around and, in his center, an eye opening, not his *tanjian* eye—or then again perhaps it was, but if so, it was of such a different aspect that he could not recognize it.

It opened fully and he saw his surroundings as if from a dimension he had never known existed. He saw the house in its many incarnations. He saw gangsters here, and the hand of God; he saw love fulfilled and love broken, hearts filled with joy and shattered; tears of pain and enormous sorrow; rage and a flash—as of heat lightning, gone almost before it had begun—of evil. . . .

His eyes opened and he found himself gazing up into Kisoko's concerned face. She was kneeling on the cool marble floor of the vestibule, cradling his head in her lap. She was rocking slightly as a mother will a sick and terrified child.

"I . . . ," he began, but a wave of dizziness stopped him.

"I know," Kisoko whispered, bending over him. "I know what you are going through, how you are suffering."

"How could you possibly—"

He stopped as he saw an image taking form in his mind. It was of Kisoko as she had been in 1947. All around her was a penumbra of darkness within which he could just discern the movement of shadows without faces or voices. It was as if reality had shifted and the past had been made to live again. He felt her love as a living thing, a jewel that radiated warmth in the palm of the hand, and he knew she had extended her psyche, cradling him as she was doing with her arms.

Then the vision was gone. But the warmth remained, and for a moment he closed his eyes.

"You are *tanjian*," he whispered.

"I know of Akshara. And Kshira. I know the darkness and the light are sweeping through you."

"The Kshira is bubbling up, threatening to drown me." Nicholas opened his eyes, stared up into hers. "What is happening to me?"

"Change. And whatever it is, you must allow it to take place."

"But I—"

"Banish fear from your heart. Trust in *kokoro*, the center of things."

"Kisoko-san, I feel as if the Kshira will take me over completely. Okami-san could not help me. Can you?"

She shook her head.

"But the darkness—"

"Linnear-san," she said in the most gentle voice imaginable, "you do not need help. Let the darkness come."

When, twenty minutes later, he left her house, the rain had returned, whipping more leaves off the trees. The sky was stained indigo and here was the sound of constant faraway drumming. The blank faces of the warehouses stared back at him with grim and unforgiving looks.

What to make of Kisoko? She was *tanjian,* of that he was certain. He recalled how still she had sat the first time he had come to her house and had a Kshira seizure. Had she even breathed? Surely she had felt what he had felt. Surely she could help him.

Let the darkness come . . .

He got back on his Kawasaki and wended his way through the traffic-choked streets to Shinjuku. A message had been left on his Kami. It was from Mikio Okami, who wanted to meet him at the Fūzoku Shiryōkan, the Shitamachi Museum, at four forty-five tomorrow afternoon. He transmitted a confirm icon to Okami's address as he waited for a light on Minami-dōri to turn green.

Let the darkness come . . .

Could he do that? Was his faith in *kokoro* absolute? He looked deep into his heart and did not know the answer.

They came for Mick Leonforte as he was leaving Both Ends Burning, an all-night S&M club in Roppongi notable for the young, full-breasted women who, slowly and one imagined quite painfully, poured hot wax all over their naked bodies as a crowd of sweaty men looked on.

The plan had been well coordinated. While Ise Ikuzo, the head of the steel and metallurgy *keiretsu* bearing his name, emerged from a gleaming white Mercedes, two burly men popped out of the front seat of the car—the driver and the man riding shotgun—and headed toward Mick at full speed. One was short and squat as a sumo, the other was younger and completely bald. The *irezumi* of a phoenix rising covered half his bare pate.

"Not so big a man here on the street, are you?" Ikuzo called. "I am here to teach you a lesson. No one causes me to lose face, Mr. Leonforte, not even you."

It was just past three A.M., but by the neon light of the Tokyo night Mick could tell the two men were, indeed, members of the Shikei clan. So the rumors of Ikuzo's Yakuza connections were true. Mick thought briefly of how sorry Jōchi—his bodyguard—would be to miss the fun.

"You're an interloper in our world." Ikuzo lounged against the Mercedes. "Worse, you're an *iteki*, a foreign maggot. I am not fooled by your silver tongue as others may be. And when they find you tomorrow morning, it will serve as an example for others who might try to follow your lead."

The two Yakuza heavyweights expected him to turn tail, but he did not. Instead, he stood his ground, whirling at the last instant to meet the squat Yakuza's charge. Mick's right hand, which had surreptitiously slipped beneath his jacket, was filled with the Damascus-steel push dagger with which he had dispatched Rodney Kurtz. He jammed it into the squat Yakuza's chest just above and to the right of the end of the sternum. After a brief scrape of bone the blade drove completely home, its tip piercing the man's heart. Then, before the Yakuza could slam into him, Mick swiveled away to face phoenix-man. Behind him, he could hear the squat Yakuza stumbling along on legs that refused to pump. Terrible sounds of labored breathing filled the small street, then a retching and the sudden stench of death.

But Mick had other matters to attend to, the most pressing of which was the snub-nosed automatic phoenix-man was pointing at him. He did the last thing phoenix-man expected him to do. While a broad smile of triumph was still on the Yakuza's face, Mick ignored the gun and stepped into point-blank range. Reaching up with astonishing speed, his cupped hands brought phoenix-man's head down against his raised knee.

Cartilage shattered with a satisfying crunch as phoenix-man's nose collapsed. The automatic fell from his grasp, and Mick kicked it into the gutter while he slammed the heel of his hand into the vulnerable spot just behind phoenix-man's right ear, home of major nerve bundles.

Phoenix-man plunged to the street as if in heavy gravity.

Mick put one foot on his shoulder, the other on his neck. Kicking out with the heel of his foot, he heard the neck vertebrae snap.

In almost the same motion Mick turned and loped down the street to the white Mercedes. Ikuzo had wisely retreated to the car's interior. He had just electronically locked the doors and was fumbling with the gearshift when Mick put his left elbow through the driver's side window. Ikuzo yelped as the safety glass collapsed onto him, and then Mick had hold of him and was hauling him out through the window. He fumbled out a small .25-caliber automatic, which Mick contemptuously slapped away.

"*Iteki* am I?" Mick breathed as he struck Ikuzo a paralyzing blow between his eyes. "Too bad. This *iteki* will be the death of you."

His push dagger was in his hand, and he made the first ritual incision, as the Nungs had taught him. There was no hurry now. The street was deserted. Tokyo watched his revenge with blank eyes.

He excised the heart, liver, and spleen, then he hefted the bloody corpse across the hood of the idling Mercedes, its white sheen bluish in the light. Blood, black as cuttlefish ink, crawled across the once-pristine hood. Mick took the spleen and, using the blade of the push dagger to open Ikuzo's jaws, jammed the glistening organ in.

"You had the right idea, setting an example. You just had the wrong victim."

Mick walked ten minutes until he came to his car, which he never left in the vicinity of the club he was patronizing. There, he crouched down as he'd done so many times in the jungles of Vietnam and Laos, setting the organs in front of him. He wiped his hands as best he could and took out his cellular phone.

Jōchi answered on the first ring, listened in silence as Mick related what had happened. "I want you to dispose of the two bodies in the street in the usual way, so no one knows they ever existed."

"Only two?"

"That's right. Leave the one on the white Mercedes. It's an ensign of a very private war."

* * *

Lew Croaker stretched out on the turquoise chair at Playa del Sol, one of the myriad beachfront restaurants that lined the newly renovated South Beach area of Miami. The sun burned bright and hot in a cloudless sky that could make the skin turn red even through high-level sunblock. In an oversized rayon shirt, peach-colored slacks, huaraches, and wraparound mirrored sunglasses, he pushed around a forkful of sausages with rice and black beans—*cristianos y moros,* as the Cubans called it—but he didn't eat it. No appetite; his stomach was doing flip-flops. He looked up just as a bronzed beach bunny in a string bikini went past him on Rollerblades on the beach side of Ocean Boulevard.

South Beach had returned to the art deco splendor it had achieved in the thirties and forties, hot tropical colors and all, due in no small measure to an influx of international models and fashion designers who had drawn the interest of jaded Europeans and wealthy South Americans alike. So new buildings were going up shoulder to shoulder with the renovated ones from decades ago. In fact, he was just down the block from Gianni Versace's ornate European villa, whose imported Italian facade stood guarded and gated against the almost constant *turista* crush.

A fire-red Camaro cruised by with a testosterone rush of music blaring from its stereo system. The two blond muscle boys inside were having a grand time ogling all the female flesh in sight. They were followed by three hard young men on Softail Harleys vrooming their way on clouds of thrumming exhaust.

Croaker's cellular phone buzzed and he picked it up. "I hope to shit what you and Vesper's got in mind'll spear Bad Clams in his tracks." It was Wade Forrest, the Anti-Cartel Task Force fed. "Otherwise we're all lookin' at a shitload of trouble."

Croaker hitched his chair closer and cocked his head forward. Previously he'd kept one eye on the lookout for Vesper and Bad Clams, who, according to their timetable, were due any minute. Early this morning, he'd sneaked out of the Marlin, the way-cool hotel on Washington Avenue where he'd been sleeping, and had driven to Bad Clams's white mansion. There, using a pair of high-powered binoculars, he'd focused on the second-story window directly over the front door and at precisely seven o'clock had seen the curtains stir, then part. He had been so relieved to see Vesper's face clearly but briefly in the window that he'd let out an audible sigh. Her appearance there at that time had been their prearranged signal that everything was on schedule. She and Bad Clams were due at South Beach by lunchtime.

"What's up?" Croaker asked the fed.

"Bad Clams's people whacked Tony D. and tried t'do the same to his old lady."

"What?" Croaker felt as if he'd been jabbed with an electric prod. "How is Margarite DeCamillo? Is she alive?"

"You know this woman?" Even through the phone line Croaker could tell Forrest was curious.

"I . . . Yes. She's important to this plan . . . in an indirect way," Croaker finished lamely. "What the hell happened?"

"Bad Clams and Vesper in sight yet?"

Croaker craned his neck. "It's clear."

"Thing is, his people missed the DeCamillo woman and he had to go to plan B."

Croaker heard the blood roaring through his ears. "Which was?" At that moment he could have strangled Forrest, who was clearly enjoying drawing this out.

"He snatched the kid, you know, what's her name . . . ?"

Croaker closed his eyes for an instant. "Francine."

"Yeah, right. Francine. Anyway, he snatches the kid, then reels mama in. Only, she's smarter than anyone thinks and she gets some homicide dick—Barnett, I think his name was—to come protect her." Forrest paused and Croaker could hear him giving orders to his team. Meanwhile, blood was pounding heavily in his temples and his stomach felt hollow. "Now it really gets goin'." Forrest was back on the line. "The city dick whacks the two punks sent to take her in, but the city dick, he gets it in the neck from the inside guy—Bad Clams's man inside the Goldoni machine—Paul Chiaramonte."

Croaker's heart flipped over. Bright sunlight spun off the crawling line of cars and rigged-out motorcycles moving like a millipede down Ocean Boulevard. A pair of bare-chested musclemen sat down at a table and, flexing their well-oiled flesh for the bored waitress, ordered Bloody Marys. A willowy young woman in a skintight red, white, and blue outfit that left nothing to the imagination led a black and tan Doberman on a thick chain leash. Everybody, gawking, gave her a wide berth as she went by.

Croaker pulled at his shirt, trying not to sweat into it, because he had to do something to calm himself down. This was explosive stuff. Bad Clams had a mole inside Margarite's outfit. How come none of them suspected as much? What the hell was he doing here while Margarite and Francie were in mortal danger? He was already planning his quick exit to the Miami airport when he said, "What did Chiaramonte do with them?"

"With the DeCamillo woman and her kid?" Forrest said as if he didn't know whom Croaker was talking about. "According to our sources, Chiaramonte stuffed 'em into a private plane."

Croaker waited for Forrest to go on, but there was only silence on the line. He *was* going to strangle this bastard. Then he asked the question Forrest was waiting for him to ask. "Where was the plane headed?"

"Here. Right here. Chiaramonte's bringing 'em into the lion's den. Sometime today they're going to meet Bad Clams on his own turf and on his own terms." Forrest waited a beat. "You still with me, Croaker."

"Yeah, sure."

"I don't know what he's after, but it doesn't look good for the DeCamillo woman. She's a Goldoni, after all, and we know what Leonfortes do to Goldonis."

Croaker knew, all too well.

"Hey." Forrest's voice in his ear buzzed with tension. "Speak of the devil and he pops up right between your fucking legs. North One reports a sighting. Heading your way on Ocean. Be careful, subject's got on a sports jacket so he must be carrying."

Croaker turned just in time to see Vesper walking arm in arm with Caesare Leonforte. Just as Forrest had said, the couple was heading in his direction. He folded up his phone and went into the restaurant, wending his way to the rest rooms, where he tried without success to lower his pulse rate.

"We have about two minutes, no more," Vesper said to Croaker. "I told him I had to tap a kidney." They were locked inside the ladies' room, which, typically, had one stall. "He's got a line into the Coast Guard." She described the meet of last night, including a description of the man named Milo and the number of the Coast Guard cutter, CGM 1176. She also told him how pissed off Caesare was about the arsenic-laced dope.

"I'll check it out," Croaker said. "This Coast Guard connection's interesting. I have a feeling he's using the cutter for more than bringing in cocaine. Maybe that's how he smuggles *out* the DARPA arms matériel."

"It's possible," Vesper said thoughtfully. "What better cover than a Coast Guard cutter that can go anywhere and everywhere. By the way, there's a meet I'm going on tomorrow. It's set for five o'clock in the afternoon."

"Great work. With the number of the cutter, we'll be able to trace its movements."

She seemed so excited about this possibility that he hated to spoil her mood. But he had no choice. Quickly, he told her about Caesare's move on the Goldoni family, about Margarite and Paul Chiaramonte. Vesper and Margarite had been friends and associates since Margarite had taken over her brother Dominic's role.

"Christ, Margarite." Her hands balled into white-knuckled fists. "We've got to find a way to get her the hell away from Caesare."

"Bad Clams is gonna make that very hard to do."

Vesper put a hand on his arm. "Leave Caesare to me. You deal with the women." She bit her lip. "So Tony D. got whacked." She shook her head. "Why didn't we see this coming?"

"My thoughts exactly. But now's not the time for recriminations."

Vesper nodded in agreement. "Bad Clams told me a friend of his named Paul would be coming in today—with his girlfriend. I'll bet anything he'll stash them in the guesthouse." She looked at Croaker. "You okay?"

He nodded. "What about you?"

"Fine." She didn't want to talk about her and Caesare. Instead, she squeezed his arm. "We'll get them back, don't worry."

"Sure."

"After this, he'll be giving me his confidence, Lew. I mean, that's the point, isn't it?" She took a deep breath. "Meanwhile, we've got the next thirty seconds to get through. Now, listen, it's just like drowning."

"Thanks a lot."

"Don't try to breathe." Someone hammered on the door. "Just relax and let it happen. Let me do everything."

He grinned fiercely. "One day, maybe I'll take you up on that."

"Dream on." She laughed, then gave his arm a last squeeze. "Anyway, you'll be too busy with Margarite and Francie. They're going to need you now more than ever." She flipped the lock behind them. "We'd better get out of here. Ready?"

He nodded.

"See you on the other side," she said, and they piled out of the toilet, past an indignant woman in winged sunglasses and orange lipstick, who muttered, "The nerve of some people!"

When Caesare saw Vesper hurrying out of the restaurant, he took note immediately. He did not like the look on her face.

"Caesare!" she called, and looked back over her shoulder.

Caesare took a step toward her. "What th' fuck—!" He saw Croaker racing out of the restaurant after her.

"Hey!" Croaker shouted. "Hey! You can't get away from me that easily. Who the fuck you think you are?"

"Get away from me!" Vesper cried as he reached out for her blouse.

The sound of ripping silk made Caesare sprint toward her. Then, everything seemed to go into fast-forward so that, even later, it all seemed one brief blur to him.

Croaker, his hand full of Vesper's rent blouse, slapped her hard across the face. She whirled and screamed.

"Hey, you washed up fucker, get the fuck offa her!" Caesare shouted as he scrabbled for the automatic in his left armpit.

People jumped, electrified at the explosion that shoved Croaker back like a giant fist. Caesare got a glimpse of the gun in Vesper's hand, the blood seeping from the left side of Croaker's chest as a table and chairs went flying. Diners shrieked, waitresses dropped trays and ran, panic escalated as the second explosion came. This time, Caesare was sure he saw the bullet slam into Croaker's chest just millimeters from the first. The ex-cop was thrown off the canted overturned table, crumpling to the ground. Weirdly, in the midst of all the madness, Caesare found himself thinking with admiration and a bit of awe what a crack shot Vesper was.

Caesare knew he had to get them out of there as he clambered over scrambling bodies, shoved and punched others out of the way. It was like trying to swim against a riptide. He was inundated with people in a frenzy to get clear. The screams of the terrified onlookers built to an eerie crescendo. Caesare ignored it all, got to her, and pulled her to him.

"That sonuvabitch," he heard her panting. "Nobody treats me like a piece of shit."

He held her, knowing she was in serious trouble and that she needed his protection, his power, that without him she was finished. This was the confidence he was now prepared to give her, the confidence he *wanted* to give her; this was what the con game was all about. By needing him, Vesper would win his complete trust and bind him to her. It was simple human nature.

He took a step toward where Croaker lay, bent and bleeding. Was he dead? Jesus, how could he not be? Vesper had pumped two bullets into his heart. Jesus, she had nerves of steel.

He grabbed Vesper up in his arms and hustled her out of there, racing down Ocean Boulevard as the wail of the police sirens could be heard over the hip-hop blasting from cruising convertibles and out of packed restaurant terraces.

8
Tokyo/South Beach

The massed wail of electronic guitars at first sounded like the sirens from a thousand ambulances. Then, as the acoustics of the vast space allowed the ululations to rise through the eight heavily glyphed columns girdling Mūdra's dance floor, sound was magically transmuted into music—an ear-piercing, pulse-pounding, adrenaline-rush type of thing, but still rife with melody, harmonies—plus, you could dance to it.

Nicholas and Tanaka Gin moved through the writhing, sweaty dancers and the sweeping laser beams of light, feeling as if they were fish in a tank. Periodically, the haunting Sanskrit glyphs and bodhisattva sculptures were lit by the passing lights, giving literal form to the enlightened beings, whose karma it was to forgo nirvana in order to help others attain that state.

Outside, though it was past four in the morning, the Kai-gon-dōri was alive with street punks with money to burn, models, singers, teenaged actors, *talentos,* and the predatory types who prowled around them in the urban forest of the night. Uncaring, they crisscrossed over the spot where Giai Kurtz had been killed by the murderous hit-and-run.

Nicholas had responded to a call from the prosecutor, who had told him there was someone he wanted Nicholas to interview, had driven into the heart of Tokyo and the Shibaura district, pushing his modified Kawasaki hard. He had been up anyway, analyzing the preliminary information Okami had provided on the personnel in the Tokyo Prosecutor's Office. He hadn't bothered to wake Koei, but had left her a note. Unlike Justine, she was not threatened by his nocturnal comings and goings. She recognized that this was part of him.

"I discovered who Kurtz left his money to." Tanaka Gin had to fairly shout above the din. "It was Sterngold, his corporate entity."

"Interesting," Nicholas said as he dodged a spinning female body, breasts all but exposed, that came at him with the speed and single-mindedness of a missile.

"Wait, it gets better." Tanaka Gin led them beyond the dance floor to a relatively safe spot near a semicircular bar that looked as if it were carved out of the side of an Angkor Wat temple. "Kurtz stipulated in his will that his share of the Denwa Partners be spun off into a separate entity, Worldtel, Inc. I spent the better part of the afternoon in the data banks checking out Worldtel. It's got a couple of small Southeast Asian wireless interests, nothing big-time. Now it's got Denwa."

Nicholas was momentarily distracted by a young woman with a series of nose rings that ran like a chain from one nostril to her cheek. She wore black lipstick and her spiky hair was pure white. "So who controls Worldtel? The Sterngold board of directors?"

"Maybe once, but not anymore," Tanaka Gin said. "Worldtel was sold so recently—within the last twenty-four hours—that I couldn't get any of the details, except for the name of the company that snapped it up, something called Tenki Associates."

Nicholas felt a stirring at the back of his neck. Tenki was the name of the *toruko* where, according to Kisoko's son, Ken, his mother and Nangi had met thirty-four years before they had actually gotten together, and where Honniko's mother had worked during the Occupation. "Tenki?" In his world there was no such thing as coincidence. "Are you sure?"

"Yes. Why?"

"You check it out?"

Tanaka Gin nodded. "Naturally. It's hollow, a holding company with an address in Sri Lanka. I called, got an answering machine, and left a message, but I'm not holding my breath for a call back."

Nicholas thought a moment. "My guess is we find out who owns Tenki Associates and we might have a direct line on the Kurtzes' murderer."

"*You* have a direct line to the murderer, Linnear-san."

The floor turned to jelly beneath Nicholas's feet and he felt himself falling, falling until Mūdra's light and sound machine arched far above him and he felt as if he were slithering through primeval ooze, sinking down farther, sound damped, light disappearing more swiftly than the blink of an eye.

The incessant buzz of the bees trapped inside his head made him dizzy. Darkness all around, the voices of the bees—for now he could determine that they *were* voices, a language forming, being translated even as he listened like a greedy and fearful observer, a young child slipping out of bed to listen to the brittle and forbidden chatter at his parents' late-night party.

Kshira was filling him with its shining face of evil. It was slipping through his unconscious like a nocturnal predator, jaws gleaming in the moonlight. It was so near dawn and he had had so little sleep during the last thirty-six hours that he did not have the strength to fight it, to claw his way back to the light and sound far above him.

Change, Kisoko had told him. *Whatever it is, you must allow it to take place. Banish fear. Trust in* kokoro.

He slipped deeper into the jellylike darkness, and as he did so, the buzzing of the ten thousand bees, the parsing of the unknown language, was reduced to a single voice:

You should be familiar with revolutionaries; you were brought up by one. . . . A voice that was as familiar as it was chilling. *I have made an exhaustive study of your father. The Colonel was the most secretive man I have come across. More secretive, even, than my own father, who changed identities so often I wondered finally if he remembered who he really was. . . .* Mick Leonforte's voice echoing in his head, at the center of his being as the dark constructs of Kshira continued to form a permanent home. But how? How? *I make it my business to ruthlessly deconstruct the past and re-create it in the image of the future....*

Nicholas's eyes snapped open into a light only he could see. Eerily, terrifyingly, Kshira was showing him its Path, a converging of possibilities all extrapolated from recent events, which, like pieces of a jigsaw puzzle, were being fit together to form the tapestry of the present . . . and the future.

And he could see now that Kshira's Path was a mirror, or at least what he had thought to be a mirror that night at the Kurtzes' when, feeling the presence of their murderer, he had stared into it and had seen himself.

But now he knew the truth: it was a window, not a mirror, and the image he saw within, that he had mistaken for his own, was in fact that of Mick Leonforte. Doppelgänger. That rather old-fashioned word sent a roll of thunder echoing through his mind. *He and I are mirror images.*

But that was absurd. Mick had murdered the Kurtzes, he was certain of that now. Why? To gain possession of Rodney Kurtz's share of Denwa? But how would murder accomplish that? It might certainly prove valuable, but enough to kill two people for? Perhaps, for a man like Mick Leonforte. But Nicholas could not dismiss the feeling that he was missing some vital part of the puzzle.

The fear had vanished, replaced by a kind of fierce and feral exhilaration. It was Kshira—not Akshara—that had shown him the truth. Why had he been so afraid of it? Had he conveniently forgotten the effect it had had on Kansatsu, his mad *sensei*, and on Okami when he had tried to access the dark path? Why bother bringing up needless memories when the truth was right in front of him. Kshira provided *chikaku*, the profound perception all mystics of whatever discipline spent their lifetime searching for.

"Linnear-san?"

He blinked, was back amid crushing sound and light. He was on his knees near the edge of the dance floor, his field of vision filled with a pair of Japanese girls with hair longer than their skirts, which were, in any case, riding so high on their thighs, the secret was out.

"I saw him," Nicholas said as Tanaka Gin pulled him to

his feet. "I know who killed the Kurtzes, Gin-san. It was Michael Leonforte."

Tanaka Gin's eyes opened wide as he led Nicholas back toward a dark area near the bar. "Leonforte, the man behind Floating City?"

"He and the dead American warlord Rock, yes."

"But I thought Mick Leonforte had been nuked in the explosion that destroyed Floating City."

"That's apparently what he wants everyone to believe, but now I think he's the one who stole the TransRim vid-byte technology from us."

Tanaka Gin looked hard at Nicholas. "It's all connected, isn't it, Linnear-san? The Kurtzes' murders, the Sato industrial espionage. Our cases have converged."

"So it would seem. But the only way to confirm it is to find out who owns Tenki Associates."

Tanaka Gin said nothing for some time. Inundated as they were by the machine of amplified music, it was as if silence had been banished to another dimension. Not a breath could be taken without the tang of slamming bodies in motion, not a sensation could be felt without the deep, bone-jarring beat of digitalized bass and synthesized percussion.

"The only way for me, you mean." Tanaka Gin stood close to Nicholas. "I am beginning to understand this about you, Linnear-san: you have your own methods of looking into matters." He nodded, almost a formal bow. "Given your talents, perhaps this is not uncalled for. But I want you to understand this: I am sworn to uphold the law, and though I am convinced that you are an honorable man in every sense of the word, still it has occurred to me that my law and yours will not always be . . . the same."

Once again, Nicholas was struck by this man's remarkable insight. He was unlike any prosecutor Nicholas had ever met before. In telling Nicholas that he was an honorable man in every sense of the word, Tanaka Gin had paid him the highest compliment. It seemed their relationship was destined to take new and unexpected turns. Nicholas returned the other man's nod. "This may be as you say, Gin-san. But I swear to you that they will always be compatible."

Now Tanaka Gin presented Nicholas with a formal bow.

In this manner was their peculiar and deepening friendship sealed for all time.

"Will you be able to talk to this individual? I need you to concentrate," Tanaka Gin asked, now all business. And when Nicholas nodded, he led him around the left side of the bar, through a door at the end of it that looked like a part of the wall. As the door shut behind them, the massive noise and heavy vibration all but disappeared. Some kind of sophisticated acoustic damping, Nicholas thought.

Almost immediately, another kind of vibration, rhythmic but much slower, became audible, rising in volume as they walked down a dim wood-floored corridor that seemed part of the original warehouse into which the dance club had been built. An old metal-grilled industrial elevator took them down into a sub-basement. Music with a slow, sensual beat rose around them like tendrils from the deep.

The elevator disgorged them into a tiny anteroom beyond which Nicholas could see on a round lighted dais a woman in buttock-length hair squatting over a prostrate male who was naked, except for a spiked dog collar around his neck. The woman wore skintight leather capri pants pockmarked with zippers, a scary-looking black latex bra, a leather hood, and six-inch spike heels. In one hand she held a cat-o'-nine-tails, in the other a leash attached to the dog collar.

A dapper-looking Japanese with slicked-back hair and a hatchet face said, "What can I do for you gentlemen?"

The woman on the dais pulled open a zipper and began to urinate on the prostrate man's face.

"Got an appointment with Tento-san."

Hatchet-face gave them both the once-over. "Tento-san?"

It was a joke, a nickname. *Tento* was slang for a hard-on. It was taken, not inappropriately, from the English word *tent*.

"He's expecting us," Tanaka Gin said.

Incredibly, on the dais the prostrate man was drinking the woman's urine.

Hatchet-face leaned forward expectantly. "And you are?"

"You don't want to know. Just tell him Gin."

Hatchet-face disappeared while in the small theater there was a smattering of applause and the lights went out while attendants mopped the dais in preparation for the next act.

Nicholas hoped they'd be out of here before then. Judging by what he'd just seen, one S&M act a night was more than enough. Men in rumpled gray suits and sweating faces trooped by on their way to the elevator.

A fat man in a sharkskin suit and with rings on every finger waddled up to them, gave them both perfunctory bows. This was Tento.

"Gin-san," he said in a high, almost feminine voice, "we will be more comfortable in back."

His office was a windowless cubicle whose only wall decoration was a filthy air vent behind which was the almost constant rustling of rodents. There was one dented and severely scarred green metal desk that looked vaguely American Army issue, a cheap swivel chair, and against the opposite wall, two sets of flimsy file cabinets. This was Tento's idea of comfort? Maybe he meant privacy.

Nicholas wisely declined the fat man's offer of a drink. While Tento blew into a dusty glass covered with greasy fingerprints, Tanaka Gin said, "Tento-san, when we last spoke, you told me you had seen the woman Giai Kurtz in your club several times before her death."

Tento fetched a bottle of Suntory Scotch from a desk drawer, poured two fingers in the glass. "That's right."

Tanaka Gin produced a photo of Giai Kurtz and placed it on the desk. "You're absolutely certain it was this woman?"

Tento glanced down at the photo, then into the prosecutor's face. "There are two things I am superb at. One is handling money. The other is faces. I can tell you with confidence I know every face that's entered my club more than once." His finger stabbed out. "She came here maybe half a dozen times."

"The dance club or here?" Nicholas asked.

"A Bas." Tento downed the Scotch. "That's the name of this place. It's French for Down There."

"So she liked this sort of thing?"

Tento inclined his head. "Who is he?"

"A friend of the family," Tanaka Gin said. "Just answer his questions, please."

The fat man pursed his lips. "I never talked to her, you understand, but if I had to make a guess, I'd say no, she didn't like S and M. She used to turn her head away, I remember. But her companion, now he was a different story altogether."

"Describe him, please," Tanaka Gin said.

"But I already—"

"Again."

Very precisely, Tento began to describe a man who very clearly was Mick Leonforte. Tanaka Gin's eyes briefly met Nicholas's in recognition.

"He liked the S-and-M show," Nicholas said when Tento was done.

"Oh, yeah." The fat man poured himself another drink. "But I mean he lapped the stuff up. You know, I got a lotta types in here so I know one when I see one."

"One what?" Tanaka Gin asked.

"A sex junkie." Tento very carefully pushed the empty glass aside. "He'd come back sometimes without the woman and he'd pay extra to take the dominatrices upstairs after the show, sometimes two, three at a time."

"What was that like?" Nicholas asked.

Tento made a face. "Shit, what d'you think I am, a pervert? I didn't ask because I didn't want to know. That kind of thing—well, every man to his own kind of meat."

"Anything else?" Tanaka Gin asked.

Tento thought a moment. "Only one: the dominatrix he liked best, Londa, left about three months ago, and I got the feeling this guy had something to do with it."

"You have an address for her?" Nicholas said.

"Yeah, well, who knows with these creatures." Tento sat down behind his desk, rummaged through his drawers. He took out a long logbook, went through it until he came to the entry he was looking for. He grabbed a pad and pen and scribbled something down, tore it off, and handed it over.

"That's it, then." Tanaka Gin took the photo of Giai Kurtz off the desk and was already halfway out the door when Nicholas turned back to Tento.

"You said this man came back sometimes without the woman."

"That's right."

"You mean he'd also come back *with* her?"

Tento nodded. "Yeah. He'd always want Londa then, and

she'd go upstairs with the two of them—the woman, I mean."

"Did you ever wonder?"

Tento was looking longingly at the bottle of Scotch. "About the three of them? Naw. Why should I?"

As they walked back to the elevator, Tanaka Gin said, "What're you thinking?"

"I'm not sure." Nicholas opened the gate and they got in. Thankfully, the next act hadn't yet taken the dais. "But somehow for Mick sex and death are inextricably linked. That was a sense I got most strongly that night at the Kurtzes'. I think it'd be worth my while to see if I can run Londa down."

Tanaka Gin shook his head. "Not without me."

"Listen, Gin-san, this dominatrix works in another world altogether." They had reached street level and they went back to the dense clamor of Mūdra. "Her work may not be illegal per se, but if she's mixed up with Mick Leonforte, she's on the other side of the law. I don't think she's going to want anything to do with you." They went past the bar. "Besides, I've got some leads for you to run down concerning the personnel in your office."

Tanaka Gin was about to reply when his pager went off. He scrolled through the LED readout and his face lit up.

"Let's go," he said with some excitement. "We've got something that may be of interest to both of us."

It had begun to rain again, the slick streets picking up the city's neon shimmer and smearing it in long pastel streaks against the blackness. Nicholas followed Tanaka Gin's Honda across town, west by northwest, from the rather dull southern boundary of establishment Tokyo into the glitter of Roppongi, high-tech ghetto of the foreigner and the roving bands of Nihonin, the motorcycle gangs who collectively had been dubbed with the Japanese street slang for nihilist.

The Honda led him into a side street that had been cordoned off by police cars, their multicolored lights swinging again and again off the buildings, the flashes running like blood reflected in the rain-slick street.

Nicholas got off his Kawasaki. Dead ahead of him was a white Mercedes across whose long hood was spread-eagled a male body. As Tanaka Gin guided him past the phalanx of uniformed cops, Nicholas got a look at the corpse's face in the lurid light. Even with the dark, glistening mass protruding from the livid lips, even with the bloody vertical crescent carved in the center of the forehead, he recognized the man.

"Ikuzo-san!"

That brought Tanaka Gin up short. "You know this man?"

"Yes. He was the head of Ikuzo Nippon Steel and Metallurgy." Nicholas moved closer to the body. "Gin-san, this man was a member of Denwa Partners."

"Heart, liver, and what else carved out of him," Tanaka Gin said. "What's that he's got in his mouth?"

"It's his spleen," a thin man who was the medical examiner said.

Tanaka Gin nodded. "Too much like Rodney Kurtz to be the work of another killer."

Nicholas let out a deep breath. "Has anyone touched the body yet?"

"It has been photographed," the ME said, "that's all. I was given instructions to wait for Gin-san's arrival."

"I want to examine the wounds."

Tanaka Gin nodded and signaled to the ME. He, in turn, spoke to several assistants, who, donning latex gloves, carefully removed the corpse from the hood of the white Mercedes and laid it on a gurney.

Nicholas asked for a flashlight and, when it was given to him, played the beam at close range over the wounds. "See here . . . and here." He pointed to several major wounds. "As with Rodney Kurtz, something with a wide blade punctured him with great force." He gestured. "Like this, straight in. There was no tearing or ripping of skin as with a knife blade."

"What was the murder weapon?"

"My guess is a push dagger."

Tanaka Gin glanced at him. "What is that?"

"The blade emanates here." Nicholas put the forefinger of his left hand between the third and fourth fingers of his right hand and jabbed outward. "And when it strikes, it does so with the full force of the body behind it. It would puncture flesh, sinew, muscle, even bone, with a force like that." He pointed. "Here you can see the puncture wound went straight in and out. That's unique to push daggers." He pointed to the place where the organs had been removed. "But here these are almost like surgical cuts. If you look closely, you can see the blade marks."

The two men stood up. Tanaka Gin glanced at Nicholas, who nodded, and the prosecutor signaled for the ME's men to take the body. "I want a full report as quickly as you can, Doctor," Gin said.

"By nine A.M.," the medical examiner said.

Tanaka Gin watched Ikuzo being loaded into the ambulance. "Showy kind of murder, don't you think?"

"Yes," Nicholas said. "And the spleen stuffed in his mouth. Almost like a warning."

"To us or to someone else?"

"Perhaps both."

They were cold and tired but entirely too wired to think about bed and sleep. Besides, it was almost dawn. They drove over to Tsukiji. The fish market was already open, its flood of light and movement a tonic from the claustrophobic darkness the two men had endured. At a nearby noodle stand, they stood out of the rain, slurping up steaming bowls of broth enriched by fresh greens and slices of roast pork as well as soba noodles.

"We must both use extreme caution," Nicholas said.

Tanaka Gin's impassive face was attentive as ever.

"The vertical crescent is a ritual symbol of a certain tribe in the Vietnamese highlands."

"The Nungs." Tanaka Gin nodded. "Yes, I know."

Nicholas's head swung around. "You knew all along."

"I wanted to trust you, Linnear-san. And I wanted you to trust me." Tanaka Gin slurped up some soba noodles, chewed thoughtfully. "It's all worked out for us, in the end, hasn't it?"

Nicholas laughed. "I suppose so." He sipped some of the delicious, rich broth. "Then you know something of the Nung ritual of absorbing an enemy's strength by eating his vital organs."

"Yes. The *ngoh-meih-yuht*, the crescent moon."

"It also has another meaning here. The ancient Messulethe used the symbol of the crescent—the Gim—for their two-edged sword. They used to paint their faces with woad to mark themselves—and the bodies of their enemies."

Tanaka Gin swallowed hard and put down his chopsticks. "Are you saying that Michael Leonforte is a Messulethe?"

"I don't know. He's lived in Vietnam and Laos on and off since 1968. And most of the time it was in the deep bush where the Nungs live. He obviously knows the ritual. Whether he was initiated by them is impossible to guess."

Tanaka Gin took up his chopsticks again, began to eat more slowly and thoughtfully.

Nicholas, who had been running this conversation back in his mind, said, "Gin-san, you didn't ask me what a Messulethe is. That means you already know."

Tanaka Gin smiled. "I spent a year in the Vietnamese highlands. It was part of my reckless youth. I had an anthropology professor at college who was mad about hands-on experience. I followed him to Vietnam one summer and didn't come back for twelve months."

"So you met the Nungs."

"We lived among them for almost all that time. Fascinating people, in touch with the spirits, the old gods of earth, or so they believe." Tanaka Gin pushed the sleeve of his coat up, unbuttoned his long-sleeve shirt, rolled it up to his elbow. There, on the inside of his left wrist, was a crude tattoo of a vertical crescent.

Nicholas took a deep breath, let it out slowly. No wonder it seemed to him as if Gin knew more than he was letting on. He himself was a Nung novitiate.

"We've got to stop Michael Leonforte from killing again," Tanaka Gin said flatly.

"Everything leads back to Denwa. Mick wants to control the partnership. He also wants the vid-byte technology." Nicholas considered a moment. "I think it's now more imperative than ever that I have a talk with Londa, the dominatrix Mick is so attached to."

"Maybe that isn't such a good idea." Tanaka Gin rolled his sleeve down over the Gim tattoo. "Has it occurred to you that Leonforte had Giai Kurtz run down in front of a club he frequented? Normally, I'd say that was a stupid thing to do, a slip-up. Most criminals are stupid, if cunning, which

is why we eventually catch them. But we already know this
man is different. This was no slip-up, was it?"

"No. He's proved he's got a deadly, shrewd mind."

"What then?"

Nicholas breathed in the salt and fish tang of the air. The
rain had taken most of the soot and carbon monoxide out
of the atmosphere, and for the moment at least, the morning
smelled good. "I suspect he's leading us along a preselected
path. What he wants is, right now, anyone's guess." He
thought a moment. "But perhaps you're right. I've been
thinking of the weapon he must have used for the murders.
If I'm right about it being a push dagger, I think I know
who made it for him. I'd better run by there first just to see
if Mick's got any other surprise weapons in store for us."

"I don't like people playing God." Tanaka Gin put down
his bowl, stacked his chopsticks across its rim. "They don't
know their place in the world."

Nicholas looked at Tanaka Gin. "That's as good a definition of Mick Leonforte as I can think of." But he could not
help wondering whether it was also the correct definition
of himself.

Mick ran his hand over Honniko's breast and she moved
like an impaled serpent. She was naked, her flesh gleaming
with fragrant oil, bound at wrists, thighs, and ankles; there
was a silk scarf tied across her eyes, two more beneath and
above her breasts, thrusting them out like ripe fruit in a
street market. Outside the small window rain beat a military
tattoo on the circular glass. The chair on which they were
fused like glass creaked with their movements. He smelled
the heat rising off her like incense.

Honniko ran her tongue along the dark blue crescent tattoo on the inside of his wrist, so primitive the bamboo needles had left permanent holes in his skin, as if this were the
one true way to identify him.

"Men like me are misunderstood," Mick said, moving on
her, slithering in the oil and their musk. "Passion frightens
society and society is in the business of protecting itself first,
last, and always." His hand found her nipple, erect and pli-
ant. "Even when that society has outlived its usefulness."

Honniko felt him deep inside her, moving easily from one

orifice to another. She was used to him speaking in this way. It was like an incantation, his philosophy, the way she imagined Apollo or Dionysus might have spoken, once, so very long ago. It was part of this ritual—he made a habit of ritualizing everything—and it made her dizzy with sensation.

"I am an inquirer after life, like Julius Caesar, Napoleon, and Nietzsche. I, like they, am feared and, when not feared, despised." In the saddle of Honniko's own making, Mick stared out of the tiny prefab apartment in the Naigai Capsule Tower. "They were true heroes. They knew how to imbue their existence with a solidity and depth of meaning that made them feared. But fear did not concern them; it was the last thing on their minds." Rain beat against the glass, turning the cityscape into crazy streamers of light that ran like frosting off a melting cake. "What concerned them was the revelation of awe of themselves fountaining upward from their very hearts." His gaze fell upon the new and beautiful high-rise three hundred feet away, upon a particular set of windows above him through whose panes he could make out a familiar figure moving. "To make this happen they needed not only to subdue tradition but the gods within themselves in order to believe." The figure switched on a lamp and he could see her face now—Koei's face. He was looking directly into the apartment she shared with Nicholas. She lifted her arms over her head, slid out of her shift. "How can this be done?" he said, staring at Koei's naked breasts and thrusting more deeply, more violently, making Honniko cry out. "King Vishvamitra discovered the truth centuries ago: the strength and fortitude to build a new heaven comes from the depths of one's own hell."

It's just like drowning, Vesper had said, and she'd been right. Eyes closed, back aching from the hit of the table edge, feeling as if he were on the verge of having a heart attack, Croaker nevertheless felt the unnatural lassitude overcome him. Vesper was doing it, but how? He'd heard stories about just this feeling from people who'd almost drowned, sinking into the depths where even semitropical seas were cold enough to chill the bones. Near death, air all but exhausted in the straining lungs, the body was seized by this same curious lassitude, carrying it downward into darkness.

Croaker heard the screams of terrified patrons as if from behind a thick concrete wall, was only dimly aware of the febrile rush of movement as Vesper used this gift that had been honed by Okami to damp Croaker's senses and give the appearance of death. His pulse rate was way down, his heart pumped at a crawl. How *did* she do it?

Then he was being lifted onto a gurney, and bright sunlight against his closed lids was replaced by dimness as he was slid into the back of the private ambulance they'd contracted, and sirens blasting, they took off.

"How's he doing?"

Croaker recognized Rico Limòn's voice. Limòn was a film special-effects expert Vesper had recruited through the Anti-Cartel Task Force, members of whom were even now posing as FBI agents as they took over the "investigation" into Croaker's "death." *Right,* Croaker thought, *I'm starting to come out of it now.*

"What about this hand, would'ja? Never saw anything like it."

Croaker tried to laugh. The paramedic was more interested in his biomechanical hand than he was in the bruises the bullets had made when they struck the Kevlar vest.

"How's it work?"

"Revive him and maybe he'll tell you," Limòn said crossly.

"Yeah, yeah, okay. Keep your briefs on," the paramedic said.

Then Croaker coughed and snorted as the paramedic held the smelling salts under his nose. "Okay, okay, enough," he muttered as his eyes fluttered open.

He saw Limòn's concerned brown face leaning over him. "How's it feel to come back from the dead?"

Croaker grunted. "I don't think I'm there just yet."

"So far, so good," said a voice from the recesses of the van. That would be Wade Forrest, the senior fed on this project. Forrest leaned into the light. "I want him in tip-top shape," he said to the interior at large. He was a large man, looked in fact like a football lineman with a neck as large as most models' waists, small ears, brush-cut, blondish hair, and what Croaker knew were light eyes hidden behind mirror glasses. He jutted his prominent jaw. "You okay, Croaker?"

For sure he had been the date of the homecoming queen each fall in college, Croaker thought. "Give me a minute, okay?"

"We don't have a minute," Forrest said in that flinty tone they taught you on the Potomac. He hunched forward as if giving quarterback signals in the huddle. "See, I've been after Caesare Leonforte for three years." He pulled at his brush cut. "I got gray hair because of this rotten sonuvabitch. I missed my daughter's graduation because I was in L.A. setting up an infiltration, and all I got for it was a man down and a bleeding ulcer. I'm missing my younger daughter's birthday today because I'm here." His hunched form was rock solid, his expression hyper as a greyhound's, his bunched muscles making him look weirdly like a gargoyle. "But this time I mean to make it count for something. I want him, Croaker, and by God you and Vesper will get him for me."

Croaker had been exposed to these fed types before and knew they were often wound up to within an inch of their lives. The best thing to do, sometimes, was to ignore them when they were venting. That was a relatively new thing, venting, suggested by fed shrinks and mandated in triplicate by their superiors, to cut down on field-agent burnout.

Croaker turned to Limón. "Get me out of this contraption, would you?"

Limón reached behind him, and as Croaker lifted his shoulders, he unsnapped the harness that held the Kevlar vest in place.

"Look at those holes!" the paramedic said in awe. "Right over his heart! And this blood looks real!"

"It *is* real," Limón said. "It's chicken blood." He poked his finger through the holes in Croaker's shirt. "How'd the impacts feel?" Given Caesare Leonforte's reach, neither Croaker nor Vesper had felt comfortable soliciting the cooperation of the Miami PD. In any event, Limón had set off tiny charges by remote control that opened the plastic sacs of blood attached to the vest that gave the illusion that the bullets Vesper had fired had penetrated Croaker's flesh instead of being repelled by the Kevlar.

Croaker grimaced. "How'd they feel? Like I was having a heart attack." He sat up slowly. "I wouldn't recommend it for a steady diet, if that's what you mean."

With his shirt off, he stayed still as the paramedic probed the left side of his chest. "These bruises are pretty deep. I'd go easy on twisting your torso for a while." The paramedic shook his head. "Skin's not even broken. Amazing!" Then he began to pack up his instruments. "You need a painkiller? Those bruises will start to smart pretty good by tonight."

"No, thanks. Those things'll only slow me down."

"Suit yourself." The paramedic was about to get up. "Uh, by the way, would you mind?" He pointed to Croaker's biomechanical hand.

"Sure. Why not?" Croaker leaned over and, balling the titanium and polycarbonate fingers, smashed his fist through the side of the ambulance.

The paramedic jumped as if stabbed and the driver yelled back at them, "What the hell was that?"

The paramedic, looking as if he had been struck by lightning, peered through the rent in the steel frame. "Jesus H. Christ."

"Okay, you've had your fun," Limòn said, elbowing the paramedic out of the way. "I got work to do." He hauled over a heavy black satchel and dug into its capacious interior. He was a young man, perhaps just thirty, slim and good-looking, with large chocolate-brown eyes, buzz-cut black hair, and a pencil-thin mustache right out of a Dick Powell movie. He knew his special effects—liked to have fun with them and so was inventive. Also, he was local, which helped.

"All righty," he said, holding up a latex nose, "when I get through with you, even your mother would walk right by you without giving you a second glance." He waggled the nose. "What do you think, ordinary enough?"

Croaker shrugged. "You're the expert."

"Damn straight. And the beauty part is there's a tiny homing device hidden in the left nostril, so I advise you against sneezing." Limòn gestured. "Now lie down on your back and keep still. I have to make a death mask out of plaster to make sure all the prostheses I make for you fit your facial size and type."

"A death mask," Croaker said, settling back on the gurney and listening to the wind whistle through the rent he'd made in the wall of the ambulance. "That seems all too appropriate."

When Tetsuo Akinaga, *oyabun* of the Shikei clan, was released from jail after his incarceration pending indictment, he returned not to his home or to his many businesses, for he thought of these all as tainted somehow by the death of Naohiro Ushiba, the chief minister of MITI. This was a death he, Akinaga, had ordered, for in the end, Ushiba had sided with Mikio Okami and had thus become Akinaga's implacable enemy.

All these familiar places were tainted not only by that murder but by the events immediately following—most notably his public arrest by the prosecutor Tanaka Gin in the *o-furo*—the public baths—his father had built, and his humiliating subsequent incarceration.

When Tetsuo Akinaga entered one of a dozen apartments he kept for himself throughout Tokyo, the first thing he did was strip off his $3,500 imported suit—in fact, all his clothes—and, piling them into the kitchen sink, poured kerosene over them and lit a match.

In the resulting white-hot flare he felt his cheeks burning with rage with the face he had lost. All the familiar things in his life had been rendered unfit for habitation. Like a priest who finds his church has been summarily desanctified, he had nowhere to go except to these hidey-holes, anonymous places with no aesthetic value, as if he were this same priest forced to conduct services in the basement of an office building.

As the fire flared and sparked, his rage burned brighter than any kerosene-fed flame. The stench of the burning fabrics, the rapid evaporation of his own stale sweat, clogged his nostrils and almost made him gag. His rage burned all the brighter. Naked, he stood on his powerful bandy legs, gripping the warm porcelain of the sink, his mind consumed by revenge. He was so thin he looked like a concentration camp inmate, with his knobby joints. He was in his midfifties, but the vicissitudes of maintaining power and influence had made him seem older. His gray hair was unfashionably long, at samurai length, pulled back from his wide, flat forehead in a traditional queue. His deep-set eyes were impenetrable. In all, he was a hard man, someone who could take blows as well as give them. A man who asked for no quarter and gave none. A man who believed in nothing—save perhaps the sanctity of being an outsider in a world gone mad.

At that moment, a key turned in the lock and he heard someone enter. He did not turn around because he knew who it must be. Only one other person had a key to this apartment besides himself.

"Shall I make you a drink?" Londa asked in that voice that made you want to be staked out across her bed.

He said nothing, continuing to stare at the flames, dying now as they ate away the last of the fabrics, the remains of the fear that had gripped him when representatives of the establishment he reviled had taken him inside, when he had heard the hard steel doors clang shut and had seen nothing but iron bars and had known his world had shrunk to the size of his cell.

Even when he killed Tanaka Gin—which he would, very soon and with a great deal of ingenuity and gusto—he would never forgive him for making him fall prey to that disabling fear. Inside, Akinaga had felt helpless, and this, above all other things, he could not abide.

Londa came up behind him and wound her long, long hair around his throat. In this way, she pulled him back from the sink, from the brink of his one true fear, from the acrid foment of his revenge.

"I need a bath," he said.

"Later. You'll stink more before I'm through with you."

He was already hard. It did not take much from her: the feel of her hair on his naked flesh, the touch of her leathergloved hand, even, sometimes, the steel-hard flash in her eye, because he knew what was in store for him and he could relax completely, forget about decisions of influence, money, corruption, and business. He could be a child in her capable hands, free from maintaining control—which was, after all, an exceptionally exhausting undertaking.

Floor-to-ceiling windows, thin as columns in a medieval church, looked out over Roppongi, an area of contemporary Japan where no one would think to look for a traditional-minded man such as Akinaga. Also, he was high enough to have an almost perfect view of the Nogi Jinja, a shrine to a modern general who had nevertheless been a true samurai, who committed seppuku—ritual suicide—in 1912 with his wife following the death of Emperor Meiji. This juxtaposition—the samurai spirit alive and abiding in foreign-dominated Roppongi—was just the kind of irony that appealed to Akinaga, whose cynical outlook on life was nothing if not ironic.

He rested his head against the rough gray Berber carpet. It did not seem odd to him to be staring down at the Nogi Jinja, lit up as if it were on fire in the night, while he knelt on the carpet with his butt in the air and his genitals dangling between his gangly legs. He could smell himself, which was not altogether unpleasant, and then he could smell Londa as she placed the spike heel of her shoe in his crack and bent over him.

Strangely, there was no indignity in this for him, only an intense relief. Indignity was being publicly arrested in his father's *o-furo* by Tanaka Gin. Indignity was being stripped by professional penal people who knew his power, perhaps had even lost money in one of his gambling parlors or had spent an idle hour with one of his girls. Once, they had feared him, but now he appeared before them with his clothes scrunched in a ball in front of his genitals, just another old man, a criminal without either power or influence enough to stay out of prison.

He had wilted. Well, it was no wonder, with the humiliation coursing through his veins like a drug. How he wished to step out of his skin and become a whole new person! Londa would see to that, as only she could. But, tonight, he wanted to go further, to blot out what had been done to him. Tonight, he wanted to *be* someone else instead of pretending for a couple of hours. He wanted, in short, what no one could give him, and he clenched his fists, beating them against the Berber in rage and frustration.

"Are you ready?" Londa reached down between his legs, fondling him. Then, at almost the same instant, came a sharp, painful crack across his butt that made the blood rush to his head in dizzying fashion. "Not yet," she crooned, "but we'll get you there, won't we?"

Of course she would. That was her specialty, why he had become addicted—yes, that was the right word: *addicted*—to her. He had met her at that club everyone had been talking about, had seen her act once, and that was it. He'd had to have her, and have her he did, though not as often as he would have liked. She was so popular with so many influential people that even he, Tetsuo Akinaga, had had to wait his turn.

But then something had happened a month or so before his arrest. She had become more available to him—he could have her almost any day he pleased, though at specific times she designated. What *did* she do at those other times when he could not have her? Better not to know, he had decided. Why destroy an illusion that was working so well for him?

Pain enough to make him moan, and his member uncoiled like a snake, all the bad and humiliating thoughts driven from his mind. The pain continued, a specific kind of pain that, more and more, edged into pleasure, until the line between them was blurred completely and it became both, pleasure *and* pain coexisting in a ball that expanded from his loins outward.

He was moaning as Londa worked him over as only she could. He felt her sweat plopping onto his naked back like droplets of hot wax, each one excruciating, intensifying his pleasure-pain. Then, crouched over him like a giant crab, she did something to him that made his eyes bulge out of their sockets. A great groan emerged from deep inside him and he was sure that he would collapse. But, as always, he did not; he would be punished for that with a cessation of her ministrations, and that he could not abide. Instead, he swayed on thighs and elbows, his trembling thighs threatening to shake his teeth loose. Just one moment more and he would . . .

He heard something foreign, something outside the sphere of pleasure-pain that Londa had created for him. It was sharp, metallic like the latch of a lock being turned.

"What is it?" he mumbled vaguely.

"Nothing," Londa said, digging in again with her high

heel until that taste came to his mouth that he associated with the end.

But he heard it again, and dimly he wondered whether he had heard her lock the door behind her when she had come in. Of course, she had. She always did. But this time— had he heard her do it, or . . . ?

His watering eyes focused on a pair of shoes—black, highly polished, expensive. Not Londa's; these were men's shoes.

"What? Who . . . ?" He tried to change position, to look up past the cuffs of the trousers, but Londa had hold of him and he was immobile, locked in her exotic embrace.

"Akinaga-san," a male voice said, "so good to meet you after all this time."

Still locked in his erotic haze, Akinaga struggled to make his mind focus, but Londa had hold of him and his blood was pounding in his veins; the testosterone was raging and it was like listening to far-off voices through the crack and spark of a forest fire.

"Who . . . ?"

"My name is Michael Leonforte. Are you familiar with it?"

Akinaga tried to shake his head, settled for a feeble "No" instead.

"No matter. I have heard a great deal about you." The shoes shifted a bit. "I think we can do business. I think we can help each other."

"I don't need . . . any help."

Mick laughed. "You should see yourself, Akinaga-san. It's a scream, the position I find you in. Are you certain you don't need help?"

"I'll kill . . . both of you."

"With her heel buried in the crack of your ass? I don't think so."

"If you know anything about me . . ."

"Yes, yes. I know all about the Yakuza. But you're not the force you once were. The Kaisho's inner council of which you were a part is gone—blown away like so many autumn leaves. And what is left? Your power's broken, never to return. You have Nicholas Linnear and your own Kaisho—Mikio Okami—to thank for that. You should never have ousted Okami. And when you put a contract out on him, you really pissed him off. You forced him to call in a debt Okami was owed by his former partner, Col. Denis Linnear. Okami recruited the Colonel's son, Nicholas. Bad move, Akinaga-san. Very bad move. Linnear has almost destroyed you totally. You're hanging on by the skin of your teeth."

"My ... what?"

"It's American slang, Akinaga-san, for terminal trouble."

"I still have my power. And my contacts. They got the prosecutor's case thrown out on technicalities, and now I'm out of jail. Could *you* have done the same under those circumstances?"

"I would never have allowed myself to be in that position."

"Talk is nothing," Akinaga spit out, "but the drool of incompetent and foolish men!"

Then, so abruptly that his teeth clashed together, Akinaga's head was jerked up by his hair and he found himself staring into Mick Leonforte's face.

"I'll tell you what's foolish," Mick said in a harsh and grating whisper, "you here with your ass in the air, being taken advantage of by a woman you hardly know."

"What ... what do you mean?"

"Londa works for me. She's a most valuable asset, don't you agree? I sent her to ensnare you when you showed such unbridled lust for her at the club." Mick shook his head. "How can anyone measure the value of things according to pleasure and pain? That kind of thinking is superficial. I, who am conscious of the formative powers of the human brain, who am aware of its awesome *potential,* can only feel scorn at the way you have managed to squander your power." He pulled Akinaga's face to him. "Don't you see? Here, in this room of *your* apartment I am shogun. *You* bow down to *me.*"

Akinaga said nothing. This man, so feral and demanding—burning almost at the point of madness—had begun to intrigue him.

"Friedrich Nietzsche wrote that in man there is united both *creature* and *creator.* Do you understand this, Akinaga-san? The *creature* in man is the raw material: the clay, fragments of other times and other lives, filth, nonsense, and chaos, the excess of pleasure and pain. But then there is the *creator:* the image maker that turns that clay, that chaos, into *something more;* the flinty hardness that forges a personality in the painful crucible of experience. The spectator-divinity that flies in the face of the common, the rote training, the done thing; that forms, breaks apart, hammers anew, burns, brings to white heat, and then purifies the *creature,* making of it through these rounds of suffering something more, something *better.*"

Mick let go of Akinaga's hair, and at the same time, Londa released him from her hold, so that he collapsed with a groan, rolled over on his back, breathing hard. He stared up into Mick Leonforte's face.

"You don't speak like an *iteki.* And you don't think or act like one." Akinaga paused a moment. "I could have you killed—right here, right now, and it would mean nothing to me—nothing."

Mick crouched down beside him. "Talk is nothing but the drool of incompetent and foolish men."

Akinaga threw his head back and laughed. His cries of mirth echoed through the apartment like peals of thunder. "I want sake," he shouted.

While Londa went to fetch some, he sat up. "You are a fascinating man. Where, I wonder, would someone like you come from?"

"The cauldron of experience."

Akinaga gave a brief nod. "An altogether appropriate answer."

Londa brought the rice wine, along with a silk robe, which Akinaga slipped on. When they had drunk three cups each, Akinaga said, "You mentioned something about us being able to help one another."

"I want something, you want something. A simple barter old as time."

Akinaga, eyeing Mick carefully, said, "I think with you nothing is ever simple." He nodded. "But go on. You have my undivided attention."

Staring into Akinaga's dark, hooded eyes, Mick said, "But it is simple. I want access into Sato International."

For a brief moment there was absolute silence in the

apartment. Then, abruptly, shockingly, Akinaga began to laugh. He laughed so hard tears came to his eyes and he was obliged to hold his sides and gasp for air. "Is that all?" he said at last. He wiped his eyes, then gestured at Londa, lounging in the shadows. "I am very much afraid you've set your elaborate scheme in the wrong part of the forest. I'd like access to Sato myself, but I don't have it."

Mick, pouring himself more sake, seemed not to have heard the *oyabun*. "Allow me tell you a story. This goes back, oh, a decade or so. A then very ambitious under-*oyabun* anxious to take control of a clan he believed—quite rightly—to be drifting without proper leadership, to be under siege from the Yamauchi clan, made a deal. It was the kind of deal that, quite frankly, is made every day of the week. Among Japanese. However, this particular deal the under-*oyabun* made was with an *iteki*. Not just any foreigner, mind you, but a very powerful industrialist who, in exchange for getting his businesses set up in Japan without having to be held up by the endless protectionist regulations, punitive tariffs, and bureaucratic red tape, agreed to make this certain under-*oyabun* rich on the Tokyo Stock Exchange."

Silence lay heavy in the apartment. Akinaga, staring out at the shrine to General Nogi, said, "This is an edifying story, but what does it have to do with me?"

"Wait, it gets better." Mick had taken on the predatory aspect of a wolf. "In order to thoroughly cover up the illegal transaction, this ambitious under-*oyabun* took all the required precautions—setting up a legitimate account at a legitimate brokerage house, engaging a legitimate broker and funneling all trades through him, putting up a small sum of his own money that was easily traceable, putting the account on margin—and then he took another: he arranged for the proceeds of the spectacular investment windfall to come to his twin sons." At the mention of those two last words Akinaga gave a small but noticeable twitch.

Mick cocked his head at an angle. "Now do you see how this concerns you, Akinaga-san?" When the *oyabun* said nothing, Mick continued, "You see, I am a most diligent student of human behavior. I know what it is you want more than anything."

"And what would that be?" A sullen note had crept into Akinaga's voice and Mick noted it.

"The continuation of your line. When you are gone, you want your sons to rule the Shikei clan, and their sons after them, on and on, until a dynasty is born to rival the two-hundred-year rule of the Tokugawa shogunate."

"I think you have grossly misunderstood me," Akinaga said quietly.

Mick shrugged. "Then it is my loss of face, eh, Akinaga-san? But, just for the hell of it, let me play out the hand. It happens that I have obtained certain records concerning the brokerage transactions. Now, they won't have any effect on the industrialist. His name is Rodney Kurtz and he met with a rather violent end earlier this week. I got close with his wife. Kurtz seriously underestimated her. While I was cuckolding him, she gave up all his secrets—happily, willingly, ecstatically." Mick waved a hand. "But that's another story. Back to you. You, well, your myriad contacts within the Japanese justice machine will eventually wriggle you out with a minimum of penalty—a stiff fine, which I have no doubt you won't even miss when you pay it. But as for your twin sons, I do believe they won't be as fortunate. Your protection may be able to extend to them—in the end—but in the interim their reputations will have been irrevocably tarnished. They'll never be made *oyabun* of the Shikei clan—or any other, for that matter."

Mick spent some time lighting up a cigar while he allowed Akinaga to come to terms with the situation in which he found himself.

"I could have you snuffed out in the wink of an eye."

"I have no doubt. But circumstance does not favor you, Akinaga-san. Tanaka Gin is after your ass and he won't stop until he puts you behind bars."

"Fuck Gin," Akinaga spat. "I'm taking care of him."

"Then there's Nicholas Linnear," Mick continued as if he hadn't been interrupted. "He's as cozy with Mikio Okami as his father ever was. And that means he'd become your enemy as well." Mick drew on his cigar. "I believe you need new allies, Akinaga-san. Allies who hate Linnear and Okami as much as you do. Allies whose philosophical outlook meshes with yours."

Akinaga's head swung around. "Allies like yourself."

Mick gave a little bow.

The *oyabun* glanced at Londa. "It seems you have played your hand well, *iteki.*" He gave a grim smile. "Well, I have thrown my lot in with one foreigner. Why not another?"

Mick held up his cup as he poured sake for the *oyabun*. "To this new alliance." The men drank while Londa looked on, silent as stone.

"All right," Mick said briskly. "About your penetration of Sato International."

Akinaga looked at him a long time. Secrets were not something he divulged so easily. At last, he said, "There is a man named Kanda Tōrin. In Nicholas Linnear's absence, he has gained Tanzan Nangi's trust. Tōrin works for me."

9
West Palm Beach/Tokyo

"Fuck you get my gun?" Caesare shouted.

"From your collection, where else?" Vesper said. "What, I'm not allowed to protect myself?"

"You don't need no fuckin' gun now," he thundered. "You got me."

He was in a towering rage, and Vesper wanted to know why.

"As it turned out, it's a damned good thing I was armed. What's your problem?"

"Problem? I'll tell you my fuckin' problem," he thundered. "It's you! Women should not be carrying, *that's* the fuckin' problem." He hit his forehead with his palm. "Jesus, a blind man could see it. There are certain *rules* inna world that shouldn't be violated. Men do men things, women do women things. Women do not go around shooting people. Christ, it's clear as black 'n' white."

They were back at the white mansion in West Palm and he had been on the phone for almost an hour straight, pulling strings, invoking privilege, and using his subtle forms of persuasion to ensure that whatever investigation into Croaker's death was made, it would be brief and perfunctory.

"This fuckin' pain in my ass Croaker was ex-NYPD," Caesare had said into the phone during the last call. "He hadda lotta enemies, right? They all do. One of them whacked 'im. Period. You tell *that* to the feds or whoever's handlin' the investigation. You make sure there're no witnesses, get me? End of investigation, end of conversation." He'd rung off. "Fuckin' cops," he'd muttered to no one in particular. "Once they make commissioner, they think they know it all."

He turned back to her, shook his head. "You're fuckin' nuts, you know that? What the hell am I gonna do with you, killing a fuckin' ex-cop like that."

"What d'you care? From what I could see, there was no love lost between the two of you."

"Loony as shit." He put his hands on his hips and glared at her.

"I got royally pissed off, okay?" Her voice softened suddenly and he saw tears glistening at the corners of her eyes. "You'll make it all right, won't you, Caesare?"

He took her into his arms, stroked her gleaming golden hair. He was filled with pride that she needed him now for protection, she was vulnerable, and giving her his confidence was something he wanted very badly. She was like a dream, every day revealed to him another side of her that delighted him, and now he would do anything to keep her at his side.

"Don't worry 'bout a fuckin' thing. I think we got it all worked out."

And the weird and awful thing was that, cradled in his powerful arms, feeling the aura of his power coming off him in waves, she *did* feel protected, safe as she'd never felt in her parents'. house, or on the street or even with Mother Madonna in the House of Marbella—safe as she'd ever felt with Okami. Nothing in her life could have prepared her for this, and so, for a moment, she was disarmed, the chink in her self-made armor pried back, exposing the starving woman beneath.

Caesare kissed her and said, "Paulie's here an' I gotta say hello to him. It's business."

She nodded.

He tipped her head back with his thumb beneath her chin. "You okay? I mean you whacked a man, an' all, an' it wasn't just some anonymous jamoke. You wanna throw up or anything?"

She smiled. "I already did that while you were on the phone."

He nodded. "Okay then. Move on from it. It's over. Go into the kitchen an' have Gino fix you something."

"I can do it myself."

"Jesus Christ, I know you can. There anything you *can't* do? But what should I do? It's Gino's job. You want I should fire him?"

She laughed. "No." And bowed her head obediently because that was what he needed to complete the picture of having her completely in his power, a woman like her. It was the most compelling aphrodisiac imaginable. "Okay, I'll get him to fix me something." She disengaged herself from his embrace. "You?"

"Nah. I'll pick something up on the way inta see Paulie. He an' his broad—what's-her-name, I never remember. Anyway, they're in the guesthouse." He took her hand kissed the palm. "I may be a while, okay?"

She smiled at him. "Okay." Then she shooed him out the door. "Go on. Take care of your business."

In fact, Caesare spent very little time with Paul Chiaramonte. He said, "How'ya doin'? Ya did a good job gettin' the broad an' her kid outta New Yawk." Then he cuffed Paulie hard behind his right ear. "You fuckin' moron, killin' an NYPD detective. Shit for brains."

"But no one saw me," Paul Chiaramonte protested, "except the broad and her kid. I used a stolen gun that's untraceable, so fuck the NYPD six times over."

"It isn't the cops I'm thinkin' of, Paulie. It's your fuckin' cover. You blew it. You were my little church mouse inside the Goldoni machine."

"But now you're takin' over, who gives a shit?"

Caesare cuffed him another one hard enough to make Paul's head ring. "Putz, don't you read your history? How d'you think the Romans extended their empire so successfully. Infiltration among the conquered. You think the Goldoni family capos are gonna just roll over an' let me scratch their stomachs? That's a sucker bet. They'll pretend to go along with me, then try to stab me in the back first chance they get. An' now I don't have you to keep me one step ahead of them."

Paul's head went down. "Sorry."

"Ah, what th' fuck, you did good with Tony D.'s wife."

Paul's head came up. "So we can forget the whole thing?"

Caesare stepped up into his face. "Fuck, no. Listen, Paulie, I want you to remember every step of this—not as a penance, unnerstand? But to *learn,* so you never make the same mistake again. Got it?"

"Sure."

Caesare reached out, drew the younger man toward him with his hand on the back of his neck. He kissed Paul's forehead. "You're a good kid. An' loyal. I put a high premium on loyalty. An', meanwhile, read some Pliny, for Christ's sake." He looked around the guesthouse, which had been furnished by some local interior designer in soothing neutral shades. He hated it, but what the fuck, he didn't have to stay here. "Where's Margarite?"

"Inna bedroom."

"Okay. You keep an eye on the kid. I don't wanna be disturbed, got me?"

Paulie nodded and headed for the bedroom, where he uncuffed Francie from the doorknob of the closet.

"C'mon, kid. Let's get some lunch."

Francie looked at Margarite bound by wrists and ankles to the corner posts of the king-size bed. "But what about my mom?"

"I'll take care of her," Caesare said, entering the room. "How ya doin', Francie?"

Francie shook her head and said nothing as Paul hustled her out of the room.

Caesare, a can of diet Coke in one hand, stood at the foot of the bed, regarding Margarite. "Now this is a sorry sight."

Margarite stared straight at him. "It was one thing to go after Tony. But by marking me and my daughter you have violated every rule of our world. You're a pariah, a marked man without respect."

Caesare scratched the side of his head with a pinkie. "You finished? Nobody's gonna buy that crap an' I'm gonna tell you why. You brought this grief on yourself, Margarite. You couldn't leave the business to Tony D. You had to stick your nose inta things that didn't concern you, taking trips to D.C. to see Dom's old pals, to maybe strike up new alliances for Tony. An' then, to top it off, you started to play stuff the bacon with Lew Croaker, an ex-NYPD detective, for the love of God." He shook his head. "Why Tony D. allowed you to run amok is one fuckin' mystery. But the fact is, you became my enemy as much as Tony D. As for your daughter—an' what a lovely creature she has become— you left me no choice. When you whacked two of my out-of-town crew, I had to reel you in as quickly as possible. An' I hadda bring Paul inta it. I didn't like that. But, again, you left me no choice; you'd become far too dangerous. In my opinion, Francine was the most reliable way to get to you." He took a sip of the drink. "I think, how things turned out, I was right."

"You're despicable."

Caesare moved around the side of the bed. "Considering the source, I'll take that as a compliment." He offered the can. "Care for a sip?"

"I'd rather die of thirst."

Caesare smiled. "Just like a woman. Overreacting and overemotional." He shook his head. "It was a mistake to make this your business, Margarite. I trust you see that now."

"I have nothing more to say to you." She turned her head to the wall.

"Oh, in that matter, like everything else, you're wrong, Margarite." He sat beside her. "I didn't bring you here for a vacation or even to dispose of you. I brought you here so that you could vomit it all up, every secret that Tony made you privy to. You see, I want what Dom had: his leverage in D.C. and overseas. I want the Nishiki files—the dirt he used t'keep so many of the really big boys under his thumb. Now, you'll do that for me, won't you, Margarite?"

"Get lost."

He stood up abruptly and smashed her across the face with the aluminum can. She cried out, but he ignored her and the blood blooming on her cheek. "You *will* tell me everything, Margarite, or by God I'll march Francine in here, and while you watch, I will take a lit cigarette to her beautiful, unblemished body and face inch by inch."

* * *

Sunlight flooded through the high windows, making of the dust motes suspended in the air tiny dancers that spun and sparked as they were struck. Far below them, in the dimness of his Vulcanlike chamber, Kaichi Toyoda bent to the task at hand. His broad, round back made him look like a tortoise, an impression that his huge shoulders, deep chest, and narrow hips and waist did nothing to dispel.

Toyoda slid a bar of layered steel into his forge, and a blast of heat seared the already uncomfortably hot workroom. The stained and flame-singed ferroconcrete walls were festooned with the tools of his trade. Toyoda was an armorer, a man who fashioned beautiful and deadly blades out of solid bars of steel. He did this by beating out the white-hot steel ingot until it was long and narrow, then folding it over, hammering it again, heating it again until the two layers formed an inseparable bond, then repeating the process again and again, some said ten thousand times, until the composite sword blade was ready to be shaped. The Japanese were unique in all peoples of the world—in that only they had perfected the art of composite swordmaking. They used ultrahard steel to shape the edge and spine of the blade, the one to hold a cutting edge so perfectly sharp it virtually disappeared, the other to create a strong backbone. They surrounded this hard spine with layers of mild steel, soft enough to absorb the shock of the hardest blows. Surrounding this were layers of semimild steel of medium hardness to give the blade flexibility. Only then did it have the requisite strength and flexibility to cleave armor and bone and to resist being broken in two.

"Push dagger," Toyoda said now in response to Nicholas's question. "I don't get too much call for that kind of weapon these days." The swordsmith was old—in his seventies, at least, Nicholas estimated, with a round face and skin as lined and leathery as an armadillo's hide. A wispy white beard floated from the point of his chin.

"But you have been asked for at least one, haven't you?"

Toyoda pulled out the steel and was about to pound it with his hammer when he apparently noticed something, a flaw forming, and he flung the now useless piece of metal into a barrel filled with cold water. Steam hissed like an angry serpent.

The swordsmith wiped his heavy, blunt-fingered hands on his thick apron, went to the front door of his shop, and locked it.

"Let's go inside," he said.

He led Nicholas into a short hallway behind the forge that was as hot as a sauna going full blast. At the end of it was an open tatami room that looked out onto a tiny garden surrounded on three sides by high walls. Still, a single hinoki cypress, dark green, flourished amid its sterile surroundings. Toyoda pulled down mottled bamboo blinds until the upper half of the wide slider out to the garden was covered. Heat rose like dizzying waves from the desert.

The room was small and as decorated as a monk's cell. Toyoda was a Zen Buddhist; as such, less was always more. It was like the single hinoki—it was all the garden he required.

The two men sat where Toyoda indicated. There was a long white scar down the inside of his left leg where a decade ago surgeons had taken out a vein to circumvent two clogged arteries in his heart. Toyoda offered him tea and he accepted. They drank in companionable silence for some time, staring out at the hinoki.

"We know each other a long time, Linnear-san." Toyoda put aside his cup, signaling the silence was over. "I have made you many weapons. Dangerous weapons. Unique weapons."

"I would not have gone to anyone else, Toyoda-san."

The swordsmith shrugged. "I was a convenient source." What he meant was he was the *only* source. He made weapons other swordsmiths could only dream of. He appeared to consider for a moment. "I made a dangerous weapon for a man."

"A push dagger."

Toyoda nodded.

"You designed it?"

Toyoda stared at the hinoki, baking in a sliver of sunlight. "That was the intriguing part, Linnear-san. I worked from his own design. It was crude, yes, but quite ingenious and altogether functional."

"Functional?"

"Oh, yes." The old head bobbed up and down. "You

could kill a wild boar with this push dagger. If you had the strength and determination."

"Could it slash as well as puncture?"

A slow sly smile enlivened Toyoda's face. "I told you the design was ingenious. Yes, it had a distinct blade signature."

Nicholas took out a pad and pen. "Like this?" He drew a weapon's blade consistent with the slashes on Ise Ikuzo's body.

The swordsmith's eyes dropped down to look at the drawing. "Yes, just like that."

Nicholas produced a copy of the U.S. Army photo showing Mick Leonforte. He was a good deal younger, clean-cut and almost formal looking, but there was no mistaking the shape of the face, the sensual lips, or the hooded look of his dark eyes.

Toyoda stared at it for a long time before answering. "This is the man."

"Did he tell you his name?"

"I did not ask."

"Why not?"

"Name leads to purpose, and in my work any purpose other than my own is a distraction."

"Did you make anything else for him, Toyoda-san?"

"No."

Nicholas put the photo and the pad and pen away. "Tell me, Toyoda-san, why did you make this weapon?"

"I would think that would be obvious. It is why I make any weapon. When it is finished, it is a work of art."

"I'm not hungry," Francie said as Paul Chiaramonte took her toward the kitchen.

"Okay." He eyed her. "You nervous about Bad Clams?" When she didn't answer, he switched tactics. "Hey, how about a swim? That pool sure looks good."

Francie shrugged. "I don't have a suit."

"No problem," he said, herding her into another bedroom. She watched, passive as a sheep, while he rummaged through bleached-wood dresser drawers. "Here." He held up a turquoise tank suit. "This looks like it'll fit."

She took it from him, padded to the door of the bathroom. In the doorway, she turned back to him and with a perfectly serious face said, "Wanna watch?"

"Jesus, kid, you're the limit," he said, immediately nervous again. Judging by the look on her face, he was beginning to think she liked doing this to him. "Get in there an' do your thing, okay?"

"What about you?"

He pulled a pair of big trunks, gaudy with tropical fish in electric colors, out of another drawer, which brought a brief giggle from her. "I'll get changed in heah," he said.

Francie closed the door behind her, and with a sigh of relief Paul collapsed on the end of the bed. This assignment was getting to him. First, he whacks an NYPD detective, then he's got to bring the Goldoni wildcat all the way down here like some caveman dragging his unwilling mate to the slaughter. Then he's got to deal with a sixteen-year-old who cracks wise and is, in all probability, smarter than he is. But a very special sixteen-year-old to him, for all that. Because there was a real chance that she had seen Jaqui, had—who knows?—even spoken to her.

Jaqui alive.

The thought sent tendrils of electricity through him. Or maybe this obsession of his was a decades-old delusion. Either way, he had to know. Somehow, he had to gain the kid's trust to get more info out of her. Besides, he really liked her. She was smart, quick, and damned funny. It was rare Paul found anyone who made him laugh. To be honest, his life was a mess, running undercover for Bad Clams, betraying the Abriola family, who had taken him in as one of their own. And as for his private life, forgeddaboutit! He'd been hung up on Jaqui from the moment they had met in '62; since then, no one could measure up to the perfect memory stuck in his head like a melody that played over and over until it made you crazy.

He began to disrobe. As he did so, he breathed out sharply several times as he'd learned to do in his yoga class. Stress busters, as it was billed; Paul knew he needed the extreme stress he was under busted or he'd for sure have a heart attack. He was already battling hypertension, and on too many occasions his doctor had cautioned him on his elevated blood pressure. The yoga was helping, for sure. Next stop, meditation.

He had his trousers and shirt off and his shorts were a puddle at his ankles when the door to the bathroom swung open and Francie stepped out.

"Madonna!" he cried, red-faced, shoving the gaudy trunks against his exposed crotch.

Francie stood in the doorway, clad in the turquoise tank suit, a look on her face like the cat who'd just swallowed the canary. The ghost of a smile that played across her lips made her look just like the *Mona Lisa.*

"You happy now?" he said, frowning.

"Like the way I look?"

She posed like some model in one of those women's magazines, *Vogue* or *Cosmo.* Very professional, very sexy. Paul had to remind himself twice that she was not yet seventeen, though with the hard evidence of her body staring him in the face, it was next to impossible to believe.

"Yeah, sure," he said sullenly. "What's not to like?"

She came and sat next to him on the end of the bed. Staring him right in the eye, she said, "Why don't you put on your suit? I want to take a swim."

"Why d'you think? You're lookin' right at me."

"So what? I've seen it before."

Paul shook his head. "For Christ's sake, kid. Turn around, at least."

She complied and he scrambled into the trunks, but he was terrified she'd turn back and watch. He had some difficulty, though. To his horror and intense shame he found he was starting to get erect. *Oh, Jesus,* he thought. *Just what I need, or what?*

"Okay."

She swung her head around and giggled. "You look cute."

"Why don't you cover yourself up?" he said, more crossly than he'd wanted.

Francie looked down at her body. "Don't you like the way I look?"

He rolled his eyes. "Kid, I like it *too* much is the problem."

She sucked her lower lip between her teeth, contemplating this. Then she stood and, in front of the mirror above the dresser, ran her hand over her flat belly and hips. "You know, last year I would have given anything—a finger, an eye, *anything*—to be thinner than thin. *Painful* is the word that comes to mind."

"That sounds kinda extreme."

She turned around to face him. "It's the truth, all the same." She had these eyes that, when she leveled them at you, were filled with an emotion so naked they made you sure she'd never learned how to lie.

"You have to understand, my body was the only thing that belonged to me. Everything else was controlled by my parents, and my parents were not getting along." She gave a rueful laugh. " 'Not getting along' doesn't begin to describe it. They were in a state of perpetual war. My mom was too smart—she's got her own company, you know—and my father decided he'd punish her for her brains. So he beat her. Continually."

"Yeah," Paul said, nodding his head in acknowledgment, "you got it."

Francie took a breath. "So, something deep inside me decided that if I stayed real, real thin, everything would work out with my parents." She kept her eyes on him, maybe to see if he would mock her. "It was like I made a deal with God. But it took me a long time to learn that what I'd really done was make a deal with the worst, darkest part of myself. I was punishing myself for my parents' war."

She plunked herself down beside him, so disconcertingly close that Paul felt as if he had been singed by a fire. "I hated myself, my body, most of all. So now it's important to me. I take pride in it. I want to show it off."

"Yeah, but, kid, you should be showin' it off t'kids your own age." She began to laugh and he immediately recognized his gaffe. "Naw, that's not what I meant. You shouldn't be showin' it off t'*anyone* right now. Like I said last night, don't be in such a hurry t'grow up. It's not all it's cracked up t'be."

He looked at his watch. "C'mon, let's take that swim."

In the water she was like the dolphins Paul had seen at the New York Aquarium at Coney Island: long and sleek and playful, in love with the water, with its buoyancy, its supportive weight, its cool, clear blue depths. She swam rings around him, her long, deep red hair streaming out behind her like an animal's tail or the dorsal fin of one of the exotic fish that decorated his trunks. He hated his voluminous swimsuit. It was nerdy, the way it kept filling up with air bubbles like a clown's trick trousers.

At last, exhausted, the pads of his fingers looking like prunes, he paddled to the side of the pool and made careful note of the patterns the guards and their dogs took around the periphery of the property and key areas of the guesthouse.

Briefly, he wondered what was happening in that back bedroom between Bad Clams and Margarite Goldoni De-Camillo. Better not to know, he decided, turning away from the guesthouse as Francie surfaced with a great whip of water.

"What happened to you? You gave up too soon."

"I guess I'm not as young as I used t'be."

She swam over to where he floated, his elbows up on the coping. She was a perfect shape for the water, tapered as a torpedo, but as she neared him, her limbs splayed out like those of a starfish, her hands and feet gripping the pool on either side of him.

"That's not it," she said. "You're not used to having fun."

He opened his mouth to say something, then closed it with a snap. She was right. Her lithe body set up warm ripples, a kind of vibration he felt deep inside like the hammering of his heart.

"Yeah, well, maybe I live a life doesn't have too much call for fun," he said defensively. "I got a lotta responsibilities, y'know. People count on me."

"Like Bad Clams." When he said nothing, she added, "Is that why you said being a grown-up isn't all it's cracked up to be?"

He waved his hands. "Where d'you come up with these nutty ideas?"

But she wouldn't budge an inch. "I'm right, aren't I? Working for Bad Clams, ratting on people who trust you and count on you, isn't so hot, right?" Those preternaturally intelligent eyes just would not let him go. "In fact, I bet it sucks."

Right again, he thought. But he'd be damned if he'd admit

it to her or anyone else, for that matter. "It's the life I chose," he said steadfastly, "because it's right for me."

"Lying, cheating, fucking decent people over, you want me to believe that's the life you chose for yourself?"

Now she was really bugging him. "Kid, I don't give a flyin' fuck what—"

"I think that kind of low life chose *you.*"

He made a scoffing sound in his throat. "Fuck does that mean?"

"I think you know."

"What, you like talkin' in riddles?" He tried to turn his head away, found he couldn't. Like a cobra going to its end at the hands of the mongoose, he was powerless to escape.

"Maybe. But I know this: you're being eaten up inside by everything you can't let out—hate, revenge, love."

"Love?" Paul was astonished. *"Love?"*

She put her head so close to his he could feel the soft beat of her eyelashes like angel's wings against his cheeks and said in a low voice, "I know about Jaqui."

Paul, who up to now had maintained at least a semblance of control over the situation, felt his heart freeze in his chest. "What did you say?" His fingertips were like icicles. He had been racking his brains about how to pry this out of her, and whammo! here it comes, right down the chute.

"I think I said that wrong," Francie whispered. "I have met her. Sister Marie Rose, as she's known. I have spoken with her, been trained by her. The woman you have been trying to find; the woman you love."

Paul was sure he was losing his mind. After so many years of digging, of coming to dead ends, of being so sure in his mind that Jaqui was alive, that someone else had been killed in that hit-and-run, and feeling increasingly paranoid as his conspiracy theory was derided by Santa Maria's mother superior. Posing as a reporter and, later, as an intern from a nearby hospital, he'd tried to weasel Jaqui's morgue shot out of the medical examiner's office during the latter half of 1962, but had been rebuffed at every turn. So he'd never stopped believing in his heart, though he had grieved for her and, certainly, had never forgotten. And now this bombshell, laid on him by a very clever slip of a girl whom he knew—just *knew*—he'd better not underestimate. But he already suspected to his lasting sorrow that she was too much for him, for in those naked eyes he already foresaw his doom. And like a sleepwalker he saw himself already too far along the path down which she was all too eager to lead him.

Gathering himself as best he could, he said, "You lying to me, kid?"

"No."

And in that single-word answer he recognized the truth, for he had already noted the lie she had told him last night on the plane when he had asked her about that one special nun with eyes the color of the deep ocean. Jaqui.

"Ah, Christ," he breathed.

"You want to see her again?" Francie whispered. "You want to talk to her?"

"More than anything." He should have hated himself for letting that slip, but all he felt was a rush of elation so strong that the tips of his fingers, so recently numb, now tingled warmly with newfound energy.

"You can," Francie whispered "I'll take you to her. But you gotta get us out of here. Me and my mom."

This was his doom, the road he was already too far down to turn back. The moment she'd uttered Jaqui's name, he knew what she would ask of him in return. She was far too smart to demand anything less. And the truly awful part was, he knew that she would make good on her end of the bargain. He could see it in her eyes, feel it in every fiber of her being. She wanted to help him, and with a heavy resignation he understood finally that he, in turn, wanted to help her.

This was a first for him, a man trained by circumstance to look out for Paul Chiaramonte first, last, and always and fuck everyone else, as he had been fucked over by his father, by Faith Goldoni, by his mother even, who by dint of being Jewish could not even keep Black Paul by her side.

He *wanted* to help Francie, even though it would most surely cost him dearly—maybe, knowing Bad Clams, even his life. But, by God, he'd have fun doing it.

Slowly, as if in a dream, his hand came up and clasped hers in the only embrace he felt comfortable giving her. It was done. The pact was silently signed. It boggled the mind.

* * *

Koei was scrolling through the computer at the Nipponshū Sake Center on Harumi-dōri, a block from the mammoth Ginza Yonchōme crossing. Everything you wanted to know about the Japanese national liquor made from fermented rice was here. Nicholas loved sake, and the computer program was helping her to locate the brands that would best suit his taste.

A shadow passed across the screen and she looked up into the face of Mick Leonforte. He had appeared as if from the ripples of a mirage, a dark and evil place in her mind.

"Hello, Koei," he said. "What a surprise running into you here." Said in that tone of voice she had come to know well during the time they had lived together—she miserable and self-castigating, he rampant all the time, filled with sinuous and disturbing suggestions regarding their sexual cojoining. A tone of voice that told her everything he wished her to know: namely, that this had been no coincidence, that he was far from surprised.

Outside, a thousand people marched by, hustling along the rain-slick streets, black umbrellas crowding each other, bobbing and weaving. Koei felt a little shudder go through her, isolated here, herded out of the moving crowd by this sinister animal she knew too well.

He smiled like a boy on the way to a prom. "Aren't you happy to see me? I mean, it's been a long time since we lived together, a long time you've been in hiding." He gave her a quizzical look, almost sad but not quite because the overhead lights were doing odd things to his features, elongating them as if they were made of tallow. "What made you change your mind?"

Koei automatically glanced around to see who was near them. A lot of people, as it happened, but no one was paying them the slightest attention.

Mick, emotions sliding like quicksilver, laughed. "You're not nervous, are you?" He spread his hands. "I mean, why should you be? Just because you were supposed to marry me and didn't? You ran to Mikio Okami, if memory serves, and he stashed you away someplace where I couldn't find you." He put his arm out, strong and menacing as a prison's steel bar, and she flinched. He saw that and it seemed to please him. "I tried, you know—to find you, I mean. I used every means at my disposal—I made a lot of people miserable, crawling all over them for information. And what did I get for my time and trouble? Not a fucking thing. You were gone, vanished like a puff of smoke. That bastard Okami's a real magician."

He moved closer to her, wedging her against the computer screen, which kept prompting her to ask the next question.

"That's not strictly speaking true," he continued, enjoying her increasing discomfort. "I *did* get something for my time and trouble. Humiliation. It got to a point where everyone I went to knew how badly I wanted you back. I sweated out that search while behind my back they must have been laughing." His face darkened suddenly. "Laughing at me."

"I'm sorry."

"Bullshit." He shook his head, his eyes boring into her. "You're not sorry. You did just what you pleased. You always did. You never cared about me, you never cared about anyone but yourself." His face was twisted with rage. "No, don't worry, I won't hurt you. But I pity the poor bastard you're with now."

He was gone before she could form a reply. Humiliated and sick to her stomach, she turned her back on the crowd inside the center and blindly scrolled through screens she did not bother to read. She could feel hot tears forming and she tried to force them back, but they dropped one by one onto the keyboard. She wanted to run home, to tell Nicholas what had happened, but she knew she must not. She remembered all too well his reaction when she had told him that Michael had fallen in love with her.

The computer beeped, and wiping away her tears, she saw that she had reached the final screen. She had found the perfect sake for Nicholas. Somehow, it seemed totally irrelevant now.

I've got to figure out why my life seems to be running in parallel with Mick Leonforte's, Nicholas thought as he drove crosstown toward the address Tento had given him for the dominatrix Londa. He had been on stakeout, parked across the street from the restaurant Pull Marine in Roppongi, on the lookout for Mick. This was the place to which Nicholas had come when he was following the trail of the stolen

TransRim CyberNet data, and it was here, he felt certain, he would eventually find Leonforte.

He felt as if Mick were a vast penumbra, a shadow mirror image of himself where all the dark forces were held in check. And this led to a truly chilling thought: Mick was the very personification of the Kshira that was rising like a tide inside him, that threatened with its increasingly powerful seizures to strip him of his sanity. Because what was Kshira but the coalescing of those dark forces, breaking the bonds that had kept them in the prison of his mind. Every man and woman walking the earth had these dark forces—evil thoughts, selfish, avaricious, jealous, rage-filled. More often than not they remained mere thoughts, passing through consciousness like clouds momentarily obscuring the sunlight. But the sun returned; it always did. Except in those individuals for whom these dark thoughts became real, metamorphosing into deed. These were the people the police hunted down like animals and shut away for the rest of their lives. This was what Mick had become—was part of him truly a reflection of what lay inside Nicholas?

A police siren's harsh on-and-off blare broke into his thoughts, and glancing in his mirror, he saw a motorcycle cop on his tail, lights flashing. Since he had been speeding, Nicholas slowed slightly, trying to find a place to weave out of the narrow lane between traffic and pull over. He found one, finally, and headed right between two Toyotas. In that moment, he glanced in the mirror to keep track of the cop and, at this closer distance, saw the cop's face and recognized it. It was Jōchi, the hulking maître d' at Pull Marine, the restaurant where Honniko worked. What was he doing impersonating a cop?

Nicholas looked for and found a gap in the traffic, and with a squeal of burning rubber and a cloud of blue exhaust, he took the Kawasaki through a scarifyingly narrow gap between vehicles, accelerating away from Jōchi on his big police motorcycle.

Slamming on his siren, Jōchi took off in pursuit. Now Nicholas would get a field test of all the modifications he'd made on the big Kawasaki engine. As soon as Jōchi got his initial clearance through the traffic, he cut the siren. That figured. His cop impersonation had been blown and he had no wish to attract real cops by keeping his siren on.

Nicholas whipped by the south exit of Shinjuku Station with Jōchi on his tail. Nicholas kept the station to his left for as long as he could, then, at the last instant, he ripped across the divider, almost colliding head-on with a red Mitsubishi. A blare of horns followed him as he bounded up on the sidewalk, scattering pedestrians, then bouncing down at street level, heading toward Shinjuku Gyoen, the park filled with both Western- and Japanese-style gardens as well as a now rather shabby pavilion in the Chinese style dating back to 1927.

Risking a glance in his mirror, he saw Jōchi right behind him, with a brief shout of his siren, rounding the corner that Nicholas had just so dangerously cut. Nicholas, grinning into the quickening wind, accelerated into the park. Because of the poor condition of the structures, it was a relatively deserted place, and the few strollers had plenty of warning, scrambling out of the way of the huge black Kawasaki and its pursuing police cycle.

Nicholas went airborne, flying over a small, rock-strewn pond filled with koi. He hit the other side, skidded briefly, recovered, and was off, heading toward the pavilion that had been built in honor of Emperor Hirohito's wedding. Jōchi made it safely across the pond, his cycle coming down with a jarring thud and almost stalling out. In expert fashion, Jōchi used his booted left foot to right the cycle while he swung it around, then, gunning it, set off after Nicholas.

The pavilion was coming up and Nicholas headed straight for it. Seeing this bit of madness, Jōchi slowed, swinging wide of the course Nicholas was on.

When it seemed that a collision was inevitable, Nicholas swerved so close to the corner of the pavilion he felt a chunk of wood fly off, striking the top of his helmet and glancing off. As it was, his head was swung hard around and pain flared momentarily in his neck. He almost missed the workman's ramp, made out of bamboo sawhorses and banged-up wooden planks. He rode along it, paralleling the side of the pavilion, Jōchi's silhouette disappearing behind the facade.

But he could hear the cop cycle's exhaust booming off the building's facade. In a moment, the cycle appeared on the other side of the pavilion, and Nicholas was obliged to turn sharply left, off the planks, the wild spin of his wheels making the boards and sawhorses fly apart like straw in the grip of a twister.

Around the side of the French-style garden he went, with Jōchi almost on his flank. Into the street, with cars spinning this way and that, more horns blaring, pedestrians screaming, onto the wide staircase that led up to a huge granite-slab plaza. He and Jōchi raced across it. Ahead of them rose the glittering spaceshiplike dome of the newly erected Tokyo-kan, the gigantic underground mall, virtual-reality center, and sports complex.

There were no doors, just a rectangular opening in the dome made to look like a gaping mouth.

Into the mouth Nicholas zoomed, jumping the magnetic-admission-card barrier, screeching down the ramp filled with people running this way and that, scrambling for whatever cover they could manage to find. Nicholas passed gymnasiums for weight lifters, sumo, sprint track, and marathon conditioning. Boutiques of all sizes and descriptions blurred away behind him. He had modified the Kawasaki to be tremendously responsive to even the most minute changes in pressure on the accelerator and brakes. This made for a supremely responsive machine that held him in good stead as he zigzagged his way around terrified people and octagonal ferroconcrete columns set in a double line down the length of the mall.

Nicholas was rocketing down the center, with the columns streaming by on either side of him. And here came Jōchi on his big cop bike. Ahead was the long ramp up toward the other entrance to the mall. At the far end were the virtual-reality parlors on the left, the largest of the gymnasiums on the right. Up there, because of the layout of the city, the mall ended at street level instead of being underground as it was here.

Now Nicholas began to weave back and forth across the width of the emptying mall, coming closer and closer to the columns. He opened his *tanjian* eye and, for the first time, summoned Kshira. The world tilted over, colors deepened to the dark and fiery hues one saw in the heart of a furnace that had been running for weeks on end.

He shot past a column, almost clipping its side as he crossed to the side of the mall. Jōchi, following him, almost crashed and was forced to drop back the space of two car lengths in order to keep his speed under control.

This is what Nicholas had been counting on. He took off up the long ramp and, at the last instant, veered to the right, banging open a set of doors. He found himself streaking along the polished wooden floor of a huge gymnasium. Athletes scattered, leaving their equipment and gym bags where they lay. Dead ahead was a wall in which was an enormous round window looking out on Shinjuku Central Park. The oriel window was perhaps twenty feet off the floor.

Nicholas, in Kshira, shifted his weight back on the Kawasaki. Then, two-thirds of the way across the gym, he lifted the front of the bike off the floor, kicked down hard on the second accelerator he had installed himself, and the Kawasaki was launched upward.

Airborne, Nicholas leaned out over the front of the bike as a ski jumper will over his skis. For an instant, he thought he was not going to make it, that he was going to hurtle headfirst into the ferroconcrete wall of the gym. Then the trajectory of the bike trued and he hit the window square on, the glass bursting upward as he broke through, the front wheel, then the back, landing on a grassy knoll, slipping, the bike almost skidding into a cypress tree, then the rear tire gripping and, as he kicked down the accelerator, the Kawasaki speeding off through the park, into the busy street, between the lines of traffic, far from Jōchi, left in his dust in the middle of the chaotic gym.

It was almost closing time at the Fūzoku Shiryōkan, the Shitamachi Museum, and with just twenty minutes left, almost everyone had left. One who remained was Mikio Okami. He liked to come to this particular museum to rest and to think because of its magnificent reproductions of Shitamachi shops from centuries past. There was a tenement, a merchant's counting house, and the shop in front of which he was sitting that sold sweets called *dagashi*.

He had come from a meeting with Jō Hitomoto, the current finance minister, who was one of the leading candidates for the vacant prime minister's position, along with the rightist Kansai Mitsui, Tetsuo Akinaga's choice. They had met in the Nakamise-dōri, the shopping street within the precincts of the Sensō-ji, the Asakusa Kannon Temple. Okami, who had been saved from alcoholism by Colonel Linnear, nevertheless had an addictive personality, and there was a two-hundred-year-old shop in the Nakamise-dōri that sold *dagashi*, which he visited whenever he could.

This was yet another reason, he reflected, why it was so good to be back home in Tokyo. It astonished him how much he missed it. But his past resided here not unlike this museum, a living treasury filled with glittering artifacts and incidents that continued to exert their influence over time.

He now had the interesting sensation of munching thoughtfully on these sweets in the almost deserted Shitamachi Museum while contemplating a painstakingly precise replica of an ancient shop that specialized in *dagashi.*

He thought about Jō Hitomoto and whether he was, in fact, the right man to take the reins of power. Better him than Mitsui, with his dangerously fascistic reminders of the war and the worst aspects of the Japanese worldview.

He thought about Nicholas Linnear and his long struggle to understand his father, his fate, and his own complex personality. But mostly, he thought about his old friend Denis Linnear. The Colonel had meant everything to him—friend, confidant, mentor, enemy. It was curious and not a little disturbing to realize that all these disparate facets could reside in one human being. But then the Colonel was a rather exceptional specimen. He had seen the future of Japan, had recognized its vast potential not only to itself but to the West. To this end, he had used Okami, manipulating elements of the Yakuza into service, eliminating those who stood in his way. He had, in the end, used the whole structure of Japan—bureaucracy, industry, and political parties—to attain his goal.

Though terribly moral, the Colonel could be a ruthless man when circumstance dictated. Envious others thought his morality mutable—that he manipulated it in the same clever manner he manipulated everyone around him. True or false? As with all things human, Okami reflected, it depended on your own point of view. Okami's point of view slid back and force in the sands of time, but of course that was for very personal reasons that he preferred not to examine. When it came to family, there was a line no one ought to cross. Colonel Linnear had done so, and even today, sitting here in this timeless place, Okami could not find it in his heart to forgive him.

"A museum is a fitting place for you, old man."

Another person had slipped onto the cool stone bench at its far end.

"Look at you," Mick Leonforte said, "the mighty Kaisho sitting here like an old homeless man eating sweets while contemplating the world as it once was." He put one hand briefly over his heart. "How touching." He pointed at the paper bag of sweets. "That's how I was able to find you, you know. I followed you here all the way from Asakusa. That monstrous sweet tooth of yours. You might have been better off with cirrhosis of the liver."

"I know you."

"Yes, you do." Mick put a forefinger up and tapped his lips. "Now let me see, what were you thinking of, being here, surrounded by the past?" He leaned toward Okami suddenly. "It was *him,* wasn't it?"

"Him?"

"Colonel Linnear. Your pal." Mick could see Okami's eyes take on a flat, dead look. "You were thinking about what he did to you." Now Okami's body went rigid, as if he had stared into Medusa's eyes and been turned to stone. "Yes," Mick said in a conversational tone, "I know." He slid closer on the bench. "What I want to know is how you could have allowed it to happen. Oh, it's true, you may not have known in the beginning. But afterward . . ." He clicked his tongue against the roof of his mouth. "What excuse could you have had, I wonder, not to take action?"

"What do you want?" Okami asked in a tone as flat and dead as his eyes. He still had not turned his head away from the model of the sweetshop.

Mick sidled farther along the bench until his thigh was almost touching Okami's. Then he leaned in and putting his lips close to Okami's ear, whispered, "The truth."

Okami seemed to come alive. "The truth!" he scoffed. "It seems to me you already know the truth—or the version of it that best suits your needs. It seems to me that you make your own truth. You chop the past up into such tiny, discrete fragments that they no longer make sense. But that loss of integrity is your very intent because you then very carefully reassemble them in your own image. What is it you call yourself?"

"A deconstructionist."

"Fascistic nihilism is more like it. Destruction is your stock-in-trade; the eradication of existing political and social institutions in order to install your own."

Mick grinned. "It takes one to know one."

"What?"

"Isn't that what Colonel Linnear set out to do in 1947 with you as his trusty sidekick? Sure it is."

"What is a sidekick?"

Mick blew air between his teeth. "An aide-de-camp, a flunky, a *pal,* depending on your point of view."

"I don't know what you're talking about."

Mick snorted. "Passive resistance isn't going to get you anywhere with me, *Kaisho.* Colonel Linnear set out to rebuild Japan almost single-handedly *in his image.* Can you deny that?"

Okami stared mutely at the replica of the sweetshop, but the taste of *dagashi* had turned bitter in his mouth.

"A more fascistic vision I cannot imagine." Mick took the half-empty bag of sweets from Okami's hand, popped one into his mouth. "So let's not be throwing stones too hastily."

"This is your special gift, is it not? To twist the truth until day becomes night, good becomes evil, and morality slips into a faceless limbo where it can no longer be recognized or depended upon."

"Okay. Let's talk morality. Let me animate like ghosts from their graves the names Seizo and Mitsuba Yamauchi, Yakuza who stood in the way of your schemes. Do you deny planning their deaths? And what of Katsuodo Kozo, the *oyabun* of the Yamauchi clan, who, in the summer of 1947, was found floating facedown in the Sumida River. Did you also not arrange his demise? Shall I go on? There are plenty of others."

"I will not play the game of morality with loaded dice."

"You also have not answered my questions. But that's okay, gramps. I didn't really think you would. I know you're guilty as charged, and since the dead cannot bear witness to the crimes you have committed, I am prosecutor, jury, and judge in this court of law."

"Law. What law?"

"The law of kiss my ass," Mick said as he placed the muzzle of a square ceramic gun to the side of Okami's head.

"I know your type." Okami was breathing in through his mouth, out through his nostrils, as if sitting so close to this noxious being was fouling the very air he breathed. "What you call morality is self-glorification. Whatever threatens you is a threat to the world at large."

"Yes. I create honor, just as I create morality. It is the common people, roaming the streets like dogs, who are the liars. Not me."

"Of course not. You are among the chosen. Like the nobles who ruled Greece, the truth resides inside you. Isn't that how you see it?"

Mick ground the ceramic muzzle into the flesh of Okami's temple. "So many people would give their right leg to be in the position I am in right now. All I have to do is pull the trigger, and *Boom!* you're just another part of history. *My* history."

"And this feeling of fulgence, of power endlessly flowing, the bliss of high tension, is what you live for. It is, in effect, your life's work, all that you are or can ever be."

Mick's cheeks expanded like the sides of a poisonous blowfish. "Do you think quoting Nietzsche at me will save you, Kaisho? Think again."

"Being so familiar with Nietzsche, you must know the essence of the Viking saga of their chief god, Wotan, because you live by it: 'Whoever has not a hard heart when young will never get it at all.'"

"How hard *your* heart must have been, old man, to have killed when you were so young."

"I killed to avenge treachery, to destroy the enemies of my father who conspired to have him murdered," Okami said in a voice without inflection, "nothing more or less. What I did I did out of filial duty."

"I was right," Mick exulted. "A hard man, indeed."

"Have you no place for compassion inside you?" Okami whispered.

"Compassion, Kaisho?" Mick sneered. "You have not been reading your Nietzsche carefully enough. Those whose hearts have been hardened by Wotan are not made for compassion. Compassion is weakness, compassion is for the lower man, the liar, the violated ones with a slave morality who run like cowering dogs amid the garbage of the back alleys; who equate power with danger, who see good versus evil when neither exists. Compassion is for the good-natured beast, the easily deceived, the little bit stupid, those overflowing with human kindness, always ready with a helping hand—in short, those whose lot in life is to do the bidding of people like me."

"How smug you are. How sure you are that you understand the equation of universal principles."

"Why not?" Mick's face was arranged in a lopsided grin. "The equation's simple enough."

"That's where you're wrong. It's far more complex than you can ever know."

Mick leered at him. "But *you* know, old man, don't you?"

"I?" Okami seemed astonished. "I know as little of the equation as anyone."

Mick made a face. "Confucian humility is really a pathetic sight to behold. But beneath your good Confucian mask I know what's in your heart."

"Of course you do. You know everything."

Mick squeezed the trigger of the ceramic gun. There was a sound, no louder than a discreet fart. Mick caught Okami before he could roll off the bench.

"Everything," Mick said as if he could stop the sands of time and make the moment last forever.

Because of the incident with Jōchi, Nicholas was forty minutes late for his rendezvous with Okami. When he got to the Shitamachi Museum, it had already closed and there was no sign of Okami. Nicholas punched in Okami's address on the CyberNet but got no response. He left a message for Okami to contact him as soon as possible. Then he called the Finance Ministry, but was told that Jō Hitomoto, Okami's candidate for prime minister, was out of the office and was not expected back today. For the moment, that was as much as Nicholas could do, and he reluctantly got back on his Kawasaki and took off.

According to Tento, the owner of the S&M club A Bas, the dominatrix Londa lived in Meguro, one of the low-lying western districts lost in Tokyo's eternal haze. It was not far from the fairy-tale castle facade of Meguro Club Sekitei, the city's most famous and easily identified love hotel.

It took some time for Nicholas to get there for he was obliged to stop several times as the Kshira he had summoned raged through him, distorting his sense of sight and touch even as it increased his perception in other, more subtle ways. He saw, for instance, the entire grid of Tokyo laid out beneath him, small as a postage stamp, intricate as a wasp's wing. Within each district he could sense the pulse of the city, the energy that pulled people from starting point to destination, not the electrical power of the city but the febrile network of psychic energy of so many people pressed together like ants in a warren. He pulsed with the energy, filled with a dark illumination, burning with Kshira's power.

At one of those stops, his Kami buzzed, and checking it, he saw he had a communication from Kanda Tōrin. He ignored it, in no mood for the young executive.

At last, with the Kshira burned from his system like adrenaline, he turned down the rate of his metabolism. He arrived at his destination and dismounted. Meguro was not an upscale district, and the narrow street on which Londa lived was not among the best of the area. Unlovely buildings from the postwar era, when housing was being thrown up at lightning speed, crammed the streets and dank back alleys, huddled and forlorn, covered in a mantle of industrial soot. A group of Nihonin, bikers in black leather and shiny chrome studs, stared at him as he pulled up in front of the building, a crumbling, ramshackle structure that looked all but condemned.

He found the super in his basement apartment. It appeared as if he had been asleep and he was thoroughly irritated at being disturbed. He claimed to know nothing of a woman named Londa who worked odd hours, mostly nights. The more Nicholas tried to query him the more hostile he became, peering at Nicholas in the low light.

"Half-breed," he finally shouted, "I have nothing to say to you!" And slammed the door in Nicholas's face.

Back out in the street, he found a couple of the Nihonin standing around his Kawasaki, admiring it.

"Bitchin' bike," said one of the youths, a small but muscular Japanese with a nose ring, spiky hair the color of snow, and jaded eyes. His practiced slouch approximated the shape of a question mark. His leather jacket had the rising-sun flag stitched across its back. He glanced sideways at Nicholas. "Looks like you did some work here."

"Two months of it, off and on."

The Nihonin nodded sagely, pointing out the many tweaks Nicholas had made to the bike. Finally, he squinted up at Nicholas. "Name's Kawa. You find who you're lookin' for?"

"No." There was no use denying why he was here. He stood out like an American at a sumo tournament. He looked at Kawa, whose name meant skin. "You hang here all the time?"

"Now and then," Kawa said noncommittally. That got a chuckle from some of his companions.

"You know a woman named Londa? She might have worked nights."

"Worked nights, hah!" Kawa sneered. "That pussy. Yeah, she used to live here. Couple months ago, at least, she split. For *high-class* digs, for sure."

"You know that?"

"Sure do."

"Know where she's living now?"

"Might." Kawa turned to his companions, who shrugged or grinned evilly, waffling their hands from side to side. He turned back to Nicholas. "You got one mean bike, brother." He sucked his lower lip into his mouth, then stuck out his tongue. It, too, was pierced by a ring. "Let's see if it's just a toy or it's part of you. If you can ride with us, we'll take you there, fair enough?"

Their gang name was WarPaint, which was important to them because, as in all Nihonin, it drew them together into a surrogate family. These were the scions of the bureaucrats and businessmen who had forged Japan Inc. in the preceding decades. Their progeny, bored, restless, rich, and so Westernized they'd rather eat a Bigu Maku than sushi, lived their lives at the Hyperspeed of the interactive video games to which they were addicted.

The Nihonin took off in formation with Nicholas on point so they could all see him. He knew what was expected of him. They wanted no part of the establishment, and if he proved a part of it, they'd peel off in a minute and leave him stranded.

He took them through a series of tricky maneuvers, weaving fearlessly in and out of traffic, jumping lights in a massed thunder of rpms, speeding the wrong way down narrow streets that left no margin for error. They liked the escalating danger well enough, but when he launched himself over three car tops, onto a deserted stretch of sidewalk cracked with neglect, he really made his bones with them. They followed him eagerly, whooping it up, grinning from ear to ear, pumped with excitement.

He'd made their day and they were as good as their word, delivering him, an hour later, to Sunshine City, a complex of buildings in Ikebukuro. Sunshine City was built on the site of the infamous Sugamo Prison, where virtually all of Japan's most prominent war criminals had been held and, in some cases, hanged. Besides apartments, the gigantic block-long complex housed a hotel, museum, cultural center, and a sixty-story office spire.

Kawa gave Nicholas the number of Londa's apartment. Apparently, he had a grudge that, like an itch, needed to be assuaged. "She used to use us as bodyguards sometimes," he told Nicholas. "But since she moved upscale, she wants no part of us."

Nicholas thanked Kawa, and as they thundered off, he saw Kawa turn around to stare at him. His snow-white hair shone like a halo. Nicholas parked the Kawasaki, went into the lobby of the building they'd indicated. There was a locked inner door and, on one wall, a sea of buzzers, each one marked with a letter and a number. No names. He pressed the one for the apartment directly above Londa's. No answer. He tried another and another without luck.

The outer door opened and an old lady with packages entered. She was grateful when he held them while she inserted her key in the lock of the inner door and he pushed it open. He gave her back her packages and she nodded.

"I'm looking for Mrs. Okushimo," he said. "Do you know her? She's in E twenty-nine."

The woman looked at him as he came through the door but said nothing. He let her take the elevator alone, preferring the stairs. He reached Londa's floor without incident, went down the anonymous-looking corridor. He could have been in any large city in the world.

He stopped in front of the door to Londa's apartment and rapped his knuckles hard and fast against it.

It was a moment before he heard a muffled voice say, "Who's there?"

He rapped again and the door opened.

Dark almond eyes and long black hair down to her buttocks. She was dressed in an informal kimono and was barefoot.

"Jesus Christ." She stared at him with a stunned expression.

She had good reason to do that. The woman who stood framed in the doorway was Honniko.

She took off the long black hair—a wig—revealing her short blond cut.

"I don't want to know how you found me here," she said, "but you should not have come."

Her eyes said something different, however.

"Will you let me in?" he said, playing to the emotion she so desperately wanted to keep hidden.

"I don't think that's such a hot idea."

But as at their first meeting, in the restaurant Pull Marine, she saw that he would not go.

She nodded mutely and stepped aside. He found himself in a bright two-bedroom apartment with typically low ceilings and small rooms. It was sparsely but expensively furnished with lacquer and cypress-wood sofa, easy chairs, dining table and chairs. There were no paintings, but a silver crucifix hung from a chain on the wall, and a small marble statue of the Virgin Mary was in one of the bookcases. The floors were a light, cool green granite, the walls stuccoed the color of pale bronze, behind a succession of bookcases filled with volumes of all sizes and descriptions. In short, it didn't look like the home of a dominatrix—or of a maître d', for that matter.

Honniko, hipsprung, arms folded across her breasts, regarded Nicholas with a slightly ironic smile. This was a woman of the shadows, used to keeping her inner thoughts and emotions tightly wrapped—perhaps once forced to do so.

"I see it written all over your face. You don't approve of what I do. Well, get lost! I'm not the poor little lost girl you thought I was back in Roppongi, someone you could feel sorry for. You forced yourself into my world, and now that you're in it, you don't like it, you're full of contempt and loathing for what I do, for what I am."

She said all of this in a breathless rush as she backed up until she was pressed hard against the wall holding the crucifix. While still facing him, she had got as far away from him as the room would permit.

"An interesting theory, but that's not at all what I think. Is it what *you* think?"

"What?"

"About yourself." He moved after her, across the room. "Maybe it's you who feels contempt and self-loathing. Do you hate yourself, Honniko? Or should I call you Londa?"

"Either." She turned her head away. "It doesn't matter."

"Oh, doesn't it?" He studied her with some curiosity. "Somewhere beneath all that cynical armor beats the heart of one woman."

"Stop it."

"One woman with a keen mind, unique insights, a worldview, likes and dislikes—"

"Stop it, I said!" she shouted.

He stopped in front of her. "Pleasure and pain. Dreams and so many, many fears she has erected an entire city of facades, personalities, and masks to protect herself. Who are you, do you even really know?"

"You bastard!" she cried. Then, reaching out, she literally pulled herself from the wall by grabbing onto him. Behind her, the crucifix jangled on its chain. She pressed her lips hard against his, her lips trembling, softening as they opened, as her hot tongue sought his. She seemed to melt against him, into him.

Then, abruptly, she hurled herself away, crashing backward, books flying as she fell, then scrambling up, staring at him as if he were a vision of her own private hell come to terrifying life.

"Ah, God, what am I doing? I care about you. I made an oath never to care for a man. I promised myself—"

Nicholas felt something from her mind, a quicksilver current purling the surface of her consciousness. "Do you have someone here? A customer, perhaps?" He strode to the door to the bedroom, opened it, and saw standing there a slender Caucasian woman with deep sea-green eyes. They were the kind of eyes in which you could see whole worlds appear and disappear in a heartbeat, intelligent, cool, kind, and something more—something in contrast, almost at odds, with the deeply ingrained empathy. She looked to be in her forties and possessed the kind of beauty one dreamt about if one were very lucky, but had no chance of finding. It was the beauty of a sort so fragile and febrile one could almost say it did not belong to this world.

She was dressed in a simple black suit and was clutching a black leather handbag. She smiled sweetly and he felt an immediate aura of serenity and determination. This was definitely not a client.

"Hello," she said, holding out her hand. He took it. "My name's Sister Marie Rose."

"Nicholas Linnear." Her hand was firm and dry and slightly callused, and he could feel her physical strength as well as her psychic mettle.

She gave him a little nod, another little smile as she slipped her hand from his. Now he could see the delicate gold chain around her neck on the end of which was a hand-carved crucifix.

"Do I know you?" Nicholas asked.

Sister Marie Rose answered him with her sea-green gaze.

"Marie Rose—" It was Honniko.

"It's okay, Honniko-san," Sister Marie Rose said in perfect idiomatic Japanese. "My presence here cannot remain a secret forever. I must get on with my work."

"And what work is that?" Nicholas asked.

"God's work."

As Sister Marie Rose brushed past him as she went into

the living room, he smelled the faint perfume of roses. Did nuns wear perfume?

"Marie Rose is mother superior of the Convent of the Sacred Heart of Santa Maria," Honniko said. "In Astoria, Queens."

"A long way from home, Mother," he said, "aren't we?"

"Mr. Linnear, I am the head of the Order of Donà di Piave," Marie Rose said in a matter-of-fact voice. "Have you heard of it?"

"Should I?"

"Perhaps not." Some flicker passed through her eyes. "I thought the Colonel might have mentioned it to you before he died."

"My father?" Nicholas shook his head. "No, he didn't."

Marie Rose smiled. "You were right, Honniko-san. I see it now, the resemblance. You look very much like your father, Mr. Linnear. That long, handsome face, the dark, brooding eyes, but your body is so different from his."

"How would either of you know what my father looked like?"

"From my mother," Honniko said. "She knew Colonel Linnear from the *toruko*."

"The soapland in Roppongi. From Tenki."

"Yes."

"Then that wasn't a lie you told at lunch. There really was a *toruko?*"

"Tenki. Oh, yes."

"I keep hearing that name. What is the significance of Tenki? It's the name of the *toruko* where your mother worked as well as what Michael Leonforte calls his shell corporation. That's no coincidence. What's his involvement with this *toruko?*"

The world canted over, the colors running like spilled paint, and he was sinking down through the crust of the earth into its molten core. Kshira turned the apartment inside out, inverted Nicholas's consciousness. He heard Mick Leonforte's voice: *I am the future. I am progress, efficiency, safety in one's own kind. I am for God and country and the family; I am evangelical; I forbid abortion and foreigners and indiscriminate immigration. I am the new Fascism unfurled. You are wrapped in my banner of war. You and I are locked in a circle that's slowly closing its circumference. Soon we will occupy the same space. But we cannot occupy the same space. What will happen then? I know. Do you?*

His eyes snapped open. He was lying on the floor of Honniko's apartment amid a welter of strewn books. Honniko's face, white and stricken, stared down at him. She had been crying, her cheeks were streaked with dried tears. Above her stood the regal figure of Marie Rose, regarding him with her serene sea-green gaze.

"When you fell, I thought you were dead," Honniko said. He felt the flat of her hand on his chest. "Then I felt your heart beating strongly, but so slowly!"

"Honniko—"

Sister Marie Rose put her hand on Honniko's shoulder. "You know your duty," she said as Honniko rocked slowly back and forth as if trying to calm herself.

"Duty?" Nicholas echoed. He was still partially stunned by the onset of Kshira. It had been far stronger this time, perhaps because he had deliberately summoned it not long ago. "What duty?"

Those sea-green eyes floated in his vision. "Honniko is a member of the Order of Donà di Piave, Mr. Linnear, just as her mother was before her. Her duty is to God and to the purpose of the order."

"The order was here, in Japan, in my father's day?"

"Yes." Marie Rose smiled. "He met my predecessor, Bernice."

"I don't understand."

"I know," Marie Rose said in her kindest voice. "But in a moment you will. Honniko will tell you everything. About Tenki. About what happened in the *toruko*. About your father and how their lives became irrevocably entwined." Marie Rose knelt and took his hand in hers. "But first I must ask you for a leap of faith. I must ask you to trust me, even though we have only just now met and you cannot know me."

This close to her he could feel her aura, strong as iron, hot as the sun, but there was a cool undercurrent—no, cold, cold as ice, cold as death. She was in mortal fear of something. What?

"I trust you, Mother."

"Yes." Her grip tightened on him. "You do." She nodded.

"Then look into my eyes, Mr. Linnear, and tell me who you see."

It was an odd question but he did as she asked. Suddenly, he remembered his own question to her: *Do I know you?* And the silent reply he had seen in her eyes. No, he didn't know her, not really, but the resemblance . . . A door opened in his mind and someone stepped through.

Sister Marie Rose saw shocked recognition forming in his eyes and she nodded. "Yes, with your extraordinary psychic powers you've intuited it, haven't you? You see the family resemblance.

"I took the name Marie Rose when I was ordained, but the name I was born with was Jaqui. I am Michael Leonforte's sister."

The Toruko

Borrowed armor, old,
getting fitted to my body—
oh, it's cold!

—Buson

Tokyo

Autumn 1949

In Col. Denis Linnear's estimation the *toruko* was the perfect candidate to become his house of secrets. An anonymous-looking building in Roppongi—Tokyo's burgeoning new pleasure district for foreigners—this Japanese take on a Turkish bath was a place for sex, pure and simple. As such, it was already a harbor for the darkest secrets. In Colonel Linnear's estimation, there was nothing like the sex act to engender secrets. No other human occupation caused the body to be so free and vulnerable—or the soul to be so mortgaged by its secret whims. Fantasy, perversion, peccadillo, infantilism, shameful memory—all took flight during sex even as they took flight *from* an act as revealing as a hot and blinding klieg light.

In such a dark and overheated atmosphere, the secrets Colonel Linnear and Mikio Okami bore were as easily hidden as bullion in a vault.

Not that their secrets had anything to do with sex; at least not in the beginning.

The woman who ran this *toruko*—which was aptly named Tenki, a profound secret—was named Eiko Shima. She was a handsome woman, small and compact, with a deceptively slow pace. At times, the Colonel felt as if she were not quite following what he was saying, but he soon found out she was almost always way ahead of him.

Okami had his people check her out. She was from Osaka, where many women did the work and the men did nothing but take their wife's surname in the Shinto marriage ceremony. She was a shrewd businesswoman as well as a keen observer of the human condition. While other *toruko* were systematically being taken over by the Yakuza, she refused to acquiesce. She had met the underworld's blandishments and threats by besting them at their own game, blackmailing them with abuses so egregious even the SCAP government could not afford to look the other way.

So, with plenty of other less thorny pickings, the Yakuza stayed away, which suited Colonel Linnear just fine. Of late, the Colonel's enemies within G-2 had been given to surveilling his known haunts, and Tenki, with no connections to his world, was an ideal place to rendezvous and hold clandestine meetings.

Eiko provided the Colonel and Okami with a suite of small rooms at the back of Tenki, and they retired there immediately. They had much to discuss. In February of 1947, they had become aware of a black market ring of alarming proportions. In those days black market rings were sprouting like wheat in a Kansas field, but this one was different. It was larger, more well-organized—and it had been run by an American who had somehow made an alliance with a Yakuza *oyabun*. This man was U.S. Army Captain Jonathan Leonard. Some diligent digging on Okami's part, however, unearthed the man's real name: Johnny Leonforte. Leonforte was working for someone named Leon Waxman, but despite exhaustive investigating neither the Colonel nor Okami could unearth anyone with that name.

When Okami had met Johnny Leonforte the following April, he'd also come in contact with his girlfriend. This woman, whose name was Faith Sawhill, was ostensibly a nurse in the U.S. Army. Okami had killed Leonforte in a violent confrontation only to discover that it was Faith who was managing the operation. She had asked him to go into partnership with her and he had agreed. According to Okami, Faith knew nothing about a man named Leon Waxman, and at last the Colonel was forced to conclude that the name was just that—a nonentity floated by Johnny Leonforte to take any investigative heat off him.

Soon after, Okami had discovered that Katsuodo Kozo, the *oyabun* of the Yamauchi clan, had been clandestinely backing the Leonforte ring. He had done this through several supposedly disenfranchised under-*oyabun*, using their *kobun*—street soldiers—so no known member of the Yamauchi could be connected with Leonforte. Over the summer, the Colonel and Okami had agreed to do away with Katsuodo Kozo, and not long after, the *oyabun* had been discovered floating facedown in the Sumida River.

Almost immediately, the ring itself had been thrust into the background, because Okami discovered that Faith's real role was as part of a pipeline back to the United States that was funneling secret intelligence on military personnel from Maj. Gen. Charles Willoughby's office. Willoughby, a thorn in the Colonel's side until he had been forced aside several months ago, was the head of G 2, the Army's Intelligence operation in the Occupation. Willoughby was a well-known fascist with powerful friends in Washington; his former adjutant Jack Donnough—the man Okami had discovered was leaking the intelligence to Faith—had stepped up in rank and office following a disaster that caused Willoughby's transfer. This disaster—the incineration of the group of war criminals Willoughby was training to spy for G-2—had been engineered by Mikio Okami.

Faith's people had a safe house that Okami had been to once—though Faith had warned him never to return there. It was in an industrial district that ran along the Sumida River, a private residence wedged between two windowless warehouses.

Okami remembered the extraordinary town house with its vaulted ceilings, crystal chandeliers, antique furniture, and floor-to-ceiling bookcases filled with fascinating volumes on warfare, histories, and most prominently, philosophical texts. Whose iconoclastic tastes did it reflect? Why did Faith consider it a dangerous place for him to be seen? And whom did Faith ultimately report to?

These were questions Okami posed to the Colonel in the *toruko*.

Colonel Linnear, with his uncanny ability to ferret out the

truth, had already made significant headway. One of the reasons he had picked Eiko's *toruko,* he now informed Okami, was that it serviced Donnough's unsavory sexual proclivities. The major was a pedophile. He liked little girls, but his preference was for prepubescent boys.

Donnough was handsome in a wispy way. With his windblown sandy hair, high forehead, green eyes, and intense thin-lipped mouth, the Colonel could imagine him commanding a yacht heading into Newport harbor. He looked as if he came from money, but that didn't make him a pushover. He was tough as nails—and as political an animal as the Army ever got. He'd outlasted his predecessor, Charles Willoughby.

He took it calmly enough when the Colonel showed him the packet of photos of him in the steamy sexual embrace of a number of obviously young Japanese boys.

"I like this one especially," Donnough said, holding one up. "Could you possibly make me a blowup?"

The Colonel, who knew the measure of things, watched as Donnough carefully pushed the photos back in their envelope and dropped them on the floor at his feet. "Is there a fire anywhere where I can stuff these?" Then he gave a little shudder and turned his sunny-cheeked face toward where the Colonel stood, silent as a cat. "What is it you want?"

The Colonel loaded his pipe, and when he had gotten it going to his satisfaction, said, "What a man does in private is his business, Major Donnough. But everything in life must be paid for and not always in the most obvious way." He let out a cloud of aromatic smoke. "I'm not here to judge you or to drum you out of the service. No, yours is to be a subtler form of payment for your pleasures."

Donnough gave the kind of wry smile only a miser would make. "I hesitate to ask, but could you give me an example?"

The Colonel thought a moment. Then he took the pipe out of his mouth and said, "This stream of information on G-2 activities—backgrounds on the Army's own men—where is it going?"

"You know an Army nurse named Faith Sawhill?"

The Colonel sighed, came and sat next to Donnough.

"This debriefing can be easy—or difficult—it's totally in your hands."

Donnough kicked the packet of photos across the room as if he could make them disappear in the baseboard. At last he said, "You ever hear of Sen. Jacklyn McCabe? . . . No, I didn't think so. Well, up until late 'forty-seven he was a captain in the Army, served well in the war. Then he went home to Minnesota and, as a self-promoted war hero and Republican candidate, beat the pants off the incumbent Democrat senator."

Donnough looked longingly at the smoke the Colonel was blowing. "McCabe's wasted no time making quite a name for himself on Capitol Hill. He's become a self-appointed defender of the American people against, as he calls it, 'the insidious and pervasive threat of Communism.' He's a lime-light hog and the Hill is a perfect forum for him. He makes speeches almost nonstop, all on the same theme." Donnough sat back and, with nothing to do with his arms, folded them across his chest. "What I think he's doing is compiling dossiers on everyone he can get his hands on. What he's going to do with them is anyone's guess."

"Give me yours."

Donnough gave him a quick glance, then shrugged. "I haven't thought about it too much, but if I had to guess, I'd say he's contemplating a witch-hunt at home—a purge of everyone with even a hint of leftist leanings. Personally, I don't think that would be a bad thing."

The Colonel thought about this for some time. "Is this how Faith bought you? The pipeline's going straight to Senator McCabe?"

"I have my views but I'm no ideologue. No, the truth is more mundane, I'm afraid. I like all the good things in life a serviceman's salary can't buy. Faith bought me with money." Donnough crossed one leg over the other. "You know, I'm dying for a smoke."

The Colonel went out of the room, came back a moment later with a pack of Chesterfields and a gunmetal Zippo lighter. Donnough took them gratefully, ripped open the packet, and tapped out a cigarette. He seemed calmer lighting up, as if his orderly mind had processed the disastrous situation in which he found himself and had made its peace with it.

"Do you know who Faith Sawhill is delivering the intelligence to?" the Colonel asked abruptly.

"No, but it's not directly to McCabe. He doesn't know she exists." He exhaled in a long, drawn-out hiss. "McCabe doesn't talk to women in that way. He's a man's man, if you know what I mean. Women have their place but that's it. He'd never listen to what one had to say for advice, that I can tell you."

The Colonel remained silent. He had learned interrogation techniques from the best in the business when he had been stationed in Singapore during the war. Silence was an underappreciated weapon in the interrogator's arsenal. So was a feeling of empathy engendered in the person being interrogated.

Donnough took a flake of tobacco off his lower lip, then took a deep drag. "Who *does* she report to?" Smoke purled out of his nostrils. "At first I thought it was this Mafia capo, Caesare Leonforte, legendary sort. He's the *patrón*—got two sons, Alphonse and John. He and this capo, oh, what is his colorful name?"—he snapped his fingers a couple of times—"Black Paul Mattaccino, that's it. Both capos want to be connected to the increasingly powerful fascist contingent in Washington." He took another drag. "I may be right that Faith reports to Caesare Leonforte. But, if so, there's someone else, someone Leonforte knows nothing about."

"You think Faith Sawhill is a double agent?"

"Oh, not in the sense you and I would think. I mean, she's not working secretly for the Communists or anything. But I get the impression that she doesn't like the Leonfortes."

"She was living with one. Did you know Captain Leonard is really Johnny Leonforte, Caesare's kid?"

"Is that so?" Donnough stared at the lit end of his cigarette. "Now that *is* interesting." He kept doggedly at his cigarette, dragging the smoke deep into his lungs. "But, you know, living and loving are two separate things. She might've hated John Leonforte's guts, for all we know."

We, that was a good sign in any interrogation. It meant

the person being interrogated had made the crucial leap from me vs. them, to us vs. them.

"True," the Colonel said. "I know next to nothing about her. Maybe I should talk to her."

"Good luck to you, then. This one is like no woman I ever met. She's hard as iron and twice as wicked. She knows her own mind." He stubbed out his butt, got another cigarette going right away. "I get the distinct impression Faith Sawhill has her whole life planned out."

The Colonel changed tack for a moment and asked Donnough if he knew anything about the house wedged between two warehouses down by the Sumida. Donnough did not. He didn't tell Donnough that Okami had been inside or that it was a safe house for Faith but not, apparently, for Okami. That was the most curious point. But if Donnough was right about Faith working for Caesare Leonforte *and* someone else, it would make sense she'd have a safe house that was insecure for Okami.

The Colonel rose. "That's it for now."

Donnough looked up at him. "You mean I'm free to go?"

"You bet."

Donnough got to his feet slowly. Almost reluctantly, his gaze slid toward the packet of photos on the floor.

"Take them if you want. I have others."

Donnough gave the Colonel that abstemious smile as he crossed to the door. "I don't think so. I have my memories, after all."

The Colonel waited until Donnough was almost out the door. "Oh, Major." He hesitated, turned back. "I would appreciate you doing your best to find out who owns that town house in the warehouse district."

Donnough's green eyes kept being drawn back to the packet of photos. He nodded and left.

Late that evening, Okami confirmed much of the Mafia background Donnough had given him. Okami, obsessed with the similarities between *omertà*—the Sicilian code of loyalty and silence—and the Yakuza code of fealty, had made the study of the Italian and American Mafia his hobby. According to Okami, there was an intense and bitter rivalry between the Leonfortes and the Mattaccinos, and the forum for their struggle was, increasingly, Washington, D.C. Both desperately wanted to extend their reach into a government in flux and therefore vulnerable to infiltration, bribes, and extortion. Sen. Jacklyn McCabe, the newest rising star, was the ultimate prize.

"I want you to go after Faith Sawhill," the Colonel said.

"In what way?" Okami asked.

"Jack Donnough thinks she's a double, working for the Leonfortes and someone else. Who?"

"Black Paul Mattaccino?"

The Colonel nodded. "Maybe."

Okami looked out the window of the *toruko*. "It's a fanciful idea, but one we're not likely to be able to pursue with Faith."

"Why not?"

"Ever since I killed Johnny Leonforte and she and I took over the network, she's kept me at arm's length. I've tried every way I know to discover what she's really up to." Okami turned back to look at the Colonel. "She's as closed up as a clam, and since Johnny's dead, she's as solitary as a nun. At least, I think so. Although I speak with her at least twice a week, I haven't see her in close to ten months."

"Where the hell is she? Sicily?"

"I have no idea. And all the inquiries I've made have led me nowhere."

"Keep at it. There must be *some* chink in this mysterious woman's armor."

Okami said in the best Confucian tradition, "I will do my best."

But two weeks later, Okami was no closer to unearthing Faith's secrets. The Colonel was staring out at the gray skyline of Tokyo, which, daily, was changing as drastically as the view through a kaleidoscope. His rooms at the *toruko* had become a kind of home away from home, as if the influence of his enemies had put him under siege. He had been thinking of Faith Sawhill's mysterious safe house down by the warehouses and who might own it, when it occurred to him that he ought to take a look at the place himself. As he went down the corridor, he passed the room where Eiko worked—filling the ledgers with her neat calligraphy, keeping track of the comings and goings of her girls—when she wasn't performing less mundane functions with the clients themselves.

"Colonel-san," she said, mangling the els in his title.

He poked his head inside. Eiko's smile was half-hidden behind the wide sleeve of her kimono. "I am about to have tea. Would you join me?"

Eiko had never before asked either the Colonel or Okami to tea, and curious as he was about the safe house, this invitation was so unusual he did not think he could afford to pass it up.

He bowed formally. "Thank you, Eiko-san."

She cleared papers off the table she was using as a desk. She possessed the tension of a coiled spring deep inside her. Was that from ambition or from having to fend off male business rivals, including the Yakuza? The Colonel did not yet know. "You work day, night, time doesn't matter to you. When do you ever have time for your wife, Cheong, or your son, Nicholas—when do you have time to rest?" She slid a tray onto the table, set about boiling water in a kettle she placed atop the hibachi set into the tatami of the floor. She had strong, slender hands and a neck like a swan. Her narrow face gave her a patrician's look. The Colonel could imagine her as the strong-willed wife of a powerful daimyo—warlord—in feudal times.

"There is much to do and too little time to do it in, I'm afraid."

"Spoken like a true Englishman," she said as she deftly distributed *macha,* the finest and most expensive of the green teas, into two cups. This interested the Colonel. *Macha* was normally prepared only for the tea ceremony or for important meetings, when the server wanted to impress his or her guest—or when there were matters of consequence to discuss.

Eiko averted her eyes and ducked her head. "I hope I haven't offended you. In many ways you are very Japanese."

He bowed. "Thank you, but I hardly deserve such praise. And, no, you haven't offended me. My soul is still at least a little British."

"But your heart is Japanese, *neh?*" She poured the boiling water into the cups, whisked the tea into a pale and delicate froth. She held out a cup and he took it in both hands. She waited until he had taken his first sip before touching her own cup.

The silence lengthened. Eiko stared into her tea as if observing an entire universe there. She asked a series of polite questions about Cheong, Nicholas, and the Colonel's garden, which she knew he loved but hardly had any time to appreciate. They finished the pot of tea and she made another. The thing was, the Colonel knew, to be patient. Whatever it was Eiko wished to speak to him about would eventually be made clear to him.

At last she said, "I am not totally unaware of your work here, Colonel-san." She shrugged. "I make no special effort to eavesdrop, but one cannot help noticing the parade of people you and Okami-san bring in here for meetings and, er, other occasions." She paused and he waited. "Personally, I applaud your efforts on behalf of my country. I am pleased that I can, in some small and insignificant way, contribute."

Eiko poured more tea. Now she placed between them a selection of pastel-colored sweets made of soybean paste carved into the shape of maple leaves. The Colonel bit into one, took some tea. The confluence of concentrated sweet and intense bitter made for a pleasing whole. So, too, the Japanese believed, in life.

"I have a certain client," Eiko said. "I work on him myself—he likes me above any of my girls."

The Colonel cocked an ear. Eiko made it a strict rule never to speak of her clients, so the fact that she was breaking that rule now was of great significance.

She seemed abruptly unsure of how to proceed. "Something about this client disturbs you, Eiko-san?"

She nodded. "Yes. That is it precisely." She extended her forefinger and touched one cheek. "He has scars."

"From the war. He's a veteran, cut by shrapnel, perhaps."

"No. I have seen such wounds. They have a particular look. Plus, the stitching is not of the finest quality in field hospitals." She shook her head again. "No, these scars are perfect, and they are almost evenly placed. Plus the skin between them—it has an ever so slightly different color." She took her finger from her cheek and held it up. "I have seen such scars before on a female acquaintance who thought she was ugly."

"Are you saying this client has had plastic surgery?"

"Hai."

"I take it this man is Caucasian. American?"

"Hai."

The Colonel looked at her. Why would she think someone who had had plastic surgery would be worth mentioning to him?

"But not just plastic surgery," Eiko continued. "It appears as if he has had his entire face remade. Bones have been broken and realigned, cartilage removed and transferred." Her fingernail tapped a staccato tattoo on the tabletop. "For instance, his cheeks have been built up, along with the ridge of his forehead. His nose has had a great deal of work—more than one operation. And the skin around his eyes has been tucked to give the eyes themselves a somewhat different shape."

"Sounds to me as if he's got something to hide."

"Yes."

The Colonel inclined his head. "Do you know what it is?"

"He asked me if I could find him a man he has been looking for. He had discovered that I am connected, that I have many friends. He offered to pay me a great deal of money if I found this man for him."

"Who does he want you to dig up?"

At last, Eiko's eyes met his and he could see a trace of anxiety there. "Okami-san."

The Colonel wanted to laugh. "Many people want to speak with Okami-san."

"This man does not want to speak with the *oyabun*. He wants to kill him."

The Colonel cocked his head. "Kill him? Did he tell you that?"

"Of course not. But I could see it in his eyes when he made his request. His hatred for Okami-san was naked as a newborn baby."

The Colonel nodded. "All right, I'll look into it. Does this client have a name?"

"Leon Waxman."

The first thing the Colonel did was swear Eiko to absolute secrecy. He wanted no one—least of all Okami—to know that a Leon Waxman, a man with extensive facial reconstruction, had suddenly surfaced two years after Johnny Leonforte had floated the name around.

In 1947 the Colonel had harbored the suspicion that Leon Waxman had been nothing more than a fiction. But if that was so, who was this flesh-and-blood Leon Waxman?

The Colonel asked Eiko to find out from her friend where she had had her plastic surgery done and started there. During the following two weeks, the Colonel visited every clinic and surgeon specializing in plastic surgery, without luck. There weren't that many, and he was beginning to toy with the notion that LeonWaxman might have had the surgery performed outside Tokyo—improbable as that seemed, given the capital's superior facilities—when he met a second time with a surgeon named Hiigata.

Their first interview had been terminated prematurely when the doctor was informed one of his new patients had begun to hemorrhage in recovery. Five days later, he agreed to meet with the Colonel again.

He was a small, intense man with iron-gray hair and a narrow, almost cadaverous face. "I've been thinking about your problem," he said as they sat in his small, cramped office. Books and skulls loomed on almost every shelf, on every horizonal surface. "You've been making the rounds of plastic surgeons because you're apparently under the impression that this man—what's his name?"

"Leon Waxman."

"Yes, Waxman. You're assuming that his surgery was voluntary." Hazy sunlight filtered through a small window that desperately needed cleaning a year ago and now seemed to be growing a lab experiment on its outer side. "Well, what if it wasn't?"

The Colonel sat forward. "What do you mean?"

Dr. Hiigata steepled his fingers. "Just this. If he had been in some kind of accident—a serious car crash or a nasty fall down a flight of stairs, for instance—he might have required extensive neural surgery as well as bone, cartilage, and skin reconstruction. Tell me, Colonel, have you tried the Hospital for Neural Surgery attached to Tōdai University?"

Another week went by before Dr. Ingawa, the doctor the

Colonel had been referred to by Dr. Hiigata, was available. He was chief surgeon for the Hospital for Neural Surgery.

"Leon Waxman? Yes, he was a patient here for upwards of, oh, ten months, I should think." Dr. Ingawa consulted his records. "Yes. Just over, actually."

The Colonel's heart turned over. "When was he discharged?"

"Last year." Dr. Ingawa looked up and smiled politely. "At cherry-blossom viewing time."

That would be mid-April of 1948. That meant he would have been admitted a little less than a year before: May 1947.

His pulse pounding in his temples, the Colonel said, "Would you by any chance have photos of Mr. Waxman before his surgery?"

"Naturally," Dr. Ingawa said, shutting the file with a defensive snap. "But they are confidential." He was a large man for a Japanese, thin as a rail, with large, bony hands on which all the joints were visible. He wore small, round glasses, which unfortunately emphasized his small, permanently pursed lips and pinched nose. His ears stuck out from his head, making them look like butterfly wings pinned to a lepidopterist's board. He exuded the professor's rather musty air of chalk dust and academic debate. In every glance and gesture he exhibited a sense of existing on a loftier plane than those around him.

"This is official business of the United States armed forces," the Colonel said in his most pleasant voice. "Mr. Waxman is wanted for questioning concerning a series of felonies including trafficking in contraband and murder in the second degree. Please don't force me to return with the military police."

Academic infighting at the university had apparently honed Dr. Ingawa's political skills. He knew when he was defeated. Even so, he hesitated just that fraction in order to let the Colonel know that this was still his territory and he was handing over confidential material of his own free will and not on the command of the U.S. Army. It was a way to save face and the Colonel let him salvage what he could from the confrontation. He waited patiently for the folder.

Only when Dr. Ingawa placed it on his desk and slid it

across to the center did the Colonel say, "Thank you for your cooperation, Doctor." He waited just that moment before reaching out for the folder, preserving his own face.

Then, placing it on his lap, he opened the cover and his blood ran cold. He found himself looking at the face of Johnny Leonforte—the supposedly late and unlamented Johnny Leonforte.

"When he was brought in here he was a mess. Frankly, I didn't think we'd be able to save him. He was—"

"Excuse me, Doctor, who brought him in?"

"I'm not sure." Dr. Ingawa hummed to himself as he thought back. "I think she said she was a nun."

"A nun?" That was curious. "Japanese?"

"No, American." Dr. Ingawa nodded. "I remember because of her eyes. They were a magnificent color. A kind of electric blue. Extraordinary, really."

"Did she give you her name?"

Dr. Ingawa shrugged. "She might have but I don't remember."

"You mean no one wrote it down?"

Dr. Ingawa cocked his head and in his most supercilious tone said, "My dear Colonel, the man she brought in was our only concern. He was near death; he'd lost a great deal of blood and his wounds were both grave and extensive. I don't know what kind of disaster befell him, but it must have been excruciating. My team and I were concentrated wholly on the patient." His thin shoulders lifted and fell. "By the time I came out of surgery for the first time, she was long gone."

"And she never returned—or rang you to ask about Mr. Waxman's condition?"

"Not to my knowledge. No one ever inquired about Mr. Waxman. And to be perfectly honest I think that was how Mr. Waxman wanted it."

The Colonel was finished going through the file. "What makes you say that, Doctor?"

"Oh, nothing concrete. But from observing the patient—well, despite the fact that he had violent nightmares almost every night, he refused to speak to the psychologist I recommended see him. He was rather rude to the man, as I recall." Dr. Ingawa paused. "Then there was the fact that he never made any calls—even when he was on the mend and mobile again. He made no friends among the patients or staff. In fact, he spoke to almost no one save for me and a couple of the nurses—and only then when it was necessary. Yes, on reflection, he seemed to be a man very much on his own."

"Isolated?"

"Why, yes. Very deliberately so."

The Colonel thought for a moment. "He had extensive reconstruction on his face."

"Yes." Dr. Ingawa nodded. "There isn't a part of it, in fact, that remains from his previous face." He said this with an unpleasant smugness, as if Waxman were a prized creation of his, which, the Colonel supposed, was not too far off the mark.

"You said his injuries were both grave and extensive."

"Correct."

"Is this why you redid his face so completely?"

"Why, no. I repaired his injuries during that first surgery. It took us, oh, fourteen hours or so because of the delicate nature of the neural work. The three subsequent operations to give him a new face were entirely at Mr. Waxman's request."

"There's another thing," Eiko said one night not long after. "Waxman's making friends here."

The Colonel, who had been filling his pipe, paused. "You mean among the clients?"

"Yes."

He knew what that meant. Tenki had become a kind of clandestine crossroads, attending to the various sexual needs of the who's who of the American Occupation staff. Not just military men, either, but the flood of technicians, economists, politicos, and businessmen who were, weekly, being flown in to assist in Japan's economic reconstruction. On any given night, a tenth of the top men in Washington were here. The Colonel had seen most of them.

"This is his real reason for being here," he mused.

Eiko nodded. "From what I have observed, I would think so."

She had brought him food—sushi from the all-night place down the street. It stayed open to service her clients, who, invariably, were famished when they exited Tenki. He ate less than he wanted, leaving a third of the raw fish and pressed rice so that she might eat as well. Eiko would never have bought enough for herself.

"Who, exactly, has he been making contact with?"

"I have made a list." Drawing a folded sheet of paper from the wide sleeve of her kimono, she handed it to him.

As he opened it, he said in his most offhanded manner, "I've eaten my fill, Eiko-san."

"I apologize. I bought too much."

The Colonel tried not to frown. "I'd consider it a favor if you would finish it."

"Oh, thank you, Colonel-san, but I am not hungry. Really."

He got his pipe going, then read the list of names she had recorded in her neat vertical calligraphy. "He's going after the cream of the crop," he observed. "What do you suppose he wants with them?"

"Contacts," Eiko said promptly. "I think he's going into business for himself."

But what kind of business? the Colonel thought. He looked up. "You've done well, Eiko-san. I'd like you to keep a record of Leon Waxman's comings and goings. When the time comes, I want to know when I can find him with you."

She took the tray of sushi and was about to leave when he said, "Oh, and Eiko-san, there is this woman, Faith Sawhill. Supposedly, she's a captain—a nurse—in the U.S. Army. But Okami-san and I have reason to believe that she is also something else. He hasn't even seen her for ten months, though she's been in contact. Would you use your contacts to see what you can find out about her?"

"It would be my pleasure, Colonel-san."

Later, when he was at last ready to go home, the Colonel went silently down the corridor. Outside Eiko's room, he paused for a moment. Aware of movement inside, he changed his position slightly so he had an angle of sight into the room. He saw Eiko at her table, bent over, eating the leftover sushi. Her look of sheer delight brought a smile to his face.

* * *

The next day, Maj. Jack Donnough asked to see him after working hours. They met at Tenki while the lights of Tokyo were being lit with the coming of night.

"I've discovered who owns that odd town house in the warehouse district," Donnough said without preamble. He stood in front of the Colonel's desk, fidgeting, so filled with excitement he could not sit down. "You won't believe this, but it's Sen. Jacklyn McCabe."

"McCabe? What the hell is he doing with property in Tokyo? Especially one that's being used as a Mafia safe house?"

Donnough shrugged. "It was a shocker, I can tell you."

The Colonel's brows knit together. "You're certain of this?"

"Absolutely. My source is unimpeachable."

"Christ." The Colonel stood, looking out the window at nothing in particular. His brain was racing a mile a minute, trying to figure the angles. But nothing made sense. Unless Donnough had said that the Leonfortes and the Mattaccinos were both hell-bent to make liaisons with the fascists in Washington. Was it possible that one of them was already in bed with Capitol Hill's chief fascist?

An hour after Donnough departed, Okami came in. By the look of him he'd had no luck tracking down Faith Sawhill. The Colonel, who had been batting around an odd coincidence, said to Okami, "I've never seen Faith. What color eyes does she have?"

"Blue," Okami said, and went out to get washed up.

Now that was interesting, the Colonel thought. It was a long shot, but these days, long shots were all that were available to him. He had been thinking of his interview with Dr. Ingawa, the neural surgeon who had worked on Leon Waxman's face. He'd said Waxman had been brought in by someone claiming to be a nun. Dr. Ingawa remembered nothing else about her except for her extraordinary blue eyes. Okami had referred to Faith Sawhill as living like a nun after Johnny Leonforte ostensibly died. She had blue eyes. Coincidence, or had she been the one to bring her lover to the hospital? Did she really hate Leonforte, as Donnough believed, or did she love him and was now protecting his new identity?

*　　*　　*

Three nights later, the Colonel went looking for Eiko. She was not in her room so he concluded she must be working on a client. He went to her table to write her a note to come see him as soon as she had a moment. He sat down and went through the stacks of paper, looking for a clean sheet on which to write. As he lifted up a partial stack on the right-hand side of the table, he saw something metallic gleaming. He put the papers aside and stared at it. It was a silver crucifix on a slender chain. Was Eiko Catholic? He'd never known it, and she had given no indication that she was anything but Buddhist. She had spoken to him several times of the *misogi*, the Shinto rite of purification by water that she periodically attended. Also, she was so traditionally Japanese in her dress and demeanor that he could not imagine that she was a convert to a Western religion. But if, in fact, she was Catholic, why was she hiding the fact?

He was about to replace the stack of papers when he heard her voice from the doorway.

"Colonel-san?"

He put the papers down. "Ah, Eiko-san, I was just about to write you a note."

She came into the room. "You wish to see me?"

"Indeed I do."

She gave a quick glance toward the still-visible crucifix. "So now you know my secret."

The Colonel stood up. "I've never considered religion a secret, Eiko-san."

She looked at him shrewdly. From this angle, her narrow face with its dark eyes, framed by her black hair, made her seem like a clever crow. "You are half-Jewish, Colonel-san, yet you go to considerable lengths to keep that part of yourself hidden."

The Colonel did not care to speculate on how she had discovered this bit of intelligence about his background. Even Okami did not know. "There are reasons, Eiko-san. Jews are considered different by many people. There is widespread discrimination, though many would deny its existence; no doubt there would be unpleasant repercussions were my Jewish heritage to become common knowledge."

"Well, you needn't worry about me being indiscreet. We

all have our secrets." Eiko went to a chair and sat down, crossing her legs in classic Western style. The Colonel could not have been more shocked had she opened her kimono and showed him a penis between her legs. She switched to her very fine English. "You see, Colonel, I, too, belong to an order that is persecuted as savagely and consistently as the Jews."

He frowned. "Catholics? I don't think—"

"I am speaking of women."

There was dead silence in the room. Now and again, he could hear through the walls the soft hiss of traffic from the street nearby, and then a soft and sexual groan wafted down the hallway like incense.

At last, the Colonel sat down. "Could you explain this, Eiko-san?"

With her forearms on the thigh crossed over her left leg, she bent slightly forward. "I have some information on your Faith Sawhill. The reason Okami-san has not seen her in close to ten months is that she is no longer in Japan."

"Where did she go, back to the States?"

"Yes. Before leaving she'd been staying down in the warehouse district."

The Colonel's insides went cold as everything started to coalesce. "In a town house wedged between two warehouses?"

Eiko nodded. If she was surprised by his question, she did not show it.

"I need to find out what's going on," he said, almost to himself. "I've got to get into that town house."

Eiko's dark eyes flicked up at his. "Would now be a convenient time?"

It had a door of stainless steel, that was first thing the Colonel noticed. It looked like a regular wooden door, but when Eiko used the knocker, the sound told the Colonel the truth.

The truth. This was why he was here now, at the town house Faith had taken Okami to but had told him was too dangerous to come back to. Who was waiting for him inside? Faith? Caesare Leonforte? Sen. Jacklyn McCabe? Even—most wildly—Leon Waxman–Johnny Leonforte?

The door swung open.

A young woman of no more than twenty, whom Eiko introduced as Anako, led them through a lovely oval vestibule dominated by a wide staircase up to the second floor, and down a corridor beautifully paneled in cherrywood and into a magnificent library. Everything about this interior was exquisite and spoke of barrels of money. As was true of the door, the homely exterior of the town house belied what was inside.

The library was made spacious by its eighteen-foot vaulted ceiling from which hung an Austrian crystal chandelier. Floor-to-ceiling mahogany shelves held thousands of volumes of books. An estate-sized Persian carpet of lush ruby, sapphire, and emerald tones was spread across the floor on which was scattered leather furniture: a brace of facing sofas, a pair of chairs with matching ottomans, several green-shaded lamps. In one corner an exceptional French secretary of gleaming pearwood stood like an exhibit in a museum. A small but ornate ormolu clock on a bronze-and-glass coffee table chimed the hour and then began to tick away the seconds toward another. Thick, dark green velvet curtains hung where he knew no windows could be.

He turned to Eiko. "What is this place?"

"It's a home away from home," a rich contralto voice said, "an oasis for strangers in a strange land."

The Colonel turned around to see a tall, stately woman with rosy cheeks, chestnut hair, and the most extraordinary eyes he had ever seen. Dr. Ingawa had been right: they were a shade that could only be described as electric blue. She stepped forward and the black skirts of her habit rustled. She extended a hand, and when the Colonel took it, he found it dry and hard and powerful. An odd kind of heat passed through him and he blinked.

The nun was smiling. "Welcome to our manor house, Colonel Linnear. My name is Bernice. I am in charge of the Convent of the Sacred Heart of Santa Maria."

"You," he stumbled, almost at a loss for words. "You saved Johnny Leonforte's life."

Bernice continued to grip his hand and smile like the sun in August. "All in good time, Colonel. All in good time." She turned to Eiko. "You were right about him, Sister."

Eiko bowed her head. "Thank you, Bernice." She said this in wholly Western style, and the Colonel had cause to remember what she had said to him: *I, too, belong to an order that is persecuted as savagely and consistently as the Jews.*

Turning back to him, Bernice said, "So, Colonel Linnear, what is your opinion of me?"

Still connected to her by her strong grip, he said the first thing that came into his mind. "I think you are the most beautiful warrior I have ever met."

Bernice laughed then and said, "By the sword of Donà di Piave, I think I am going to like you, Colonel Linnear!"

She indicated one of the high-backed leather chairs. "Please make yourself comfortable." She took a seat on the chair that accompanied the French secretary. She sat, perched on the edge like a wren poised to take flight, her back ramrod-straight, her white, long-fingered hands folded in her lap. She had the fingernails, the Colonel saw, of a field-worker. Whatever else this nun might be, he decided, she was not an administrator. In chess terms, she was more the knight or the bishop; the one who spearheaded the attacks.

"Colonel, may I offer you anything? Tea? Coffee? Brandy?"

He opted for tea and she joined him. Eiko disappeared and short moments thereafter Anako arrived with a chased-silver tea service. Tea was done English style, down to the thin rounds of fresh lemon, whole milk, fresh-baked scones, and clotted cream, all presumably on his account. It was an astonishing, unexpected treat and he set about enjoying himself.

At last, sated and content, he sat back. "Sister, I am in need of explanations."

Her eyes darted his way, quick as a bird's, and she spread her hands. "How can I help?"

"What are you doing here in a house being used as a Mafia safe house and which is owned by Sen. Jacklyn McCabe?"

"An excellent question, Colonel," came a booming baritone voice. The Colonel shifted in his seat just enough to get a look at the figure standing in the doorway to the library. He was a good deal over six feet. A broad-shouldered man in a beautiful chalk-stripe suit that made the Colonel long momentarily for civilian life. He wore a crisp white shirt, a cravat at his throat. Gleaming black handmade brogues were on his feet.

"And one I intend to answer."

He had a dark olive complexion, curling, thick black hair, and a thin mustache. His eyes were alive and dancing, as if he found life the most delicious and intoxicating game imaginable. He was good-looking, in his early thirties with sharp cheeks, a strong jaw, and a wide forehead. He looked both intelligent and formidable.

He strode toward them with the carriage of a man who had seen the world and had rightly recognized it as his oyster. "The simple truth is that we are in bed with the devil."

He gave a wide smile that encompassed Bernice as well as the Colonel. "I don't mean the Devil with a capital *D*, though Bernice here might not agree." He stopped in front of the chased-silver tray, dipped his pinky in the clotted cream, and putting it between his rather sensual lips, sucked it off. With unaffected nonchalance he transformed a rather rude act into a perfectly natural one. Natural for him. Here was a true force of nature, and this fact was not lost on the Colonel.

The man took out a linen handkerchief and wiped his hand. "I mean a devil as in an evil man." He sat abruptly on an ottoman, pulled it to a spot midway between them. "That's what this man, Sen. Jacklyn McCabe is. He's a righteous sonuvabitch—sorry, Bernice—sure what he's doing is good work, and that makes him all the more dangerous."

"God puts blinders on fanatics," Bernice said, "and that's a fact."

The man shot out a hand, and when the Colonel took it, pumped it enthusiastically. "Name's Paul Mattaccino. But everyone calls me Black Paul"—he laughed delightedly, pulling on his cheek—"on account of this dark skin of mine. Moors, maybe, from Africa, coming through Agrigento, who knows that far back in history."

"You're digressing, Paul," Bernice said softly. "The Colonel is a busy man."

"Sure he is!" Black Paul boomed. "I know that." He gave the Colonel a wink. "Reason he's here now is 'cause he's such a high-muck-a-muck."

"Paul . . . ," Bernice said in the tone a nanny uses to curtail the more egregious activities of an obstreperous charge.

"Okay, okay." Black Paul sighed, knowing it was time to get down to business. "I've been using a network my family established over here to get close with McCabe. He, in turn, has gotten me tight with a lotta the big shots in D.C. To do that, though, I had to pay a high price. My network's been feeding him the dish on everyone in SCAP command through me."

"Senator McCabe is compiling dossiers on everyone high up in the military," Bernice said. "He's recently confided in Paul that through the military personnel he now has under his thumb, he is beginning to compile the same kind of dossiers on State Department personnel."

"Damned braggart," Black Paul barked.

The Colonel looked at Bernice, but she seemed unperturbed by the capo's blasphemous remark. An odd kind of nun, he thought.

"McCabe has had his uses," Black Paul continued. "Through him I'm in with the people who count in running the nation. That's jake with me, far as it goes. But now I've been hearing rumors that McCabe's thinking of asking for congressional hearings on un-Americanism in the government. If it's true, that's nasty business and I want no part of it."

"You already are," the Colonel pointed out.

"Perhaps we have been guilty of a kind of overzealousness," Bernice said.

There's an understatement, the Colonel thought. "Which brings me to another point. What are *you* doing in bed with the Mafia?"

"Hey, bud," Black Paul said, "you'll damn well be respectful to the sister when you speak to her."

"Paul, hush now," Bernice admonished.

"I meant no disrespect," the Colonel said. "But, from where I sit, this is as . . . bizarre an alliance as I could imagine."

Bernice smiled. "Perhaps *unholy* was a word that came to mind."

The Colonel matched her smile. "It did occur to me."

"Hey, hey." Black Paul jabbed a forefinger threateningly. "I'll have you know my family goes way back with the Order of Donà di Piave." He leaned forward, putting creases in his magnificent suit. "The Mattaccinos have *ties*, Colonel." He clasped his hands tight together in front of his face. "Ties you can't even imagine."

"People like the Mattaccinos have their uses, Colonel." Bernice spread her hands. "We are an order of women—and women have all the limitations of gender working against them. We have been persecuted in one form or another down through the centuries." Her electric blue eyes would not let his go, and the Colonel found himself wondering whether she knew of his Jewish heritage. "God in His infinite wisdom gave Donà di Piave a mandate that has survived the centuries. We do God's work in the manner He chooses for us." She smiled. "Where we are weak, He provides strength."

"Which is, presumably, where the Mattaccinos come in. Are you telling me God wants you to befriend gangsters—mafiosi?"

"All are God's children, Colonel," Bernice said. "Would you turn from those who sin? All are in need of redemption. Because of our influence, they contribute to the Church, to the neighborhood in which they live. They keep many people safe from harm."

"And prey on just as many others."

"I told you!" Black Paul exploded. He jumped up. "I don't hafta hear this kinda—" He bit his lip to choke off the expletive. "This was a goddamned mistake an' I knew it!"

Bernice kept her eyes on the Colonel and remained calm. When Black Paul had run out of blasphemies, she said, "Who among us are not sinners, Colonel? Will you throw the first stone?"

The Colonel, chastened, said nothing. Bernice was right. How could he, a man who had broken laws, murdered, even, in the name of his overriding vision—who had gotten in bed with the Yakuza—how could he take the moral high ground with these people?

"What is it you want?" he said at length.

Black Paul stared down at him, then switched his gaze to Bernice. Clearly, he was amazed.

"We need your help to reverse course. We've gotten what we wanted from Senator McCabe. But now, with the increasing risk of his radical anticommunist witch-hunts, he's become a threat," Bernice said with astonishing pragmatism.

Bending over between them, Black Paul made a fist. "It's time to crush him inna ground."

"And you want me to help you?" the Colonel asked.

"McCabe is scheduled to arrive here in Tokyo the beginning of next week," Bernice said.

"Excellent," the Colonel said, rising, "I'll take out my gun and shoot him dead."

"Madonna!" Black Paul clapped the heel of his hand against his forehead. "Whatta we need this jamoke for, Bernice?"

She turned her gaze on him for a moment. "Because we can't do it without him. Neither you nor I can be seen anywhere near Senator McCabe."

"Devil or no," the Colonel said, "I won't be a party to his murder."

"What murder?" Black Paul's hands whirled like dervishes. "Who said anything 'bout murder?"

The Colonel rounded on him. " 'It's time to crush him into the ground,' you said."

"Yeah, but—"

"Sit down, both of you."

The men sat at Bernice's command.

"Colonel," she said in her deep, calming voice, "we need to find a way to neutralize Senator McCabe, nothing more. We want to strip him of his influence, not kill him."

The Colonel thought about this a long time. He dug out his pipe and spent precious moments filling it, lighting it, and getting it going to his satisfaction. At last, he said, "It may be possible. For a price."

"Money's no object," Black Paul interjected.

"Oh, don't be ridiculous, Paul," Bernice said. "The Colonel is a highly pragmatic man. I'm certain money will play no part in our bargain."

"Yeah?" Black Paul said uncertainly. "Then what?"

The Colonel looked at both of them. "First, I want to speak with Faith—"

"No!" Black Jack shouted. "Absofuckin'lutely not! I will not have it! Faith's outta this discussion!"

The Colonel turned to Bernice.

"The fact is Paul's right. Faith is no longer here. She has returned to the States."

"She could verify everything," the Colonel said.

"Y'see?" Black Paul's hands spun like windmills. "The bastard doesn't believe a word of what we've told 'im. He's like every outsider I came in contact with." He turned to the Colonel, outraged. "You have her word. She's a fuckin' nun, for chrissake!"

"That will be quite enough, Paul!"

Black Paul turned away, stalked on stiff legs to the curtains, and stood staring at them.

"Colonel, I'm afraid this point is nonnegotiable," Bernice said firmly. "Faith is gone, you'll have to accept that."

"You know what you're asking me to get involved in, Sister. Is this so different from murder? You're asking me to take Senator McCabe's *life* away from him. Without his career, with his reputation ruined, he may put a gun to his head."

"The bettah for alla us," Black Paul said from across the room. "The maniac's a devil. Take it from me, I've broken bread with the sonuvabitch an' almost choked on it."

Bernice and the Colonel ignored the outburst.

"You know what McCabe could do to America if he gets his way," Bernice said. "Rip it right apart. Friends, families, reputations, careers, all ruined. Tens, hundreds. And for what?"

"Speculation is not enough," the Colonel said. "What it boils down to is you want me to clean up the mess you had a hand in making."

Bernice shook her head. "That's not it at all." Then she half-turned her head and in a louder voice said, "Eiko-san."

Eiko came in. She was carrying a buff-colored folder and she would not meet the Colonel's eyes. She handed the folder to Bernice and hurried out the way people flee the site of a catastrophe.

Bernice silently handed over the folder. The Colonel took it and it seemed to burn his hands.

"Whatta you doing?" Black Paul said, coming back from his exile at the curtains. "I thought we agreed—"

Bernice held up her hand and now her creamy contralto had a steely note to it. "He deserves to know."

The Colonel, filled with trepidation, opened the folder. It was his G-2 file, all familiar stuff, and he relaxed. Then he got to the end. Two pages had been added as a confidential addendum. They were on plain paper but bore the official G-2 seal. With mounting horror, the Colonel read details of his partnership with Mikio Okami. He turned to the second page. OF JEWISH HERITAGE. There was no point in going on. The words stuck out on the page as if they had been written in fire instead of on an Army typewriter. Lines from Shakespeare's *Richard III* came into his mind: *Murder, stern murder in the direct degree, All several sins, all used in each degree, Throng to the bar, crying all, "Guilty! Guilty!"*

"That is the G-2 office copy," Bernice said softly. "A duplicate was passed on, through Paul, to Senator McCabe." The Colonel looked up to meet her steady gaze. "You know what will happen, don't you, Colonel? Jew. McCabe will brand you a Communist conspirator simply because several well-known Jews were known to sympathize with the Soviet Union. And you're a British national, to boot, serving in SCAP. That fact alone has made you powerful enemies in Washington. These people would dance a jig around your funeral pyre." Bernice took the file from him. "Now the threat of careers, reputations ruined does not seem so remote, does it, Colonel? It has hit home in the most personal way."

The Colonel cleared his throat. "What about G-2? Has intelligence seen this file?"

"Not since it was updated." Bernice slipped out the last two pages and held them up. "Shall we?"

The Colonel nodded numbly. He took up a heavy silver lighter, put it to the lower corner of the papers. Flames flared, eating the evidence. *My conscience hath a thousand several tongue, And every tongue brings in a several tale, And every tale condemns me for a villain.* Richard III was so right, the Colonel thought as he watched Bernice drop the gray ash onto the chased-silver tea tray.

Bernice crossed herself. "The deed is done. Now what are we going to do about it?"

Maj. Jack Donnough was in a jovial mood when he entered the Colonel's rooms at the back of the *toruko*. "You'll never guess who's going to be G-2's special guest come next week. It's classified, so when I tell you—"

He gave a squawk like a chicken about to get its neck wrung. His eyes bulged, sensing his dire fate as the Colonel hurled him against the back wall. His head slammed back painfully, his teeth rattled, and he saw stars. Before he knew what was happening, the Colonel had kicked over a chair and had jammed him onto it. He squeezed his eyes shut, hoping to make this nightmare go away, but a hard metallic click made his eyes snap open.

"Wha—?"

Then the barrel of his own service revolver was filling his mouth. Its taste and length made him gag. *Christ*, he wanted to say. *Christ on the cross!*

"Now I am going to count to three," the Colonel said with his face close to Donnough's, "and then I am going to splatter your brains all over the wall. Is that clear enough for you, Donnough?" The major froze, as if this extreme lack of motion might somehow save him. "Then I am going to place this gun in your hand and I will spread those photos of you all around and put in a call to the MPs. Let them make of it what they will."

Donnough began to retch.

"Go ahead, do it." The Colonel ground the muzzle of the revolver into Donnough's palate. "You'll choke on your own vomit."

Donnough caught himself, tried to stop retching.

"You did it to me, didn't you, Donnough? What made you take such a desperate chance? Did you think I wouldn't get a look at how you doctored my G-2 file? Fascist bastard."

Abruptly, he withdrew the pistol, slapped the major so hard across the face he flew off the chair. Huddled in a corner, his head down, he drew his knees up to his chest and began to cry.

The Colonel, disgusted by this breakdown, dragged the chair over and sat down on it backward. With his forearms loosely draped over the chairback he peered down at Donnough. "Well? I'm waiting, Major."

Donnough sniffled, wiped his running nose on his sleeve. "I—I was scared. I didn't know what else to do. I had to try to save myself."

"That's it?"

He nodded dumbly.

Why not? the Colonel thought. The mundane answers were most often the truth.

"All right, listen up," the Colonel said briskly. "I know Senator McCabe is coming into town the beginning of next week under an intelligence blackout. I also know some of his peculiar sexual proclivities." He paused a beat. "I also know about *you,* Donnough." When the major's head came up and his bloodshot eyes met the Colonel's, he said, "You and McCabe were an item when he was in service, weren't you? That's how you know so much about him." Another tidbit provided by McCabe's former partners. One thing you had to say about them, they were filled with bits of useful information.

The Colonel stood and, wheeling the chair away, grabbed the front of Donnough's uniform blouse and hauled him upright. The major's mouth was rank with terror. "Now you're going to do exactly what I tell you." He lifted the pistol so that Donnough's head shied away. "And let me tell you, if you fuck up in any way, I *will* put this into your mouth and pull the trigger. Is that clear?"

Donnough, still half-stunned, nodded.

"And one other thing," the Colonel said. "My G-2 file has been replaced without those addenda you wrote. If you attempt to alter it again—"

"I—I won't. I swear."

"So sorry, but the plumbing in my usual room is under repair," Eiko said to Leon Waxman when he arrived at the *toruko.* "We will have to use another."

Waxman shrugged. He was thinking about what deal he

could consummate after he got hosed down by the Jap broad.

Eiko led him to the rear of the building. As they passed by the Colonel's office, Waxman heard a voice. "I don't give a good goddamn what you think is best. I'm handling this." Silence. The man was obviously on the phone. Johnny slowed his pace. "That's right," the Colonel said. "Now you bloody well listen to me, Mr. Mattaccino—"

"Oh, shit!" Waxman softly hit the side of his head, and Eiko turned around. "I left the lights on in my car." He gave her a smile that made his scars burn white. "I tell you what, honey. You go on ahead and get everything ready and I'll be right along."

"Hai." Eiko pointed out the room to him, then gave him a little bow and trotted off down the hall.

Waxman turned and took a couple of steps back down the hall. But when he heard the door to the room slide shut, he went back to stand outside the Colonel's rooms to overhear more of the conversation with that lying sonuvabitch Black Paul Mattaccino.

"Mr. Mattaccino, you're sorely trying my patience.... Is that so? . . . I don't take kindly to threats like that.... See here, I'll have you picked up and— Hello? Hello?" Sound of the receiver slamming onto its pips. "Sodding hell!"

Johnny Leonforte had heard enough. A sly, secret smile broadened his mouth. He knocked on the door, and when a voice muttered, "Come in," he did just that.

The Colonel looked up. "Can I help you? I think you've come to the wrong place."

"Nah, I don't think so." Johnny hooked an ankle around a chair leg, brought it under him, and sank into it.

"And you are?"

A limey, Johnny thought. And a colonel to boot. "Leon Waxman." He did not extend a hand, remembering vaguely how formal limeys were.

"Col. Denis Linnear." The Colonel gave him a curt nod and, closing a file in which he had been writing, slipped it into the top left-hand drawer of a desk. He slid it firmly shut, then clasped his hands across the desktop. "How may I be of help, Mr. Waxman?"

"I think you got it the wrong way around," Johnny said with a little grin.

The Colonel's eyebrows shot up. "Is that so?"

"Yeah. I hear you got problems with a man named Black Paul Mattaccino."

"Never heard of him."

"Yeah, well, I have. Fact is, I know the bastard inside out. Bettah maybe than his own mama."

"That's all very interesting but—"

At that moment, Eiko burst in, breathless and sweating. "Colonel-san," she cried, "please come quick. A fight between two clients. One is bleeding and the other—"

"Excuse me, Mr. Waxman, I'll be right back," the Colonel said, leaping up. In two strides he was out of the room. Johnny could hear the two of them racing down the hall.

"That's all right," he said to the empty room, "take your time." Then he got up and, after taking a peek at the empty hallway, sat down behind the Colonel's desk. He slid open the top left-hand drawer and took out the file in which the Colonel had been writing. It had a TOP SECRET G-2 stamp. American military intelligence, Johnny thought. He opened it, found the plans to bring Sen. Jacklyn McCabe to Tokyo early the next week. In the left-hand margin was handwritten in hurried script: *Donnough bringing McC here 2300 hrs, tues. Use rm 7. Mk sure security airtight.*

Johnny's heart was hammering hard in his chest. Senator McCabe was going to be here at Tenki. Johnny knew everything: date, time, place. He knew this was the break of a lifetime. Neither his father nor his brother Alphonse had been able to get to see McCabe. Now he had his chance. The Leonforte family had a great deal to offer the senator, and McCabe was nothing if not a pragmatic man. Johnny glanced up. *Thank you, Colonel Linnear,* he thought. Then, as he heard voices in the hall, he closed the file, shoved it into the drawer, and slid it shut. He got up and was just settling himself in the chair across the desk when the Colonel came in.

"You still here?" The Colonel, clearly annoyed, sat down behind his desk and began making hurried notes.

"Trouble?" Johnny asked nonchalantly.

"Nothing I can't handle."

"Take it from me, it won't be so easy with Black Paul Mattaccino."

The Colonel's eyes flicked up. "I told you, I don't know the man."

"Yeah, right."

"Listen, Mr. . . ."

"Waxman."

"Mr. Waxman, we're wasting each other's time here."

Johnny put up his palms and rose. "Okay. Maybe you're right." He flashed the Colonel a brief smile. "See you around."

That Tuesday night, the Colonel was nervous. So much was riding on a plan that was as fragile as it was audacious. So many vectors heading toward one nexus point, so many variables, so much to go wrong.

"Fragile," Eiko said, turning the word over in her mouth as the Colonel voiced his fears. Then she shook her head. "I don't think so. It's all a matter of human nature, isn't it? And that's the surest thing in the world." She flashed him a smile. "Don't worry, Colonel-san. What is the worst that can happen?"

"McCabe gets away scot-free and crucifies me for being a Communist-loving Jew and Okami finds out I'm hiding Johnny Leonforte from him." He looked at her over his pipe. "Two greater personal catastrophes I cannot imagine."

"Well, at least now you have it in perspective," Eiko said quietly, and in her tone and the look on her face the Colonel knew that she was proud to be involved in what he was doing. This gave him the flash of added confidence he needed.

"Thank you, Eiko-san."

Her eyes lowered before his gaze. "I have done nothing, Colonel-san."

He put the flat of his hands on his desk and stood up. "Either way this goes, Eiko-san, I'm going to take you out tonight for the best sushi you've ever had."

She said nothing, which, for her, was as good as acceptance.

* * *

At precisely 2300 hours—eleven P.M. civilian time—Donnough brought Jacklyn McCabe to Tenki. McCabe was a heavyset, balding man with a slab of a forehead, heavy jowls, blue with permanent stubble, and a thick roll of fat above the collar of his shirt. He smelled of cologne and sweat and he glowered at the world with equal amounts of distrust and hostility from out of piggish eyes set too close together.

But he had an undeniable force of personality and a sonorous speaking voice that could make the phone book interesting, and that, apparently, was what mattered most.

McCabe took a look around the operation as if he were a field commander inspecting the troops. The Colonel could almost see him licking his chops.

"We sure can't get this kind of service at home," McCabe said to Donnough. "The most I can expect is to poke a bull when no one's looking." He roared with laughter.

At last, he was introduced to Eiko. "You got any boys in this rattrap? I mean real fine upstanding youths." McCabe guffawed again, enjoying himself immensely. Perhaps the freedom of the *toruko* after the intensive round of high-level meetings at SCAP HQ made him feel giddy.

"All first-rate," Eiko said in her best imitation of pidgin English. "All up—up—"

"Upstanding!" McCabe roared, making a lewd gesture with one loosely held fist. And when she nodded vigorously and led him to room seven, he turned to Donnough as if she were not there and said, "This looks to be the highlight of a very acrimonious trip, Jack." He put his hand on the door and said in a dismissive tone, "Now you run along and wait till I'm done. Then, maybe we'll get some chow."

Room seven was set up and waiting for him. Through the two-way mirror, the Colonel snapped picture after picture of the senator's hairy, overweight body performing a series of truly astonishing sexual gymnastics with a sleek-bodied Japanese boy of no more than twelve. The Colonel had been in the Orient far too long to be squeamish about such things. Still, he never failed to feel a deep pang of frustration that there was nothing to be done about such practices. He felt no anger and he had some time before he put away prejudices that brought to mind the word *abuse*. Sex was a cultural thing and he had no jurisdiction—either legal or moral—to interfere.

When a naked Johnny Leonforte entered room seven, the Colonel allowed himself a small smile of satisfaction. Human nature, as Eiko said. The young boy was slumped on the floor asleep, but the senator, still filled with energy, had rung for another.

"Jesus Mother," he said when he saw Johnny, "you're too fuckin' old."

Johnny laughed, stuck out his hand, and introduced himself. "Senator Jacklyn, you and I have a lot t'talk about."

"We do?" McCabe gave a nervous glance at the Japanese youth.

"Yes, indeed." Johnny gave him his broadest grin. "I, personally, will see to it you get blotto on sex and whatever else it is you want every night of the week."

McCabe looked skeptical. "I live in the United States, Mr. Waxman, in Washington, D.C., to be exact. Folks over there don't take too kindly to what gives me pleasure."

"But that's the beauty part, Senator Jack. I'm in the business of, er, procurement." Johnny made a deep bow. "I'm your personal genie. Your wish is my command."

The Colonel, watching this first contact through the two-way mirror, had to admire Johnny Leonforte's nerve. This had been the most difficult part of his plan because he had no part in it. He'd had to rely on Leonforte to make contact with McCabe, to form a liaison close enough to bring him—and the entire Leonforte family—down when pictures of McCabe in the embrace of a twelve-year-old boy were circulated to every member of the Congressional Ethics Committee.

Peering through the mirror at the parade of young Japanese boys Johnny now ushered through the door, the Colonel could see he needn't have worried. Johnny Leonforte was a clever and resourceful soul.

"It's over," Eiko said as she happily ate a huge plateful of sushi. "You took care of Senator McCabe *and* the Leonfortes. Bernice and Paul are very grateful."

"I trust you to make sure they fulfill their part of the

bargain," the Colonel said. Her unabashed delight in the food made him happy.

"Of that you can be assured." Eiko gripped a piece of fatty toro with the end of her chopsticks and, after dipping it delicately in soy sauce, popped it into her mouth. Her eyes closed as she chewed slowly and methodically. "This *is* the best sushi I've ever had. Where did you find this place?"

"Okami owns it."

"Ah, Okami." She wiped her lips. "You have successfully kept all of this from him?"

"It wasn't easy and, to be honest, I'm not happy about it. I can only hope this deception doesn't come back to haunt me one day." The Colonel looked past her. "But with his hot temper I knew the moment I told him that Leon Waxman was Johnny Leonforte, he'd go after him again and this time finish the job. That wouldn't have fit into my plans. I needed Johnny to take all the Leonfortes down."

"I hope it was worth keeping him alive. In my estimation he's a very dangerous man."

Prophetic words, but the Colonel would never know that. In the autumn of 1963 he died, and everything he had worked for slowly started to come undone.

Book 4

Beyond Good and Evil

"I did this," says my memory. "I cannot have done this," says my pride, remaining inexorable. Eventually, my memory yields.

—Friedrich Nietzsche

10
Tokyo

Nicholas found Tanzan Nangi in a back room of Kisoko's town house. It was on the top floor, a place of musty smells from long disuse. Cobwebs crisscrossed the windows like bars in a prison. Somewhere a clock with an enormous pendulum was ticking sonorously. The pendulum's shadow was cast across the dusty wooden floor like an admonishing finger.

Nangi was draped across an antique sleigh bed of bitter black ebony. The white sheets in which he was tangled were heavily stained, and when Nicholas approached, he could see blood, black as night, black as the ebony of the bed.

He called Nangi's name but it was as if something in the walls absorbed his voice. The ticking of the clock. Or was it Nangi's heart? He bent down and, scooping Nangi up, turned to take him away.

The ticking turned metallic. In the semidarkness, he saw another shadow cut through the swinging blade of the pendulum. He went slowly back across the room the way he had come. It seemed a very long way; with each step Nangi's gray body grew heavier.

"Who is it?" Nicholas called. "Who's there?" But, again, the walls caught his voice and absorbed it.

Then, he saw movement, and the shadow of the pendulum

was blotted out. Someone—he could not see who—seemed to be sitting cross-legged on the floor. He was blocking the only exit from the room.

Nicholas opened his *tanjian* eye, extending his psyche outward to get a sense of who was blocking the way.

That won't work here.

Then, inexplicably, Akshara shut down. He gave a little cry, just as if he had extended his arm into unknown blackness only to have it lopped off at the shoulder. A cold shudder ran through him as, unbidden, his *tanjian* eye closed.

And, in that instant of panic, he saw the seated figure levitate off the floor. Floating, floating, a soft laughter echoing, bouncing off walls that absorbed his own voice. And then the figure shot toward him with such malignant intent Nicholas threw one arm reflexively across his face . . .

And awoke sitting bolt upright.

"Nicholas, are you all right?"

He looked up into Honniko's anxious face. "Where am I?"

"In my apartment in Sunshine City. You had a—I don't know what to call it—a seizure like the ones you had just before and at lunch. Marie Rose and I managed to get you to my futon before you passed out altogether." Honniko knelt on the bed, wiped his forehead. "You're sweating. Maybe you're sick?"

He shook his head. "No. It's just a nightmare." But such a real nightmare, he thought. He put his head in his hands, went into prana to cleanse his respiratory system. The bouts with Kshira were getting worse; he had no memory of this one. It seemed clear to him now that deliberately summoning Kshira was making the involuntary seizures more acute.

"Where is the mother superior?"

"She left. I don't know where." Honniko said it in a tone that made him understand she was not supposed to ask.

He looked up at her. "That story you told me—about your mother, Eiko, my father, and Johnny Leonforte—"

"It's not a story. It's the truth."

"Why did you tell me now? You must have known who I was the first time we met. Why didn't you tell me then?"

"I wanted to but—" She stopped abruptly, turned her head away. "I have too many secrets," she whispered.

"Like being Londa."

She nodded, her blond hair gleaming. "I didn't want you to know—or even suspect." She took a ragged breath, as if she were holding something mean and nasty tight to her breast. "I didn't want you to misunderstand—to hate me."

"Why do you do it? You don't have to be involved in the sex club scene."

"Have to?" She almost laughed. "I *want* to." Her smile faded. "Now I *have* shocked you." He said nothing and her eyes held his, their gaze probing. "But maybe not. I'm like my mother—she got involved in the *toruko* because she wanted to. Also, it was what the order required of her. She did God's work and so do I."

"I don't understand. God requires you to perform sex acts on men?"

"God requires me to gather secrets. God asks me to help the order amass power. In this world, a woman's work is done in prescribed ways. Not so much has changed over the centuries."

"Then it's not so tough a life after all."

Honniko laughed. "You know, I liked you right away. There's a difference. A—" She leaned across impulsively and kissed him hard on the lips.

Nicholas took her by the shoulders and looked deep into her eyes. "I liked you, too. From the moment I first saw you in the restaurant." She kissed him again with a naked hunger that pulled on his heart. He disengaged himself. "But this isn't such a good idea."

"I'm not a whore." That defiant look again.

"It wouldn't matter to me if you were." He looked at the small statue of the Madonna on a high shelf. "You haven't lost your faith."

"Not in God," she said, following his gaze. "But men can be such bastards." She reached out and touched him. He thought the naked hunger would be in her eyes, but perhaps he still underestimated her. It wasn't sex she wanted from him; from her vantage point, sex was a devalued commodity.

He smiled and took her hand in his, kissed her palm once,

then let it go. "It's after eight." He got off the futon and she swiveled around to look at him. "I've got to get going."

"You'd better wash up first," she said. "You look like you've been in a war."

He stared down at her a moment. *I have too many secrets,* she had told him. How many more was she hiding? he wondered. "By the way, do you have any idea why Jōchi, your fellow maître d' at Pull Marine, would want to kill me?"

"What do you mean?"

"I played a very dangerous game of motorcycle tag with him earlier today. He was on a police cycle and, judging by the way he kept on my tail, he was a very determined man."

"No, I—" She looked surprised—shocked even. "What happened?"

"I made it through a hole in the wall and he didn't."

"I'm glad you weren't hurt." Her shock seemed to deepen. "But as for Jōchi, I have no idea what he was up to."

She didn't, but Nicholas certainly did. Honniko, Jōchi, Pull Marine, were all intimately connected to Mick Leonforte. Perhaps Mick even owned the restaurant. This little game of charades Nicholas had played with Honniko told him one thing: she genuinely did not know about Jōchi's most recent actions. Maybe he couldn't yet trust her fully, but he knew now that though she was in the enemy's camp, she was not the enemy.

"The Denwa Partners want an immediate meeting," Kanda Tōrin said as Nicholas strode into his office at Sato International. The night staff was in place and the place hummed as if it were the middle of the morning. "I have been trying to contact you via your Kami while working on possible responses. I didn't want to leave until I spoke with you."

"Put Denwa off," Nicholas said, running quickly through the electronic messages that had not been automatically forwarded to his Kami. More problems in the Saigon operation. Continuing instability in South America. And three messages—the last one urgent—from Terrence McNaughton, the company's D.C. lobbyist. Nicholas saw that McNaughton had reduced to three the candidates for president of Sato-

Tomkin, the American company Nicholas had merged with Nangi's Sato International.

"I can't put them off," Tōrin was saying. "The contract we signed with them stipulates we must brief them in person every thirty days. We're five days overdue."

"Put them off a couple of days more. We can't have much to report yet on the CyberNet. It's only been on-line in Japan for four days."

"Linnear-san, they have requested this meeting because they have grave doubts about Sato International's long-term viability as a *keiretsu*. The CyberNet, along with our fiber-optic businesses in South America, have drained us dry."

Nicholas looked up, concentrating fully for the first time. "They're overreacting. All we need is an infusion of short-term capital to get us through the next six months."

Tōrin hesitated, a look of obvious pain in his eyes.

"Go on. Spit it out."

"Pardon me for saying this, Linnear-san, but in their minds you are gaijin—and as such unreliable to be in charge of their investment. They have one hundred fifteen billion yen tied up in Sato through Denwa." That was more or less the equivalent of $2 billion. "Unless we meet with them as soon as possible, they are threatening to seek legal remedy." Tōrin's eyes looked bleak. "They will sue for control of the CyberNet."

"That would just about kill Sato. Christ, how did we get into such a mess?" But Nicholas knew. He should have been here. With Nangi so infirm, there had been only Tōrin to take up the slack. Ambitious Tōrin, who, he reminded himself, was behind the CyberNet deal with Denwa. He thought for a moment. "Okay, set the meeting for ten tomorrow morning."

He put his eyes back on his notes, read through them twice before he realized he could not remember a word of what he'd read. Tōrin was cooling his heels, patient as sand. Let him wait, Nicholas decided.

He tried McNaughton but the time was wrong and he got his voice mail. There was a note for him to press in his code to download the files on the job candidates. Nicholas plugged in his Kami and downloaded the data. While he was doing that, he searched for a message from Okami.

Nothing. What had happened to him? The phone rang. The night manager of the Osaka field office had a problem with his fiber-optic contracts, and by the time Nicholas solved it Tōrin was back. With no time to review the McNaughton data, Nicholas pocketed his Kami, put an expectant look on his face as he looked up. Tōrin was still dutifully standing there.

"You came up with the Denwa Partners notion, which may turn out to be brilliant or a catastrophe," Nicholas said, "but how could you allow Nangi-san to sign a contract with such onerous clauses?"

"I did nothing," Tōrin said in true Japanese fashion. "The Denwa Partners left us no leeway for negotiation. They knew we were desperate to get the CyberNet on-line and that we had nowhere else to turn."

"If I were here, I could have found American partners not quite so eager to squeeze our nuts into a tin can."

"I wish you had been here. We could have used your wisdom and experience. I admit I might have been influenced in no small part by Nangi-san's overriding enthusiasm." Tōrin ducked his head deferentially. "But, again, that had a great deal to do with you. The vid-byte technology our American R-and-D division provided us fired him up. This recession has been a long, grinding affair and, along with the ongoing political destabilization, I think people of his age have had a fear that the country was on the verge of disintegration."

"Something new is forming beneath the slough of the old like a second skin. We should not be afraid of what it represents." It was only after Nicholas said it that he realized the same sentiment could be applied to his personal situation.

Let the darkness come.

Kshira.

His eyes flicked up at Tōrin and he made a decision. "Nangi-san has made it clear that I should trust you, so I am going to tell you what I plan to do tomorrow at the Denwa Partners meeting. From what I have been able to gather, I think they are going to make a run at wresting control of the CyberNet from us. We cannot allow that to happen. I am going to need your help if we are to defeat the Denwa Partners."

Tōrin nodded. "I am honored that you are taking me into your confidence, Linnear-san. Rest assured I will do my utmost to prove worthy of your trust."

Kanda Tōrin did not go home after work. He went, instead, to his car and made a brief call to a coded address on his Kami. Then he drove through rain-slick streets in an almost aimless pattern. More than twice, he doubled back on his route, watching in his side mirror for any cars that stayed with him. There were none.

At last, he arrived at a ferroconcrete building in Toshima-ku studded with antennas and a satellite dish. A large and incongruous mirror jutted from one corner, angled to catch the sun and reflect its rays onto a minuscule and otherwise shadow-stifled garden beside the building's entrance. At the far corner of the block a bar's neon sign flickered like an eyelid with a nervous twitch.

Glancing at the car's clock, he saw that he was early. He turned on the radio and listened to the latest political news. The smart money had the reactionary Kansai Mitsui in the lead for prime minister. Hitomoto, the finance minister, looked as if he couldn't muster coalition support. And while all the warring political parties dithered, the economy was going to hell. Dead meat, Tōrin thought.

Cars hissed by his window, throwing up brief sprays, rainbowed in the overbright urban night. A pair of headlights split the rain and streetlights flared off the hood of a large van as it passed by. Silence.

Tōrin looked at the dial of the illuminated clock and got out of the Lexus. He went up the block and into the bar. He took the last stool and ordered a Suntory Scotch and water. It was placed down on the dark wood bar on top of a small piece of folded paper. Someone was singing badly and drunkenly along with a karaoke version of Frank Sinatra's "My Way." Tōrin regarded this man with a certain amount of envy. He was a typical Japanese salaryman, with a boring job, a good salary, benefits, a wife and no doubt children at home. What did he know of high-stakes intrigue, industrial espionage, a man so formidable as Nicholas Linnear peering suspiciously at his every move? Life was simple for him; at the end of the day he could afford to sing kara-oke and get blind drunk.

Tōrin took the tiniest sip of his Scotch, set the glass down, aware of the well of self-pity that had opened up inside him. *Keep calm,* he thought. *Big ambitions mean taking big risks. That's what you wanted, isn't it?* He took another sip of his drink. As he put the glass down on the bartop, he slipped his hand over the paper. Unfolding it in his lap, he read the instructions. He left the Scotch on the bartop. The drunken man had segued into "Strangers in the Night" and it was painful. Tōrin paid for his drink and left the bar.

The Nogi Jinja was lit up like a stage set, but then, Tōrin reflected, all of Roppongi was, in many ways, a stage set. By day, it gleamed with the newest fashions, the most expensive jewelry, the most extravagant art. By night, it glittered between the raindrops, throbbing to the beat of hip-hop, way-cool acid jazz, and the massed guttural roar of sleekly painted motorcycles. It was a bit of living sculpture, an ultra-modern torso on which could be placed many heads, depending on the time of day and the zeitgeist of the times.

He found Akinaga's hideaway without difficulty and took the stainless-steel and cut-glass elevator to the top floor of the narrow high-rise. The door to the just-released *oyabun*'s apartment was open as he stepped into the hallway. This should have made him wary.

The darkness inside seemed alive, waiting for him. It was hot and sticky, as close as the inside of a coffin. He breathed shallowly through his mouth. There was a stench in here, like rotting flowers, like death reaching out its hand. It all but made him shudder. Then the lights blazed on, making Tōrin blink rapidly.

"Good evening, Tōrin-san," Mick Leonforte said as Tōrin came into the apartment. Someone closed and locked the door behind him, then disappeared into another room. It was Jōchi. He had recovered from his high-speed motorcycle pursuit of Nicholas. Mick had sent him after Nicholas to keep him from making his rendezvous with Mikio Okami at the Shitamachi Museum. Mick, who, as a Denwa partner, had access to a Kami communicator and the TransRim Cyber-Net, had "read" Okami's vid-mail to Nicholas setting up the meet. He had sent Jōchi out to keep Nicholas away from the rendezvous site long enough for Mick to snatch Okami.

"Pardon me," Tōrin said to Mick, "but do I know you?"

Mick gave a mock-bow, an offensive parody of Japanese custom, said, "I can imagine your surprise and confusion, Tōrin-san. You had been expecting Akinaga-san to greet you at the door." He smiled an unpleasant smile. "The great *oyabun* is otherwise occupied, but he kindly informed me of your imminent arrival." Mick ushered him into the living room. "He offers his apologies and asked me to take his place. He and I have come to a certain arrangement."

"And you are?" Tōrin stopped in his tracks, all the breath going out of him. "Good God."

He stood, rooted to the spot, staring at an old man who, naked, was hanging upside down from a chain from the ceiling. His skin was as white as milk, except for his neck and face, which were ruddy with blood. Over almost all his body great swaths of intricate *irezumi* spread like tapestries in a great hall. Mythical creatures, female sirens, great mailed warriors brandishing gleaming weapons, fire, ice, and wind-whipped rain, all painstakingly tattooed into the skin, spoke eloquently of the Japanese idea of machismo: violence turned inward, an exotic display of masochism.

At the old man's side was a stainless-steel IV stand from which hung a soft plastic bag filled with a pale amber liquid that was by drips entering a vein on the inside of his left wrist, which was curled up like the claw of an animal.

"What is this?" Tōrin whispered hoarsely without taking his eyes from the terrible but irresistible sight of a human being so grotesquely trussed and demeaned.

"This," said Mick with the grand flourish of a ringmaster at a circus, "is Mikio Okami, *oyabun of oyabun,* the Kaisho."

"The Kaisho," Tōrin said, unable to wrench his gaze away. "I thought he was a myth."

"So was the concept of a round earth, once upon a time."

At last, Tōrin tore his eyes away from the Kaisho and stared at Mick. He could see this man was clearly enjoying himself. "I don't understand any of this."

Mick was grinning madly. "All in good time." He gave

that mock-bow again. "Michael Leonforte. I am in the process of making a leveraged buyout of Akinaga's business."

Tōrin goggled. "Akinaga-san is Yakuza. Even if I could believe he would willingly give up his leadership of the Shikei clan—which is quite out of the question—he could never designate you as *oyabun* to succeed him. You are gaijin."

"Fuck that. This is a brave new world—and a brave new world order. Wake up. You guys are no longer *ichiban,* no longer number one. The game is global now, buddy. Fuck, *everything's* interconnected. Which means, if you're clever enough, anything's possible!" Mick came and slung his arm around Tōrin's shoulder, another horrendous breach of etiquette from which Tōrin literally cringed. Mick liked his discomfort just fine. "You better be ready to make alliances. Strategic partners are the only things that will save you." He squeezed Tōrin's shoulder hard. "And, believe me, I'm not offended. When you get to know me better, you'll understand that anything *is* possible for me."

Tōrin broke free of Mick's vile embrace and pointed to Mikio Okami. "Why have you done this?"

"All part of the master plan, Tōrin-san, don't you worry about that. You just concentrate on your part."

Tōrin turned. "My part?"

"Sure." Mick bobbed his head. "That's why you're here, isn't it?"

"I came to see Akinaga-san."

"Yessir, you did. You work for the great *oyabun,* don't you." Mick spread his hands. "Which means you work for me now."

"Where is Akinaga-san?" Tōrin asked, looking around. "I want to—"

He stopped, his heart a trip-hammer in his chest. The muzzle of a .38-caliber automatic was pressed hard against his temple.

"Let's get the ground rules straight. You don't *want* anything anymore except to do what I tell you. Is that clear?"

Tōrin nodded.

"You have been rising like a phoenix on Akinaga-san's money and by his benevolent hand," Mick continued in a calm and studied tone. It was nothing short of miraculous, Tōrin thought dizzily, how Mick's voice could change like the skin of a chameleon, evoking different and compelling emotions. "The hand that took you off the street, out of the Nihonin, the nouveau nihilists whose daddies worked too hard, made too much money, became too successful for their offspring to possibly emulate. So rather than compete with daddy and fail, you dropped out, joined mindless thrill-kill cults, slept days, drove endlessly through the nights, did drugs and sex, believed in nothing and tore yourself to shreds."

There was a pause during which Tōrin tried unsuccessfully not to look at Mikio Okami's tattooed body.

"I would say that pretty well defined you when Akinaga-san took you off the streets, *neh?*"

Tōrin, horrified, said nothing.

"He gave you a home, provided you with an education and a purpose." Mick shrugged. "What more could you want or need?" Then he laughed harshly. "I'll tell you what. Fucking Akinaga's a miser. Think he cares about you? Shit, no. He doesn't care whether you live or die, as long as you're of use to him. With me, the sky's the limit, get me? You can make a fortune, and I mean that literally. You can even run things, if you've got the right attitude." He clutched Tōrin's crotch. "And the balls for it. Interested?"

Tōrin nodded again.

Mick made the gun disappear.

"Okay, then," Mick said, seemingly mollified. "Here's the deal. You're inside Sato International, which means you're valuable to me. I control Denwa Partners." He laughed. "You should see your face, Tōrin-san. Don't look so surprised. I've been manipulating events for quite some time. I whacked Rodney Kurtz, but not before I fucked his wife in as many places and positions as I could think of. Giai Kurtz despised her husband and she was all too pleased to vomit up all his secrets. I got Kurtz's cut of Denwa from his estate, I overruled the one piece of opposition inside Denwa—"

"You murdered Ise Ikuzo."

"Yah." Mick licked his chops. "And I did a fine job of it, too." He laughed. "Who d'you think called for tomorrow's meeting between Linnear and the Denwa Partners? Yours truly. That's when I take control of everything—Denwa, the CyberNet, Sato International."

Tōrin's eyes followed Mick as he began to move. "I don't believe you."

Mick went to a sideboard. As he passed Okami, he punched him casually in the stomach. Okami gave a low groan. Mick went to a small metal surgical table on which were a line of vials and test tubes. He poured some liquids into two small teacups, brought them over to where Tōrin stood. He held them out.

"Okay. One's got colored water in it. The other has some of what was fed to Kappa Watanabe, your tech." He hooked a thumb. "Also the great Kaisho here." He smiled benignly. "It's called Banh Tom. Care to try some?"

Tōrin recoiled. "What is it?"

"As I said, it's only colored water."

"No, the other one."

Mick shrugged. "You said you didn't believe me when I told you I was going to take control of Sato tomorrow."

"I *can't* believe it."

"You mean you *won't* believe it." Mick frowned, turning pensive. "Why is it human beings refuse to believe the evidence in front of their eyes? What makes the mind create safe little kingdoms of its own when the world is such a *very* dangerous place?" Again, he offered the two cups. "Okami-san's being slowly poisoned with a very nasty brew I discovered in Vietnam. You don't believe me and it's important that you do. So drink up!"

"I believe you," Tōrin said, not making a move. He was wide-eyed and his pulse was jumpy.

"No you don't. I see that look in your eyes and I *know*." Quick as a wink he flipped one wrist, downed the contents of one cup. He let it drop to the floor and smacked his lips. Then his hand whipped out and, strong as wound leather, gripped Tōrin's wrist.

Slowly, inexorably, he drew Tōrin toward him. "Drink," he said, shoving the second cup into Tōrin's face. *"Drink!"* he commanded. The porcelain of the cup clicked against Tōrin's front teeth.

"It's join or be trampled underfoot, Tōrin-san." Mick

grinned. "It's now or never. I am the future. What do you say?"

Tōrin opened his mouth, either in protest or in acquiescence, and with a little practiced flip Mick dumped the pale amber liquid down his throat. Tōrin coughed and almost choked. He wanted to vomit but Mick clamped his jaws tightly shut.

"You're not gonna die from this, stupid," Mick hissed into Tōrin's ear. "But you *will* become a believer."

Abruptly, he let go, and Tōrin stood swaying slightly, staring at Mick as he went in and out of focus. Tōrin blinked heavily. He wanted to move but his legs felt like lead weights. He lifted an arm instead, found to his horror that it was trembling in palsy. It was as if he had aged fifty years. The thought was terrifying. He stood, trying only to breathe, hearing the labored pulse of his blood pumping through his arteries and veins, slowing like a grandfather clock someone had forgotten to wind down.

And then, with an almost audible *pop!* he snapped back to normal. His pulse increased, his blood raced through his veins, and he could move again. He looked inquiringly, mutely, at Mick, who winked and nodded at him.

"Yup. Take too much of that baby and you don't come back, get me?"

Tōrin, petrified with fear, stared at Mick as if he'd just grown another head.

"Now you know there's no turning back. Nangi and Linnear aren't going to return to their cochairmanship of Sato International. Not ever. Have you got that fixed in your mind?"

Tōrin swallowed hard and nodded. "Linnear has a plan for the Denwa Partners meeting tomorrow morning. He believes we will lose control of the CyberNet and perhaps even the *keiretsu* itself."

"In that he is quite correct. But he has already lost control of the situation; nothing he can do now will stop the inevitable from occurring." Mick pulled Tōrin close. " 'Cause here's my intention come tomorrow morning. I have Denwa Partners sewed up, so whatever I propose they'll go along with, but I need someone inside Sato to back me. You have Nangi's confidence, everyone knows that. The division vice presidents have no real power outside their own *kobun*. That's the way Nangi and Linnear set things up and I don't blame them. But the bottom line is the vice presidents have no power tø fight me. And when you approve of my becoming interim chairman—"

"Haven't you forgotten Nicholas Linnear?"

"No," Mick said, grinning like a wolf, "I haven't forgotten him." He threw his arms wide to encompass the surreal-looking apartment with Mikio Okami hanging upside down like a side of Kobe beef. "That's what this is all about, genius. It's all about Nicholas Linnear."

Nicholas and Tanaka Gin were walking down a street in Jimbōchō, the booksellers district of Shitamachi. During business hours every kind of book could be found here, from the most erudite scientific text to the greatest of literature to pure pornography.

It was raining lightly, almost a mist that floated straight down as if from heaven. It gave the streetlamps an almost surreal aura, as if they weren't real at all but had been imagined by René Magritte.

"It's a lock. Mick Leonforte killed Ise Ikuzo," Nicholas said. "Which means he killed Rodney Kurtz and had Giai Kurtz killed as well." He told Tanaka Gin about his visit with Toyoda, the armorer.

"Is it enough to arrest him?"

"That's more your expertise than mine. But we have this: Toyoda positively ID'd Mick from the Army photo you dug up, he made the push dagger from Mick's own design, and he told me the thing was built so it could slash as well as puncture. I drew the blade signature for him and he confirmed that, as well. By the way, he said this thing could bring down a wild boar at full charge."

Tanaka Gin gave a low whistle. "Just the right instrument for a Messulethe ritual."

Nicholas nodded. "You bet."

"Then we have him."

"Maybe. If we can find him."

"Oh, we will." Tanaka Gin's eyes were alight. "We'll find him because he wants us to. He left the first clue at Mūdra by having Giai Kurtz killed outside. As I said, he had all of

Tokyo to play with, why have her hit just outside a club he frequented? And why use a very special weapon to ritually slaughter his victims?" Tanaka Gin stopped. "See, he knows you, Linnear-san. He knew you'd take a long hard look at Ikuzo's wounds, and you'd know. I think he had the push dagger made by Toyoda-san *because* you know him."

Nicholas nodded. "Go on."

"He's playing a dark game, dancing all around you, getting closer and closer, like a moth to a flame."

"And when he gets too close?"

Tanaka Gin shrugged. "Who knows?"

Nicholas thought this over while they continued to walk. At last, he said, "There's something else. Just before I met you, I followed Kanda Tōrin, the young executive at Sato, to a bar in Toshima-ku, and then to a building in Roppongi that overlooked the Nogi Jinja. Tōrin went into it," He described in detail the location and appearance of the building, there being no actual addresses in Tokyo.

"We've caught a break. I know who he went to see," Tanaka Gin said. "It was Tetsuo Akinaga."

"Are you certain?"

Tanaka Gin nodded. "I have made a study of his life. He owns many businesses, most under false identities or shell corporate names. About three years ago, another of these phony companies came to our attention. This one, however, seemed to have no particular use. Until that is, I probed a bit more deeply. It seems as if Akinaga has been using it to buy a series of apartments all over the city. He uses them all from time to time. This is one of them."

"So I was right to distrust Tōrin. He's working for Akinaga."

"It would seem so."

Nicholas shook his head. "How did he fool Nangi-san so thoroughly? Nangi-san is such a good judge of character."

"It's not all bad news. At least now you know the face of the enemy."

"The faces, you mean." Nicholas looked at Tanaka Gin. "It seems, my friend, we are faced with many enemies."

Guided by the information he had gotten from Mikio Okami, Nicholas led them to a side street. Bright lights glowed from windows. In people's homes, TVs were on, everyone sitting around after dinner, watching the news or one of those silly game shows where every contestant was eager to humiliate himself in front of 10 million people.

It was an ordinary street in every way, just like thousands of others throughout the city, and Tanaka Gin felt a brief but distinct pang. How easily this could have been his life—a small apartment on a quiet side street, a wife and two children, dinners home every night, weekend outings, two vacations a year—skiing in Hokkaido, sunning in Hawaii—a bond fund for his children's education. Simple, neat, comfortable.

Tanaka Gin found that he had broken out into a cold sweat. He imagined animals in their zoo cages felt much the same way—just as he imagined his enigmatic companion also felt.

They reached the address he had been given and rang the bell beneath which was a neatly lettered name: J. KANA-GAWA. They were buzzed in and, a moment later, were outside the door to Kanagawa's apartment.

Kanagawa turned out to be a distinguished-looking gentleman in his midsixties, with silver hair and mustache, a round face, and robust body. He greeted them formally, introduced them to his wife and his twelve-year-old grandson, who was visiting them, and then led Nicholas and Tanaka Gin into his study.

The apartment was larger than Tanaka Gin had expected—three bedrooms, plus another room Kanagawa had turned into his sanctuary. And it was expensively furnished. Kanagawa's wife served them green tea and soybean sweets, then departed as silently as she had arrived. Through the walls of the study, painted a pleasingly serene green-gray, they could hear the muffled voice of the television.

Kanagawa had filled his sanctuary with books, and the walls were festooned with degrees and awards of merit from Tōdai—Tokyo University, the country's most prestigious institute of learning. Also, photos of Kanagawa with a vast array of dignitaries and VIPs. Some of them—former prime ministers, the new emperor—Tanaka Gin recognized, others he did not.

They sat and had tea. After the rituals of niceties had been dispensed with, Kanagawa said, "In your phone call you said your business was of some urgency. May I inquire what the Bank of Japan could want with me?"

This had been Tanaka Gin's cover story. He had not wanted to alert Kanagawa to the true nature of the interview by prematurely giving away his identity.

Nicholas crossed his arms over his chest as Tanaka Gin flipped open his notebook. "You are head bursar for Tōdai, Kanagawa-san."

"Yes."

"And how long have you had this position?"

"Fifteen years."

"And before that?"

"I was assistant bursar." Kanagawa's eyes narrowed. "Look here, all this is a matter of public record. I imagine you knew it before you came here."

"Indeed." Tanaka Gin looked around him. "And how much do you pay in rent for this apartment?"

"Pardon me?"

A look of alarm had dawned on Kanagawa's face. Tanaka Gin would have felt sorry for him under other circumstances. His life had no doubt been placid as a calm lake before tonight. Too bad.

"And all these furnishings," Tanaka Gin continued relentlessly, "very expensive, I imagine. Tell me, what do you earn as chief bursar?" He flipped closed his notebook and stared hard into Kanagawa's flushed and astonished face. "Never mind. I already know." He displayed his credentials, and when Kanagawa's eyes dropped to read them, he said, "I'm afraid you're in serious trouble, Kanagawa-san."

The older man looked back at him, frightened. Tanaka Gin imagined he could see all Kanagawa's sins fluttering in his eyes, coming back to haunt him.

"How serious?" Kanagawa managed to say. His eyes, betraying him completely, strayed to the door to his sanctuary, beyond which his wife and grandchild sat, oblivious to the darkness that had suddenly crept into the apartment.

"That depends," Nicholas said sharply, "on how willingly and completely you are willing to help us."

"And if I plead ignorance?"

Tanaka Gin leaned forward. "Let me lay it all out for you, Kanagawa-san. You have been systematically taking money from Tetsuo Akinaga in exchange for admitting certain young men to Tokyo University who, over the years, Akinaga has sent to you. In addition, you have seen that these people have graduated, falsifying their grades if and when necessary. This is not speculation on my part; I have obtained records, transcripts. I have gained access to your bank accounts—all six of them. Over and above the obvious penalties for tax evasion, serious criminal charges can and will be filed against you for aiding and abetting a known Yakuza *oyabun*." Tanaka Gin very deliberately looked around the room. "All this, Kanagawa-san—your comfort, security, and standing in the academic community—will be stripped from you."

Kanagawa shuddered. He seemed on the verge of tears. Tanaka Gin could very well understand. For a man like him, comfort, security, and especially his reputation were everything.

"You made a stupid mistake," Nicholas said in that same hard and commanding tone of voice. "Don't compound it now by making another one."

"What is it you wish to know?"

"There is a man within my own office," Tanaka Gin said, "who, like you, is on Tetsuo Akinaga's payroll. Tell me who he is."

"And then?"

"Don't try to bargain with us," Nicholas snapped. "It is beginning to smell bad in here."

Kanagawa's eyes swung away from Nicholas and he licked his lips. "You must understand, Prosecutor, this . . . information is the only thing I have of value. Give me something for it. Please."

"Give me the name.

"Hatta." Kanagawa spat it out almost convulsively. "The man you want is Takuo Hatta."

Tanaka Gin sat very still for several moments, then uncoiled like a tightly wound spring as he stood. He waited for Nicholas to join him. "Very well, Kanagawa-san. As of this moment, you will sever all ties with the *oyabun* Tetsuo Akinaga. You will have no contact with him whatsoever. If you do, I will know and I will expose your connection with him and you will be ruined."

"But—" Kanagawa looked up at the two men with terror. "If I break off now, he will know what I have done."

"By then it will be too late for him," Tanaka Gin said. "Those are my terms, take them or leave them."

"I want my life back," Kanagawa said softly.

"Then take possession of it," Nicholas said as they went to the door. "And think about how you almost lost it."

The staircase smelled of concrete dust and rain. They followed many damp footprints down concrete stairs.

"What do you think?" Tanaka Gin asked. "Is he sufficiently frightened to put his past behind him?"

"I think he'd rather cut off his arm than talk to Akinaga again."

Outside, the street was splattered with rain. A large black Toyota sedan was sitting at the curb. When Nicholas and Tanaka Gin emerged from Kanagawa's building, all four car doors opened simultaneously and out came four men: two uniformed policemen, one plainclothes detective, and Ginjirō Machida, chief prosecutor and Tanaka Gin's boss.

"Machida-san!"

Tanaka Gin's greeting was almost a martial salute. Nicholas, positioned just behind and to the right of his friend, could see that Tanaka Gin had taken in the entire scene with a single glance.

"Gin-san." Machida bowed perfunctorily. The uniforms spread out on either side of him, the detective immediately behind. This man had the hungrily expectant aspect of a second in an old-fashioned western duel.

Machida spread his hands, as if apologetically. "I waited as long as I could." A car went hissing by behind them, but there was a silent space between them, deep as a chasm. "Tetsuo Akinaga is no longer in custody. His lawyers destroyed your brief against him." With a sinking heart Tanaka Gin noted that he had said "your brief" not "our brief." Machida was here on damage control, no doubt about it.

"Gin-san, will you come voluntarily with me?"

"Where are you taking me?"

"To police headquarters." It was the plainclothes detective who spoke, and as he did so, the two uniformed cops took one step forward.

"Certainly. But what for?"

419

The detective was about to answer, but a small motion from Machida silenced him. "There are suspicions, Gin-san. And more—allegations that someone in *my* department is on Akinaga's payroll."

Two more cars went by with the benign sounds of a woman's skirt swishing. Between the men, the chasm only deepened.

At last, Tanaka Gin said softly, "You believe *I* am guilty?"

"It is the errors in your brief that got Akinaga sprung." Machida shrugged. "You see how it looks."

"But I was the one who arrested him in the first place." Even as Tanaka Gin said it, he knew how foolish it sounded. He saw contempt in the detective's eyes, and Machida was looking at a point just past his left shoulder, and ignoring Nicholas completely.

"A case is pending against you," Machida said. Then he walked to the far side of the black Toyota, as if disassociating himself from what was to come.

"Would you step into the car, please, Gin-san," the detective said in a neutral tone. Tanaka Gin glanced at his boss. He had not even offered the tiniest expression of confidence.

Nicholas, sensing Tanaka Gin was about to move, hooked two fingers into the prosecutor's right rear pocket, deftly lifted his wallet. It looked as if Tanaka Gin wouldn't need it anytime soon, and where Nicholas was headed, he might be in need of an official identity.

"Stand tall," Nicholas whispered in Tanaka Gin's ear, but the prosecutor did not reply. Rain began to drum across the top of the Toyota as Tanaka Gin ducked inside. The uniforms were already flanking the car, waiting for the detective.

"I know you," he said to Nicholas. But there was nothing in his voice. Nothing at all.

11

West Palm Beach/Tokyo

When Margarite heard the gunshot, she screamed and jumped out of the chair in which she had been sitting.

She was still in the same room where Paul Chiaramonte had tied her spread-eagle on the bed. She had slept fitfully for several hours following Caesare's first interrogation. He untied her, had allowed her to use the facilities as often as she needed, even let her take a shower. God, how she had stunk. It sickened and humiliated her to smell the stench of terror on her, and she had soaped herself as obsessively as Lady Macbeth had washed her hands to rid herself of imaginary blood. But then it was back to the interrogation—though not, thank God, the bed and the ropes binding her at wrists and ankles. And, though she begged him for it, not even an instant's glimpse of Francine. Her heart ached with a black and awful pain. Her baby. Was Francine all right? If it came down to choosing between her child and giving up the secrets of the Nishiki network, she knew what she would do. She could delay a certain amount of time, but then Caesare would run out of patience and when he brought Francie in and put a gun to her head, she would tell him everything.

She had begun to cry. Maybe Dominic would have handled it differently. No doubt, he would have found a way out of this bind, but she was a mother, and her first—and only—imperative was to save her daughter's life.

In the night, in between her bouts of fitful sleep, she had chafed in the clothes Caesare had brought for her after her shower, not new clothes, someone else's—his current mistress's? That would be ironic. But there was something familiar here in the darkness, not the clothes themselves—they were of colors better suited to a blonde than someone with her dark hair. But something definitely was familiar about them. What?

Her nostrils had flared wide. The scent. Whose? Someone she knew, someone close to her. Who? She could not think, though she spent the early-morning hours racking her brain. But her thoughts felt encased in a lead-lined box marked PANIC.

Then, in the morning, Caesare had come himself with food and coffee, and humiliated again, she had eaten like the starving animal she was becoming. She was aware of him watching her like a trainer will his charge in a zoo.

Then, with her sitting unbound in a chair, they had begun the interrogations again, and he had quickly come to the end of his patience. Throwing the coffeepot across the room, he had stormed out.

And a moment later, she had heard the single pistol shot.

She had leapt up and stupidly, irrationally, had rattled the locked doorknob like a berserk gorilla. All she could think of was him putting the gun to Francie's head. Then, crying, "No! No! No!" she had begun to slam her shoulder into the door, shuddering painfully at each impact, but keeping at it nonetheless. Until she had heard the key in the door turning and she had stepped back, had, in one last lucid moment, sat back down in the chair where he had left her, her body coiled as tightly as a spring, her shoulder and ribs white with pain.

But the moment Caesare appeared in the open doorway, a gun in his hand, she lost it completely, hurtling from the chair with such speed and ferocity he had no chance to sidestep her. She barreled into him, heedless of the weapon, and together they crashed back into the living room. She clawed at him, pummeled him, and at last got her knee between his legs and drove it up into his crotch.

She was up and running as his breath came out of him in a *whoosh!*—her eyes wide and staring, screaming, "Francie! Francie!"—bounding through the house, frantically searching every room, finding them all empty, blessedly devoid of her body. Until at last she found herself, sweat-streaked and panting, back in the living room, staring at a newly made bullet hole in one of the sofas.

She swung around to where Caesare, disheveled, holding on to a chair back with one hand, while pressing his groin with the other, stood staring darkly at her.

"You *bastard!*" She wanted to scream but she had no strength left. The adrenaline fit of terror that had ripped through her when he had made her think he had shot Francie had run its course, leaving her weak and shaken. She collapsed onto the sofa, her head in her hands.

"Oh, dear God," she whispered.

"You're playing in the wrong arena," Caesare said. "Foolish, really, to think you could keep the family together after I whacked Tony. You should have raised the white flag."

"When should I have done that," she asked without looking at him, "before or after your wiseguys whacked my driver right in front of my face?"

"Fuck you talkin' about. It was your call to bring in the cop. And Paul tells me you blew away one of my men yourself. I think he admires you for that."

Her head came up and Caesare was momentarily startled by the dark, feral look in her eyes. "Stop dicking me around. You had your campaign against me planned well before you knew whether I would give up or not. You stole my company out from under me."

"That was business, Margarite." He shrugged. "I saw a good opportunity and I took it."

"Bullshit." She swiped her hair from her face. "You knew what that company meant to me. I built it from the ground up."

He spread his hands. "It's only a company, for chrissake."

"It was my fucking *legs,* you moron." Her hands closed into fists. "It defined me, made me what I was. Besides my daughter it was the only thing in my life I've ever been proud of." She waved a hand. "Oh, why am I bothering? You wouldn't understand in a million years."

But the truth was Caesare did understand. The truth was that he respected her more than he had ever respected that *gavonne* Tony D. What Dominic saw in him Caesare would never figure out. But this woman had stood up to him, had taken whatever he had dished out. She had been shot at, had reacted with courage in firing back at her assailants, had further been bold enough to enlist the help of an NYPD detective, and if not for Paul Chiaramonte, would have gotten away from his machine. Then she had withstood the assault of psychological torture.

But now, looking at her curled on the sofa, he knew he had her. All he had to do was drag in the kid and openly threaten her with bodily harm and Margarite would fold like cards in the wind.

It was time to call Paul out of the guesthouse and get the kid over here. He went painfully over to the intercom. After buzzing Paul three times with no response, he called in a couple of the guards and ordered them to hustle over to investigate.

It seemed an eternity before the intercom buzzed. Hitting the button with the butt of his pistol, Caesare barked, "Yeah?"

"They're gone," came the metallic voice.

"Fuck d'you mean?"

"We searched everywhere," the voice came back, raspy and devoid of emotion. "The house, the grounds, everywhere. Chiaramonte and the girl have split."

"How the fuck's that possible?"

"I dunno, boss. They just—"

Caesare pointed the muzzle of his pistol at the intercom and, with a deep roar of rage, fired.

"He'll kill my mom."

Paul Chiaramonte stared into those keenly intelligent eyes and said with every ounce of sincerity he could muster, "No, he won't."

"Bullshit." Francie was sitting, staring out the window at the soft parade of semidressed people along South Beach's Ocean Boulevard.

"It ain't bullshit. You were the leverage, see? Why he wanted you inna first place. Your mama will do anything for you—even betray her own people. Bad Clams knows that." Paul flailed his arms. "And, hey, get outta the window. Whatta you, a sign?" He shook his head. "Like I was sayin', without you—"

"Without me, she's of no use to him." Francie turned back into the hotel room, which was decorated in high-tone art deco fashion, with blues, greens, and purples that made the eyeballs ache. "We should never have gone without her."

"We got the chance an' we took it. That's what life is all about."

Francie shook her head. "Life's not about running out on people you love—not for any reason."

"Tell that to my father," Paul said darkly. "He ran out on me 'n' my mom when the shit came down."

"So that's your reason for doing the same thing to the members of the Abriola family who treated you like one of their sons?"

He jammed his hands in his pockets and said nothing.

Francie cocked her head. "Don't you get it?" she said softly. "Without me Mom won't tell Caesare anything and he'll turn on her. He won't care if she lives or dies."

Paul, damning her to six kinds of hell, was staring at her fixedly. "You don't give your mama half enough credit."

"Maybe. But what if you're wrong?" Her eyes caught his. "I think Caesare is out of her league."

He was just thinking she might be right when she said, "We gotta go back."

" 'Scuse me?" He shook his head. "I got wax inna ears. I thought you said we gotta go back."

"Right." Francie nodded. "We gotta go back and get my mom."

Paul goggled at her. "We'll all get shot to death, is what we'll get."

She shook her head. "No, we won't. Caesare wants me."

"Sure he does." Paul rolled his eyes and said slowly and carefully, "But we don't want him to get you, an' if we go back, guess what?" He threw up his hands, as if to say, Kids!

"Not necessarily."

"Wha'?" Paul's head turned so quickly his vertebrae made a cracking sound.

"Listen to me," Francie said, slipping from her perch on the windowsill. "I've got an idea."

"Yeah, well, I don' wanna hear it. You wanted t'go straight t'the airport. Bad Clams woulda been able to track us for sure."

"Okay, so maybe that was a bum idea." Francie pulled him down onto the bed. It was covered in a spread whose pattern was reminiscent of something Frank Lloyd Wright would have designed. "But going back isn't."

"You're nuts, you know that? The place is crawling with button men. How we gonna get past 'em?"

"No problem. They're going to let us in." Francie was grinning. "You put a gun to my head and tell them I escaped and you caught me. You're just bringing me back is all."

Paul rested his hands on his thighs. "Okay, genius. Then what?"

"Then we get my mom and split."

Paul sighed. "An' I s'pose Bad Clams will sit back an' let me do that."

"Of course he won't." Francie pointed her forefinger and cocked her thumb like a gun. "But when he tries to stop us, you'll shoot him."

Paul laughed. "Kid, you give me too much credit."

She jutted her chin. "Don't have the balls for it, huh?"

Paul jumped up. "Would you, for the love of God, stop talking like, like . . ."

"Like what?" There was a defiant tone to her voice, hard as brass.

His hands flew in small circles. "Like a guy, damn it! Why don't you act like what you are?"

"Did Jaqui?"

He pursed his lips, spurted air through them. "Did she what?"

"Act like a girl?"

"Sure she did." But it was a lie and they both knew it. Paul raked a hand through his hair, sat down abruptly. "Ah, nuts." He glanced at her. "My life went to shit the moment I met you."

"It already *was* shit." She went to the minibar and opened it. "Want something?"

"Nah, ever notice the prices they put on that crap? Six bucks for a Coke? What a rip-off."

"What do you care?" She threw him a can of Coke, took a diet Coke for herself. "Chances are you're not going to pay for it."

He laughed and they popped the tops at almost the same time. He took a swig. It felt almost as good as a beer going down. Thing was, he didn't like to drink around her. It was probably stupid, he knew, but he couldn't help himself. He felt proprietary toward her, as if she were his own daughter.

"How come you're so smart?"

"I'm not so smart." She ran her tongue around the beaded top of the can. "I just wised up pretty quickly. But I have to say I had some help. My mom, once she straightened herself up. Uncle Lew. And, the more I think about it, Sister Marie Rose—Jaqui, I mean." She crossed one leg over the other, rocked it gently, watching her toes bounce up and down. "I used to hate her. What a little Hitler she is, I used to tell my mom. Rules, discipline, the law of God. 'You should've been a watchmaker,' I once told her. 'Or a drill instructor.' Her eyes rose to meet Paul's. You know what she said to me? 'It's about time you paid me a compliment.' " Francie shook her head in disbelief. "I think I threw something, a plaster statue of the Virgin Mary or something. Shattered it into a million pieces."

"Uh-oh. That's bad."

Francie drank some diet Coke. "You'd think so. But Sister Marie Rose never got angry with me no matter what nasty stuff I pulled. That was smart, now I think of it. I guess I was trying to get her mad, and when I found out she wasn't going to bite, I lost interest in being a beast around her." She took another swallow. "That was half of it. The other half was when I discovered she never told Mom how badly I acted with her. 'Sister Marie Rose says you're such an angel,' Mom said to me one day. 'I wish I knew her secret.' " Francie drained the can, put it aside. "Right then I knew. Sister Marie Rose was on my side, no matter what. That made such a difference. My mother first took me to see her when I was eight, and I saw her regularly. Then, later, when I was sick with bulimia and everything—I mean, really sick in my head, you know?—I needed someone who wasn't going to judge me."

"Yeah, but all those rules she laid on you."

"But, see, they weren't *hers*. They were God's rules." Francie put her hands together as if in prayer. "Then I found out that Sister Marie Rose had no rules of her own and I fell in love with her. She was my kind of person." She laughed somewhat embarrassedly. "Imagine, a nun—and she was the only one I could talk to—until Uncle Lew."

"That would be Lew Croaker, the ex-cop."

"You know him?"

He shook his head. "Only what I've picked up from Bad Clams." Paul paused a moment. "You think he's a good guy, huh?"

Francie's eyes lit up. "Yeah."

He got up and put his half-finished Coke on top of the minibar, then rubbed his palms down the sides of his trousers. He took out his gun, checked the cartridge. Then he replaced it, turned around to face her. "I may be nuts myself for sayin' this but—" He nodded and gave her a lopsided grin she decided she liked a whole lot. "Okay, let's go back an' get your mom outta that den of thieves."

"You are so very beautiful."

Nicholas smiled at the slim European man with short hair and sensual lips.

"Care to accompany me? There's a love hotel right around the corner."

"Sorry," Nicholas said. "I've already got a date."

"Some other time, maybe." The European slinked off toward another candidate on his predatory quest.

Nicholas went to the bar and ordered a Scotch and soda. He was in Twenty-One Roses, a gay bar in Shinjuku 2-chome. Many eyes wandered in his direction. He did not feel threatened in this atmosphere. *Nanshoku,* the idea of lust between males, had a long and hallowed history in Japan, where among samurai, showing any affinity toward women was considered a sign of weakness. Taking a young man or, even, a boy as a lover had its roots in the culture of ancient Greece, where the male form was revered. In

Japan, the practice was widely attributed to the influx of Buddhist monks from China.

Nicholas paid for his drink, turned, and scanned the room for any sign of Takuo Hatta. The prosecutor was notorious for spending a couple of nights a week in one gay bar or another in this district. Nicholas had confirmed with Hatta's wife that he was not at home. Twenty-One Roses was the fourth bar Nicholas had been in that night. Male couples were slow-dancing on the packed and minuscule dance floor, the bar was three deep, and everywhere bodies pressed lasciviously against one another. The place was dark and smoky, with a vaguely thirties look of seedy decadence that was at once evocative and comforting to its habitués.

Nicholas was propositioned twice more, was groped once intimately, and had made up his mind that this place was a real meat market when he saw someone who looked like Hatta emerging from the men's room. With some difficulty he made his way through the shifting, sweaty throng. Someone grabbed his ass, and as he slithered through the dance floor, a Japanese salaryman with a wedding ring kissed him hard on the lips.

Nicholas survived it all and, arriving on the other side of the barely controlled melee, discovered that the figure was indeed Takuo Hatta. Unfortunately, Hatta spotted him. His eyes opened wide behind his spectacles and, shoving aside a pair of young men pawing each other, broke into an ungainly run.

Slick as an eel, he made it to the front door before Nicholas could get to him. He darted out the door. Nicholas, feeling as if he were stuck in a dream, made progress as slowly as if he were in quicksand. Using his elbows, he wedged himself into one of the two main traffic lanes and was whirled, possibly by centrifugal force, toward the door.

Gaining the street, he saw Hatta opening the rear door of a big black Mercedes sedan idling at the curb. Nicholas shouted as he sprinted toward the car, and Hatta jerked his head around, his eyes opened wide in fear. He dove into the backseat of the Mercedes as the driver threw the car in gear and depressed the accelerator.

With a harsh squeal of rubber, the Mercedes peeled away

from the curb, banged to a temporary halt as it hit the front fender of a cruising taxi. It lurched, swung out in a wider arc.

Nicholas, who had been gaining on it, threw his body forward just as the driver accelerated the car again. He lunged out, extending his body fully, and grabbed onto the open window frame as the Mercedes hurtled into the rain-slicked street.

A wiry Yakuza *kobun* was driving the Mercedes. Now the *kobun* spun the wheel hard over, almost rocketing the Mercedes into the stainless-steel grille of an oncoming truck. Nicholas's body slammed hard against the side of the car as he hung on. The Mercedes rocked on its shocks as, amid the shrill blare of an air horn, the *kobun* righted it and hurtled it down the street. As he did so, he swerved back and forth. Every time he jerked the car to the right Nicholas's shoes would be flayed by the tarmac; and on each leftward cut the prosecutor would be thrown hard against the door. And when the *kobun* took a skidding left turn, it seemed just another evasive maneuver.

Nicholas was reaching into the interior for a better hold when something black and looming caught in the periphery of his vision. He turned his head slightly, saw the narrow blackness of the alley coming up fast and knew he could not remain where he was—there was hardly enough room for the Mercedes itself to squeeze through.

A whump! and crackle as the near-side headlight smashed against a soot-encrusted wall presaged the car's entrance into the alley. With no time to spare, Nicholas dropped his legs, let his heels hit painfully on the tarmac, bump up, did it again, this time harder, and used the more powerful bump upward as momentum to swing his body up over the open window and onto the roof of the car.

The Mercedes rocketed down the alley in a squeal of protesting body metal and occasional bright blue showers of sparks at the contact. Nicholas, on his stomach, was holding on with the curled tips of his fingers to the trim at the top of the windshield.

An explosion close to his ears caused him to twist his body, almost losing his fingerhold. Another one and he saw a chunk of the roof disintegrate, and he thought, *The bas-*

tard's shooting at me! He rolled back across the roof the other way as a third shot took a chunk of metal off.

Behind the wheel, the *kobun* dropped the gun on the seat beside him so he could grip the wheel with both hands, then slammed on the brakes. He was gratified to see Nicholas hurtling off the roof into the alley in front of him. He grabbed for the gun, but by that time Nicholas was running directly at him. The *kobun* stamped on the accelerator. In this cramped spot there was nowhere for Nicholas to hide. In a tenth of a second, Nicholas would be plowed under the vehicle. The *kobun* liked the sound rushing steel made when it hit a human body, but he liked the feel of it even more. There was a rush of power so strong . . .

Then he jerked back reflexively as Nicholas slammed heels first into the windshield. The safety glass spider-webbed, collapsing inward but holding together. The *kobun* heard Hatta screaming from the backseat and was distracted long enough for Nicholas to make a second powerful kick that broke through the safety film and showered the *kobun* with glass fragments. His finger closed around the trigger of the gun and he fired point-blank at the figure coming at him.

Nicholas felt the searing heat of the bullet even while his ears rang from the percussion of the shot. He felt something tear through the shoulder of his jacket, just as if he'd snagged it on barbed wire. Then he had slid halfway into the seat. The *kobun* slammed on the brakes, as much for self-preservation as for an offensive maneuver, hurtling Nicholas into the padded dashboard. The back of his head smashed into the CD player, and his legs got tangled up in the gearshift.

Pain exploded in his ribs and he grunted. There was a metallic taste in his mouth, and he felt the second blow through a veil of pain and growing numbness creeping up his side. He tried to roll out of the way of the blows, fetched up hard against the glove compartment for his efforts.

The *kobun*'s eyes were glossy, fever bright as he brought more and more adrenaline into his system. He was a young man in his early twenties, with a shaven head and veins popping along the curve of his shiny skull. Nicholas could see by the dilation of his pupils that he was on something, possibly cocaine. His strength was superhuman.

Another blow descended, this one more vicious, intended to crack a couple of vertebrae. Nicholas did not try to evade or ward off the blow, but instead reached out and caught the *kobun*'s hand. In the process, the sleeve of the *kobun*'s jacket rode up to his forearm, and Nicholas could see the beginning of the complex *irezumi,* the tattooing almost all Yakuza wore like a uniform. If he could see more of it, he'd know to which clan this man belonged.

Right now, however, he had other, more immediate considerations. The *kobun* bent forward from the waist, using the superior leverage of his position to pin Nicholas on his side back into the footwell of the front seat. He applied more and more pressure, exerting it slowly, inexorably, with the full knowledge of his advantage.

An expression almost of curiosity crossed his face as Nicholas uncoiled his upper leg, smashing his kneecap into the leading point of the *kobun*'s ribs. There was a sharp cracking sound. Curiosity metamorphosed into disbelief and then into a kind of disappointment bordering on astonishment as the *kobun* realized that his ribs were broken.

A bloom of pure rage shot through him, aided and abetted by the drugs he had ingested. He clamped down on the pain, went after Nicholas with the switchblade he kept in his waistband.

Nicholas took a slash to his shoulder before jamming an elbow into the *kobun*'s Adam's apple. He twisted away as the *kobun,* already beginning to gag, stabbed out in desperate reflex. The gearshift moved and the blade, bouncing off, buried itself in the polished leather of the seatback. Then Nicholas used his lower body against the *kobun.*

It was a mistake. The *kobun*'s foot slipped off the brake, pushed down spastically on the accelerator. The Mercedes shot forward with a ragged spray of blue and white sparks, careening off one wall, then another, hurtling out of the alley with terrifying speed.

Hatta screamed from the backseat. Nicholas made a desperate grab to take control of the wheel, and the *kobun* managed to jerk the switchblade free and make another attempt to disembowel Nicholas.

The Mercedes, more or less out of control, slammed into the rear end of a Nissan. Careening sideways, its tires screeching, it hit the opposite curb and, half-righted, kept on going, jumping the sidewalk. Pedestrians scattered, shouting through the massed blare of horns.

The edge of the blade came so close to Nicholas's neck it felt as hot as a furnace. Then, with a ragged wrench, Nicholas broke the *kobun*'s wrist. As he yelped in pain, Nicholas used his elbow to smash the *kobun*'s nose flat against his cheeks. The *kobun* rocketed back in the seat in a welter of blood, collapsing upon the wheel.

Nicholas hauled the *kobun*'s torso backward, trying to kick his foot clear of the accelerator. He managed to steer the Mercedes back onto the street, but it was no safer there, since they were now headed down the street the wrong way, toward oncoming traffic and an intersection with the wide Meiji-dōri.

Sweat broke out on Nicholas's face as he tried to get to the accelerator or brake, but the *kobun*'s feet were wedged tight. Nicholas felt dizzy, a buzzing in his brain. *No!* he screamed silently. *Not now!* He fought down the oncoming Kshira seizure. Had he blacked out for an instant? The broad side of a trailer truck coming into the intersection rushed up at them with frightening speed. Nicholas abandoned his efforts to get to the pedals, instead threw the gearshift into neutral, switched off the engine.

The side of the truck looked as large as a building facade as they shot toward it. The engine was off but the momentum of the car continued to propel it forward. Nicholas pulled hard on the wheel and the Mercedes did a one-eighty. Blood rushed to his head as centrifugal force kicked in. Hatta continued his terrified screaming from the backseat, and the world became one long blur. Colors streaked by, then merged, images elongating, then disappearing altogether into this new and curiously exhilarating reality. All of this happened in a tenth of a second, but the sense of being so out of control was liberating. Nicholas felt his heart beating fast and close inside his chest. No sense of danger or of imminent death occurred to him.

Then the car came out of it, they were rear-ended, not hard but enough to throw Hatta against the back of the front seats and to make Nicholas's molars click together. But now, with the engine dead, much of their momentum was dissipated, and Nicholas was able, at last, to guide the Mercedes to a gradual stop curbside.

There was a sour stench inside the car. The sound of the hot engine ticking over was slowly overtaken by the scream of sirens, the pounding of running feet. With an effort, Nicholas turned around, saw Hatta crouched half-off the seat, heaving. He had vomited all over the backseat.

The sound of the sirens was increasing. Quickly, Nicholas took up the knife and slit open the *kobun*'s jacket and shirt to reveal the fantastic *irezumi*. Noting the *kobun*'s clan affiliation, he got out of the car, went around to the back, opened the door. By this time, the cops had arrived and he produced Tanaka Gin's wallet and flashed them the credentials. Invoking prosecutor's privilege, he hauled the cowering Hatta out of the backseat.

Rain light as an angel's kiss fell on Nicholas's face, clearing his mind. The police lights were flashing, merry as a carnival in full swing, and a crowd had begun to form. Some of the officers went to disperse the onlookers and to direct traffic, which was backed up all along the avenue. Others were waiting for Nicholas to make a statement. An ambulance drew up, its lights adding to the dark carnival atmosphere, but no one suggested Nicholas get in. Paramedics disembarked and, peering into the Mercedes, prepared to extract the twisted form of the *kobun* from behind the wheel.

Nicholas noticed skid marks on the tarmac, dark as scars against the rain-slicked surface, and only slowly realized they had been made by him. His mind was beginning to function normally again. He sucked deeply of the night air. As he did so, he leaned in toward Hatta and whispered, "You're mine now, traitor. Unless you want me to hand you over to the police this instant, you'll do and say exactly as I tell you. Is that clear?"

Hatta nodded, white-faced and utterly spent, and Nicholas turned to the patiently waiting sergeant. "I'm ready to make my statement now."

12

West Palm Beach/Tokyo

Two burly men with .38 revolvers in their armpits burst into Room 421 of the Aquamarine Hotel in South Beach. By the time they had taken a single step into the room, their guns were drawn. One took the bathroom, the other the closets. One looked under the bed while the other stepped into the hallway and gave a signal.

Caesare Leonforte strode into the room, Vesper just behind him. "Where's that little weasel?"

None of them, not even Vesper, knew whether he was referring to the kid or Paul Chiaramonte.

"Fuck they get past you?" Caesare asked one of the burly men. He had oily, curly hair and eyes too close together.

"He told us the kid wanted a diet Coke an' she slipped him inna kitchen of the guesthouse," the man said. He was still panting from having taken four flights of stairs while his boss and the girlfriend took the elevator. He was sweating heavily and was pissed off they had found no one. He waved his pistol around as if looking for someone to plug.

"Put that fuckin' heat away," Caesare said. "What're you gonna shoot, the fuckin' roaches?"

"Okay, so we start inna kitchen ova guesthouse," the man said, sliding his .38 into his sweaty armpit. "We find nothin' inna kitchen so we go outside. The guys, the dogs, no one's seen shit." He threw out his arms at the same time he hunched his shoulders. "So whatta we s'posed t'do?"

Caesare couldn't be bothered replying to this sad tale; he was staring at the empties atop the minibar. "Cokes and diet Cokes," he said softly. "They were here, all right."

"But no one saw them leave," Vesper said.

"Yeah." Caesare nodded. His brow furrowed. "Fuck they're in such a hurry now?"

"Let's get after them," one of the burly men said. He was itching to use his pistol.

"We got the airports, the bus terminals, train stations, all covered," Caesare said as if to himself. "The rental cars know t'call if a man of Paul's description tries t'rent. The only other possibilities—stealing wheels or buying a used one—I'd rule out. Paul'd be an idiot to risk the cops, an' I know he doesn't have the bread to buy."

"You don't even know whether he's taken the kid or he's trying to find her," Vesper said.

Caesare pointed to the empty cans. "They're t'gether all right," he said in his nastiest voice. "I don't know what the fuck Paul thinks he's up to, but you can be damn sure I'll make him wish he'd never thought of it." He made a curt gesture. "You two take to the streets round here. Make sure you check the cans in alla bars an' restaurants. Also, the hotels. Stick to an eight-block square. If the hotel still thinks they're holed up here, they haven't been gone long."

"Akinaga isn't taking calls; he can't be disturbed," Hatta said, putting down the public phone. He jammed his hands in his pockets, hunching his shoulders as his shoes scuffed against the sidewalk. "That means he's at Both Ends Burning."

"I want Akinaga and I want him tonight," Nicholas said. "And believe me, I won't let you out of my sight until you've gotten me near him."

Nicholas, standing near the Shinjuku intersection of Meiji-dōri and Yasukunidōri, was watching the rain distort the neon colors in the wide avenues, sending them floating off the dark surfaces like kites on Boys' Day. "What is Both Ends Burning, S-and-M club, gay bar?"

Hatta hesitated until Nicholas swung around, shot him a

menacing glance. "S-and-M membership-only club, yes, but it's a very special place. All the top people are members."

Nicholas was on the lookout for big shiny cars driven by Yakuza *kobun*. Having encountered one tonight had been more than enough, but he was taking no chances. Hatta was being protected, and now that the primary protection had broken down, perhaps a backup was somewhere out there waiting for a chance to take him back. Nicholas was also thinking of the name Both Ends Burning. That was the club outside which Ise Ikuzo had been slaughtered as an example, perhaps by Michael Leonforte. An odd kind of coincidence. "Top people?" Nicholas echoed.

That tiny hesitation again. Hatta's appearance was disheveled and he smelled terrible. By design, Nicholas had given him no opportunity to clean himself up. There were times, Nicholas believed, when humiliation cleansed the soul as nothing else could.

Then Hatta nodded his head. "You know. Politicos, bureaucrats, businessmen. No salarymen allowed." Meaning no low- or middle-level management people. "Both Ends Burning skims off the very top, and everyone with influence wants in. That's why Akinaga makes it a kind of unofficial home away from home."

Nicholas was thinking. Something had been nagging at him ever since Hatta had confessed his sleazy relationship with Tetsuo Akinaga. Akinaga was *oyabun* of the Shikei clan, but as he noted from the pattern of the *irezumi*, the *kobun* who had been protecting Hatta was from the Yamauchi clan. Ever since its last *oyabun*, Tachi Shidare, had been killed, the Yamauchi had been run by a triumvirate of under-*oyabun* because none of them had enough backing within the clan to consolidate power. Was Akinaga making a bid to take over the Yamauchi? There had been rumors that he had been trying to run Shidare. In any event, Akinaga had tried at least once to have Nicholas killed. Nicholas now said, "If Akinaga hangs out at Both Ends Burning, what about other Yakuza *oyabun?*"

Hatta nodded. "Of course. Almost all of them. But only *oyabun* and under-*oyabun.*"

Pieces, floating in darkness, coming together, perhaps. "Are you a member?"

Hatta hesitated once more, then nodded his head in assent.

Nicholas was silent, watching the silver rain fall between the glass behemoths of Shinjuku. "You're important enough to have a pipeline to Akinaga. You know where he hangs out, so let's see how well they know you there."

Hatta was, indeed, a member. And so well known he didn't even have to produce his card, they knew him on sight. As a guest, Nicholas was required to sign in. He used Mick Leonforte's name. They were both given plastic cards with laser-printed emblems.

"Why do you want me here?" Hatta whined as they descended a long flight of stone stairs, slick and uneven from decades of wear. "This can only end badly."

"I have no doubt." Nicholas prodded him on. "But you were there at the beginning, you were willing to destroy Tanaka Gin; now it's only fitting you be there at the end."

The stairway was lit by a line of flickering fluorescent tubes recessed into niches covered with the kind of metal grilles found in prisons. The unpleasant monochromatic illumination turned their skin as pale and waxen as that of a two-week-old corpse. Bone-jarring rock music made its way through the stone flooring, the soles of their feet, rising like needles up their legs.

A long, narrow passageway lay before them. The end was smothered in darkness. The floor was a series of flat stones slightly raised from a stream of black, purling water that appeared to drop off precipitously on both sides before the curving stone walls rose to meet in a kind of gothically arched ceiling. Wan disks of light filtered down from weak bulbs in wire cages. They looked to be traversing an underground cavern, possibly just above the level of the subway.

At length, they came to a metal gate, not unlike the portcullis in a castle. Behind it sat a moonlighting sumo of gargantuan proportions. He rose as they approached, took the plastic cards they slipped through the bars, ran them through a machine. The portcullis opened silently and smoothly on hidden gimbals, and he handed them back the cards.

The music was palpably louder now, a frenzied tribal tattoo, insistent as a heartbeat. They were confronted with a short, cramped entryway, dense with moving bodies. Squeezing through the mob, they found themselves in a long, low room. The heat and humidity of hundreds of human bodies made a dense, tropical fog. Colored lights flashed, strobes popped off at irregular intervals, and complex acid-jazz—a combination of jazz tonalities, hip-hop beat, and the occasional rap voice—blew through the swaying bodies like a moist wind through a forest of bamboo.

As he and Hatta moved slowly through the mob, Nicholas saw the minister of finance, the minister of commerce and industry, the ministers of the Textiles Bureau, the Commercial Affairs Bureau, the International Trade Promotion Bureau. After he spotted the superintendent of international trade, he stopped counting. Then there were the members of the Liberal Democratic Party, the Socialist Party, the New Lands Party, the deputy justice minister—the list was virtually endless. Members of the top ten industrial *keiretsu* were, here and there, in evidence, as were a number of Yakuza *oyabun*.

Nicholas headed in their direction, looking for Tetsuo Akinaga. He saw a youngish *oyabun* he did not recognize talking to the chief of the Consumer Goods Industries Bureau and wondered what deal was being born. Hatta was trying to drift off, but Nicholas kept him close.

"Where is Akinaga?" Nicholas hissed.

"I don't know," Hatta almost shouted over the din.

They passed a circular bar, six deep with clamoring men, all commanders of industry, bureaus, or illegal activities. It was curious and unsettling to see them scrabbling for drinks, shouting and gesticulating like commodities traders in the pits.

"Is it like this every night?" Nicholas asked.

Hatta nodded.

How many deals were consummated in the shadows? Nicholas asked himself. Each night, more of Japan's future was decided here than in the chambers of the Diet, the parliament. Here was the nexus of power, the great, dark engine that kept Japan chugging along in the traditional ways. Forget all the talk of reform, the lip service paid to clearing away the traditional abuses, finding new ways to conduct business among the steel triangle of business, bureaucracy, and politics. Too much money passed hands here, too many accommodations were made, too complex a web of friendship and favoritism that extended in all directions out of the light of public scrutiny. The people here—and not only the Yakuza—had grown too comfortable in this humid darkness where power was passed as an amulet from hand to hand, and all things were possible.

Nicholas, scanning the human cacophony, felt Hatta stiffen slightly, and without turning his head, Nicholas shifted his gaze. He looked where Hatta had looked. At first he saw nothing but a haze composed of smoke, heat, sound waves, superimposed over a kind of chain-mail curtain of human bodies. He probed the semidarkness with his eyes and then with his psyche. He opened his *tanjian* eye and felt something slippery as a tadpole skitter away from his consciousness. He tried to follow it, but there were too much sensory data sweeping over him and he began to close his *tanjian*.

At that instant, something odd happened. As the light from his *tanjian* eye faded, he became aware not of the familiar darkness but of a maelstrom. Ten thousand bees buzzed, a rising chorus, and he instinctively recoiled from the onset of Kshira.

But this time he felt himself cradled as into his mind came Kisoko's whispered words: *Let the darkness come.*

The darkness was coming, a black orb opening, the veil of darkness shielding him from the psychic clatter of hundreds of other souls. Silence. And then, in one corner of that silence, a silver flash, as if from the tail of a fish breaking the skin of the water, a ripple in the darkness, a trail of phosphorescence along which he found himself moving, gliding between closely pressed people in earnest consultations, in amorous embraces, in meaningless conversations, in sweaty transactions, in venal quid pro quos, in malicious double crosses, in dangerous alliances.

Through this thorny lexicon of human endeavor Nicholas dragged Hatta, the traducer, the craven, as if he were a bleating sheep Nicholas was taking to market.

Through the black silence of Kshira, Nicholas identified Tetsuo Akinaga, not with his eyes but with his mind. The dark eye of Kshira had marked him just as if Nicholas had shot him with a quiverful of arrows. Nicholas honed in on him, quartering the room, coming toward him at an angle that would make escape that much more difficult. When he was near enough to Akinaga to glimpse him through the throng, he said to Hatta, "This is the end."

He was almost close enough to the *oyabun* to reach out and touch him. He drew Hatta closer to him so that he would not make a sudden break. Akinaga was deep in a strategy session with a high-ranking member of the New Lands Party and Kansai Mitsui, the *oyabun*'s candidate for prime minister. It was clear Akinaga had not spotted Nicholas, who was maneuvering in to give him no room to run, and Nicholas wanted to keep it that way.

He was fully concentrated on Akinaga when he heard his name being called, felt a lunge to his left, and swinging his gaze, saw Honniko.

"Nicholas!" she cried. "Nicholas!"

At that moment, there was a rush on his immediate right and Hatta slammed into him, crying out as he was literally lifted off his feet. Nicholas felt a hot spray of blood, whirled to feel Jōchi's hot breath on his face. Hatta was squirming like a fish caught by a boat hook, and another spray of blood flew up.

Jōchi grunted and rushed Hatta, jamming him harder against Nicholas's right side. At the same time, the dark eye of Kshira told Nicholas that Akinaga was slithering away from the commotion, eeling backward into the shadows, heading for one of the rear exits almost directly behind him.

Nicholas swiveled away from Jōchi's attack, bringing Hatta with him. The long knife blade came free of Hatta's side, and he began to bleed like a stuck pig. All around, people locked into their hermetically sealed worlds were oblivious. They continued to dance and jostle and bob up and down, drink and smoke and talk and negotiate deals.

"Honniko!" Nicholas cried, letting Hatta go. He grabbed her wrists, pulled her to him through the thicket of bodies. "Hatta-san's been hurt—stabbed by Jōchi."

Her eyes were wide.

"I think he was after me." Nicholas turned, saw the tall, slender woman cradling Hatta. There was blood all over her lap. As he stared down, her head came up and he was fixed in the gaze of those wide-apart green eyes. What was the mother superior doing here? he wondered.

"Take care of him," Nicholas said to Honniko. "Get a doctor or an ambulance, preferably both."

Honniko looked up from where she knelt beside the stricken Hatta and Sister Marie Rose. "Where are you—?"

But he had already been swallowed up by the crowd.

Lew Croaker, looking ten years younger and as unprepossessing as a florist's assistant should, entered Caesare Leonforte's compound in the back of the green and yellow Amazonia Florist van that daily delivered fresh flowers to the white mansion. Rico Limòn, the F/X guru, had been right: even his mother wouldn't recognize him. The latex prostheses—nose, cheeks, forehead, and the small but crucial areas at the sides of his mouth—were perfect, having been designed off the death mask Rico had made of his face.

"These babies are made to withstand the glare of hot lights, but not without almost constant touch-ups," he had warned Croaker of the prostheses, "so my best advice is stay out of the noonday sun. And whatever you do, don't press the left side of the nose until you want reinforcements."

As usual, the van was stopped just inside the gate so guards could visually examine the contents and the dogs could get a good sniff at everyone and everything. For one terrible, irrational moment, as one of the dogs came up to him, Croaker was afraid it could sense the latex. But, as it turned out, the guard with the hairy hands was more interested in him because Croaker's was a new face among the regular tradespeople.

"Morty's on vacation," the driver of the van said.

"Yeah?" Hairy-hands said, staring at Croaker as if this were a contest of wills. "Where'd Morty go? Fuckin' Alaska t'get outta this heat?" He guffawed.

"He took his kids to Disney World."

"Fuck you talkin'?" Hairy-hands's eyebrows shot up. "Seemed t'me ol' Morty was a little light in the loafers."

"Nah," the driver said, obviously used to this kind of cross-examination, "that'd be me."

They both had a good laugh at that. Croaker risked a smile at Hairy-hands and was rewarded with a scowl. The other guard pulled the dog back, and Hairy-hands slammed the van door shut. "Get on up there. Boss don't like the smell a dyin' flowahs."

With a profound sense of relief Croaker took his biomechanical hand out of his pocket where he had kept it hidden throughout the visual check.

"C'mon, c'mon," he urged the driver.

It was just after two P.M. and he was both anxious and annoyed. He had been all set to penetrate Bad Clamsville at eight this morning in La Petite Bakery's truck, which daily delivered fresh croissants, rolls, and baguettes, when by sheer good fortune he had discovered the dispatcher trying to make a call into the compound. Subsequent interrogation by the backup team of federal agents Vesper had requested had revealed that the dispatcher was on Bad Clams's payroll. It had given everyone involved—including Croaker—a queasy feeling. How much of the area infrastructure was under Bad Clams's thumb? There was no way of telling, but when they invaded the Amazonia premises, all outgoing calls were carefully monitored.

They spent the next forty minutes removing yesterday's flower arrangements and replacing them with the load they had trucked in. Croaker was upstairs in a sitting room, putting the finishing touches on a tropical-looking centerpiece when Hairy-hands sauntered in.

"Where's your dog?" Croaker said, placing a fiery-red bird-of-paradise in place.

"Very fuckin' funny," Hairy-hands said. He was so close Croaker could smell the sour remnants of lunch on his breath. He stuck out a sausagelike finger, the top of which was a forest of curly black hair. "What's zis?"

Croaker looked at him.

"Zis?" Hairy-hands pointed more emphatically to a white flower. "What'sa name?"

Croaker had no idea. "Delphinium," he said. "Where's the can? I gotta pee."

Hairy-hands glowered at him. "Downa hall. I'll take ya."

Croaker dutifully went out into the hall at Hairy-hands's direction, feeling him like a brick wall at his back. He opened the door to the bathroom inward. At the same moment, he jammed his left elbow in Hairy-hands's solar plexus. He whirled, but before he could get his biomechanical hand around Hairy-hands's throat, the big man slammed the heel of his hand into the point of Croaker's chin.

He flew backward, hitting the cool tile bathroom floor on

one hip. In one stride, Hairy-hands was on top of him, shaking him this way and that, then slamming him back against the side of the porcelain tub. Croaker felt lances of pain radiate from his side as he made an inarticulate sound.

Hairy-hands bent over him, grinning, and Croaker, his biomechanical hand balled up, drove his fist into the big man's clavicle. It cracked beneath the force of the blow, and Croaker's stainless-steel and polycarbonate fingers opened like the petals of a poisonous flower, pressing against the carotid artery in the side of Hairy-hands's neck. The big man slipped to his knees, his huge hands flailing, still trying to do damage, and Croaker chopped down with his other hand onto the bridge of Hairy-hands's nose. He collapsed amid a welter of blood.

Croaker tried to stand up, slipped on the tiles, righted himself by grabbing onto the sink. He saw himself in the mirror and did not like what he saw. He was breathing hard and his side hurt like hell. He wanted to splash cold water on his face, but what with the prostheses and the makeup, it was out of the question. His nose was slightly askew and he fixed it as best he could.

He turned back to Hairy-hands. Quickly, he undressed him, then with a grunt got him into the tub. He took out several plastic notched ties, bound his ankles and wrists. Then Croaker emptied the pockets of his green and yellow Amazonia overalls, took them off, and balling them up, threw them into the tub. He drew closed the plastic shower curtain on which was imprinted a French lawn-party scene à la Toulouse-Lautrec.

He climbed into Hairy-hands's clothes and immediately began to smell like onions and peppers. He studied himself in the mirror. The trousers were too big, but by notching the belt tighter he judged they didn't look too bad.

He stuffed all his paraphernalia into his new clothes, took Hairy-hands's snub-nosed .38 in its shoulder holster, and swung it into place. All set. He checked the room one last time, neatening knickknacks here and there. Then he went out into the upstairs hallway, shutting the door behind him.

There was a commotion behind him, people coming up the stairs. He turned and almost ran right into Caesare Leonforte.

*　　*　　*

"Hot as a fuckin' furnace out there," Caesare Leonforte said as he strode down the second-floor hallway of his house. When he brushed by one of his men standing there, he was already calling for Vesper, who hurried behind him. It wasn't exactly as if Caesare remembered the man—he had only given him the most cursory of glances—but, like a ribbon of paper fetched up against a stanchion, something stuck in his mind, fluttering there.

Caesare went into his office, immediately turned down to tundra level the thermostat that controlled the central air-conditioning.

"That fuckin' Paul," he said. "I give him everything a man could ask for—money, opportunity, a chance to show his smarts—an' what does he do? He turns around an' fucks me inna ass." As usual when he was agitated, the shell of sophistication he had carefully crafted cracked, and more of his street accent came out. "But I don't want any a this to fuck with our rendezvous with Milo," he said over his shoulder to Vesper as he checked his gold Patek Philippe. "I gotta make that pickup in less than an hour an' I gotta settle a score." His huge fists struck his desk with a resounding thud, and he stared out the window. "I haven't heard from the boys in South Beach an' I don't like leavin' loose ends."

He took out a cellular phone, auto-dialed a number. "Fuck!" he shouted, throwing the phone onto his desk. "No answer. Out of range or out of brains. Either way, they haven't found Paul an' the kid."

Vesper waited a beat. "You haven't told me why your friend Paul would kidnap his girlfriend's kid."

"An' I appreciate you keepin' your nose outta it." Caesare was still staring blankly out the window, as if by sheer force of will he could bring them back. "Actually, you're right. The story I told you makes no sense now." He sighed. "The broad isn't Paul's dish, she's a business rival a mine. She got a little, you know, overambitious, stepped outta line. I had Paul bring her an' her kid here."

"Why the kid?"

"Persuasion. The kid's more important to her than her business."

"That's pretty low, isn't it? I mean, the Sicilians have rules against that sort of thing, don't they?"

"Fuck th' rules!" Caesare shouted. "The rules're for old men with black suits an' arthritis." He pounded his chest. "*I* make the rules around here an' fuck anybody who doesn't like it."

Suddenly, Vesper saw his whole body stiffen like a hunting dog on point.

"Well, holy shit, will you look at that!"

Vesper came up behind him, stared over his shoulder at the scene unfolding outside. Her heart skipped a beat. Through the window she could see Paul Chiaramonte leading Francie through the compound. He was accompanied by two of Caesare's thugs. One of the dogs, at the extreme end of its chain, was sniffing at Francie's knees. As they came toward the house, Vesper and Caesare could see that Paul had tight hold of Francie by the back of her blouse.

"Now what d'you suppose *that's* all about?" Caesare said as he drew a .38 from his desk drawer and checked the cylinder.

"It looks like he's bringing her back. Maybe you were wrong about him."

"Yeah?" Caesare snapped the chamber back in place. "We'll see about that."

As he turned away from the window, his cellular phone rang. For an instant he thought about ignoring it, then he snatched it up, yelled into it, "Yeah! What?"

"It's White Wolf."

Caesare rolled his eyes. The chief of police, who was on his payroll, read too many spy novels. He insisted on using code names and something he called a parole—an exchange of these secret names, changed periodically, that identified two otherwise anonymous voices over the phone.

"Green Dolphin," Caesare said, his mind on Paul Chiaramonte and whether or not he had crossed him.

"On the matter of the killing of that ex-NYPD cop, Lewis Croaker."

"Yeah, what about it? I told you to make sure the investi—"

"Forget the investigation, It was the most cursory thing I've ever seen, and there's a good reason why, Croaker never was admitted to any area hospital."

"Course not. I croaked Croaker." Caesare laughed at that.

"I wouldn't be so sure of that. I just spoke with the coroner and he has no record of the body, either. I went through the prelim crime-scene reports. The team that secures the crime scene is required to get the particulars of anyone in or around it. That includes the ambulance crew. I called the hospital and got an official runaround. Then I made some unofficial calls, if you get my drift, and I came up with this kick in the head: the ambulance dispatched to the crime scene was a phony."

All thoughts of Paul Chiaramonte and Francine Goldoni DeCamillo evaporated. Caesare slowly swung around until he was looking right at Vesper. Two things were now possible and he didn't like the feel of either of them. Either Croaker was dead and the feds had him, which meant a thorough clandestine investigation that might or might not be beyond his reach, or it was all a setup and Croaker was still alive. Which meant that Vesper, who had after all shot him, wasn't what she was pretending to be.

"So who picked him up?"

"I don't know. Believe me, that was as far as I could get."

Caesare took a deep breath. "You sure about everything you've told me?"

"As sure as anyone can be in this uncertain world."

Caesare nodded slowly. "Thanks. You've been a big help."

"A word to the wise. I have no control over whatever is happening, so until this blows over, I'd rather we didn't have any further communication." The chief of police laughed, but with an ambivalent note. "Remember me in your will."

As Caesare broke the connection, a memory fluttered in his mind like that ribbon of paper caught on a stanchion. The man he had bumped into in the hallway. Caesare could just about see his face: nothing remarkable about it at all—except he was sure he'd never seen it before.

With a growl of disgust and rage, he yanked open the door and kicked it back so that it banged against the rubber doorstop, twanging like a bow.

"That guy!" Caesare burst out into the hallway, Vesper just behind him. "Where's that fuckin' guy!"

The goon who was standing guard on the landing looked at his boss and said, "What guy?"

"The *guy!*" Caesare screamed, gesticulating madly. "You know, the jamoke who I bumped into a minute ago."

"What guy? Mikey? Joey? Fredo? Who?"

"Not any one of those, you moron!" Caesare shouted, pushing past him and thundering down the stairs. Caesare wanted to describe the guy, but he realized there was nothing to describe. He was just a guy—big, muscular, but featureless. "The fuckin' *guy!*" he screamed in frustration. "One a you morons musta seen him! Fuck do I pay you for? Stand around an' scratch your nuts?"

He pushed past two more men on the first floor just as the front door opened. He whirled with the grace of a ballet dancer, his .38 coming up, expecting to confront Paul and Francie, but instead, Joey loped in. He looked flushed and worried, which wasn't Joey's normal state.

"Boss, there's a copter headin' our way!"

Caesare lifted his hands. "So fuckin' what? We get choppers in here alla time!"

"I put the specs on it," Joey said, meaning binoculars. "This one's a fed."

"A fed copter?" Caesare couldn't believe it, but Joey's head was bobbing up and down like one of those annoying plastic dogs in the back window of a car. A small, almost reverent hush filled the grand foyer of the mansion, as if the shadow of the red death had entered.

"Yeah," Joey said, a little more breathlessly. "It's like a fuckin' Nam gunship, fulla cammos wit' sniper rifles an' semiautomatics. It's comin' in low, right ovah the tops a the trees."

"C'mon!" Caesare grabbed Vesper and headed through the now crowded foyer into a back corridor leading to the kitchen. His head felt as if a balloon were inflating inside it, and he could not control a throbbing in his temples.

"This way," he hissed as he grabbed her arm and pulled her bodily into the walk-in pantry. It was cool and dark and that was good. Like a blind man in his own house, Caesare knew every inch of this room because he had personally overseen its construction. He felt his way to the right rear corner. At the bottom of the floor-to-ceiling shelving, he pushed aside two cans. His fingertip depressed a button, and as he was rearranging the cans, a breath of sulfurous air wafted up at them like the exhalation of a demon.

"Down," he whispered, placing a hand on the back of Vesper's head. He went down the shallow steps behind her, then felt for another button, and the sliding panel closed just over his head.

Down here, it stunk like the pits of hell. The mansion had no basement. This was typical of Florida houses because the water table was so near the surface. But after one of his holding companies had bought this compound, he had had this shallow escape route trenched in. He had told the builders that it was for existing and future fiber-optic cable bundles and auxiliary electrical lines, but he'd made sure it was wide enough for him to traverse.

He guided Vesper through the darkness, one hand firmly on her to keep her bent over in the low space, but also to keep control of her. She was the only immediate element in his life he now had control over, and this was important to him either way—whether she was who she said she was or whether she had betrayed him, was part of the conspiracy Croaker and the feds had launched against him.

On the most basic level, there was no difference, he reflected, as he crawled through the damp, sulfurous PVC piping, away from the house, the compound, and the feds. What mattered was that she was with him. She was like a magic amulet, his protection against, as the chief of police had said, an uncertain world. Either he would have her as his lover or as a hostage. Croaker and the feds could go fuck themselves till they turned blue.

Croaker, feeling stiff and uncomfortable in his prostheses, hurried out the front door and into the broiling Florida sun. He immediately began to sweat, and remembering Rico Limòn's admonition regarding heat's effects on his disguise, he began to sweat all the more.

He approached the two goons who were riding herd on the dark-skinned man who had a gun pressed into Francie's side. He'd always found the best defense to be an offense, so he shouted, "What the hell's going on here?"

"I let the brat outta my sight for a minute," the dark-skinned man said, "an' you can tell Bad Clams I found 'er. My fault, but all's well that ends well."

"Who the fuck're you?" the goon with the dog on the chain said.

"Joey Hand," Croaker said, displaying his biomechanical hand. He studiously ignored Francie's brief wide-eyed look, but he wondered why she dug her elbow into the dark-skinned man's stomach while the goons were staring at him.

"Don't know no Joey Hand," the goon said. The dog did not care for his agitation and was whining at the end of its leash. It looked as if it was itching to get its teeth into Croaker's thigh.

"From the New York machine," Croaker said, verbally dancing as fast as he could. "The boss brought me down to help 'im deal with the DeCamillo broad an' the brat."

"This here's Paul Chiaramonte," the other goon said. "He's from the New York machine. He brought the broad an' the brat down." He looked from one to the other. "How 'bout it? You two know each other, or what?"

Croaker saw Paul Chiaramonte open his mouth and al-most make a sound as Francie stepped on his instep. He smiled, his eyes watering a bit. "Sure. Who doesn't know Joey Hand in New Yawk?" He shot out a hand, which Croaker gripped as their eyes locked. "We met—where was it? In Bensonhurst, must've been—the Donelli wedding."

"Right," Croaker said, feeling a line of sweat creep down his spine. "The Donelli wedding. Helluva affair, wasn't it?" How did actors keep this ton of shit on their faces without its melting like candle wax? he wondered.

"Jesus," Paul said, getting with the program, "was it not? Remember Rose?" He pushed out his chest.

"And Sophia singing like a drunken lunatic."

"Okay," the goon with the dog said, "enough of *This Is Your Life.*" He turned to Croaker. "The boss ain't sure about Chiaramonte. What does he want we should do with these two for the time being? Inna main house?"

"I wanna see my mom!" Francie cried, and began pulling Paul toward the guesthouse.

Croaker blessed her for her quick wit. "No," he said. "He wants the broad and the brat together so we can keep a better eye on 'em."

The second goon nodded. "Sounds good t'me. We don't want a repeat ova escape. The boss'll roast us alive."

They went across the emerald lawn, past high privet hedges and neat lines of boxwood interspersed with flower beds. Their soles made a hollow sound against the brickwork around the pool, and Croaker was acutely aware of the quick clicking of the dog's long nails. Above their heads, a bird flitted among the cool leaves, free from the cruelty of man-made crises.

Croaker saw the guesthouse, shining brilliant white, and he imagined Margarite inside. What kind of shape was she in? Was she all right? He wanted to break into a run and he could feel the adrenaline pumping through him.

They were on the brick path to the front door when they heard the *thwop-thwop-thwop!* of a helicopter's rotors and, looking up, saw what looked like a military gunship coming in low and fast.

"Fuck is that?" the first goon said as his dog began to bark, leaping in the air as if possessed.

Croaker smashed his biomechanical fist into the goon's side and he crumpled over. The dog whirled almost in mid-air, its eyes bright, its jaws snapping. Grabbing the plastic snap-guard from his pocket, Croaker jammed it over the dog's muzzle, then pressed the point of a tiny tranquilizer dart into its neck.

"Hey—!" Croaker heard the second goon cry out and, turning, saw the goon, a bloody gash in his temple, going down from a blow from the butt of Paul Chiaramonte's gun.

Paul looked at Croaker. "You know who I am, but who the fuck're you?" He had to shout over the growing noise of the chopper.

"Uncle Lew!" Francie cried, running into his arms. "I knew you'd come find us!"

Paul looked at the two of them with what Croaker sensed was a kind of sadness. At that moment, Paul seemed very much apart from this goonish world, as isolated as an arctic ice floe.

As they huddled in the doorway, Croaker said, "I know all about you, buddy."

"No, Uncle Lew, you don't," Francie said.

Paul tousled her hair. "I fucked up big time, I know. But

I made a deal with Francie. I promised t'get her and her mom outta here an' I aim t'do that."

Leaves were whipping all over the place and eddies of wind rattled the glass panes of the windows. Croaker glanced from Paul to the lowering copter. "You still have some way to go." Croaker gestured with his head. "How many guards inside?"

"Two. But that was before I split with the kid. May be more now."

"Okay," Croaker said, the gun he had taken from the goon upstairs in the main house at the ready. "Let's do it."

As Paul knocked on the door, he turned to Francie, placed her out of harm's way. "Now just stay there, will you promise me?"

She stared at him, then at the copter out of which men in camouflage outfits were leaping. "Uncle Lew, what's going on?"

"Just stay here," Croaker said as the front door opened and Paul slammed it back on its hinges as hard as he could.

Croaker bulled his way into the hallway, saw a goon coming out of a back bedroom, skidded sideways as the goon aimed and squeezed off a shot that slammed into a cabinet. Croaker, landing on one shoulder, fired three times, and the goon was knocked backward into the doorframe. He went down and stayed down.

Croaker turned in time to see Paul struggling with the goon who had opened the door. The goon used a right cross to deck Paul, and Croaker took up a chair and threw it. The goon ducked right into Paul's fist. He went down on one knee and Paul chopped him viciously across the neck.

Croaker went through room after room and found them empty. He waved Paul back, then cautiously entered the back bedroom through the open door. The king-size bed was to the right, the door to the room, a dresser and mirror to the left. Straight ahead was a bathroom.

To his right, he saw Margarite kneeling on the bed, her eyes wide and staring, her mouth opened in a soundless scream. At almost the same instant, he saw the dark splotch in the corner of his vision, reflected in the mirror—someone standing hidden behind the open door. As he took a step toward Margarite, he fired back over his left shoulder point-blank at the door. The bullets broke through the hollow-core door and he heard a heavy thump. Stepping around the door, he pulled it toward him, saw the body of a third goon who'd been hiding there. He used the front of his shoe to pull the gun from the goon's hand, then bent to check his pulse. There wasn't any.

"Who—?"

He came around from behind the door, already pulling off his prosthetic nose. "It's me, Margarite. Lew."

"Oh, my God!" She scrambled off the bed and into his arms. "Lew."

He kissed the side of her neck as she clung to him. It had been a long time since he had held her, and he savored the moment.

"It's all over," he said. "You're safe and so is Francie."

Tetsuo Akinaga was nowhere to be seen, but Nicholas glimpsed the figure of Jōchi disappearing through the exit door in the left rear of Both Ends Burning.

The exit opened not onto a back alley or the street but onto a lightless and stifling corridor at the end of which was another door slightly ajar. Nicholas moved carefully through the darkness until he reached the door, which was painted metal, a fire door. He pushed it slightly open, peered out into an alley. It was deserted. He wondered whether Jōchi and Akinaga had come this way.

Back in the corridor, he opened his dark eye—and the blackness fell away. He became aware of the square outline in the ceiling, the trapdoor and the cord hanging down from it. Pulling it, he saw a set of steel steps slide down. He went up them, ducking over to make it through the small trapdoor.

He found himself in the back room of a video-game parlor. Making his way past stacked cartons and the hulks of older machines, he opened a door onto rows of machines spewing the complex graphics and elemental noises of ultraviolent computerized confrontations. Hunched over the pixel-dominated screens were mesmerized teenagers—many of them Nihonin in their black leather outfits, tattoos and body piercings, their hair buzz-cut or maned, their eyes heavy with the attitude of menace forged from the excess of empty leisure.

Nicholas scanned the room, which was as large as any pachinko parlor. Strings of neon lights ran around the walls where they met the ceiling, often spelling out the brand names of the game manufacturers in brilliant starburst patterns.

Here was their life in its figurative nutshell: the control of little men on little screens, life and death played out in concentrated bursts of color, light, and sound, all played at amphetamine speed. They had dropped out of their fathers' highly controlled life and dropped into another, one without any sense of responsibility or decay. Here among the machines that re-created the lives of their combatants over and over without ever missing a beat, they were immortal, suspended in time. With one night identical to the last, the future had been obliterated as effectively as the past.

Nicholas went through the video-game parlor, seeing nothing, hearing nothing, searching for Jōchi. He passed the cashier in her tower of neon and plastic and went up a steep flight of stairs. A jammed, raucous bar decked out as one dazzlingly colored screen from a popular video game led into another room, quieter, almost hushed. Muted shades of charcoal-gray and wood-brown bare walls were hung with huge black-and-white photographs of Jack Kerouac, Alan Ginsberg, Lawrence Ferlinghetti, an achingly young Marlon Brando in his role in *The Wild One,* a ferocious Jim Morrison onstage in full leather regalia, clutching a microphone, a softly lit, expertly retouched studio publicity still of Lawrence Harvey, a sultry James Dean exuding the scary longeur of the temporarily sated predator, a grainy shot of T. E. Lawrence, his desert-seared teak skin contrasting sharply with the white Arab burnoose he wore.

A number of tiny tables were scattered around the cool, dimly lit room, and on a small platform that hardly deserved the name *stage,* a young man slouched in black boots, knife-blade-narrow trousers, T-shirt, and leather vest. A half-smoked cigarette lounged at a corner of his mouth as he recited what many in the room mistakenly thought of as poetry. Everyone was drinking coffee or an ornate variation thereof. The atmosphere was thick with cigarette smoke and resuscitated beat attitude.

Nicholas entered a stainless-steel kitchen as long and narrow as a hallway. He squinted through the bright fluorescent lights, ignored the questions put to him by one of the cooks, and made a thorough search. It looked like a dead end, and back in the coffee bar he took a long, penetrating look around.

He saw neither Akinaga nor Jōchi, but he did see some-one he knew. He went over, took a spare chair from the back of the room, slid it next to the Nihonin and his pals.

Kawa looked languidly over at him. "Hey," he said, and gripped Nicholas's hand in a firm American bikers' grip. His snow-white hair looked eerie in the half-light.

Nicholas nodded his head toward the minuscule stage. "You like this stuff?"

"It sucks," Kawa said, and his table snickered. He shrugged. "But, hey, the atmosphere's right for the moment."

Nicholas put his head close to Kawa's. He smelled of cloves and pot. Nicholas wondered whether he was on any other drugs. "You see someone—maybe two people—hur-rying through here a short time ago?" He gave them a brief description of Akinaga and Jōchi.

Kawa's eyes opened wide. "Hunt?" he inquired in his odd kind of shorthand.

When Nicholas nodded, he conferred with his compatri-ots. The knot broke and he said to Nicholas, "Maya might have seen something of the sort, but she wasn't paying too much attention. The rest of us, no sale."

Nicholas turned to Maya, a Japanese girl with dyed-blond hair and fever-bright eyes, but Kawa was right, whatever she might have seen lay light-years away behind those stoned eyes.

"Hey, don't sweat it." Kawa winked at Nicholas. "If they *did* come this way, I have an idea where."

"Show me."

Nicholas followed Kawa back into the kitchen. The smell of freshly brewed espresso was a sharp tang, mingling with the released zest of fresh lemons. A *latte* machine was hiss-ing like a nest of vipers. Past the stinking toilet was the space used to stack garbage in neat plastic bags. Beyond that, as Nicholas had already seen, was a blank wall.

But now Nicholas could see that none of the bags were resting against this back wall, and as he watched, Kawa depressed a hidden stud. The plasterboard wall slid back, revealing a small elevator.

Nicholas stared at it for a moment much the way he would an asp showing its fangs. "Where does this go? The street?"

"No," Kawa said. "It goes up to a high-rent restaurant."

Nicholas felt the undercurrent of a premonition. "Do you know the name?"

"Yeah, sure. Pull Marine."

The restaurant where Honniko and Jōchi worked as part-time maître d's while toiling in the service of Mick Leonforte. Pull Marine, the nexus point. He looked at Kawa. "You think the manager of this place is around?"

"I saw him a while ago. He was on his way out, but take a minute and I'll check."

Kawa disappeared through the steam of *latte* and coffee. In a moment, he had returned with a short, balding man with sharp features and cunning eyes. "This is Suta-san," he said, and the short man bowed.

Nicholas, returning the bow, whipped out Tanaka Gin's prosecutor's credentials before Kawa could introduce him. He saw the Nihonin's eyes flick over the opened wallet. If he was surprised, he didn't show it.

"How may I be of service?" Suta said.

"The Prosecutor's Office is investigating a multiple homicide," Nicholas said not untruthfully. "The trail has led us back to this building. Can you tell me who owns it?"

Suta rubbed his hands together, happy that it wasn't he who was somehow under investigation. "Firstly, this is a series of buildings—three linked together by a warren of very old subterranean corridors—or so I am told." His hands made little washing gestures. Nicholas was prepared for him to say that the buildings were owned by a corporation he would be able to trace back to Tetsuo Akinaga.

"The history is perhaps interesting," Suta continued, "though, I suppose, only to a select few. A corporation owned it for many years—perhaps ten. Sterngold Associates. Recently, it was bought by a company named Tenki."

Nicholas's mind was reeling. Sterngold had been owned by Rodney Kurtz, the German industrialist whom Mick had ritually murdered. Tenki was Mick's own company.

"I imagine Sterngold bought up the three buildings," Nicholas said.

Suta shook his head. "No, they were already a parcel when Sterngold bought in."

"May I ask how you know all this?"

"Certainly." The bald head nodded. "My father built up a modest real estate business, which I now run." Suta gestured. "This club is a hobby for me. My wife died several years ago and I find my life—more pleasant—when it is filled."

"So your office did all these transactions?"

Suta nodded. *"Hai."*

Nicholas's mind was racing. "Who did Sterngold buy the three buildings from?"

Suta shifted from one foot to another as if his feet hurt. "I really shouldn't say."

This was interesting. "Why? There are no secrets from the Prosecutor's Office."

"No, no, nothing like that." The hands were washing again. "But I hesitate to intrude on an individual's—"

"The entire parcel was owned by an individual?"

Suta nodded. "Yes, dating back a long time, to before the war in the Pacific. An individual by the name of Okami-san."

Nicholas felt as if he had been punched in the stomach. Taking a careful breath, he said, "Mikio Okami, the Yakuza *oyabun?*"

"No. His sister. Kisoko."

Dark shards spinning in his mind, wheels within wheels within . . . "You mean it was sold by the family?"

"No. I was required to inspect the deed prior to the closing. It was in the name of Kisoko Okami."

Nicholas was lost in thought. What did Rodney Kurtz, Mick Leonforte, and Kisoko Okami have in common? He could not imagine. All of a sudden, reality had been turned ninety degrees, all the disparate pieces upended out of their assigned slots. Nothing was what it had appeared to be five minutes ago. In a moment, Nicholas realized that Suta was watching him expectantly.

Nicholas bowed. "You have been extremely helpful, Suta-san," he said formally. "I will make note of that in my report."

Again, relief flooded Suta's face. He could not stop bowing, but at length he left them in the kitchen, standing by the closed door to the elevator.

"Hunt just got a little more interesting," Kawa said, and Nicholas could see a spark of interest briefly illumine Kawa's icy nihilistic facade.

"You could say that."

Kawa inclined his head. "You going up there?" He meant Pull Marine.

"I've got no choice." Nicholas reached out, pressed the single button, and they could hear the whir of machinery over the hiss and pop of the kitchen.

"Coming down," Kawa said.

The door opened and Nicholas stepped in. When he turned around to face the closing door, he saw the Nihonin with one thumb upraised.

"Hey," Kawa said. "Blood tonight."

The door shut and Nicholas rode up in darkness. The tiny cabin smelled faintly of a woman's spicy-sweet perfume and a gamey, masculine odor. Whatever lights the elevator had weren't working. Nicholas had not pressed a button but he was ascending. Was the elevator on automatic, rising and descending between the coffee bar and Pull Marine like the tide?

Nicholas felt a whiff of air on his cheek. Were they passing vents in the shaft? Unlikely in this maze of three interlinked buildings. His eyes seemed to go out of focus and he lost his balance.

Kshira?

But no, he did not hear the telltale buzzing of ten thousand bees in his head. In fact, his mind seemed completely unruffled, still as a summer pond, devoid of volition and decision.

His last thought, disconnected, as out of context as a clown at a funeral, was the word *gas*.

Then the world dropped far and fast into a pit of utter blackness.

13
West Palm Beach/Tokyo

Caesare pushed away a pile of accumulated dirt, silt, sand, and rotting leaves that was rapidly decomposing into humus. The far end of the PVC pipe debouched more than a city block away from the house, beside a private dock on Lake Worth. He wriggled out, brushing off a dark coating of detritus and insects, then turned back and gave Vesper a hand.

While Caesare climbed into the Cigarette, Vesper looked back at the compound, which now looked like the grounds of a military training exercise. The moment the fed copter had touched down the agents dismounted from its landing struts and a voice over an amplified loudspeaker had cautioned those inside the compound to lay down their arms and stand still with their hands in the air.

Vesper, wondering about her friends, said, "Aren't you the least bit interested in what's going on there?"

Caesare, having made sure the tank was topped off, cast off the bow line. "If my life has taught me anything, it is never to look back."

"But these are your people. They put their lives on the line for you. Don't you owe them something?"

Caesare glanced at her. "To a man they're greedy and stupid and, essentially, lazy."

"But they're loyal."

Caesare raised a hand. "I could getta a dog t'do that." He gestured. "C'mon, c'mon. An' cast off the stern line as you come aboard."

A moment later, he had started the engine and they eased out of the dock, swinging first east, then south in a perfect arc, their wake churning white and foamy. When they were past the small island that housed the U.S. Coast Guard Reservation, he put on speed. The Cigarette went up onto plane, the huge arcing wake forming almost immediately, the sound booming across the lake, and soon they had left the lights and sounds of encroaching chaos far behind.

Wade Forrest came off the copter with his heart beating fast. He was dressed in full cammo and he held a machine pistol in his right hand. He had lifted off the moment he had received the electronic signal from Croaker's homing device.

Already his people were rounding up these Italian goons, who stood awestruck at the firepower of the United States government. Forrest, bent over and squinting against the rotor's wash, spoke authoritatively into the headset built into his helmet. In truth, he felt overlarge and bulky in his bulletproof clothes, but regs were regs and he was not about to make an exception. He had spoken to his daughter yesterday. He had interrupted her birthday party, could hear the music and the noise in the background, and he had felt a certain sinking feeling in the pit of his stomach. They had talked for five minutes, but after he had hung up, he realized he couldn't remember a thing she'd said to him. He'd been too busy wishing he'd been there, wishing he'd been to even one of the milestones in his daughters' lives. But his job being what it was, he hadn't made any. And now he didn't even have this snippet of conversation to keep with him. On impulse, he'd called back, but his daughter was somewhere outside. A friend promised to retrieve her, but after five minutes of listening to music and bursts of laughter and nothing else, he'd hung up. Anyway, he'd had a great deal of work to do.

Now he was busy deploying his men. He strode through the grounds of the compound like Lee at Chancellorsville, an armed aide at his side. Men were pouring out of the main house under armed guard, others were being led from the perimeter of the fencing where they had been hiding or trying to make a run for it. Not a shot had been fired.

On the other hand, there was no sign of Caesare Leonforte, and Forrest ordered an immediate thorough search of the main house. He found Croaker in the guesthouse, where he had subdued three men who had been guarding a handsome but disheveled woman with dark hair and light eyes. Forrest recognized her immediately. She was standing with her arm around a girl of eighteen or so, her daughter, Forrest guessed. There was another man in the room, whom Forrest didn't know and didn't care about.

"Margarite Goldoni DeCamillo," he said in the formal voice he had learned to evoke in the Virginia academy where he had received his advanced training, "you are hereby charged with the murder of one Franco 'the Fish' Bondini." He took out the cuffs. "Three separate eyewitnesses have identified you as the woman who shot Mr. Bondini dead on Park Avenue and—"

"What?" Margarite had a stunned look on her face. "But that was self-defense."

"Maybe, maybe not." Forrest snapped the cuffs on her, read her her Miranda rights.

"But I'm not guilty!" Margarite cried. She looked from Forrest to Croaker. "Lew," she implored.

Croaker, who was in the midst of ditching the rest of his prostheses, said, "Forrest, what the hell d'you think you're doing? This is utter bullshit and you know it. They killed her driver—"

"Bodyguard." Forrest leered. "What kind of business d'you think she's in?"

Croaker took a step toward the fed. "They shot to death the man standing beside her and were about to execute her." Light glinted off his makeup. "No jury in this country will convict. In fact, no D.A. will charge. Under the law, she's entitled to defend herself if she's in fear for her life. It's just like she said, self-defense."

"You've done your bit, now kindly let me do mine. Get the hell out of my face."

"Like hell I will."

"Look, Croaker, I have a federal mandate to make cases against the remaining Families and she's Goldoni."

"This isn't a case, it's a farce. Do you really believe the government will allow itself to end up with egg on its face? They're gonna need a patsy, and you are it. Your fast-track career's going in the shitter."

The cords on the sides of Forrest's bull neck were popping. "Like I said, get the hell out of my way."

Croaker took another step toward Forrest, lowered his voice. "For God's sake, take the cuffs off her, man. She's been through hell here. Bad Clams had her and her daughter kidnapped."

Forrest's eyes flickered like one of those exhibits in a house-of-horrors exhibit. "Step aside, I tell you, or by God I'll arrest you along with Mrs. DeCamillo." He reached out, grabbed the chain between the cuffs, jerked it so that Margarite stumbled forward.

"Mom!"

"Easy, kid." Paul tried to hold her, but Francie ducked her shoulder and broke past him on an end run. She slammed into Forrest, her arms flailing.

"Get her off me, will ya?" Forrest cried, but before the other feds could act, Croaker snatched her up and whispered in her ear, "Stop it. This won't do any good."

Francie was crying, turning in Croaker's arms until she had buried her face in the crook of his shoulder. He saw that Margarite's heart was breaking, and his with it. Had she ever contemplated the physical reality of being arrested? he wondered. If she had, she had certainly never considered the possibility of its happening in front of her daughter. After making it this far, Margarite almost lost it as Forrest led her out the door into the secured compound.

Nicholas heard a humming, but it was coming from a long way off. The humming went on, a disembodied sound that gradually became a melody wafting in darkness. The melody unfurled like a black sail, complex and strangely familiar. Nicholas had heard it before. It was a piece of Richard Wagner's *Die Lieder von der Erde*.

Coming up like a skin diver from the depths, he felt an enormous need to take a breath. He tried to do so but nothing happened. His lungs refused to work. He tried to focus his mind, to open his *tanjian* eye, but something was holding him back, like the web of a spider, and he could not find *kokoro,* the center of all things. His mind felt encased in amber. Putting one thought after another was enormously difficult.

His lids felt glued shut and he opened his eyes with some difficulty. He found himself in a bare room and he had a moment of blind panic. Then he realized he was hanging upside down. His heart thudded heavily in his chest. Across from him, against the opposite wall, Mikio Okami hung from a chain in what he assumed was an identical position. An IV dripped into the inside of Okami's left wrist, and by turning his head just slightly Nicholas could see a similar contraption dripping liquid into his own vein. In this position, he could see the wall at a right angle to him, saw a third chain and an IV rig. This spot was, however, empty.

"Okami-san," he whispered, and then more urgently: "Okami-san!"

The Kaisho opened eyes turned rheumy. He blinked several times, like an owl in bright light.

"Linnear-san." He sighed heavily, his words slurred by drugs. "Caught in the same trap."

"Don't give up hope. We'll get out of this."

The look Okami gave him sent a shiver down his spine.

"Death waits for all of us," the Kaisho said slowly. "Our sole duty is to see that it has meaning."

"There will be no death here," Nicholas vowed.

Mikio Okami tried to smile. "Give it meaning," he rasped, his eyelids already closing in drug-induced stupor.

"Okami-san!"

There was no response. Nicholas himself was struggling with thought. What had happened? He had been in the S&M club Both Ends Burning, Hatta had been knifed by Jōchi, and Nicholas had taken off in pursuit. Corridors, sounds, bright lights, shadows shifting, the rich smell of coffee brewing—all these and more were a jumble in his mind. Then, like a flare in the darkness, he remembered ascending in the coffinlike elevator, the whiff of air brushing his cheek. He'd been gassed; it had been a trap. Honniko, Kawa, Suta, were they all in on it?

Flash of Kawa's grinning face, his thumbs-up sign, and his enigmatic farewell, *Blood tonight.*

The German lied recommenced, and now Nicholas became aware of someone else in the room. This person was moving, working busily and humming industriously all the while. At that precise moment, the figure turned and stared directly into Nicholas's face. He came over, lifted Nicholas's head by the hair.

"Had a nice nap?" He rattled Nicholas's IV. "Comfy in our little den?"

A shaft of pale light filtering down from above picked out features on the figure's face, and Nicholas recognized Mick Leonforte.

"And it *is* our little den. This is Tenki, the old *toruko* where Colonel Linnear spun his busy little spiderwebs just after the war." Mick was grinning. "Quite an odyssey you took getting here, I must say." He pursed his lips in mock sorrow and shook his head. "Too bad unlike Odysseus you didn't have a goddess to advise you." He spread his arms. "There's no Athena here, no one to get you out of this. So here you will stay while I make my bloodless coup against your vast, far-flung empire." He stroked the side of Nicholas's face. "Sweet, sweet revenge."

The hand withdrew, and abruptly, his tone changed, becoming declamatory. "I must say you've done well by yourself. Marrying into money and power and Tomkin Industries, merging it with Sato at just the right time, expanding from computer chips to hardware design, to fiber optics, moving into every emerging market you could stick your fingers into. And then there's your crowning achievement: the TransRim CyberNet." Mick nodded. "Oh, yes, you've done well indeed. Almost as well as I would have done had I not been forced into the shadows to escape the long arm of the law." He guffawed. "What law? What am I thinking of? *I* am the law."

He let Nicholas's head go. "But you overextended." He nodded toward Okami. "And then you get caught up in old grandpa's own nightmare, and guarding him against assassins took you out of the Sato program for fifteen months. Too long in this day and age. Hell, in your business two *months* is too long to be away. You lose the feel, the flow of the changes. You forget your abilities, your predictive capacities become impaired." He grinned again, adjusting something on IV. "You created your own soft spot, Nicky boy, and I sank my jaws into it like the predatory animal I am."

"It felt good, but . . ." Mick frowned. "I must say it was something I had to get used to. In a way it was like getting myself bloody. You and me, you know, we have a special bond. And why? Because our fathers fucked with one another's lives. They toyed and tinkered and brought each other such misery. Just like I am doing with you. I slept with your woman, over and over and over, and no matter what she tells you, she enjoyed it."

He snapped his fingers. "Hey, but don't take my word for it." He turned, rummaging around before pulling out a portable tape recorder. He popped in a cassette, pressed the play button, and put the machine next to Nicholas's ear.

"Listen . . ."

Nicholas tried to turn his mind away, to blank it out, but the drug was all through his system now, and he had had no time to try to hypermetabolize it out. Besides, more was entering his open vein with every drip of the IV. So he heard in agony the pants and moans, the whispered endearments, and then the slow, obscene crescendo of moans, cries, and screams. Was that Koei's voice? How could he know through the distortion of the tape and the drugs? But it might be, and that was what Mick intended and it was enough.

"Ah, I see it in your face, the knife thrust has been felt." Mick switched off the tape recorder and knelt down in front of Nicholas's face. "But I want you to know something—and it is the most important *thing* in this little construct of mine: What I do here to you—to those you love, to everything you have spent so many years building, to you—I do not because of what happened between our fathers." He gestured as if waving to an unseen crowd. "Let their ghosts, whatever hell they may inhabit, continue their enmity on their own terms. I refuse to be bound by what went on before me. I am a deconstructionist, after all. I repudiate the past." He made a slow fist. "I use history for my own ends, I correctly interpret what went before, torching to ash the so-called *facts* cited by the cabal of criminals who seditiously call themselves *historians*. Sedition, certainly, because their lies serve to undercut the transformation of mankind."

Mick's head tilted back and his features rose into the wan

light like a dark and dangerous sea creature disturbing the surface for the first time. "We are, after all, merely heralds, imprecisely marked dice cast in the great game of chance by Zeus, Jove, Odin, whatever name you wish to put to Heraclitus's divine child. We, too, are children of the great philosopher Heraclitus, Nicky boy, because we know what he did: the change and strife are the natural order of the universe."

Mick's head whipped forward as his lips pulled back from shining teeth. "I cannot—I will not—seek revenge for what Colonel Linnear did to my father because that would require a conscience, and the plain fact is I have none. The social compact, Nicky boy, so revered by civilization, is the single worst transformation human beings were ever forced to undergo. I would willingly submit myself to the fictionalized 'horrors' of a concentration camp, so ubiquitously and falsely disseminated—if anything like them had ever existed—rather than give up the best part of my humanity to society.

"To become a sociable and pacific creature is like asking a fish to adapt to the land. What you have taken away is the very *essence*, the primordial ichor gifted us by the gods. Nietzsche taught me this: we once were happily adapted to an existence closest to godliness—we roamed free in the primordial wilderness, we went to war and gorged ourselves on adventure and conflict."

Mick peered into Nicholas's drug-fogged eyes. "All these things, you understand, were in our innate nature—they were instinctual. And what did the social contract do? It instantly said, 'Fuck you,' to those instincts, branding them evil, shameful, insane. The social contract not only castrated man, but forced him into a straitjacket. But here's the thing, the very essence of the deed: society could only muzzle our instincts; it could not kill them."

He wiped his hands on his trousers as he stood up. "So began the subtle game of sublimation, of small covert satisfactions, venal and perverted, in place of the overt ones to which we were accustomed and to which we were entitled. But it got worse. Confinement and the lack of a constant supply of external enemies turned man in upon himself, persecuting, terrorizing himself. There is, I am sure you are aware, having lived in Japan for so long, a peculiar kind of violence that builds up in humans who are heavily repressed.

And when at last it is released, it is terrible, awesome to behold. This is what happened. Bereft of his natural hunting grounds, told that his natural predatory instincts were criminal, man went slowly mad." Mick's arms swept out in a grand gesture, again as if he were surrounded by an audience. "You have only to look at the world to know what I say is the truth. Where should we look? Bosnia, Rwanda, Cambodia, Russia, Ukraine, Iraq, Haiti, Colombia, Italy, Germany, the United States. Shall I go on?" He turned his head. "What would be the point? Hatred is running like poisoned blood all across the globe. Madness stalks us. Total, complete madness."

Mick slipped on his push dagger. The Damascus blade was dark as night, filmed with a thin sheen of oil. He flexed the push dagger so the blade caught the light, showing its striations. "So, you see, here we are, the two of us, mirror images, the darkness and the light, sunshine and shadow." He cocked an ear at an imaginary response. "What, you say, good and evil?" He shook his head sagely. "No, Nicky boy, that particular comparison's meaningless. The two of us have transcended such notions. We have gone beyond good and evil into another realm entirely. For there to be good and evil we would have to hate one another, and we don't, do we?" He shrugged. "At least, I don't hate you. God alone knows what you think of me." He laughed, a brutal, eerie sound bouncing off the walls like a hardball with a load of spin. "Not that it matters, because a portion of the essential paradigm is missing. We're opposite but unequal, and d'you know why, Nicky boy?"

With his free hand, Mick grabbed Nicholas's hair again, this time, yanked his head back and forth viciously. "Because you're a Jew. Your father was dogged by this fatal flaw—in fact, I believe he hid it often enough—and so are you. Jeez, what were you thinking? You could get so oriental your skin turned yellow, but it wouldn't be worth a damn. You can't outrun heritage no matter how hard you try. So, you see, I *can't* hate you because you're inferior, too far beneath me to evoke such a strong emotion."

Without another word, he turned on his heel, and crossing the room, he stood in front of Mikio Okami, staring up at him with opaque eyes. A curious stillness settled over him, and something deep inside Nicholas's drugged mind shouted, *No! You can't!* Because Nicholas recognized this as the first stages of the shaman's ritual. It was the summoning of power that would bring about an act of primeval magic.

Nicholas drove himself into a frenzy, willing himself to overcome the drug being pumped into him. He knew what was coming as surely as if he could see into the future. His mind was screaming for his body to react, but all he could manage was a soft tinkling of his chain.

Across the room, Mick was smiling gently. "It's coming. You know it's coming."

Nicholas did. He had some experience with the Messulethe, the ancient psycho-mages; he had seen firsthand the grisly remains of Mick's incantatory rituals. *Think!* Nicholas's mind screamed. *It's just like walking. Put one thought in front of the other.* From the symptoms, he had begun to zero in on what the drug was not. It was a nerve toxin as well as a vascular inhibitor. Given that it was being administered by Mick Leonforte, the chances were good it was Banh Tom venom, the same toxin used on Kappa Watanabe. He knew how to hypermetabolize its chemical constituents because he had done it with Watanabe and had saved his life, but this was an altogether different situation. He was held virtually spellbound by the slow drip of the poison into his bloodstream.

All the same, he had to try. Mentally gritting his teeth, he began the hypermetabolic process, but he was so slowed down by the drug the chemical changes had little or no effect.

Meanwhile, the atmosphere in the room had turned dank and dark, as if swirls of black mist were crawling up the walls, whorling into the wan light, turning it as ashy gray as a shroud.

"It comes!"

Mick's cry was a howl of triumph, of the wolf pouncing upon the exposed underbelly of the deer.

No!

All at once, Mick was in motion. His daggered fist drove forward, and the dark blade of Damascus steel plunged to its guard into Mikio Okami's chest. There was a rending as of a soul in torment or a door too long shut being pried open. The offal stench of the abattoir rose like a miasma, and blood, dark as oil, began to flood the room.

14
Florida Coast/Tokyo

Out on the high seas Caesare Leonforte was a different person. Like a shark returned to open water, his movements were connected to a deeper, one might even say more primeval, imperative. Seeing him drive the sleek Cigarette, consulting charts, navigating surely and deftly, legs spread and slightly flexed against the pitch and roll, Vesper had the feeling he had left all his cares behind him.

At least, this is what she would have thought if Caesare had been any other person. But he was not. Over the course of days and nights with him she had come to know him better, perhaps, than she had ever wanted to. The fact was, Caesare had no cares. Not a one. He had no loyalty, he cared about nothing and no one but himself. If there had ever been in him the human capacity to love, it had been squeezed out of him by circumstance and this studiedly perverse nature. He despised his father while yearning to emulate him; he was openly contemptuous of his sister, Jaqui, while in some way needing her approval. He was a seething mass of contradictions that, far from canceling one another out, were perpetually at war. That made for a volatile and unpredictable mix.

"Fucking feds," he said as he drove the Cigarette toward its inevitable rendezvous with Coast Guard cutter CGM

1176. "Alla time on my ass. I thought I had 'em buffaloed, thought I had 'em in my back pocket. But the feds have more heads than a fucking Hydra." He spoke quietly, fiercely, as if talking to himself. Vesper, standing just behind the wind- and spray-whipped cowling, wondered if he was aware of her presence. "Gotta regroup, gotta call in the favors, pull the strings, set 'em to dancing my tune again."

Vesper shaded her eyes. In the distance, she could see a Coast Guard cutter. It seemed to be lying still on the ocean, idling its engines. Caesare saw it, too, because he changed course to port, heading toward it. He came down off of plane, ran on another hundred yards or so and cut the engines. He directed Vesper to drop anchor and she activated the electronic winch. With a soft plash, the anchor slipped out of its resting place forward.

The Coast Guard cutter was near enough for Vesper to make out its designation: CGM 1176. The boat Milo captained. She could hear the throaty gurgle of its diesels, and with a puff of blue smoke from its stern, the cutter headed slowly toward them.

They boarded it without incident and Milo ordered the cutter to reverse engines. Caesare did not acknowledge Milo's presence at all, except to say, "Things are fucked back at the house. We won't be coming back to the Cigarette."

Milo nodded. He looked trim as a greyhound ready to race in his crisp white uniform and close-clipped beard. His eyes strayed momentarily to Vesper's as if searching for further explanation. She smiled at him, and while Caesare went aft to check on the arms shipment they would exchange for the cocaine, she slipped into the cabin near Milo.

"What's the hell's up with him?" Milo asked out of the corner of his mouth. Up close you could see a fine webwork of wrinkles at the corners of his eyes and mouth. As usual, his eyes were hidden behind reflective sunglasses.

"Feds raided the compound," she said softly. "Came in by armored copter. They threw the whole nine yards at us. We escaped by a hairsbreadth."

Milo's thin lips went even thinner, which, for him, connoted grave concern. "I better talk to him. The pipeline could be in jeopardy." But he stopped as Vesper put a hand on his arm.

"I wouldn't go anywhere near him right now if I were you. He'll take your head clear off."

"I hear ya." Milo paused to give a course correction to the pilot. Then he nodded to Vesper and she followed him to a more private part of the cockpit. "Listen," he hissed, putting his face close to hers, "I got my whole career—shit, whatam I saying? My entire *life* wrapped up in this operation."

"The arms pipeline into DARPA, you mean?" She was talking about the highly secret government advanced weapons project from which Caesare was diverting product to sell to the highest bidder overseas.

"Yeah, yeah." He looked at her and sneered. "You think I'd waste my time with cocaine smuggling? No fucking way, man. Too many Latino types wound tighter than a duck's ass on machismo. They'd blow an Anglo away as soon as look at you. No, I got into this for the weapons. Hobby of mine, you know."

Vesper didn't but she made approving noises.

"Anyway," Milo said, licking his lips, "I gotta stake inna pipeline. A *big* stake, know what I mean? Shit, it's my contacts that got the big guy inta it in the first place, so I get a cut of all the action. I'm a player, see, not a fucking mule, and now that the shit's come down I don't want any of it sticking to me."

"In other words, you want denial of accountability."

She could see the squint lines around Milo's eyes deepen. "I want to smell clean all the way through this, that's what I fucking want."

She could sense how frightened he was, a man on the fringe of lawlessness, loving his job, but having gotten bored maybe, wanting something more, and being given a chance at it, had jumped without looking how far down he could fall. He'd said it himself—he was a player not a mule. That's what Milo had wanted all along, but now that the shit had hit the fan, he wasn't prepared.

"Don't do the crime if you can't serve the time."

Milo jumped as if he'd come in contact with an electric current. "What the fuck? I'm not serving any time."

"I can arrange that."

"Yeah? Who the fuck are you, the queen of fucking Sheba?"

"I'm the one who can provide you with a denial of accountability." She looked at him. "You *do* want to save your own ass, right, Milo?"

She could hear his exhalation of breath, and his head moved so that even without being able to see his eyes, she knew he was looking at Caesare. She knew he was going to jump ship even before he said it. Why not? Caesare had no loyalty to his people, so when push came to shove, why should they be loyal to him?

"If he knew . . ."

Milo was speaking of Caesare and she knew it. "He won't. You leave him to me." She waited a beat. "Are you signed on?"

Milo moved his head again and sunlight flashed across his mirrored lenses. "I do no time. Is that solid?"

"Guaranteed."

Milo licked his lips and nodded.

Vesper had decided to pump him right then and there for the details of how they had penetrated the government safeguards when Caesare called her aft. She went with the obedience of a dog without even a glance at Milo.

Caesare was waving his arms around wildly. "Will ya look at this?" he shouted over the roar of the engines. He pointed down to where he'd pried open the top of a crate covered with government seals and official warning stickers.

Vesper bent to take a look and he grabbed her by the back of the neck so hard that she saw stars. Before she could catch her breath, he jammed her head into the edge of the open box of weapons. Forward, Milo, who had been watching from the shadows at the edge of the cockpit, turned away.

Half-dazed and hurting, she heard a metallic click, felt the cool metal muzzle of his gun worming its way painfully into her ear.

"You fucking little bitch," he spat. His face was a twisted mask of rage. "Did you think you'd get away with it?"

She had a hard time forming words, but at last she managed to answer, "Get away with what?"

Caesare cuffed the back of her head. "You fucking ratted me out to the feds."

The vaguely triangular shape, glistening, dark as death, hung before Nicholas's eyes. He could smell it, and even through the drugs, his stomach quailed. He was hypermetabolizing the Banh Tom toxin, but it wasn't fast enough.

"Here it is! Power!"

Mick Leonforte held Mikio Okami's heart in his hand, and as Nicholas watched, horrified, he bit into it. Like the butcher he had become, Mick was covered in blood. Mikio Okami's blood. Nicholas did not want to look at the swaying corpse across the room, the lifeless husk that had once been the Kaisho of all the Yakuza, now mortal as the next man. Worse, he had been reduced to a slab of meat.

Mick chewed slowly, thoughtfully, ecstatically, wordlessly. The time for speechmaking was over, Nicholas knew; the time for deeds had arrived. Nicholas knew a great deal about shamanism. He knew, for instance, of the power of human organs to instill superhuman strength and endurance into the eater. The greater the warrior whose organs you ingested, the more strength and endurance you achieved. But there was more. In taking from your enemy his vital organs, in destroying them utterly by eating them, you deprived him of his place on the mandala of life, of being born again.

Mick finished the heart. He strolled to the corpse, made another slash in it with a precise but offhand flick of his wrist. He returned to Nicholas carrying a darkly purple, slithery object. Okami's liver. This Mick thrust against Nicholas's chest like a poultice. Mick began to chant in a strange Vietnamese dialect.

"You are ill. Terminally ill. It is your Jewishness. It's like a blood disorder; it has damaged you, turning you into a lower order of life. I can save you, perhaps, if that is what pleases me." He gave a laugh that was part bubbling chortle. His lips and chin were dark with blood.

He resumed his chanting, his eyes closed to slits, his body swaying slightly in trance. Then he snatched away the liver and, with a growl, bit off a piece, then another. Curiously, he did not chew but held them in his mouth.

He put his stinking face close to Nicholas's and said with a half-full mouth, "Eat! Eat!"

He offered up the liver but Nicholas held his lips firmly shut. Mick smiled, almost benignly, and slammed his fist into Nicholas's solar plexus. Air escaped Nicholas's mouth as it gaped open. Mick put his lips over Nicholas's in a terrifying kind of kiss, spat the bits of liver into his throat.

Nicholas's jaw snapped shut and he gagged. Mick clamped his hands across Nicholas's mouth and whispered in his ear, "Swallow, Nicky boy, or Okami will choke you to death."

Nicholas swallowed convulsively.

"Better." Mick nodded. "Much better." He finished eating the liver, tearing at it with bared teeth and feral eyes. When he was done, he said, "I'm not through with you yet. There's another chapter that needs to be played before it's done."

He touched Nicholas gently, almost lovingly. "Rest now," he said, his voice utterly calm, still and brittle as glass. "You will need all your reserves of strength in the hours to come."

"Deal? What kind of deal?"

But Wade Forrest was not even looking at Croaker when he said this. They were in the middle of the compound and Forrest was busy absorbing the status reports from his officers. The news was all bad: Caesare Leonforte was nowhere in evidence and no one had any idea how he had escaped. Everyone in the general vicinity was treated to a choice five minutes of Wade Forrest's unbridled wrath. Even the hardened fieldmen, armed to the teeth, seemed to cringe.

By dint of sheer willpower, Croaker kept his mouth shut long enough to find this out and to learn that Vesper was also missing. He knew where she was, but then again he knew where Bad Clams was. Or, more accurately, where he would be in just over an hour: aboard Coast Guard cutter CGM 1176. This was Croaker's last best shot to save Margarite, and somewhere deep inside him he knew he was saying his prayers just as he had every night when he had been a child.

All around them was the sanctified chaos only the United States government could generate during emergencies or declarations of war. Armed men in cammo and painted faces hustled to and fro, shouting orders or receiving updated intelligence. The Leonforte button men were being led away under guard, hands on their heads. The field radio on the chopper was feeding blasts of static-laden sound into the general cacophony. Forrest stood in the center of it all, back straight, directing and conducting with all the aplomb of a tuxedoed maestro. Croaker could feel the waves of satisfaction coming off him, as if saying, *What a thrill! It's war again.*

But like all wars, this one had its downside: despite their best efforts the main quarry had eluded the elite troops.

"I got a deal for you, Forrest," Croaker repeated into the teeth of the din.

"I don't make deals," Forrest said simply.

"Sure you do, you just don't know it yet."

Forrest dismissed one of his men, turned to look at Croaker, who had been in court enough hours to pick up the most effective psychological tactics of defense attorneys as well as assistant DAs. He pulled Francine close against him. She was weeping, and he could feel her shivering against him and knew her eyes were locked on her manacled mother. He hated to use her like this, but it was for all their good.

Forrest grunted his disbelief. "You're dreaming, brother."

"Maybe, but I don't think so." Croaker stepped closer so he could lower his voice, making sure he kept Francie at his side. "See, Forrest, you and I have the makings for a perfect deal. You have what I want: Margarite DeCamillo."

"Yeah, I got her and she's staying with me." Forrest's cool skepticism could not completely mask a kernel of interest. "Now what could you possibly have that would interest me."

"Caesare Leonforte."

Forrest's all-American face clouded over. "Let me tell you right now, buddy, if you have any information pertaining to the whereabouts of Leonforte, you'd best tell me now, otherwise I'll slap you with a federal warrant for obstruction of justice."

"Don't threaten me, Wade," Croaker said softly. "Whatever you do don't try that."

Forrest, reacting perhaps to Croaker's tone or his use of

Forrest's first name, pulled in his horns slightly. "I'm not giving Mrs. DeCamillo up, so forget it."

But Croaker could see Forrest making sure he didn't look directly at Francie's teary-eyed face. "Then you'll let Leonforte walk."

"If I have to." Forrest was choking back bile.

"And with him his cocaine connection."

"Fuck it." Forrest hung tough. "We'll find others to bust."

"And his pipeline into the DARPA weapons cache."

At the mention of DARPA, Forrest winced. He bit his lip. He was about to say something when one of his idiots reported in. Forrest almost took his head off and the man backed away, ashen-faced. Forrest returned to chewing his lips, as if he were a maddened animal in a too-small cage, ready to rend itself from limb to limb. At last, his restless eyes alighted on Francine and stayed there for a very long time.

"Shit," he said. "Shit, shit, shit."

"I think you've lost your mind," Maya said. "What d'you know about him anyway?"

"He can ride a fucking bike," Kawa said.

He was standing just outside the tiny elevator that had whisked Nicholas upstairs to Pull Marine minutes ago. Kawa had gone back to the coffee bar, listened without really hearing the beat poetry. He kept thinking of Nicholas and where he might be headed. Someone laughed, asked him a question, but he paid no attention. He did not notice Maya looking at him from across the table. When he had abruptly got up and gone into the kitchen, she followed him.

Now Kawa pressed the button and the elevator hummed.

"So what he can ride a fucking bike," Maya said. "Why should you get involved?"

"'Cause it's there. Also, that poet sucks." He grinned at her.

The elevator door slid open and he stuck his head cautiously inside.

"Shit," Maya said. "It smells in there." She turned to him. "You're going, aren't you?"

He stared at her and she shook her head, placed something in the palm of his hand. He looked down at it, closed his fingers around it. "Hey," he said.

Kawa took a deep breath, held it, and stepped inside. When he turned around, all he could see were Maya's zonked-out eyes. Then the door closed and he went up.

The door opened and Jōchi almost took his head off with one giant swing. Kawa ducked, felt the fist graze his temple and strip off three layers of skin. He bent forward, flicked open the blade of the knife, and went for it.

Jōchi grabbed his arm and nearly broke it. The knife clattered to the floor. Kawa, realizing this was no joke, no way-cool hipster happening he was creating for himself in the video arcade, did the only thing he could think of: he bit into Jōchi's cheek. The agonizing pressure on his arm let up just enough for him to use his knee. That seemed to have little or no effect as Jōchi grunted and pinned him to the wall.

Kawa grunted, Jōchi grinned, and Kawa saw his death reflected in the older man's eyes. Jōchi slammed the heel of his hand into Kawa's solar plexus and the Nihonin doubled over. He bucked his knees and slid to the floor. As he reached out for the knife, Jōchi's shoe trod hard on his hand, making him cry out.

Kawa, truly pissed off now, cleared his head of the residual pot he had smoked earlier and, using all the strength in his coiled legs, butted Jōchi under the chin. Jōchi's head snapped back and he took one stumbling step away. Kawa grabbed the knife and, crying a little bit, plunged the blade between two of Jōchi's ribs.

Jōchi made an inarticulate sound and he tried to grab the knife. He whipped backward, wrenching away Kawa's grip on the handle. He stared down, wide-eyed, at his chest. He looked up at Kawa. He mumbled something, took a shambling step toward the Nihonin, and promptly fell onto his face.

He lay unmoving for a long time. Kawa was breathing hard, crying still and unaware of it. He bit his lip and ran a trembling hand through his snow-white hair. He continued to stare down at Jōchi. Why wasn't he moving? Then he got it. Understanding flashed like lightning across his face and he vomited. He kept on retching even after there was nothing left to throw up.

Eventually, he felt better. He thought of Maya, waiting for him down below, and he almost turned back, almost reached out for the button to open the elevator door and take him back down to his familiar, anarchic world. But now something had changed, because he suddenly understood that what he and his pals had believed was rebellious anarchy had its own grooved pattern. It was actually as safe and tame as going to work five days a week, and now it seemed empty.

He thought about why he had come, and he went in search of Nicholas. He found him, eventually, in a back room of the restaurant, a place that looked as if it hadn't been used in decades—until tonight.

Walking into the charnel house, Kawa was perversely grateful he had had to kill a man that night, otherwise the sights and smells in there would surely have blown his mind to smithereens.

"What if you're wrong?"

"I'll tell you what, babe, the world doesn't function on *what if,* and because of that I don't go around second-guessing myself."

Vesper felt her pulse heavy in her temples even over the deep throb of the cutter's diesels. She smelled the ocean, briny and fish-laden, full of life. Spots of spume settled on her hair. She knew she was at a nexus point. He wanted to kill her, she knew that as surely as if he had said it. The coiled-spring tension in his body told her. It was anger, pure and simple; his empire was coming apart. And she had become the lodestone for his rage. But, as was typical with him, she sensed something else as well, and she knew she must capitalize on it if she had any chance of staying alive.

"Shoot me now." She spat. "Go ahead, it's what your father would have done."

She felt the momentary hesitation ripple through him, and she extended her psyche to its limits, trying to redirect his towering rage.

He jammed the muzzle of his gun so hard into her ear she cried out. "What does my father have to do with it?"

"I used to work for him, remember? I was one of his elite agents in the field." She was growing dizzy from a combination of mortal tension and using her limited gift. She gritted her teeth and went on. "He was so obsessed with his secret identity he became paranoid. Field executions became the rule rather than the exception. When you get like this, you remind me of him."

Again a ripple, this time more pronounced. "What do you mean, 'like this'?"

"You know," she said in her most offhand voice, "irrational."

It was a risk and she knew it. But she sensed she was teetering on the brink. Either she would fall into the eternal abyss or she would survive. There was no middle course.

"Irrational." He said the word as if it were food he was tasting. "Yeah, right, my father could be fucking irrational. Not that I'd remember what he was like 'cause he was never around when we were growin' up." He nodded. "Yeah, he could be a fuckin' pig, all right. But he was also smart. Smart enough to fool the feds for decades."

Vesper concentrated. She could hear it now—the darkness and the light, the two sides, the rage and the admiration he felt toward his father that he could not reconcile. She could almost hear in her mind the clash of swords as the two opinions continued their endless war. No wonder he had to see the world at large as black and white. Anything else would be for him utter and complete chaos.

"Yeah, he was smart, all right," Vesper said. "So smart that you could never control him, though I imagine you tried." Her back was aching from being bent over and her head hurt where her cheek was pressed hard against the wooden box that held the stolen DARPA weapons.

"Fuck you talkin'? I never—"

"Sure you did. You wanted to show the old man what he had missed out on by running off and leaving the family. You wanted to push his nose in your accomplishments."

Caesare grunted. "That's crap. Why the fuck would I wanta do that?" Another ripple and unconsciously he let up on the pressure of the gun muzzle in her ear.

"To show him you were better, smarter than he was."

"I wasn't in competition with Pop."

"Oh, but you were, and it was the worst kind. It poisoned you through and through. You wanted revenge, Caesare. You wanted to hurt him, to pay him back for abandoning you."

"He had no choice," Caesare shouted. "He'd made a commitment; it was for the good of the family."

"That's bullshit and you know it." Vesper kept up the pressure. "He was ambitious—*too* ambitious for him to consider the good of the family. He got married, had kids, but by that time he knew it was a mistake. A family, being a loving husband and father, was not what he wanted. He had no need for stability; he worshiped change. He wanted power and money, he wanted to live at the pinnacle."

"No, no, you're wrong." The gun swung away. "I *know* you're wrong!"

Vesper stood up painfully and saw he was looking at her differently. She was no longer the lodestone. She had carefully manipulated his rage away from her, turning it back on himself.

"I'm not wrong, Caesare." Her voice was calm and clear. "Your father fucked his way through Tokyo. In 1947, he was sleeping with Faith Goldoni. Then, when that ended, after he got out of hospital, there were so many others. Woman after woman, a long succession of skirts—that was what he called them."

Caesare was white-faced, paralyzed by confronting his greatest fear, which he had been able to suppress for so many years. Jaqui had been right all along: he *was* just like his father. But isn't that what he had wanted? Yes and no. He'd idolized a father he'd never known when he was growing up. He'd made up stories—long, involved tales that he'd never shared with anyone about his father's exploits undercover. He'd needed those stories to make certain he wouldn't come to hate his father—as Jaqui had come to—for walking out on all of them.

Woman after woman—a long succession of skirts. John and Caesare Leonforte, father and son—two of a kind. Jesus!

The emotional storm was building. Vesper could feel it like the first strike of far-off lightning, a slight rumble that would soon and perhaps without warning turn into a collapse of the universe.

"You're lying." It was a hoarse whisper and there was no conviction in it; his eyes told her he believed every word. He was guided by his own intuition now. She had disarmed him, if not literally then figuratively. That part of his mind that had for so long suppressed his intuition had been mortally weakened by his thundering anger. "You're so young. How would you know?"

Vesper took a step toward him. "Because he told me, Caesare. He *bragged* about his conquests. It was the verbal equivalent of notching his belt; telling me—a woman—confirmed his stature in his own eyes."

Caesare stared into her face; he wasn't looking at her but through her to another time, another place.

Vesper took another step closer and kept her voice calm and without inflection. "If I learned one thing about your father, it was that he cared about nothing and nobody. It was almost as if he wasn't human."

Caesare blinked. "Wasn't human?" He swayed slightly as if in a semitrance.

She was close to him now. "He was incapable of feeling love, of giving it or receiving it. Love was as alien to him as breathing water."

He stumbled backward and she followed him, relentless, taking on the final role in this twisted passion play—the accusatory finger of his conscience. "And you are just like him, Caesare."

"No!"

"But, yes." She came on, her eyes electric, her hair fanning out behind her in the wind like some avenging goddess. "You have no God, no loyalty, nothing. Stripped bare, you're just what your father was—all ego. I look at you and I see empty space—a pit—the void."

He shook his head, words beyond him now. His eyes were wide and staring, fascinated by her, yet repelled by what she represented.

"Why do you think your sister stopped talking to you? Just because you hit her?"

"I wish I knew." It was a pathetic whisper, slapped away by the salt wind.

"But you *do* know, Caesare. You knew all along. She saw all this in you and it horrified her. She could have loved you, Caesare—I'm sure she did, at one time. But your indifference and callousness killed that love. Even then you were becoming your father and she could not bear it." She pointed a finger. "It was you. You drove Jaqui away and now she's dead."

Out of the corner of her eye, Vesper saw Milo emerge from the cockpit. He was about to shout something when she waved him off. Instead, he pointed aft, into the sun-whitened sky. She risked a look, saw the copter winging its way toward them.

Croaker, she thought, and she barely held back a sob of relief. *I know it's him.*

In that instant, she heard the gunshot and she jumped. Milo was running from his position and Vesper looked down at her feet. Caesare was on his knees, his gun to his head. He was swaying and she thought for an instant that he had shot himself. But no, there was still too much ego. Vesper slipped to her knees and put her hands on him. Her heart thundered, seemed about to break. His great and powerful aura had shrunk to the size of a fist, buried now so deeply within him she knew it would never again emerge.

"I want to do it," he whispered. His finger was tremoring on the trigger. "I want to."

"No. You don't." Vesper could feel the blackness within him, the bitter sense of being a pariah, and the familiarity of it momentarily sickened her. All the falcons inside her were loosed like a handful of rice at a wedding. She was bound to him, all right, but not in the way she feared. It was the wildness inside her, the call of her own shrieking falcons that he heard now as she used all of her charisma to reach out to him, pull him back from the brink of oblivion. The sound of the copter's rotors was louder now, and the sea around the cutter had begun to flatten in a sun-drenched disk. She pulled the falcons down around her, around him, until even the hard shattering of the copter was obliterated. If she could do this, then she knew she would fulfill all the promise Mikio Okami had seen in her. Movement all around her on the cutter, movement she held back from them like Moses with the Red Sea. A connection was forming, she could feel it. That certain tension went out of him. Something inside him responded, recognizing a kinship beyond his comprehension. She glanced up. "The feds are coming," she told Milo. "Cut your engines. Tell the crew to surrender quietly." Milo nodded grimly.

She turned back to Caesare. His eyes had a milky quality she had seen before in the eyes of the newly dead. Where had his mind gone?

"Jaqui?"

And then she knew. She answered him as he desperately needed her to do. "I'm here, Caesare."

"Jaqui, I'm ... sorry."

"I know you are."

She pried his fingers one by one from the grips of the gun and took possession of it. The air was thundering as if with the beat of angel's wings.

"Jaqui ..." He took a shuddering breath.

"It's all right, Caesare." She took his head in her hands and held him to her breast, rocking gently. "It's all right now."

"You look like you died and nobody came to resurrect you."

"You resurrected me." Nicholas smiled briefly and gripped Kawa's hand. "Thank you for coming."

"No big thing."

They were squatting in one of the back storerooms of the restaurant Pull Marine. Neither of them mentioned the charnel house in the rearmost room. It was just as well. Kawa didn't want to know why the mutilated corpse of an old man was hanging there, and right now, Nicholas did not want to remember. There would be many nights, he suspected, of remembering.

"Think I oughta get you to a hospital, man."

Nicholas shook his head. Now that Kawa had taken him off the drip, he was feeling better, he was hypermetabolizing the Banh Tom venom as quickly as he could, but he was far from being himself again.

"There's something I have to do and it can't wait."

Flash of bloody-faced Mick. *I'm not through with you yet.*

There's another chapter that needs to be played before it's done.

Flash of the Banh Tom venom dripping into his open vein from the IV. And beyond that the third chain hanging from the ceiling, empty; the third IV stand with its plastic bag of pale amber poison and its curling, needle-tipped line, ready for another victim.

"Hey, man, no offense," the Nihonin said, "but you look too strung out to go anywhere but bed."

I'm not through with you yet.

Through the haze of the venom Nicholas had worked it out. He knew where Mick was headed. He stood up and felt as if he were in an elevator in free fall. Kawa jumped up, grabbed him around the waist, supporting him as his knees gave out.

"See? What'd I tell you?"

Nicholas turned to the Nihonin. "Kawa-san, the man who did *that* is on the loose and I am very much afraid he is going to kill again."

Kawa stared at him. "Kill like that?" His snow-white hair lent him a ghostly air, and Nicholas could imagine he was living a Japanese myth, a warrior being saved from death by an impish demon.

"Yes."

Kawa shuddered.

"I'm going to need some help."

"Hey," Kawa said with a lopsided grin, "this night's already turned out to be the trip of a lifetime. I figure why stop now, right?"

Koei was asleep. It was not a deep sleep. Contrary to what Nicholas believed, she did not sleep well when he was out. Resting on her back, she stared out at the Tokyo night reflected like a dream on the bedroom ceiling. She tried counting the lights, then seeing what patterns they formed. She closed her eyes and opened them again. It was almost five and Nicholas had not yet returned. She wasn't worried; he often stayed out all night, especially since the crisis with the CyberNet a week ago.

She sat up, saw that she had forgotten to draw the drapes. Perhaps the lights of the city had kept her up. She rose and went to the high window and looked out. She could see the Naigai Capsule Tower just below her, seeming close enough to reach out and touch. Its steel scaffolding looked like the home of a gigantic spider. She remembered the Metabolism movement of the 1970s and had always found its insistence on segregating parts of the urban landscape as a sinister attempt to further disconnect people from their environment. She wondered what it would be like to live in one of those metallic-skinned capsules, then thought she was better off not knowing.

She sighed. Sleep was impossible now. The sky had turned an oyster gray; perhaps today the sun would burn its way through the overcast. She pulled on a short cotton *yukata* and, drawing it closed around her waist, padded to the top of the stairs. At that moment, she heard a sound.

"Nicholas?"

Silence and darkness were the stillborn replies.

She stood very still, her hand on the top of the handrail, which curved dark and cool, down into the unknown shadows. What had the noise sounded like? A chink, as of metal, a rustle, as of clothes, a soft tread, as of footsteps? Or was it only the drapes being moved by the air coming from the floor registers? She couldn't remember. She couldn't tell.

Slowly, silently, she descended the stairs. It was like sinking into an ocean trench. All the drapes had been drawn down here against the night lights of the city. Had she done that before she had gone up to bed? As with most acts repeated so often they had become unconscious, she could not recall.

Down in the shadows she felt her breath flutter in her throat. She stood at the bottom of the stairs, staring so hard into the pitch blackness her eyes began to hurt. Someone was in the apartment with her; she knew it with a certainty that made her heart constrict painfully in her chest.

Sound came to her then, as if clothing against flesh.

"Koei . . ."

She shivered and lunged for a lamp.

"Don't turn on the light. Please."

Something in the voice caused her to draw her hand back from the switch.

"It is better for us in the darkness now." It was a female

voice, clear and rich. In the comfortable softness of her tones Koei recognized a person used to being obeyed.

"My name is Marie Rose. But Michael Leonforte knows me as Jaqui."

Koei gasped and, feeling the strength go out of her legs, felt behind her with her outstretched hand for the edge of an upholstered chair on which to sit. "Jaqui, his sister?" She perched on the edge as if she were a bird about to take flight.

"That's right."

Koei could barely manage her voice. "But he told me you died . . . a long time ago."

"Someone died, but it was not me." By straining, Koei could just make out a partial outline of her face. "You see, I was chosen by God to become the mother superior of the Order of Donà di Piave."

Koei's breath was a gentle exhalation. "The Order . . ."

"You know it. It is funded—and has been so since they brought the order over from Italy—by the Goldonis. However, since I am a Leonforte, a ruse had to be used so I could be installed. That was done." She shifted slightly, a brief rustle of garments the only sound. "The order has been in Japan since just after the war. Kisoko Okami, Eiko Shima and her daughter, Honniko, many others were initiated. They all became tiles in a vast mosaic."

"But why are you here now? It's five in the morning. You frightened me half to death." Koei frowned. "And how did you get in here?"

"To answer your last question first, I picked the lock." Her voice had changed modulation, as if she picked up the timbre and intonations of Koei's speech. "I have many such unexpected talents. As to why I am here now, I will tell you. My brother needs me."

"Michael? Is he coming here? But how do you know that?"

"God has told me." Koei sensed Jaqui moving through the darkness toward the curtains.

With a great crack of thunder, the windowpane blew inward and the thick drapes were hurled backward. Koei jumped up with a little scream. She was brought up short as she saw Mick crouched on the windowsill. He was outfitted in strange matte-black garb, girdled by a wide leather cinch that seemed bound by ropes that dropped into the oyster-gray darkness beyond the building.

"Michael, what—?"

Koei started as she heard Jaqui speaking perfectly accented Japanese. She felt as if she were in a dream, hearing herself speak. Another of Jaqui's so-called unexpected talents.

"Time to pay all debts, Koei," Michael said in a guttural voice.

Koei stifled a scream as he grabbed Jaqui and, pulling once on one of the ropes, disappeared out of the shattered window. In that brief glimpse through the wildly swinging curtains, Koei had seen that Jaqui had hair just like her own and was wearing some of Koei's clothes.

"Michael!" Koei cried, hurling herself across the welter of broken glass and leaning out the window. She could see him, with Jaqui over his shoulder, sliding down the system of ropes and pulleys he had connected from the top of the Naigai Capsule Tower. Now she knew the truth: Jaqui had deliberately placed herself in harm's way. She had fooled Michael into thinking she was Koei.

When, eleven minutes later, Nicholas stormed into the apartment, followed by a strange-looking Nihonin with hair the color of snow, she had much to tell him.

The energy of the Kaisho, residing like an imploding star within his stomach and intestines, had honed Mick's senses to superhuman pitch. It synthesized with the drug he'd ingested without which the Nung ritual was ineffectual. The drug was made from herbs and the ground shell of a horned beetle indigenous to the hills of Vietnam. The insect, as large as a child's hand, was trapped, hung in the sun for a week, where it turned black as obsidian. Then its carapace was carefully stripped off and ground to grit by stone mortar and pestle. Its horns were used in the insides of the shaman's sacred rattle.

It was with these heightened powers that Mick sensed he was being stalked. Rappelling down from the top of the Capsule Tower, he hardly missed a beat as he thought of Nicholas Linnear and reached up over his head to unsnap a metal clip. This was what he wanted, after all, a chance to take away everything Nicholas held dear, and then to defeat him one on one. That was important because Nicholas was everything that Mick was not; he was everything that Mick, as a lovesick young man in the meditation garden of the Convent of the Sacred Heart of Santa Maria, had longed to be. Denied by blood and evil circumstance the love of the one woman he would gladly have died for, he had tried to outrun memory, love, his past, everything that he had been and would always be. He had tried to bury all of that in the wilds of Vietnam by creating an entirely new Michael Leonforte, but all that he had concocted was a wicked shaman's stew, a walking, talking nightmare, a golem, a hollow-eyed and hollow-souled doppelgänger. Because no matter how hard he tried, the old Michael Leonforte would not stay buried. That Michael Leonforte had looked into his young heart and had found it filled with the unthinkable: a soulmate whom he could never have and never even love as he so desperately longed to love her.

As he had said to Nicholas, you can't outrun heritage no matter how hard you try.

He reached the first capsule and, ducking through a lozenge-shaped interstice between steel girders, clambered onto the black metal grid landing. He unbuckled himself from his mountaineering rig and, with his heavy bundle over his shoulder, took off down the landing.

He was eighteen floors up, and as he loped along, he passed through thick blades of shadow and wan flowers of light that seemed to have drifted into the tower from another time. The wind soughed with a peculiarly childlike cry through the webwork. It was punctuated by the humming and gurgling of the tower's machinery—for the elevators, the heat and air-conditioning, plumbing and sanitation, the electricity, phone lines, and television hookups. The conduits for these services ran in thickly cabled bundles of flexible PVC throughout the levels, looking much like the veins and arteries of a cut-open body. His head whipped around as a bird fluttered through the structure, panicking in a flurry of wing beats, until it found its way. He wiped sweat away from his eyes and listened.

* * *

Nicholas had taken a towel from the bathroom and, looping it over the nylon rappelling line that ran from a spot just beneath his broken-out living-room window to the top of the Naigai Capsule Tower, gripped its ends on either side of the line and dropped to into the pearly light of dawn.

With this crude method of sliding down the line he had no way of slowing or otherwise controlling his momentum. A third of the way down he began to smell charring fabric and, glancing up, saw an ominous tendril of gray smoke whipping away from the center of the towel. The abrasion against the nylon was causing the towel to combust.

He was halfway across when the first flame sparked, licking at the cotton cloth. The very speed at which he was sliding caused it to flicker out, but almost immediately, more flames burst through the fabric and he could feel some of its support give way. He was now approximately three-quarters of the way down to the tower. Below him was nothing but humid air for hundreds of feet until the roofs of other buildings rose far below, needled with antennas, satellite dishes, and the like. It would certainly be a fatal fall.

The stench of burning fabric was thick in his nostrils and he began to sway back and forth beneath the nylon line, clutching at the fast-disintegrating towel. He looked ahead and knew he was not going to make it. He sensed the final rending of the cotton seconds before it happened and, swinging his torso and legs backward to gain momentum, lifted his legs in an arc up, over his head, until the side of his shoes clamped the nylon line down which he was speeding. He could feel the intense friction almost immediately eating away at his thin shoes, but more than half his weight came off the flaming towel and it bought him two seconds, three, precious time at this stage.

Below and ahead, the top of the Capsule Tower loomed large, the soft light of incipient dawn creeping through the geometric gaps between the girders. It looked momentarily beautiful, a powerful atavistic puzzle of a structure like a Mayan pyramid rising in a precise urban cityscape. He was coming down to it fast. Only a few seconds more, that's all he needed . . .

He didn't get it. The flames ate through the center of the towel and it came apart in his hands. His head, shoulders, and torso dropped down until he was hanging vertically off the nylon line, held to it only by the power in his legs as he clamped the line between his feet. He slid down, faster and faster, the muscles of his legs and feet hard as rock and beginning to cramp. There was pain there already, as the friction burned through the leather and thin cotton lisle of his socks. The skin on the insides of his feet began to blister.

He had no other choice and was readying himself to leap off when he passed the clip that Mick had unfastened and the line collapsed, swinging wildly away from the tower. Nicholas scissored his legs open, leaped for an oblique girder, missed it, slammed his shoulder against another, and reaching out, wrapped his arms around a third.

He swung like a pendulum, fighting the pain, the fatigue of a long, virtually sleepless week, the delayed shock of Mikio Okami's horrific death, and the residue of the Banh Tom venom he was still hypermetabolizing out of his system. Slowly, he steadied himself, fighting the pounding in his head, a combination of being inverted and having a host of toxins breaking down inside him.

He drew inward and at the core of himself rejected his *tanjian* eye, opting for Kshira. The dark eye opened onto a violently changed world. He saw the Capsule Tower for what it was: an unsuccessful attempt to integrate the permanent and the impermanent, the darkness and the light. He saw the city all around as a gray ocean, vast and remote. Only the tower existed now, black as a crow's head—and the three people climbing upon it like ants crawling up Mt. Fuji.

The dark eye swung upward, inward, through the interstices of the tower, and he located Mick. He began to climb.

"Michael . . ."

Mick paused, crouched upon the metal grille of an outside walkway. He had been concentrating on Nicholas, on his approach. He was on the tower, he knew that much. He had survived the booby-trapped rappelling line.

"Michael . . ."

That voice. It was not Koei's at all, and yet he knew it as well as he knew anything in his life. He turned, his heart flipping over in his chest even before his mind had begun to work it out. In shock he stared at the woman taking off a wig. She was dressed in Koei's clothes but she was not Koei.

He stared into those deep sea-green eyes that out of self-defense his mind had set adrift in the sea of forgotten memory. Some memories were too painful and had to be set aside, relegated to the shadows. They rose up now like specters in a graveyard. His eyes opened wide.

"Yes." She nodded. "It's me, Michael. Jaqui."

"Jesus, it can't be." He felt as if he had been dipped in ice, as if someone had reached inside him and turned him inside out. He felt raw with disbelief. "You're dead."

She took a step toward him. "Am I?"

He cringed as she reached out to touch him.

"Agghh!" he cried. "My God, what's happening?"

"It's God that's brought us together." Jaqui's voice was soft, soothing, blending into the eerie susurrus of the wind and the workings of the tower. "See, Michael"—she pinched the flesh of her arm—"I'm alive and well. My 'death' was a ruse to allow me to enter the order, which was owned by the Goldonis."

He was pressed back against the railing that ran along the outside of the walkways. "But why?"

"Because of the enmity between the Goldonis and the Leonfortes. No one really knows how it began. Like all such vendettas it was perpetuated by terrible stories handed down from one generation to another, and each time they were retold the stories became more horrible until they passed into the realm of myth.

"Grandpa Caesare knew this and wanted very badly to end it, but until I came along, he did not know how. He was close with the order's previous mother superiors, and as he observed me growing up, he saw in me the kernel of an answer.

"It was he who convinced Mom to take me to the convent when I turned a certain age, and he was right. God had chosen me to enter the order—and more. After my staged death, I began to be trained under the name Sister Marie Rose to replace the existing mother superior. None of that would have been possible had I not 'died.' The Goldonis would not have allowed it and neither would Uncle Alphonse."

"I remember . . ." Mick's voice had taken on a certain dreamlike quality. "Alphonse was pissed when he came back from the convent. He was sure he could get you back and he vowed he would someday. Not long after, you died."

Jaqui nodded. "That was how it was." She took another step toward him, holding out her arms. "Michael, I'm here to end once and for all the vendetta. I'm here to heal you."

"Ah, no!" Mick clapped his hands to his ears as he slipped to his knees. "God protect me from my own thoughts."

Seeing his anguish, Jaqui knelt beside him. "I'm here to protect you, too, Michael. You have done terrible things, evil things. You are not the brother with whom I spent evenings on our rooftop, sharing dreams."

Mick's head whipped from side to side. "Don't you see it? We shared nothing. What we spoke about was all bullshit."

"Why do you say that? We shared the same dream. To fly as far away from the life of the Leonfortes as we could. You remember, don't you?"

"Ah, Jaqui. The only dream I ever had that meant anything to me I never shared with you. I couldn't." His eyes flicked up to that wondrous sea-green gaze that had so captivated him.

"What was it? Tell me. I'm here now. Tell me."

His face twisted up. "I . . . can't."

"Yes, you can. God will give you the strength."

"God." His face twisted further. "I have fallen so far from God He no longer exists."

Jaqui reached out. "He exists, Michael. I am here now because of Him. Believe me, He exists."

"You're so pure, so good, holy even, like a shaman who has touched the underside of heaven." His eyes squeezed shut. "God exists for you."

"He exists for everyone, Michael, you included."

He felt her touch him and his desire to shrink away and hide his face vanished. "Oh, Jaqui, I'm like a leper. Be careful. There must be poison in my sweat." She only held him tighter. The wind rushed around them as dawn rose, speaking in tongues.

"Tell me the dream," she whispered.

He shuddered. "If I tell you, I'll die."

"You cannot die while I am holding you. You have nothing to fear, Michael."

"But I do. I fear myself and . . . oh, God, help me, I fear you."

"Me? Why?"

"What you will think of me if I tell you the dream." He was trembling as if with the ague. "You'll hate me."

"Then say nothing and just listen." She gathered him to her. "When we were younger, I had a crush on you. One night I dreamed you came into my room. It was very still, as if we were far away from Ozone Park. Perhaps I heard the distant boom of the surf, I don't know. You came into my room and though it was pitch-black, I knew it was you. I felt your skin burning mine as you lay down beside me. You whispered my name and I whispered yours, and we made love."

Mick had gone limp in her arms as she spoke. He felt as if he had turned to liquid. There was a heat inside him he could no longer control. Tears burned his cheeks even as he squeezed his eyes tightly shut. It was too much, hearing what he had longed to hear from her for so many years. He felt as if he had found his heart again only to have it shattered to pieces.

When he was able, he told her his dream of them together dancing at the lantern-lighted terrace on some unnamed part of the Mediterranean seacoast. "I loved you, I wanted you, I could not have you," he concluded. "It was impossible, terrible and terrifying. I was certain I would fry in hell, and yet it held me in such thrall I could not walk away from it, much less stop thinking about it. Then you went into the convent and I knew I had to get as far away from you as possible."

"Oh, Michael, how I've failed you." She was weeping.

"No, no." After all this time he was astonished how tender he felt toward her, how powerful a force she remained in his life—the only force, he realized with a painful lurch of his heart. The second skin he had so painstakingly constructed upon the ashes of his old personality disintegrated, leaving him breathless and vulnerable.

She kissed him then—with passion or with a sisterly tenderness? He could not tell, realized he did not want to know, and his torment began all over again.

With an animal cry, he thrust her away from him—perhaps too roughly, because she fell back and he saw a shadow standing there on the walkway, as familiar as his own. It was Nicholas, his doppelgänger.

Mick ran at Nicholas in a headlong rush, even as Jaqui screamed at him to stop. But why stop? Mick was already doomed, damned by emotions he was powerless to change or control. He loved Jaqui with all his heart and soul, he knew that now with the kind of giddy elation one feels in a speeding car that has gone out of control. In that split instant before impact, all things seem possible. The laws of the universe have been suspended, even life and death have reduced meaning in the maelstrom of this cosmic free fall.

He hit Nicholas as hard as he could, rocking him backward. Or so he thought. He slammed against the railing, saw that Nicholas had stepped to the side, avoiding the brunt of the blow. Then he felt the dark eye of Kshira and he smiled. It was the smile of an ancient god awaking from a long slumber, the smile of the satyr called to revel in the darkness of the night.

He sent his psyche outward, like a missile thrown into the ether, and as he saw the surprise register on Nicholas's face, he smashed him across the face with both fists, did it again, a third time, until Nicholas was bent backward over the railing. He teetered there for a moment as Mick tried to flip him over the top rail.

Nicholas, battling Mick both mentally and physically, felt under siege. Many of his defenses were down at the moment he felt the implosion of Mick's psychic attack. The last of the Banh Tom venom was working its way out of his system, but the hypermetabolizing had exhausted much of Nicholas's psychic energy. That inner engine had been hard at work on mortal problems for hours. Even he had his limits, and he had now overreached them.

As Mick levered him over the rail, Nicholas lost all sense of balance and the dark eye of Kshira blinked. Sensing this, Mick pushed all the harder, and Nicholas knew he was going over, down into the void, to be impaled on some rooftop equipment far below.

In that instant when he hung almost upside down, while Mick pushed him farther over the rail, he felt something. It was not Kshira, not Akshara, but it was psychic. Perhaps it was the hand of God, reaching down through Tokyo's industrial dawn to steady him. At that instant, he had no more time to analyze it. He used it.

His legs came up and clamped around Mick's hips. Then he slammed the knuckles of his fists into the sides of Mick's neck. Mick let out a shocked sound and his grip weakened. Nicholas pushed, and Mick staggered back against a bundle of thickly coiled PVC pipes. He took out a small blade, held it in front of him.

"Michael, no!" Jaqui cried.

He ignored her, rushing Nicholas, who sidestepped him. He turned and ran at Nicholas again, feinting to the right this time, then coming in from the left, slashing Nicholas's forearm, getting inside his guard and going for the throat.

Nicholas reached up, hauled mightily on one of the PVC pipes, which split at a joint. Steam burst out in a stinging cloud and he directed it at Mick. The vapor struck Mick full in the face. He screamed, lurching backward so hard he bounced hard off the railing, lost his footing, and when he slammed against it a second time, was hurled over the rail with such force that he was thrown out and away from the tower, tumbling head over heels down, down into the city below.

Jaqui did not cry out, she did not move for a long time. She bit down on her knuckle hard enough to draw blood. The steam continued to hiss from the broken pipe, sending vapor climbing through the bulwark of the tower's exoskeleton and into the white sky. Somewhere not far away, the sounds of police sirens knifed through the small city noises.

Nicholas crouched against the wall where Mick had made his last stand and tried to gather himself. He was dizzy and sick at heart. At last he looked up at Jaqui and said, "I'm sorry I couldn't save him."

She took her bloody knuckle out of her mouth and her sea-green eyes swung around to him. "That wasn't your responsibility." Something had gone out of those astonishing eyes, the peculiar light he had noticed when he had seen her at Honniko's and again briefly at Both Ends Burning. And it was at that moment he realized something.

He stood up shakily, using the wall as support. His forearm ached where Mick had sliced it. "You saved me, didn't you?"

She came to him and, ripping off a sleeve of her blouse, tied it tightly just above his wound. "I don't know what you mean."

"Oh, I think you do," he said, watching her. "At the moment when your brother was about to push me over the rail, I felt something. A hand steadying me, something."

"Perhaps it was Michael himself," she said as she walked to the railing. "He apparently collected some extraordinary powers in his travels."

"How could it have been him? He wanted so desperately to destroy me."

She was looking out and down at the line of police cars crawling along the avenue far below, making their way to the base of the tower. A pink glow, softened by distance, illumined her face. She shook her head. "It wasn't you he wanted to destroy, Mr. Linnear. It was a part of himself he could no longer tolerate."

"Maybe you don't know the crimes he committed."

Her mouth twitched in an ironic smile. "Mr. Linnear, I know more than that. I know everything Michael was capable of."

He looked from her down to the spot where Mick lay like a dark star, spent of its incredible energy, that had until recently burned so bright in the night. "His death was like his life, wasn't it? Spectacular, theatrical, a kind of work of art—just as is prescribed in the *Kagakure,* the book of the samurai."

He said nothing more for some time. What must she be feeling? She had not shed a tear for her brother. How deeply had she cared for him?

She turned to him, pressed her back against the railing. The wind, freshening over the Sumida River, tousled her hair, and now he could see the extreme sorrow etched in her face and knew she would never look the same again.

Would those sea-green eyes ever sparkle as they once had? he wondered.

"I'll tell you what's funny, Mr. Linnear. Funny in an ironic and tragic kind of way. Michael was so sure I was pure and untainted. Holy, he called me. That was his dream of me, his fantasy. And, of course, it was false." She crossed her arms over her breasts, hugging herself. "Will you hear my confession?"

"I am no priest. I don't think—"

"Please!"

"All right." How could he deny those eyes anything? "As you wish."

"Not as I wish, Mr. Linnear. As God wills it." She closed her eyes and took a deep breath. "Michael committed terrible crimes and so have I."

"Excuse me, Mother, but your brother was a murderer."

"And so am I."

Those sea-green eyes captured his and would not let them go.

"Mother—"

"You remember Nguyen Van Truc, the man who was to take the stolen CyberNet data to Honniko and then to my brother?"

Nicholas blinked. "How would you know about the stolen data and Nguyen—" And then he realized that it had been through Honniko.

"You followed Van Truc and you caught him," Jaqui went on. "You switched the floppy disc and then you hypnotized him so he would not remember being caught. But something went wrong and hours after he delivered the disc to Honniko, he told her he began to remember what had happened."

Nicholas could not take his gaze off her. "So Honniko told you."

"Yes."

"And?"

"And I did what I had to do. I couldn't allow Michael to find out about your ruse prematurely. Plans were already in motion."

"What plans?"

"You will know, in time."

He continued to look at her. "You killed Van Truc, didn't you?"

"As I said, I did what I had to do." There was something in her eyes, something new. "Van Truc had to be silenced." It spun there, dark and mysterious, like the inscribed tablet of an unknown race.

Nicholas knew what it was and he was already stretching for her as she went over the railing. She collapsed like a paper doll as she slipped over the top rail and began to fall.

Nicholas reached the railing and bent, grabbing her wrist.

"Mother, this is not the way."

She looked up at him, her eyes dimmed and clouded. "I came here to save Michael and to heal him, and I failed. I failed my order and my sacred oath to God."

She looked so fragile, dangling there at the end of his arm, and touching his psyche to hers, he felt just how deeply she had been scarred. "Whatever you have done, Mother, I cannot believe God wishes you to give up your life—and your eternal soul—for it."

Her hair whipped about her face, partially obscuring her sea-green eyes. Light was coming now, hard and jangly, flashbulbs popping in the skyrise windows as it muscled through the clouds. "I haven't confessed it all. The worst part remains."

"Then confess and be done with it. Live."

"Let me go, I beg you. God cannot want me to live with what I carry in my heart."

"Surely that is for God to decide," he said as he slowly and deliberately pulled her back over the rail to safety. "Not you."

Harvest Night

Where
are you hurrying to?
You will see
the same moon tonight
wherever you go!

—Izumi Shikibu

Tokyo/New York

Tetsuo Akinaga came to the Kaisho's funeral. Brazenly, he entered the Nichiren Buddhist temple while a full retinue of twenty *kobun* and under-*oyabun* assembled outside in the afternoon sunshine. It was more than a sign of respect. It was a show of strength. After the internal struggle between Mikio Okami and his inner circle of *oyabun*, only Akinaga remained, and the tall, cadaverous Yakuza wanted everyone to know that he was consolidating his power.

In the lull between the service and the burial, he planted himself squarely in front of Nicholas Linnear, and they commenced the ritual Yakuza greeting by stating their names, rank, and clan affiliation. That done, Akinaga wasted no time: "I understand you have been looking for me."

The red and gold splendor of the temple interior seemed hollow, and at the same time as bright and garish as a Ginza neon sign. Although Akinaga had chosen his moment carefully, when the few mourners allowed at the service had filed outside, Nicholas could see Honniko standing to one side, watching the confrontation, listening intently as these two males locked horns. Koei, seeing Nicholas, as if trapped on a promontory at high tide, had made a move toward him, but he had signaled her with his hand and she had reluctantly turned into the sunshine, her outline as indistinct as the image in an old and overexposed print.

"Tanaka Gin was compiling the last of the evidence against you," Nicholas said, carefully keeping his enmity hidden. "All of it is entrusted to me. As soon as Okami-san is buried, I will present it to the chief prosecutor himself."

"Yes, yes, I know all this." Akinaga seemed unconcerned. "A pretty fairy tale is still a fairy tale."

"I *do* have the evidence."

Akinaga inclined his head. "Of this I have no doubt. And I know of your appointment with Ginjirō Machida. However, I strenuously advise you to cancel that appointment and turn your evidence over to me."

"You are insane."

"Far from it. Hatta-san is dead and, with him, his testimony that he, not your misbegotten friend Tanaka Gin, was on my payroll. Without Hatta, Tanaka Gin will rot in jail for a very long time. In this day and age of public outrage, the government cannot afford to take kindly to one of its own crawling into bed with the Yakuza."

"The case against Tanaka Gin is not strong," Nicholas said, but already he sensed where this was going and his heart sank. He wished for sunshine, for Koei's warm and knowing presence beside him.

Akinaga shrugged. "Perhaps not, but it does not really matter. The government has a duty to assuage the public. As usual, truth doesn't enter into it. Rest assured they'll make a scapegoat of Gin; and they'll throw the maximum sentence at him after he is convicted. I know. I have my sources."

Nicholas was aware of the priests and mourners—Kisoko, Nangi, Koei—drifting farther away toward the cemetery like water flowing downhill. Only he and Akinaga remained, and Honniko, still as a statue in the shadows of a corner of the temple.

"And if I hand over the evidence?"

"Not if, Linnear-san, when. Then I make a public statement, exonerating Gin."

"Who will believe you?"

"A witness of unimpeachable character will come forward

to corroborate every word I say. Tanaka Gin will be set free within four hours. This I guarantee."

Tanaka Gin's life for Akinaga's. It was not a fair exchange, Nicholas thought, but then what in life was?

"I will see you an hour after the burial," Nicholas said. "At the Nogi Jinja in Roppongi."

"A fitting site." Akinaga inclined his head. "I am pleased." At that moment, one of Akinaga's retinue, ranged on either side of the temple's main entrance, entered, handing him his cellular phone. He spoke into it in terse, one-word sentences, then handed it back to his *kobun*, who withdrew outside.

"You will leave now, won't you, Akinaga-san?"

Akinaga turned his narrow, skull-like head as if annoyed at a songbird's incessant chittering. "This chat has been so pleasant I would wish to prolong it, but as it happens my presence is required elsewhere."

Akinaga made the minimal bow, almost an insult, turned, and was about to depart when something made him turn back. "My apologies, but I never paid my condolence for the death of your wife."

"That was more than a year ago."

"Yes, I know." Akinaga seemed lost in contemplation for a moment. "It is said in some quarters, Linnear-san, that nothing will make you react. Is that true? I wonder. You did not weep at your wife's funeral, and I dare say you won't weep here today." He lifted a knobby forefinger. "But, if you indulge me for a moment, I would dearly like to see further evidence of such *Japanese* stoicism." His eyes were alight. "Your wife—Justine, wasn't it?—died in an automobile accident."

Nicholas's heart closed up. "That's right."

Akinaga leaned in a little so that Nicholas could smell the fish and soy paste on his breath. "Actually, no. She was being followed by one of my people. She saw him and panicked. Ran right into the front of that truck."

Nicholas felt the rage building inside him. He knew Akinaga was baiting him; it had galled him that Nicholas was so easily resigned to the deal he had set out. He wanted to punish Nicholas, to exact a response, another pound of flesh from him before the deal was consummated.

Akinaga shook his head. "That must have been tough to take. I admire a man who takes a blow to his bowels and doesn't flinch. Good for you." He smiled thinly. "And here's another. That friend of hers who was in the car with her when it burst into flames—who was it again? Oh, yes, Rick Millar, her former boss. They had just come from an all-night session in his hotel room. They fucked their brains out." He was staking out Nicholas's face like a wolf in enemy territory. "That's right, she was cheating on you, so maybe after all I did you a favor." Then he turned on his heel and left with the swagger of a modern-day shogun, trailing his men in his wake like a comet heated by sunlight forming an incandescent tail.

Nicholas stood beside Kisoko in the library of her town house. It appeared stark with the shelves bare. Boxes were stacked neatly on the scarred wood floor, and the Persian carpet had been rolled, wrapped, and tied. The artwork had been crated and the furniture was either already gone or covered with white dustcloths. Light from a bare bulb where the cut-glass chandelier had been spilled down, its harshness melancholy, making the room seem cavernous. Already, it had the slightly musty smell of departure.

"The meeting with the Denwa Partners went well, I hope?"

"Yes," Nicholas said. "Without Mick to cow them, they agreed to give us more time. Although, I imagine Nangi-san's appearance had something to do with it. And Kanda Tōrin proved a big help. He knows these people better than I do."

"That's good," Kisoko said. "You and Tōrin-san should come to some form of working relationship."

"We will now." Nicholas studied her face. "Did you know that Tōrin was in Akinaga's debt, that he had been working for the *oyabun* since before he came to work at Sato."

"No." She shook her head. "I had no idea, and neither did Okami-san or Nangi-san."

"I found out about Tōrin and told him I knew. He despises Akinaga but lived in fear of him." Nicholas smiled. "I believe he's more frightened of me now. As I said, he's been very cooperative."

Kisoko seemed paler than usual in the dusty light. "Do you think you should fire him?"

"Possibly, but perhaps not. Tōrin knows more about Akinaga than I could ever find out on my own. I can use that. Plus, Nangi-san was right about him—he's got a sharp mind."

He turned away, no longer wishing to talk about Kanda Tōrin. He had other things on his mind. With little life left, the house seemed inhabited by ghosts. Nicholas imagined his father here. Better to think of the Colonel now, than of what Akinaga had told him. Better to think of Koei or Nangi or Tanaka Gin or Tōrin, anything but the horror of Akinaga's boast—yes, damn him, it *was* a boast—that he had been ultimately responsible for Justine's death, had known so much about their lives that he knew the relationship between Justine and Millar better than Nicholas did. What if he was right? Nicholas asked himself. What if Justine had been cheating on him? She had been so unhappy, so lost, and he had all but abandoned her to Tokyo while he fulfilled his debt of honor to protect Mikio Okami. She had begged him not to go. He had called her twice that night and had gotten no answer. Had she been out or had she been so upset she had not wanted to talk to him? Had she been in bed with Rick? It could have happened that way, he knew. The truth. What was the truth? He'd never know, but then again he didn't want to know. Honniko had seen that, had had the good sense not to approach him in the deathly silence of the Nichiren temple after Akinaga had sucked all the oxygen, all the holiness, from the place. She had stared, silent as an image of Buddha, feeling the white-hot cinders of rage and grief sparking off him like fireworks.

Now, hours later, standing in a place that was a pasture of grave memories, it occurred to him for the first time that honor was a cruel and willful mistress.

Kisoko crossed to a sideboard on which stood a tray with a half-empty bottle of Scotch and two cut-crystal glasses, and his uneasy musings were shattered.

"Where will you and Nangi-san go?" he asked.

"Anywhere he can rest completely," Kisoko said, splashing Scotch into two glasses. "My son, Ken, has left for the United States, so nothing is keeping me here for the time being." She brought the glasses back to him, her heels clicking across the wooden boards. He wasn't surprised she hadn't brewed tea; the occasion called for something more fortifying. She was dressed in white, the color of mourning: Shantung silk suit, gloves, a pillbox hat with a veil that had been in fashion in the sixties and was so again. She looked very chic in Western garb. He gazed into her sad eyes as they clinked glasses. They drank to the memory of Mikio Okami.

"Well, hell," she said, throwing her empty glass across the room, "he had a long and fascinating life."

Nicholas, looking at the shattered glass, said, "I wish I could have saved him."

"You did in a way. At least you redeemed him. He came to love you, Linnear-san, as he had loved no other, including me." There was no jealousy in her voice, certainly no envy. "He could be a difficult man. He certainly was a thorny brother. I wanted to look after him, you see, because from a very early age danger swirled around him like a whirlpool, but that kind of behavior only infuriated him. He adored the danger, thrived on it, really. So I tried to do what I could from the shadows"—she smiled—"when he wasn't looking."

"With Tau-tau."

"Yes."

"Did he know you were a *tanjian?*"

"I have no idea. That was not a topic we would have discussed. Possibly he did."

"About Kshira—"

"Yes. I thought you'd get around to that." She went to the sideboard, her high heels click-clacking along the floor, saw there were no more glasses. Nicholas offered her his and she took it gratefully, splashing in more Scotch, drinking it more slowly than the first glass. "I must be careful. I imagine alcoholism runs in the family."

She perched on a covered chair, crossed her legs. She might have been posing for a portrait, and Nicholas felt Nangi was a lucky man. "All the dark stories about Kshira turning people mad—"

"I've seen it happen."

She glanced up at him. "I have no doubt you have. Kshira is not for every *tanjian*. Between Akshara and Kshira, it's by far the more potent of the two forms of Tau-tau. And because of that, little is understood of it." She decided to abandon her own warning and downed the remainder of the Scotch in one long gulp. "I am a Kshira adept, Linnear-san, so believe me when I tell you Kshira turns mad those who cannot control it. Do not turn away from it and it will not harm you. Learn from what is inside you. Explore carefully and you will be richly rewarded." She gave him an enigmatic smile. "But I believe you have already learned this lesson."

"And Shuken—the Dominion—the combination of Akshara and Kshira, does it exist? I have heard conflicting opinions."

Kisoko's eyes regarded him silently, slyly. "And what do you think?"

"I think I don't know enough about it to make a judgment."

"Oh, you know far more than most *tanjian*, Linnear-san." She rose, replaced the glass on the sideboard. He wondered if the glance she gave the Scotch bottle, almost as empty as this house, was one of longing. She turned to face him. "You see, you hold the answer to your own question inside you."

"What do you mean?"

Click-clack, she came across the room to where he stood. For a long moment, she stood, regarding him solemnly. She was filled with sudden emotion, he could tell that much, and he felt the two of them on the brink of a personal revelation, a shared intimacy he could not even guess at. "Akshara and Kshira coexist in *you*, Linnear-san."

He stood stunned, pinned to the spot. Of course she was right. The answer to Shuken's existence had been inside him all this time. He was living proof that the integration of the two sides of Tau-tau was possible. Kansatsu, his *sensei*, had miscalculated. He had not believed Nicholas strong enough to handle Kshira because he himself had been driven mad by it. A kind of relief flooded Nicholas and he wished Koei were here at this moment to share it.

Dust motes floated in the air and each one seemed to him to have a history, a tale to tell, a bright spark in the ocean of time.

"Kisoko," he said at length, "you have been very kind to me."

"My brother loved you as a son, and that is how I think of you." She had a direct gaze that reminded him of Koei's. He felt unaccountably comfortable with her and was suddenly sorry she was leaving. "You have a special destiny, a significant karma. I feel it like the beating of the sun's rays on my back."

"Like my father."

"Oh, no." She seemed shocked. "Not like his at all. Your father was an architect and like all architects he was a dreamer. That was why he and my brother made such a good team. The Colonel dreamed the future and Okami-san made it so. He was the doer. But your father's plan for a peaceful and powerful new Japan was always doomed to partial failure."

"Why?"

"Only God can imagine the future and make it so." Kisoko stared into a column of light slanting in through a window. So dense was it that it seemed solid enough to walk on. "Men are only men, after all," she went on in the dreamy voice of reminiscence, "no matter how extraordinary they may be. They cannot imagine all possibilities—there were too many variables even in the monolithic structure that the Colonel created here of the Liberal Democratic Party, the bureaucracy, big business, and the Yakuza. Human nature undid him."

She turned to stare into Nicholas's face, and for an instant her features were so aflame that Nicholas saw her as she had been in her magnificent youth. "You see, your father was not a greedy man so he could not imagine his grand scheme being undone by greed. But humans are a greedy lot—money, property, debts of honor, influence, and power—they want to amass them all. Greed is what brought the LDP down, greed is what made our current recession, greed has stymied our government, made weaklings of strong politicians pushed into an awkward coalition where no one has control and compromise blocks every effort."

Nicholas thought a moment. "But it was a magnificent scheme my father imagined and to a great extent it succeeded."

"Yes, it did." She took out her compact and began to

apply lipstick, by which gesture he divined that the subject was closed.

He waited a moment while she blotted her crimson lips. He watched her as she moved around the room, touching the edges of things—bookcases, moldings—as if they were old friends who needed her reassurance. Or perhaps it was she who needed the reassurance.

"I have some questions," he said.

She paused, her hand on polished wood.

"Mother Superior said you were a member of the order."

Her hand found every curve and turning of the carved wood, dark and mysterious with age. "That's right."

"And it was you, not your brother, who owned the buildings once housing the *toruko* known as Tenki and which now contains Pull Marine and Both Ends Burning, among other establishments."

Kisoko's eyes flicked up at him, "The property was in my name, yes, but the money came from the order."

Nicholas shook his head. "I don't get it. What was the order doing here during the Occupation?"

"I need some air," Kisoko said, abruptly disengaging herself from the room. "Will you join me?"

Nicholas followed her as she went to one of the curtains behind which was a brick wall. She pushed on the center and it swung open on a central post. Nicholas stepped through and found himself in a truly astonishing space.

Swirling gravel paths, still damp from days of rain, led through a series of dwarf maples and conifers like stops on a mountain road. Water burbled in a small pool within which spotted carp swam in indolent circles. Obviously, the warehouse abutting the dwelling was nothing more than a hollow shell within which this jewellike garden had been planted.

"Do you like it?" Kisoko asked with a sudden and sweet shyness.

"Very much."

She seemed pleased. "There is so little space in Tokyo in which to breathe." She sighed. "This is the one place I will be sorry to leave behind."

She sat on a backless stone bench, and something about her posture or the brave stoicism that set the features of her face reminded him of photos of Jacqueline Kennedy at the funeral of her husband. Outside, in the afternoon's custardy light, the years seemed to slip off her like old skin, revealing the young woman the Colonel had known, the person she still was.

"In all ways the order attempts to serve God." She looked down at her gloved hands composed in her lap. "It came into being to do His will." Her head turned in a direction that led him to believe she was staring into the past. "This is not often easy. God moves in mysterious ways; he has, on occasion, given signs to the chosen of the order. These invariably come in visions. But the visions are open to interpretation. And sometimes—" She halted abruptly and she passed a hand across her face. "Sometimes there are false visions."

Her eyes met Nicholas's and they were absolutely unreadable. "Such a vision came to Mary Margaret, who was the order's mother superior in 1947, and she dispatched Bernice to Tokyo on a difficult and dangerous mission. The vision had indicated that an Army officer in the Occupation would return to the States, turn to politics, and become a demagogue, building on hate and fear and paranoia to become president. The vision was apocalyptic: he was a kind of Antichrist, pushing the country into war with the Soviet Union."

Nicholas thought of the story Honniko had told him. "You researched, identified, and targeted Jacklyn McCabe."

Kisoko nodded. "He fit every aspect of the vision, but while we were concentrating on him, the real danger was left undiscovered."

"Sen. Joe McCarthy."

She nodded. "When we discovered our error, we were mortified. You must understand, Nicholas-san, in those days the threat of Soviet infiltration and control was all too real. This is what gave McCarthy his credibility among a large segment of government and the population; it took us some time to break that down, and by then a great deal of damage had been done."

The long afternoon had grown increasingly steamy and uncomfortable, and Kisoko took off her gloves, smoothing them with long, rhythmic strokes of her fingers. A bumblebee buzzed somewhere nearby. "The true danger was that *some* of what McCarthy was fighting against was real. We decided to help your father in his quest to make Japan strong again. Japan stood as a bulwark against the spread of Communism in the Pacific. The Soviet Union already had under their control the Kurils, islands that belong to Japan. What else would they take?" Kisoko brushed a tendril of hair from her cheek, wrapped it behind one ear. "The old fascism of Hitler and Mussolini was dead, but a new form of it was condoned and abetted abroad by the United States government. It was, in its own way, fashionable." She lifted a hand. "Now, as the wheel of life continues to turn, it has become fashionable again, in the guise of religious righteousness and ethnic intolerance."

She stood up, brushed off the skirt of her suit. The sun had gone in and night was fast coming. "We allowed Michael Leonforte to play all his cards, not knowing which ones he held and which he would play. It was God's will and there were terrible consequences, but there are always terrible consequences when such dark forces are set in motion."

For an instant, as she went by him, his psyche brushed hers, and he felt a dark current, swirling, a cold spot, deep and dark, in a corner of a children's summertime swimming hole. "Kisoko-san . . ."

"Yes?" She turned, expectant, but when her eyes met his, a veil was lifted from in front of her emotions. She stopped cold.

"There's more, isn't there, when it comes to Mick Leonforte."

A lark began to sing, hidden somewhere in the foliage of the garden. Kisoko drew on her spotless white gloves with the care and precision of a surgeon entering the operating theater.

"You're right, of course." Her head came up. "Long ago, Michael's grandfather invested a small sum of his money with the order. On his death, a great deal more was added to it. Michael's grandfather had pegged him for great things, and he wanted the future prepared for his grandson's arrival."

"But Mick got rich on drug money he stole from the U.S. government-sponsored pipeline in Laos. He didn't need the order's money."

"But he needed our influence, and this is what the money was used to procure for him without his ever knowing the source. In the Army; before he went AWOL and began his career as a renegade. How else do you think he was able to outwit the military for so long? By that time he'd cemented the necessary liaisons that kept him one step ahead of military justice." Her eyes slid away from his. "So you see, the order had a very personal reason for wanting Michael neutralized."

"Then Mother Superior—"

Kisoko nodded. "Was obliged to plot her own brother's demise."

Back inside, the house was as echoey as a cathedral. "It was all the worse because Marie Rose—well, her relationship with Michael was, as I believe you saw, quite special. She came here to try one last time to save him, though I am quite sure in her heart she knew there was no chance." She gave him a partial smile. "Still, there is always hope, *neh?* It is the pain and elation of being human."

"God, I've missed you!" Margarite hugged Croaker to her.

He kissed her cheek and put his arms around her, constrained by the garden in which they stood. All around them the white walls of the Convent of the Sacred Heart of Santa Maria rose around them, shining in the sunlight as if newly washed. Birds flitted among the trees and the drone of the bees among the rose canes was a lazy and nostalgic sound.

"Francie always adored it here," Margarite said. "As a child she saw it as a safe haven, but later, when she was so ill and Tony and I were at our worst, I think she rejected everything that was safe."

They lapsed into a comfortable silence. There had been plenty of time on the flight north from Ft. Lauderdale to think about their lives and how much they meant to each other. Margarite had also had time to decide what was most important to her. She wanted to reclaim her company, even if that meant a court fight. Because of Vesper's diligent work and Milo's testimony, Caesare was behind bars facing an airtight case against him for smuggling arms, drugs, and multiple violations of the RICO act. Vesper had been promoted to head her own unit of the Anti-Cartel Task Force, reporting to its director, Spaulding Gunn. She had put Margarite in touch with the assistant attorney general attached to the ACTF, who had assured Margarite that she had an excellent chance of getting a judge to annul Caesare's takeover of her company on grounds of misrepresentation. And with Caesare's apparent mental breakdown she had nothing more to fear from him. As far as her brother's business was concerned, it would have to run without her. She had already put the mechanism in motion by creating a commission of the three Family capos most loyal to the Goldonis. These men were not used to decision by committee, it was true, but it seemed clear to Margarite that everyone, including them, was going to have to learn to live by new rules.

Croaker saw her at last turn her head toward the chapel with its tall, narrow windows so like a fortified castle.

"Are you worried?" he asked.

"Worried? No." She gave him a small smile and gathered his hands in hers. "Well, maybe a little." Her face darkened. "What if I lose Francie, Lew? It wouldn't be fair, would it? Now that she and I have found each other again. Now that you're here. She never really had a proper father."

Croaker took their joined hands and kissed the back of hers. "I think you have to trust her just a little. She's been through enough to begin to know herself. Her life is just beginning, Margarite. After all that's happened to her, something has changed inside her, something new to replace the old. Let whatever will emerge, emerge."

Paul Chiaramonte stood alone in the stone chapel of the Convent of the Sacred Heart of Santa Maria and nervously shifted from one foot to another. The chapel smelled faintly of stone dust and incense. It was cool and dim, but Paul found himself sweating. The Latin he heard faintly spoken and echoing made him nervous. Religious places made him think of confession, and confession brought up all the sins he had committed.

"Paul."

He turned at the sound of her voice, and his heart skipped a beat. Jaqui looked almost regal in the black and white robes of the mother superior. Behind her, like a medieval lady in waiting, he was surprised to see Francie. She wore a plain black dress that covered her from neck to knee. Her pink-cheeked face at first looked solemn, but as she came closer, he saw that it was composed. She gave him a tiny serene smile.

"I knew," Paul said, gazing into Jaqui's sea-green eyes, which had haunted him for so long. "All these years I knew you were alive."

Jaqui extended her hands and he took them briefly. They did not kiss, but Francie could feel an extraordinary current pass between them, like a heat ripple coming up from hot pavement in August.

"I must apologize, Paul."

"For what?"

"For that night—in the garden shed when we—"

"No," he said emphatically, "don't apologize. Even then I knew I couldn't have you forever, but I wanted you that night, and it was right, Jaqui. It was right."

She moved a little at his use of her secular name. It was not that she hadn't anticipated it, but the reality of it possessed more power than she had expected. It made her think of her brother Michael, of them dancing together on the rooftop of their apartment building in Ozone Park. Or had that been Michael's dream? Her dream? She couldn't remember now; they were melded, memory and dream one seamless whole.

"Thank you. Yes," she said. "It was."

Despite her vow, in her heart part of her was still Jaqui Leonforte and always would be. Was it always so with the mother superiors of the order? She put her arm around Francie, allowed the warmth of her charisma to enfold the girl, as well as Paul. Was Francie of the chosen? Was she an agent of change as those before her had been? If so, she was about to tread a challenging and difficult path. Perhaps, Jaqui reflected, that was precisely what she needed.

Paul cleared his throat. "It was good of you to see me."

"For a time, you were her protector." He knew Jaqui was speaking of Francie. "That makes you important to this order. I thank you from the bottom of my heart."

Her eyes were a world in which he could still become lost. Paul spent a long time thinking about what he had lost—

and what he had found in the odyssey of his life. It seemed to him now that the most important lessons were to be learned closest to home, where the knife clove closest to the bone.

Staring into Jaqui's eyes, he already knew the answer to the question he was about to ask, but he asked it anyway: "Will I see you again?"

"You'll see Francine again, I'm sure." He was leaving her, perhaps forever, and Jaqui knew it. "God bless you."

Damaged light leaked through the rent in clouds dark as a bruise. Mist rose off the leaf-strewn ground, the pockmarked stone markers, as if it were morning.

"Say something." Koei stood at his right shoulder like a sentinel. "Your silence terrifies me."

The cemetery within which the Kaisho lay was still save for the low chanting of the Heart Sutra, weaving itself on an invisible loom of light. A breeze ruffled Koei's hair and then collapsed into the wet heat of the afternoon.

"Akinaga told me everything about the last days, when I wasn't around." Nicholas said it almost as a sigh, and the tender regret made her heart constrict. "And it was the truth."

Almost against her will she said, "What did he tell you?"

Exhausted shadows, broken by tree roots and small markers, lengthened along the pathways, pooled beneath the dark cryptomeria.

"That Justine's death was no accident, that she was having an affair with her former boss."

"And now you're thinking, how could she betray me?"

"Part of me."

"But she didn't." Koei moved so that she was in front of him, waited until his wandering gaze intersected with hers. "Whatever you had with her is in here"—she tapped his head—"and in here"—tapped his heart. "If she had an affair at the very end, it was because your relationship was already dead. She knew it; the problem is you only realized it after the fact. That is where the source of your guilt lies."

"But Akinaga—"

"Forget Akinaga." She would not allow his eyes to wander. "Forget everything for a moment and let yourself be."

"I cannot forget Mikio Okami. He was—"

"You must accept Justine's death before you can mourn him, or anyone else."

A plover canted down through light lacerated by planks of cloud, alit upon Okami's marker, stayed for a brief moment, then departed in a small clatter. And in an instant Nicholas saw that she was right. He could not allow Akinaga to destroy whatever he and Justine had had when they had been happy. Those memories dwelled solely within him now, like dreams, a landscape apart, full of symbols and portents. Akinaga could not touch them.

Whatever circumstances had driven them apart could not be boiled down into so easy a syrup as guilt, not any one thing or even ten, rather a vast web growing within each of them, pushing them inexorably apart. He could have turned himself inside out and the result would have been the same. What happened could not be helped. Karma.

He reached out and Koei put her hand in his. "I'll miss her."

"Yes. I imagine you will."

Together they knelt by the side of the marker. Together they recited the prayer for the dead. Then they rose.

He turned to her. "Koei, you're magic."

The Heart Sutra had finished, but its spell seemed to hang in the trees like glittering tears. Koei put her head against his shoulder. "Nicholas, you have been isolated inside yourself so long." And she felt with an intense sense of relief his body and his mind—all of him—melt into her.

A glowing moon the color of a persimmon broke through indigo clouds hanging low on the horizon. From where he lay, naked and relaxed, Tetsuo Akinaga could see the full moon of Harvest Night illumine the snow on the crest of Mt. Fuji, white tinged the palest shade of blue.

Akinaga loved Harvest Night. It had great significance for him because on a Harvest Night many years ago he had been in a vicious street fight with a *kobun* of a rival family. Both had been grievously wounded. Crawling in the gutter on bleeding hands, he had managed to strangle his barely conscious antagonist with fingers clawed with hatred, seeing with immense satisfaction the tongue emerge between bloody lips, hearing the terrible thick gurgling of lungs deprived of oxygen, the heavy stench of fresh fecal matter.

Behind him, Akinaga heard Londa's sweet alto, as she sang a song unfamiliar to him. *"Watching the moon at dawn,"* she sang softly as a breath of breeze at sunrise, *"solitary, midsky, I knew myself completely"*—he felt her coming up behind him where he was staring at the persimmon moon—*"no part left out."*

As her strong and knowing hands flowed over him like oil, he said, "It's a luxury to have you with me. And a reminder. I have had many enemies in my time, but none of them have lived long." He sighed as her hands did wonders for his mind and body. "All have come with one thought—to destroy me. All have tried, in more ways than I can now count." He chuckled. "And here I am, the sole survivor. Even Mikio Okami, the Kaisho, is dead. Yes, indeed, I went to his funeral. Well, why not? He deserved to be honored, if not in life then certainly in death." He cackled like an old woman whom the gods have made mad. "And I must say it was a pleasure to confront Nicholas Linnear, to know he cannot touch me. He has no proof against me, he knows nothing but what I have told him. I played with him like a monkey in a zoo. Poor bastard." Akinaga sighed. "Londa, you are worth your weight in—"

"Shut up."

Honniko, in her guise as Londa the dominatrix, pulled the silken cord tight around his neck. A shudder of sexual arousal went through him, and suddenly, he was as hard as a bar of iron. Ah, the sheer ecstasy of being helpless. Like a child again at his mother's breast, soft and warm and cozy and helpless. He sniffed the air for the flowery, milky scent of her. His mother. He closed his eyes.

The cord tightened, and with the pain, the near asphyxia, he felt ecstasy coming, creeping along his spine to his groin, pooling there like liquid iron. He could feel the power of his erection thundering through him, vibrating like a stroke of lightning landing between his feet. Sweet pain. She was good, very good. Oh, yes!

His eyes flew open, blinking like a child's in the sun. Was it his imagination or was the cord just a bit too tight? He opened his mouth to say something and gagged as the cord was tightened still further. His head jerked up, the veins at the sides of his neck popping. He tried to scrabble up, but she had planted her knee firmly in the small of his back, and like an adder that can be picked up once impaled just behind its head, he could thrash but not get up or roll over.

What was going on? He tried to force air into his burning lungs, but he could not. If he did not get oxygen soon ...

He saw the persimmon moon grow larger and larger, like a balloon filling with air, expanding until its very outline became distorted, until it no longer looked like the moon at all.

Honniko, watching Akinaga's hateful face fill with blood and darken like the harvest moon, felt her blood singing. When he was dead, she, too, stared up at the moon and, thinking of Nicholas Linnear, of his grief and his rage, of him standing alone and empty on the stage of the temple, sang again the last refrain of the song: *"I knew myself completely—no part left out."*

Her voice, soft and ineffably sweet, carried up into the inky sky like a plover, suffused with the divine animation of God.